Scenes from a Courtesan's Life

A Note About the Author

Sinclair Lewis (1885–1951) was an American author and playwright. As a child, Lewis struggled to fit in with both his peers and family. He was much more sensitive and introspective than his brothers, so he had a difficult time connecting to his father. Lewis' troubling childhood was one of the reasons he was drawn to religion, though he would struggle with it throughout most of his young adult life, until he became an atheist. Known for his critical views of American capitalism and materialism, Lewis was often praised for his authenticity as a writer. With over twenty novels, four plays, and around seventy short stories, Lewis was a very prolific author. In 1930, Sinclair Lewis became the first American to receive the Nobel Prize for literature, setting an inspiring precedent for future American writers.

A Note from the Publisher

Spanning many genres, from non-fiction essays to literature classics to children's books and lyric poetry, Mint Edition books showcase the master works of our time in a modern new package. The text is freshly typeset, is clean and easy to read, and features a new note about the author in each volume. Many books also include exclusive new introductory material. Every book boasts a striking new cover, which makes it as appropriate for collecting as it is for gift giving. Mint Edition books are only printed when a reader orders them, so natural resources are not wasted. We're proud that our books are never manufactured in excess and exist only in the exact quantity they need to be read and enjoyed.

bookfinity™

Discover more of your favorite classics with Bookfinity™.

- Track your reading with custom book lists.
- Get great book recommendations for your personalized Reader Type.
- Add reviews for your favorite books.
- AND MUCH MORE!

Visit **bookfinity.com** and take the fun Reader Type quiz to get started.

Enjoy our classic and modern companion pairings!

Printed in the USA
CPSIA information can be obtained
at www.ICGtesting.com
JSHW022331140824
68134JS00019B/1412

CONTENTS

Esther Happy; or, How a Courtesan Can Love

I n 1824, at the last opera ball of the season, several masks were struck by the beauty of a youth who was wandering about the passages and greenroom with the air of a man in search of a woman kept at home by unexpected circumstances. The secret of this behavior, now dilatory and again hurried, is known only to old women and to certain experienced loungers. In this immense assembly the crowd does not trouble itself much to watch the crowd; each one's interest is impassioned, and even idlers are preoccupied.

The young dandy was so much absorbed in his anxious quest that he did not observe his own success; he did not hear, he did not see the ironical exclamations of admiration, the genuine appreciation, the biting gibes, the soft invitations of some of the masks. Though he was so handsome as to rank among those exceptional persons who come to an opera ball in search of an adventure, and who expect it as confidently as men looked for a lucky coup at roulette in Frascati's day, he seemed quite philosophically sure of his evening; he must be the hero of one of those mysteries with three actors which constitute an opera ball, and are known only to those who play a part in them; for, to young wives who come merely to say, "I have seen it," to country people, to inexperienced youths, and to foreigners, the opera house must on those nights be the palace of fatigue and dulness. To these, that black swarm, slow and serried—coming, going, winding, turning, returning, mounting, descending, comparable only to ants on a pile of wood—is no more intelligible than the Bourse to a Breton peasant who has never heard of the Grand livre.

With a few rare exceptions, men wear no masks in Paris; a man in a domino is thought ridiculous. In this the spirit of the nation betrays itself. Men who want to hide their good fortune can enjoy the opera ball without going there; and masks who are absolutely compelled to go in come out again at once. One of the most amusing scenes is the crush at the doors produced as soon as the dancing begins, by the rush of persons getting away and struggling with those who are pushing in. So the men who wear masks are either jealous husbands who come to watch their wives, or husbands on the loose who do not wish to be watched by them—two situations equally ridiculous.

Now, our young man was followed, though he knew it not, by a man in a mask, dogging his steps, short and stout, with a rolling gait, like a barrel. To every one familiar with the opera this disguise betrayed a stock-broker, a banker, a lawyer, some citizen soul suspicious of infidelity. For in fact, in really high society, no one courts such humiliating proofs. Several masks had laughed as they pointed this preposterous figure out to each other; some had spoken to him, a few young men had made game of him, but his stolid manner showed entire contempt for these aimless shafts; he went on whither the young man led him, as a hunted wild boar goes on and pays no heed to the bullets whistling about his ears, or the dogs barking at his heels.

Though at first sight pleasure and anxiety wear the same livery—the noble black robe of Venice—and though all is confusion at an opera ball, the various circles composing Parisian society meet there, recognize, and watch each other. There are certain ideas so clear to the initiated that this scrawled medley of interests is as legible to them as any amusing novel. So, to these old hands, this man could not be here by appointment; he would infallibly have worn some token, red, white, or green, such as notifies a happy meeting previously agreed on. Was it a case of revenge?

Seeing the domino following so closely in the wake of a man apparently happy in an assignation, some of the gazers looked again at the handsome face, on which anticipation had set its divine halo. The youth was interesting; the longer he wandered, the more curiosity he excited. Everything about him proclaimed the habits of refined life. In obedience to a fatal law of the time we live in, there is not much difference, physical or moral, between the most elegant and best bred son of a duke and peer and this attractive youth, whom poverty had not long since held in its iron grip in the heart of Paris. Beauty and youth might cover him in deep gulfs, as in many a young man who longs to play a part in Paris without having the capital to support his pretensions, and who, day after day, risks all to win all, by sacrificing to the god who has most votaries in this royal city, namely, Chance. At the same time, his dress and manners were above reproach; he trod the classic floor of the opera house as one accustomed there. Who can have failed to observe that there, as in every zone in Paris, there is a manner of being which shows who you are, what you are doing, whence you come, and what you want?

"What a handsome young fellow; and here we may turn round to look at him," said a mask, in whom accustomed eyes recognized a lady of position.

"Do you not remember him?" replied the man on whose arm she was leaning. "Madame du Chatelet introduced him to you—"

"What, is that the apothecary's son she fancied herself in love with, who became a journalist, Mademoiselle Coralie's lover?"

"I fancied he had fallen too low ever to pull himself up again, and I cannot understand how he can show himself again in the world of Paris," said the Comte Sixte du Chatelet.

"He has the air of a prince," the mask went on, "and it is not the actress he lived with who could give it to him. My cousin, who understood him, could not lick him into shape. I should like to know the mistress of this Sargine; tell me something about him that will enable me to mystify him."

This couple, whispering as they watched the young man, became the object of study to the square-shouldered domino.

"Dear Monsieur Chardon," said the Prefet of the Charente, taking the dandy's hand, "allow me to introduce you to some one who wishes to renew acquaintance with you—"

"Dear Comte Chatelet," replied the young man, "that lady taught me how ridiculous was the name by which you address me. A patent from the king has restored to me that of my mother's family—the Rubempres. Although the fact has been announced in the papers, it relates to so unimportant a person that I need not blush to recall it to my friends, my enemies, and those who are neither—You may class yourself where you will, but I am sure you will not disapprove of a step to which I was advised by your wife when she was still only Madame de Bargeton."

This neat retort, which made the Marquise smile, gave the Prefet of la Charente a nervous chill. "You may tell her," Lucien went on, "that I now bear gules, a bull raging argent on a meadow vert."

"Raging argent," echoed Chatelet.

"Madame la Marquise will explain to you, if you do not know, why that old coat is a little better than the chamberlain's key and Imperial gold bees which you bear on yours, to the great despair of Madame Chatelet, nee Negrepelisse d'Espard," said Lucien quickly.

"Since you recognize me, I cannot puzzle you; and I could never tell you how much you puzzle me," said the Marquise d'Espard, amazed at the coolness and impertinence to which the man had risen whom she had formerly despised.

"Then allow me, madame, to preserve my only chance of occupying your thoughts by remaining in that mysterious twilight," said he, with the smile of a man who does not wish to risk assured happiness.

"I congratulate you on your changed fortunes," said the Comte du Chatelet to Lucien.

"I take it as you offer it," replied Lucien, bowing with much grace to the Marquise.

"What a coxcomb!" said the Count in an undertone to Madame d'Espard. "He has succeeded in winning an ancestry."

"With these young men such coxcombry, when it is addressed to us, almost always implies some success in high places," said the lady; "for with you older men it means ill-fortune. And I should very much like to know which of my grand lady friends has taken this fine bird under her patronage; then I might find the means of amusing myself this evening. My ticket, anonymously sent, is no doubt a bit of mischief planned by a rival and having something to do with this young man. His impertinence is to order; keep an eye on him. I will take the Duc de Navarrein's arm. You will be able to find me again."

Just as Madame d'Espard was about to address her cousin, the mysterious mask came between her and the Duke to whisper in her ear:

"Lucien loves you; he wrote the note. Your Prefet is his greatest foe; how can he speak in his presence?"

The stranger moved off, leaving Madame d'Espard a prey to a double surprise. The Marquise knew no one in the world who was capable of playing the part assumed by this mask; she suspected a snare, and went to sit down out of sight. The Comte Sixte du Chatelet— whom Lucien had abridged of his ambitious *du* with an emphasis that betrayed long meditated revenge—followed the handsome dandy, and presently met a young man to whom he thought he could speak without reserve.

"Well, Rastignac, have you seen Lucien? He has come out in a new skin."

"If I were half as good looking as he is, I should be twice as rich," replied the fine gentleman, in a light but meaning tone, expressive of keen raillery.

"No!" said the fat mask in his ear, repaying a thousand ironies in one by the accent he lent the monosyllable.

Rastignac, who was not the man to swallow an affront, stood as if struck by lightning, and allowed himself to be led into a recess by a grasp of iron which he could not shake off.

"You young cockerel, hatched in Mother Vauquer's coop—you, whose heart failed you to clutch old Taillefer's millions when the hardest part of the business was done—let me tell you, for your personal safety, that if you do not treat Lucien like the brother you love, you are in our power, while we are not in yours. Silence and submission! or I shall join your game and upset the skittles. Lucien de Rubempre is under the protection of the strongest power of the day—the Church. Choose between life and death—Answer."

Rastignac felt giddy, like a man who has slept in a forest and wakes to see by his side a famishing lioness. He was frightened, and there was no one to see him; the boldest men yield to fear under such circumstances.

"No one but HE can know—or would dare—" he murmured to himself.

The mask clutched his hand tighter to prevent his finishing his sentence.

"Act as if I were *he*," he said.

Rastignac then acted like a millionaire on the highroad with a brigand's pistol at his head; he surrendered.

"My dear Count," said he to du Chatelet, to whom he presently returned, "if you care for your position in life, treat Lucien de Rubempre as a man whom you will one day see holding a place far above where you stand."

The mask made a imperceptible gesture of approbation, and went off in search of Lucien.

"My dear fellow, you have changed your opinion of him very suddenly," replied the Prefet with justifiable surprise.

"As suddenly as men change who belong to the centre and vote with the right," replied Rastignac to the Prefet-Depute, whose vote had for a few days failed to support the Ministry.

"Are there such things as opinions nowadays? There are only interests," observed des Lupeaulx, who had heard them. "What is the case in point?"

"The case of the Sieur de Rubempre, whom Rastignac is setting up as a person of consequence," said du Chatelet to the Secretary-General.

"My dear Count," replied des Lupeaulx very seriously, "Monsieur de Rubempre is a young man of the highest merit, and has such good interest at his back that I should be delighted to renew my acquaintance with him."

"There he is, rushing into the wasps' nest of the rakes of the day," said Rastignac.

THE THREE SPEAKERS LOOKED TOWARDS a corner where a group of recognized wits had gathered, men of more or less celebrity, and several men of fashion. These gentlemen made common stock of their jests, their remarks, and their scandal, trying to amuse themselves till something should amuse them. Among this strangely mingled party were some men with whom Lucien had had transactions, combining ostensibly kind offices with covert false dealing.

"Hallo! Lucien, my boy, why here we are patched up again—new stuffing and a new cover. Where have we come from? Have we mounted the high horse once more with little offerings from Florine's boudoir? Bravo, old chap!" and Blondet released Finot to put his arm affectionately around Lucien and press him to his heart.

Andoche Finot was the proprietor of a review on which Lucien had worked for almost nothing, and to which Blondet gave the benefit of his collaboration, of the wisdom of his suggestions and the depth of his views. Finot and Blondet embodied Bertrand and Raton, with this difference—that la Fontaine's cat at last showed that he knew himself to be duped, while Blondet, though he knew that he was being fleeced, still did all he could for Finot. This brilliant condottiere of the pen was, in fact, long to remain a slave. Finot hid a brutal strength of will under a heavy exterior, under polish of wit, as a laborer rubs his bread with garlic. He knew how to garner what he gleaned, ideas and crown-pieces alike, in the fields of the dissolute life led by men engaged in letters or in politics.

Blondet, for his sins, had placed his powers at the service of Finot's vices and idleness. Always at war with necessity, he was one of the race of poverty-stricken and superior men who can do everything for the fortune of others and nothing for their own, Aladdins who let other men borrow their lamp. These excellent advisers have a clear and penetrating judgment so long as it is not distracted by personal interest. In them it is the head and not the arm that acts. Hence the looseness of their morality, and hence the reproach heaped upon them by inferior minds. Blondet would share his purse with a comrade he had affronted the day before; he would dine, drink, and sleep with one whom he would demolish on the morrow. His amusing paradoxes excused everything. Accepting the whole world as a jest, he did not want to be taken seriously; young, beloved, almost famous and contented, he did not devote himself, like Finot, to acquiring the fortune an old man needs.

The most difficult form of courage, perhaps, is that which Lucien needed at this moment to get rid of Blondet as he had just got rid of Madame d'Espard and Chatelet. In him, unfortunately, the joys of vanity hindered the exercise of pride—the basis, beyond doubt, of many great things. His vanity had triumphed in the previous encounter; he had shown himself as a rich man, happy and scornful, to two persons who had scorned him when he was poor and wretched. But how could a poet, like an old diplomate, run the gauntlet with two self-styled friends, who had welcomed him in misery, under whose roof he had slept in the worst of his troubles? Finot, Blondet, and he had groveled together; they had wallowed in such orgies as consume something more than money. Like soldiers who find no market for their courage, Lucien had just done what many men do in Paris: he had still further compromised his character by shaking Finot's hand, and not rejecting Blondet's affection.

Every man who has dabbled, or still dabbles, in journalism is under the painful necessity of bowing to men he despises, of smiling at his dearest foe, of compounding the foulest meanness, of soiling his fingers to pay his aggressors in their own coin. He becomes used to seeing evil done, and passing it over; he begins by condoning it, and ends by committing it. In the long run the soul, constantly strained by shameful and perpetual compromise, sinks lower, the spring of noble thoughts grows rusty, the hinges of familiarity wear easy, and turn of their own accord. Alceste becomes Philinte, natures lose their firmness, talents are perverted, faith in great deeds evaporates. The man who yearned to be proud of his work wastes himself in rubbishy articles which his conscience regards, sooner or later, as so many evil actions. He started, like Lousteau or Vernou, to be a great writer; he finds himself a feeble scrivener. Hence it is impossible to honor too highly men whose character stands as high as their talent—men like d'Arthez, who know how to walk surefooted across the reefs of literary life.

Lucien could make no reply to Blondet's flattery; his wit had an irresistible charm for him, and he maintained the hold of the corrupter over his pupil; besides, he held a position in the world through his connection with the Comtesse de Montcornet.

"Has an uncle left you a fortune?" said Finot, laughing at him.

"Like you, I have marked some fools for cutting down," replied Lucien in the same tone.

"Then Monsieur has a review—a newspaper of his own?" Andoche Finot retorted, with the impertinent presumption of a chief to a subordinate.

"I have something better," replied Lucien, whose vanity, nettled by the assumed superiority of his editor, restored him to the sense of his new position.

"What is that, my dear boy?"

"I have a party."

"There is a Lucien party?" said Vernou, smiling

"Finot, the boy has left you in the lurch; I told you he would. Lucien is a clever fellow, and you never were respectful to him. You used him as a hack. Repent, blockhead!" said Blondet.

Blondet, as sharp as a needle, could detect more than one secret in Lucien's air and manner; while stroking him down, he contrived to tighten the curb. He meant to know the reasons of Lucien's return to Paris, his projects, and his means of living.

"On your knees to a superiority you can never attain to, albeit you are Finot!" he went on. "Admit this gentleman forthwith to be one of the great men to whom the future belongs; he is one of us! So witty and so handsome, can he fail to succeed by your quibuscumque viis? Here he stands, in his good Milan armor, his strong sword half unsheathed, and his pennon flying!—Bless me, Lucien, where did you steal that smart waistcoat? Love alone can find such stuff as that. Have you an address? At this moment I am anxious to know where my friends are domiciled; I don't know where to sleep. Finot has turned me out of doors for the night, under the vulgar pretext of 'a lady in the case.'"

"My boy," said Lucien, "I put into practice a motto by which you may secure a quiet life: Fuge, late, tace. I am off."

"But I am not off till you pay me a sacred debt—that little supper, you know, heh?" said Blondet, who was rather too much given to good cheer, and got himself treated when he was out of funds.

"What supper?" asked Lucien with a little stamp of impatience.

"You don't remember? In that I recognize my prosperous friend; he has lost his memory."

"He knows what he owes us; I will go bail for his good heart," said Finot, taking up Blondet's joke.

"Rastignac," said Blondet, taking the young dandy by the arm as he came up the room to the column where the so-called friends were standing. "There is a supper in the wind; you will join us—unless," he added gravely, turning to Lucien, "Monsieur persists in ignoring a debt of honor. He can."

"Monsieur de Rubempre is incapable of such a thing; I will answer for him," said Rastignac, who never dreamed of a practical joke.

"And there is Bixiou, he will come too," cried Blondet; "there is no fun without him. Without him champagne cloys my tongue, and I find everything insipid, even the pepper of satire."

"My friends," said Bixiou, "I see you have gathered round the wonder of the day. Our dear Lucien has revived the Metamorphoses of Ovid. Just as the gods used to turn into strange vegetables and other things to seduce the ladies, he has turned the Chardon (the Thistle) into a gentleman to bewitch—whom? Charles X!—My dear boy," he went on, holding Lucien by his coat button, "a journalist who apes the fine gentleman deserves rough music. In their place," said the merciless jester, as he pointed to Finot and Vernou, "I should take you up in my society paper; you would bring in a hundred francs for ten columns of fun."

"Bixiou," said Blondet, "an Amphitryon is sacred for twenty-four hours before a feast and twelve hours after. Our illustrious friend is giving us a supper."

"What then!" cried Bixiou; "what is more imperative than the duty of saving a great name from oblivion, of endowing the indigent aristocracy with a man of talent? Lucien, you enjoy the esteem of the press of which you were a distinguished ornament, and we will give you our support.—Finot, a paragraph in the 'latest items'!—Blondet, a little butter on the fourth page of your paper!—We must advertise the appearance of one of the finest books of the age, *l'Archer de Charles IX*! We will appeal to Dauriat to bring out as soon as possible *les Marguerites*, those divine sonnets by the French Petrarch! We must carry our friend through on the shield of stamped paper by which reputations are made and unmade."

"If you want a supper," said Lucien to Blondet, hoping to rid himself of this mob, which threatened to increase, "it seems to me that you need not work up hyperbole and parable to attack an old friend as if he were a booby. To-morrow night at Lointier's—" he cried, seeing a woman come by, whom he rushed to meet.

"Oh! oh! oh!" said Bixiou on three notes, with a mocking glance, and seeming to recognize the mask to whom Lucien addressed himself. "This needs confirmation."

He followed the handsome pair, got past them, examined them keenly, and came back, to the great satisfaction of all the envious crowd, who were eager to learn the source of Lucien's change of fortune.

"Friends," said Bixiou, "you have long known the goddess of the Sire de Rubempré's fortune: She is des Lupeaulx's former 'rat.'"

A form of dissipation, now forgotten, but still customary at the beginning of this century, was the keeping of "rats." The "rat"—a slang word that has become old-fashioned—was a girl of ten or twelve in the chorus of some theatre, more particularly at the opera, who was trained by young roués to vice and infamy. A "rat" was a sort of demon page, a tomboy who was forgiven a trick if it were but funny. The "rat" might take what she pleased; she was to be watched like a dangerous animal, and she brought an element of liveliness into life, like Scapin, Sganarelle, and Frontin in old-fashioned comedy. But a "rat" was too expensive; it made no return in honor, profit, or pleasure; the fashion of rats so completely went out, that in these days few people knew anything of this detail of fashionable life before the Restoration till certain writers took up the "rat" as a new subject.

"What! after having seen Coralie killed under him, Lucien means to rob us of La Torpille?" (the torpedo fish) said Blondet.

As he heard the name the brawny mask gave a significant start, which, though repressed, was understood by Rastignac.

"It is out of the question," replied Finot; "La Torpille has not a sou to give away; Nathan tells me she borrowed a thousand francs of Florine."

"Come, gentlemen, gentlemen!" said Rastignac, anxious to defend Lucien against so odious an imputation.

"Well," cried Vernou, "is Coralie's kept man likely to be so very particular?"

"Oh!" replied Bixiou, "those thousand francs prove to me that our friend Lucien lives with La Torpille—"

"What an irreparable loss to literature, science, art, and politics!" exclaimed Blondet. "La Torpille is the only common prostitute in whom I ever found the stuff for a superior courtesan; she has not been spoiled by education—she can neither read nor write, she would have understood us. We might have given to our era one of those magnificent Aspasias without which there can be no golden age. See how admirably Madame du Barry was suited to the eighteenth century, Ninon de l'Enclos to the seventeenth, Marion Delorme to the sixteenth, Imperia to the fifteenth, Flora to Republican Rome, which she made her heir, and which paid off the public debt with her fortune! What would Horace be without Lydia, Tibullus without Delia, Catullus without Lesbia, Propertius without Cynthia, Demetrius without Lamia, who is his glory at this day?"

"Blondet talking of Demetrius in the opera house seems to me rather too strong of the *Debats*," said Bixiou in his neighbor's ears.

"And where would the empire of the Caesars have been but for these queens?" Blondet went on; "Lais and Rhodope are Greece and Egypt. They all indeed are the poetry of the ages in which they lived. This poetry, which Napoleon lacked—for the Widow of his Great Army is a barrack jest, was not wanting to the Revolution; it had Madame Tallien! In these days there is certainly a throne to let in France which is for her who can fill it. We among us could make a queen. I should have given La Torpille an aunt, for her mother is too decidedly dead on the field of dishonor; du Tillet would have given her a mansion, Lousteau a carriage, Rastignac her footmen, des Lupeaulx a cook, Finot her hats"—Finot could not suppress a shrug at standing the point-blank fire of this epigram—"Vernou would have composed her advertisements, and Bixiou her repartees! The aristocracy would have come to enjoy themselves with our Ninon, where we would have got artists together, under pain of death by newspaper articles. Ninon the second would have been magnificently impertinent, overwhelming in luxury. She would have set up opinions. Some prohibited dramatic masterpiece should have been read in her drawing-room; it should have been written on purpose if necessary. She would not have been liberal; a courtesan is essentially monarchical. Oh, what a loss! She ought to have embraced her whole century, and she makes love with a little young man! Lucien will make a sort of hunting-dog of her."

"None of the female powers of whom you speak ever trudged the streets," said Finot, "and that pretty little 'rat' has rolled in the mire."

"Like a lily-seed in the soil," replied Vernou, "and she has improved in it and flowered. Hence her superiority. Must we not have known everything to be able to create the laughter and joy which are part of everything?"

"He is right," said Lousteau, who had hitherto listened without speaking; "La Torpille can laugh and make others laugh. That gift of all great writers and great actors is proper to those who have investigated every social deep. At eighteen that girl had already known the greatest wealth, the most squalid misery—men of every degree. She bears about her a sort of magic wand by which she lets loose the brutal appetites so vehemently suppressed in men who still have a heart while occupied with politics or science, literature or art. There is not in Paris another woman who can say to the beast as she does: 'Come out!' And the beast leaves his lair and wallows in excesses. She feeds you up to the chin, she helps you to drink and smoke. In short, this woman is the salt of which Rabelais writes, which, thrown on matter, animates it and elevates it to the marvelous realms of art; her robe displays unimagined splendor, her fingers drop gems as her lips shed smiles; she gives the spirit of the occasion to every little thing; her chatter twinkles with bright sayings, she has the secret of the quaintest onomatopoeia, full of color, and giving color; she—"

"You are wasting five francs' worth of copy," said Bixiou, interrupting Lousteau. "La Torpille is something far better than all that; you have all been in love with her more or less, not one of you can say that she ever was his mistress. She can always command you; you will never command her. You may force your way in and ask her to do you a service—"

"Oh, she is more generous than a brigand chief who knows his business, and more devoted than the best of school-fellows," said Blondet. "You may trust her with your purse or your secrets. But what made me choose her as queen is her Bourbon-like indifference for a fallen favorite."

"She, like her mother, is much too dear," said des Lupeaulx. "The handsome Dutch woman would have swallowed up the income of the Archbishop of Toledo; she ate two notaries out of house and home—"

"And kept Maxime de Trailles when he was a court page," said Bixiou.

"La Torpille is too dear, as Raphael was, or Careme, or Taglioni, or Lawrence, or Boule, or any artist of genius is too dear," said Blondet.

"Esther never looked so thoroughly a lady," said Rastignac, pointing to the masked figure to whom Lucien had given his arm. "I will bet on its being Madame de Serizy."

"Not a doubt of it," cried du Chatelet, "and Monsieur du Rubempre's fortune is accounted for."

"Ah, the Church knows how to choose its Levites; what a sweet ambassador's secretary he will make!" remarked des Lupeaulx.

"All the more so," Rastignac went on, "because Lucien is a really clever fellow. These gentlemen have had proof of it more than once," and he turned to Blondet, Finot, and Lousteau.

"Yes, the boy is cut out of the right stuff to get on," said Lousteau, who was dying of jealousy. "And particularly because he has what we call independent ideas. . ."

"It is you who trained him," said Vernou.

"Well," replied Bixiou, looking at des Lupeaulx, "I trust to the memory of Monsieur the Secretary-General and Master of Appeals—that mask is La Torpille, and I will stand a supper on it."

"I will hold the stakes," said du Chatelet, curious to know the truth.

"Come, des Lupeaulx," said Finot, "try to identify your rat's ears."

"There is no need for committing the crime of treason against a mask," replied Bixiou. "La Torpille and Lucien must pass us as they go up the room again, and I pledge myself to prove that it is she."

"So our friend Lucien has come above water once more," said Nathan, joining the group. "I thought he had gone back to Angoumois for the rest of his days. Has he discovered some secret to ruin the English?"

"He has done what you will not do in a hurry," retorted Rastignac; "he has paid up."

The burly mask nodded in confirmation.

"A man who has sown his wild oats at his age puts himself out of court. He has no pluck; he puts money in the funds," replied Nathan.

"Oh, that youngster will always be a fine gentleman, and will always have such lofty notions as will place him far above many men who think themselves his betters," replied Rastignac.

At this moment journalists, dandies, and idlers were all examining the charming subject of their bet as horse-dealers examine a horse for sale. These connoisseurs, grown old in familiarity with every form of Parisian depravity, all men of superior talent each his own way, equally corrupt, equally corrupting, all given over to unbridled ambition, accustomed to assume and to guess everything, had their eyes centered on a masked woman, a woman whom no one else could identify. They, and certain habitual frequenters of the opera balls, could alone recognize under the long shroud of the black domino, the hood and falling ruff which make the wearer unrecognizable, the rounded form, the individuality of figure and gait, the sway of the waist, the carriage of the head—the most intangible trifles to ordinary eyes, but to them the easiest to discern.

In spite of this shapeless wrapper they could watch the most appealing of dramas, that of a woman inspired by a genuine passion. Were she La Torpille, the Duchesse de Maufrigneuse, or Madame de

Serizy, on the lowest or highest rung of the social ladder, this woman was an exquisite creature, a flash from happy dreams. These old young men, like these young old men, felt so keen an emotion, that they envied Lucien the splendid privilege of working such a metamorphosis of a woman into a goddess. The mask was there as though she had been alone with Lucien; for that woman the thousand other persons did not exist, nor the evil and dust-laden atmosphere; no, she moved under the celestial vault of love, as Raphael's Madonnas under their slender oval glory. She did not feel herself elbowed; the fire of her glance shot from the holes in her mask and sank into Lucien's eyes; the thrill of her frame seemed to answer to every movement of her companion. Whence comes this flame that radiates from a woman in love and distinguishes her above all others? Whence that sylph-like lightness which seems to negative the laws of gravitation? Is the soul become ambient? Has happiness a physical effluence?

The ingenuousness of a girl, the graces of a child were discernible under the domino. Though they walked apart, these two beings suggested the figures of Flora and Zephyr as we see them grouped by the cleverest sculptors; but they were beyond sculpture, the greatest of the arts; Lucien and his pretty domino were more like the angels busied with flowers or birds, which Gian Bellini has placed beneath the effigies of the Virgin Mother. Lucien and this girl belonged to the realm of fancy, which is as far above art as cause is above effect.

When the domino, forgetful of everything, was within a yard of the group, Bixiou exclaimed:

"Esther!"

The unhappy girl turned her head quickly at hearing herself called, recognized the mischievous speaker, and bowed her head like a dying creature that has drawn its last breath.

A sharp laugh followed, and the group of men melted among the crowd like a knot of frightened field-rats whisking into their holes by the roadside. Rastignac alone went no further than was necessary, just to avoid making any show of shunning Lucien's flashing eye. He could thus note two phases of distress equally deep though unconfessed; first, the hapless Torpille, stricken as by a lightning stroke, and then the inscrutable mask, the only one of the group who had remained. Esther murmured a word in Lucien's ear just as her knees gave way, and Lucien, supporting her, led her away.

Rastignac watched the pretty pair, lost in meditation.

"How did she get her name of La Torpille?" asked a gloomy voice that struck to his vitals, for it was no longer disguised.

"*He* again—he has made his escape!" muttered Rastignac to himself.

"Be silent or I murder you," replied the mask, changing his voice. "I am satisfied with you, you have kept your word, and there is more than one arm ready to serve you. Henceforth be as silent as the grave; but, before that, answer my question."

"Well, the girl is such a witch that she could have magnetized the Emperor Napoleon; she could magnetize a man more difficult to influence—you yourself," replied Rastignac, and he turned to go.

"One moment," said the mask; "I will prove to you that you have never seen me anywhere."

The speaker took his mask off; for a moment Rastignac hesitated, recognizing nothing of the hideous being he had known formerly at Madame Vauquer's.

"The devil has enabled you to change in every particular, excepting your eyes, which it is impossible to forget," said he.

The iron hand gripped his arm to enjoin eternal secrecy.

At three in the morning des Lupeaulx and Finot found the elegant Rastignac on the same spot, leaning against the column where the terrible mask had left him. Rastignac had confessed to himself; he had been at once priest and pentient, culprit and judge. He allowed himself to be led away to breakfast, and reached home perfectly tipsy, but taciturn.

THE RUE DE LANGLADE AND the adjacent streets are a blot on the Palais Royal and the Rue de Rivoli. This portion of one of the handsomest quarters of Paris will long retain the stain of foulness left by the hillocks formed of the middens of old Paris, on which mills formerly stood. These narrow streets, dark and muddy, where such industries are carried on as care little for appearances wear at night an aspect of mystery full of contrasts. On coming from the well-lighted regions of the Rue Saint-Honore, the Rue Neuve-des-Petits-Champs, and the Rue de Richelieu, where the crowd is constantly pushing, where glitter the masterpieces of industry, fashion, and art, every man to whom Paris by night is unknown would feel a sense of dread and melancholy, on finding himself in the labyrinth of little streets which lie round that blaze of light reflected even from the sky. Dense blackness is here, instead of floods of gaslight; a dim oil-lamp here and there sheds its doubtful and smoky gleam, and many blind alleys are not lighted at all. Foot passengers are few, and walk fast. The shops are shut, the few that are open are of a squalid kind; a dirty, unlighted wineshop, or a seller of underclothing and eau-de-Cologne. An unwholesome chill lays a clammy cloak over your shoulders. Few carriages drive past. There are sinister places here, especially the Rue de Langlade, the entrance to the Passage Saint-Guillaume, and the turnings of some streets.

The municipal council has not yet been to purge this vast lazar-place, for prostitution long since made it its headquarters. It is, perhaps, a good thing for Paris that these alleys should be allowed to preserve their filthy aspect. Passing through them by day, it is impossible to imagine what they become by night; they are pervaded by strange creatures of no known world; white, half-naked forms cling to the walls—the darkness is alive. Between the passenger and the wall a dress steals by—a dress that moves and speaks. Half-open doors suddenly shout with laughter. Words fall on the ear such as Rabelais speaks of as frozen and melting. Snatches of songs come up from the pavement. The noise is not vague; it means something. When it is hoarse it is a voice; but if it suggests a song, there is nothing human about it, it is more like a croak. Often you hear a sharp whistle, and then the tap of boot-heels has a peculiarly aggressive and mocking ring. This medley of things makes you giddy. Atmospheric conditions are reversed there—it is warm in winter and cool in summer.

Still, whatever the weather, this strange world always wears the same aspect; it is the fantastic world of Hoffmann of Berlin. The most mathematical of clerks never thinks of it as real, after returning through the straits that lead into decent streets, where there are passengers, shops, and taverns. Modern administration, or modern policy, more scornful or more shamefaced than the queens and kings of past ages, no longer dare look boldly in the face of this plague of our capitals. Measures, of course, must change with the times, and such as bear on individuals and on their liberty are a ticklish matter; still, we ought, perhaps, to show some breadth and boldness as to merely material measures—air, light, and construction. The moralist, the artist, and the sage administrator alike must regret the old wooden galleries of the Palais Royal, where the lambs were to be seen who will always be found where there are loungers; and is it not best that the loungers should go where they are to be found? What is the consequence? The gayest parts of the Boulevards, that delightfulest of promenades, are impossible in the evening for a family party. The police has failed to take advantage of the outlet afforded by some small streets to purge the main street.

The girl whom we have seen crushed by a word at the opera ball had been for the last month or two living in the Rue de Langlade, in a very poor-looking house. This structure, stuck on to the wall of an enormously large one, badly stuccoed, of no depth, and immensely high, has all its windows on the street, and bears some resemblance to a parrot's perch. On each floor are two rooms, let as separate flats. There is a narrow staircase clinging to the wall, queerly lighted by windows which mark its ascent on the outer wall, each landing being indicated by a stink, one of the most odious peculiarities of Paris. The shop and entresol at that time were tenanted by a tinman; the landlord occupied the first floor; the four upper stories were rented by very decent working girls, who were treated by the portress and the proprietor with some consideration and an obligingness called forth by the difficulty of letting a house so oddly constructed and situated. The occupants of the quarter are accounted for by the existence there of many houses of the same character, for which trade has no use, and which can only be rented by the poorer kinds of industry, of a precarious or ignominious nature.

At three in the afternoon the portress, who had seen Mademoiselle Esther brought home half dead by a young man at two in the morning, had just held council with the young woman of the floor above, who, before setting out in a cab to join some party of pleasure, had expressed her uneasiness about Esther; she had not heard her move. Esther was, no doubt, still asleep, but this slumber seemed suspicious. The portress, alone in her cell, was regretting that she could not go to see what was happening on the fourth floor, where Mademoiselle Esther lodged.

Just as she had made up her mind to leave the tinman's son in charge of her room, a sort of den in a recess on the entresol floor, a cab stopped at the door. A man stepped out, wrapped from head to foot in a cloak evidently intended to conceal his dress or his rank in life, and asked for Mademoiselle Esther. The portress at one felt relieved; this accounted for Esther's silence and quietude. As the stranger mounted the stairs above the portress' room, she noticed silver buckles in his shoes, and fancied she caught sight of the black fringe of a priest's sash; she went downstairs and catechised the driver, who answered without speech, and again the woman understood.

The priest knocked, received no answer, heard a slight gasp, and forced the door open with a thrust of his shoulder; charity, no doubt lent him strength, but in any one else it would have been ascribed to practice. He rushed to the inner room, and there found poor Esther in front of an image of the Virgin in painted plaster, kneeling, or rather doubled up, on the floor, her hands folded. The girl was dying. A brazier of burnt charcoal told the tale of that dreadful morning. The domino cloak and hood were lying on the ground. The bed was undisturbed. The unhappy creature, stricken to the heart by a mortal thrust, had, no doubt, made all her arrangements on her return from the opera. A candle-wick, collapsed in the pool of grease that filled the candle-sconce, showed how completely her last meditations had absorbed her. A handkerchief soaked with tears proved the sincerity of the Magdalen's despair, while her classic attitude was that of the irreligious courtesan. This abject repentance made the priest smile.

Esther, unskilled in dying, had left the door open, not thinking that the air of two rooms would need a larger amount of charcoal to make it suffocating; she was only stunned by the fumes; the fresh air from the staircase gradually restored her to a consciousness of her woes.

The priest remained standing, lost in gloomy meditation, without being touched by the girl's divine beauty, watching her first movements as if she had been some animal. His eyes went from the crouching figure to the surrounding objects with evident indifference. He looked at the furniture in the room; the paved floor, red, polished, and cold, was poorly covered with a shabby carpet worn to the string. A little bedstead, of painted wood and old-fashioned shape, was hung with yellow cotton printed with red stars, one armchair and two small chairs, also of painted wood, and covered with the same cotton print of which the window-curtains were also made; a gray wall-paper sprigged with flowers blackened and greasy with age; a fireplace full of kitchen utensils of the vilest kind, two bundles of fire-logs; a stone shelf, on which lay some jewelry false and real, a pair of scissors, a dirty pincushion, and some white scented gloves; an exquisite hat perched on the water-jug, a Ternaux shawl stopping a hole in the window, a handsome gown hanging from a nail; a little hard sofa, with no cushions; broken clogs and dainty slippers, boots that a queen might have coveted; cheap china plates, cracked or chipped, with fragments of a past meal, and nickel forks—the plate of the Paris poor; a basket full of potatoes and dirty linen, with a smart gauze cap on the top; a rickety wardrobe, with a glass door, open and empty, and on the shelves sundry pawn-tickets,—this was the medley of things, dismal or pleasing, abject and handsome, that fell on his eye.

These relics of splendor among the potsherds, these household belongings—so appropriate to the bohemian existence of the girl who knelt stricken in her unbuttoned garments, like a horse dying in harness under the broken shafts entangled in the reins—did the whole strange scene suggest any thoughts to the priest? Did he say to himself that this erring creature must at least be disinterested to live in such poverty when her lover was young and rich? Did he ascribe the disorder of the room to the disorder of her life? Did he feel pity or terror? Was his charity moved?

To see him, his arms folded, his brow dark, his lips set, his eye harsh, any one must have supposed him absorbed in morose feelings of hatred, considerations that jostled each other, sinister schemes. He was certainly insensible to the soft roundness of a bosom almost crushed under the weight of the bowed shoulders, and to the beautiful modeling of the crouching Venus that was visible under the black petticoat, so closely was the dying girl curled up. The drooping head which, seen from behind, showed the white, slender, flexible neck and the fine shoulders of a well-developed figure, did not appeal to him. He did not raise Esther, he did not seem to hear the agonizing gasps which showed that she was returning to life; a fearful sob and a terrifying glance from the girl were needed before he condescended to lift her, and he carried her to the bed with an ease that revealed enormous strength.

"Lucien!" she murmured.

"Love is there, the woman is not far behind," said the priest with some bitterness.

The victim of Parisian depravity then observed the dress worn by her deliverer, and said, with a smile like a child's when it takes possession of something longed for:

"Then I shall not die without being reconciled to Heaven?"

"You may yet expiate your sins," said the priest, moistening her forehead with water, and making her smell at a cruet of vinegar he found in a corner.

"I feel that life, instead of departing, is rushing in on me," said she, after accepting the Father's care and expressing her gratitude by simple gestures. This engaging pantomime, such as the Graces might have used to charm, perfectly justified the nickname given to this strange girl.

"Do you feel better?" said the priest, giving her a glass of sugar and water to drink.

This man seemed accustomed to such queer establishments; he knew all about it. He was quite at home there. This privilege of being everywhere at home is the prerogative of kings, courtesans, and thieves.

"When you feel quite well," this strange priest went on after a pause, "you must tell me the reasons which prompted you to commit this last crime, this attempted suicide."

"My story is very simple, Father," replied she. "Three months ago I was living the evil life to which I was born. I was the lowest and vilest of creatures; now I am only the most unhappy. Excuse me from telling you the history of my poor mother, who was murdered—"

"By a Captain, in a house of ill-fame," said the priest, interrupting the penitent. "I know your origin, and I know that if a being of your sex can ever be excused for leading a life of shame, it is you, who have always lacked good examples."

"Alas! I was never baptized, and have no religious teaching."

"All may yet be remedied then," replied the priest, "provided that your faith, your repentance, are sincere and without ulterior motive."

"Lucien and God fill my heart," said she with ingenuous pathos.

"You might have said God and Lucien," answered the priest, smiling. "You remind me of the purpose of my visit. Omit nothing that concerns that young man."

"You have come from him?" she asked, with a tender look that would have touched any other priest! "Oh, he thought I should do it!"

"No," replied the priest; "it is not your death, but your life that we are interested in. Come, explain your position toward each other."

"In one word," said she.

The poor child quaked at the priest's stern tone, but as a woman quakes who has long ceased to be surprised at brutality.

"Lucien is Lucien," said she, "the handsomest young man, the kindest soul alive; if you know him, my love must seem to you quite natural. I met him by chance, three months ago, at the Porte-Saint-Martin theatre, where I went one day when I had leave, for we had a day a week at Madame Meynardie's, where I then was. Next day, you understand, I went out without leave. Love had come into my heart, and had so completely changed me, that on my return from the theatre I did not know myself: I had a horror of myself. Lucien would never have known. Instead of telling him what I was, I gave him my address at these rooms, where a friend of mine was then living, who was so kind as to give them up to me. I swear on my sacred word—"

"You must not swear."

"Is it swearing to give your sacred word?—Well, from that day I have worked in this room like a lost creature at shirt-making at twenty-eight sous apiece, so as to live by honest labor. For a month I have had nothing to eat but potatoes, that I might keep myself a good girl and worthy of Lucien, who loves me and respects me as a pattern of virtue. I have made my declaration before the police to recover my rights, and submitted to two years' surveillance. They are ready enough to enter your name on the lists of disgrace, but make every difficulty about scratching it out again. All I asked of Heaven was to enable me to keep my resolution.

"I shall be nineteen in the month of April; at my age there is still a chance. It seems to me that I was never born till three months ago.—I prayed to God every morning that Lucien might never know what my former life had been. I bought that Virgin you see there, and I prayed to her in my own way, for I do not know any prayers; I cannot read nor write, and I have never been into a church; I have never seen anything of God excepting in processions, out of curiosity."

"And what do you say to the Virgin?"

"I talk to her as I talk to Lucien, with all my soul, till I make him cry."

"Oh, so he cries?"

"With joy," said she eagerly, "poor dear boy! We understand each other so well that we have but one soul! He is so nice, so fond, so sweet in heart and mind and manners! He says he is a poet; I say he is god.—Forgive me! You priests, you see, don't know what love is. But, in fact, only girls like me know enough of men to appreciate such as Lucien. A Lucien, you see, is as rare as a woman without sin. When you come across him you can love no one else; so there! But such a being must have his fellow; so I want to be worthy to be loved by my Lucien. That is where my trouble began. Last evening, at the opera, I was recognized by some young men who have no more feeling than a tiger has pity—for that matter, I could come round the tiger! The veil of innocence I had tried to wear was worn off; their laughter pierced my brain and my heart. Do not think you have saved me; I shall die of grief."

"Your veil of innocence?" said the priest. "Then you have treated Lucien with the sternest severity?"

"Oh, Father, how can you, who know him, ask me such a question!" she replied with a smile. "Who can resist a god?"

"Do not be blasphemous," said the priest mildly. "No one can be like God. Exaggeration is out of place with true love; you had not a pure and genuine love for your idol. If you had undergone the conversion you boast of having felt, you would have acquired the virtues which are a part of womanhood; you would have known the charm of chastity, the refinements of modesty, the two virtues that are the glory of a maiden.—You do not love."

Esther's gesture of horror was seen by the priest, but it had no effect on the impassibility of her confessor.

"Yes; for you love him for yourself and not for himself, for the temporal enjoyments that delight you, and not for love itself. If he has thus taken possession of you, you cannot have felt that sacred thrill that is inspired by a being on whom God has set the seal of the most adorable perfections. Has it never occurred to you that you would degrade him by your past impurity, that you would corrupt a child by the overpowering seductions which earned you your nickname glorious in infamy? You have been illogical with yourself, and your passion of a day—"

"Of a day?" she repeated, raising her eyes.

"By what other name can you call a love that is not eternal, that does not unite us in the future life of the Christian, to the being we love?"

"Ah, I will be a Catholic!" she cried in a hollow, vehement tone, that would have earned her the mercy of the Lord.

"Can a girl who has received neither the baptism of the Church nor that of knowledge; who can neither read, nor write, nor pray; who cannot take a step without the stones in the street rising up to accuse her; noteworthy only for the fugitive gift of beauty which sickness may destroy to-morrow; can such a vile, degraded creature, fully aware too of her degradation—for if you had been ignorant of it and less devoted, you would have been more excusable—can the intended victim to suicide and hell hope to be the wife of Lucien de Rubempre?"

Every word was a poniard thrust piercing the depths of her heart. At every word the louder sobs and abundant tears of the desperate girl showed the power with which light had flashed upon an intelligence as pure as that of a savage, upon a soul at length aroused, upon a nature over which depravity had laid a sheet of foul ice now thawed in the sunshine of faith.

"Why did I not die!" was the only thought that found utterance in the midst of a torrent of ideas that racked and ravaged her brain.

"My daughter," said the terrible judge, "there is a love which is unconfessed before men, but of which the secret is received by the angels with smiles of gladness."

HONORÉ DE BALZAC

"What is that?"

"Love without hope, when it inspires our life, when it fills us with the spirit of sacrifice, when it ennobles every act by the thought of reaching some ideal perfection. Yes, the angels approve of such love; it leads to the knowledge of God. To aim at perfection in order to be worthy of the one you love, to make for him a thousand secret sacrifices, adoring him from afar, giving your blood drop by drop, abnegating your self-love, never feeling any pride or anger as regards him, even concealing from him all knowledge of the dreadful jealousy he fires in your heart, giving him all he wishes were it to your own loss, loving what he loves, always turning your face to him to follow him without his knowing it—such love as that religion would have forgiven; it is no offence to laws human or divine, and would have led you into another road than that of your foul voluptuousness."

As she heard this horrible verdict, uttered in a word—and such a word! and spoken in such a tone!—Esther's spirit rose up in fairly legitimate distrust. This word was like a thunder-clap giving warning of a storm about to break. She looked at the priest, and felt the grip on her vitals which wrings the bravest when face to face with sudden and imminent danger. No eye could have read what was passing in this man's mind; but the boldest would have found more to quail at than to hope for in the expression of his eyes, once bright and yellow like those of a tiger, but now shrouded, from austerities and privations, with a haze like that which overhangs the horizon in the dog-days, when, though the earth is hot and luminous, the mist makes it indistinct and dim—almost invisible.

The gravity of a Spaniard, the deep furrows which the myriad scars of virulent smallpox made hideously like broken ruts, were ploughed into his face, which was sallow and tanned by the sun. The hardness of this countenance was all the more conspicuous, being framed in the meagre dry wig of a priest who takes no care of his person, a black wig looking rusty in the light. His athletic frame, his hands like an old soldier's, his broad, strong shoulders were those of the Caryatides which the architects of the Middle Ages introduced into some Italian palaces, remotely imitated in those of the front of the Porte-Saint-Martin theatre. The least clear-sighted observer might have seen that fiery passions or some unwonted accident must have thrown this man into the bosom of the Church; certainly none but the most tremendous shocks of lightning could have changed him, if indeed such a nature were susceptible of change.

Women who have lived the life that Esther had so violently repudiated come to feel absolute indifference as to the critics of our day, who may be compared with them in some respects, and who feel at last perfect disregard of the formulas of art; they have read so many books, they see so many pass away, they are so much accustomed to written pages, they have gone through so many plots, they have seen so many dramas, they have written so many articles without saying what they meant, and have so often been treasonable to the cause of Art in favor of their personal likings and aversions, that they acquire a feeling of disgust of everything, and yet continue to pass judgment. It needs a miracle to make such a writer produce sound work, just as it needs another miracle to give birth to pure and noble love in the heart of a courtesan.

The tone and manner of this priest, who seemed to have escaped from a picture by Zurbaran, struck this poor girl as so hostile, little as externals affected her, that she perceived herself to be less the object of his solitude than the instrument he needed for some scheme. Being unable to distinguish between the insinuating tongue of personal interest and the unction of true charity, for we must be acutely awake to recognize false coin when it is offered by a friend, she felt herself, as it were, in the talons of some fierce and monstrous bird of prey who, after hovering over her for long, had pounced down on her; and in her terror she cried in a voice of alarm:

"I thought it was a priest's duty to console us, and you are killing me!"

At this innocent outcry the priest started and paused; he meditated a moment before replying. During that instant the two persons so strangely brought together studied each other cautiously. The priest understood the girl, though the girl could not understand the priest.

He, no doubt, put aside some plan which had threatened the unhappy Esther, and came back to his first ideas.

"We are physicians of the soul," said he, in a mild voice, "and we know what remedies suit their maladies."

"Much must be forgiven to the wretched," said Esther.

She fancied she had been wrong; she slipped off the bed, threw herself at the man's feet, kissed his gown with deep humility, and looked up at him with eyes full of tears.

"I thought I had done so much!" she said.

"Listen, my child. Your terrible reputation has cast Lucien's family into grief. They are afraid, and not without reason, that you may lead him into dissipation, into endless folly—"

"That is true; it was I who got him to the ball to mystify him."

"You are handsome enough to make him wish to triumph in you in the eyes of the world, to show you with pride, and make you an object for display. And if he wasted money only!—but he will waste his time, his powers; he will lose his inclination for the fine future his friends can secure to him. Instead of being some day an ambassador, rich, admired and triumphant, he, like so many debauchees who choke their talents in the mud of Paris, will have been the lover of a degraded woman.

"As for you, after rising for a time to the level of a sphere of elegance, you will presently sink back to your former life, for you have not in you the strength bestowed by a good education to enable you to resist vice and think of the future. You would no more be able to break with the women of your own class than you have broken with the men who shamed you at the opera this morning. Lucien's true friends, alarmed by his passion for you, have dogged his steps and know all. Filled with horror, they have sent me to you to sound your views and decide your fate; but though they are powerful enough to clear a stumbling-stone out of the young man's way, they are merciful. Understand this, child: a girl whom Lucien loves has claims on their regard, as a true Christian worships the slough on which, by chance, the divine light falls. I came to be the instrument of a beneficent purpose;—still, if I had found you utterly reprobate, armed with effrontery and astuteness, corrupt to the marrow, deaf to the voice of repentance, I should have abandoned you to their wrath.

"The release, civil and political, which it is so hard to win, which the police is so right to withhold for a time in the interests of society, and which I heard you long for with all the ardor of true repentance—is here," said the priest, taking an official-looking paper out of his belt. "You were seen yesterday, this letter of release is dated to-day. You see how powerful the people are who take an interest in Lucien."

At the sight of this document Esther was so ingenuously overcome by the convulsive agitation produced by unlooked-for joy, that a fixed smile parted her lips, like that of a crazy creature. The priest paused, looking at the girl to see whether, when once she had lost the horrible strength which corrupt natures find in corruption itself, and was thrown back on her frail and delicate primitive nature, she could endure so much excitement. If she had been a deceitful courtesan, Esther would have acted a part; but now that she was innocent and herself once more, she might perhaps die, as a blind man cured may lose his sight again if he is exposed to too bright a light. At this moment this man looked into the very depths of human nature, but his calmness was terrible in its rigidity; a cold alp, snow-bound and near to heaven, impenetrable and frowning, with flanks of granite, and yet beneficent.

Such women are essentially impressionable beings, passing without reason from the most idiotic distrust to absolute confidence. In this respect they are lower than animals. Extreme in everything—in their joy and despair, in their religion and irreligion—they would almost all go mad if they were not decimated by the mortality peculiar to their class, and if happy chances did not lift one now and then from the slough in which they dwell. To understand the very depths of the wretchedness of this horrible existence, one must know how far in madness a creature can go without remaining there, by studying La Torpille's violent ecstasy at the priest's feet. The poor girl gazed at the paper of release with an expression which Dante has overlooked, and which surpassed the inventiveness of his Inferno. But a reaction came with tears. Esther rose, threw her arms round the priest's neck, laid her head on his breast, which she wetted with her weeping, kissing the coarse stuff that covered that heart of steel as if she fain would touch it. She seized hold of him; she covered his hands with kisses; she poured out in a sacred effusion of gratitude her most coaxing caresses, lavished fond names on him, saying again and again in the midst of her honeyed words, "Let me have it!" in a thousand different tones of voice; she wrapped him in tenderness, covered him with her looks with a swiftness that found him defenceless; at last she charmed away his wrath.

The priest perceived how well the girl had deserved her nickname; he understood how difficult it was to resist this bewitching creature; he suddenly comprehended Lucien's love, and just what must have fascinated the poet. Such a passion hides among a thousand temptations a dart-like hook which is most apt to catch the lofty soul of an artist. These passions, inexplicable to the vulgar, are perfectly accounted for by the thirst for ideal beauty, which is characteristic of a creative mind. For are we not, in some degree, akin to the angels, whose task it is to bring the guilty to a better mind? are we not creative when we purify such a creature? How delightful it is to harmonize moral with physical beauty! What joy and pride if we succeed! How noble a task is that which has no instrument but love!

Such alliances, made famous by the example of Aristotle, Socrates, Plato, Alcibiades, Cethegus, and Pompey, and yet so monstrous in the eyes of the vulgar, are based on the same feeling that prompted Louis XIV to build Versailles, or that makes men rush into any ruinous enterprise—into converting the miasma of a marsh into a mass of fragrance surrounded by living waters; placing a lake at the top of a hill, as the Prince de Conti did at Nointel; or producing Swiss scenery at Cassan, like Bergeret, the farmer-general. In short, it is the application of art in the realm of morals.

The priest, ashamed of having yielded to this weakness, hastily pushed Esther away, and she sat down quite abashed, for he said:

"You are still the courtesan." And he calmly replaced the paper in his sash.

Esther, like a child who has a single wish in its head, kept her eyes fixed on the spot where the document lay hidden.

"My child," the priest went on after a pause, "your mother was a Jewess, and you have not been baptized; but, on the other hand, you have never been taken to the synagogue. You are in the limbo where little children are—"

"Little children!" she echoed, in a tenderly pathetic tone.

"As you are on the books of the police, a cipher outside the pale of social beings," the priest went on, unmoved. "If love, seen as it swept past, led you to believe three months since that you were then born, you must feel that since that day you have been really an infant. You must, therefore, be led as if you were a child; you must be completely changed, and I will undertake to make you unrecognizable. To begin with, you must forget Lucien."

The words crushed the poor girl's heart; she raised her eyes to the priest and shook her head; she could not speak, finding the executioner in the deliverer again.

"At any rate, you must give up seeing him," he went on. "I will take you to a religious house where young girls of the best families are educated; there you will become a Catholic, you will be trained in the practice of Christian exercises, you will be taught religion. You may come out an accomplished young lady, chaste, pure, well brought up, if—" The man lifted up a finger and paused.

"If," he went on, "you feel brave enough to leave the 'Torpille' behind you here."

"Ah!" cried the poor thing, to whom each word had been like a note of some melody to which the gates of Paradise were slowly opening. "Ah! if it were possible to shed all my blood here and have it renewed!"

"Listen to me."

She was silent.

"Your future fate depends on your power of forgetting. Think of the extent to which you pledge yourself. A word, a gesture, which betrays La Torpille will kill Lucien's wife. A word murmured in a dream, an involuntary thought, an immodest glance, a gesture of impatience, a reminiscence of dissipation, an omission, a shake of the head that might reveal what you know, or what is known about you for your woes—"

"Yes, yes, Father," said the girl, with the exaltation of a saint. "To walk in shoes of red-hot iron and smile, to live in a pair of stays set with nails and maintain the grace of a dancer, to eat bread salted with ashes, to drink wormwood,—all will be sweet and easy!"

She fell again on her knees, she kissed the priest's shoes, she melted into tears that wetted them, she clasped his knees, and clung to them, murmuring foolish words as she wept for joy. Her long and beautiful light hair waved to the ground, a sort of carpet under the feet of the celestial messenger, whom she saw as gloomy and hard as ever when she lifted herself up and looked at him.

"What have I done to offend you?" cried she, quite frightened. "I have heard of a woman, such as I am, who washed the feet of Jesus with perfumes. Alas! virtue has made me so poor that I have nothing but tears to offer you."

"Have you not understood?" he answered, in a cruel voice. "I tell you, you must be able to come out of the house to which I shall take you so completely changed, physically and morally, that no man or woman you have ever known will be able to call you 'Esther' and make you look round. Yesterday your love could not give you strength enough so completely to bury the prostitute that she could never reappear; and again to-day she revives in adoration which is due to none but God."

"Was it not He who sent you to me?" said she.

"If during the course of your education you should even see Lucien, all would be lost," he went on; "remember that."

"Who will comfort him?" said she.

"What was it that you comforted him for?" asked the priest, in a tone in which, for the first time during this scene, there was a nervous quaver.

"I do not know; he was often sad when he came."

"Sad!" said the priest. "Did he tell you why?"

"Never," answered she.

"He was sad at loving such a girl as you!" exclaimed he.

"Alas! and well he might be," said she, with deep humility. "I am the most despicable creature of my sex, and I could find favor in his eyes only by the greatness of my love."

"That love must give you the courage to obey me blindly. If I were to take you straight from hence to the house where you are to be educated, everybody here would tell Lucien that you had gone away to-day, Sunday, with a priest; he might follow in your tracks. In the course of a week, the portress, not seeing me again, might suppose me to be what I am not. So, one evening—this day week—at seven o'clock, go out quietly and get into a cab that will be waiting for you at the bottom of the Rue des Frondeurs. During this week avoid Lucien, find excuses, have him sent from the door, and if he should come in, go up to some friend's room. I shall know if you have seen him, and in that event all will be at an end. I shall not even come back. These eight days you will need to make up some suitable clothing and to hide your look of a prostitute," said he, laying a purse on the chimney-shelf. "There is something in your manner, in your clothes— something indefinable which is well known to Parisians, and proclaims you what you are. Have you never met in the streets or on the Boulevards a modest and virtuous girl walking with her mother?"

"Oh yes, to my sorrow! The sight of a mother and daughter is one of our most cruel punishments; it arouses the remorse that lurks in the innermost folds of our hearts, and that is consuming us.—I know too well all I lack."

"Well, then, you know how you should look next Sunday," said the priest, rising.

"Oh!" said she, "teach me one real prayer before you go, that I may pray to God."

It was a touching thing to see the priest making this girl repeat Ave *Maria* and *Paternoster* in French.

"That is very fine!" said Esther, when she had repeated these two grand and universal utterances of the Catholic faith without making a mistake.

"What is your name?" she asked the priest when he took leave of her.

"Carlos Herrera; I am a Spaniard banished from my country."

Esther took his hand and kissed it. She was no longer the courtesan; she was an angel rising after a fall.

IN A RELIGIOUS INSTITUTION, FAMOUS for the aristocratic and pious teaching imparted there, one Monday morning in the beginning of

March 1824 the pupils found their pretty flock increased by a newcomer, whose beauty triumphed without dispute not only over that of her companions, but over the special details of beauty which were found severally in perfection in each one of them. In France it is extremely rare, not to say impossible, to meet with the thirty points of perfection, described in Persian verse, and engraved, it is said, in the Seraglio, which are needed to make a woman absolutely beautiful. Though in France the whole is seldom seen, we find exquisite parts. As to that imposing union which sculpture tries to produce, and has produced in a few rare examples like the Diana and the Callipyge, it is the privileged possession of Greece and Asia Minor.

Esther came from that cradle of the human race; her mother was a Jewess. The Jews, though so often deteriorated by their contact with other nations, have, among their many races, families in which this sublime type of Asiatic beauty has been preserved. When they are not repulsively hideous, they present the splendid characteristics of Armenian beauty. Esther would have carried off the prize at the Seraglio; she had the thirty points harmoniously combined. Far from having damaged the finish of her modeling and the freshness of her flesh, her strange life had given her the mysterious charm of womanhood; it is no longer the close, waxy texture of green fruit and not yet the warm glow of maturity; there is still the scent of the flower. A few days longer spent in dissolute living, and she would have been too fat. This abundant health, this perfection of the animal in a being in whom voluptuousness took the place of thought, must be a remarkable fact in the eyes of physiologists. A circumstance so rare, that it may be called impossible in very young girls, was that her hands, incomparably fine in shape, were as soft, transparent, and white as those of a woman after the birth of her second child. She had exactly the hair and the foot for which the Duchesse de Berri was so famous, hair so thick that no hairdresser could gather it into his hand, and so long that it fell to the ground in rings; for Esther was of that medium height which makes a woman a sort of toy, to be taken up and set down, taken up again and carried without fatigue. Her skin, as fine as rice-paper, of a warm amber hue showing the purple veins, was satiny without dryness, soft without being clammy.

Esther, excessively strong though apparently fragile, arrested attention by one feature that is conspicuous in the faces in which Raphael has shown his most artistic feeling, for Raphael is the painter who has most studied and best rendered Jewish beauty. This remarkable effect was produced by the depth of the eye-socket, under which the eye moved free from its setting; the arch of the brow was so accurate as to resemble the groining of a vault. When youth lends this beautiful hollow its pure and diaphanous coloring, and edges it with closely-set eyebrows, when the light stealing into the circular cavity beneath lingers there with a rosy hue, there are tender treasures in it to delight a lover, beauties to drive a painter to despair. Those luminous curves, where the shadows have a golden tone, that tissue as firm as a sinew and as mobile as the most delicate membrane, is a crowning achievement of nature. The eye at rest within is like a miraculous egg in a nest of silken wings. But as time goes on this marvel acquires a dreadful melancholy, when passions have laid dark smears on those fine forms, when grief had furrowed that network of delicate veins. Esther's nationality proclaimed itself in this Oriental modeling of her eyes with their Turkish lids; their color was a slate-gray which by night took on the blue sheen of a raven's wing. It was only the extreme tenderness of her expression that could moderate their fire.

Only those races that are native to deserts have in the eye the power of fascinating everybody, for any woman can fascinate some one person. Their eyes preserve, no doubt, something of the infinitude they have gazed on. Has nature, in her foresight, armed their retina with some reflecting background to enable them to endure the mirage of the sand, the torrents of sunshine, and the burning cobalt of the sky? or, do human beings, like other creatures, derive something from the surroundings among which they grow up, and preserve for ages the qualities they have imbibed from them? The great solution of this problem of race lies perhaps in the question itself. Instincts are living facts, and their cause dwells in past necessity. Variety in animals is the result of the exercise of these instincts.

To convince ourselves of this long-sought-for truth, it is enough to extend to the herd of mankind the observation recently made on flocks of Spanish and English sheep which, in low meadows where pasture is abundant, feed side by side in close array, but on mountains, where grass is scarce, scatter apart. Take these two kinds of sheep, transfer them to Switzerland or France; the mountain breeds will feed apart even in a lowland meadow of thick grass, the lowland sheep will keep together even on an alp. Hardly will a succession of generations eliminate acquired and transmitted instincts. After a century the highland spirit reappears in a refractory lamb, just as, after eighteen centuries of exile, the spirit of the East shone in Esther's eyes and features.

Her look had no terrible fascination; it shed a mild warmth, it was pathetic without being startling, and the sternest wills were melted in its flame. Esther had conquered hatred, she had astonished the depraved souls of Paris; in short, that look and the softness of her skin had earned her the terrible nickname which had just led her to the verge of the grave. Everything about her was in harmony with these characteristics of the Peri of the burning sands. Her forehead was firmly and proudly molded. Her nose, like that of the Arab race, was delicate and narrow, with oval nostrils well set and open at the base. Her mouth, fresh and red, was a rose unblemished by a flaw, dissipation had left no trace there. Her chin, rounded as though some amorous sculptor had polished its fulness, was as white as milk. One thing only that she had not been able to remedy betrayed the courtesan fallen very low: her broken nails, which needed time to recover their shape, so much had they been spoiled by the vulgarest household tasks.

The young boarders began by being jealous of these marvels of beauty, but they ended by admiring them. Before the first week was at an end they were all attached to the artless Jewess, for they were interested in the unknown misfortunes of a girl of eighteen who could neither read nor write, to whom all knowledge and instruction were new, and who was to earn for the Archbishop the triumph of having converted a Jewess to Catholicism and giving the convent a festival in her baptism. They forgave her beauty, finding themselves her superiors in education.

Esther very soon caught the manners, the accent, the carriage and attitudes of these highly-bred girls; in short, her first nature reasserted itself. The change was so complete that on his first visit Herrera was astonished as it would seem—and the Mother Superior congratulated him on his ward. Never in their existence as teachers had these sisters met with a more charming nature, more Christian meekness, true modesty, nor a greater eagerness to learn. When a girl has suffered such misery as had overwhelmed this poor child, and looks forward to such a reward as the Spaniard held out to Esther, it is hard if she does not realize the miracles of the early Church which the Jesuits revived in Paraguay.

"She is edifying," said the Superior, kissing her on the brow.

And this essentially Catholic word tells all.

In recreation hours Esther would question her companions, but discreetly, as to the simplest matters in fashionable life, which to her were like the first strange ideas of life to a child. When she heard that she was to be dressed in white on the day of her baptism and first Communion, that she should wear a white satin fillet, white bows, white shoes, white gloves, and white rosettes in her hair, she melted into tears, to the amazement of her companions. It was the reverse of the scene of Jephtha on the mountain. The courtesan was afraid of being understood; she ascribed this dreadful dejection to the joy with which she looked forward to the function. As there is certainly as wide a gulf between the habits she had given up and the habits she was acquiring as there is between the savage state and civilization, she had the grace and simplicity and depth which distinguished the wonderful heroine of the American Puritans. She had too, without knowing it, a love that was eating out her heart—a strange love, a desire more violent in her who knew everything than it can be in a maiden who knows nothing, though the two forms of desire have the same cause, and the same end in view.

During the first few months the novelty of a secluded life, the surprises of learning, the handiworks she was taught, the practices of religion, the fervency of a holy resolve, the gentle affections she called forth, and the exercise of the faculties of her awakened intelligence, all helped to repress her memory, even the effort she made to acquire a new one, for she had as much to unlearn as to learn. There is more than one form of memory: the body and mind have each their own; home-sickness, for instance, is a malady of the physical memory. Thus, during the third month, the vehemence of this virgin soul, soaring to Paradise on outspread wings, was not indeed quelled, but fettered by a dull rebellion, of which Esther herself did not know the cause. Like the Scottish sheep, she wanted to pasture in solitude, she could not conquer the instincts begotten of debauchery.

Was it that the foul ways of the Paris she had abjured were calling her back to them? Did the chains of the hideous habits she had renounced cling to her by forgotten rivets, and was she feeling them, as old soldiers suffer still, the surgeons tell us, in the limbs they have lost? Had vice and excess so soaked into her marrow that holy waters had not yet exorcised the devil lurking there? Was the sight of him for whom her angelic efforts were made, necessary to the poor soul, whom God would surely forgive for mingling human and sacred love? One had led to the other. Was there some transposition of the vital force in her involving her in inevitable suffering? Everything is doubtful and obscure in a case which science scorns to study, regarding the subject as too immoral and too compromising, as if the physician and the writer, the priest and the political student, were not above all suspicion. However, a doctor who was stopped by death had the courage to begin an investigation which he left unfinished.

Perhaps the dark depression to which Esther fell a victim, and which cast a gloom over her happy life, was due to all these causes; and perhaps, unable as she was to suspect them herself, she suffered as sick creatures suffer who know nothing of medicine or surgery.

The fact is strange. Wholesome and abundant food in the place of bad and inflammatory nourishment did not sustain Esther. A pure and regular life, divided between recreation and studies intentionally abridged, taking the place of a disorderly existence of which the pleasures and the pains were equally horrible, exhausted the convent-boarder. The coolest rest, the calmest nights, taking the place of crushing fatigue and the most torturing agitation, gave her low fever, in which the common symptoms were imperceptible to the nursing Sister's eye or finger. In fact, virtue and happiness following on evil and misfortune, security in the stead of anxiety, were as fatal to Esther as her past wretchedness would have been to her young companions. Planted in corruption, she had grown up in it. That infernal home still had a hold on her, in spite of the commands of a despotic will. What she loathed was life to her, what she loved was killing her.

Her faith was so ardent that her piety was a delight to those about her. She loved to pray. She had opened her spirit to the lights of true religion, and received it without an effort or a doubt. The priest who was her director was delighted with her. Still, at every turn her body resisted the spirit.

To please a whim of Madame de Maintenon's, who fed them with scraps from the royal table, some carp were taken out of a muddy pool and placed in a marble basin of bright, clean water. The carp perished. The animals might be sacrificed, but man could never infect them with the leprosy of flattery. A courtier remarked at Versailles on this mute resistance. "They are like me," said the uncrowned queen; "they pine for their obscure mud."

This speech epitomizes Esther's story.

At times the poor girl was driven to run about the splendid convent gardens; she hurried from tree to tree, she rushed into the darkest nooks—seeking? What? She did not know, but she fell a prey to the demon; she carried on a flirtation with the trees, she appealed to them in unspoken words. Sometimes, in the evening, she stole along under the walls, like a snake, without any shawl over her bare shoulders. Often in chapel, during the service, she remained with her eyes fixed on the Crucifix, melted to tears; the others admired her; but she was crying with rage. Instead of the sacred images she hoped to see, those glaring nights when she had led some orgy as Habeneck leads a Beethoven symphony at the Conservatoire—nights of laughter and lasciviousness, with vehement gestures, inextinguishable laughter, rose before her, frenzied, furious, and brutal. She was as mild to look upon as a virgin that clings to earth only by her woman's shape; within raged an imperial Messalina.

She alone knew the secret of this struggle between the devil and the angel. When the Superior reproved her for having done her hair more fashionably than the rule of the House allowed, she altered it with prompt and beautiful submission; she would have cut her hair off if the Mother had required it of her. This moral home-sickness was truly pathetic in a girl who would rather have perished than have returned to the depths of impurity. She grew pale and altered and thin. The Superior gave her shorter lessons, and called the interesting creature to her room to question her. But Esther was happy; she enjoyed the society of her companions; she felt no pain in any vital part; still, it was vitality itself that was attacked. She regretted nothing; she wanted nothing. The Superior, puzzled by her boarder's answers, did not know what to think when she saw her pining under consuming debility.

The doctor was called in when the girl's condition seemed serious; but this doctor knew nothing of Esther's previous life, and could not guess it; he found every organ sound, the pain could not be localized. The invalid's replies were such as to upset every hypothesis. There remained one way of clearing up the learned man's doubts, which now lighted on a frightful suggestion; but Esther obstinately refused to submit to a medical examination.

In this difficulty the Superior appealed to the Abbe Herrera. The Spaniard came, saw that Esther's condition was desperate, and took the physician aside for a moment. After this confidential interview, the man of science told the man of faith that the only cure lay in a journey to Italy. The Abbe would not hear of such a journey before Esther's baptism and first Communion.

"How long will it be till then?" asked the doctor.

"A month," replied the Superior.

"She will be dead," said the doctor.

"Yes, but in a state of grace and salvation," said the Abbe.

In Spain the religious question is supreme, above all political, civil, or vital considerations; so the physician did not answer the Spaniard. He turned to the Mother Superior, but the terrible Abbe took him by the arm and stopped him.

"Not a word, monsieur!" said he.

The doctor, though a religious man and a Monarchist, looked at Esther with an expression of tender pity. The girl was as lovely as a lily drooping on its stem.

"God help her, then!" he exclaimed as he went away.

On the very day of this consultation, Esther was taken by her protector to the *Rocher de Cancale*, a famous restaurant, for his wish to save her had suggested strange expedients to the priest. He tried the effect of two excesses—an excellent dinner, which might remind the poor child of past orgies; and the opera, which would give her mind some images of worldliness. His despotic authority was needed to tempt the young saint to such profanation. Herrera disguised himself so effectually as a military man, that Esther hardly recognized him; he took care to make his companion wear a veil, and put her in a box where she was hidden from all eyes.

This palliative, which had no risks for innocence so sincerely regained, soon lost its effect. The convent-boarder viewed her protector's dinners with disgust, had a religious aversion for the theatre, and relapsed into melancholy.

"She is dying of love for Lucien," said Herrera to himself; he had wanted to sound the depths of this soul, and know how much could be exacted from it.

So the moment came when the poor child was no longer upheld by moral force, and the body was about to break down. The priest calculated the time with the hideous practical sagacity formerly shown by executioners in the art of torture. He found his protegee in the garden, sitting on a bench under a trellis on which the April sun fell gently; she seemed to be cold and trying to warm herself; her companions looked with interest at her pallor as of a folded plant, her eyes like those of a dying gazelle, her drooping attitude. Esther rose and went to meet the Spaniard with a lassitude that showed how little life there was in her, and, it may be added, how little care to live. This hapless outcast, this wild and wounded swallow, moved Carlos Herrera to compassion for the second time. The gloomy minister, whom God should have employed only to carry out His revenges, received the sick girl with a smile, which expressed, indeed, as much bitterness as sweetness, as much vengeance as charity. Esther, practised in meditation, and used to revulsions of feeling since she had led this almost monastic life, felt on her part, for the second time, distrust of her protector; but, as on the former occasion, his speech reassured her.

"Well, my dear child," said he, "and why have you never spoken to me of Lucien?"

"I promised you," she said, shuddering convulsively from head to foot; "I swore to you that I would never breathe his name."

"And yet you have not ceased to think of him."

"That, monsieur, is the only fault I have committed. I think of him always; and just as you came, I was saying his name to myself."

"Absence is killing you?"

Esther's only answer was to hang her head as the sick do who already scent the breath of the grave.

"If you could see him—?" said he.

"It would be life!" she cried.

"And do you think of him only spiritually?"

"Ah, monsieur, love cannot be dissected!"

"Child of an accursed race! I have done everything to save you; I send you back to your fate.—You shall see him again."

"Why insult my happiness? Can I not love Lucien and be virtuous? Am I not ready to die here for virtue, as I should be ready to die for him? Am I not dying for these two fanaticisms—for virtue, which was to make me worthy of him, and for him who flung me into the embrace of virtue? Yes, and ready to die without seeing him or to live by seeing him. God is my Judge."

The color had mounted to her face, her whiteness had recovered its amber warmth. Esther looked beautiful again.

"The day after that on which you are washed in the waters of baptism you shall see Lucien once more; and if you think you can live in virtue by living for him, you shall part no more."

The priest was obliged to lift up Esther, whose knees failed her; the poor child dropped as if the ground had slipped from under her feet.

The Abbe seated her on a bench; and when she could speak again she asked him:

"Why not to-day?"

"Do you want to rob Monseigneur of the triumph of your baptism and conversion? You are too close to Lucien not to be far from God."

"Yes, I was not thinking—"

"You will never be of any religion," said the priest, with a touch of the deepest irony.

"God is good," said she; "He can read my heart."

Conquered by the exquisite artlessness and gestures, Herrera kissed her on the forehead for the first time.

"Your libertine friends named you well; you would bewitch God the Father.—A few days more must pass, and then you will both be free."

"Both!" she echoed in an ecstasy of joy.

This scene, observed from a distance, struck pupils and superiors alike; they fancied they had looked on at a miracle as they compared Esther with herself. She was completely changed; she was alive. She reappeared her natural self, all love, sweet, coquettish, playful, and gay; in short, it was a resurrection.

HERRERA LIVED IN THE RUE Cassette, near Saint-Sulpice, the church to which he was attached. This building, hard and stern in style, suited this Spaniard, whose discipline was that of the Dominicans. A lost son of Ferdinand VII's astute policy, he devoted himself to the cause of the constitution, knowing that this devotion could never be rewarded till the restoration of the *Rey netto*. Carlos Herrera had thrown himself body and soul into the *Camarilla* at the moment when the Cortes seemed likely to stand and hold their own. To the world this conduct seemed to proclaim a superior soul. The Duc d'Angouleme's expedition had been carried out, King Ferdinand was on the throne, and Carlos Herrera did not go to claim the reward of his services at Madrid. Fortified against curiosity by his diplomatic taciturnity, he assigned as his reason for remaining in Paris his strong affection for Lucien de Rubempre, to which the young man already owed the King's patent relating to his change of name.

Herrera lived very obscurely, as priests employed on secret missions traditionally live. He fulfilled his religious duties at Saint-Sulpice, never went out but on business, and then after dark, and in a hackney cab. His day was filled up with a siesta in the Spanish fashion, which arranges for sleep between the two chief meals, and so occupies the hours when Paris is in a busy turmoil. The Spanish cigar also played its part, and consumed time as well as tobacco. Laziness is a mask as gravity is, and that again is laziness.

Herrera lived on the second floor in one wing of the house, and Lucien occupied the other wing. The two apartments were separated and joined by a large reception room of antique magnificence, suitable equally to the grave priest and to the young poet. The courtyard was gloomy; large, thick trees shaded the garden. Silence and reserve are always found in the dwellings chosen by priests. Herrera's lodging may be described in one word—a cell. Lucien's, splendid with luxury, and furnished with every refinement of comfort, combined everything that the elegant life of a dandy demands—a poet, a writer, ambitious and dissipated, at once vain and vainglorious, utterly heedless, and yet wishing for order, one of those incomplete geniuses who have some power to wish, to conceive—which is perhaps the same thing—but no power at all to execute.

These two, Lucien and Herrera, formed a body politic. This, no doubt, was the secret of their union. Old men in whom the activities of life have been uprooted and transplanted to the sphere of interest, often feel the need of a pleasing instrument, a young and impassioned actor, to carry out their schemes. Richelieu, too late, found a handsome pale face with a young moustache to cast in the way of women whom he wanted to amuse. Misunderstood by giddy-pated younger men, he was compelled to banish his master's mother and terrify the Queen, after having tried to make each fall in love with him, though he was not cut out to be loved by queens.

Do what we will, always, in the course of an ambitious life, we find a woman in the way just when we least expect such an obstacle. However great a political man may be, he always needs a woman to set against a woman, just as the Dutch use a diamond to cut a diamond. Rome at the height of its power yielded to this necessity. And observe how immeasurably more imposing was the life of Mazarin, the Italian cardinal, than that of Richelieu, the French cardinal. Richelieu met with opposition from the great nobles, and he applied the axe; he died in the flower of his success, worn out by this duel, for which he had only a Capuchin monk as his second. Mazarin was repulsed by the citizen class and the nobility, armed allies who sometimes victoriously put royalty to flight; but Anne of Austria's devoted servant took off no heads, he succeeded in vanquishing the whole of France, and trained Louis XIV, who completed Richelieu's work by strangling the nobility with gilded cords in the grand Seraglio of Versailles. Madame de Pompadour dead, Choiseul fell!

Had Herrera soaked his mind in these high doctrines? Had he judged himself at an earlier age than Richelieu? Had he chosen Lucien to be his Cinq-Mars, but a faithful Cinq-Mars? No one could answer these questions or measure this Spaniard's ambition, as no one could foresee what his end might be. These questions, asked by those who were able to see anything of this coalition, which was long kept a secret, might have unveiled a horrible mystery which Lucien himself had known but a few days. Carlos was ambitious for two; that was what his conduct made plain to those persons who knew him, and who all imagined that Lucien was the priest's illegitimate son.

Fifteen months after Lucien's reappearance at the opera ball, which led him too soon into a world where the priest had not wished to see him till he should have fully armed him against it, he had three fine horses in his stable, a coupe for evening use, a cab and a tilbury to drive by day. He dined out every day. Herrera's foresight was justified; his pupil was carried away by dissipation; he thought it necessary to effect some diversion in the frenzied passion for Esther that the young man still cherished in his heart. After spending something like forty thousand francs, every folly had brought Lucien back with increased eagerness to La Torpille; he searched for her persistently; and as he could not find her, she became to him what game is to the sportsman.

Could Herrera understand the nature of a poet's love?

When once this feeling has mounted to the brain of one of these great little men, after firing his heart and absorbing his senses, the poet becomes as far superior to humanity through love as he already is through the power of his imagination. A freak of intellectual heredity has given him the faculty of expressing nature by imagery, to which he gives the stamp both of sentiment and of thought, and he lends his love the wings of his spirit; he feels, and he paints, he acts and meditates, he multiplies his sensations by thought, present felicity becomes threefold through aspiration for the future and memory of the past; and with it he mingles the exquisite delights of the soul, which makes him the prince of artists. Then the poet's passion becomes a fine poem in which human proportion is often set at nought. Does not the poet then place his mistress far higher than women crave to sit? Like the sublime Knight of la Mancha, he transfigures a peasant girl to be a princess. He uses for his own behoof the wand with which he touches everything, turning it into a wonder, and thus enhances the pleasure of loving by the glorious glamour of the ideal.

Such a love is the very essence of passion. It is extreme in all things, in its hopes, in its despair, in its rage, in its melancholy, in its joy; it flies, it leaps, it crawls; it is not like any of the emotions known to ordinary men; it is to everyday love what the perennial Alpine torrent is to the lowland brook.

These splendid geniuses are so rarely understood that they spend themselves in hopes deceived; they are exhausted by the search for their ideal mistress, and almost always die like gorgeous insects splendidly adorned for their love-festival by the most poetical of nature's inventions, and crushed under the foot of a passer-by. But there is another danger! When they meet with the form that answers to their soul, and which not unfrequently is that of a baker's wife, they do as Raphael did, as the beautiful insect does, they die in the Fornarina's arms.

Lucien was at this pass. His poetical temperament, excessive in all things, in good as in evil, had discerned the angel in this girl, who was tainted by corruption rather than corrupt; he always saw her white, winged, pure, and mysterious, as she had made herself for him, understanding that he would have her so.

Towards the end of the month of May 1825 Lucien had lost all his good spirits; he never went out, dined with Herrera, sat pensive, worked, read volumes of diplomatic treatises, squatted Turkish-fashion on a divan, and smoked three or four hookahs a day. His groom had more to do in cleaning and perfuming the tubes of this noble pipe than in currying and brushing down the horses' coats, and dressing them with cockades for driving in the Bois. As soon as the Spaniard saw Lucien pale, and detected a malady in the frenzy of suppressed passion, he determined to read to the bottom of this man's heart on which he founded his life.

One fine evening, when Lucien, lounging in an armchair, was mechanically contemplating the hues of the setting sun through the trees in the garden, blowing up the mist of scented smoke in slow, regular clouds, as pensive smokers are wont, he was roused from his reverie by hearing a deep sigh. He turned and saw the Abbe standing by him with folded arms.

"You were there!" said the poet.

"For some time," said the priest, "my thoughts have been following the wide sweep of yours." Lucien understood his meaning.

"I have never affected to have an iron nature such as yours is. To me life is by turns paradise and hell; when by chance it is neither, it bores me; and I am bored—"

"How can you be bored when you have such splendid prospects before you?"

"If I have no faith in those prospects, or if they are too much shrouded?"

"Do not talk nonsense," said the priest. "It would be far more worthy of you and of me that you should open your heart to me. There is now that between us which ought never to have come between us—a secret. This secret has subsisted for sixteen months. You are in love."

"And what then?"

"A foul hussy called La Torpille—"

"Well?"

"My boy, I told you you might have a mistress, but a woman of rank, pretty, young, influential, a Countess at least. I had chosen Madame d'Espard for you, to make her the instrument of your fortune without scruple; for she would never have perverted your heart, she would have left you free.—To love a prostitute of the lowest class when you have not, like kings, the power to give her high rank, is a monstrous blunder."

"And am I the first man who had renounced ambition to follow the lead of a boundless passion?"

"Good!" said the priest, stooping to pick up the mouthpiece of the hookah which Lucien had dropped on the floor. "I understand the retort. Cannot love and ambition be reconciled? Child, you have a mother in old Herrera—a mother who is wholly devoted to you—"

"I know it, old friend," said Lucien, taking his hand and shaking it.

"You wished for the toys of wealth; you have them. You want to shine; I am guiding you into the paths of power, I kiss very dirty hands to secure your advancement, and you will get on. A little while yet and you will lack nothing of what can charm man or woman. Though effeminate in your caprices, your intellect is manly. I have dreamed all things of you; I forgive you all. You have only to speak to have your ephemeral passions gratified. I have aggrandized your life by introducing into it that which makes it delightful to most people—the stamp of political influence and dominion. You will be as great as you now are small; but you must not break the machine by which we coin money. I grant you all you will excepting such blunders as will destroy your future prospects. When I can open the drawing-rooms of the Faubourg Saint-Germain to you, I forbid your wallowing in the gutter. Lucien, I mean to be an iron stanchion in your interest; I will endure everything from you, for you. Thus I have transformed your lack of tact in the game of life into the shrewd stroke of a skilful player—"

Lucien looked up with a start of furious impetuosity.

"I carried off La Torpille!"

"You?" cried Lucien.

In a fit of animal rage the poet jumped up, flung the jeweled mouthpiece in the priest's face, and pushed him with such violence as to throw down that strong man.

"I," said the Spaniard, getting up and preserving his terrible gravity.

His black wig had fallen off. A bald skull, as shining as a death's head, showed the man's real countenance. It was appalling. Lucien sat on his divan, his hands hanging limp, overpowered, and gazing at the Abbe with stupefaction.

"I carried her off," the priest repeated.

"What did you do with her? You took her away the day after the opera ball."

"Yes, the day after I had seen a woman who belonged to you insulted by wretches whom I would not have condescended to kick downstairs."

"Wretches!" interrupted Lucien, "say rather monsters, compared with whom those who are guillotined are angels. Do you know what the unhappy Torpille had done for three of them? One of them was her lover for two months. She was poor, and picked up a living in the gutter; he had not a sou; like me, when you rescued me, he was very near the river; this fellow would get up at night and go to the cupboard where the girl kept the remains of her dinner and eat it. At last she discovered the trick; she understood the shameful thing, and took care to leave a great deal; then she was happy. She never told any one but me, that night, coming home from the opera.

"The second had stolen some money; but before the theft was found out, she lent him the sum, which he was enabled to replace, and which he always forgot to repay to the poor child.

"As to the third, she made his fortune by playing out a farce worthy of Figaro's genius. She passed as his wife and became the mistress of a man in power, who believed her to be the most innocent of good citizens. To one she gave life, to another honor, to the third fortune—what does it all count for to-day? And this is how they reward her!"

"Would you like to see them dead?" said Herrera, in whose eyes there were tears.

"Come, that is just like you! I know you by that—"

"Nay, hear all, raving poet," said the priest. "La Torpille is no more."

Lucien flew at Herrera to seize him by the throat, with such violence that any other man must have fallen backwards; but the Spaniard's arm held off his assailant.

"Come, listen," said he coldly. "I have made another woman of her, chaste, pure, well bred, religious, a perfect lady. She is being educated. She can, if she may, under the influence of your love, become a Ninon, a Marion Delorme, a du Barry, as the journalist at the opera ball remarked. You may proclaim her your mistress, or you may retire behind a curtain of your own creating, which will be wiser. By either method you will gain profit and pride, pleasure and advancement; but if you are as great a politician as you are a poet, Esther will be no more to you than any other woman of the town; for, later, perhaps she may help us out of difficulties; she is worth her weight in gold. Drink, but do not get tipsy.

"If I had not held the reins of your passion, where would you be now? Rolling with La Torpille in the slough of misery from which I dragged you. Here, read this," said Herrera, as simply as Talma in *Manlius*, which he had never seen.

A sheet of paper was laid on the poet's knees, and startled him from the ecstasy and surprise with which he had listened to this astounding speech; he took it, and read the first letter written by Mademoiselle Esther:—

To Monsieur l'Abbe Carlos Herrera
My Dear Protector,

Will you not suppose that gratitude is stronger in me than love, when you see that the first use I make of the power of expressing my thoughts is to thank you, instead of devoting it to pouring forth a passion that Lucien has perhaps forgotten. But to you, divine man, I can say what I should not dare to tell him, who, to my joy, still clings to earth.

"Yesterday's ceremony has filled me with treasures of grace, and I place my fate in your hands. Even if I must die far away from my beloved, I shall die purified like the Magdalen, and my soul will become to him the rival of his guardian angel. Can I ever forget yesterday's festival? How could I wish to abdicate the glorious throne to which I was raised? Yesterday I washed away every stain in the waters of baptism, and received the Sacred Body of my Redeemer; I am become one of His tabernacles. At that moment I heard the songs of angels, I was more than a woman, born to a life of light amid the acclamations of the whole earth, admired by the world in a cloud of incense and prayers that were intoxicating, adorned like a virgin for the Heavenly Spouse.

"Thus finding myself worthy of Lucien, which I had never hoped to be, I abjured impure love and vowed to walk only in the paths of virtue. If my flesh is weaker than my spirit, let it perish. Be the arbiter of my destiny; and if I die, tell Lucien that I died to him when I was born to God."

Lucien looked up at the Abbe with eyes full of tears.

"You know the rooms fat Caroline Bellefeuille had, in the Rue Taitbout," the Spaniard said. "The poor creature, cast off by her magistrate, was in the greatest poverty; she was about to be sold up. I bought the place all standing, and she turned out with her clothes. Esther, the angel who aspired to heaven, has alighted there, and is waiting for you."

At this moment Lucien heard his horses pawing the ground in the courtyard; he was incapable of expressing his admiration for a devotion which he alone could appreciate; he threw himself into the arms of the man he had insulted, made amends for all by a look and the speechless effusion of his feelings. Then he flew downstairs, confided Esther's address to his tiger's ear, and the horses went off as if their master's passion had lived in their legs.

THE NEXT DAY A MAN, who by his dress might have been mistaken by the passers-by for a gendarme in disguise, was passing the Rue Taitbout, opposite a house, as if he were waiting for some one to come out; he walked with an agitated air. You will often see in Paris such vehement promenaders, real gendarmes watching a recalcitrant National Guardsman, bailiffs taking steps to effect an arrest, creditors planning a trick on the debtor who has shut himself in, lovers, or jealous and suspicious husbands, or friends doing sentry for a friend; but rarely do you meet a face portending such coarse and fierce thoughts as animated that of the gloomy and powerful man who paced to and fro under

Mademoiselle Esther's windows with the brooding haste of a bear in its cage.

At noon a window was opened, and a maid-servant's hand was put out to push back the padded shutters. A few minutes later, Esther, in her dressing-gown, came to breathe the air, leaning on Lucien; any one who saw them might have taken them for the originals of some pretty English vignette. Esther was the first to recognize the basilisk eyes of the Spanish priest; and the poor creature, stricken as if she had been shot, gave a cry of horror.

"There is that terrible priest," said she, pointing him out to Lucien.

"He!" said Lucien, smiling, "he is no more a priest than you are."

"What then?" she said in alarm.

"Why, an old villain who believes in nothing but the devil," said Lucien.

This light thrown on the sham priest's secrets, if revealed to any one less devoted than Esther, might have ruined Lucien for ever.

As they went along the corridor from their bedroom to the dining-room, where their breakfast was served, the lovers met Carlos Herrera.

"What have you come here for?" said Lucien roughly.

"To bless you," replied the audacious scoundrel, stopping the pair and detaining them in the little drawing-room of the apartment. "Listen to me, my pretty dears. Amuse yourselves, be happy—well and good! Happiness at any price is my motto.—But you," he went on to Esther, "you whom I dragged from the mud, and have soaped down body and soul, you surely do not dream that you can stand in Lucien's way?—As for you, my boy," he went on after a pause, looking at Lucien, "you are no longer poet enough to allow yourself another Coralie. This is sober prose. What can be done with Esther's lover? Nothing. Can Esther become Madame de Rubempre? No.

"Well, my child," said he, laying his hand on Esther's, and making her shiver as if some serpent had wound itself round her, "the world must never know of your existence. Above all, the world must never know that a certain Mademoiselle Esther loves Lucien, and that Lucien is in love with her.—These rooms are your prison, my pigeon. If you wish to go out—and your health will require it—you must take exercise at night, at hours when you cannot be seen; for your youth and beauty, and the style you have acquired at the Convent, would at once be observed in Paris. The day when any one in the world, whoever it be," he added in an awful voice, seconded by an awful look, "learns that Lucien is your lover, or that

HONORÉ DE BALZAC

you are his mistress, that day will be your last but one on earth. I have procured that boy a patent permitting him to bear the name and arms of his maternal ancestors. Still, this is not all; we have not yet recovered the title of Marquis; and to get it, he must marry a girl of good family, in whose favor the King will grant this distinction. Such an alliance will get Lucien on in the world and at Court. This boy, of whom I have made a man, will be first Secretary to an Embassy; later, he shall be Minister at some German Court, and God, or I—better still—helping him, he will take his seat some day on the bench reserved for peers—"

"Or on the bench reserved for—" Lucien began, interrupting the man.

"Hold your tongue!" cried Carlos, laying his broad hand on Lucien's mouth. "Would you tell such a secret to a woman?" he muttered in his ear.

"Esther! A woman!" cried the poet of *Les Marguerites*.

"Still inditing sonnets!" said the Spaniard. "Nonsense! Sooner or later all these angels relapse into being women, and every woman at moments is a mixture of a monkey and a child, two creatures who can kill us for fun.—Esther, my jewel," said he to the terrified girl, "I have secured as your waiting-maid a creature who is as much mine as if she were my daughter. For your cook, you shall have a mulatto woman, which gives style to a house. With Europe and Asie you can live here for a thousand-franc note a month like a queen—a stage queen. Europe has been a dressmaker, a milliner, and a stage super; Asie has cooked for an epicure Milord. These two women will serve you like two fairies."

Seeing Lucien go completely to the wall before this man, who was guilty at least of sacrilege and forgery, this woman, sanctified by her love, felt an awful fear in the depths of her heart. She made no reply, but dragged Lucien into her room, and asked him:

"Is he the devil?"

"He is far worse to me!" he vehemently replied. "But if you love me, try to imitate that man's devotion to me, and obey him on pain of death!—"

"Of death!" she exclaimed, more frightened than ever.

"Of death," repeated Lucien. "Alas! my darling, no death could be compared with that which would befall me if—"

Esther turned pale at his words, and felt herself fainting.

"Well, well," cried the sacrilegious forger, "have you not yet spelt out your daisy-petals?"

Esther and Lucien came out, and the poor girl, not daring to look at the mysterious man, said:

"You shall be obeyed as God is obeyed, monsieur."

"Good," said he. "You may be very happy for a time, and you will need only nightgowns and wrappers—that will be very economical."

The two lovers went on towards the dining-room, but Lucien's patron signed to the pretty pair to stop. And they stopped.

"I have just been talking of your servants, my child," said he to Esther. "I must introduce them to you."

The Spaniard rang twice. The women he had called Europe and Asie came in, and it was at once easy to see the reason of these names.

Asie, who looked as if she might have been born in the Island of Java, showed a face to scare the eye, as flat as a board, with the copper complexion peculiar to Malays, with a nose that looked as if it had been driven inwards by some violent pressure. The strange conformation of the maxillary bones gave the lower part of this face a resemblance to that of the larger species of apes. The brow, though sloping, was not deficient in intelligence produced by habits of cunning. Two fierce little eyes had the calm fixity of a tiger's, but they never looked you straight in the face. Asie seemed afraid lest she might terrify people. Her lips, a dull blue, were parted over prominent teeth of dazzling whiteness, but grown across. The leading expression of this animal countenance was one of meanness. Her black hair, straight and greasy-looking like her skin, lay in two shining bands, forming an edge to a very handsome silk handkerchief. Her ears were remarkably pretty, and graced with two large dark pearls. Small, short, and squat, Asie bore a likeness to the grotesque figures the Chinese love to paint on screens, or, more exactly, to the Hindoo idols which seem to be imitated from some non-existent type, found, nevertheless, now and again by travelers. Esther shuddered as she looked at this monstrosity, dressed out in a white apron over a stuff gown.

"Asie," said the Spaniard, to whom the woman looked up with a gesture that can only be compared to that of a dog to its master, "this is your mistress."

And he pointed to Esther in her wrapper.

Asie looked at the young fairy with an almost distressful expression; but at the same moment a flash, half hidden between her thick, short eyelashes, shot like an incendiary spark at Lucien, who, in a magnificent dressing-gown thrown open over a fine Holland linen shirt and red trousers, with a fez on his head, beneath which his fair hair fell in thick curls, presented a godlike appearance.

Italian genius could invent the tale of Othello; English genius could put it on the stage; but Nature alone reserves the power of throwing into a single glance an expression of jealousy grander and more complete than England and Italy together could imagine. This look, seen by Esther, made her clutch the Spaniard by the arm, setting her nails in it as a cat sets its claws to save itself from falling into a gulf of which it cannot see the bottom.

The Spaniard spoke a few words, in some unfamiliar tongue, to the Asiatic monster, who crept on her knees to Esther's feet and kissed them.

"She is not merely a good cook," said Herrera to Esther; "she is a past-master, and might make Careme mad with jealousy. Asie can do everything by way of cooking. She will turn you out a simple dish of beans that will make you wonder whether the angels have not come down to add some herb from heaven. She will go to market herself every morning, and fight like the devil she is to get things at the lowest prices; she will tire out curiosity by silence.

"You are to be supposed to have been in India, and Asie will help you to give effect to this fiction, for she is one of those Parisians who are born to be of any nationality they please. But I do not advise that you should give yourself out to be a foreigner.—Europe, what do you say?"

Europe was a perfect contrast to Asie, for she was the smartest waiting-maid that Monrose could have hoped to see as her rival on the stage. Slight, with a scatter-brain manner, a face like a weasel, and a sharp nose, Europe's features offered to the observer a countenance worn by the corruption of Paris life, the unhealthy complexion of a girl fed on raw apples, lymphatic but sinewy, soft but tenacious. One little foot was set forward, her hands were in her apron-pockets, and she fidgeted incessantly without moving, from sheer excess of liveliness. Grisette and stage super, in spite of her youth she must have tried many trades. As full of evil as a dozen Madelonnettes put together, she might have robbed her parents, and sat on the bench of a police-court.

Asie was terrifying, but you knew her thoroughly from the first; she descended in a straight line from Locusta; while Europe filled you with uneasiness, which could not fail to increase the more you had to do with her; her corruption seemed boundless. You felt that she could set the devils by the ears.

"Madame might say she had come from Valenciennes," said Europe in a precise little voice. "I was born there—Perhaps monsieur," she added to Lucien in a pedantic tone, "will be good enough to say what name he proposes to give to madame?"

"Madame van Bogseck," the Spaniard put in, reversing Esther's name. "Madame is a Jewess, a native of Holland, the widow of a merchant, and suffering from a liver-complaint contracted in Java. No great fortune—not to excite curiosity."

"Enough to live on—six thousand francs a year; and we shall complain of her stinginess?" said Europe.

"That is the thing," said the Spaniard, with a bow. "You limbs of Satan!" he went on, catching Asie and Europe exchanging a glance that displeased him, "remember what I have told you. You are serving a queen; you owe her as much respect as to a queen; you are to cherish her as you would cherish a revenge, and be as devoted to her as to me. Neither the door-porter, nor the neighbors, nor the other inhabitants of the house—in short, not a soul on earth is to know what goes on here. It is your business to balk curiosity if any should be roused.—And madame," he went on laying his broad hairy hand on Esther's arm, "madame must not commit the smallest imprudence; you must prevent it in case of need, but always with perfect respect.

"You, Europe, are to go out for madame in anything that concerns her dress, and you must do her sewing from motives of economy. Finally, nobody, not even the most insignificant creature, is ever to set foot in this apartment. You two, between you, must do all there is to be done.

"And you, my beauty," he went on, speaking to Esther, "when you want to go out in your carriage by night, you can tell Europe; she will know where to find your men, for you will have a servant in livery, of my choosing, like those two slaves."

Esther and Lucien had not a word ready. They listened to the Spaniard, and looked at the two precious specimens to whom he gave his orders. What was the secret hold to which he owed the submission and servitude that were written on these two faces—one mischievously recalcitrant, the other so malignantly cruel?

He read the thoughts of Lucien and Esther, who seemed paralyzed, as Paul and Virginia might have been at the sight of two dreadful snakes, and he said in a good-natured undertone:

"You can trust them as you can me; keep no secrets from them; that will flatter them.—Go to your work, my little Asie," he added to the cook.—"And you, my girl, lay another place," he said to Europe; "the children cannot do less than ask papa to breakfast."

When the two women had shut the door, and the Spaniard could hear Europe moving to and fro, he turned to Lucien and Esther, and opening a wide palm, he said:

"I hold them in the hollow of my hand."

The words and gesture made his hearers shudder.

"Where did you pick them up?" cried Lucien.

"What the devil! I did not look for them at the foot of the throne!" replied the man. "Europe has risen from the mire, and is afraid of sinking into it again. Threaten them with Monsieur Abbe when they do not please you, and you will see them quake like mice when the cat is mentioned. I am used to taming wild beasts," he added with a smile.

"You strike me as being a demon," said Esther, clinging closer to Lucien.

"My child, I tried to win you to heaven; but a repentant Magdalen is always a practical joke on the Church. If ever there were one, she would relapse into the courtesan in Paradise. You have gained this much: you are forgotten, and have acquired the manners of a lady, for you learned in the convent what you never could have learned in the ranks of infamy in which you were living.—You owe me nothing," said he, observing a beautiful look of gratitude on Esther's face. "I did it all for him," and he pointed to Lucien. "You are, you will always be, you will die a prostitute; for in spite of the delightful theories of cattle-breeders, you can never, here below, become anything but what you are. The man who feels bumps is right. You have the bump of love."

The Spaniard, it will be seen, was a fatalist, like Napoleon, Mahomet, and many other great politicians. It is a strange thing that most men of action have a tendency to fatalism, just as most great thinkers have a tendency to believe in Providence.

"What I am, I do not know," said Esther with angelic sweetness; "but I love Lucien, and shall die worshiping him."

"Come to breakfast," said the Spaniard sharply. "And pray to God that Lucien may not marry too soon, for then you would never see him again."

"His marriage would be my death," said she.

She allowed the sham priest to lead the way, that she might stand on tiptoe and whisper to Lucien without being seen.

"Is it your wish," said she, "that I should remain in the power of this man who sets two hyenas to guard me?"

Lucien bowed his head.

The poor child swallowed down her grief and affected gladness, but she felt cruelly oppressed. It needed more than a year of constant and devoted care before she was accustomed to these two dreadful creatures whom Carlos Herrera called the two watch-dogs.

LUCIEN'S CONDUCT SINCE HIS RETURN to Paris had borne the stamp of such profound policy that it excited—and could not fail to excite—the jealousy of all his former friends, on whom he took no vengeance but by making them furious at his success, at his exquisite "get up," and his way of keeping every one at a distance. The poet, once so communicative, so genial, had turned cold and reserved. De Marsay, the model adopted by all the youth of Paris, did not make a greater display of reticence in speech and deed than did Lucien. As to brains, the journalist had ere now proved his mettle. De Marsay, against whom many people chose to pit Lucien, giving a preference to the poet, was small-minded enough to resent this.

Lucien, now in high favor with men who secretly pulled the wires of power, was so completely indifferent to literary fame, that he did not care about the success of his romance, republished under its real title, L'*Archer de Charles IX*, or the excitement caused by his volume of sonnets called *Les Marguerites*, of which Dauriat sold out the edition in a week.

"It is posthumous fame," said he, with a laugh, to Mademoiselle des Touches, who congratulated him.

The terrible Spaniard held his creature with an iron hand, keeping him in the road towards the goal where the trumpets and gifts of victory await patient politicians. Lucien had taken Beaudenord's bachelor quarters on the Quai Malaquais, to be near the Rue Taitbout, and his adviser was lodging under the same roof on the fourth floor. Lucien kept only one horse to ride and drive, a man-servant, and a groom. When he was not dining out, he dined with Esther.

Carlos Herrera kept such a keen eye on the service in the house on the Quai Malaquais, that Lucien did not spend ten thousand francs a year, all told. Ten thousand more were enough for Esther, thanks to the unfailing and inexplicable devotion of Asie and Europe. Lucien took the utmost precautions in going in and out at the Rue Taitbout. He never came but in a cab, with the blinds down, and always drove into the courtyard. Thus his passion for Esther and the very existence of the establishment in the Rue Taitbout, being unknown to the world, did him no harm in his connections or undertakings. No rash word ever escaped him on this delicate subject. His mistakes of this sort with regard to Coralie, at the time of his first stay in Paris, had given him experience.

In the first place, his life was marked by the correct regularity under which many mysteries can be hidden; he remained in society every night till one in the morning; he was always at home from ten till one in the afternoon; then he drove in the Bois de Boulogne and paid calls till five. He was rarely seen to be on foot, and thus avoided old acquaintances. When some journalist or one of his former associates waved him a greeting, he responded with a bow, polite enough to avert annoyance, but significant of such deep contempt as killed all French geniality. He thus had very soon got rid of persons whom he would rather never have known.

An old-established aversion kept him from going to see Madame d'Espard, who often wished to get him to her house; but when he met her at those of the Duchesse de Maufrigneuse, of Mademoiselle des Touches, of the Comtesse de Montcornet or elsewhere, he was always exquisitely polite to her. This hatred, fully reciprocated by Madame d'Espard, compelled Lucien to act with prudence; but it will be seen how he had added fuel to it by allowing himself a stroke of revenge, which gained him indeed a severe lecture from Carlos.

"You are not yet strong enough to be revenged on any one, whoever it may be," said the Spaniard. "When we are walking under a burning sun we do not stop to gather even the finest flowers."

Lucien was so genuinely superior, and had so fine a future before him, that the young men who chose to be offended or puzzled by his return to Paris and his unaccountable good fortune were enchanted whenever they could do him an ill turn. He knew that he had many enemies, and was well aware of those hostile feelings among his friends. The Abbe, indeed, took admirable care of his adopted son, putting him on his guard against the treachery of the world and the fatal imprudence of youth. Lucien was expected to tell, and did in fact tell the Abbe each evening, every trivial incident of the day. Thanks to his Mentor's advice, he put the keenest curiosity—the curiosity of the world—off the scent. Entrenched in the gravity of an Englishman, and fortified by the redoubts cast up by diplomatic circumspection, he never gave any one the right or the opportunity of seeing a corner even of his concerns. His handsome young face had, by practice, become as expressionless in society as that of a princess at a ceremonial.

Towards the middle of 1829 his marriage began to be talked of to the eldest daughter of the Duchesse de Grandlieu, who at that time had no less than four daughters to provide for. No one doubted that in honor of such an alliance the King would revive for Lucien the title of Marquis. This distinction would establish Lucien's fortune as a diplomate, and he would probably be accredited as Minister to some German Court. For the last three years Lucien's life had been regular and above reproach; indeed, de Marsay had made this remarkable speech about him:

"That young fellow must have a very strong hand behind him."

Thus Lucien was almost a person of importance. His passion for Esther had, in fact, helped him greatly to play his part of a serious man. A habit of this kind guards an ambitious man from many follies; having no connection with any woman of fashion, he cannot be caught by the reactions of mere physical nature on his moral sense.

As to happiness, Lucien's was the realization of a poet's dreams—a penniless poet's, hungering in a garret. Esther, the ideal courtesan in love, while she reminded Lucien of Coralie, the actress with whom he had lived for a year, completely eclipsed her. Every loving and devoted woman invents seclusion, incognito, the life of a pearl in the depths of the sea; but to most of them this is no more than one of the delightful whims which supply a subject for conversation; a proof of love which they dream of giving, but do not give; whereas Esther, to whom her first enchantment was ever new, who lived perpetually in the glow of Lucien's first incendiary glance, never, in four yours, had an impulse of curiosity. She gave her whole mind to the task of adhering to the terms of the programme prescribed by the sinister Spaniard. Nay, more! In the midst of intoxicating happiness she never took unfair advantage of the unlimited power that the constantly revived desire of a lover gives to the woman he loves to ask Lucien a single question regarding Herrera, of whom indeed she lived in constant awe; she dared not even think of him. The elaborate benefactions of that extraordinary man, to whom Esther undoubtedly owed her feminine accomplishment and her well-bred manner, struck the poor girl as advances on account of hell.

"I shall have to pay for all this some day," she would tell herself with dismay.

Every fine night she went out in a hired carriage. She was driven with a rapidity no doubt insisted on by the Abbe, in one or another of the beautiful woods round Paris, Boulogne, Vincennes, Romainville, or Ville-d'Avray, often with Lucien, sometimes alone with Europe. There she could walk about without fear; for when Lucien was not with her, she was attended by a servant dressed like the smartest of outriders, armed with a real knife, whose face and brawny build alike proclaimed him a ruthless athlete. This protector was also provided, in the fashion of English footmen, with a stick, but such as single-stick players use, with which they can keep off more than one assailant. In obedience to an order of the Abbe's, Esther had never spoken a word to this escort. When madame wished to go home, Europe gave a call; the man in waiting whistled to the driver, who was always within hearing.

When Lucien was walking with Esther, Europe and this man remained about a hundred paces behind, like two of the infernal minions that figure in the *Thousand and One Nights*, which enchanters place at the service of their devotees.

The men, and yet more the women of Paris, know nothing of the charm of a walk in the woods on a fine night. The stillness, the moonlight effects, the solitude, have the soothing effect of a bath. Esther usually went out at ten, walked about from midnight till one o'clock, and came in at half-past two. It was never daylight in her rooms till eleven. She then bathed and went through an elaborate toilet which is unknown to most women, for it takes up too much time, and is rarely carried out by any but courtesans, women of the town, or fine ladies who have the day before them. She was only just ready when Lucien came, and appeared before him as a newly opened flower. Her only care was that her poet should be happy; she was his toy, his chattel; she gave him entire liberty. She never cast a glance beyond the circle where she shone. On this the Abbe had insisted, for it was part of his profound policy that Lucien should have gallant adventures.

Happiness has no history, and the story-tellers of all lands have understood this so well that the words, "They are happy," are the end of every love tale. Hence only the ways and means can be recorded of this really romantic happiness in the heart of Paris. It was happiness in its loveliest form, a poem, a symphony, of four years' duration. Every woman will exclaim, "That was much!" Neither Esther nor Lucien had ever said, "This is too much!" And the formula, "They were happy," was more emphatically true, than even in a fairy tale, for "they had *no* children."

So Lucien could coquet with the world, give way to his poet's caprices, and, it may be plainly admitted, to the necessities of his position. All this time he was slowly making his way, and was able to render secret service to certain political personages by helping them in their work. In such matters he was eminently discreet. He cultivated Madame de Serizy's circle, being, it was rumored, on the very best terms with that lady. Madame de Serizy had carried him off from the Duchesse de Maufrigneuse, who, it was said, had "thrown him over," one of the phrases by which women avenge themselves on happiness they envy. Lucien was in the lap, so to speak, of the High Almoner's set, and intimate with women who were the Archbishop's personal friends. He was modest and reserved; he waited patiently. So de Marsay's speech—de Marsay was now married, and made his wife live as retired a life as Esther—was significant in more ways that one.

But the submarine perils of such a course as Lucien's will be sufficiently obvious in the course of this chronicle.

MATTERS WERE IN THIS POSITION when, one fine night in August, the Baron de Nucingen was driving back to Paris from the country residence of a foreign banker, settled in France, with whom he had been dining. The estate lay at eight leagues from Paris in the district of la Brie. Now, the Baron's coachman having undertaken to drive his master there and back with his own horses, at nightfall ventured to moderate the pace.

As they entered the forest of Vincennes the position of beast, man, and master was as follows:—The coachman, liberally soaked in the kitchen of the aristocrat of the Bourse, was perfectly tipsy, and slept soundly, while still holding the reins to deceive other wayfarers. The footman, seated behind, was snoring like a wooden top from Germany—the land of little carved figures, of large wine-vats, and of humming-tops. The Baron had tried to think; but after passing the bridge at Gournay, the soft somnolence of digestion had sealed his eyes. The horses understood the coachman's plight from the slackness of the reins; they heard the footman's basso continuo from his perch behind; they saw that they were masters of the situation, and took advantage of their few minutes' freedom to make their own pace. Like intelligent slaves, they gave highway robbers the chance of plundering one of the richest capitalists in France, the most deeply cunning of the race which, in France, have been energetically styled lynxes—loups-cerviers. Finally, being independent of control, and tempted by the curiosity which every one must have remarked in domestic animals, they stopped where four roads met, face to face with some other horses, whom they, no doubt, asked in horses' language: "Who may you be? What are you doing? Are you comfortable?"

When the chaise stopped, the Baron awoke from his nap. At first he fancied that he was still in his friend's park; then he was startled by a celestial vision, which found him unarmed with his usual weapon—self-interest. The moonlight was brilliant; he could have read by it—even an evening paper. In the silence of the forest, under this pure light, the Baron saw a woman, alone, who, as she got into a hired chaise, looked at the strange spectacle of this sleep-stricken carriage. At the sight of this angel the Baron felt as though a light had flashed into glory within him. The young lady, seeing herself admired, pulled down her veil with terrified haste. The man-servant gave a signal which the driver perfectly understood, for the vehicle went off like an arrow.

The old banker was fearfully agitated; the blood left his feet cold and carried fire to his brain, his head sent the flame back to his heart; he was chocking. The unhappy man foresaw a fit of indigestion, but in spite of that supreme terror he stood up.

"Follow qvick, fery qvick.—Tam you, you are ashleep!" he cried. "A hundert franc if you catch up dat chaise."

At the words "A hundred francs," the coachman woke up. The servant behind heard them, no doubt, in his dreams. The baron reiterated his orders, the coachman urged the horses to a gallop, and at the Barriere du Trone had succeeded in overtaking a carriage resembling that in which Nucingen had seen the divine fair one, but which contained a swaggering head-clerk from some first-class shop and a lady of the Rue Vivienne.

This blunder filled the Baron with consternation.

"If only I had prought Chorge inshtead of you, shtupid fool, he should have fount dat voman," said he to the servant, while the excise officers were searching the carriage.

"Indeed, Monsieur le Baron, the devil was behind the chaise, I believe, disguised as an armed escort, and he sent this chaise instead of hers."

"Dere is no such ting as de Teufel," said the Baron.

The Baron de Nucingen owned to sixty; he no longer cared for women, and for his wife least of all. He boasted that he had never known such love as makes a fool of a man. He declared that he was happy to have done with women; the most angelic of them, he frankly said, was not worth what she cost, even if you got her for nothing. He was supposed to be so entirely blasé, that he no longer paid two thousand francs a month for the pleasure of being deceived. His eyes looked coldly down from his opera box on the corps de ballet; never a glance was shot at the capitalist by any one of that formidable swarm of old young girls, and young old women, the cream of Paris pleasure.

Natural love, artificial and love-of-show love, love based on self-esteem and vanity, love as a display of taste, decent, conjugal love, eccentric love—the Baron had paid for them all, had known them all excepting real spontaneous love. This passion had now pounced down on him like an eagle on its prey, as it did on Gentz, the confidential friend of His Highness the Prince of Metternich. All the world knows what follies the old diplomate committed for Fanny Elssler, whose rehearsals took up a great deal more of his time than the concerns of Europe.

The woman who had just overthrown that iron-bound money-box, called Nucingen, had appeared to him as one of those who are unique in their generation. It is not certain that Titian's mistress, or Leonardo da Vinci's Monna Lisa, or Raphael's Fornarina were as beautiful as this exquisite Esther, in whom not the most practised eye of the most experienced Parisian could have detected the faintest trace of the ordinary courtesan. The Baron was especially startled by the noble and stately air, the air of a well-born woman, which Esther, beloved, and lapped in luxury, elegance, and devotedness, had in the highest degree. Happy love is the divine unction of women; it makes them all as lofty as empresses.

For eight nights in succession the Baron went to the forest of Vincennes, then to the Bois de Boulogne, to the woods of Ville-d'Avray, to Meudon, in short, everywhere in the neighborhood of Paris, but failed to meet Esther. That beautiful Jewish face, which he called "a face out of te Biple," was always before his eyes. By the end of a fortnight he had lost his appetite.

Delphine de Nucingen, and her daughter Augusta, whom the Baroness was now taking out, did not at first perceive the change that had come over the Baron. The mother and daughter only saw him at breakfast in the morning and at dinner in the evening, when they all dined at home, and this was only on the evenings when Delphine received company. But by the end of two months, tortured by a fever of impatience, and in a state like that produced by acute home-sickness, the Baron, amazed to find his millions impotent, grew so thin, and seemed so seriously ill, that Delphine had secret hopes of finding herself a widow. She pitied her husband, somewhat hypocritically, and kept her daughter in seclusion. She bored her husband with questions; he answered as Englishmen answer when suffering from spleen, hardly a word.

Delphine de Nucingen gave a grand dinner every Sunday. She had chosen that day for her receptions, after observing that no people of fashion went to the play, and that the day was pretty generally an open one. The emancipation of the shopkeeping and middle classes makes Sunday almost as tiresome in Paris as it is deadly in London. So the Baroness invited the famous Desplein to dinner, to consult him in spite of the sick man, for Nucingen persisted in asserting that he was perfectly well.

Keller, Rastignac, de Marsay, du Tillet, all their friends had made the Baroness understand that a man like Nucingen could not be allowed to die without any notice being taken of it; his enormous business transactions demanded some care; it was absolutely necessary to know where he stood. These gentlemen also were asked to dinner, and the Comte de Gondreville, Francois Keller's father-in-law, the Chevalier d'Espard, des Lupeaulx, Doctor Bianchon—Desplein's best beloved pupil—Beaudenord and his wife, the Comte and Comtesse de Montcornet, Blondet, Mademoiselle des Touches and Conti, and finally, Lucien de Rubempre, for whom Rastignac had for the last five years manifested the warmest regard—by order, as the advertisements have it.

"We shall not find it easy to get rid of that young fellow," said Blondet to Rastignac, when he saw Lucien come in handsomer than ever, and uncommonly well dressed.

"It is wiser to make friends with him, for he is formidable," said Rastignac.

"He?" said de Marsay. "No one is formidable to my knowledge but men whose position is assured, and his is unattacked rather than attackable! Look here, what does he live on? Where does his money come from? He has, I am certain, sixty thousand francs in debts."

"He has found a friend in a very rich Spanish priest who has taken a fancy to him," replied Rastignac.

"He is going to be married to the eldest Mademoiselle de Grandlieu," said Mademoiselle des Touches.

"Yes," said the Chevalier d'Espard, "but they require him to buy an estate worth thirty thousand francs a year as security for the fortune he is to settle on the young lady, and for that he needs a million francs, which are not to be found in any Spaniard's shoes."

"That is dear, for Clotilde is very ugly," said the Baroness.

Madame de Nucingen affected to call Mademoiselle de Grandlieu by her Christian name, as though she, nee Goriot, frequented that society.

"No," replied du Tillet, "the daughter of a duchess is never ugly to the like of us, especially when she brings with her the title of Marquis and a diplomatic appointment. But the great obstacle to the marriage is Madame de Serizy's insane passion for Lucien. She must give him a great deal of money."

"Then I am not surprised at seeing Lucien so serious; for Madame de Serizy will certainly not give him a million francs to help him to marry Mademoiselle de Grandlieu. He probably sees no way out of the scrape," said de Marsay.

"But Mademoiselle de Grandlieu worships him," said the Comtesse de Montcornet; "and with the young person's assistance, he may perhaps make better terms."

"And what will he do with his sister and brother-in-law at Angouleme?" asked the Chevalier d'Espard.

"Well, his sister is rich," replied Rastignac, "and he now speaks of her as Madame Sechard de Marsac."

"Whatever difficulties there may be, he is a very good-looking fellow," said Bianchon, rising to greet Lucien.

"How 'do, my dear fellow?" said Rastignac, shaking hands warmly with Lucien.

De Marsay bowed coldly after Lucien had first bowed to him.

Before dinner Desplein and Bianchon, who studied the Baron while amusing him, convinced themselves that this malady was entirely nervous; but neither could guess the cause, so impossible did it seem that the great politician of the money market could be in love. When Bianchon, seeing nothing but love to account for the banker's condition, hinted as much to Delphine de Nucingen, she smiled as a woman who has long known all her husband's weaknesses. After dinner, however, when they all adjourned to the garden, the more intimate of the party gathered round the banker, eager to clear up this extraordinary case when they heard Bianchon pronounce that Nucingen must be in love.

"Do you know, Baron," said de Marsay, "that you have grown very thin? You are suspected of violating the laws of financial Nature."

"Ach, nefer!" said the Baron.

"Yes, yes," replied de Marsay. "They dare to say that you are in love."

"Dat is true," replied Nucingen piteously; "I am in lof for somebody I do not know."

"You, in love, you? You are a coxcomb!" said the Chevalier d'Espard.

"In lof, at my aje! I know dat is too ridiculous. But vat can I help it! Dat is so."

"A woman of the world?" asked Lucien.

"Nay," said de Marsay. "The Baron would not grow so thin but for a hopeless love, and he has money enough to buy all the women who will or can sell themselves!"

"I do not know who she it," said the Baron. "And as Motame de Nucingen is inside de trawing-room, I may say so, dat till now I have nefer known what it is to lof. Lof! I tink it is to grow tin."

"And where did you meet this innocent daisy?" asked Rastignac.

"In a carriage, at mitnight, in de forest of Fincennes."

"Describe her," said de Marsay.

"A vhite gaze hat, a rose gown, a vhite scharf, a vhite feil—a face just out of de Biple. Eyes like Feuer, an Eastern color—"

"You were dreaming," said Lucien, with a smile.

"Dat is true; I vas shleeping like a pig—a pig mit his shkin full," he added, "for I vas on my vay home from tinner at mine friend's—"

"Was she alone?" said du Tillet, interrupting him.

"Ja," said the Baron dolefully; "but she had ein heiduque behind dat carriage and a maid-shervant—"

"Lucien looks as if he knew her," exclaimed Rastignac, seeing Esther's lover smile.

"Who doesn't know the woman who would go out at midnight to meet Nucingen?" said Lucien, turning on his heel.

"Well, she is not a woman who is seen in society, or the Baron would have recognized the man," said the Chevalier d'Espard.

"I have nefer seen him," replied the Baron. "And for forty days now I have had her seeked for by de Police, and dey do not find her."

"It is better that she should cost you a few hundred francs than cost you your life," said Desplein; "and, at your age, a passion without hope is dangerous, you might die of it."

"Ja, ja," replied the Baron, addressing Desplein. "And vat I eat does me no goot, de air I breade feels to choke me. I go to de forest of Fincennes to see de place vat I see her—and dat is all my life. I could not tink of de last loan—I trust to my partners vat haf pity on me. I could pay one million franc to see dat voman—and I should gain by dat, for I do nothing on de Bourse.—Ask du Tillet."

"Very true," replied du Tillet; "he hates business; he is quite unlike himself; it is a sign of death."

"A sign of lof," replied Nucingen; "and for me, dat is all de same ting."

The simple candor of the old man, no longer the stock-jobber, who, for the first time in his life, saw that something was more sacred and more precious than gold, really moved these world-hardened men; some exchanged smiles; other looked at Nucingen with an expression that plainly said, "Such a man to have come to this!"—And then they all returned to the drawing-room, talking over the event.

For it was indeed an event calculated to produce the greatest sensation. Madame de Nucingen went into fits of laughter when Lucien betrayed her husband's secret; but the Baron, when he heard his wife's sarcasms, took her by the arm and led her into the recess of a window.

"Motame," said he in an undertone, "have I ever laughed at all at your passions, that you should laugh at mine? A goot frau should help her husband out of his difficulty vidout making game of him like vat you do."

From the description given by the old banker, Lucien had recognized his Esther. Much annoyed that his smile should have been observed, he took advantage of a moment when coffee was served, and the conversation became general, to vanish from the scene.

"What has become of Monsieur de Rubempre?" said the Baroness.

"He is faithful to his motto: Quid me continebit?" said Rastignac.

"Which means, 'Who can detain me?' or 'I am unconquerable,' as you choose," added de Marsay.

"Just as Monsieur le Baron was speaking of his unknown lady, Lucien smiled in a way that makes me fancy he may know her," said Horace Bianchon, not thinking how dangerous such a natural remark might be.

"Goot!" said the banker to himself.

Like all incurables, the Baron clutched at everything that seemed at all hopeful; he promised himself that he would have Lucien watched by some one besides Louchard and his men—Louchard, the sharpest commercial detective in Paris—to whom he had applied about a fortnight since.

Before going home to Esther, Lucien was due at the Hotel Grandlieu, to spend the two hours which made Mademoiselle Clotilde Frederique de Grandlieu the happiest girl in the Faubourg Saint-Germain. But the prudence characteristic of this ambitious youth warned him to inform Carlos Herrera forthwith of the effect resulting from the smile wrung from him by the Baron's description of Esther. The banker's passion for Esther, and the idea that had occurred to him of setting the police to seek the unknown beauty, were indeed events of sufficient importance to be at once communicated to the man who had sought, under a priest's robe, the shelter which criminals of old could find in a church. And Lucien's road from the Rue Saint-Lazare, where Nucingen at that time lived, to the Rue Saint-Dominique, where was the Hotel Grandlieu, led him past his lodgings on the Quai Malaquais.

Lucien found his formidable friend smoking his breviary—that is to say, coloring a short pipe before retiring to bed. The man, strange rather than foreign, had given up Spanish cigarettes, finding them too mild.

"Matters look serious," said the Spaniard, when Lucien had told him all. "The Baron, who employs Louchard to hunt up the girl, will certainly be sharp enough to set a spy at your heels, and everything will come out. To-night and to-morrow morning will not give me more than enough time to pack the cards for the game I must play against the Baron; first and foremost, I must prove to him that the police cannot help him. When our lynx has given up all hope of finding his ewe-lamb, I will undertake to sell her for all she is worth to him—"

"Sell Esther!" cried Lucien, whose first impulse was always the right one.

"Do you forget where we stand?" cried Carlos Herrera.

"No money left," the Spaniard went on, "and sixty thousand francs of debts to be paid! If you want to marry Clotilde de Grandlieu, you must invest a million of francs in land as security for that ugly creature's settlement. Well, then, Esther is the quarry I mean to set before that lynx to help us to ease him of that million. That is my concern."

"Esther will never—"

"That is my concern."

"She will die of it."

"That is the undertaker's concern. Besides, what then?" cried the savage, checking Lucien's lamentations merely by his attitude. "How many generals died in the prime of life for the Emperor Napoleon?" he asked, after a short silence. "There are always plenty of women. In 1821 Coralie was unique in your eyes; and yet you found Esther. After her will come—do you know who?—the unknown fair. And she of all women is the fairest, and you will find her in the capital where the Duc de Grandlieu's son-in-law will be Minister and representative of the King of France.—And do you tell me now, great Baby, that Esther will die of it? Again, can Mademoiselle de Grandlieu's husband keep Esther?

"You have only to leave everything to me; you need not take the trouble to think at all; that is my concern. Only you must do without Esther for a week or two; but go to the Rue Taitbout, all the same.— Come, be off to bill and coo on your plank of salvation, and play your part well; slip the flaming note you wrote this morning into Clotilde's hand, and bring me back a warm response. She will recompense herself for many woes in writing. I take to that girl.

"You will find Esther a little depressed, but tell her to obey. We must display our livery of virtue, our doublet of honesty, the screen behind which all great men hide their infamy.—I must show off my handsomer self—you must never be suspected. Chance has served us better than my brain, which has been beating about in a void for these two months past."

All the while he was jerking out these dreadful sentences, one by one, like pistol shots, Carlos Herrera was dressing himself to go out.

"You are evidently delighted," cried Lucien. "You never liked poor Esther, and you look forward with joy to the moment when you will be rid of her."

"You have never tired of loving her, have you? Well, I have never tired of detesting her. But have I not always behaved as though I were sincerely attached to the hussy—I, who, through Asie, hold her life in my hands? A few bad mushrooms in a stew—and there an end. But Mademoiselle Esther still lives!—and is happy!—And do you know why? Because you love her. Do not be a fool. For four years we have been waiting for a chance to turn up, for us or against us; well, it will take something more than mere cleverness to wash the cabbage luck has flung at us now. There are good and bad together in this turn of the wheel—as there are in everything. Do you know what I was thinking of when you came in?"

"No."

"Of making myself heir here, as I did at Barcelona, to an old bigot, by Asie's help."

"A crime?"

"I saw no other way of securing your fortune. The creditors are making a stir. If once the bailiffs were at your heels, and you were turned out of the Hotel Grandlieu, where would you be? There would be the devil to pay then."

And Carlos Herrera, by a pantomimic gesture, showed the suicide of a man throwing himself into the water; then he fixed on Lucien one of those steady, piercing looks by which the will of a strong man is injected, so to speak, into a weak one. This fascinating glare, which relaxed all Lucien's fibres of resistance, revealed the existence not merely of secrets of life and death between him and his adviser, but also of feelings as far above ordinary feeling as the man himself was above his vile position.

Carlos Herrera, a man at once ignoble and magnanimous, obscure and famous, compelled to live out of the world from which the law had banned him, exhausted by vice and by frenzied and terrible struggles, though endowed with powers of mind that ate into his soul, consumed especially by a fever of vitality, now lived again in the elegant person of Lucien de Rubempre, whose soul had become his own. He was represented in social life by the poet, to whom he lent his tenacity and iron will. To him Lucien was more than a son, more than a woman beloved, more than a family, more than his life; he was his revenge; and as souls cling more closely to a feeling than to existence, he had bound the young man to him by insoluble ties.

After rescuing Lucien's life at the moment when the poet in desperation was on the verge of suicide, he had proposed to him one of those infernal bargains which are heard of only in romances, but of which the hideous possibility has often been proved in courts of justice by celebrated criminal dramas. While lavishing on Lucien all the delights of Paris life, and proving to him that he yet had a great future before him, he had made him his chattel.

But, indeed, no sacrifice was too great for this strange man when it was to gratify his second self. With all his strength, he was so weak to this creature of his making that he had even told him all his secrets. Perhaps this abstract complicity was a bond the more between them.

Since the day when La Torpille had been snatched away, Lucien had known on what a vile foundation his good fortune rested. That priest's robe covered Jacques Collin, a man famous on the hulks, who ten years since had lived under the homely name of Vautrin in the Maison Vauquer, where Rastignac and Bianchon were at that time boarders.

Jacques Collin, known as *Trompe-la-Mort*, had escaped from Rochefort almost as soon as he was recaptured, profiting by the example of the famous Comte de Sainte-Helene, while modifying all that was ill planned in Coignard's daring scheme. To take the place of an honest man and carry on the convict's career is a proposition of which the two terms are too contradictory for a disastrous outcome not to be inevitable, especially in Paris; for, by establishing himself in a family, a convict multiplies tenfold the perils of such a substitution. And to be safe from all investigation, must not a man assume a position far above the ordinary interests of life. A man of the world is subject to risks such as rarely trouble those who have no contact with the world; hence the priest's gown is the safest disguise when it can be authenticated by an exemplary life in solitude and inactivity.

"So a priest I will be," said the legally dead man, who was quite determined to resuscitate as a figure in the world, and to satisfy passions as strange as himself.

The civil war caused by the Constitution of 1812 in Spain, whither this energetic man had betaken himself, enabled him to murder secretly the real Carlos Herrera from an ambush. This ecclesiastic, the bastard son of a grandee, long since deserted by his father, and not knowing to what woman he owed his birth, was intrusted by King Ferdinand VII, to whom a bishop had recommended him, with a political mission to France. The bishop, the only man who took any interest in Carlos Herrera, died while this foundling son of the Church was on his journey from Cadiz to Madrid, and from Madrid to France. Delighted to have met with this longed-for opportunity, and under the most desirable conditions, Jacques Collin scored his back to efface the fatal letters, and altered his complexion by the use of chemicals. Thus metamorphosing himself face to face with the corpse, he contrived to achieve some likeness to his Sosia. And to complete a change almost as marvelous as that related in the Arabian tale, where a dervish has acquired the power, old as he is, of entering into a young body, by a magic spell, the convict, who spoke Spanish, learned as much Latin as an Andalusian priest need know.

As banker to three hulks, Collin was rich in the cash intrusted to his known, and indeed enforced, honesty. Among such company a mistake is paid for by a dagger thrust. To this capital he now added the money given by the bishop to Don Carlos Herrera. Then, before leaving Spain, he was able to possess himself of the treasure of an old bigot at Barcelona, to whom he gave absolution, promising that he would make restitution of the money constituting her fortune, which his penitent had stolen by means of murder.

Jacques Collin, now a priest, and charged with a secret mission which would secure him the most brilliant introductions in Paris, determined to do nothing that might compromise the character he had assumed, and had given himself up to the chances of his new life, when he met Lucien on the road between Angouleme and Paris. In this youth the sham priest saw a wonderful instrument for power; he saved him from suicide saying:

"Give yourself over to me as to a man of God, as men give themselves over to the devil, and you will have every chance of a new career. You will live as in a dream, and the worst awakening that can come to you will be death, which you now wish to meet."

The alliance between these two beings, who were to become one, as it were, was based on this substantial reasoning, and Carlos Herrera cemented it by an ingeniously plotted complicity. He had the very genius of corruption, and undermined Lucien's honesty by plunging him into cruel necessity, and extricating him by obtaining his tacit consent to bad or disgraceful actions, which nevertheless left him pure, loyal, and noble in the eyes of the world. Lucien was the social magnificence under whose shadow the forger meant to live.

"I am the author, you are the play; if you fail, it is I who shall be hissed," said he on the day when he confessed his sacrilegious disguise.

Carlos prudently confessed only a little at a time, measuring the horrors of his revelations by Lucien's progress and needs. Thus *Trompe-la-Mort* did not let out his last secret till the habit of Parisian pleasures and success, and gratified vanity, had enslaved the weak-minded poet body and soul. Where Rastignac, when tempted by this demon, had stood firm, Lucien, better managed, and more ingeniously compromised, succumbed, conquered especially by his satisfaction in having attained an eminent position. Incarnate evil, whose poetical embodiment is called the Devil, displayed every delightful seduction before this youth, who was half a woman, and at first gave much and asked for little. The great argument used by Carlos was the eternal secret promised by Tartufe to Elmire.

The repeated proofs of absolute devotion, such as that of Said to Mahomet, put the finishing touch to the horrible achievement of Lucien's subjugation by a Jacques Collin.

At this moment not only had Esther and Lucien devoured all the funds intrusted to the honesty of the banker of the hulks, who, for their sakes, had rendered himself liable to a dreadful calling to account, but the dandy, the forger, and the courtesan were also in debt. Thus, as the very moment of Lucien's expected success, the smallest pebble under the foot of either of these three persons might involve the ruin of the fantastic structure of fortune so audaciously built up.

At the opera ball Rastignac had recognized the man he had known as Vautrin at Madame Vauquer's; but he knew that if he did not hold his tongue, he was a dead man. So Madame de Nucingen's lover and Lucien had exchanged glances in which fear lurked, on both sides, under an expression of amity. In the moment of danger, Rastignac, it is clear, would have been delighted to provide the vehicle that should convey Jacques Collin to the scaffold. From all this it may be understood that Carlos heard of the Baron's passion with a glow of sombre satisfaction, while he perceived in a single flash all the advantage a man of his temper might derive by means of a hapless Esther.

"Go on," said he to Lucien. "The Devil is mindful of his chaplain."

"You are smoking on a powder barrel."

"Incedo per ignes," replied Carlos with a smile. "That is my trade."

THE HOUSE OF GRANDLIEU DIVIDED into two branches about the middle of the last century: first, the ducal line destined to lapse, since the present duke has only daughters; and then the Vicomtes de Grandlieu, who will now inherit the title and armorial bearings of the elder branch. The ducal house bears gules, three broad axes or in fess, with the famous motto: Caveo non timeo, which epitomizes the history of the family.

The coat of the Vicomtes de Grandlieu is the same quartered with that of Navarreins: gules, a fess crenelated or, surmounted by a knight's helmet, with the motto: Grands faits, grand lieu. The present Viscountess, widowed in 1813, has a son and a daughter. Though she returned from the Emigration almost ruined, she recovered a considerable fortune by the zealous aid of Derville the lawyer.

The Duc and Duchesse de Grandlieu, on coming home in 1804, were the object of the Emperor's advances; indeed, Napoleon, seeing them come to his court, restored to them all of the Grandlieu estates that had been confiscated to the nation, to the amount of about forty thousand francs a year. Of all the great nobles of the Faubourg Saint-Germain who allowed themselves to be won over by Napoleon, this Duke and Duchess—she was an Ajuda of the senior branch, and connected with the Braganzas—were the only family who afterwards never disowned him and his liberality. When the Faubourg Saint-Germain remembered this as a crime against the Grandlieus, Louis XVIII respected them for it; but perhaps his only object was to annoy *Monsieur*.

A marriage was considered likely between the young Vicomte de Grandlieu and Marie-Athenais, the Duke's youngest daughter, now nine years old. Sabine, the youngest but one, married the Baron du Guenic after the revolution of July 1830; Josephine, the third, became Madame d'Ajuda-Pinto after the death of the Marquis' first wife, Mademoiselle de Rochefide, or Rochegude. The eldest had taken the veil in 1822. The second, Mademoiselle Clotilde Frederique, at this time seven-and-twenty years of age, was deeply in love with Lucien de Rubempre. It need not be asked whether the Duc de Grandlieu's mansion, one of the finest in the Rue Saint-Dominique, did not exert a thousand spells over Lucien's imagination. Every time the heavy gate turned on its hinges to admit his cab, he experienced the gratified vanity to which Mirabeau confessed.

"Though my father was a mere druggist at l'Houmeau, I may enter here!" This was his thought.

And, indeed, he would have committed far worse crimes than allying himself with a forger to preserve his right to mount the steps of that entrance, to hear himself announced, "Monsieur de Rubempre" at the door of the fine Louis XIV drawing-room, decorated in the time of the grand monarque on the pattern of those at Versailles, where that choicest circle met, that cream of Paris society, called then le petit chateau.

The noble Portuguese lady, one of those who never care to go out of their own home, was usually the centre of her neighbors' attentions—the Chaulieus, the Navarreins, the Lenoncourts. The pretty Baronne de Macumer—nee de Chaulieu—the Duchesse de Maufrigneuse, Madame d'Espard, Madame de Camps, and

Mademoiselle des Touches—a connection of the Grandlieus, who are a Breton family—were frequent visitors on their way to a ball or on their return from the opera. The Vicomte de Grandlieu, the Duc de Rhetore, the Marquis de Chaulieu—afterwards Duc de Lenoncourt-Chaulieu—his wife, Madeleine de Mortsauf, the Duc de Lenoncourt's grand-daughter, the Marquis d'Ajuda-Pinto, the Prince de Blamont-Chauvry, the Marquis de Beauseant, the Vidame de Pamiers, the Vandenesses, the old Prince de Cadignan, and his son the Duc de Maufrigneuse, were constantly to be seen in this stately drawing-room, where they breathed the atmosphere of a Court, where manners, tone, and wit were in harmony with the dignity of the Master and Mistress whose aristocratic mien and magnificence had obliterated the memory of their servility to Napoleon.

The old Duchesse d'Uxelles, mother of the Duchesse de Maufrigneuse, was the oracle of this circle, to which Madame de Serizy had never gained admittance, though nee de Ronquerolles.

Lucien was brought thither by Madame de Maufrigneuse, who had won over her mother to speak in his favor, for she had doted on him for two years; and the engaging young poet had kept his footing there, thanks to the influence of the high Almoner of France, and the support of the Archbishop of Paris. Still, he had not been admitted till he had obtained the patent restoring to him the name and arms of the Rubempre family. The Duc de Rhetore, the Chevalier d'Espard, and some others, jealous of Lucien, periodically stirred up the Duc de Grandlieu's prejudices against him by retailing anecdotes of the young man's previous career; but the Duchess, a devout Catholic surrounded by the great prelates of the Church, and her daughter Clotilde would not give him up.

Lucien accounted for these hostilities by his connection with Madame de Bargeton, Madame d'Espard's cousin, and now Comtesse du Chatelet. Then, feeling the importance of allying himself to so powerful a family, and urged by his privy adviser to win Clotilde, Lucien found the courage of the parvenu; he came to the house five days in the week, he swallowed all the affronts of the envious, he endured impertinent looks, and answered irony with wit. His persistency, the charm of his manners, and his amiability, at last neutralized opposition and reduced obstacles. He was still in the highest favor with Madame de Maufrigneuse, whose ardent letters, written under the influence of her passion, were preserved by Carlos Herrera; he was idolized by Madame de Serizy, and stood well in Mademoiselle des Touches' good graces; and well content with being received in these houses, Lucien was instructed by the Abbe to be as reserved as possible in all other quarters.

"You cannot devote yourself to several houses at once," said his Mentor. "The man who goes everywhere finds no one to take a lively interest in him. Great folks only patronize those who emulate their furniture, whom they see every day, and who have the art of becoming as necessary to them as the seat they sit on."

Thus Lucien, accustomed to regard the Grandlieus' drawing-room as his arena, reserved his wit, his jests, his news, and his courtier's graces for the hours he spent there every evening. Insinuating, tactful, and warned by Clotilde of the shoals he should avoid, he flattered Monsieur de Grandlieu's little weaknesses. Clotilde, having begun by envying Madame de Maufrigneuse her happiness, ended by falling desperately in love with Lucien.

Perceiving all the advantages of such a connection, Lucien played his lover's part as well as it could have been acted by Armand, the latest *jeune premier* at the *Comedie Francaise*.

He wrote to Clotilde, letters which were certainly masterpieces of literary workmanship; and Clotilde replied, vying with him in genius in the expression of perfervid love on paper, for she had no other outlet. Lucien went to church at Saint-Thomas-d'Aquin every Sunday, giving himself out as a devout Catholic, and he poured forth monarchical and pious harangues which were a marvel to all. He also wrote some exceedingly remarkable articles in papers devoted to the "Congregation," refusing to be paid for them, and signing them only with an "L." He produced political pamphlets when required by King Charles X or the High Almoner, and for these he would take no payment.

"The King," he would say, "has done so much for me, that I owe him my blood."

For some days past there had been an idea of attaching Lucien to the prime minister's cabinet as his private secretary; but Madame d'Espard brought so many persons into the field in opposition to Lucien, that Charles X's *Maitre Jacques* hesitated to clinch the matter. Nor was Lucien's position by any means clear; not only did the question, "What does he live on?" on everybody's lips as the young man rose in life, require an answer, but even benevolent curiosity—as much as malevolent curiosity—went on from one inquiry to another, and found more than one joint in the ambitious youth's harness.

Clotilde de Grandlieu unconsciously served as a spy for her father and mother. A few days since she had led Lucien into a recess and told him of the difficulties raised by her family.

"Invest a million francs in land, and my hand is yours: that is my mother's ultimatum," Clotilde had explained.

"And presently they will ask you where you got the money," said Carlos, when Lucien reported this last word in the bargain.

"My brother-in-law will have made his fortune," remarked Lucien; "we can make him the responsible backer."

"Then only the million is needed," said Carlos. "I will think it over."

To be exact as to Lucien's position in the Hotel Grandlieu, he had never dined there. Neither Clotilde, nor the Duchesse d'Uxelles, nor Madame de Maufrigneuse, who was always extremely kind to Lucien, could ever obtain this favor from the Duke, so persistently suspicious was the old nobleman of the man that he designated as "le Sire de Rubempre." This shade of distinction, understood by every one who visited at the house, constantly wounded Lucien's self-respect, for he felt that he was no more than tolerated. But the world is justified in being suspicious; it is so often taken in!

To cut a figure in Paris with no known source of wealth and no recognized employment is a position which can by no artifice be long maintained. So Lucien, as he crept up in the world, gave more and more weight to the question, "What does he live on?" He had been obliged indeed to confess to Madame de Serizy, to whom he owed the patronage of Monsieur Granville, the Public Prosecutor, and of the Comte Octave de Bauvan, a Minister of State, and President of one of the Supreme Courts: "I am dreadfully in debt."

As he entered the courtyard of the mansion where he found an excuse for all his vanities, he was saying to himself as he reflected on *Trompe-la-Mort's* scheming:

"I can hear the ground cracking under my feet!"

He loved Esther, and he wanted to marry Mademoiselle de Grandlieu! A strange dilemma! One must be sold to buy the other.

Only one person could effect this bargain without damage to Lucien's honor, and that was the supposed Spaniard. Were they not bound to be equally secret, each for the other? Such a compact, in which each is in turn master and slave, is not to be found twice in any one life.

Lucien drove away the clouds that darkened his brow, and walked into the Grandlieu drawing-room gay and beaming. At this moment the windows were open, the fragrance from the garden scented the room, the flower-basket in the centre displayed its pyramid of flowers. The Duchess, seated on a sofa in the corner, was talking to the Duchesse de Chaulieu. Several women together formed a group remarkable for their various attitudes, stamped with the different expression which each strove to give to an affected sorrow. In the fashionable world nobody takes any interest in grief or suffering; everything is talk. The men were walking up and down the room or in the garden. Clotilde and Josephine were busy at the tea-table. The Vidame de Pamiers, the Duc de Grandlieu, the Marquis d'Ajuda-Pinto, and the Duc de Maufrigneuse were playing Wisk, as they called it, in a corner of the room.

When Lucien was announced he walked across the room to make his bow to the Duchess, asking the cause of the grief he could read in her face.

"Madame de Chaulieu has just had dreadful news; her son-in-law, the Baron de Macumer, ex-duke of Soria, is just dead. The young Duc de Soria and his wife, who had gone to Chantepleurs to nurse their brother, have written this sad intelligence. Louise is heart-broken."

"A women is not loved twice in her life as Louise was loved by her husband," said Madeleine de Mortsauf.

"She will be a rich widow," observed the old Duchesse d'Uxelles, looking at Lucien, whose face showed no change of expression.

"Poor Louise!" said Madame d'Espard. "I understand her and pity her."

The Marquise d'Espard put on the pensive look of a woman full of soul and feeling. Sabine de Grandlieu, who was but ten years old, raised knowing eyes to her mother's face, but the satirical glance was repressed by a glance from the Duchess. This is bringing children up properly.

"If my daughter lives through the shock," said Madame de Chaulieu, with a very maternal manner, "I shall be anxious about her future life. Louise is so very romantic."

"It is so difficult nowadays," said a venerable Cardinal, "to reconcile feeling with the proprieties."

Lucien, who had not a word to say, went to the tea-table to do what was polite to the demoiselles de Grandlieu. When the poet had gone a few yards away, the Marquise d'Espard leaned over to whisper in the Duchess' ear:

"And do you really think that that young fellow is so much in love with your Clotilde?"

The perfidy of this question cannot be fully understood but with the help of a sketch of Clotilde. That young lady was, at this moment, standing up. Her attitude allowed the Marquise d'Espard's mocking eye to take in Clotilde's lean, narrow figure, exactly like an asparagus stalk; the poor girl's bust was so flat that it did not allow of the artifice known to dressmakers as *fichus menteurs*, or padded habitshirts. And Clotilde, who knew that her name was a sufficient advantage in life, far from trying to conceal this defect, heroically made a display of it. By wearing plain, tight dresses she achieved the effect of that stiff prim shape which medieval sculptors succeeded in giving to the statuettes whose profiles are conspicuous against the background of the niches in which they stand in cathedrals.

Clotilde was more than five feet four in height; if we may be allowed to use a familiar phrase, which has the merit at any rate of being perfectly intelligible—she was all legs. These defective proportions gave her figure an almost deformed appearance. With a dark complexion, harsh black hair, very thick eyebrows, fiery eyes, set in sockets that were already deeply discolored, a side face shaped like the moon in its first quarter, and a prominent brow, she was the caricature of her mother, one of the handsomest women in Portugal. Nature amuses herself with such tricks. Often we see in one family a sister of wonderful beauty, whose features in her brother are absolutely hideous, though the two are amazingly alike. Clotilde's lips, excessively thin and sunken, wore a permanent expression of disdain. And yet her mouth, better than any other feature of her face, revealed every secret impulse of her heart, for affection lent it a sweet expression, which was all the more remarkable because her cheeks were too sallow for blushes, and her hard, black eyes never told anything. Notwithstanding these defects, notwithstanding her board-like carriage, she had by birth and education a grand air, a proud demeanor, in short, everything that has been well named le je ne sais quoi, due partly, perhaps, to her uncompromising simplicity of dress, which stamped her as a woman of noble blood. She dressed her hair to advantage, and it might be accounted to her for a beauty, for it grew vigorously, thick and long.

She had cultivated her voice, and it could cast a spell; she sang exquisitely. Clotilde was just the woman of whom one says, "She has fine eyes," or, "She has a delightful temper." If any one addressed her in the English fashion as "Your Grace," she would say, "You mean 'Your leanness.'"

"Why should not my poor Clotilde have a lover?" replied the Duchess to the Marquise. "Do you know what she said to me yesterday? 'If I am loved for ambition's sake, I undertake to make him love me for my own sake.'—She is clever and ambitious, and there are men who like those two qualities. As for him—my dear, he is as handsome as a vision; and if he can but repurchase the Rubempre estates, out of regard for us the King will reinstate him in the title of Marquis.—After all, his mother was the last of the Rubempres."

"Poor fellow! where is he to find a million francs?" said the Marquise.

"That is no concern of ours," replied the Duchess. "He is certainly incapable of stealing the money.—Besides, we would never give Clotilde to an intriguing or dishonest man even if he were handsome, young, and a poet, like Monsieur de Rubempre."

"You are late this evening," said Clotilde, smiling at Lucien with infinite graciousness.

"Yes, I have been dining out."

"You have been quite gay these last few days," said she, concealing her jealousy and anxiety behind a smile.

"Quite gay?" replied Lucien. "No—only by the merest chance I have been dining every day this week with bankers; to-day with the Nucingens, yesterday with du Tillet, the day before with the Kellers—"

Whence, it may be seen, that Lucien had succeeded in assuming the tone of light impertinence of great people.

"You have many enemies," said Clotilde, offering him—how graciously!—a cup of tea. "Some one told my father that you have debts to the amount of sixty thousand francs, and that before long Sainte-Pelagie will be your summer quarters.—If you could know what all these calumnies are to me!—It all recoils on me.—I say nothing of my own suffering—my father has a way of looking that crucifies me—but of what you must be suffering if any least part of it should be the truth."

"Do not let such nonsense worry you; love me as I love you, and give me time—a few months—" said Lucien, replacing his empty cup on the silver tray.

"Do not let my father see you; he would say something disagreeable; and as you could not submit to that, we should be done for.—That odious Marquise d'Espard told him that your mother had been a monthly nurse and that your sister did ironing—"

"We were in the most abject poverty," replied Lucien, the tears rising to his eyes. "That is not calumny, but it is most ill-natured gossip. My sister now is a more than millionaire, and my mother has been dead two years.—This information has been kept in stock to use just when I should be on the verge of success here—"

"But what have you done to Madame d'Espard?"

"I was so rash, at Madame de Serizy's, as to tell the story, with some added pleasantries, in the presence of Mm. de Bauvan and de Granville, of her attempt to get a commission of lunacy appointed to sit on her husband, the Marquis d'Espard. Bianchon had told it to me. Monsieur de Granville's opinion, supported by those of Bauvan and Serizy, influenced the decision of the Keeper of the Seals. They all were afraid of the *Gazette des Tribunaux*, and dreaded the scandal, and the Marquise got her knuckles rapped in the summing up for the judgment finally recorded in that miserable business.

"Though M. de Serizy by his tattle has made the Marquise my mortal foe, I gained his good offices, and those of the Public Prosecutor, and Comte Octave de Bauvan; for Madame de Serizy told them the danger in which I stood in consequence of their allowing the source of their information to be guessed at. The Marquis d'Espard was so clumsy as to call upon me, regarding me as the first cause of his winning the day in that atrocious suit."

"I will rescue you from Madame d'Espard," said Clotilde.

"How?" cried Lucien.

"My mother will ask the young d'Espards here; they are charming boys, and growing up now. The father and sons will sing your praises, and then we are sure never to see their mother again."

"Oh, Clotilde, you are an angel! If I did not love you for yourself, I should love you for being so clever."

"It is not cleverness," said she, all her love beaming on her lips. "Goodnight. Do not come again for some few days. When you see me in church, at Saint-Thomas-d'Aquin, with a pink scarf, my father will be in a better temper.—You will find an answer stuck to the back of the chair you are sitting in; it will comfort you perhaps for not seeing me. Put the note you have brought under my handkerchief—"

This young person was evidently more than seven-and-twenty.

Lucien took a cab in the Rue de la Planche, got out of it on the Boulevards, took another by the Madeleine, and desired the driver to have the gates opened and drive in at the house in the Rue Taitbout.

On going in at eleven o'clock, he found Esther in tears, but dressed as she was wont to dress to do him honor. She awaited her Lucien reclining on a sofa covered with white satin brocaded with yellow flowers, dressed in a bewitching wrapper of India muslin with cherry-colored bows; without her stays, her hair simply twisted into a knot, her feet in little velvet slippers lined with cherry-colored satin; all the candles were burning, the hookah was prepared. But she had not smoked her own, which stood beside her unlighted, emblematical of her loneliness. On hearing the doors open she sprang up like a gazelle, and threw her arms round Lucien, wrapping him like a web caught by the wind and flung about a tree.

"Parted.—Is it true?"

"Oh, just for a few days," replied Lucien.

Esther released him, and fell back on her divan like a dead thing.

In these circumstances, most women babble like parrots. Oh! how they love! At the end of five years they feel as if their first happiness were a thing of yesterday, they cannot give you up, they are magnificent in their indignation, despair, love, grief, dread, dejection, presentiments. In short, they are as sublime as a scene from Shakespeare. But make no mistake! These women do not love. When they are really all that they profess, when they love truly, they do as Esther did, as children do, as true love does; Esther did not say a word, she lay with her face buried in the pillows, shedding bitter tears.

Lucien, on his part, tried to lift her up, and spoke to her.

"But, my child, we are not to part. What, after four years of happiness, is this the way you take a short absence.—What on earth do I do to all these girls?" he added to himself, remembering that Coralie had loved him thus.

"Ah, monsieur, you are so handsome," said Europe.

The senses have their own ideal. When added to this fascinating beauty we find the sweetness of nature, the poetry, that characterized Lucien, it is easy to conceive of the mad passion roused in such women, keenly alive as they are to external gifts, and artless in their admiration. Esther was sobbing quietly, and lay in an attitude expressive of the deepest distress.

"But, little goose," said Lucien, "did you not understand that my life is at stake?"

At these words, which he chose on purpose, Esther started up like a wild animal, her hair fell, tumbling about her excited face like wreaths of foliage. She looked steadily at Lucien.

"Your life?" she cried, throwing up her arms, and letting them drop with a gesture known only to a courtesan in peril. "To be sure; that friend's note speaks of serious risk."

She took a shabby scrap of paper out of her sash; then seeing Europe, she said, "Leave us, my girl."

When Europe had shut the door she went on—"Here, this is what he writes," and she handed to Lucien a note she had just received from Carlos, which Lucien read aloud:—

> "You must leave to-morrow at five in the morning; you will be taken to a keeper's lodge in the heart of the Forest of Saint-Germain, where you will have a room on the first floor. Do not quit that room till I give you leave; you will want for nothing. The keeper and his wife are to be trusted. Do not write to Lucien. Do not go to the window during daylight; but you may walk by night with the keeper if you wish for exercise. Keep the carriage blinds down on the way. Lucien's life is at stake.
>
> "Lucien will go to-night to bid you good-bye; burn this in his presence."

Lucien burned the note at once in the flame of a candle.

"Listen, my own Lucien," said Esther, after hearing him read this letter as a criminal hears the sentence of death; "I will not tell you that I love you; it would be idiotic. For nearly five years it has been as natural to me to love you as to breathe and live. From the first day when my happiness began under the protection of that inscrutable being, who placed me here as you place some little curious beast in a cage, I have known that you must marry. Marriage is a necessary factor in your career, and God preserve me from hindering the development of your fortunes.

"That marriage will be my death. But I will not worry you; I will not do as the common girls do who kill themselves by means of a brazier of charcoal; I had enough of that once; twice raises your gorge, as Mariette says. No, I will go a long way off, out of France. Asie knows the secrets of her country; she will help me to die quietly. A prick—whiff, it is all over!

"I ask but one thing, my dearest, and that is that you will not deceive me. I have had my share of living. Since the day I first saw you, in 1824, till this day, I have known more happiness than can be put into the lives of ten fortunate wives. So take me for what I am—a woman as strong as I am weak. Say 'I am going to be married.' I will ask no more of you than a fond farewell, and you shall never hear of me again."

HONORÉ DE BALZAC

There was a moment's silence after this explanation as sincere as her action and tone were guileless.

"Is it that you are going to be married?" she repeated, looking into Lucien's blue eyes with one of her fascinating glances, as brilliant as a steel blade.

"We have been toiling at my marriage for eighteen months past, and it is not yet settled," replied Lucien. "I do not know when it can be settled; but it is not in question now, child!—It is the Abbe, I, you.— We are in real peril. Nucingen saw you—"

"Yes, in the wood at Vincennes," said she. "Did he recognize me?"

"No," said Lucien. "But he has fallen so desperately in love with you, that he would sacrifice his coffers. After dinner, when he was describing how he had met you, I was so foolish as to smile involuntarily, and most imprudently, for I live in a world like a savage surrounded by the traps of a hostile tribe. Carlos, who spares me the pains of thinking, regards the position as dangerous, and he has undertaken to pay Nucingen out if the Baron takes it into his head to spy on us; and he is quite capable of it; he spoke to me of the incapacity of the police. You have lighted a flame in an old chimney choked with soot."

"And what does your Spaniard propose to do?" asked Esther very softly.

"I do not know in the least," said Lucien; "he told me I might sleep soundly and leave it to him;"—but he dared not look at Esther.

"If that is the case, I will obey him with the dog-like submission I profess," said Esther, putting her hand through Lucien's arm and leading him into her bedroom, saying, "At any rate, I hope you dined well, my Lulu, at that detestable Baron's?"

"Asie's cooking prevents my ever thinking a dinner good, however famous the chef may be, where I happen to dine. However, Careme did the dinner to-night, as he does every Sunday."

Lucien involuntarily compared Esther with Clotilde. The mistress was so beautiful, so unfailingly charming, that she had as yet kept at arm's length the monster who devours the most perennial loves— Satiety.

"What a pity," thought he, "to find one's wife in two volumes. In one—poetry, delight, love, devotion, beauty, sweetness—"

Esther was fussing about, as women do, before going to bed; she came and went and fluttered round, singing all the time; you might have thought her a humming-bird.

"In the other—a noble name, family, honors, rank, knowledge of the world!—And no earthly means of combining them!" cried Lucien to himself.

Next morning, at seven, when the poet awoke in the pretty pink-and-white room, he found himself alone. He rang, and Europe hurried in.

"What are monsieur's orders?"

"Esther?"

"Madame went off this morning at a quarter to five. By Monsieur l'Abbe's order, I admitted a new face—carriage paid."

"A woman?"

"No, sir, an English woman—one of those people who do their day's work by night, and we are ordered to treat her as if she were madame. What can you have to say to such hack!—Poor Madame, how she cried when she got into the carriage. 'Well, it has to be done!' cried she. 'I left that poor dear boy asleep,' said she, wiping away her tears; 'Europe, if he had looked at me or spoken my name, I should have stayed—I could but have died with him.'—I tell you, sir, I am so fond of madame, that I did not show her the person who has taken her place; some waiting maids would have broken her heart by doing so."

"And is the stranger there?"

"Well, sir, she came in the chaise that took away madame, and I hid her in my room in obedience to my instructions—"

"Is she nice-looking?"

"So far as such a second-hand article can be. But she will find her part easy enough if you play yours, sir," said Europe, going to fetch the false Esther.

THE NIGHT BEFORE, ERE GOING to bed, the all-powerful banker had given his orders to his valet, who, at seven in the morning, brought in to him the notorious Louchard, the most famous of the commercial police, whom he left in a little sitting-room; there the Baron joined him, in a dressing gown and slippers.

"You haf mate a fool of me!" he said, in reply to this official's greeting.

"I could not help myself, Monsieur le Baron. I do not want to lose my place, and I had the honor of explaining to you that I could not meddle in a matter that had nothing to do with my functions. What did I promise you? To put you into communication with one of our agents, who, as it seemed to me, would be best able to serve you. But you know, Monsieur le Baron, the sharp lines that divide men of different trades: if you build a house, you do not set a carpenter to do smith's work. Well, there are two branches of the police—the political police and the judicial police. The political police never interfere with the other branch, and vice versa. If you apply to the chief of the political police, he must get permission from the Minister to take up our business, and you would not dare to explain it to the head of the police throughout the kingdom. A police-agent who should act on his own account would lose his place.

"Well, the ordinary police are quite as cautious as the political police. So no one, whether in the Home Office or at the Prefecture of Police, ever moves excepting in the interests of the State or for the ends of Justice.

"If there is a plot or a crime to be followed up, then, indeed, the heads of the corps are at your service; but you must understand, Monsieur le Baron, that they have other fish to fry than looking after the fifty thousand love affairs in Paris. As to me and my men, our only business is to arrest debtors; and as soon as anything else is to be done, we run enormous risks if we interfere with the peace and quiet of any man or woman. I sent you one of my men, but I told you I could not answer for him; you instructed him to find a particular woman in Paris; Contenson bled you of a thousand-franc note, and did not even move. You might as well look for a needle in the river as for a woman in Paris, who is supposed to haunt Vincennes, and of whom the description answers to every pretty woman in the capital."

"And could not Contenson haf tolt me de truf, instead of making me pleed out one tousand franc?"

"Listen to me, Monsieur le Baron," said Louchard. "Will you give me a thousand crowns? I will give you—sell you—a piece of advice?"

"Is it vort one tousand crowns—your atvice?" asked Nucingen.

"I am not to be caught, Monsieur le Baron," answered Louchard. "You are in love, you want to discover the object of your passion; you are getting as yellow as a lettuce without water. Two physicians came to see you yesterday, your man tells me, who think your life is in danger; now, I alone can put you in the hands of a clever fellow.—But the deuce is in it! If your life is not worth a thousand crowns—"

"Tell me de name of dat clefer fellow, and depent on my generosity—"

Louchard took up his hat, bowed, and left the room.

"Wat ein teufel!" cried Nucingen. "Come back—look here—"

"Take notice," said Louchard, before taking the money, "I am only selling a piece of information, pure and simple. I can give you the name and address of the only man who is able to be of use to you—but he is a master—"

"Get out mit you," cried Nucingen. "Dere is not no name dat is vort one tousant crown but dat von Varschild—and dat only ven it is sign at the bottom of a bank-bill.—I shall gif you one tousant franc."

Louchard, a little weasel, who had never been able to purchase an office as lawyer, notary, clerk, or attorney, leered at the Baron in a significant fashion.

"To you—a thousand crowns, or let it alone. You will get them back in a few seconds on the Bourse," said he.

"I will gif you one tousant franc," repeated the Baron.

"You would cheapen a gold mine!" said Louchard, bowing and leaving.

"I shall get dat address for five hundert franc!" cried the Baron, who desired his servant to send his secretary to him.

Turcaret is no more. In these days the smallest banker, like the greatest, exercises his acumen in the smallest transactions; he bargains over art, beneficence, and love; he would bargain with the Pope for a dispensation. Thus, as he listened to Louchard, Nucingen had hastily concluded that Contenson, Louchard's right-hand man, must certainly know the address of that master spy. Contenson would tell him for five hundred francs what Louchard wanted to see a thousand crowns for. The rapid calculation plainly proves that if the man's heart was in possession of love, his head was still that of the lynx stock-jobber.

"Go your own self, mensieur," said the Baron to his secretary, "to Contenson, dat spy of Louchart's de bailiff man—but go in one capriolette, very qvick, and pring him here qvick to me. I shall vait.— Go out trough de garten.—Here is dat key, for no man shall see dat man in here. You shall take him into dat little garten-house. Try to do dat little business very clefer."

Visitors called to see Nucingen on business; but he waited for Contenson, he was dreaming of Esther, telling himself that before long he would see again the woman who had aroused in him such unhoped-for emotions, and he sent everybody away with vague replies and double-edged promises. Contenson was to him the most important person in Paris, and he looked out into the garden every minute. Finally, after giving orders that no one else was to be admitted, he had his breakfast served in the summer-house at one corner of the garden. In the banker's office the conduct and hesitancy of the most knowing, the most clearsighted, the shrewdest of Paris financiers seemed inexplicable.

"What ails the chief?" said a stockbroker to one of the head-clerks.

"No one knows; they are anxious about his health, it would seem. Yesterday, Madame la Baronne got Desplein and Bianchon to meet."

One day, when Sir Isaac Newton was engaged in physicking one of his dogs, named "Beauty" (who, as is well known, destroyed a vast amount of work, and whom he reproved only in these words, "Ah! Beauty, you little know the mischief you have done!"), some strangers called to see him; but they at once retired, respecting the great man's occupation. In every more or less lofty life, there is a little dog "Beauty." When the Marechal de Richelieu came to pay his respects to Louis XV after taking Mahon, one of the greatest feats of arms of the eighteenth century, the King said to him, "Have you heard the great news? Poor Lansmatt is dead."—Lansmatt was a gatekeeper in the secret of the King's intrigues.

The bankers of Paris never knew how much they owed to Contenson. That spy was the cause of Nucingen's allowing an immense loan to be issued in which his share was allotted to him, and which he gave over to them. The stock-jobber could aim at a fortune any day with the artillery of speculation, but the man was a slave to the hope of happiness.

The great banker drank some tea, and was nibbling at a slice of bread and butter, as a man does whose teeth have for long been sharpened by appetite, when he heard a carriage stop at the little garden gate. In a few minutes his secretary brought in Contenson, whom he had run to earth in a cafe not far from Sainte-Pelagie, where the man was breakfasting on the strength of a bribe given to him by an imprisoned debtor for certain allowances that must be paid for.

Contenson, you must know, was a whole poem—a Paris poem. Merely to see him would have been enough to tell you that Beaumarchais' *Figaro*, Moliere's *Mascarille*, Marivaux's *Frontin*, and Dancourt's *Lafleur*—those great representatives of audacious swindling, of cunning driven to bay, of stratagem rising again from the ends of its broken wires—were all quite second-rate by comparison with this giant of cleverness and meanness. When in Paris you find a real type, he is no longer a man, he is a spectacle; no longer a factor in life, but a whole life, many lives.

Bake a plaster cast four times in a furnace, and you get a sort of bastard imitation of Florentine bronze. Well, the thunderbolts of numberless disasters, the pressure of terrible necessities, had bronzed Contenson's head, as though sweating in an oven had three times over stained his skin. Closely-set wrinkles that could no longer be relaxed made eternal furrows, whiter in their cracks. The yellow face was all wrinkles. The bald skull, resembling Voltaire's, was as parched as a death's-head, and but for a few hairs at the back it would have seemed doubtful whether it was that of a living man. Under a rigid brow, a pair of Chinese eyes, like those of an image under a glass shade in a tea-shop—artificial eyes, which sham life but never vary—moved but expressed nothing. The nose, as flat as that of a skull, sniffed at fate; and the mouth, as thin-lipped as a miser's, was always open, but as expressionless as the grin of a letterbox.

Contenson, as apathetic as a savage, with sunburned hands, affected that Diogenes-like indifference which can never bend to any formality of respect.

And what a commentary on his life was written on his dress for any one who can decipher a dress! Above all, what trousers! made, by long wear, as black and shiny as the camlet of which lawyers' gowns are made! A waistcoat, bought in an old clothes shop in the Temple, with a deep embroidered collar! A rusty black coat!—and everything well brushed, clean after a fashion, and graced by a watch and an imitation gold chain. Contenson allowed a triangle of shirt to show, with pleats in which glittered a sham diamond pin; his black velvet stock set stiff like a gorget, over which lay rolls of flesh as red as that of a Caribbee. His silk hat was as glossy as satin, but the lining would have yielded grease enough for two street lamps if some grocer had bought it to boil down.

But to enumerate these accessories is nothing; if only I could give an idea of the air of immense importance that Contenson contrived to impart to them! There was something indescribably knowing in the collar of his coat, and the fresh blacking on a pair of boots with gaping soles, to which no language can do justice. However, to give some notion of this medley of effect, it may be added that any man of intelligence would have felt, only on seeing Contenson, that if instead of being a spy he had been a thief, all these odds and ends, instead of raising a smile, would have made one shudder with horror. Judging only from his dress, the observer would have said to himself, "That is a scoundrel; he gambles, he drinks, he is full of vices; but he does not get drunk, he does not cheat, he is neither a thief nor a murderer." And Contenson remained inscrutable till the word spy suggested itself.

This man had followed as many unrecognized trades as there are recognized ones. The sly smile on his lips, the twinkle of his green eyes, the queer twitch of his snub nose, showed that he was not deficient in humor. He had a face of sheet-tin, and his soul must probably be like his face. Every movement of his countenance was a grimace wrung from him by politeness rather than by any expression of an inmost impulse. He would have been alarming if he had not seemed so droll.

Contenson, one of the most curious products of the scum that rises to the top of the seething Paris caldron, where everything ferments, prided himself on being, above all things, a philosopher. He would say, without any bitter feeling:

"I have great talents, but of what use are they? I might as well have been an idiot."

And he blamed himself instead of accusing mankind. Find, if you can, many spies who have not had more venom about them than Contenson had.

"Circumstances are against me," he would say to his chiefs. "We might be fine crystal; we are but grains of sand, that is all."

His indifference to dress had some sense. He cared no more about his everyday clothes than an actor does; he excelled in disguising himself, in "make-up"; he could have given Frederic Lemaitre a lesson, for he could be a dandy when necessary. Formerly, in his younger days, he must have mingled in the out-at-elbows society of people living on a humble scale. He expressed excessive disgust for the criminal police corps; for, under the Empire, he had belonged to Fouche's police, and looked upon him as a great man. Since the suppression of this Government department, he had devoted his energies to the tracking of commercial defaulters; but his well-known talents and acumen made him a valuable auxiliary, and the unrecognized chiefs of the political police had kept his name on their lists. Contenson, like his fellows, was only a super in the dramas of which the leading parts were played by his chief when a political investigation was in the wind.

"Go 'vay," said Nucingen, dismissing his secretary with a wave of the hand.

"Why should this man live in a mansion and I in a lodging?" wondered Contenson to himself. "He has dodged his creditors three times; he has robbed them; I never stole a farthing; I am a cleverer fellow than he is—"

"Contenson, mein freund," said the Baron, "you haf vat you call pleed me of one tousand-franc note."

"My girl owed God and the devil—"

"Vat, you haf a girl, a mistress!" cried Nucingen, looking at Contenson with admiration not unmixed with envy.

"I am but sixty-six," replied Contenson, as a man whom vice has kept young as a bad example.

"And vat do she do?"

"She helps me," said Contenson. "When a man is a thief, and an honest woman loves him, either she becomes a thief or he becomes an honest man. I have always been a spy."

"And you vant money—alvays?" asked Nucingen.

"Always," said Contenson, with a smile. "It is part of my business to want money, as it is yours to make it; we shall easily come to an understanding. You find me a little, and I will undertake to spend it. You shall be the well, and I the bucket."

"Vould you like to haf one note for fife hundert franc?"

"What a question! But what a fool I am!—You do not offer it out of a disinterested desire to repair the slights of Fortune?"

"Not at all. I gif it besides the one tousand-franc note vat you pleed me off. Dat makes fifteen hundert franc vat I gif you."

"Very good, you give me the thousand francs I have had and you will add five hundred francs."

"Yust so," said Nucingen, nodding.

"But that still leaves only five hundred francs," said Contenson imperturbably.

"Dat I gif," added the Baron.

"That I take. Very good; and what, Monsieur le Baron, do you want for it?"

"I haf been told dat dere vas in Paris one man vat could find the voman vat I lof, and dat you know his address. . . A real master to spy."

"Very true."

"Vell den, gif me dat address, and I gif you fife hundert franc."

"Where are they?" said Contenson.

"Here dey are," said the Baron, drawing a note out of his pocket.

"All right, hand them over," said Contenson, holding out his hand.

"Noting for noting! Le us see de man, and you get de money; you might sell to me many address at dat price."

Contenson began to laugh.

"To be sure, you have a right to think that of me," said he, with an air of blaming himself. "The more rascally our business is, the more honesty is necessary. But look here, Monsieur le Baron, make it six hundred, and I will give you a bit of advice."

"Gif it, and trust to my generosity."

"I will risk it," Contenson said, "but it is playing high. In such matters, you see, we have to work underground. You say, 'Quick march!'—You are rich; you think that money can do everything. Well, money is something, no doubt. Still, money can only buy men, as the two or three best heads in our force so often say. And there are many things you would never think of which money cannot buy.—You cannot buy good luck. So good police work is not done in this style. Will you show yourself in a carriage with me? We should be seen. Chance is just as often for us as against us."

"Really-truly?" said the Baron.

"Why, of course, sir. A horseshoe picked up in the street led the chief of the police to the discovery of the infernal machine. Well, if we were to go to-night in a hackney coach to Monsieur de Saint-Germain, he would not like to see you walk in any more than you would like to be seen going there."

"Dat is true," said the Baron.

"Ah, he is the greatest of the great! such another as the famous Corentin, Fouche's right arm, who was, some say, his natural son, born while he was still a priest; but that is nonsense. Fouche knew how to be a priest as he knew how to be a Minister. Well, you will not get this man to do anything for you, you see, for less than ten thousand-franc notes—think of that.—But he will do the job, and do it well. Neither seen nor heard, as they say. I ought to give Monsieur de Saint-Germanin notice, and he will fix a time for your meeting in some place where no one can see or hear, for it is a dangerous game to play policeman for private interests. Still, what is to be said? He is a good fellow, the king of good fellows, and a man who has undergone much persecution, and for having saving his country too!—like me, like all who helped to save it."

"Vell den, write and name de happy day," said the Baron, smiling at his humble jest.

"And Monsieur le Baron will allow me to drink his health?" said Contenson, with a manner at once cringing and threatening.

"Shean," cried the Baron to the gardener, "go and tell Chorge to sent me one twenty francs, and pring dem to me—"

"Still, Monsieur le Baron, if you have no more information than you have just given me, I doubt whether the great man can be of any use to you."

"I know off oders!" replied the Baron with a cunning look.

"I have the honor to bid you good-morning, Monsieur le Baron," said Contenson, taking the twenty-franc piece. "I shall have the honor of calling again to tell Georges where you are to go this evening, for we never write anything in such cases when they are well managed."

"It is funny how sharp dese rascals are!" said the Baron to himself; "it is de same mit de police as it is in buss'niss."

WHEN HE LEFT THE BARON, Contenson went quietly from the Rue Saint-Lazare to the Rue Saint-Honore, as far as the Cafe David. He looked in through the windows, and saw an old man who was known there by the name of le Pere Canquoelle.

The Cafe David, at the corner of the Rue de la Monnaie and the Rue Saint-Honore, enjoyed a certain celebrity during the first thirty years of the century, though its fame was limited to the quarter known as that of the Bourdonnais. Here certain old retired merchants, and large shopkeepers still in trade, were wont to meet—the Camusots, the Lebas, the Pilleraults, the Popinots, and a few house-owners like little old Molineux. Now and again old Guillaume might be seen there, coming from the Rue du Colombier. Politics were discussed in a quiet way, but cautiously, for the opinions of the Cafe David were liberal. The gossip of the neighborhood was repeated, men so urgently feel the need of laughing at each other!

This cafe, like all cafes for that matter, had its eccentric character in the person of the said Pere Canquoelle, who had been regular in his attendance there since 1811, and who seemed to be so completely in harmony with the good folks who assembled there, that they all talked politics in his presence without reserve. Sometimes this old fellow, whose guilelessness was the subject of much laughter to the customers, would disappear for a month or two; but his absence never surprised anybody, and was always attributed to his infirmities or his great age, for he looked more than sixty in 1811.

"What has become of old Canquoelle?" one or another would ask of the manageress at the desk.

"I quite expect that one fine day we shall read in the advertisement-sheet that he is dead," she would reply.

Old Canquoelle bore a perpetual certificate of his native province in his accent. He spoke of *une estatue* (a statue), *le peuble* (the people), and said *ture* for *turc*. His name was that of a tiny estate called les Canquoelles, a word meaning cockchafer in some districts, situated in the department of Vaucluse, whence he had come. At last every one had fallen into the habit of calling him Canquoelle, instead of des Canquoelles, and the old man took no offence, for in his opinion the nobility had perished in 1793; and besides, the land of les Canquoelles did not belong to him; he was a younger son's younger son.

Nowadays old Canquoelle's costume would look strange, but between 1811 and 1820 it astonished no one. The old man wore shoes with cut-steel buckles, silk stockings with stripes round the leg, alternately blue and white, corded silk knee-breeches with oval buckles cut to match those on his shoes. A white embroidered waistcoat, an old coat of olive-brown with metal buttons, and a shirt with a flat-pleated frill completed his costume. In the middle of the shirt-frill twinkled a small gold locket, in which might be seen, under glass, a little temple worked in hair, one of those pathetic trifles which give men confidence, just as a scarecrow frightens sparrows. Most men, like other animals, are frightened or reassured by trifles. Old Canquoelle's breeches were kept in place by a buckle which, in the fashion of the last century, tightened them across the stomach; from the belt hung on each side a short steel chain, composed of several finer chains, and ending in a bunch of seals. His white neckcloth was fastened behind by a small gold buckle. Finally, on his snowy and powdered hair, he still, in 1816, wore the municipal cocked hat which Monsieur Try, the President of the Law Courts, also used to wear. But Pere Canquoelle had recently substituted for this hat, so dear to old men, the undignified top-hat, which no one dares to rebel against. The good man thought he owed so much as this to the spirit of the age. A small pigtail tied with a ribbon had traced a semicircle on the back of his coat, the greasy mark being hidden by powder.

If you looked no further than the most conspicuous feature of his face, a nose covered with excrescences red and swollen enough to figure in a dish of truffles, you might have inferred that the worthy man had an easy temper, foolish and easy-going, that of a perfect gaby; and you would have been deceived, like all at the Cafe David, where no one had ever remarked the studious brow, the sardonic mouth, and the cold eyes of this old man, petted by his vices, and as calm as Vitellius, whose imperial and portly stomach reappeared in him palingenetically, so to speak.

In 1816 a young commercial traveler named Gaudissart, who frequented the Cafe David, sat drinking from eleven o'clock till midnight with a half-pay officer. He was so rash as to discuss a conspiracy against the Bourbons, a rather serious plot then on the point of execution. There was no one to be seen in the cafe but Pere Canquoelle, who seemed to be asleep, two waiters who were dozing, and the accountant at the desk. Within four-and-twenty hours Gaudissart was arrested, the plot was discovered. Two men perished on the scaffold. Neither Gaudissart nor any one else ever suspected that worthy old Canquoelle of having peached. The waiters were dismissed; for a year they were all on their guard and afraid of the police—as Pere Canquoelle was too; indeed, he talked of retiring from the Cafe David, such horror had he of the police.

Contenson went into the cafe, asked for a glass of brandy, and did not look at Canquoelle, who sat reading the papers; but when he had gulped down the brandy, he took out the Baron's gold piece, and called the waiter by rapping three short raps on the table. The lady at the desk and the waiter examined the coin with a minute care that was not flattering to Contenson; but their suspicions were justified by the astonishment produced on all the regular customers by Contenson's appearance.

"Was that gold got by theft or by murder?"

This was the idea that rose to some clear and shrewd minds as they looked at Contenson over their spectacles, while affecting to read the news. Contenson, who saw everything and never was surprised at anything, scornfully wiped his lips with a bandana, in which there were but three darns, took his change, slipped all the coppers into his side pocket, of which the lining, once white, was now as black as the cloth of the trousers, and did not leave one for the waiter.

"What a gallows-bird!" said Pere Canquoelle to his neighbor Monsieur Pillerault.

"Pshaw!" said Monsieur Camusot to all the company, for he alone had expressed no astonishment, "it is Contenson, Louchard's right-hand man, the police agent we employ in business. The rascals want to nab some one who is hanging about perhaps."

It would seem necessary to explain here the terrible and profoundly cunning man who was hidden under the guise of Pere Canquoelle, as Vautrin was hidden under that of the Abbe Carlos.

Born at Canquoelles, the only possession of his family, which was highly respectable, this Southerner's name was Peyrade. He belonged, in fact, to the younger branch of the Peyrade family, an old but impoverished house of Franche Comte, still owning the little estate of la Peyrade. The seventh child of his father, he had come on foot to Paris in 1772 at the age of seventeen, with two crowns of six francs in his pocket, prompted by the vices of an ardent spirit and the coarse desire to "get on," which brings so many men to Paris from the south as soon as they understand that their father's property can never supply them with means to gratify their passions. It is enough to say of Peyrade's youth that in 1782 he was in the confidence of chiefs of the police and the hero of the department, highly esteemed by Mm. Lenoir and d'Albert, the last Lieutenant-Generals of Police.

The Revolution had no police; it needed none. Espionage, though common enough, was called public spirit.

The Directorate, a rather more regular government than that of the Committee of Public Safety, was obliged to reorganize the Police, and the first Consul completed the work by instituting a Prefect of Police and a department of police supervision.

Peyrade, a man knowing the traditions, collected the force with the assistance of a man named Corentin, a far cleverer man than Peyrade, though younger; but he was a genius only in the subterranean ways of police inquiries. In 1808 the great services Peyrade was able to achieve were rewarded by an appointment to the eminent position of Chief Commissioner of Police at Antwerp. In Napoleon's mind this sort of Police Governorship was equivalent to a Minister's post, with the duty of superintending Holland. At the end of the campaign of 1809, Peyrade was removed from Antwerp by an order in Council from the Emperor, carried in a chaise to Paris between two gendarmes, and imprisoned in la Force. Two months later he was let out on bail furnished by his friend Corentin, after having been subjected to three examinations, each lasting six hours, in the office of the head of the Police.

Did Peyrade owe his overthrow to the miraculous energy he displayed in aiding Fouche in the defence of the French coast when threatened by what was known at the time as the Walcheren expedition, when the Duke of Otranto manifested such abilities as alarmed the Emperor? Fouche thought it probable even then; and now, when everybody knows what went on in the Cabinet Council called together by Cambaceres, it is absolutely certain. The Ministers, thunderstruck by the news of England's attempt, a retaliation on Napoleon for the Boulogne expedition, and taken by surprise when the Master was entrenched in the island of Lobau, where all Europe believed him to be lost, had not an idea which way to turn. The general opinion was in favor of sending post haste to the Emperor; Fouche alone was bold enough to sketch a plan of campaign, which, in fact, he carried into execution.

"Do as you please," said Cambaceres; "but I, who prefer to keep my head on my shoulders, shall send a report to the Emperor."

It is well known that the Emperor on his return found an absurd pretext, at a full meeting of the Council of State, for discarding his Minister and punishing him for having saved France without the Sovereign's help. From that time forth, Napoleon had doubled the hostility of Prince de Talleyrand and the Duke of Otranto, the only two great politicians formed by the Revolution, who might perhaps have been able to save Napoleon in 1813.

To get rid of Peyrade, he was simply accused of connivance in favoring smuggling and sharing certain profits with the great merchants. Such an indignity was hard on a man who had earned the Marshal's baton of the Police Department by the great services he had done. This man, who had grown old in active business, knew all the secrets of every Government since 1775, when he had entered the service. The Emperor, who believed himself powerful enough to create men for his own uses, paid no heed to the representations subsequently laid before him in favor of a man who was reckoned as one of the most trustworthy, most capable, and most acute of the unknown genii whose task it is to watch over the safety of a State. He thought he could put Contenson in Peyrade's place; but Contenson was at that time employed by Corentin for his own benefit.

Peyrade felt the blow all the more keenly because, being greedy and a libertine, he had found himself, with regard to women, in the position of a pastry-cook who loves sweetmeats. His habits of vice had become to him a second nature; he could not live without a good dinner, without gambling, in short, without the life of an unpretentious fine gentleman, in which men of powerful faculties so generally indulge when they have allowed excessive dissipation to become a necessity. Hitherto, he had lived in style without ever being expected to entertain; and living well, for no one ever looked for a return from him, or from his friend Corentin. He was cynically witty, and he liked his profession; he was a philosopher. And besides, a spy, whatever grade he may hold in the machinery of the police, can no more return to a profession regarded as honorable or liberal, than a prisoner from the hulks can. Once branded, once matriculated, spies and convicts, like deacons, have assumed an indelible character. There are beings on whom social conditions impose an inevitable fate.

Peyrade, for his further woe, was very fond of a pretty little girl whom he knew to be his own child by a celebrated actress to whom he had done a signal service, and who, for three months, had been grateful to him. Peyrade, who had sent for his child from Antwerp, now found himself without employment in Paris and with no means beyond a pension of twelve hundred francs a year allowed him by the Police Department as Lenoir's old disciple. He took lodgings in the Rue des Moineaux on the fourth floor, five little rooms, at a rent of two hundred and fifty francs.

If any man should be aware of the uses and sweets of friendship, is it not the moral leper known to the world as a spy, to the mob as a *mouchard*, to the department as an "agent"? Peyrade and Corentin were such friends as Orestes and Pylades. Peyrade had trained Corentin as Vien trained David; but the pupil soon surpassed his master. They had carried out more than one undertaking together. Peyrade, happy at having discerned Corentin's superior abilities, had started him in his career by preparing a success for him. He obliged his disciple to make use of a mistress who had scorned him as a bait to catch a man (see *The Chouans*). And Corentin at that time was hardly five-and-twenty.

Corentin, who had been retained as one of the generals of whom the Minister of Police is the High Constable, still held under the Duc de Rovigo the high position he had filled under the Duke of Otranto. Now at that time the general police and the criminal police were managed on similar principles. When any important business was on hand, an account was opened, as it were, for the three, four, five, really capable agents. The Minister, on being warned of some plot, by whatever means, would say to one of his colonels of the police force:

"How much will you want to achieve this or that result?"

Corentin or Contenson would go into the matter and reply:

"Twenty, thirty, or forty thousand francs."

Then, as soon as the order was given to go ahead, all the means and the men were left to the judgment of Corentin or the agent selected. And the criminal police used to act in the same way to discover crimes with the famous Vidocq.

Both branches of the police chose their men chiefly from among the ranks of well-known agents, who have matriculated in the business, and are, as it were, as soldiers of the secret army, so indispensable to a government, in spite of the public orations of philanthropists or narrow-minded moralists. But the absolute confidence placed in two men of the temper of Peyrade and Corentin conveyed to them the right of employing perfect strangers, under the risk, moreover, of being responsible to the Minister in all serious cases. Peyrade's experience and acumen were too valuable to Corentin, who, after the storm of 1820 had blown over, employed his old friend, constantly consulted him, and contributed largely to his maintenance. Corentin managed to put about a thousand francs a month into Peyrade's hands.

Peyrade, on his part, did Corentin good service. In 1816 Corentin, on the strength of the discovery of the conspiracy in which the Bonapartist Gaudissart was implicated, tried to get Peyrade reinstated in his place in the police office; but some unknown influence was working against Peyrade. This was the reason why.

In their anxiety to make themselves necessary, Peyrade, Corentin, and Contenson, at the Duke of Otranto's instigation, had organized for the benefit of Louis XVIII a sort of opposition police in which very capable agents were employed. Louis XVIII died possessed of secrets which will remain secrets from the best informed historians. The struggle between the general police of the kingdom, and the King's opposition police, led to many horrible disasters, of which a certain number of executions sealed the secrets. This is neither the place nor the occasion for entering into details on this subject, for these "Scenes of Paris Life" are not "Scenes of Political Life." Enough has been said to show what were the means of living of the man who at the Cafe David was known as good old Canquoelle, and by what threads he was tied to the terrible and mysterious powers of the police.

Between 1817 and 1822, Corentin, Contenson, Peyrade, and their myrmidons, were often required to keep watch over the Minister of Police himself. This perhaps explains why the Minister declined to employ Peyrade and Contenson, on whom Corentin contrived to cast the Minister's suspicions, in order to be able to make use of his friend when his reinstatement was evidently out of the question. The Ministry put their faith in Corentin; they enjoined him to keep an eye on Peyrade, which amused Louis XVIII Corentin and Peyrade were then masters of the position. Contenson, long attached to Peyrade, was still at his service. He had joined the force of the commercial police (the Gardes du Commerce) by his friend's orders. And, in fact, as a result of the sort of zeal that is inspired by a profession we love, these two chiefs liked to place their best men in those posts where information was most likely to flow in.

And, indeed, Contenson's vices and dissipated habits, which had dragged him lower than his two friends, consumed so much money, that he needed a great deal of business.

Contenson, without committing any indiscretion, had told Louchard that he knew the only man who was capable of doing what the Baron de Nucingen required. Peyrade was, in fact, the only police-agent who could act on behalf of a private individual with impunity. At the death of Louis XVIII, Peyrade had not only ceased to be of consequence, but had lost the profits of his position as spy-in-ordinary to His Majesty. Believing himself to be indispensable, he had lived fast. Women, high feeding, and the club, the *Cercle des Etrangers*, had prevented this man from saving, and, like all men cut out for debauchery, he enjoyed an iron constitution. But between 1826 and 1829, when he was nearly seventy-four years of age, he had stuck half-way, to use his own expression. Year by year he saw his comforts dwindling. He followed the police department to its grave, and saw with regret that Charles X's government was departing from its good old traditions. Every session saw the estimates pared down which were necessary to keep up the police, out of hatred for that method of government and a firm determination to reform that institution.

"It is as if they thought they could cook in white gloves," said Peyrade to Corentin.

In 1822 this couple foresaw 1830. They knew how bitterly Louis XVIII hated his successor, which accounts for his recklessness with regard to the younger branch, and without which his reign would be an unanswerable riddle.

As Peyrade grew older, his love for his natural daughter had increased. For her sake he had adopted his citizen guise, for he intended that his Lydie should marry respectably. So for the last three years he had been especially anxious to find a corner, either at the Prefecture of Police, or in the general Police Office—some ostensible and recognized post. He had ended by inventing a place, of which the necessity, as he told Corentin, would sooner or later be felt. He was anxious to create an inquiry office at the Prefecture of Police, to be intermediate between the Paris police in the strictest sense, the criminal police, and the superior general police, so as to enable the supreme board to profit by the various scattered forces. No one but Peyrade, at his age, and after fifty-five years of confidential work, could be the connecting link between the three branches of the police, or the keeper of the records to whom political and judicial authority alike could apply for the elucidation of certain cases. By this means Peyrade hoped, with Corentin's assistance, to find a husband and scrape together a portion for his little Lydie. Corentin had already mentioned the matter to the Director-General of the police forces of the realm, without naming Peyrade; and the Director-General, a man from the south, thought it necessary that the suggestion should come from the chief of the city police.

At the moment when Contenson struck three raps on the table with the gold piece, a signal conveying, "I want to speak to you," the senior was reflecting on this problem: "By whom, and under what pressure can the Prefet of Police be made to move?"—And he looked like a noodle studying his *Courrier Francais*.

"Poor Fouche!" thought he to himself, as he made his way along the Rue Saint-Honore, "that great man is dead! our go-betweens with Louis XVIII are out of favor. And besides, as Corentin said only yesterday, nobody believes in the activity or the intelligence of a man of seventy. Oh, why did I get into a habit of dining at Very's, of drinking choice wines, of singing *La Mere Godichon*, of gambling when I am in funds? To get a place and keep it, as Corentin says, it is not enough to be clever, you must have the gift of management. Poor dear M. Lenoir was right when he wrote to me in the matter of the Queen's necklace, 'You will never do any good,' when he heard that I did not stay under that slut Oliva's bed."

If the venerable Pere Canquoelle—he was called so in the house—lived on in the Rue des Moineaux, on a fourth floor, you may depend on it he had found some peculiarity in the arrangement of the premises which favored the practice of his terrible profession.

The house, standing at the corner of the Rue Saint-Roch, had no neighbors on one side; and as the staircase up the middle divided it into two, there were on each floor two perfectly isolated rooms. Those two rooms looked out on the Rue Saint-Roch. There were garret rooms above the fourth floor, one of them a kitchen, and the other a bedroom for Pere Canquoelle's only servant, a Fleming named Katt, formerly Lydie's wet-nurse. Old Canquoelle had taken one of the outside rooms for his bedroom, and the other for his study. The study ended at the party-wall, a very thick one. The window opening on the Rue des Moineaux looked on a blank wall at the opposite corner. As this study was divided from the stairs by the whole width of Peyrade's bedroom, the friends feared no eye, no ear, as they talked business in this study made on purpose for his detestable trade.

Peyrade, as a further precaution, had furnished Katt's room with a thick straw bed, a felt carpet, and a very heavy rug, under the pretext of making his child's nurse comfortable. He had also stopped up the chimney, warming his room by a stove, with a pipe through the wall to the Rue Saint-Roch. Finally, he laid several rugs on his floor to prevent the slightest sound being heard by the neighbors beneath. An expert himself in the tricks of spies, he sounded the outer wall, the ceiling, and the floor once a week, examining them as if he were in search of noxious insects. It was the security of this room from all witnesses or listeners that had made Corentin select it as his council-chamber when he did not hold a meeting in his own room.

Where Corentin lived was known to no one but the Chief of the Superior Police and to Peyrade; he received there such personages as the Ministry or the King selected to conduct very serious cases; but no agent or subordinate ever went there, and he plotted everything connected with their business at Peyrade's. In this unpretentious room schemes were matured, and resolutions passed, which would have furnished strange records and curious dramas if only walls could talk. Between 1816 and 1826 the highest interests were discussed there. There first germinated the events which grew to weigh on France. There Peyrade and Corentin, with all the foresight, and more than all the information of Bellart, the Attorney-General, had said even in 1819: "If Louis XVIII does not consent to strike such or such a blow, to make away with such or such a prince, is it because he hates his brother? He must wish to leave him heir to a revolution."

Peyrade's door was graced with a slate, on which very strange marks might sometimes be seen, figures scrawled in chalk. This sort of devil's algebra bore the clearest meaning to the initiated.

Lydie's rooms, opposite to Peyrade's shabby lodging, consisted of an ante-room, a little drawing-room, a bedroom, and a small dressing-room. The door, like that of Peyrade's room, was constructed of a plate of sheet-iron three lines thick, sandwiched between two strong oak planks, fitted with locks and elaborate hinges, making it as impossible to force it as if it were a prison door. Thus, though the house had a public passage through it, with a shop below and no doorkeeper, Lydie lived there without a fear. The dining-room, the little drawing-room, and her bedroom—every window-balcony a hanging garden—were luxurious in their Dutch cleanliness.

The Flemish nurse had never left Lydie, whom she called her daughter. The two went to church with a regularity that gave the royalist grocer, who lived below, in the corner shop, an excellent opinion of the worthy Canquoelle. The grocer's family, kitchen, and counter-jumpers occupied the first floor and the entresol; the landlord inhabited the second floor; and the third had been let for twenty years past to a lapidary. Each resident had a key of the street door. The grocer's wife was all the more willing to receive letters and parcels addressed to these three quiet households, because the grocer's shop had a letter-box.

Without these details, strangers, or even those who know Paris well, could not have understood the privacy and quietude, the isolation and safety which made this house exceptional in Paris. After midnight, Pere Canquoelle could hatch plots, receive spies or ministers, wives or hussies, without any one on earth knowing anything about it.

Peyrade, of whom the Flemish woman would say to the grocer's cook, "He would not hurt a fly!" was regarded as the best of men. He grudged his daughter nothing. Lydie, who had been taught music by Schmucke, was herself a musician capable of composing; she could wash in a sepia drawing, and paint in gouache and water-color. Every Sunday Peyrade dined at home with her. On that day this worthy was wholly paternal.

Lydie, religious but not a bigot, took the Sacrament at Easter, and confessed every month. Still, she allowed herself from time to time to be treated to the play. She walked in the Tuileries when it was fine. These were all her pleasures, for she led a sedentary life. Lydie, who worshiped her father, knew absolutely nothing of his sinister gifts and dark employments. Not a wish had ever disturbed this pure child's pure life. Slight and handsome like her mother, gifted with an exquisite voice, and a delicate face framed in fine fair hair, she looked like one of those angels, mystical rather than real, which some of the early painters grouped in the background of the Holy Family. The glance of her blue eyes seemed to bring a beam from the sky on those she favored with a look. Her dress, quite simple, with no exaggeration of fashion, had a delightful middle-class modesty. Picture to yourself an old Satan as the father of an angel, and purified in her divine presence, and you will have an idea of Peyrade and his daughter. If anybody had soiled this jewel, her father would have invented, to swallow him alive, one of those dreadful plots in which, under the Restoration, the unhappy wretches were trapped who were designate to die on the scaffold. A thousand crowns were ample maintenance for Lydie and Katt, whom she called nurse.

As Peyrade turned into the Rue des Moineaux, he saw Contenson; he outstripped him, went upstairs before him, heard the man's steps on the stairs, and admitted him before the woman had put her nose out of the kitchen door. A bell rung by the opening of a glass door, on the third story where the lapidary lived warned the residents on that and the fourth floors when a visitor was coming to them. It need hardly be said that, after midnight, Peyrade muffled this bell.

"What is up in such a hurry, Philosopher?"

Philosopher was the nickname bestowed on Contenson by Peyrade, and well merited by the Epictetus among police agents. The name of Contenson, alas! hid one of the most ancient names of feudal Normandy.

"Well, there is something like ten thousand francs to be netted."

"What is it? Political?"

"No, a piece of idiocy. Baron de Nucingen, you know, the old certified swindler, is neighing after a woman he saw in the Bois de Vincennes, and she has got to be found, or he will die of love.—They had a consultation of doctors yesterday, by what his man tells me.—I have already eased him of a thousand francs under pretence of seeking the fair one."

And Contenson related Nucingen's meeting with Esther, adding that the Baron had now some further information.

"All right," said Peyrade, "we will find his Dulcinea; tell the Baron to come to-night in a carriage to the Champs-Elysees—the corner of the Avenue de Gabriel and the Allee de Marigny."

Peyrade saw Contenson out, and knocked at his daughter's rooms, as he always knocked to be let in. He was full of glee; chance had just offered the means, at last, of getting the place he longed for.

He flung himself into a deep armchair, after kissing Lydie on the forehead, and said:

"Play me something."

Lydie played him a composition for the piano by Beethoven.

"That is very well played, my pet," said he, taking Lydie on his knees. "Do you know that we are one-and-twenty years old? We must get married soon, for our old daddy is more than seventy—"

"I am quite happy here," said she.

"You love no one but your ugly old father?" asked Peyrade.

"Why, whom should I love?"

"I am dining at home, my darling; go and tell Katt. I am thinking of settling, of getting an appointment, and finding a husband worthy of you; some good young man, very clever, whom you may some day be proud of—"

"I have never seen but one yet that I should have liked for a husband—"

"You have seen one then?"

"Yes, in the Tuileries," replied Lydie. "He walked past me; he was giving his arm to the Comtesse de Serizy."

"And his name is?"

"Lucien de Rubempre.—I was sitting with Katt under a lime-tree, thinking of nothing. There were two ladies sitting by me, and one said to the other, 'There are Madame de Serizy and that handsome Lucien de Rubempre.'—I looked at the couple that the two ladies were watching. 'Oh, my dear!' said the other, 'some women are very lucky! That woman is allowed to do everything she pleases just because she was a de Ronquerolles, and her husband is in power.'—'But, my dear,' said the other lady, 'Lucien costs her very dear.'—What did she mean, papa?"

"Just nonsense, such as people of fashion will talk," replied Peyrade, with an air of perfect candor. "Perhaps they were alluding to political matters."

"Well, in short, you asked me a question, so I answer you. If you want me to marry, find me a husband just like that young man."

"Silly child!" replied her father. "The fact that a man is handsome is not always a sign of goodness. Young men gifted with an attractive appearance meet with no obstacles at the beginning of life, so they make no use of any talent; they are corrupted by the advances made to them by society, and they have to pay interest later for their attractiveness!—

What I should like for you is what the middle classes, the rich, and the fools leave unholpen and unprotected—"

"What, father?"

"An unrecognized man of talent. But, there, child; I have it in my power to hunt through every garret in Paris, and carry out your programme by offering for your affection a man as handsome as the young scamp you speak of; but a man of promise, with a future before him destined to glory and fortune.—By the way, I was forgetting. I must have a whole flock of nephews, and among them there must be one worthy of you!—I will write, or get some one to write to Provence."

A strange coincidence! At this moment a young man, half-dead of hunger and fatigue, who had come on foot from the department of Vaucluse—a nephew of Pere Canquoelle's in search of his uncle, was entering Paris through the Barriere de l'Italie. In the day-dreams of the family, ignorant of this uncle's fate, Peyrade had supplied the text for many hopes; he was supposed to have returned from India with millions! Stimulated by these fireside romances, this grand-nephew, named Theodore, had started on a voyage round the world in quest of this eccentric uncle.

AFTER ENJOYING FOR SOME HOURS the joys of paternity, Peyrade, his hair washed and dyed—for his powder was a disguise—dressed in a stout, coarse, blue frock-coat buttoned up to the chin, and a black cloak, shod in strong, thick-soled boots, furnished himself with a private card and walked slowly along the Avenue Gabriel, where Contenson, dressed as an old costermonger woman, met him in front of the gardens of the Elysee-Bourbon.

"Monsieur de Saint-Germain," said Contenson, giving his old chief the name he was officially known by, "you have put me in the way of making five hundred pieces (francs); but what I came here for was to tell you that that damned Baron, before he gave me the shiners, had been to ask questions at the house (the Prefecture of Police)."

"I shall want you, no doubt," replied Peyrade. "Look up numbers 7, 10, and 21; we can employ those men without any one finding it out, either at the Police Ministry or at the Prefecture."

Contenson went back to a post near the carriage in which Monsieur de Nucingen was waiting for Peyrade.

"I am Monsieur de Saint-Germain," said Peyrade to the Baron, raising himself to look over the carriage door.

"Ver' goot; get in mit me," replied the Baron, ordering the coachman to go on slowly to the Arc de l'Etoile.

"You have been to the Prefecture of Police, Monsieur le Baron? That was not fair. Might I ask what you said to M. le Prefet, and what he said in reply?" asked Peyrade.

"Before I should gif fife hundert francs to a filain like Contenson, I vant to know if he had earned dem. I simply said to the Prefet of Police dat I vant to employ ein agent named Peyrate to go abroat in a delicate matter, an' should I trust him—unlimited!—The Prefet telt me you vas a very clefer man an' ver' honest man. An' dat vas everything."

"And now that you have learned my true name, Monsieur le Baron, will you tell me what it is you want?"

When the Baron had given a long and copious explanation, in his hideous Polish-Jew dialect, of his meeting with Esther and the cry of the man behind the carriage, and his vain efforts, he ended by relating what had occurred at his house the night before, Lucien's involuntary smile, and the opinion expressed by Bianchon and some other young dandies that there must be some acquaintance between him and the unknown fair.

"Listen to me, Monsieur le Baron; you must, in the first instance, place ten thousand francs in my hands, on account for expenses; for, to you, this is a matter of life or death; and as your life is a business-manufactory, nothing must be left undone to find this woman for you. Oh, you are caught!—"

"Ja, I am caught!"

"If more money is wanted, Baron, I will let you know; put your trust in me," said Peyrade. "I am not a spy, as you perhaps imagine. In 1807 I was Commissioner-General of Police at Antwerp; and now that Louis XVIII is dead, I may tell you in confidence that for seven years I was the chief of his counter-police. So there is no beating me down. You must understand, Monsieur le Baron, that it is impossible to make any estimate of the cost of each man's conscience before going into the details of such an affair. Be quite easy; I shall succeed. Do not fancy that you can satisfy me with a sum of money; I want something for my reward—"

"So long as dat is not a kingtom!" said the Baron.

"It is less than nothing to you."

"Den I am your man."

"You know the Kellers?"

"Oh! ver' well."

"Francois Keller is the Comte de Gondreville's son-in-law, and the Comte de Gondreville and his son-in-law dined with you yesterday."

"Who der teufel tolt you dat?" cried the Baron. "Dat vill be Georche; he is always a gossip." Peyrade smiled, and the banker at once formed strange suspicions of his man-servant.

"The Comte de Gondreville is quite in a position to obtain me a place I covet at the Prefecture of Police; within forty-eight hours the prefet will have notice that such a place is to be created," said Peyrade in continuation. "Ask for it for me; get the Comte de Gondreville to interest himself in the matter with some degree of warmth—and you will thus repay me for the service I am about to do you. I ask your word only; for, if you fail me, sooner or later you will curse the day you were born—you have Peyrade's word for that."

"I gif you mein vort of honor to do vat is possible."

"If I do no more for you than is possible, it will not be enough."

"Vell, vell, I vill act qvite frankly."

"Frankly—that is all I ask," said Peyrade, "and frankness is the only thing at all new that you and I can offer to each other."

"Frankly," echoed the Baron. "Vere shall I put you down."

"At the corner of the Pont Louis XVI."

"To the Pont de la Chambre," said the Baron to the footman at the carriage door.

"Then I am to get dat unknown person," said the Baron to himself as he drove home.

"What a queer business!" thought Peyrade, going back on foot to the Palais-Royal, where he intended trying to multiply his ten thousand francs by three, to make a little fortune for Lydie. "Here I am required to look into the private concerns of a very young man who has bewitched my little girl by a glance. He is, I suppose, one of those men who have an eye for a woman," said he to himself, using an expression of a language of his own, in which his observations, or Corentin's, were summed up in words that were anything rather than classical, but, for that very reason, energetic and picturesque.

The Baron de Nucingen, when he went in, was an altered man; he astonished his household and his wife by showing them a face full of life and color, so cheerful did he feel.

"Our shareholders had better look out for themselves," said du Tillet to Rastignac.

They were all at tea, in Delphine de Nucingen's boudoir, having come in from the opera.

"Ja," said the Baron, smiling; "I feel ver' much dat I shall do some business."

"Then you have seen the fair being?" asked Madame de Nucingen.

"No," said he; "I have only hoped to see her."

"Do men ever love their wives so?" cried Madame de Nucingen, feeling, or affecting to feel, a little jealous.

"When you have got her, you must ask us to sup with her," said du Tillet to the Baron, "for I am very curious to study the creature who has made you so young as you are."

"She is a *cheff-d'oeufre* of creation!" replied the old banker.

"He will be swindled like a boy," said Rastignac in Delphine's ear.

"Pooh! he makes quite enough money to—"

"To give a little back, I suppose," said du Tillet, interrupting the Baroness.

Nucingen was walking up and down the room as if his legs had the fidgets.

"Now is your time to make him pay your fresh debts," said Rastignac in the Baroness' ear.

At this very moment Carlos was leaving the Rue Taitbout full of hope; he had been there to give some last advice to Europe, who was to play the principal part in the farce devised to take in the Baron de Nucingen. He was accompanied as far as the Boulevard by Lucien, who was not at all easy at finding this demon so perfectly disguised that even he had only recognized him by his voice.

"Where the devil did you find a handsomer woman than Esther?" he asked his evil genius.

"My boy, there is no such thing to be found in Paris. Such a complexion is not made in France."

"I assure you, I am still quite amazed. Venus Callipyge has not such a figure. A man would lose his soul for her. But where did she spring from?"

"She was the handsomest girl in London. Drunk with gin, she killed her lover in a fit of jealousy. The lover was a wretch of whom the London police are well quit, and this woman was packed off to Paris for a time to let the matter blow over. The hussy was well brought up—the daughter of a clergyman. She speaks French as if it were her mother tongue. She does not know, and never will know, why she is here. She was told that if you took a fancy to her she might fleece you of millions, but that you were as jealous as a tiger, and she was told how Esther lived."

"But supposing Nucingen should prefer her to Esther?"

"Ah, it is out at last!" cried Carlos. "You dread now lest what dismayed you yesterday should not take place after all! Be quite easy. That fair and fair-haired girl has blue eyes; she is the antipodes of the beautiful Jewess, and only such eyes as Esther's could ever stir a man so rotten as Nucingen. What the devil! you could not hide an ugly woman. When this puppet has played her part, I will send her off in safe custody to Rome or to Madrid, where she will be the rage."

"If we have her only for a short time," said Lucien, "I will go back to her—"

"Go, my boy, amuse yourself. You will be a day older to-morrow. For my part, I must wait for some one whom I have instructed to learn what is going on at the Baron de Nucingen's."

"Who?"

"His valet's mistress; for, after all, we must keep ourselves informed at every moment of what is going on in the enemy's camp."

At midnight, Paccard, Esther's tall chasseur, met Carlos on the Pont des Arts, the most favorable spot in all Paris for saying a few words which no one must overhear. All the time they talked the servant kept an eye on one side, while his master looked out on the other.

"The Baron went to the Prefecture of Police this morning between four and five," said the man, "and he boasted this evening that he should find the woman he saw in the Bois de Vincennes—he had been promised it—"

"We are watched!" said Carlos. "By whom?"

"They have already employed Louchard the bailiff."

"That would be child's play," replied Carlos. "We need fear nothing but the guardians of public safety, the criminal police; and so long as that is not set in motion, we can go on!"

"That is not all."

"What else?"

"Our chums of the hulks.—I saw Lapouraille yesterday—He has choked off a married couple, and has bagged ten thousand five-franc pieces—in gold."

"He will be nabbed," said Jacques Collin. "That is the Rue Boucher crime."

"What is the order of the day?" said Paccard, with the respectful demeanor a marshal must have assumed when taking his orders from Louis XVIII.

"You must get out every evening at ten o'clock," replied Herrera. "Make your way pretty briskly to the Bois de Vincennes, the Bois de Meudon, and de Ville-d'Avray. If any one should follow you, let them do it; be free of speech, chatty, open to a bribe. Talk about Rubempre's jealousy and his mad passion for madame, saying that he would not on any account have it known that he had a mistress of that kind."

"Enough.—Must I have any weapons?"

"Never!" exclaimed Carlos vehemently. "A weapon? Of what use would that be? To get us into a scrape. Do not under any circumstances use your hunting-knife. When you know that you can break the strongest man's legs by the trick I showed you—when you can hold your own against three armed warders, feeling quite sure that you can account for two of them before they have got out flint and steel, what is there to be afraid of? Have not you your cane?"

"To be sure," said the man.

Paccard, nicknamed The Old Guard, Old Wide-Awake, or The Right Man—a man with legs of iron, arms of steel, Italian whiskers, hair like an artist's, a beard like a sapper's, and a face as colorless and immovable as Contenson's, kept his spirit to himself, and rejoiced in a sort of drum-major appearance which disarmed suspicion. A fugitive from Poissy or Melun has no such serious self-consciousness and belief in his own merit. As Giafar to the Haroun el Rasheed of the hulks, he served him with the friendly admiration which Peyrade felt for Corentin.

This huge fellow, with a small body in proportion to his legs, flat-chested, and lean of limb, stalked solemnly about on his two long pins. Whenever his right leg moved, his right eye took in everything around him with the placid swiftness peculiar to thieves and spies. The left eye followed the right eye's example. Wiry, nimble, ready for anything at any time, but for a weakness of Dutch courage Paccard would have been perfect, Jacques Collin used to say, so completely was he endowed with the talents indispensable to a man at war with society; but the master had succeeded in persuading his slave to drink only in the evening. On going home at night, Paccard tippled the liquid gold poured into small glasses out of a pot-bellied stone jar from Danzig.

"We will make them open their eyes," said Paccard, putting on his grand hat and feathers after bowing to Carlos, whom he called his Confessor.

These were the events which had led three men, so clever, each in his way, as Jacques Collin, Peyrade, and Corentin, to a hand-to-hand fight on the same ground, each exerting his talents in a struggle for his own passions or interests. It was one of those obscure but terrible conflicts on which are expended in marches and countermarches, in strategy, skill, hatred, and vexation, the powers that might make a fine fortune. Men and means were kept absolutely secret by Peyarde, seconded in this business by his friend Corentin—a business they thought but a trifle. And so, as to them, history is silent, as it is on the true causes of many revolutions.

But this was the result.

Five days after Monsieur de Nucingen's interview with Peyrade in the Champs Elysees, a man of about fifty called in the morning, stepping out of a handsome cab, and flinging the reins to his servant. He had the dead-white complexion which a life in the "world" gives to diplomates, was dressed in blue cloth, and had a general air of fashion—almost that of a Minister of State.

He inquired of the servant who sat on a bench on the steps whether the Baron de Nucingen were at home; and the man respectfully threw open the splendid plate-glass doors.

"Your name, sir?" said the footman.

"Tell the Baron that I have come from the Avenue Gabriel," said Corentin. "If anybody is with him, be sure not to say so too loud, or you will find yourself out of place!"

A minute later the man came back and led Corentin by the back passages to the Baron's private room.

Corentin and the banker exchanged impenetrable glances, and both bowed politely.

"Monsieur le Baron," said Corentin, "I come in the name of Peyrade—"

"Ver' gott!" said the Baron, fastening the bolts of both doors.

"Monsieur de Rubempre's mistress lives in the Rue Taitbout, in the apartment formerly occupied by Mademoiselle de Bellefeuille, M. de Granville's ex-mistress—the Attorney-General—"

"Vat, so near to me?" exclaimed the Baron. "Dat is ver' strange."

"I can quite understand your being crazy about that splendid creature; it was a pleasure to me to look at her," replied Corentin. "Lucien is so jealous of the girl that he never allows her to be seen; and she loves him devotedly; for in four years, since she succeeded la Bellefeuille in those rooms, inheriting her furniture and her profession, neither the neighbors, nor the porter, nor the other tenants in the house have ever set eyes on her. My lady never stirs out but at night. When she sets out, the blinds of the carriage are pulled down, and she is closely veiled.

"Lucien has other reasons besides jealousy for concealing this woman. He is to be married to Clotilde de Grandlieu, and he is at this moment Madame de Serizy's favorite fancy. He naturally wishes to keep a hold on his fashionable mistress and on his promised bride. So, you are master of the position, for Lucien will sacrifice his pleasure to his interests and his vanity. You are rich; this is probably your last chance of happiness; be liberal. You can gain your end through her waiting-maid. Give the slut ten thousand francs; she will hide you in her mistress' bedroom. It must be quite worth that to you."

No figure of speech could describe the short, precise tone of finality in which Corentin spoke; the Baron could not fail to observe it, and his face expressed his astonishment—an expression he had long expunged from his impenetrable features.

"I have also to ask you for five thousand francs for my friend Peyrade, who has dropped five of your thousand-franc notes—a tiresome accident," Corentin went on, in a lordly tone of command. "Peyrade knows his Paris too well to spend money in advertising, and he trusts entirely to you. But this is not the most important point," added Corentin, checking himself in such a way as to make the request for money seem quite a trifle. "If you do not want to end your days miserably, get the place for Peyrade that he asked you to procure for him—and it is a thing you can easily do. The Chief of the General Police must have had notice of the matter yesterday. All that is needed is to get Gondreville to speak to the Prefet of Police.—Very well, just say to Malin, Comte de Gondreville, that it is to oblige one of the men who relieved him of Mm. de Simeuse, and he will work it—"

"Here den, mensieur," said the Baron, taking out five thousand-franc notes and handing them to Corentin.

"The waiting-maid is great friends with a tall chasseur named Paccard, living in the Rue de Provence, over a carriage-builder's; he goes out as heyduque to persons who give themselves princely airs. You can get at Madame van Bogseck's woman through Paccard, a brawny Piemontese, who has a liking for vermouth."

This information, gracefully thrown in as a postscript, was evidently the return for the five thousand francs. The Baron was trying to guess Corentin's place in life, for he quite understood that the man was rather a master of spies than a spy himself; but Corentin remained to him as mysterious as an inscription is to an archaeologist when three-quarters of the letters are missing.

"Vat is dat maid called?" he asked.

"Eugenie," replied Corentin, who bowed and withdrew.

The Baron, in a transport of joy, left his business for the day, shut up his office, and went up to his rooms in the happy frame of mind of a young man of twenty looking forward to his first meeting with his first mistress.

The Baron took all the thousand-franc notes out of his private cash-box—a sum sufficient to make the whole village happy, fifty-five thousand francs—and stuffed them into the pocket of his coat. But a millionaire's lavishness can only be compared with his eagerness for gain. As soon as a whim or a passion is to be gratified, money is dross to a Croesus; in fact, he finds it harder to have whims than gold. A keen pleasure is the rarest thing in these satiated lives, full of the excitement that comes of great strokes of speculation, in which these dried-up hearts have burned themselves out.

For instance, one of the richest capitalists in Paris one day met an extremely pretty little working-girl. Her mother was with her, but the girl had taken the arm of a young fellow in very doubtful finery, with a very smart swagger. The millionaire fell in love with the girl at first sight; he followed her home, he went in; he heard all her story, a record of alternations of dancing at Mabille and days of starvation, of play-going and hard work; he took an interest in it, and left five thousand-franc notes under a five-franc piece—an act of generosity abused. Next day a famous upholsterer, Braschon, came to take the damsel's orders, furnished rooms that she had chosen, and laid out twenty thousand francs. She gave herself up to the wildest hopes, dressed her mother to match, and flattered herself she would find a place for her ex-lover in an insurance office. She waited—a day, two days—then a week, two weeks. She thought herself bound to be faithful; she got into debt. The capitalist, called away to Holland, had forgotten the girl; he never went once to the Paradise where he had placed her, and from which she fell as low as it is possible to fall even in Paris.

Nucingen did not gamble, Nucingen did not patronize the Arts, Nucingen had no hobby; thus he flung himself into his passion for

Esther with a headlong blindness, on which Carlos Herrera had confidently counted.

After his breakfast, the Baron sent for Georges, his body-servant, and desired him to go to the Rue Taitbout and ask Mademoiselle Eugenie, Madame van Bogseck's maid, to come to his office on a matter of importance.

"You shall look out for her," he added, "an' make her valk up to my room, and tell her I shall make her fortune."

Georges had the greatest difficulty in persuading Europe-Eugenie to come.

"Madame never lets me go out," said she; "I might lose my place," and so forth; and Georges sang her praises loudly to the Baron, who gave him ten louis.

"If madame goes out without her this evening," said Georges to his master, whose eyes glowed like carbuncles, "she will be here by ten o'clock."

"Goot. You shall come to dress me at nine o'clock—and do my hair. I shall look so goot as possible. I belief I shall really see dat mistress—or money is not money any more."

The Baron spent an hour, from noon till one, in dyeing his hair and whiskers. At nine in the evening, having taken a bath before dinner, he made a toilet worthy of a bridegroom and scented himself—a perfect Adonis. Madame de Nucingen, informed of this metamorphosis, gave herself the treat of inspecting her husband.

"Good heavens!" cried she, "what a ridiculous figure! Do, at least, put on a black satin stock instead of that white neckcloth which makes your whiskers look so black; besides, it is so 'Empire,' quite the old fogy. You look like some super-annuated parliamentary counsel. And take off these diamond buttons; they are worth a hundred thousand francs apiece—that slut will ask you for them, and you will not be able to refuse her; and if a baggage is to have them, I may as well wear them as earrings."

The unhappy banker, struck by the wisdom of his wife's reflections, obeyed reluctantly.

"Ridikilous, ridikilous! I hafe never telt you dat you shall be ridikilous when you dressed yourself so smart to see your little Mensieur de Rastignac!"

"I should hope that you never saw me make myself ridiculous. Am I the woman to make such blunders in the first syllable of my dress?

Come, turn about. Button your coat up to the neck, all but the two top buttons, as the Duc de Maufrigneuse does. In short, try to look young."

"Monsieur," said Georges, "here is Mademoiselle Eugenie."

"Adie, motame," said the banker, and he escorted his wife as far as her own rooms, to make sure that she should not overhear their conference.

On his return, he took Europe by the hand and led her into his room with a sort of ironical respect.

"Vell, my chilt, you are a happy creature, for you are de maid of dat most beautiful voman in de vorlt. And your fortune shall be made if you vill talk to her for me and in mine interests."

"I would not do such a thing for ten thousand francs!" exclaimed Europe. "I would have you to know, Monsieur le Baron, that I am an honest girl."

"Oh yes. I expect to pay dear for your honesty. In business dat is vat ve call curiosity."

"And that is not everything," Europe went on. "If you should not take madame's fancy—and that is on the cards—she would be angry, and I am done for!—and my place is worth a thousand francs a year."

"De capital to make ein tousant franc is twenty tousand franc; and if I shall gif you dat, you shall not lose noting."

"Well, to be sure, if that is the tone you take about it, my worthy old fellow," said Europe, "that is quite another story.—Where is the money?"

"Here," replied the Baron, holding up the banknotes, one at a time.

He noted the flash struck by each in turn from Europe's eyes, betraying the greed he had counted on.

"That pays for my place, but how about my principles, my conscience?" said Europe, cocking her crafty little nose and giving the Baron a serio-comic leer.

"Your conscience shall not be pait for so much as your place; but I shall say fife tousand franc more," said he adding five thousand-franc notes.

"No, no. Twenty thousand for my conscience, and five thousand for my place if I lose it—"

"Yust vat you please," said he, adding the five notes. "But to earn dem you shall hite me in your lady's room by night ven she shall be 'lone."

"If you swear never to tell who let you in, I agree. But I warn you of one thing.—Madame is as strong as a Turk, she is madly in love with Monsieur de Rubempre, and if you paid a million francs in banknotes she would never be unfaithful to him. It is very silly, but that is her way when she is in love; she is worse than an honest woman, I tell you! When she goes out for a drive in the woods at night, monsieur very seldom stays at home. She is gone out this evening, so I can hide you in my room. If madame comes in alone, I will fetch you; you can wait in the drawing-room. I will not lock the door into her room, and then—well, the rest is your concern—so be ready."

"I shall pay you the twenty-fife tousand francs in dat drawing-room.—You gife—I gife!"

"Indeed!" said Europe, "you are so confiding as all that? On my word!"

"Oh, you will hafe your chance to fleece me yet. We shall be friends."

"Well, then, be in the Rue Taitbout at midnight; but bring thirty thousand francs about you. A waiting-woman's honesty, like a hackney cab, is much dearer after midnight."

"It shall be more prudent if I gif you a cheque on my bank—"

"No, no" said Europe. "Notes, or the bargain is off."

So at one in the morning the Baron de Nucingen, hidden in the garret where Europe slept, was suffering all the anxieties of a man who hopes to triumph. His blood seemed to him to be tingling in his toe-nails, and his head ready to burst like an overheated steam engine.

"I had more dan one hundert tousand crowns' vort of enjoyment—in my mind," he said to du Tillet when telling him the story.

He listened to every little noise in the street, and at two in the morning he heard his mistress' carriage far away on the boulevard. His heart beat vehemently under his silk waistcoat as the gate turned on its hinges. He was about to behold the heavenly, the glowing face of his Esther!—the clatter of the carriage-step and the slam of the door struck upon his heart. He was more agitated in expectation of this supreme moment than he would have been if his fortune had been at stake.

"Ah, ha!" cried he, "dis is vat I call to lif—it is too much to lif; I shall be incapable of everything."

"Madame is alone; come down," said Europe, looking in. "Above all, make no noise, great elephant."

"Great Elephant!" he repeated, laughing, and walking as if he trod on red-hot iron.

Europe led the way, carrying a candle.

"Here—count dem!" said the Baron when he reached the drawing-room, holding out the notes to Europe.

Europe took the thirty notes very gravely and left the room, locking the banker in.

Nucingen went straight to the bedroom, where he found the handsome Englishwoman.

"Is that you, Lucien?" said she.

"Nein, my peauty," said Nucingen, but he said no more.

He stood speechless on seeing a woman the very antipodes to Esther; fair hair where he had seen black, slenderness where he had admired a powerful frame! A soft English evening where he had looked for the bright sun of Arabia.

"Heyday! were have you come from?—who are you?—what do you want?" cried the Englishwoman, pulling the bell, which made no sound.

"The bells dey are in cotton-vool, but hafe not any fear—I shall go 'vay," said he. "Dat is dirty tousant franc I hafe tron in de vater. Are you dat mistress of Mensieur Lucien de Rubempre?"

"Rather, my son," said the lady, who spoke French well, "But vat vas you?" she went on, mimicking Nucingen's accent.

"Ein man vat is ver' much took in," replied he lamentably.

"Is a man took in ven he finds a pretty voman?" asked she, with a laugh.

"Permit me to sent you to-morrow some chewels as a soufenir of de Baron von Nucingen."

"Don't know him!" said she, laughing like a crazy creature. "But the chewels will be welcome, my fat burglar friend."

"You shall know him. Goot night, motame. You are a tidbit for ein king; but I am only a poor banker more dan sixty year olt, and you hafe made me feel vat power the voman I lofe hafe ofer me since your difine beauty hafe not make me forget her."

"Vell, dat is ver' pretty vat you say," replied the Englishwoman.

"It is not so pretty vat she is dat I say it to."

"You spoke of thirty thousand francs—to whom did you give them?"

"To dat hussy, your maid—"

The Englishwoman called Europe, who was not far off.

"Oh!" shrieked Europe, "a man in madame's room, and he is not monsieur—how shocking!"

"Did he give you thirty thousand francs to let him in?"

"No, madame, for we are not worth it, the pair of us."

And Europe set to screaming "Thief" so determinedly, that the banker made for the door in a fright, and Europe, tripping him up, rolled him down the stairs.

"Old wretch!" cried she, "you would tell tales to my mistress! Thief! thief! stop thief!"

The enamored Baron, in despair, succeeded in getting unhurt to his carriage, which he had left on the boulevard; but he was now at his wits' end as to whom to apply to.

"And pray, madame, did you think to get my earnings out of me?" said Europe, coming back like a fury to the lady's room.

"I know nothing of French customs," said the Englishwoman.

"But one word from me to-morrow to monsieur, and you, madame, would find yourself in the streets," retorted Europe insolently.

"Dat dam' maid!" said the Baron to Georges, who naturally asked his master if all had gone well, "hafe do me out of dirty tousant franc—but it vas my own fault, my own great fault—"

"And so monsieur's dress was all wasted. The deuce is in it, I should advise you, Monsieur le Baron, not to have taken your tonic for nothing—"

"Georches, I shall be dying of despair. I hafe cold—I hafe ice on mein heart—no more of Esther, my good friend."

Georges was always the Baron's friend when matters were serious.

Two days after this scene, which Europe related far more amusingly than it can be written, because she told it with much mimicry, Carlos and Lucien were breakfasting tete-a-tete.

"My dear boy, neither the police nor anybody else must be allowed to poke a nose into our concerns," said Herrera in a low voice, as he lighted his cigar from Lucien's. "It would not agree with us. I have hit on a plan, daring but effectual, to keep our Baron and his agents quiet. You must go to see Madame de Serizy, and make yourself very agreeable to her. Tell her, in the course of conversation, that to oblige Rastignac, who has long been sick of Madame de Nucingen, you have consented to play fence for him to conceal a mistress. Monsieur de Nucingen, desperately in love with this woman Rastignac keeps hidden—that will make her laugh—has taken it into his head to set the police to keep an eye on you—on you, who are innocent of all his tricks, and whose interest with the Grandlieus may be seriously compromised. Then you must beg the Countess to secure her husband's support, for he is a Minister of State, to carry you to the Prefecture of Police.

"When you have got there, face to face with the Prefet, make your complaint, but as a man of political consequence, who will sooner or later be one of the motor powers of the huge machine of government. You will speak of the police as a statesman should, admiring everything, the Prefet included. The very best machines make oil-stains or splutter. Do not be angry till the right moment. You have no sort of grudge against Monsieur le Prefet, but persuade him to keep a sharp lookout on his people, and pity him for having to blow them up. The quieter and more gentlemanly you are, the more terrible will the Prefet be to his men. Then we shall be left in peace, and we may send for Esther back, for she must be belling like the does in the forest."

The Prefet at that time was a retired magistrate. Retired magistrates make far too young Prefets. Partisans of the right, riding the high horse on points of law, they are not light-handed in arbitary action such as critical circumstances often require; cases in which the Prefet should be as prompt as a fireman called to a conflagration. So, face to face with the Vice-President of the Council of State, the Prefet confessed to more faults than the police really has, deplored its abuses, and presently was able to recollect the visit paid to him by the Baron de Nucingen and his inquiries as to Peyrade. The Prefet, while promising to check the rash zeal of his agents, thanked Lucien for having come straight to him, promised secrecy, and affected to understand the intrigue.

A few fine speeches about personal liberty and the sacredness of home life were bandied between the Prefet and the Minister; Monsieur de Serizy observing in conclusion that though the high interests of the kingdom sometimes necessitated illegal action in secret, crime began when these State measures were applied to private cases.

Next day, just as Peyrade was going to his beloved Cafe David, where he enjoyed watching the bourgeois eat, as an artist watches flowers open, a gendarme in private clothes spoke to him in the street.

"I was going to fetch you," said he in his ear. "I have orders to take you to the Prefecture."

Peyrade called a hackney cab, and got in without saying a single word, followed by the gendarme.

The Prefet treated Peyrade as though he were the lowest warder on the hulks, walking to and fro in a side path of the garden of the Prefecture, which at that time was on the Quai des Orfevres.

"It is not without good reason, monsieur, that since 1830 you have been kept out of office. Do not you know to what risk you expose us, not to mention yourself?"

The lecture ended in a thunderstroke. The Prefet sternly informed poor Peyrade that not only would his yearly allowance be cut off, but that he himself would be narrowly watched. The old man took the shock with an air of perfect calm. Nothing can be more rigidly expressionless than a man struck by lightning. Peyrade had lost all his stake in the game. He had counted on getting an appointment, and he found himself bereft of everything but the alms bestowed by his friend Corentin.

"I have been the Prefet of Police myself; I think you perfectly right," said the old man quietly to the functionary who stood before him in his judicial majesty, and who answered with a significant shrug.

"But allow me, without any attempt to justify myself, to point out that you do not know me at all," Peyrade went on, with a keen glance at the Prefet. "Your language is either too severe to a man who has been the head of the police in Holland, or not severe enough for a mere spy. But, Monsieur le Prefet," Peyrade added after a pause, while the other kept silence, "bear in mind what I now have the honor to telling you: I have no intention of interfering with your police nor of attempting to justify myself, but you will presently discover that there is some one in this business who is being deceived; at this moment it is your humble servant; by and by you will say, 'It was I.'"

And he bowed to the chief, who sat passive to conceal his amazement.

Peyrade returned home, his legs and arms feeling broken, and full of cold fury with the Baron. Nobody but that burly banker could have betrayed a secret contained in the minds of Contenson, Peyrade, and Corentin. The old man accused the banker of wishing to avoid paying now that he had gained his end. A single interview had been enough to enable him to read the astuteness of this most astute of bankers.

"He tries to compound with every one, even with us; but I will be revenged," thought the old fellow. "I have never asked a favor of Corentin; I will ask him now to help me to be revenged on that imbecile money-box. Curse the Baron!—Well, you will know the stuff I am made of one fine morning when you find your daughter disgraced!—But does he love his daughter, I wonder?"

By the evening of the day when this catastrophe had upset the old man's hopes he had aged by ten years. As he talked to his friend Corentin, he mingled his lamentations with tears wrung from him by the thought of the melancholy prospects he must bequeath to his daughter, his idol, his treasure, his peace-offering to God.

"We will follow the matter up," said Corentin. "First of all, we must be sure that it was the Baron who peached. Were we wise in enlisting Gondreville's support? That old rascal owes us too much not to be anxious to swamp us; indeed, I am keeping an eye on his son-in-law Keller, a simpleton in politics, and quite capable of meddling in some conspiracy to overthrow the elder Branch to the advantage of the younger.—I shall know to-morrow what is going on at Nucingen's, whether he has seen his beloved, and to whom we owe this sharp pull up.—Do not be out of heart. In the first place, the Prefet will not hold his appointment much longer; the times are big with revolution, and revolutions make good fishing for us."

A peculiar whistle was just then heard in the street.

"That is Contenson," said Peyrade, who put a light in the window, "and he has something to say that concerns me."

A minute later the faithful Contenson appeared in the presence of the two gnomes of the police, whom he revered as though they were two genii.

"What is up?" asked Corentin.

"A new thing! I was coming out of 113, where I lost everything, when whom do I spy under the gallery? Georges! The man has been dismissed by the Baron, who suspects him of treachery."

"That is the effect of a smile I gave him," said Peyrade.

"Bah! when I think of all the mischief I have known caused by smiles!" said Corentin.

"To say nothing of that caused by a whip-lash," said Peyrade, referring to the Simeuse case. (In *Une Tenebreuse affaire*.) "But come, Contenson, what is going on?"

"This is what is going on," said Contenson. "I made Georges blab by getting him to treat me to an endless series of liqueurs of every color—I left him tipsy; I must be as full as a still myself!—Our Baron has been to the Rue Taitbout, crammed with Pastilles du Serail. There he found the fair one you know of; but—a good joke! The English beauty is not his fair unknown!—And he has spent thirty thousand francs to bribe the lady's-maid, a piece of folly!

"That creature thinks itself a great man because it does mean things with great capital. Reverse the proposition, and you have the problem of which a man of genius is the solution.—The Baron came home in a pitiable condition. Next day Georges, to get his finger in the pie, said to his master:

"'Why, Monsieur le Baron, do you employ such blackguards? If you would only trust to me, I would find the unknown lady, for your description of her is enough. I shall turn Paris upside down.'—'Go ahead,' says the Baron; 'I shall reward you handsomely!'—Georges told me the whole story with the most absurd details. But—man is born to be rained upon!

"Next day the Baron received an anonymous letter something to this effect: 'Monsieur de Nucingen is dying of love for an unknown lady; he has already spent a great deal utterly in vain; if he will repair at midnight to the end of the Neuilly Bridge, and get into the carriage behind which the chasseur he saw at Vincennes will be standing, allowing himself to be blindfolded, he will see the woman he loves. As his wealth may lead him to suspect the intentions of persons who proceed in such a fashion, he may bring, as an escort, his faithful Georges. And there will be nobody in the carriage.'—Off the Baron goes, taking Georges with him, but telling him nothing. They both submit to have their eyes bound up and their heads wrapped in veils; the Baron recognizes the man-servant.

"Two hours later, the carriage, going at the pace of Louis XVIII—God rest his soul! He knew what was meant by the police, he did!—pulled up in the middle of a wood. The Baron had the handkerchief off, and saw, in a carriage standing still, his adored fair—when, whiff! she vanished. And the carriage, at the same lively pace, brought him back to the Neuilly Bridge, where he found his own.

"Some one had slipped into Georges' hand a note to this effect: 'How many banknotes will the Baron part with to be put into communication with his unknown fair? Georges handed this to his master; and the Baron, never doubting that Georges was in collusion with me or with you, Monsieur Peyrade, to drive a hard bargain, turned him out of the house. What a fool that banker is! He ought not to have sent away Georges before he had known the unknown!"

"Then Georges saw the woman?" said Corentin.

"Yes," replied Contenson.

"Well," cried Peyrade, "and what is she like?"

"Oh," said Contenson, "he said but one word—'A sun of loveliness.'"

"We are being tricked by some rascals who beat us at the game," said Peyrade. "Those villains mean to sell their woman very dear to the Baron."

"Ja, mein Herr," said Contenson. "And so, when I heard you got slapped in the face at the Prefecture, I made Georges blab."

"I should like very much to know who it is that has stolen a march on me," said Peyrade. "We would measure our spurs!"

"We must play eavesdropper," said Contenson.

"He is right," said Peyrade. "We must get into chinks to listen, and wait—"

"We will study that side of the subject," cried Corentin. "For the present, I am out of work. You, Peyrade, be a very good boy. We must always obey Monsieur le Prefet!"

"Monsieur de Nucingen wants bleeding," said Contenson; "he has too many banknotes in his veins."

"But it was Lydie's marriage-portion I looked for there!" said Peyrade, in a whisper to Corentin.

"Now, come along, Contenson, let us be off, and leave our daddy to by-bye, by-bye!"

"Monsieur," said Contenson to Corentin on the doorstep, "what a queer piece of brokerage our good friend was planning! Heh!—What, marry a daughter with the price of—Ah, ha! It would make a pretty little play, and very moral too, entitled 'A Girl's Dower.'"

"You are highly organized animals, indeed," replied Corentin. "What ears you have! Certainly Social Nature arms all her species with the qualities needed for the duties she expects of them! Society is second nature."

"That is a highly philosophical view to take," cried Contenson. "A professor would work it up into a system."

"Let us find out all we can," replied Corentin with a smile, as he made his way down the street with the spy, "as to what goes on at Monsieur de Nucingen's with regard to this girl—the main facts; never mind the details—"

"Just watch to see if his chimneys are smoking!" said Contenson.

"Such a man as the Baron de Nucingen cannot be happy incognito," replied Corentin. "And besides, we for whom men are but cards, ought never to be tricked by them."

"By gad! it would be the condemned jail-bird amusing himself by cutting the executioner's throat."

"You always have something droll to say," replied Corentin, with a dim smile, that faintly wrinkled his set white face.

This business was exceedingly important in itself, apart from its consequences. If it were not the Baron who had betrayed Peyrade, who could have had any interest in seeing the Prefet of Police? From

Corentin's point of view it seemed suspicious. Were there any traitors among his men? And as he went to bed, he wondered what Peyrade, too, was considering.

"Who can have gone to complain to the Prefet? Whom does the woman belong to?"

And thus, without knowing each other, Jacques Collin, Peyrade, and Corentin were converging to a common point; while the unhappy Esther, Nucingen, and Lucien were inevitably entangled in the struggle which had already begun, and of which the point of pride, peculiar to police agents, was making a war to the death.

Thanks to Europe's cleverness, the more pressing half of the sixty thousand francs of debt owed by Esther and Lucien was paid off. The creditors did not even lose confidence. Lucien and his evil genius could breathe for a moment. Like some pool, they could start again along the edge of the precipice where the strong man was guiding the weak man to the gibbet or to fortune.

"We are staking now," said Carlos to his puppet, "to win or lose all. But, happily, the cards are beveled, and the punters young."

For some time Lucien, by his terrible Mentor's orders, had been very attentive to Madame de Serizy. It was, in fact, indispensable that Lucien should not be suspected of having kept a woman for his mistress. And in the pleasure of being loved, and the excitement of fashionable life, he found a spurious power of forgetting. He obeyed Mademoiselle Clotilde de Grandlieu by never seeing her excepting in the Bois or the Champs-Elysees.

On the day after Esther was shut up in the park-keeper's house, the being who was to her so enigmatic and terrible, who weighed upon her soul, came to desire her to sign three pieces of stamped paper, made terrible by these fateful words: on the first, accepted payable for sixty thousand francs; on the second, accepted payable for a hundred and twenty thousand francs; on the third, accepted payable for a hundred and twenty thousand francs—three hundred thousand francs in all. By writing *Bon pour*, you simply promise to pay. The word *accepted* constitutes a bill of exchange, and makes you liable to imprisonment. The word entails, on the person who is so imprudent as to sign, the risk of five years' imprisonment—a punishment which the police magistrate hardly ever inflicts, and which is reserved at the assizes for confirmed rogues. The law of imprisonment for debt is a relic of the days of barbarism, which combines with its stupidity the rare merit of being useless, inasmuch as it never catches swindlers.

"The point," said the Spaniard to Esther, "is to get Lucien out of his difficulties. We have debts to the tune of sixty thousand francs, and with these three hundred thousand francs we may perhaps pull through."

Having antedated the bills by six months, Carlos had had them drawn on Esther by a man whom the county court had "misunderstood," and whose adventures, in spite of the excitement they had caused, were soon forgotten, hidden, lost, in the uproar of the great symphony of July 1830.

This young fellow, a most audacious adventurer, the son of a lawyer's clerk of Boulogne, near Paris, was named Georges Marie Destourny. His father, obliged by adverse circumstances to sell his connection, died in 1824, leaving his son without the means of living, after giving him a brilliant education, the folly of the lower middle class. At twenty-three the clever young law-student had denied his paternity by printing on his cards

Georges d'Estourny.

This card gave him an odor of aristocracy; and now, as a man of fashion, he was so impudent as to set up a tilbury and a groom and haunt the clubs. One line will account for this: he gambled on the Bourse with the money intrusted to him by the kept women of his acquaintance. Finally he fell into the hands of the police, and was charged with playing at cards with too much luck.

He had accomplices, youths whom he had corrupted, his compulsory satellites, accessory to his fashion and his credit. Compelled to fly, he forgot to pay his differences on the Bourse. All Paris—the Paris of the Stock Exchange and Clubs—was still shaken by this double stroke of swindling.

In the days of his splendor Georges d'Estourny, a handsome youth, and above all, a jolly fellow, as generous as a brigand chief, had for a few months "protected" La Torpille. The false Abbe based his calculations on Esther's former intimacy with this famous scoundrel, an incident peculiar to women of her class.

Georges d'Estourny, whose ambition grew bolder with success, had taken under his patronage a man who had come from the depths of the country to carry on a business in Paris, and whom the Liberal party were anxious to indemnify for certain sentences endured with much courage in the struggle of the press with Charles X's government, the persecution being relaxed, however, during the Martignac administration. The Sieur Cerizet had then been pardoned, and he was henceforth known as the Brave Cerizet.

Cerizet then, being patronized for form's sake by the bigwigs of the Left, founded a house which combined the business of a general agency with that of a bank and a commission agency. It was one of those concerns which, in business, remind one of the servants who advertise in the papers as being able and willing to do everything. Cerizet was very glad to ally himself with Georges d'Estourny, who gave him hints.

Esther, in virtue of the anecdote about Nonon, might be regarded as the faithful guardian of part of Georges d'Estourny's fortune. An endorsement in the name of Georges d'Estourny made Carlos Herrera master of the money he had created. This forgery was perfectly safe so long as Mademoiselle Esther, or some one for her, could, or was bound to pay.

After making inquiries as to the house of Cerizet, Carlos perceived that he had to do with one of those humble men who are bent on making a fortune, but—lawfully. Cerizet, with whom d'Estourny had really deposited his moneys, had in hand a considerable sum with which he was speculating for a rise on the Bourse, a state of affairs which allowed him to style himself a banker. Such things are done in Paris; a man may be despised,—but money, never.

Carlos went off to Cerizet intending to work him after his manner; for, as it happened, he was master of all this worthy's secrets—a meet partner for d'Estourny.

Cerizet the Brave lived in an entresol in the Rue du Gros-Chenet, and Carlos, who had himself mysteriously announced as coming from Georges d'Estourny, found the self-styled banker quite pale at the name. The Abbe saw in this humble private room a little man with thin, light hair; and recognized him at once, from Lucien's description, as the Judas who had ruined David Sechard.

"Can we talk here without risk of being overheard?" said the Spaniard, now metamorphosed into a red-haired Englishman with blue spectacles, as clean and prim as a Puritan going to meeting.

"Why, monsieur?" said Cerizet. "Who are you?"

"Mr. William Barker, a creditor of M. d'Estourny's; and I can prove to you the necessity for keeping your doors closed if you wish it.

We know, monsieur, all about your connections with the Petit-Clauds, the Cointets, and the Sechards of Angouleme—"

On hearing these words, Cerizet rushed to the door and shut it, flew to another leading into a bedroom and bolted it; then he said to the stranger:

"Speak lower, monsieur," and he studied the sham Englishman as he asked him, "What do you want with me?"

"Dear me," said William Barker, "every one for himself in this world. You had the money of that rascal d'Estourny.—Be quite easy, I have not come to ask for it; but that scoundrel, who deserves hanging, between you and me, gave me these bills, saying that there might be some chance of recovering the money; and as I do not choose to prosecute in my own name, he told me you would not refuse to back them."

Cerizet looked at the bills.

"But he is no longer at Frankfort," said he.

"I know it," replied Barker, "but he may still have been there at the date of those bills—"

"I will not take the responsibility," said Cerizet.

"I do not ask such a sacrifice of you," replied Barker; "you may be instructed to receive them. Endorse them, and I will undertake to recover the money."

"I am surprised that d'Estourny should show so little confidence in me," said Cerizet.

"In his position," replied Barker, "you can hardly blame him for having put his eggs in different baskets."

"Can you believe—" the little broker began, as he handed back to the Englishman the bills of exchange formally accepted.

"I believe that you will take good care of his money," said Barker. "I am sure of it! It is already on the green table of the Bourse."

"My fortune depends—"

"On your appearing to lose it," said Barker.

"Sir!" cried Cerizet.

"Look here, my dear Monsieur Cerizet," said Barker, coolly interrupting him, "you will do me a service by facilitating this payment. Be so good as to write me a letter in which you tell me that you are sending me these bills receipted on d'Estourny's account, and that the collecting officer is to regard the holder of the letter as the possessor of the three bills."

"Will you give me your name?"

"No names," replied the English capitalist. "Put 'The bearer of this letter and these bills.'—You will be handsomely repaid for obliging me."

"How?" said Cerizet.

"In one word—You mean to stay in France, do not you?"

"Yes, monsieur."

"Well, Georges d'Estourny will never re-enter the country."

"Pray why?"

"There are five persons at least to my knowledge who would murder him, and he knows it."

"Then no wonder he is asking me for money enough to start him trading to the Indies?" cried Cerizet. "And unfortunately he has compelled me to risk everything in State speculation. We already owe heavy differences to the house of du Tillet. I live from hand to mouth."

"Withdraw your stakes."

"Oh! if only I had known this sooner!" exclaimed Cerizet. "I have missed my chance!"

"One last word," said Barker. "Keep your own counsel, you are capable of that; but you must be faithful too, which is perhaps less certain. We shall meet again, and I will help you to make a fortune."

Having tossed this sordid soul a crumb of hope that would secure silence for some time to come, Carlos, still disguised as Barker, betook himself to a bailiff whom he could depend on, and instructed him to get the bills brought home to Esther.

"They will be paid all right," said he to the officer. "It is an affair of honor; only we want to do the thing regularly."

Barker got a solicitor to represent Esther in court, so that judgment might be given in presence of both parties. The collecting officer, who was begged to act with civility, took with him all the warrants for procedure, and came in person to seize the furniture in the Rue Taitbout, where he was received by Europe. Her personal liability once proved, Esther was ostensibly liable, beyond dispute, for three hundred and more thousand francs of debts.

In all this Carlos displayed no great powers of invention. The farce of false debts is often played in Paris. There are many sub-Gobsecks and sub-Gigonnets who, for a percentage, will lend themselves to this subterfuge, and regard the infamous trick as a jest. In France everything—even a crime—is done with a laugh. By this means refractory parents are made to pay, or rich mistresses who might drive a hard bargain, but who, face to face with flagrant necessity, or some impending dishonor, pay up, if with a bad grace. Maxime de Trailles had often used such means, borrowed from the comedies of the old stage. Carlos Herrera, who wanted to save the honor of his gown, as well as Lucien's, had worked the spell by a forgery not dangerous for him, but now so frequently practised that Justice is beginning to object. There is, it is said, a Bourse for falsified bills near the Palais Royal, where you may get a forged signature for three francs.

BEFORE ENTERING ON THE QUESTION of the hundred thousand crowns that were to keep the door of the bedroom, Carlos determined first to extract a hundred thousand more from M. de Nucingen.

And this was the way: By his orders Asie got herself up for the Baron's benefit as an old woman fully informed as to the unknown beauty's affairs.

Hitherto, novelists of manners have placed on the stage a great many usurers; but the female money-lender has been overlooked, the Madame la Ressource of the present day—a very singular figure, euphemistically spoken of as a "ward-robe purchaser"; a part that the ferocious Asie could play, for she had two old-clothes shops managed by women she could trust—one in the Temple, and the other in the Rue Neuve-Saint-Marc.

"You must get into the skin of Madame de Saint-Esteve," said he.

Herrera wished to see Asie dressed.

The go-between arrived in a dress of flowered damask, made of the curtains of some dismantled boudoir, and one of those shawls of Indian design—out of date, worn, and valueless, which end their career on the backs of these women. She had a collar of magnificent lace, though torn, and a terrible bonnet; but her shoes were of fine kid, in which the flesh of her fat feet made a roll of black-lace stocking.

"And my waist buckle!" she exclaimed, displaying a piece of suspicious-looking finery, prominent on her cook's stomach, "There's style for you! and my front!—Oh, Ma'me Nourrisson has turned me out quite spiff!"

"Be as sweet as honey at first," said Carlos; "be almost timid, as suspicious as a cat; and, above all, make the Baron ashamed of having employed the police, without betraying that you quake before the constable. Finally, make your customer understand in more or less plain terms that you defy all the police in the world to discover his jewel. Take care to destroy your traces.

"When the Baron gives you a right to tap him on the stomach, and call him a pot-bellied old rip, you may be as insolent as you please, and make him trot like a footman."

Nucingen—threatened by Asie with never seeing her again if he attempted the smallest espionage—met the woman on his way to the Bourse, in secret, in a wretched entresol in the Rue Nueve-Saint-Marc. How often, and with what rapture, have amorous millionaires trodden these squalid paths! the pavements of Paris know. Madame de Saint-Esteve, by tossing the Baron from hope to despair by turns, brought him to the point when he insisted on being informed of all that related to the unknown beauty at ANY COST. Meanwhile, the law was put in force, and with such effect that the bailiffs, finding no resistance from Esther, put in an execution on her effects without losing a day.

Lucien, guided by his adviser, paid the recluse at Saint-Germain five or six visits. The merciless author of all these machinations thought this necessary to save Esther from pining to death, for her beauty was now their capital. When the time came for them to quit the park-keeper's lodge, he took Lucien and the poor girl to a place on the road whence they could see Paris, where no one could overhear them. They all three sat down in the rising sun, on the trunk of a felled poplar, looking over one of the finest prospects in the world, embracing the course of the Seine, with Montmartre, Paris, and Saint-Denis.

"My children," said Carlos, "your dream is over.—You, little one, will never see Lucien again; or if you should, you must have known him only for a few days, five years ago."

"Death has come upon me then," said she, without shedding a tear.

"Well, you have been ill these five years," said Herrera. "Imagine yourself to be consumptive, and die without boring us with your lamentations. But you will see, you can still live, and very comfortably too.—Leave us, Lucien—go and gather sonnets!" said he, pointing to a field a little way off.

Lucien cast a look of humble entreaty at Esther, one of the looks peculiar to such men—weak and greedy, with tender hearts and cowardly spirits. Esther answered with a bow of her head, which said: "I will hear the executioner, that I may know how to lay my head under the axe, and I shall have courage enough to die decently."

The gesture was so gracious, but so full of dreadful meaning, that the poet wept; Esther flew to him, clasped him in her arms, drank away the tears, and said, "Be quite easy!" one of those speeches that are spoken with the manner, the look, the tones of delirium.

Carlos then explained to her quite clearly, without attenuation, often with horrible plainness of speech, the critical position in which Lucien found himself, his connection with the Hotel Grandlieu, his splendid prospects if he should succeed; and finally, how necessary it was that Esther should sacrifice herself to secure him this triumphant future.

"What must I do?" cried she, with the eagerness of a fanatic.

"Obey me blindly," said Carlos. "And what have you to complain of? It rests with you to achieve a happy lot. You may be what Tullia is, what your old friends Florine, Mariette, and la Val-Noble are—the mistress of a rich man whom you need not love. When once our business is settled, your lover is rich enough to make you happy."

"Happy!" said she, raising her eyes to heaven.

"You have lived in Paradise for four years," said he. "Can you not live on such memories?"

"I will obey you," said she, wiping a tear from the corner of her eye. "For the rest, do not worry yourself. You have said it; my love is a mortal disease."

"That is not enough," said Carlos; "you must preserve your looks. At a little past two-and-twenty you are in the prime of your beauty, thanks to your past happiness. And, above all, be the 'Torpille' again. Be roguish, extravagant, cunning, merciless to the millionaire I put in your power. Listen to me! That man is a robber on a grand scale; he has been ruthless to many persons; he has grown fat on the fortunes of the widow and the orphan; you will avenge them!

"Asie is coming to fetch you in a hackney coach, and you will be in Paris this evening. If you allow any one to suspect your connection with Lucien, you may as well blow his brains out at once. You will be asked where you have been for so long. You must say that you have been traveling with a desperately jealous Englishman.—You used to have wit enough to humbug people. Find such wit again now."

Have you ever seen a gorgeous kite, the giant butterfly of childhood, twinkling with gilding, and soaring to the sky? The children forget the string that holds it, some passer-by cuts it, the gaudy toy turns head over heels, as the boys say, and falls with terrific rapidity. Such was Esther as she listened to Carlos.

What Love Costs an Old Man

For a whole week Nucingen went almost every day to the shop in the Rue Nueve-Saint-Marc to bargain for the woman he was in love with. Here, sometimes under the name of Saint-Esteve, sometimes under that of her tool, Madame Nourrisson, Asie sat enthroned among beautiful clothes in that hideous condition when they have ceased to be dresses and are not yet rags.

The setting was in harmony with the appearance assumed by the woman, for these shops are among the most hideous characteristics of Paris. You find there the garments tossed aside by the skinny hand of Death; you hear, as it were, the gasping of consumption under a shawl, or you detect the agonies of beggery under a gown spangled with gold. The horrible struggle between luxury and starvation is written on filmy laces; you may picture the countenance of a queen under a plumed turban placed in an attitude that recalls and almost reproduces the absent features. It is all hideous amid prettiness! Juvenal's lash, in the hands of the appraiser, scatters the shabby muffs, the ragged furs of courtesans at bay.

There is a dunghill of flowers, among which here and there we find a bright rose plucked but yesterday and worn for a day; and on this an old hag is always to be seen crouching—first cousin to Usury, the skinflint bargainer, bald and toothless, and ever ready to sell the contents, so well is she used to sell the covering—the gown without the woman, or the woman without the gown!

Here Asie was in her element, like the warder among convicts, like a vulture red-beaked amid corpses; more terrible than the savage horrors that made the passer-by shudder in astonishment sometimes, at seeing one of their youngest and sweetest reminiscences hung up in a dirty shop window, behind which a Saint-Esteve sits and grins.

From vexation to vexation, a thousand francs at a time, the banker had gone so far as to offer sixty thousand francs to Madame de Saint-Esteve, who still refused to help him, with a grimace that would have outdone any monkey. After a disturbed night, after confessing to himself that Esther completely upset his ideas, after realizing some unexpected turns of fortune on the Bourse, he came to her one day, intending to give the hundred thousand francs on which Asie insisted, but he was determined to have plenty of information for the money.

"Well, have you made up your mind, old higgler?" said Asie, clapping him on the shoulder.

The most dishonoring familiarity is the first tax these women levy on the frantic passions or griefs that are confided to them; they never rise to the level of their clients; they make them seem squat beside them on their mudheap. Asie, it will be seen, obeyed her master admirably.

"Need must!" said Nucingen.

"And you have the best of the bargain," said Asie. "Women have been sold much dearer than this one to you—relatively speaking. There are women and women! De Marsay paid sixty thousand francs for Coralie, who is dead now. The woman you want cost a hundred thousand francs when new; but to you, you old goat, it is a matter of agreement."

"But vere is she?"

"Ah! you shall see. I am like you—a gift for a gift! Oh, my good man, your adored one has been extravagant. These girls know no moderation. Your princess is at this moment what we call a fly by night—"

"A fly—?"

"Come, come, don't play the simpleton.—Louchard is at her heels, and I—I—have lent her fifty thousand francs—"

"Twenty-fife say!" cried the banker.

"Well, of course, twenty-five for fifty, that is only natural," replied Asie. "To do the woman justice, she is honesty itself. She had nothing left but herself, and says she to me: 'My good Madame Saint-Esteve, the bailiffs are after me; no one can help me but you. Give me twenty thousand francs. I will pledge my heart to you.' Oh, she has a sweet heart; no one but me knows where it lies. Any folly on my part, and I should lose my twenty thousand francs.

"Formerly she lived in the Rue Taitbout. Before leaving—(her furniture was seized for costs—those rascally bailiffs—You know them, you who are one of the great men on the Bourse)—well, before leaving, she is no fool, she let her rooms for two months to an Englishwoman, a splendid creature who had a little thingummy—Rubempre—for a lover, and he was so jealous that he only let her go out at night. But as the furniture is to be seized, the Englishwoman has cut her stick, all the more because she cost too much for a little whipper-snapper like Lucien."

"You cry up de goots," said Nucingen.

"Naturally," said Asie. "I lend to the beauties; and it pays, for you get two commissions for one job."

Asie was amusing herself by caricaturing the manners of a class of women who are even greedier but more wheedling and mealy-mouthed than the Malay woman, and who put a gloss of the best motives on the trade they ply. Asie affected to have lost all her illusions, five lovers, and some children, and to have submitted to be robbed by everybody in spite of her experience. From time to time she exhibited some pawn-tickets, to prove how much bad luck there was in her line of business. She represented herself as pinched and in debt, and to crown all, she was so undisguisedly hideous that the Baron at last believed her to be all she said she was.

"Vell den, I shall pay the hundert tousant, and vere shall I see her?" said he, with the air of a man who has made up his mind to any sacrifice.

"My fat friend, you shall come this evening—in your carriage, of course—opposite the Gymnase. It is on the way," said Asie. "Stop at the corner of the Rue Saint-Barbe. I will be on the lookout, and we will go and find my mortgaged beauty, with the black hair.—Oh, she has splendid hair, has my mortgage. If she pulls out her comb, Esther is covered as if it were a pall. But though you are knowing in arithmetic, you strike me as a muff in other matters; and I advise you to hide the girl safely, for if she is found she will be clapped into Sainte-Pelagie the very next day.—And they are looking for her."

"Shall it not be possible to get holt of de bills?" said the incorrigible bill-broker.

"The bailiffs have got them—but it is impossible. The girl has had a passion, and has spent some money left in her hands, which she is now called upon to pay. By the poker!—a queer thing is a heart of two and-twenty."

"Ver' goot, ver' goot, I shall arrange all dat," said Nucingen, assuming a cunning look. "It is qvite settled dat I shall protect her."

"Well, old noodle, it is your business to make her fall in love with you, and you certainly have ample means to buy sham love as good as the real article. I will place your princess in your keeping; she is bound to stick to you, and after that I don't care.—But she is accustomed to luxury and the greatest consideration. I tell you, my boy, she is quite the lady.—If not, should I have given her twenty thousand francs?"

"Ver' goot, it is a pargain. Till dis efening."

The Baron repeated the bridal toilet he had already once achieved; but this time, being certain of success, he took a double dose of pillules.

At nine o'clock he found the dreadful woman at the appointed spot, and took her into his carriage.

HONORÉ DE BALZAC

"Vere to?" said the Baron.

"Where?" echoed Asie. "Rue de la Perle in the Marais—an address for the nonce; for your pearl is in the mud, but you will wash her clean."

Having reached the spot, the false Madame de Saint-Esteve said to Nucingen with a hideous smile:

"We must go a short way on foot; I am not such a fool as to have given you the right address."

"You tink of eferytink!" said the baron.

"It is my business," said she.

Asie led Nucingen to the Rue Barbette, where, in furnished lodgings kept by an upholsterer, he was led up to the fourth floor.

On finding Esther in a squalid room, dressed as a work-woman, and employed on some embroidery, the millionaire turned pale. At the end of a quarter of an hour, while Asie affected to talk in whispers to Esther, the young old man could hardly speak.

"Montemisselle," said he at length to the unhappy girl, "vill you be so goot as to let me be your protector?"

"Why, I cannot help myself, monsieur," replied Esther, letting fall two large tears.

"Do not veep. I shall make you de happiest of vomen. Only permit that I shall lof you—you shall see."

"Well, well, child, the gentleman is reasonable," said Asie. "He knows that he is more than sixty, and he will be very kind to you. You see, my beauty, I have found you quite a father—I had to say so," Asie whispered to the banker, who was not best pleased. "You cannot catch swallows by firing a pistol at them.—Come here," she went on, leading Nucingen into the adjoining room. "You remember our bargain, my angel?"

Nucingen took out his pocketbook and counted out the hundred thousand francs, which Carlos, hidden in a cupboard, was impatiently waiting for, and which the cook handed over to him.

"Here are the hundred thousand francs our man stakes on Asie. Now we must make him lay on Europe," said Carlos to his confidante when they were on the landing.

And he vanished after giving his instruction to the Malay who went back into the room. She found Esther weeping bitterly. The poor girl, like a criminal condemned to death, had woven a romance of hope, and the fatal hour had tolled.

"My dear children," said Asie, "where do you mean to go?—For the Baron de Nucingen—"

Esther looked at the great banker with a start of surprise that was admirably acted.

"Ja, mein kind, I am dat Baron von Nucingen."

"The Baron de Nucingen must not, cannot remain in such a room as this," Asie went on. "Listen to me; your former maid Eugenie."

"Eugenie, from the Rue Taitbout?" cried the Baron.

"Just so; the woman placed in possession of the furniture," replied Asie, "and who let the apartment to that handsome Englishwoman—"

"Hah! I onderstant!" said the Baron.

"Madame's former waiting-maid," Asie went on, respectfully alluding to Esther, "will receive you very comfortably this evening; and the commercial police will never think of looking for her in her old rooms which she left three months ago—"

"Feerst rate, feerst rate!" cried the Baron. "An' besides, I know dese commercial police, an' I know vat sorts shall make dem disappear."

"You will find Eugenie a sharp customer," said Asie. "I found her for madame."

"Hah! I know her!" cried the millionaire, laughing. "She haf fleeced me out of dirty tousant franc."

Esther shuddered with horror in a way that would have led a man of any feeling to trust her with his fortune.

"Oh, dat vas mein own fault," the Baron said. "I vas seeking for you."

And he related the incident that had arisen out of the letting of Esther's rooms to the Englishwoman.

"There, now, you see, madame, Eugenie never told you all that, the sly thing!" said Asie.—"Still, madame is used to the hussy," she added to the Baron. "Keep her on, all the same."

She drew Nucingen aside and said:

"If you give Eugenie five hundred francs a month, which will fill up her stocking finely, you can know everything that madame does: make her the lady's-maid. Eugenie will be all the more devoted to you since she has already done you.—Nothing attaches a woman to a man more than the fact that she has once fleeced him. But keep a tight rein on Eugenie; she will do any earthly thing for money; she is a dreadful creature!"

"An' vat of you?"

"I," said Asie, "I make both ends meet."

Nucingen, the astute financier, had a bandage over his eyes; he allowed himself to be led like a child. The sight of that spotless and adorable Esther wiping her eyes and pricking in the stitches of her embroidery as demurely as an innocent girl, revived in the amorous old man the sensations he had experienced in the Forest of Vincennes; he would have given her the key of his safe. He felt so young, his heart was so overflowing with adoration; he only waited till Asie should be gone to throw himself at the feet of this Raphael's Madonna.

This sudden blossoming of youth in the heart of a stockbroker, of an old man, is one of the social phenomena which must be left to physiology to account for. Crushed under the burden of business, stifled under endless calculations and the incessant anxieties of million-hunting, young emotions revive with their sublime illusions, sprout and flower like a forgotten cause or a forgotten seed, whose effects, whose gorgeous bloom, are the sport of chance, brought out by a late and sudden gleam of sunshine.

The Baron, a clerk by the time he was twelve years old in the ancient house of Aldrigger at Strasbourg, had never set foot in the world of sentiment. So there he stood in front of his idol, hearing in his brain a thousand modes of speech, while none came to his lips, till at length he acted on the brutal promptings of desire that betrayed a man of sixty-six.

"Vill you come to Rue Taitbout?" said he.

"Wherever you please, monsieur," said Esther, rising.

"Vherever I please!" he echoed in rapture. "You are ein anchel from de sky, and I lofe you more as if I was a little man, vile I hafe gray hairs—"

"You had better say white, for they are too fine a black to be only gray," said Asie.

"Get out, foul dealer in human flesh! You hafe got your moneys; do not slobber no more on dis flower of lofe!" cried the banker, indemnifying himself by this violent abuse for all the insolence he had submitted to.

"You old rip! I will pay you out for that speech!" said Asie, threatening the banker with a gesture worthy of the Halle, at which the Baron merely shrugged his shoulders. "Between the lip of the pot and that of the guzzler there is often a viper, and you will find me there!" she went on, furious at Nucingen's contempt.

Millionaires, whose money is guarded by the Bank of France, whose mansions are guarded by a squad of footmen, whose person in the streets is safe behind the rampart of a coach with swift English horses, fear no ill; so the Baron looked calmly at Asie, as a man who had just given her a hundred thousand francs.

This dignity had its effect. Asie beat a retreat, growling down the stairs in highly revolutionary language; she spoke of the guillotine!

"What have you said to her?" asked the Madonna a la broderie, "for she is a good soul."

"She hafe solt you, she hafe robbed you—"

"When we are beggared," said she, in a tone to rend the heart of a diplomate, "who has ever any money or consideration for us?"

"Poor leetle ting!" said Nucingen. "Do not stop here ein moment longer."

The Baron offered her his arm; he led her away just as she was, and put her into his carriage with more respect perhaps than he would have shown to the handsome Duchesse de Maufrigneuse.

"You shall hafe a fine carriage, de prettiest carriage in Paris," said Nucingen, as they drove along. "Everyting dat luxury shall sopply shall be for you. Not any qveen shall be more rich dan vat you shall be. You shall be respected like ein Cherman Braut. I shall hafe you to be free.—Do not veep! Listen to me—I lofe you really, truly, mit de purest lofe. Efery tear of yours breaks my heart."

"Can one truly love a woman one has bought?" said the poor girl in the sweetest tones.

"Choseph vas solt by his broders for dat he was so comely. Dat is so in de Bible. An' in de Eastern lants men buy deir wifes."

On arriving at the Rue Taitbout, Esther could not return to the scene of her happiness without some pain. She remained sitting on a couch, motionless, drying away her tears one by one, and never hearing a word of the crazy speeches poured out by the banker. He fell at her feet, and she let him kneel without saying a word to him, allowing him to take her hands as he would, and never thinking of the sex of the creature who was rubbing her feet to warm them; for Nucingen found that they were cold.

This scene of scalding tears shed on the Baron's head, and of ice-cold feet that he tried to warm, lasted from midnight till two in the morning.

"Eugenie," cried the Baron at last to Europe, "persvade your mis'ess that she shall go to bet."

"No!" cried Esther, starting to her feet like a scared horse. "Never in this house!"

"Look her, monsieur, I know madame; she is as gentle and kind as a lamb," said Europe to the Baron. "Only you must not rub her the wrong way, you must get at her sideways—she had been so miserable here.—You see how worn the furniture is.—Let her go her own way.

"Furnish some pretty little house for her, very nicely. Perhaps when she sees everything new about her she will feel a stranger there, and think you better looking than you are, and be angelically sweet.—Oh! madame has not her match, and you may boast of having done a very good stroke of business: a good heart, genteel manners, a fine instep—and a skin, a complexion! Ah!—

"And witty enough to make a condemned wretch laugh. And madame can feel an attachment.—And then how she can dress!—Well, if it is costly, still, as they say, you get your money's worth.—Here all the gowns were seized, everything she has is three months old.—But madame is so kind, you see, that I love her, and she is my mistress!—But in all justice—such a woman as she is, in the midst of furniture that has been seized!—And for whom? For a young scamp who has ruined her. Poor little thing, she is not at all herself."

"Esther, Esther; go to bet, my anchel! If it is me vat frighten you, I shall stay here on dis sofa—" cried the Baron, fired by the purest devotion, as he saw that Esther was still weeping.

"Well, then," said Esther, taking the "lynx's" hand, and kissing it with an impulse of gratitude which brought something very like a tear to his eye, "I shall be grateful to you—"

And she fled into her room and locked the door.

"Dere is someting fery strange in all dat," thought Nucingen, excited by his pillules. "Vat shall dey say at home?"

He got up and looked out of the window. "My carriage still is dere. It shall soon be daylight." He walked up and down the room.

"Vat Montame de Nucingen should laugh at me ven she should know how I hafe spent dis night!"

He applied his ear to the bedroom door, thinking himself rather too much of a simpleton.

"Esther!"

No reply.

"Mein Gott! and she is still veeping!" said he to himself, as he stretched himself on the sofa.

About ten minutes after sunrise, the Baron de Nucingen, who was sleeping the uneasy slumbers that are snatched by compulsion in an awkward position on a couch, was aroused with a start by Europe from one of those dreams that visit us in such moments, and of which the swift complications are a phenomenon inexplicable by medical physiology.

"Oh, God help us, madame!" she shrieked. "Madame!—the soldiers—gendarmes—bailiffs! They have come to take us."

At the moment when Esther opened her door and appeared, hurriedly, wrapped in her dressing-gown, her bare feet in slippers, her hair in disorder, lovely enough to bring the angel Raphael to perdition, the drawing-room door vomited into the room a gutter of human mire that came on, on ten feet, towards the beautiful girl, who stood like an angel in some Flemish church picture. One man came foremost. Contenson, the horrible Contenson, laid his hand on Esther's dewy shoulder.

"You are Mademoiselle van—" he began. Europe, by a back-handed slap on Contenson's cheek, sent him sprawling to measure his length on the carpet, and with all the more effect because at the same time she caught his leg with the sharp kick known to those who practise the art as a coup de savate.

"Hands off!" cried she. "No one shall touch my mistress."

"She has broken my leg!" yelled Contenson, picking himself up; "I will have damages!"

From the group of bumbailiffs, looking like what they were, all standing with their horrible hats on their yet more horrible heads, with mahogany-colored faces and bleared eyes, damaged noses, and hideous mouths, Louchard now stepped forth, more decently dressed than his men, but keeping his hat on, his expression at once smooth-faced and smiling.

"Mademoiselle, I arrest you!" said he to Esther. "As for you, my girl," he added to Europe, "any resistance will be punished, and perfectly useless."

The noise of muskets, let down with a thud of their stocks on the floor of the dining-room, showing that the invaders had soldiers to bake them, gave emphasis to this speech.

"And what am I arrested for?" said Esther.

"What about our little debts?" said Louchard.

"To be sure," cried Esther; "give me leave to dress."

"But, unfortunately, mademoiselle, I am obliged to make sure that you have no way of getting out of your room," said Louchard.

All this passed so quickly that the Baron had not yet had time to intervene.

"Well, and am I still a foul dealer in human flesh, Baron de Nucingen?" cried the hideous Asie, forcing her way past the sheriff's officers to the couch, where she pretended to have just discovered the banker.

HONORÉ DE BALZAC

"Contemptible wretch!" exclaimed Nucingen, drawing himself up in financial majesty.

He placed himself between Esther and Louchard, who took off his hat as Contenson cried out, "Monsieur le Baron de Nucingen."

At a signal from Louchard the bailiffs vanished from the room, respectfully taking their hats off. Contenson alone was left.

"Do you propose to pay, Monsieur le Baron?" asked he, hat in hand.

"I shall pay," said the banker; "but I must know vat dis is all about."

"Three hundred and twelve thousand francs and some centimes, costs paid; but the charges for the arrest not included."

"Three hundred thousand francs," cried the Baron; "dat is a fery 'xpensive vaking for a man vat has passed the night on a sofa," he added in Europe's ear.

"Is that man really the Baron de Nucingen?" asked Europe to Louchard, giving weight to the doubt by a gesture which Mademoiselle Dupont, the low comedy servant of the Francais, might have envied.

"Yes, mademoiselle," said Louchard.

"Yes," replied Contenson.

"I shall be answerable," said the Baron, piqued in his honor by Europe's doubt. "You shall 'llow me to say ein vort to her."

Esther and her elderly lover retired to the bedroom, Louchard finding it necessary to apply his ear to the keyhole.

"I lofe you more as my life, Esther; but vy gife to your creditors moneys vich shall be so much better in your pocket? Go into prison. I shall undertake to buy up dose hundert tousant crowns for ein hundert tousant francs, an' so you shall hafe two hundert tousant francs for you—"

"That scheme is perfectly useless," cried Louchard through the door. "The creditor is not in love with mademoiselle—not he! You understand? And he means to have more than all, now he knows that you are in love with her."

"You dam' sneak!" cried Nucingen, opening the door, and dragging Louchard into the bedroom; "you know not dat vat you talk about. I shall gife you, you'self, tventy per cent if you make the job."

"Impossible, M. le Baron."

"What, monsieur, you could have the heart to let my mistress go to prison?" said Europe, intervening. "But take my wages, my savings; take them, madame; I have forty thousand francs—"

"Ah, my good girl, I did not really know you!" cried Esther, clasping Europe in her arms.

Europe proceeded to melt into tears.

"I shall pay," said the Baron piteously, as he drew out a pocket-book, from which he took one of the little printed forms which the Bank of France issues to bankers, on which they have only to write a sum in figures and in words to make them available as cheques to bearer.

"It is not worth the trouble, Monsieur le Baron," said Louchard; "I have instructions not to accept payment in anything but coin of the realm—gold or silver. As it is you, I will take banknotes."

"Der Teufel!" cried the Baron. "Well, show me your papers."

Contenson handed him three packets covered with blue paper, which the Baron took, looking at the man, and adding in an undertone:

"It should hafe been a better day's vork for you ven you had gife me notice."

"Why, how should I know you were here, Monsieur le Baron?" replied the spy, heedless whether Louchard heard him. "You lost my services by withdrawing your confidence. You are done," added this philosopher, shrugging his shoulders.

"Qvite true," said the baron. "Ah, my chilt," he exclaimed, seeing the bills of exchange, and turning to Esther, "you are de fictim of a torough scoundrel, ein highway tief!"

"Alas, yes," said poor Esther; "but he loved me truly."

"Ven I should hafe known—I should hafe made you to protest—"

"You are off your head, Monsieur le Baron," said Louchard; "there is a third endorsement."

"Yes, dere is a tird endorsement—Cerizet! A man of de opposition."

"Will you write an order on your cashier, Monsieur le Baron?" said Louchard. "I will send Contenson to him and dismiss my men. It is getting late, and everybody will know that—"

"Go den, Contenson," said Nucingen. "My cashier lives at de corner of Rue des Mathurins and Rue de l'Arcate. Here is ein vort for dat he shall go to du Tillet or to de Kellers, in case ve shall not hafe a hundert tousant franc—for our cash shall be at de Bank.—Get dress', my anchel," he said to Esther. "You are at liberty.—An' old vomans," he went on, looking at Asie, "are more dangerous as young vomans."

"I will go and give the creditor a good laugh," said Asie, "and he will give me something for a treat to-day.—We bear no malice, Monsieur le Baron," added Saint-Esteve with a horrible courtesy.

Louchard took the bills out of the Baron's hands, and remained alone with him in the drawing-room, whither, half an hour later, the cashier came, followed by Contenson. Esther then reappeared in a bewitching, though improvised, costume. When the money had been counted by Louchard, the Baron wished to examine the bills; but Esther snatched them with a cat-like grab, and carried them away to her desk.

"What will you give the rabble?" said Contenson to Nucingen.

"You hafe not shown much consideration," said the Baron.

"And what about my leg?" cried Contenson.

"Louchard, you shall gife ein hundert francs to Contenson out of the change of the tousand-franc note."

"De lady is a beauty," said the cashier to the Baron, as they left the Rue Taitbout, "but she is costing you ver' dear, Monsieur le Baron."

"Keep my segret," said the Baron, who had said the same to Contenson and Louchard.

Louchard went away with Contenson; but on the boulevard Asie, who was looking out for him, stopped Louchard.

"The bailiff and the creditor are there in a cab," said she. "They are thirsty, and there is money going."

While Louchard counted out the cash, Contenson studied the customers. He recognized Carlos by his eyes, and traced the form of his forehead under the wig. The wig he shrewdly regarded as suspicious; he took the number of the cab while seeming quite indifferent to what was going on; Asie and Europe puzzled him beyond measure. He thought that the Baron was the victim of excessively clever sharpers, all the more so because Louchard, when securing his services, had been singularly close. And besides, the twist of Europe's foot had not struck his shin only.

"A trick like that is learned at Saint-Lazare," he had reflected as he got up.

Carlos dismissed the bailiff, paying him liberally, and as he did so, said to the driver of the cab, "To the Perron, Palais Royal."

"The rascal!" thought Contenson as he heard the order. "There is something up!" Carlos drove to the Palais Royal at a pace which precluded all fear of pursuit. He made his way in his own fashion through the arcades, took another cab on the Place du Chateau d'Eau, and bid the man go "to the Passage de l'Opera, the end of the Rue Pinon."

A quarter of a hour later he was in the Rue Taitbout. On seeing him, Esther said:

"Here are the fatal papers."

Carlos took the bills, examined them, and then burned them in the kitchen fire.

"We have done the trick," he said, showing her three hundred and ten thousand francs in a roll, which he took out of the pocket of his coat. "This, and the hundred thousand francs squeezed out by Asie, set us free to act."

"Oh God, oh God!" cried poor Esther.

"But, you idiot," said the ferocious swindler, "you have only to be ostensibly Nucingen's mistress, and you can always see Lucien; he is Nucingen's friend; I do not forbid your being madly in love with him."

Esther saw a glimmer of light in her darkened life; she breathed once more.

"Europe, my girl," said Carlos, leading the creature into a corner of the boudoir where no one could overhear a word, "Europe, I am pleased with you."

Europe held up her head, and looked at this man with an expression which so completely changed her faded features, that Asie, witnessing the interview, as she watched her from the door, wondered whether the interest by which Carlos held Europe might not perhaps be even stronger than that by which she herself was bound to him.

"That is not all, my child. Four hundred thousand francs are a mere nothing to me. Paccard will give you an account for some plate, amounting to thirty thousand francs, on which money has been paid on account; but our goldsmith, Biddin, has paid money for us. Our furniture, seized by him, will no doubt be advertised to-morrow. Go and see Biddin; he lives in the Rue de l'Arbre Sec; he will give you Mont-de-Piete tickets for ten thousand francs. You understand, Esther ordered the plate; she had not paid for it, and she put it up the spout. She will be in danger of a little summons for swindling. So we must pay the goldsmith the thirty thousand francs, and pay up ten thousand francs to the Mont-de-Piete to get the plate back. Forty-three thousand francs in all, including the costs. The silver is very much alloyed; the Baron will give her a new service, and we shall bone a few thousand francs out of that. You owe—what? two years' account with the dressmaker?"

"Put it at six thousand francs," replied Europe.

"Well, if Madame Auguste wants to be paid and keep our custom, tell her to make out a bill for thirty thousand francs over four years. Make a similar arrangement with the milliner. The jeweler, Samuel Frisch the

Jew, in the Rue Saint-Avoie, will lend you some pawn-tickets; we must owe him twenty-five thousand francs, and we must want six thousand for jewels pledged at the Mont-de-Piete. We will return the trinkets to the jeweler, half the stones will be imitation, but the Baron will not examine them. In short, you will make him fork out another hundred and fifty thousand francs to add to our nest-eggs within a week."

"Madame might give me a little help," said Europe. "Tell her so, for she sits there mumchance, and obliges me to find more inventions than three authors for one piece."

"If Esther turns prudish, just let me know," said Carlos. "Nucingen must give her a carriage and horses; she will have to choose and buy everything herself. Go to the horse-dealer and the coachmaker who are employed by the job-master where Paccard finds work. We shall get handsome horses, very dear, which will go lame within a month, and we shall have to change them."

"We might get six thousand francs out of a perfumer's bill," said Europe.

"Oh!" said he, shaking his head, "we must go gently. Nucingen has only got his arm into the press; we must have his head. Besides all this, I must get five hundred thousand francs."

"You can get them," replied Europe. "Madame will soften towards the fat fool for about six hundred thousand, and insist on four hundred thousand more to love him truly!"

"Listen to me, my child," said Carlos. "The day when I get the last hundred thousand francs, there shall be twenty thousand for you."

"What good will they do me?" said Europe, letting her arms drop like a woman to whom life seems impossible.

"You could go back to Valenciennes, buy a good business, and set up as an honest woman if you chose; there are many tastes in human nature. Paccard thinks of settling sometimes; he has no encumbrances on his hands, and not much on his conscience; you might suit each other," replied Carlos.

"Go back to Valenciennes! What are you thinking of, monsieur?" cried Europe in alarm.

Europe, who was born at Valenciennes, the child of very poor parents, had been sent at seven years of age to a spinning factory, where the demands of modern industry had impaired her physical strength, just as vice had untimely depraved her. Corrupted at the age of twelve, and a mother at thirteen, she found herself bound to the most degraded of human creatures. On the occasion of a murder case, she had been as a witness before the Court. Haunted at sixteen by a remnant of rectitude, and the terror inspired by the law, her evidence led to the prisoner being sentenced to twenty years of hard labor.

The convict, one of those men who have been in the hands of justice more than once, and whose temper is apt at terrible revenge, had said to the girl in open court:

"In ten years, as sure as you live, Prudence" (Europe's name was Prudence Servien), "I will return to be the death of you, if I am scragged for it."

The President of the Court tried to reassure the girl by promising her the protection and the care of the law; but the poor child was so terror-stricken that she fell ill, and was in hospital nearly a year. Justice is an abstract being, represented by a collection of individuals who are incessantly changing, whose good intentions and memories are, like themselves, liable to many vicissitudes. Courts and tribunals can do nothing to hinder crimes; their business is to deal with them when done. From this point of view, a preventive police would be a boon to a country; but the mere word Police is in these days a bugbear to legislators, who no longer can distinguish between the three words—Government, Administration, and Law-making. The legislator tends to centralize everything in the State, as if the State could act.

The convict would be sure always to remember his victim, and to avenge himself when Justice had ceased to think of either of them.

Prudence, who instinctively appreciated the danger—in a general sense, so to speak—left Valenciennes and came to Paris at the age of seventeen to hide there. She tried four trades, of which the most successful was that of a "super" at a minor theatre. She was picked up by Paccard, and to him she told her woes. Paccard, Jacques Collin's disciple and right-hand man, spoke of this girl to his master, and when the master needed a slave he said to Prudence:

"If you will serve me as the devil must be served, I will rid you of Durut."

Durut was the convict; the Damocles' sword hung over Prudence Servien's head.

But for these details, many critics would have thought Europe's attachment somewhat grotesque. And no one could have understood the startling announcement that Carlos had ready.

"Yes, my girl, you can go back to Valenciennes. Here, read this."

And he held out to her yesterday's paper, pointing to this paragraph:

Toulon

Yesterday, Jean Francois Durut was executed here. Early
in the morning the garrison," etc.

Prudence dropped the paper; her legs gave way under the weight of her body; she lived again; for, to use her own words, she never liked the taste of her food since the day when Durut had threatened her.

"You see, I have kept my word. It has taken four years to bring Durut to the scaffold by leading him into a snare.—Well, finish my job here, and you will find yourself at the head of a little country business in your native town, with twenty thousand francs of your own as Paccard's wife, and I will allow him to be virtuous as a form of pension."

Europe picked up the paper and read with greedy eyes all the details, of which for twenty years the papers have never been tired, as to the death of convicted criminals: the impressive scene, the chaplain—who has always converted the victim—the hardened criminal preaching to his fellow convicts, the battery of guns, the convicts on their knees; and then the twaddle and reflections which never lead to any change in the management of the prisons where eighteen hundred crimes are herded.

"We must place Asie on the staff once more," said Carlos.

Asie came forward, not understanding Europe's pantomime.

"In bringing her back here as cook, you must begin by giving the Baron such a dinner as he never ate in his life," he went on. "Tell him that Asie has lost all her money at play, and has taken service once more. We shall not need an outdoor servant. Paccard shall be coachman. Coachmen do not leave their box, where they are safe out of the way; and he will run less risk from spies. Madame must turn him out in a powdered wig and a braided felt cocked hat; that will alter his appearance. Besides, I will make him us."

"Are we going to have men-servants in the house?" asked Asie with a leer.

"All honest folks," said Carlos.

"All soft-heads," retorted the mulatto.

"If the Baron takes a house, Paccard has a friend who will suit as the lodge porter," said Carlos. "Then we shall only need a footman and a kitchen-maid, and you can surely keep an eye on two strangers—"

As Carlos was leaving, Paccard made his appearance.

"Wait a little while, there are people in the street," said the man.

This simple statement was alarming. Carlos went up to Europe's room, and stayed there till Paccard came to fetch him, having called a hackney cab that came into the courtyard. Carlos pulled down the blinds, and was driven off at a pace that defied pursuit.

Having reached the Faubourg Saint-Antoine, he got out at a short distance from a hackney coach stand, to which he went on foot, and thence returned to the Quai Malaquais, escaping all inquiry.

"Here, child," said he to Lucien, showing him four hundred banknotes for a thousand francs, "here is something on account for the purchase of the estates of Rubempre. We will risk a hundred thousand. Omnibuses have just been started; the Parisians will take to the novelty; in three months we shall have trebled our capital. I know the concern; they will pay splendid dividends taken out of the capital, to put a head on the shares—an old idea of Nucingen's revived. If we acquire the Rubempre land, we shall not have to pay on the nail.

"You must go and see des Lupeaulx, and beg him to give you a personal recommendation to a lawyer named Desroches, a cunning dog, whom you must call on at his office. Get him to go to Rubempre and see how the land lies; promise him a premium of twenty thousand francs if he manages to secure you thirty thousand francs a year by investing eight hundred thousand francs in land round the ruins of the old house."

"How you go on—on! on!"

"I am always going on. This is no time for joking.—You must then invest a hundred thousand crowns in Treasury bonds, so as to lose no interest; you may safely leave it to Desroches, he is as honest as he is knowing.—That being done, get off to Angouleme, and persuade your sister and your brother-in-law to pledge themselves to a little fib in the way of business. Your relations are to have given you six hundred thousand francs to promote your marriage with Clotilde de Grandlieu; there is no disgrace in that."

"We are saved!" cried Lucien, dazzled.

"You are, yes!" replied Carlos. "But even you are not safe till you walk out of Saint-Thomas d'Aquin with Clotilde as your wife."

"And what have you to fear?" said Lucien, apparently much concerned for his counselor.

"Some inquisitive souls are on my track—I must assume the manners of a genuine priest; it is most annoying. The Devil will cease to protect me if he sees me with a breviary under my arm."

AT THIS MOMENT THE BARON de Nucingen, who was leaning on his cashier's arm, reached the door of his mansion.

"I am ver' much afrait," said he, as he went in, "dat I hafe done a bat day's vork. Vell, we must make it up some oder vays."

"De misfortune is dat you shall hafe been caught, mein Herr Baron," said the worthy German, whose whole care was for appearances.

"Ja, my miss'ess en titre should be in a position vody of me," said this Louis XIV of the counting-house.

Feeling sure that sooner or later Esther would be his, the Baron was now himself again, a masterly financier. He resumed the management of his affairs, and with such effect that his cashier, finding him in his office room at six o'clock next morning, verifying his securities, rubbed his hands with satisfaction.

"Ah, ha! mein Herr Baron, you shall hafe saved money last night!" said he, with a half-cunning, half-loutish German grin.

Though men who are as rich as the Baron de Nucingen have more opportunities than others for losing money, they also have more chances of making it, even when they indulge their follies. Though the financial policy of the house of Nucingen has been explained elsewhere, it may be as well to point out that such immense fortunes are not made, are not built up, are not increased, and are not retained in the midst of the commercial, political, and industrial revolutions of the present day but at the cost of immense losses, or, if you choose to view it so, of heavy taxes on private fortunes. Very little newly-created wealth is thrown into the common treasury of the world. Every fresh accumulation represents some new inequality in the general distribution of wealth. What the State exacts it makes some return for; but what a house like that of Nucingen takes, it keeps.

Such covert robbery escapes the law for the reason which would have made a Jacques Collin of Frederick the Great, if, instead of dealing with provinces by means of battles, he had dealt in smuggled goods or transferable securities. The high politics of money-making consist in forcing the States of Europe to issue loans at twenty or at ten per cent, in making that twenty or ten per cent by the use of public funds, in squeezing industry on a vast scale by buying up raw material, in throwing a rope to the first founder of a business just to keep him above water till his drowned-out enterprise is safely landed—in short, in all the great battles for money-getting.

The banker, no doubt, like the conqueror, runs risks; but there are so few men in a position to wage this warfare, that the sheep have no business to meddle. Such grand struggles are between the shepherds. Thus, as the defaulters are guilty of having wanted to win too much, very little sympathy is felt as a rule for the misfortunes brought about by the coalition of the Nucingens. If a speculator blows his brains out, if a stockbroker bolts, if a lawyer makes off with the fortune of a hundred families—which is far worse than killing a man—if a banker is insolvent, all these catastrophes are forgotten in Paris in few months, and buried under the oceanic surges of the great city.

The colossal fortunes of Jacques Coeur, of the Medici, of the Angos of Dieppe, of the Auffredis of la Rochelle, of the Fuggers, of the Tiepolos, of the Corners, were honestly made long ago by the advantages they had over the ignorance of the people as to the sources of precious products; but nowadays geographical information has reached the masses, and competition has so effectually limited the profits, that every rapidly made fortune is the result of chance, or of a discovery, or of some legalized robbery. The lower grades of mercantile enterprise have retorted on the perfidious dealings of higher commerce, especially during the last ten years, by base adulteration of the raw material. Wherever chemistry is practised, wine is no longer procurable; the vine industry is consequently waning. Manufactured salt is sold to avoid the excise. The tribunals are appalled by this universal dishonesty. In short, French trade is regarded with suspicion by the whole world, and England too is fast being demoralized.

With us the mischief has its origin in the political situation. The Charter proclaimed the reign of Money, and success has become the supreme consideration of an atheistic age. And, indeed, the corruption of the higher ranks is infinitely more hideous, in spite of the dazzling display and specious arguments of wealth, than that ignoble and more personal corruption of the inferior classes, of which certain details lend a comic element—terrible, if you will—to this drama. The Government, always alarmed by a new idea, has banished these materials of modern comedy from the stage. The citizen class, less liberal than Louis XIV, dreads the advent of its *Mariage de Figaro*, forbids the appearance of a political *Tartuffe*, and certainly would not allow *Turcaret* to be represented, for Turcaret is king. Consequently, comedy has to be narrated, and a book is now the weapon—less swift, but no more sure—that writers wield.

In the course of this morning, amid the coming and going of callers, orders to be given, and brief interviews, making Nucingen's private office a sort of financial lobby, one of his stockbrokers announced to him the disappearance of a member of the Company, one of the richest and cleverest too—Jacques Falleix, brother of Martin Falleix, and the successor of Jules Desmarets. Jacques Falleix was stockbroker in ordinary to the house of Nucingen. In concert with du Tillet and the Kellers, the Baron had plotted the ruin of this man in cold blood, as if it had been the killing of a Passover lamb.

"He could not hafe helt on," replied the Baron quietly.

Jacques Falleix had done them immense service in stock-jobbing. During a crisis a few months since he had saved the situation by acting boldly. But to look for gratitude from a money-dealer is as vain as to try to touch the heart of the wolves of the Ukraine in winter.

"Poor fellow!" said the stockbroker. "He so little anticipated such a catastrophe, that he had furnished a little house for his mistress in the Rue Saint-Georges; he has spent one hundred and fifty thousand francs in decorations and furniture. He was so devoted to Madame du Val-Noble! The poor woman must give it all up. And nothing is paid for."

"Goot, goot!" thought Nucingen, "dis is de very chance to make up for vat I hafe lost dis night!—He hafe paid for noting?" he asked his informant.

"Why," said the stockbroker, "where would you find a tradesman so ill informed as to refuse credit to Jacques Falleix? There is a splendid cellar of wine, it would seem. By the way, the house is for sale; he meant to buy it. The lease is in his name.—What a piece of folly! Plate, furniture, wine, carriage-horses, everything will be valued in a lump, and what will the creditors get out of it?"

"Come again to-morrow," said Nucingen. "I shall hafe seen all dat; and if it is not a declared bankruptcy, if tings can be arranged and compromised, I shall tell you to offer some reasonaple price for dat furniture, if I shall buy de lease—"

"That can be managed," said his friend. "If you go there this morning, you will find one of Falleix's partners there with the tradespeople, who want to establish a first claim; but la Val-Noble has their accounts made out to Falleix."

The Baron sent off one of his clerks forthwith to his lawyer. Jacques Falleix had spoken to him about this house, which was worth sixty thousand francs at most, and he wished to be put in possession of it at once, so as to avail himself of the privileges of the householder.

The cashier, honest man, came to inquire whether his master had lost anything by Falleix's bankruptcy.

"On de contrar' mein goot Volfgang, I stant to vin ein hundert tousant francs."

"How vas dat?"

"Vell, I shall hafe de little house vat dat poor Teufel Falleix should furnish for his mis'ess this year. I shall hafe all dat for fifty tousant franc to de creditors; and my notary, Maitre Cardot, shall hafe my orders to buy de house, for de lan'lord vant de money—I knew dat, but I hat lost mein head. Ver' soon my difine Esther shall life in a little palace. . . I hafe been dere mit Falleix—it is close to here.—It shall fit me like a glofe."

Falleix's failure required the Baron's presence at the Bourse; but he could not bear to leave his house in the Rue Saint-Lazare without going to the Rue Taitbout; he was already miserable at having been away from Esther for so many hours. He would have liked to keep her at his elbow. The profits he hoped to make out of his stockbrokers' plunder made the former loss of four hundred thousand francs quite easy to endure.

Delighted to announce to his "anchel" that she was to move from the Rue Taitbout to the Rue Saint-Georges, where she was to have "ein little palace" where her memories would no longer rise up in antagonism to their happiness, the pavement felt elastic under his feet; he walked like a young man in a young man's dream. As he turned the corner of the Rue des Trois Freres, in the middle of his dream, and of the road, the Baron beheld Europe coming towards him, looking very much upset.

"Vere shall you go?" he asked.

"Well, monsieur, I was on my way to you. You were quite right yesterday. I see now that poor madame had better have gone to prison for a few days. But how should women understand money matters? When madame's creditors heard that she had come home, they all came down upon us like birds of prey.—Last evening, at seven o'clock, monsieur, men came and stuck terrible posters up to announce a sale of furniture on Saturday—but that is nothing.—Madame, who is all heart, once upon a time to oblige that wretch of a man you know—"

"Vat wretch?"

"Well, the man she was in love with, d'Estourny—well, he was charming! He was only a gambler—"

"He gambled with beveled cards!"

"Well—and what do you do at the Bourse?" said Europe. "But let me go on. One day, to hinder Georges, as he said, from blowing out his brains, she pawned all her plate and her jewels, which had never been paid for. Now on hearing that she had given something to one of her creditors, they came in a body and made a scene. They threaten her with the police-court—your angel at that bar! Is it not enough to make a wig stand on end? She is bathed in tears; she talks of throwing herself into the river—and she will do it."

"If I shall go to see her, dat is goot-bye to de Bourse; an' it is impossible but I shall go, for I shall make some money for her—you shall compose her. I shall pay her debts; I shall go to see her at four o'clock. But tell me, Eugenie, dat she shall lofe me a little—"

"A little?—A great deal!—I tell you what, monsieur, nothing but generosity can win a woman's heart. You would, no doubt, have saved a hundred thousand francs or so by letting her go to prison. Well, you would never have won her heart. As she said to me—'Eugenie, he has been noble, grand—he has a great soul.'"

"She hafe said dat, Eugenie?" cried the Baron.

"Yes, monsieur, to me, myself."

"Here—take dis ten louis."

"Thank you.—But she is crying at this moment; she has been crying ever since yesterday as much as a weeping Magdalen could have cried in six months. The woman you love is in despair, and for debts that are not even hers! Oh! men—they devour women as women devour old fogies—there!"

"Dey all is de same!—She hafe pledge' herself.—Vy, no one shall ever pledge herself.—Tell her dat she shall sign noting more.—I shall pay; but if she shall sign something more—I—"

"What will you do?" said Europe with an air.

"Mein Gott! I hafe no power over her.—I shall take de management of her little affairs—Dere, dere, go to comfort her, and you shall say that in ein mont she shall live in a little palace."

"You have invested heavily, Monsieur le Baron, and for large interest, in a woman's heart. I tell you—you look to me younger. I am but a waiting-maid, but I have often seen such a change. It is happiness—happiness gives a certain glow. . . If you have spent a little money, do not let that worry you; you will see what a good return it will bring. And I said to madame, I told her she would be the lowest of the low, a perfect hussy, if she did not love you, for you have picked her out of hell.—When once she has nothing on her mind, you will see. Between you and me, I may tell you, that night when she cried so much—What is to be said, we value the esteem of the man who maintains us—and she did not dare tell you everything. She wanted to fly."

"To fly!" cried the Baron, in dismay at the notion. "But the Bourse, the Bourse!—Go 'vay, I shall not come in.—But tell her that I shall see her at her window—dat shall gife me courage!"

Esther smiled at Monsieur de Nucingen as he passed the house, and he went ponderously on his way, saying:

"She is ein anchel!"

This was how Europe had succeeded in achieving the impossible. At about half-past two Esther had finished dressing, as she was wont to dress when she expected Lucien; she was looking charming. Seeing this, Prudence, looking out of the window, said, "There is monsieur!"

The poor creature flew to the window, thinking she would see Lucien; she saw Nucingen.

"Oh! how cruelly you hurt me!" she said.

"There is no other way of getting you to seem to be gracious to a poor old man, who, after all, is going to pay your debts," said Europe. "For they are all to be paid."

"What debts?" said the girl, who only cared to preserve her love, which dreadful hands were scattering to the winds.

"Those which Monsieur Carlos made in your name."

"Why, here are nearly four hundred and fifty thousand francs," cried Esther.

"And you owe a hundred and fifty thousand more. But the Baron took it all very well.—He is going to remove you from hence, and place you in a little palace.—On my honor, you are not so badly off. In your place, as you have got on the right side of this man, as soon as Carlos is satisfied, I should make him give me a house and a settled income. You are certainly the handsomest woman I ever saw, madame, and the most attractive, but we so soon grow ugly! I was fresh and good-looking, and look at me! I am twenty-three, about the same age as madame, and I look ten years older. An illness is enough.—Well, but when you have a house in Paris and investments, you need never be afraid of ending in the streets."

Esther had ceased to listen to Europe-Eugenie-Prudence Servien. The will of a man gifted with the genius of corruption had thrown Esther back into the mud with as much force as he had used to drag her out of it.

Those who know love in its infinitude know that those who do not accept its virtues do not experience its pleasures. Since the scene in the den in the Rue de Langlade, Esther had utterly forgotten her former existence. She had since lived very virtuously, cloistered by her passion. Hence, to avoid any obstacle, the skilful fiend had been clever enough to lay such a train that the poor girl, prompted by her devotion, had merely to utter her consent to swindling actions already done, or on the point of accomplishment. This subtlety, revealing the mastery of the tempter, also characterized the methods by which he had subjugated Lucien. He created a terrible situation, dug a mine, filled it with powder, and at the critical moment said to his accomplice, "You have only to nod, and the whole will explode!"

Esther of old, knowing only the morality peculiar to courtesans, thought all these attentions so natural, that she measured her rivals only by what they could get men to spend on them. Ruined fortunes are the conduct-stripes of these creatures. Carlos, in counting on Esther's memory, had not calculated wrongly.

These tricks of warfare, these stratagems employed a thousand times, not only by these women, but by spendthrifts too, did not disturb Esther's mind. She felt nothing but her personal degradation; she loved Lucien, she was to be the Baron de Nucingen's mistress "by appointment"; this was all she thought of. The supposed Spaniard might absorb the earnest-money, Lucien might build up his fortune with the stones of her tomb, a single night of pleasure might cost the old banker so many thousand-franc notes more or less, Europe might extract a few hundred thousand francs by more or less ingenious trickery,—none of these things troubled the enamored girl; this alone was the canker that ate into her heart. For five years she had looked upon herself as being as white as an angel. She loved, she was happy, she had never committed the smallest infidelity. This beautiful pure love was now to be defiled.

There was, in her mind, no conscious contrasting of her happy isolated past and her foul future life. It was neither interest nor sentiment that moved her, only an indefinable and all powerful feeling that she had been white and was now black, pure and was now impure, noble and was now ignoble. Desiring to be the ermine, moral taint seemed to her unendurable. And when the Baron's passion had threatened her, she had really thought of throwing herself out of the window. In short, she loved Lucien wholly, and as women very rarely love a man. Women who say they love, who often think they love best, dance, waltz, and flirt with other men, dress for the world, and look for a harvest of concupiscent glances; but Esther, without any sacrifice, had achieved miracles of true love. She had loved Lucien for six years as actresses love and courtesans—women who, having rolled in mire and impurity, thirst for something noble, for the self-devotion of true love, and who practice exclusiveness—the only word for an idea so little known in real life.

Vanished nations, Greece, Rome, and the East, have at all times kept women shut up; the woman who loves should shut herself up. So it may easily be imagined that on quitting the palace of her fancy, where this poem had been enacted, to go to this old man's "little palace," Esther felt heartsick. Urged by an iron hand, she had found herself waist-deep in disgrace before she had time to reflect; but for the past two days she had been reflecting, and felt a mortal chill about her heart.

At the words, "End in the street," she started to her feet and said:

"In the street!—No, in the Seine rather."

"In the Seine? And what about Monsieur Lucien?" said Europe.

This single word brought Esther to her seat again; she remained in her armchair, her eyes fixed on a rosette in the carpet, the fire in her brain drying up her tears.

At four o'clock Nucingen found his angel lost in that sea of meditations and resolutions whereon a woman's spirit floats, and whence she emerges with utterances that are incomprehensible to those who have not sailed it in her convoy.

"Clear your brow, meine Schöne," said the Baron, sitting down by her. "You shall hafe no more debts—I shall arrange mit Eugenie, an' in ein mont you shall go 'vay from dese rooms and go to dat little palace.—Vas a pretty hant.—Gife it me dat I shall kiss it." Esther gave him her hand as a dog gives a paw. "Ach, ja! You shall gife de hant, but not de heart, and it is dat heart I lofe!"

The words were spoken with such sincerity of accent, that poor Esther looked at the old man with a compassion in her eyes that almost maddened him. Lovers, like martyrs, feel a brotherhood in their sufferings! Nothing in the world gives such a sense of kindred as community of sorrow.

"Poor man!" said she, "he really loves."

As he heard the words, misunderstanding their meaning, the Baron turned pale, the blood tingled in his veins, he breathed the airs of heaven. At his age a millionaire, for such a sensation, will pay as much gold as a woman can ask.

"I lofe you like vat I lofe my daughter," said he. "An' I feel dere"—and he laid her hand over his heart—"dat I shall not bear to see you anyting but happy."

"If you would only be a father to me, I would love you very much; I would never leave you; and you would see that I am not a bad woman, not grasping or greedy, as I must seem to you now—"

"You hafe done some little follies," said the Baron, "like all dose pretty vomen—dat is all. Say no more about dat. It is our pusiness to make money for you. Be happy! I shall be your fater for some days yet, for I know I must make you accustom' to my old carcase."

"Really!" she exclaimed, springing on to Nucingen's knees, and clinging to him with her arm round his neck.

"Really!" repeated he, trying to force a smile.

She kissed his forehead; she believed in an impossible combination— she might remain untouched and see Lucien.

She was so coaxing to the banker that she was La Torpille once more. She fairly bewitched the old man, who promised to be a father to her for forty days. Those forty days were to be employed in acquiring and arranging the house in the Rue Saint-Georges.

When he was in the street again, as he went home, the Baron said to himself, "I am an old flat."

But though in Esther's presence he was a mere child, away from her he resumed his lynx's skin; just as the gambler (in *le Joueur*) becomes affectionate to Angelique when he has not a liard.

"A half a million francs I hafe paid, and I hafe not yet seen vat her leg is like.—Dat is too silly! but, happily, nobody shall hafe known it!" said he to himself three weeks after.

And he made great resolutions to come to the point with the woman who had cost him so dear; then, in Esther's presence once more, he spent all the time he could spare her in making up for the roughness of his first words.

"After all," said he, at the end of a month, "I cannot be de fater eternal!"

Towards the end of the month of December 1829, just before installing Esther in the house in the Rue Saint-Georges, the Baron begged du Tillet to take Florine there, that she might see whether everything was suitable to Nucingen's fortune, and if the description of "a little palace" were duly realized by the artists commissioned to make the cage worthy of the bird.

Every device known to luxury before the Revolution of 1830 made this residence a masterpiece of taste. Grindot the architect considered it his greatest achievement as a decorator. The staircase, which had been reconstructed of marble, the judicious use of stucco ornament, textiles, and gilding, the smallest details as much as the general effect, outdid everything of the kind left in Paris from the time of Louis XV.

"This is my dream!—This and virtue!" said Florine with a smile. "And for whom are you spending all this money?"

"For a voman vat is going up there," replied the Baron.

"A way of playing Jupiter?" replied the actress. "And when is she on show?"

"On the day of the house-warming," cried du Tillet.

"Not before dat," said the Baron.

"My word, how we must lace and brush and fig ourselves out," Florine went on. "What a dance the women will lead their dressmakers and hairdressers for that evening's fun!—And when is it to be?"

"Dat is not for me to say."

"What a woman she must be!" cried Florine. "How much I should like to see her!"

"An' so should I," answered the Baron artlessly.

"What! is everything new together—the house, the furniture, and the woman?"

"Even the banker," said du Tillet, "for my old friend seems to me quite young again."

"Well, he must go back to his twentieth year," said Florine; "at any rate, for once."

In the early days of 1830 everybody in Paris was talking of Nucingen's passion and the outrageous splendor of his house. The poor Baron, pointed at, laughed at, and fuming with rage, as may easily be imagined, took it into his head that on the occasion of giving the house-warming he would at the same time get rid of his paternal disguise, and get the price of so much generosity. Always circumvented by "La Torpille," he determined to treat of their union by correspondence, so as to win from her an autograph promise. Bankers have no faith in anything less than a promissory note.

So one morning early in the year he rose early, locked himself into his room, and composed the following letter in very good French; for though he spoke the language very badly, he could write it very well:—

DEAR ESTHER, the flower of my thoughts and the only joy of my life, when I told you that I loved you as I love my daughter, I deceived you, I deceived myself. I only wished to express the holiness of my sentiments, which are unlike those felt by other men, in the first place, because I am an old man, and also because I have never loved till now. I love you so much, that if you cost me my fortune I should not love you the less.

"Be just! Most men would not, like me, have seen the angel in you; I have never even glanced at your past. I love you both as I love my daughter, Augusta, and as I might love my wife, if my wife could have loved me. Since the only excuse for an old man's love is that he should be happy, ask yourself if I am not playing a too ridiculous part. I have taken you to be the consolation and joy of my declining days. You know that till I die you will be as happy as a woman can be; and you know, too, that after my death you will be rich enough to be the envy of many women. In every stroke of business I have effected since I have had the happiness of your acquaintance, your share is set apart, and you have a standing account with Nucingen's bank. In a few days you will move into a house, which sooner or later, will be your own if you like it. Now, plainly, will you still receive me then as a father, or will you make me happy?

"Forgive me for writing so frankly, but when I am with you I lose all courage; I feel too keenly that you are indeed my mistress. I have no wish to hurt you; I only want to tell you how much I suffer, and how hard it is to wait at my age, when every day takes with it some hopes and some pleasures. Besides, the delicacy of my conduct is a guarantee of the sincerity of my intentions. Have I ever behaved as your creditor? You are like a citadel, and I am not a young man. In answer to my appeals, you say your life is at stake, and when I hear you, you make me believe it; but here I sink into dark melancholy and doubts dishonorable to us both. You seemed to me as sweet and innocent as you are lovely; but you insist on destroying my convictions. Ask yourself!—You tell me you bear a passion in your heart, an indomitable passion, but you refuse to tell me the name of the man you love.—Is this natural?

"You have turned a fairly strong man into an incredibly weak one. You see what I have come to; I am induced to ask you at the end of five months what future hope there is for my passion. Again, I must know what part I am to play at the opening of your house. Money is nothing to me when it is spent for you; I will not be so absurd as to make a merit to you of this contempt; but though my love knows no limits, my fortune is limited, and I care for it only for your sake. Well, if by giving you everything I possess I might, as a poor man, win your affection, I would rather be poor and loved than rich and scorned by you.

"You have altered me so completely, my dear Esther, that no one knows me; I paid ten thousand francs for a picture by Joseph Bridau because you told me that he was clever and unappreciated. I give every beggar I meet five francs in your name. Well, and what does the poor man ask, who regards himself as your debtor when you do him the honor of accepting anything he can give you? He asks only for a hope—and what a hope, good God! Is it not rather the certainty of never having anything from you but what my passion may seize? The fire in my heart will abet your cruel deceptions. You find me ready to submit to every condition you can impose on my happiness, on my few pleasures; but promise me at least that on the day when you take possession of your house you will accept the heart and service of him who, for the rest of his days, must sign himself your slave,

FREDERIC DE NUCINGEN.

"Faugh! how he bores me—this money bag!" cried Esther, a courtesan once more. She took a small sheet of notepaper and wrote all over it, as close as it could go, Scribe's famous phrase, which has become a proverb, "Prenez mon ours."

A quarter of an hour later, Esther, overcome by remorse, wrote the following letter:—

MONSIEUR LE BARON,

"Pay no heed to the note you have just received from me; I had relapsed into the folly of my youth. Forgive, monsieur, a poor girl who ought to be your slave. I never more keenly felt the degradation of my position than on the day when I was handed over to you. You have paid; I owe myself to you. There is nothing more sacred than a debt of dishonor. I have no right to compound it by throwing myself into the Seine.

"A debt can always be discharged in that dreadful coin which is good only to the debtor; you will find me yours to command. I will pay off in one night all the sums for which that fatal hour has been mortgaged; and I am sure that such an hour with me is worth millions—all the more because it will be the only one, the last. I shall then have paid the debt, and may get away from life. A good woman has a chance of restoration after a fall; but we, the like of us, fall too low.

"My determination is so fixed that I beg you will keep this letter in evidence of the cause of death of her who remains, for one day,

your servant,
ESTHER

Having sent this letter, Esther felt a pang of regret. Ten minutes after she wrote a third note, as follows:—

"Forgive me, dear Baron—it is I once more. I did not mean either to make game of you or to wound you; I only want you to reflect on this simple argument: If we were to continue in the position towards each other of father and daughter, your pleasure would be small, but it would be enduring. If you insist on the terms of the bargain, you will live to mourn for me.

"I will trouble you no more: the day when you shall choose pleasure rather than happiness will have no morrow for me.

Your daughter,
ESTHER

On receiving the first letter, the Baron fell into a cold fury such as a millionaire may die of; he looked at himself in the glass and rang the bell.

"An hot bat for mein feet," said he to his new valet.

While he was sitting with his feet in the bath, the second letter came; he read it, and fainted away. He was carried to bed.

When the banker recovered consciousness, Madame de Nucingen was sitting at the foot of the bed.

"The hussy is right!" said she. "Why do you try to buy love? Is it to be bought in the market!—Let me see your letter to her."

The Baron gave her sundry rough drafts he had made; Madame de Nucingen read them, and smiled. Then came Esther's third letter.

"She is a wonderful girl!" cried the Baroness, when she had read it.

"Vat shall I do, montame?" asked the Baron of his wife.

"Wait."

"Wait? But nature is pitiless!" he cried.

"Look here, my dear, you have been admirably kind to me," said Delphine; "I will give you some good advice."

"You are a ver' goot voman," said he. "Ven you hafe any debts I shall pay."

"Your state on receiving these letters touches a woman far more than the spending of millions, or than all the letters you could write, however fine they may be. Try to let her know it, indirectly; perhaps she will be yours! And—have no scruples, she will not die of that," added she, looking keenly at her husband.

But Madame de Nucingen knew nothing whatever of the nature of such women.

"Vat a clefer voman is Montame de Nucingen!" said the Baron to himself when his wife had left him.

Still, the more the Baron admired the subtlety of his wife's counsel, the less he could see how he might act upon it; and he not only felt that he was stupid, but he told himself so.

The stupidity of wealthy men, though it is almost proverbial, is only comparative. The faculties of the mind, like the dexterity of the limbs, need exercise. The dancer's strength is in his feet; the blacksmith's in his arms; the market porter is trained to carry loads; the singer works his larynx; and the pianist hardens his wrist. A banker is practised in business matters; he studies and plans them, and pulls the wires of various interests, just as a playwright trains his intelligence in combining situations, studying his actors, giving life to his dramatic figures.

We should no more look for powers of conversation in the Baron de Nucingen than for the imagery of a poet in the brain of a mathematician. How many poets occur in an age, who are either good prose writers, or as witty in the intercourse of daily life as Madame Cornuel? Buffon was dull company; Newton was never in love; Lord Byron loved nobody but himself; Rousseau was gloomy and half crazy; La Fontaine absent-minded. Human energy, equally distributed, produces dolts, mediocrity in all; unequally bestowed it gives rise to those incongruities to whom the name of Genius is given, and which, if we only could see them, would look like deformities. The same law governs the body; perfect beauty is generally allied with coldness or silliness. Though Pascal was both a great mathematician and a great writer, though Beaumarchais was a good man of business, and Zamet a profound courtier, these rare exceptions prove the general principle of the specialization of brain faculties.

Within the sphere of speculative calculations the banker put forth as much intelligence and skill, finesse and mental power, as a practised diplomatist expends on national affairs. If he were equally remarkable outside his office, the banker would be a great man. Nucingen made one with the Prince de Ligne, with Mazarin or with Diderot, is a human formula that is almost inconceivable, but which has nevertheless been known as Pericles, Aristotle, Voltaire, and Napoleon. The splendor of the Imperial crown must not blind us to the merits of the individual; the Emperor was charming, well informed, and witty.

Monsieur de Nucingen, a banker and nothing more, having no inventiveness outside his business, like most bankers, had no faith in anything but sound security. In matters of art he had the good sense to go, cash in hand, to experts in every branch, and had recourse to the best architect, the best surgeon, the greatest connoisseur in pictures or statues, the cleverest lawyer, when he wished to build a house, to attend to his health, to purchase a work of art or an estate. But as there are no recognized experts in intrigue, no connoisseurs in love affairs, a banker finds himself in difficulties when he is in love, and much puzzled as to the management of a woman. So Nucingen could think of no better method than that he had hitherto pursued—to give a sum of money to some Frontin, male or female, to act and think for him.

Madame de Saint-Esteve alone could carry out the plan imagined by the Baroness. Nucingen bitterly regretted having quarreled with the odious old clothes-seller. However, feeling confident of the attractions of his cash-box and the soothing documents signed Garat, he rang for his man and told him in inquire for the repulsive widow in the Rue Saint-Marc, and desire her to come to see him.

In Paris extremes are made to meet by passion. Vice is constantly binding the rich to the poor, the great to the mean. The Empress consults Mademoiselle Lenormand; the fine gentleman in every age can always find a Ramponneau.

The man returned within two hours.

"Monsieur le Baron," said he, "Madame de Saint-Esteve is ruined."

"Ah! so much de better!" cried the Baron in glee. "I shall hafe her safe den."

"The good woman is given to gambling, it would seem," the valet went on. "And, moreover, she is under the thumb of a third-rate actor in a suburban theatre, whom, for decency's sake, she calls her godson. She is a first-rate cook, it would seem, and wants a place."

"Dose teufel of geniuses of de common people hafe alvays ten vays of making money, and ein dozen vays of spending it," said the Baron to himself, quite unconscious that Panurge had thought the same thing.

He sent his servant off in quest of Madame de Saint-Esteve, who did not come till the next day. Being questioned by Asie, the servant revealed to this female spy the terrible effects of the notes written to Monsieur le Baron by his mistress.

"Monsieur must be desperately in love with the woman," said he in conclusion, "for he was very near dying. For my part, I advised him never to go back to her, for he will be wheedled over at once. A woman who has already cost Monsieur le Baron five hundred thousand francs, they say, without counting what he has spent on the house in the Rue Saint-Georges! But the woman cares for money, and for money only.— As madame came out of monsieur's room, she said with a laugh: 'If this goes on, that slut will make a widow of me!'"

"The devil!" cried Asie; "it will never do to kill the goose that lays the golden eggs."

"Monsieur le Baron has no hope now but in you," said the valet.

"Ay! The fact is, I do know how to make a woman go."

"Well, walk in," said the man, bowing to such occult powers.

"Well," said the false Saint-Esteve, going into the sufferer's room with an abject air, "Monsieur le Baron has met with some difficulties? What can you expect! Everybody is open to attack on his weak side. Dear me, I have had my troubles too. Within two months the wheel of Fortune has turned upside down for me. Here I am looking out for a place!—We have neither of us been very wise. If Monsieur le Baron would take me as cook to Madame Esther, I would be the most devoted of slaves. I should be useful to you, monsieur, to keep an eye on Eugenie and madame."

"Dere is no hope of dat," said the Baron. "I cannot succeet in being de master, I am let such a tance as—"

"As a top," Asie put in. "Well, you have made others dance, daddy, and the little slut has got you, and is making a fool of you.—Heaven is just!"

"Just?" said the Baron. "I hafe not sent for you to preach to me—"

"Pooh, my boy! A little moralizing breaks no bones. It is the salt of life to the like of us, as vice is to your bigots.—Come, have you been generous? You have paid her debts?"

"Ja," said the Baron lamentably.

"That is well; and you have taken her things out of pawn, and that is better. But you must see that it is not enough. All this gives her no occupation, and these creatures love to cut a dash—"

"I shall hafe a surprise for her, Rue Saint-Georches—she knows dat," said the Baron. "But I shall not be made a fool of."

"Very well then, let her go."

"I am only afrait dat she shall let me go!" cried the Baron.

"And we want our money's worth, my boy," replied Asie. "Listen to me. We have fleeced the public of some millions, my little friend? Twenty-five millions I am told you possess."

The Baron could not suppress a smile.

"Well, you must let one go."

"I shall let one go, but as soon as I shall let one go, I shall hafe to give still another."

"Yes, I understand," replied Asie. "You will not say B for fear of having to go on to Z. Still, Esther is a good girl—"

"A ver' honest girl," cried the banker. "An' she is ready to submit; but only as in payment of a debt."

"In short, she does not want to be your mistress; she feels an aversion.—Well, and I understand it; the child has always done just what she pleased. When a girl has never known any but charming young men, she cannot take to an old one. You are not handsome; you are as big as Louis XVIII, and rather dull company, as all men are who try to cajole fortune instead of devoting themselves to women.—Well, if you don't think six hundred thousand francs too much," said Asie, "I pledge myself to make her whatever you can wish."

"Six huntert tousant franc!" cried the Baron, with a start. "Esther is to cost me a million to begin with!"

"Happiness is surely worth sixteen hundred thousand francs, you old sinner. You must know, men in these days have certainly spent more than one or two millions on a mistress. I even know women who have cost men their lives, for whom heads have rolled into the basket.—You know the doctor who poisoned his friend? He wanted the money to gratify a woman."

"Ja, I know all dat. But if I am in lofe, I am not ein idiot, at least vile I am here; but if I shall see her, I shall gife her my pocket-book—"

"Well, listen Monsieur le Baron," said Asie, assuming the attitude of a Semiramis. "You have been squeezed dry enough already. Now, as sure as my name is Saint-Esteve—in the way of business, of course—I will stand by you."

"Goot, I shall repay you."

"I believe you, my boy, for I have shown you that I know how to be revenged. Besides, I tell you this, daddy, I know how to snuff out your Madame Esther as you would snuff a candle. And I know my lady! When the little huzzy has once made you happy, she will be even more necessary to you than she is at this moment. You paid me well; you have allowed yourself to be fooled, but, after all, you have forked out.—I have fulfilled my part of the agreement, haven't I? Well, look here, I will make a bargain with you."

"Let me hear."

"You shall get me the place as cook to Madame, engage me for ten years, and pay the last five in advance—what is that? Just a little earnest-money. When once I am about madame, I can bring her to these terms. Of course, you must first order her a lovely dress from Madame Auguste, who knows her style and taste; and order the new carriage to be at the door at four o'clock. After the Bourse closes, go to her rooms and take her for a little drive in the Bois de Boulogne. Well, by that act the woman proclaims herself your mistress; she has advertised herself to the eyes and knowledge of all Paris: A hundred thousand francs.—You must dine with her—I know how to cook such a dinner!—You must take her to the play, to the Varietes, to a stage-box, and then all Paris will say, 'There is that old rascal Nucingen with his mistress.' It is very flattering to know that such things are said.—Well, all this, for I am not grasping, is included for the first hundred thousand francs.—In a week, by such conduct, you will have made some way—"

"But I shall hafe paid ein hundert tousant franc."

"In the course of the second week," Asie went on, as though she had not heard this lamentable ejaculation, "madame, tempted by these preliminaries, will have made up her mind to leave her little apartment and move to the house you are giving her. Your Esther will have seen the world again, have found her old friends; she will wish to shine and do the honors of her palace—it is in the nature of things: Another hundred thousand francs!—By Heaven! you are at home there, Esther compromised—she must be yours. The rest is a mere trifle, in which you must play the principal part, old elephant. (How wide the monster opens his eyes!) Well, I will undertake that too: Four hundred thousand—and that, my fine fellow, you need not pay till the day after. What do you think of that for honesty? I have more confidence in you than you have in me. If I persuade madame to show herself as your mistress, to compromise herself, to take every gift you offer her,—perhaps this very day, you will believe that I am capable of inducing her to throw open the pass of the Great Saint Bernard. And it is a hard job, I can tell you; it will take as much pulling to get your artillery through as it took the first Consul to get over the Alps."

"But vy?"

"Her heart is full of love, old shaver, rasibus, as you say who know Latin," replied Asie. "She thinks herself the Queen of Sheba, because she has washed herself in sacrifices made for her lover—an idea that that sort of woman gets into her head! Well, well, old fellow, we must be just.—It is fine! That baggage would die of grief at being your mistress—I really should not wonder. But what I trust to, and I tell you to give you courage, is that there is good in the girl at bottom."

"You hafe a genius for corruption," said the Baron, who had listened to Asie in admiring silence, "just as I hafe de knack of de banking."

"Then it is settled, my pigeon?" said Asie.

"Done for fifty tousant franc insteat of ein hundert tousant!—An' I shall give you fife hundert tousant de day after my triumph."

"Very good, I will set to work," said Asie. "And you may come, monsieur," she added respectfully. "You will find madame as soft already as a cat's back, and perhaps inclined to make herself pleasant."

"Go, go, my goot voman," said the banker, rubbing his hands.

And after seeing the horrible mulatto out of the house, he said to himself:

"How vise it is to hafe much money."

He sprang out of bed, went down to his office, and resumed the conduct of his immense business with a light heart.

NOTHING COULD BE MORE FATAL to Esther than the steps taken by Nucingen. The hapless girl, in defending her fidelity, was defending her life. This very natural instinct was what Carlos called prudery. Now Asie, not without taking such precautions as usual in such cases, went off to report to Carlos the conference she had held with the Baron, and all the profit she had made by it. The man's rage, like himself, was terrible; he came forthwith to Esther, in a carriage with the blinds drawn, driving into the courtyard. Still almost white with fury, the double-dyed forger went straight into the poor girl's room; she looked at him—she was standing up—and she dropped on to a chair as though her legs had snapped.

"What is the matter, monsieur?" said she, quaking in every limb.

"Leave us, Europe," said he to the maid.

Esther looked at the woman as a child might look at its mother, from whom some assassin had snatched it to murder it.

"Do you know where you will send Lucien?" Carlos went on when he was alone with Esther.

"Where?" asked she in a low voice, venturing to glance at her executioner.

"Where I come from, my beauty." Esther, as she looked at the man, saw red. "To the hulks," he added in an undertone.

Esther shut her eyes and stretched herself out, her arms dropped, and she turned white. The man rang, and Prudence appeared.

"Bring her round," he said coldly; "I have not done."

He walked up and down the drawing-room while waiting. Prudence-Europe was obliged to come and beg monsieur to lift Esther on to the bed; he carried her with the ease that betrayed athletic strength.

They had to procure all the chemist's strongest stimulants to restore Esther to a sense of her woes. An hour later the poor girl was able to listen to this living nightmare, seated at the foot of her bed, his eyes fixed and glowing like two spots of molten lead.

"My little sweetheart," said he, "Lucien now stands between a splendid life, honored, happy, and respected, and the hole full of water, mud, and gravel into which he was going to plunge when I met him. The house of Grandlieu requires of the dear boy an estate worth a million francs before securing for him the title of Marquis, and handing over to him that may-pole named Clotilde, by whose help he will rise to power. Thanks to you, and me, Lucien has just purchased his maternal manor, the old Chateau de Rubempre, which, indeed, did not cost much—thirty thousand francs; but his lawyer, by clever negotiations, has succeeded in adding to it estates worth a million, on which three hundred thousand francs are paid. The chateau, the expenses, and percentages to the men who were put forward as a blind to conceal the transaction from the country people, have swallowed up the remainder.

"We have, to be sure, a hundred thousand francs invested in a business here, which a few months hence will be worth two to three hundred thousand francs; but there will still be four hundred thousand francs to be paid.

"In three days Lucien will be home from Angouleme, where he has been, because he must not be suspected of having found a fortune in remaking your bed—"

"Oh no!" cried she, looking up with a noble impulse.

"I ask you, then, is this a moment to scare off the Baron?" he went on calmly. "And you very nearly killed him the day before yesterday; he fainted like a woman on reading your second letter. You have a fine style—I congratulate you! If the Baron had died, where should we be now?—When Lucien walks out of Saint-Thomas d'Aquin son-in-law to the Duc de Grandlieu, if you want to try a dip in the Seine—Well, my beauty, I offer you my hand for a dive together. It is one way of ending matters.

"But consider a moment. Would it not be better to live and say to yourself again and again 'This fine fortune, this happy family'—for he will have children—children!—Have you ever thought of the joy of running your fingers through the hair of his children?"

Esther closed her eyes with a little shiver.

"Well, as you gaze on that structure of happiness, you may say to yourself, 'This is my doing!'"

There was a pause, and the two looked at each other.

"This is what I have tried to make out of such despair as saw no issue but the river," said Carlos. "Am I selfish? That is the way to love! Men show such devotion to none but kings! But I have anointed Lucien king. If I were riveted for the rest of my days to my old chain, I fancy I could stay there resigned so long as I could say, 'He is gay, he is at Court.' My soul and mind would triumph, while my carcase was given over to the jailers! You are a mere female; you love like a female! But in a courtesan, as in all degraded creatures, love should be a means to motherhood, in spite of Nature, which has stricken you with barrenness!

"If ever, under the skin of the Abbe Carlos Herrera, any one were to detect the convict I have been, do you know what I would do to avoid compromising Lucien?"

Esther awaited the reply with some anxiety.

"Well," he said after a brief pause, "I would die as the Negroes do—without a word. And you, with all your airs will put folks on my traces. What did I require of you?—To be La Torpille again for six months—for six weeks; and to do it to clutch a million.

"Lucien will never forget you. Men do not forget the being of whom they are reminded day after day by the joy of awaking rich every morning. Lucien is a better fellow than you are. He began by loving Coralie. She died—good; but he had not enough money to bury her; he did not do as you did just now, he did not faint, though he is a poet; he wrote six rollicking songs, and earned three hundred francs, with which he paid for Coralie's funeral. I have those songs; I know them by heart. Well, then do you too compose your songs: be cheerful, be wild, be irresistible and—insatiable! You hear me?—Do not let me have to speak again.

"Kiss papa. Good-bye."

When, half an hour after, Europe went into her mistress' room, she found her kneeling in front of a crucifix, in the attitude which the most religious of painters has given to Moses before the burning bush on Horeb, to depict his deep and complete adoration of Jehovah. After saying her prayers, Esther had renounced her better life, the honor she had created for herself, her glory, her virtue, and her love.

She rose.

"Oh, madame, you will never look like that again!" cried Prudence Servien, struck by her mistress' sublime beauty.

She hastily turned the long mirror so that the poor girl should see herself. Her eyes still had a light as of the soul flying heavenward. The Jewess' complexion was brilliant. Sparkling with tears unshed in the fervor of prayer, her eyelashes were like leaves after a summer shower, for the last time they shone with the sunshine of pure love. Her lips seemed to preserve an expression as of her last appeal to the angels, whose palm of martyrdom she had no doubt borrowed while placing in their hands her past unspotted life. And she had the majesty which Mary Stuart must have shown at the moment when she bid adieu to her crown, to earth, and to love.

"I wish Lucien could have seen me thus!" she said with a smothered sigh. "Now," she added, in a strident tone, "now for a fling!"

Europe stood dumb at hearing the words, as though she had heard an angel blaspheme.

"Well, why need you stare at me to see if I have cloves in my mouth instead of teeth? I am nothing henceforth but a vile, foul creature, a thief—and I expect milord. So get me a hot bath, and put my dress out. It is twelve o'clock; the Baron will look in, no doubt, when the Bourse closes; I shall tell him I was waiting for him, and Asie is to prepare us dinner, first-chop, mind you; I mean to turn the man's brain.—Come, hurry, hurry, my girl; we are going to have some fun—that is to say, we must go to work."

She sat down at the table and wrote the following note:—

My Friend,

If the cook you have sent me had not already been in my service, I might have thought that your purpose was to let me know how often you had fainted yesterday on receiving my three notes. (What can I say? I was very nervous that day; I was thinking over the memories of my miserable existence.) But I know how sincere Asie is. Still, I cannot repent of having caused you so much pain, since it has availed to prove to me how much you love me. This is how we are made, we luckless and despised creatures; true affection touches us far more deeply than finding ourselves the objects of lavish liberality. For my part, I have always rather dreaded being a peg on which you would hang your vanities. It annoyed me to be nothing else to you. Yes, in spite of all your protestations, I fancied you regarded me merely as a woman paid for.

"Well, you will now find me a good girl, but on condition of your always obeying me a little.

"If this letter can in any way take the place of the doctor's prescription, prove it by coming to see me after the Bourse closes. You will find me in full fig, dressed in your gifts, for I am for life your pleasure-machine,

Esther

At the Bourse the Baron de Nucingen was so gay, so cheerful, seemed so easy-going, and allowed himself so many jests, that du Tillet and the Kellers, who were on 'change, could not help asking him the reason of his high spirits.

"I am belofed. Ve shall soon gife dat house-varming," he told du Tillet.

"And how much does it cost you?" asked Francois Keller rudely—it was said that he had spent twenty-five thousand francs a year on Madame Colleville.

"Dat voman is an anchel! She never has ask' me for one sou."

"They never do," replied du Tillet. "And it is to avoid asking that they have always aunts or mothers."

Between the Bourse and the Rue Taitbout seven times did the Baron say to his servant:

"You go so slow—vip de horse!"

He ran lightly upstairs, and for the first time he saw his mistress in all the beauty of such women, who have no other occupation than the care of their person and their dress. Just out of her bath the flower was quite fresh, and perfumed so as to inspire desire in Robert d'Arbrissel.

Esther was in a charming toilette. A dress of black corded silk trimmed with rose-colored gimp opened over a petticoat of gray satin, the costume subsequently worn by Amigo, the handsome singer, in *I Puritani*. A Honiton lace kerchief fell or floated over her shoulders. The sleeves of her gown were strapped round with cording to divide the puffs, which for some little time fashion has substituted for the large sleeves which had grown too monstrous. Esther had fastened a Mechlin lace cap on her magnificent hair with a pin, *a la folle*, as it is called, ready to fall, but not really falling, giving her an appearance of being tumbled and in disorder, though the white parting showed plainly on her little head between the waves of her hair.

"Is it not a shame to see madame so lovely in a shabby drawing-room like this?" said Europe to the Baron, as she admitted him.

"Vel, den, come to the Rue Saint-Georches," said the Baron, coming to a full stop like a dog marking a partridge. "The veather is splendit, ve shall drife to the Champs Elysees, and Montame Saint-Estefe and Eugenie shall carry dere all your clo'es an' your linen, an' ve shall dine in de Rue Saint-Georches."

"I will do whatever you please," said Esther, "if only you will be so kind as to call my cook Asie, and Eugenie Europe. I have given those names to all the women who have served me ever since the first two. I do not love change—"

"Asie, Europe!" echoed the Baron, laughing. "How ver' droll you are.—You hafe infentions.—I should hafe eaten many dinners before I should hafe call' a cook Asie."

"It is our business to be droll," said Esther. "Come, now, may not a poor girl be fed by Asia and dressed by Europe when you live on the whole world? It is a myth, I say; some women would devour the earth, I only ask for half.—You see?"

"Vat a voman is Montame Saint-Estefe!" said the Baron to himself as he admired Esther's changed demeanor.

"Europe, my girl, I want my bonnet," said Esther. "I must have a black silk bonnet lined with pink and trimmed with lace."

"Madame Thomas has not sent it home.—Come, Monsieur le Baron; quick, off you go! Begin your functions as a man-of-all-work—that is to say, of all pleasure! Happiness is burdensome. You have your carriage here, go to Madame Thomas," said Europe to the Baron. "Make your servant ask for the bonnet for Madame van Bogseck.—And, above all," she added in his ear, "bring her the most beautiful bouquet to be had in Paris. It is winter, so try to get tropical flowers."

The Baron went downstairs and told his servants to go to "Montame Thomas."

The coachman drove to a famous pastrycook's.

"She is a milliner, you damn' idiot, and not a cake-shop!" cried the Baron, who rushed off to Madame Prevot's in the Palais-Royal, where he had a bouquet made up for the price of ten louis, while his man went to the great modiste.

A superficial observer, walking about Paris, wonders who the fools can be that buy the fabulous flowers that grace the illustrious bouquetiere's shop window, and the choice products displayed by Chevet of European fame—the only purveyor who can vie with the *Rocher de Cancale* in a real and delicious *Revue des deux Mondes*.

Well, every day in Paris a hundred or more passions a la Nucingen come into being, and find expression in offering such rarities as queens dare not purchase, presented, kneeling, to baggages who, to use Asie's word, like to cut a dash. But for these little details, a decent citizen would be puzzled to conceive how a fortune melts in the hands of these women, whose social function, in Fourier's scheme, is perhaps to rectify the disasters caused by avarice and cupidity. Such squandering is, no doubt, to the social body what a prick of the lancet is to a plethoric subject. In two months Nucingen had shed broadcast on trade more than two hundred thousand francs.

By the time the old lover returned, darkness was falling; the bouquet was no longer of any use. The hour for driving in the Champs-Elysees in winter is between two and four. However, the carriage was of use to convey Esther from the Rue Taitbout to the Rue Saint-Georges, where she took possession of the "little palace." Never before had Esther been the object of such worship or such lavishness, and it amazed her; but, like all royal ingrates, she took care to express no surprise.

When you go into St. Peter's at Rome, to enable you to appreciate the extent and height of this queen of cathedrals, you are shown the little finger of a statue which looks of a natural size, and which measures I know not how much. Descriptions have been so severely criticised, necessary as they are to a history of manners, that I must here follow the example of the Roman Cicerone. As they entered the dining-room, the Baron could not resist asking Esther to feel the stuff of which the window curtains were made, draped with magnificent fulness, lined with white watered silk, and bordered with a gimp fit to trim a Portuguese princess' bodice. The material was silk brought from Canton, on which Chinese patience had painted Oriental birds with a perfection only to be seen in mediaeval illuminations, or in the Missal of Charles V, the pride of the Imperial library at Vienna.

"It hafe cost two tousand franc' an ell for a milord who brought it from Intia—"

"It is very nice, charming," said Esther. "How I shall enjoy drinking champagne here; the froth will not get dirty here on a bare floor."

"Oh! madame!" cried Europe, "only look at the carpet!"

"Dis carpet hafe been made for de Duc de Torlonia, a frient of mine, who fount it too dear, so I took it for you who are my qveen," said Nucingen.

By chance this carpet, by one of our cleverest designers, matched with the whimsicalities of the Chinese curtains. The walls, painted by Schinner and Leon de Lora, represented voluptuous scenes, in carved ebony frames, purchased for their weight in gold from Dusommerard, and forming panels with a narrow line of gold that coyly caught the light.

From this you may judge of the rest.

"You did well to bring me here," said Esther. "It will take me a week to get used to my home and not to look like a parvenu in it—"

"*My* home! Den you shall accept it?" cried the Baron in glee.

"Why, of course, and a thousand times of course, stupid animal," said she, smiling.

"Animal vas enough—"

"Stupid is a term of endearment," said she, looking at him.

The poor man took Esther's hand and pressed it to his heart. He was animal enough to feel, but too stupid to find words.

"Feel how it beats—for ein little tender vort—"

And he conducted his goddess to her room.

"Oh, madame, I cannot stay here!" cried Eugenie. "It makes me long to go to bed."

"Well," said Esther, "I mean to please the magician who has worked all these wonders.—Listen, my fat elephant, after dinner we will go to the play together. I am starving to see a play."

It was just five years since Esther had been to a theatre. All Paris was rushing at that time to the Porte-Saint-Martin, to see one of those pieces to which the power of the actors lends a terrible expression of reality, *Richard Darlington*. Like all ingenuous natures, Esther loved to feel the thrills of fear as much as to yield to tears of pathos.

"Let us go to see Frederick Lemaitre," said she; "he is an actor I adore."

"It is a horrible piece," said Nucingen foreseeing the moment when he must show himself in public.

He sent his servant to secure one of the two stage-boxes on the grand tier.—And this is another strange feature of Paris. Whenever success, on feet of clay, fills a house, there is always a stage-box to be had ten minutes before the curtain rises. The managers keep it for themselves, unless it happens to be taken for a passion a la Nucingen. This box, like Chevet's dainties, is a tax levied on the whims of the Parisian Olympus.

It would be superfluous to describe the plate and china. Nucingen had provided three services of plate—common, medium, and best; and the best—plates, dishes, and all, was of chased silver gilt. The banker, to avoid overloading the table with gold and silver, had completed the array of each service with porcelain of exquisite fragility in the style of Dresden china, which had cost more than the plate. As to the linen— Saxony, England, Flanders, and France vied in the perfection of flowered damask.

At dinner it was the Baron's turn to be amazed on tasting Asie's cookery.

"I understant," said he, "vy you call her Asie; dis is Asiatic cooking."

"I begin to think he loves me," said Esther to Europe; "he has said something almost like a *bon mot*."

"I said many vorts," said he.

"Well! he is more like Turcaret than I had heard he was!" cried the girl, laughing at this reply, worthy of the many artless speeches for which the banker was famous.

The dishes were so highly spiced as to give the Baron an indigestion, on purpose that he might go home early; so this was all he got in the way of pleasure out of his first evening with Esther. At the theatre he was obliged to drink an immense number of glasses of eau sucrée, leaving Esther alone between the acts.

By a coincidence so probable that it can scarcely be called chance, Tullia, Mariette, and Madame du Val-Noble were at the play that evening. *Richard Darlington* enjoyed a wild success—and a deserved success—such as is seen only in Paris. The men who saw this play all came to the conclusion that a lawful wife might be thrown out of window, and the wives loved to see themselves unjustly persecuted.

The women said to each other: "This is too much! we are driven to it—but it often happens!"

Now a woman as beautiful as Esther, and dressed as Esther was, could not show off with impunity in a stage-box at the Porte-Saint-Martin. And so, during the second act, there was quite a commotion in the box where the two dancers were sitting, caused by the undoubted identity of the unknown fair one with La Torpille.

"Heyday! where has she dropped from?" said Mariette to Madame du Val-Noble. "I thought she was drowned."

"But is it she? She looks to me thirty-seven times younger and handsomer than she was six years ago."

"Perhaps she has preserved herself in ice like Madame d'Espard and Madame Zayonchek," said the Comte de Brambourg, who had brought the three women to the play, to a pit-tier box. "Isn't she the 'rat' you meant to send me to hocus my uncle?" said he, addressing Tullia.

"The very same," said the singer. "Du Bruel, go down to the stalls and see if it is she."

"What brass she has got!" exclaimed Madame du Val-Noble, using an expressive but vulgar phrase.

"Oh!" said the Comte de Brambourg, "she very well may. She is with my friend the Baron de Nucingen—I will go—"

"Is that the immaculate Joan of Arc who has taken Nucingen by storm, and who has been talked of till we are all sick of her, these three months past?" asked Mariette.

HONORÉ DE BALZAC

"Good-evening, my dear Baron," said Philippe Bridau, as he went into Nucingen's box. "So here you are, married to Mademoiselle Esther.—Mademoiselle, I am an old officer whom you once on a time were to have got out of a scrape—at Issoudun—Philippe Bridau—"

"I know nothing of it," said Esther, looking round the house through her opera-glasses.

"Dis lady," said the Baron, "is no longer known as 'Esther' so short! She is called Montame de Champy—ein little estate vat I have bought for her—"

"Though you do things in such style," said the Comte, "these ladies are saying that Madame de Champy gives herself too great airs.—If you do not choose to remember me, will you condescend to recognize Mariette, Tullia, Madame du Val-Noble?" the parvenu went on—a man for whom the Duc de Maufrigneuse had won the Dauphin's favor.

"If these ladies are kind to me, I am willing to make myself pleasant to them," replied Madame de Champy drily.

"Kind! Why, they are excellent; they have named you Joan of Arc," replied Philippe.

"Vell den, if dese ladies vill keep you company," said Nucingen, "I shall go 'vay, for I hafe eaten too much. Your carriage shall come for you and your people.—Dat teufel Asie!"

"The first time, and you leave me alone!" said Esther. "Come, come, you must have courage enough to die on deck. I must have my man with me as I go out. If I were insulted, am I to cry out for nothing?"

The old millionaire's selfishness had to give way to his duties as a lover. The Baron suffered but stayed.

Esther had her own reasons for detaining "her man." If she admitted her acquaintance, she would be less closely questioned in his presence than if she were alone. Philippe Bridau hurried back to the box where the dancers were sitting, and informed them of the state of affairs.

"Oh! so it is she who has fallen heir to my house in the Rue Saint-Georges," observed Madame du Val-Noble with some bitterness; for she, as she phrased it, was on the loose.

"Most likely," said the Colonel. "Du Tillet told me that the Baron had spent three times as much there as your poor Falleix."

"Let us go round to her box," said Tullia.

"Not if I know it," said Mariette; "she is much too handsome, I will call on her at home."

"I think myself good-looking enough to risk it," remarked Tullia.

So the much-daring leading dancer went round between the acts and renewed acquaintance with Esther, who would talk only on general subjects.

"And where have you come back from, my dear child?" asked Tullia, who could not restrain her curiosity.

"Oh, I was for five years in a castle in the Alps with an Englishman, as jealous as a tiger, a nabob; I called him a nabot, a dwarf, for he was not so big as le bailli de Ferrette.

"And then I came across a banker—from a savage to salvation, as Florine might say. And now here I am in Paris again; I long so for amusement that I mean to have a rare time. I shall keep open house. I have five years of solitary confinement to make good, and I am beginning to do it. Five years of an Englishman is rather too much; six weeks are the allowance according to the advertisements."

"Was it the Baron who gave you that lace?"

"No, it is a relic of the nabob.—What ill-luck I have, my dear! He was as yellow as a friend's smile at a success; I thought he would be dead in ten months. Pooh! he was a strong as a mountain. Always distrust men who say they have a liver complaint. I will never listen to a man who talks of his liver.—I have had too much of livers—who cannot die. My nabob robbed me; he died without making a will, and the family turned me out of doors like a leper.—So, then, I said to my fat friend here, 'Pay for two!'—You may as well call me Joan of Arc; I have ruined England, and perhaps I shall die at the stake—"

"Of love?" said Tullia.

"And burnt alive," answered Esther, and the question made her thoughtful.

The Baron laughed at all this vulgar nonsense, but he did not always follow it readily, so that his laughter sounded like the forgotten crackers that go off after fireworks.

We all live in a sphere of some kind, and the inhabitants of every sphere are endowed with an equal share of curiosity.

Next evening at the opera, Esther's reappearance was the great news behind the scenes. Between two and four in the afternoon all Paris in the Champs-Elysees had recognized La Torpille, and knew at last who was the object of the Baron de Nucingen's passion.

"Do you know," Blondet remarked to de Marsay in the greenroom at the opera-house, "that La Torpille vanished the very day after the evening when we saw her here and recognized her in little Rubempre's mistress."

In Paris, as in the provinces, everything is known. The police of the Rue de Jerusalem are not so efficient as the world itself, for every one is a spy on every one else, though unconsciously. Carlos had fully understood the danger of Lucien's position during and after the episode of the Rue Taitbout.

No position can be more dreadful than that in which Madame du Val-Noble now found herself; and the phrase to be on the loose, or, as the French say, left on foot, expresses it perfectly. The recklessness and extravagance of these women precludes all care for the future. In that strange world, far more witty and amusing than might be supposed, only such women as are not gifted with that perfect beauty which time can hardly impair, and which is quite unmistakable—only such women, in short, as can be loved merely as a fancy, ever think of old age and save a fortune. The handsomer they are, the more improvident they are.

"Are you afraid of growing ugly that you are saving money?" was a speech of Florine's to Mariette, which may give a clue to one cause of this thriftlessness.

Thus, if a speculator kills himself, or a spendthrift comes to the end of his resources, these women fall with hideous promptitude from audacious wealth to the utmost misery. They throw themselves into the clutches of the old-clothes buyer, and sell exquisite jewels for a mere song; they run into debt, expressly to keep up a spurious luxury, in the hope of recovering what they have lost—a cash-box to draw upon. These ups and downs of their career account for the costliness of such connections, generally brought about as Asie had hooked (another word of her vocabulary) Nucingen for Esther.

And so those who know their Paris are quite aware of the state of affairs when, in the Champs-Elysees—that bustling and mongrel bazaar—they meet some woman in a hired fly whom six months or a year before they had seen in a magnificent and dazzling carriage, turned out in the most luxurious style.

"If you fall on Sainte-Pelagie, you must contrive to rebound on the Bois de Boulogne," said Florine, laughing with Blondet over the little Vicomte de Portenduere.

Some clever women never run the risk of this contrast. They bury themselves in horrible furnished lodgings, where they expiate their extravagance by such privations as are endured by travelers lost in a

Sahara; but they never take the smallest fancy for economy. They venture forth to masked balls; they take journeys into the provinces; they turn out well dressed on the boulevards when the weather is fine. And then they find in each other the devoted kindness which is known only among proscribed races. It costs a woman in luck no effort to bestow some help, for she says to herself, "I may be in the same plight by Sunday!"

However, the most efficient protector still is the purchaser of dress. When this greedy money-lender finds herself the creditor, she stirs and works on the hearts of all the old men she knows in favor of the mortgaged creature in thin boots and a fine bonnet.

In this way Madame du Val-Noble, unable to foresee the downfall of one of the richest and cleverest of stockbrokers, was left quite unprepared. She had spent Falleix's money on her whims, and trusted to him for all necessaries and to provide for the future.

"How could I have expected such a thing in a man who seemed such a good fellow?"

In almost every class of society the good fellow is an open-handed man, who will lend a few crowns now and again without expecting them back, who always behaves in accordance with a certain code of delicate feeling above mere vulgar, obligatory, and commonplace morality. Certain men, regarded as virtuous and honest, have, like Nucingen, ruined their benefactors; and certain others, who have been through a criminal court, have an ingenious kind of honesty towards women. Perfect virtue, the dream of Moliere, an Alceste, is exceedingly rare; still, it is to be found everywhere, even in Paris. The "good fellow" is the product of a certain facility of nature which proves nothing. A man is a good fellow, as a cat is silky, as a slipper is made to slip on to the foot. And so, in the meaning given to the word by a kept woman, Falleix ought to have warned his mistress of his approaching bankruptcy and have given her enough to live upon.

D'Estourny, the dashing swindler, was a good fellow; he cheated at cards, but he had set aside thirty thousand francs for his mistress. And at carnival suppers women would retort on his accusers: "No matter. You may say what you like, Georges was a good fellow; he had charming manners, he deserved a better fate."

These girls laugh laws to scorn, and adore a certain kind of generosity; they sell themselves, as Esther had done, for a secret ideal, which is their religion.

After saving a few jewels from the wreck with great difficulty, Madame du Val-Noble was crushed under the burden of the horrible report: "She ruined Falleix." She was almost thirty; and though she was in the prime of her beauty, still she might be called an old woman, and all the more so because in such a crisis all a woman's rivals are against her. Mariette, Florine, Tullia would ask their friend to dinner, and gave her some help; but as they did not know the extent of her debts, they did not dare to sound the depths of that gulf. An interval of six years formed rather too long a gap in the ebb and flow of the Paris tide, between La Torpille and Madame du Val-Noble, for the woman "on foot" to speak to the woman in her carriage; but La Val-Noble knew that Esther was too generous not to remember sometimes that she had, as she said, fallen heir to her possessions, and not to seek her out by some meeting which might seem accidental though arranged. To bring about such an accident, Madame du Val-Noble, dressed in the most lady-like way, walked out every day in the Champs-Elysees on the arm of Theodore Gaillard, who afterwards married her, and who, in these straits, behaved very well to his former mistress, giving her boxes at the play, and inviting her to every spree. She flattered herself that Esther, driving out one fine day, would meet her face to face.

Esther's coachman was Paccard—for her household had been made up in five days by Asie, Europe, and Paccard under Carlos' instructions, and in such a way that the house in the Rue Saint-Georges was an impregnable fortress.

Peyrade, on his part, prompted by deep hatred, by the thirst for vengeance, and, above all, by his wish to see his darling Lydie married, made the Champs-Elysees the end of his walks as soon as he heard from Contenson that Monsieur de Nucingen's mistress might be seen there. Peyrade could dress so exactly like an Englishman, and spoke French so perfectly with the mincing accent that the English give the language; he knew England itself so well, and was so familiar with all the customs of the country, having been sent to England by the police authorities three times between 1779 and 1786, that he could play his part in London and at ambassadors' residences without awaking suspicion. Peyrade, who had some resemblance to Musson the famous juggler, could disguise himself so effectually that once Contenson did not recognize him.

Followed by Contenson dressed as a mulatto, Peyrade examined Esther and her servants with an eye which, seeming heedless, took everything in. Hence it quite naturally happened that in the side alley where the carriage-company walk in fine dry weather, he was on the spot one day when Esther met Madame du Val-Noble. Peyrade, his mulatto in livery at his heels, was airing himself quite naturally, like a nabob who is thinking of no one but himself, in a line with the two women, so as to catch a few words of their conversation.

"Well, my dear child," said Esther to Madame du Val-Noble, "come and see me. Nucingen owes it to himself not to leave his stockbroker's mistress without a sou—"

"All the more so because it is said that he ruined Falleix," remarked Theodore Gaillard, "and that we have every right to squeeze him."

"He dines with me to-morrow," said Esther; "come and meet him." Then she added in an undertone:

"I can do what I like with him, and as yet he has not that!" and she put the nail of a gloved finger under the prettiest of her teeth with the click that is familiarly known to express with peculiar energy: "Just nothing."

"You have him safe—"

"My dear, as yet he has only paid my debts."

"How mean!" cried Suzanne du Val-Noble.

"Oh!" said Esther, "I had debts enough to frighten a minister of finance. Now, I mean to have thirty thousand a year before the first stroke of midnight. Oh! he is excellent, I have nothing to complain of. He does it well.—In a week we give a house-warming; you must come.—That morning he is to make me a present of the lease of the house in the Rue Saint-Georges. In decency, it is impossible to live in such a house on less than thirty thousand francs a year—of my own, so as to have them safe in case of accident. I have known poverty, and I want no more of it. There are certain acquaintances one has had enough of at once."

"And you, who used to say, 'My face is my fortune!'—How you have changed!" exclaimed Suzanne.

"It is the air of Switzerland; you grow thrifty there.—Look here; go there yourself, my dear! Catch a Swiss, and you may perhaps catch a husband, for they have not yet learned what such women as we are can be. And, at any rate, you may come back with a passion for investments in the funds—a most respectable and elegant passion!—Good-bye."

Esther got into her carriage again, a handsome carriage drawn by the finest pair of dappled gray horses at that time to be seen in Paris.

"The woman who is getting into the carriage is handsome," said Peyrade to Contenson, "but I like the one who is walking best; follow her, and find out who she is."

"That is what that Englishman has just remarked in English," said Theodore Gaillard, repeating Peyrade's remark to Madame du Val-Noble.

Before making this speech in English, Peyrade had uttered a word or two in that language, which had made Theodore look up in a way that convinced him that the journalist understood English.

Madame du Val-Noble very slowly made her way home to very decent furnished rooms in the Rue Louis-le-Grand, glancing round now and then to see if the mulatto were following her.

This establishment was kept by a certain Madame Gerard, whom Suzanne had obliged in the days of her splendor, and who showed her gratitude by giving her a suitable home. This good soul, an honest and virtuous citizen, even pious, looked on the courtesan as a woman of a superior order; she had always seen her in the midst of luxury, and thought of her as a fallen queen; she trusted her daughters with her; and—which is a fact more natural than might be supposed—the courtesan was as scrupulously careful in taking them to the play as their mother could have been, and the two Gerard girls loved her. The worthy, kind lodging-house keeper was like those sublime priests who see in these outlawed women only a creature to be saved and loved.

Madame du Val-Noble respected this worth; and often, as she chatted with the good woman, she envied her while bewailing her own ill-fortune.

"Your are still handsome; you may make a good end yet," Madame Gerard would say.

But, indeed, Madame du Val-Noble was only relatively impoverished. This woman's wardrobe, so extravagant and elegant, was still sufficiently well furnished to allow of her appearing on occasion—as on that evening at the Porte-Saint-Martin to see *Richard Darlington*—in much splendor. And Madame Gerard would most good-naturedly pay for the cabs needed by the lady "on foot" to go out to dine, or to the play, and to come home again.

"Well, dear Madame Gerard," said she to this worthy mother, "my luck is about to change, I believe."

"Well, well, madame, so much the better. But be prudent; do not run into debt any more. I have such difficulty in getting rid of the people who are hunting for you."

"Oh, never worry yourself about those hounds! They have all made no end of money out of me.—Here are some tickets for the Varietes for your girls—a good box on the second tier. If any one should ask for me this evening before I come in, show them up all the same. Adele, my old maid, will be here; I will send her round."

Madame du Val-Noble, having neither mother nor aunt, was obliged to have recourse to her maid—equally on foot—to play the part of a Saint-Esteve with the unknown follower whose conquest was to enable her to rise again in the world. She went to dine with Theodore Gaillard, who, as it happened, had a spree on that day, that is to say, a dinner given by Nathan in payment of a bet he had lost, one of those orgies when a man says to his guests, "You can bring a woman."

It was not without strong reasons that Peyrade had made up his mind to rush in person on to the field of this intrigue. At the same time, his curiosity, like Corentin's, was so keenly excited, that, even in the absence of reasons, he would have tried to play a part in the drama.

At this moment Charles X's policy had completed its last evolution. After confiding the helm of State to Ministers of his own choosing, the King was preparing to conquer Algiers, and to utilize the glory that should accrue as a passport to what has been called his *Coup d'Etat*. There were no more conspiracies at home; Charles X believed he had no domestic enemies. But in politics, as at sea, a calm may be deceptive.

Thus Corentin had lapsed into total idleness. In such a case a true sportsman, to keep his hand in, for lack of larks kills sparrows. Domitian, we know, for lack of Christians, killed flies. Contenson, having witnessed Esther's arrest, had, with the keen instinct of a spy, fully understood the upshot of the business. The rascal, as we have seen, did not attempt to conceal his opinion of the Baron de Nucingen.

"Who is benefiting by making the banker pay so dear for his passion?" was the first question the allies asked each other. Recognizing Asie as a leader in the piece, Contenson hoped to find out the author through her; but she slipped through his fingers again and again, hiding like an eel in the mud of Paris; and when he found her again as the cook in Esther's establishment, it seemed to him inexplicable that the half-caste woman should have had a finger in the pie. Thus, for the first time, these two artistic spies had come on a text that they could not decipher, while suspecting a dark plot to the story.

After three bold attempts on the house in the Rue Taitbout, Contenson still met with absolute dumbness. So long as Esther dwelt there the lodge porter seemed to live in mortal terror. Asie had, perhaps, promised poisoned meat-balls to all the family in the event of any indiscretion.

On the day after Esther's removal, Contenson found this man rather more amenable; he regretted the lady, he said, who had fed him with the broken dishes from her table. Contenson, disguised as a broker, tried to bargain for the rooms, and listened to the porter's lamentations while he fooled him, casting a doubt on all the man said by a questioning "Really?"

"Yes, monsieur, the lady lived here for five years without ever going out, and more by token, her lover, desperately jealous though she was beyond reproach, took the greatest precautions when he came in or went out. And a very handsome young man he was too!"

Lucien was at this time still staying with his sister, Madame Sechard; but as soon as he returned, Contenson sent the porter to the Quai Malaquais to ask Monsieur de Rubempre whether he were willing to part with the furniture left in the rooms lately occupied by Madame van Bogseck. The porter then recognized Lucien as the young widow's mysterious lover, and this was all that Contenson wanted. The deep but suppressed astonishment may be imagined with which Lucien and Carlos received the porter, whom they affected to regard as a madman; they tried to upset his convictions.

Within twenty-four hours Carlos had organized a force which detected Contenson red-handed in the act of espionage. Contenson, disguised as a market-porter, had twice already brought home the provisions purchased in the morning by Asie, and had twice got into the little mansion in the Rue Saint-Georges. Corentin, on his part, was making a stir; but he was stopped short by recognizing the certain identity of Carlos Herrera; for he learned at once that this Abbe, the secret envoy of Ferdinand VII, had come to Paris towards the end of 1823. Still, Corentin thought it worth while to study the reasons which had led the Spaniard to take an interest in Lucien de Rubempre. It was soon clear to him, beyond doubt, that Esther had for five years been Lucien's mistress; so the substitution of the Englishwoman had been effected for the advantage of that young dandy.

Now Lucien had no means; he was rejected as a suitor for Mademoiselle de Grandlieu; and he had just bought up the lands of Rubempre at the cost of a million francs.

Corentin very skilfully made the head of the General Police take the first steps; and the Prefet de Police a propos to Peyrade, informed his chief that the appellants in that affair had been in fact the Comte de Serizy and Lucien de Rubempre.

"We have it!" cried Peyrade and Corentin.

The two friends had laid plans in a moment.

"This hussy," said Corentin, "has had intimacies; she must have some women friends. Among them we shall certainly find one or another who is down on her luck; one of us must play the part of a rich foreigner and take her up. We will throw them together. They always want something of each other in the game of lovers, and we shall then be in the citadel."

Peyrade naturally proposed to assume his disguise as an Englishman. The wild life he should lead during the time that he would take to disentangle the plot of which he had been the victim, smiled on his fancy; while Corentin, grown old in his functions, and weakly too, did not care for it. Disguised as a mulatto, Contenson at once evaded Carlos' force. Just three days before Peyrade's meeting with Madame du Val-Noble in the Champs-Elysees, this last of the agents employed by Mm. de Sartine and Lenoir had arrived, provided with a passport, at the Hotel Mirabeau, Rue de la Paix, having come from the Colonies via le Havre, in a traveling chaise, as mud-splashed as though it had really come from le Havre, instead of no further than by the road from Saint-Denis to Paris.

Carlos Herrera, on his part, had his passport *vise* at the Spanish Embassy, and arranged everything at the Quai Malaquais to start for Madrid. And this is why. Within a few days Esther was to become the owner of the house in the Rue Saint-Georges and of shares yielding thirty thousand francs a year; Europe and Asie were quite cunning enough to persuade her to sell these shares and privately transmit the money to Lucien. Thus Lucien, proclaiming himself rich through his sister's liberality, would pay the remainder of the price of the Rubempre estates. Of this transaction no one could complain. Esther alone could betray herself; but she would die rather than blink an eyelash.

Clotilde had appeared with a little pink kerchief round her crane's neck, so she had won her game at the Hotel de Grandlieu. The shares in the Omnibus Company were already worth thrice their initial value. Carlos, by disappearing for a few days, would put malice off the scent. Human prudence had foreseen everything; no error was possible. The false Spaniard was to start on the morrow of the day when Peyrade met Madame du Val-Noble. But that very night, at two in the morning, Asie came in a cab to the Quai Malaquais, and found the stoker of the machine smoking in his room, and reconsidering all the points of the situation here stated in a few words, like an author going over a page in his book to discover any faults to be corrected. Such a man would not allow himself a second time such an oversight as that of the porter in the Rue Taitbout.

"Paccard," whispered Asie in her master's ear, "recognized Contenson yesterday, at half-past two, in the Champs-Elysees, disguised as a mulatto servant to an Englishman, who for the last three days has been seen walking in the Champs-Elysees, watching Esther. Paccard knew the hound by his eyes, as I did when he dressed up as a market-porter. Paccard drove the girl home, taking a round so as not to lose sight of the wretch. Contenson is at the Hotel Mirabeau; but he exchanged so many signs of intelligence with the Englishman, that Paccard says the other cannot possibly be an Englishman."

"We have a gadfly behind us," said Carlos. "I will not leave till the day after to-morrow. That Contenson is certainly the man who sent the porter after us from the Rue Taitbout; we must ascertain whether this sham Englishman is our foe."

At noon Mr. Samuel Johnson's black servant was solemnly waiting on his master, who always breakfasted too heartily, with a purpose. Peyrade wished to pass for a tippling Englishman; he never went out till he was half-seas over. He wore black cloth gaiters up to his knees, and padded to make his legs look stouter; his trousers were lined with the thickest fustian; his waistcoat was buttoned up to his cheeks; a red scratch wig hid half his forehead, and he had added nearly three inches to his height; in short, the oldest frequenter of the Cafe David could not have recognized him. From his squarecut coat of black cloth with full skirts he might have been taken for an English millionaire.

Contenson made a show of the cold insolence of a nabob's confidential servant; he was taciturn, abrupt, scornful, and uncommunicative, and indulged in fierce exclamations and uncouth gestures.

Peyrade was finishing his second bottle when one of the hotel waiters unceremoniously showed in a man in whom Peyrade and Contenson both at once discerned a gendarme in mufti.

"Monsieur Peyrade," said the gendarme to the nabob, speaking in his ear, "my instructions are to take you to the Prefecture."

Peyrade, without saying a word, rose and took down his hat.

"You will find a hackney coach at the door," said the man as they went downstairs. "The Prefet thought of arresting you, but he decided on sending for you to ask some explanation of your conduct through the peace-officer whom you will find in the coach."

"Shall I ride with you?" asked the gendarme of the peace-officer when Peyrade had got in.

"No," replied the other; "tell the coachman quietly to drive to the Prefecture."

Peyrade and Carlos were now face to face in the coach. Carlos had a stiletto under his hand. The coach-driver was a man he could trust, quite capable of allowing Carlos to get out without seeing him, or being surprised, on arriving at his journey's end, to find a dead body in his cab. No inquiries are ever made about a spy. The law almost always leaves such murders unpunished, it is so difficult to know the rights of the case.

Peyrade looked with his keenest eye at the magistrate sent to examine him by the Prefet of Police. Carlos struck him as satisfactory: a bald head, deeply wrinkled at the back, and powdered hair; a pair of very light gold spectacles, with double-green glasses over weak eyes, with red rims, evidently needing care. These eyes seemed the trace of some squalid malady. A cotton shirt with a flat-pleated frill, a shabby black satin waistcoat, the trousers of a man of law, black spun silk stockings, and shoes tied with ribbon; a long black overcoat, cheap gloves, black, and worn for ten days, and a gold watch-chain—in every point the lower grade of magistrate known by a perversion of terms as a peace-officer.

"My dear Monsieur Peyrade, I regret to find such a man as you the object of surveillance, and that you should act so as to justify it. Your disguise is not to the Prefet's taste. If you fancy that you can thus escape our vigilance, you are mistaken. You traveled from England by way of Beaumont-sur-Oise, no doubt."

"Beaumont-sur-Oise?" repeated Peyrade.

"Or by Saint-Denis?" said the sham lawyer.

Peyrade lost his presence of mind. The question must be answered. Now any reply might be dangerous. In the affirmative it was farcical; in the negative, if this man knew the truth, it would be Peyrade's ruin.

"He is a sharp fellow," thought he.

He tried to look at the man and smile, and he gave him a smile for an answer; the smile passed muster without protest.

"For what purpose have you disguised yourself, taken rooms at the Mirabeau, and dressed Contenson as a black servant?" asked the peace-officer.

"Monsieur le Prefet may do what he chooses with me, but I owe no account of my actions to any one but my chief," said Peyrade with dignity.

"If you mean me to infer that you are acting by the orders of the General Police," said the other coldly, "we will change our route, and drive to the Rue de Grenelle instead of the Rue de Jerusalem. I have clear instructions with regard to you. But be careful! You are not in any deep disgrace, and you may spoil your own game in a moment. As for me—I owe you no grudge.—Come; tell me the truth."

"Well, then, this is the truth," said Peyrade, with a glance at his Cerberus' red eyes.

The sham lawyer's face remained expressionless, impassible; he was doing his business, all truths were the same to him, he looked as though he suspected the Prefet of some caprice. Prefets have their little tantrums.

"I have fallen desperately in love with a woman—the mistress of that stockbroker who is gone abroad for his own pleasure and the displeasure of his creditors—Falleix."

"Madame du Val-Noble?"

"Yes," replied Peyrade. "To keep her for a month, which will not cost me more than a thousand crowns, I have got myself up as a nabob and taken Contenson as my servant. This is so absolutely true, monsieur, that if you like to leave me in the coach, where I will wait for you, on my honor as an old Commissioner-General of Police, you can go to the hotel and question Contenson. Not only will Contenson confirm what I have the honor of stating, but you may see Madame du Val-Noble's waiting-maid, who is to come this morning to signify her mistress' acceptance of my offers, or the conditions she makes.

"An old monkey knows what grimaces mean: I have offered her a thousand francs a month and a carriage—that comes to fifteen hundred; five hundred francs' worth of presents, and as much again in some outings, dinners and play-going; you see, I am not deceiving you by a centime when I say a thousand crowns.—A man of my age may well spend a thousand crowns on his last fancy."

"Bless me, Papa Peyrade! and you still care enough for women to—? But you are deceiving me. I am sixty myself, and I can do without 'em.— However, if the case is as you state it, I quite understand that you should have found it necessary to get yourself up as a foreigner to indulge your fancy."

"You can understand that Peyrade, or old Canquoelle of the Rue des Moineaux—"

"Ay, neither of them would have suited Madame du Val-Noble," Carlos put in, delighted to have picked up Canquoelle's address. "Before the Revolution," he went on, "I had for my mistress a woman who had previously been kept by the gentleman-in-waiting, as they then called the executioner. One evening at the play she pricked herself with a pin, and cried out—a customary ejaculation in those days—'Ah! Bourreau!' on which her neighbor asked her if this were a reminiscence?—Well, my dear Peyrade, she cast off her man for that speech.

"I suppose you have no wish to expose yourself to such a slap in the face.—Madame du Val-Noble is a woman for gentlemen. I saw her once at the opera, and thought her very handsome.

"Tell the driver to go back to the Rue de la Paix, my dear Peyrade. I will go upstairs with you to your rooms and see for myself. A verbal report will no doubt be enough for Monsieur le Prefet."

Carlos took a snuff-box from his side-pocket—a black snuff-box lined with silver-gilt—and offered it to Peyrade with an impulse of delightful good-fellowship. Peyrade said to himself:

"And these are their agents! Good Heavens! what would Monsieur Lenoir say if he could come back to life, or Monsieur de Sartines?"

"That is part of the truth, no doubt, but it is not all," said the sham lawyer, sniffing up his pinch of snuff. "You have had a finger in the Baron de Nucingen's love affairs, and you wish, no doubt, to entangle him in some slip-knot. You missed fire with the pistol, and you are aiming at him with a field-piece. Madame du Val-Noble is a friend of Madame de Champy's—"

"Devil take it. I must take care not to founder," said Peyrade to himself. "He is a better man than I thought him. He is playing me; he talks of letting me go, and he goes on making me blab."

"Well?" asked Carlos with a magisterial air.

"Monsieur, it is true that I have been so foolish as to seek a woman in Monsieur de Nucingen's behoof, because he was half mad with love. That is the cause of my being out of favor, for it would seem that quite unconsciously I touched some important interests."

The officer of the law remained immovable.

"But after fifty-two years' experience," Peyrade went on, "I know the police well enough to have held my hand after the blowing up I had from Monsieur le Prefet, who, no doubt, was right—"

"Then you would give up this fancy if Monsieur le Prefet required it of you? That, I think, would be the best proof you could give of the sincerity of what you say."

"He is going it! he is going it!" thought Peyrade. "Ah! by all that's holy, the police to-day is a match for that of Monsieur Lenoir."

"Give it up?" said he aloud. "I will wait till I have Monsieur le Prefet's orders.—But here we are at the hotel, if you wish to come up."

"Where do you find the money?" said Carlos point-blank, with a sagacious glance.

"Monsieur, I have a friend—"

"Get along," said Carlos; "go and tell that story to an examining magistrate!"

This audacious stroke on Carlos' part was the outcome of one of those calculations, so simple that none but a man of his temper would have thought it out.

At a very early hour he had sent Lucien to Madame de Serizy's. Lucien had begged the Count's private secretary—as from the Count—to go and obtain from the Prefet of Police full particulars concerning the agent employed by the Baron de Nucingen. The secretary came back provided with a note concerning Peyrade, a copy of the summary noted on the back of his record:—

"In the police force since 1778, having come to Paris from Avignon two years previously.

"Without money or character; possessed of certain State secrets.

"Lives in the Rue des Moineaux under the name of Canquoelle, the name of a little estate where his family resides in the department of Vaucluse; very respectable people.

"Was lately inquired for by a grand-nephew named Theodore de la Peyrade. (See the report of an agent, No. 37 of the Documents.)"

"He must be the man to whom Contenson is playing the mulatto servant!" cried Carlos, when Lucien returned with other information besides this note.

Within three hours this man, with the energy of a Commander-in-Chief, had found, by Paccard's help, an innocent accomplice capable of playing the part of a gendarme in disguise, and had got himself up as a peace-officer. Three times in the coach he had thought of killing Peyrade, but he had made it a rule never to commit a murder with his own hand; he promised himself that he would get rid of Peyrade all in good time by pointing him out as a millionaire to some released convicts about the town.

Peyrade and his Mentor, as they went in, heard Contenson's voice arguing with Madame du Val-Noble's maid. Peyrade signed to Carlos to remain in the outer room, with a look meant to convey: "Thus you can assure yourself of my sincerity."

"Madame agrees to everything," said Adele. "Madame is at this moment calling on a friend, Madame de Champy, who has some rooms in the Rue Taitbout on her hands for a year, full of furniture, which she will let her have, no doubt. Madame can receive Mr. Johnson more suitably there, for the furniture is still very decent, and monsieur might buy it for madame by coming to an agreement with Madame de Champy."

"Very good, my girl. If this is not a job of fleecing, it is a bit of the wool," said the mulatto to the astonished woman. "However, we will go shares—"

"That is your darkey all over!" cried Mademoiselle Adele. "If your nabob is a nabob, he can very well afford to give madame the furniture. The lease ends in April 1830; your nabob may renew it if he likes."

"I am quite willing," said Peyrade, speaking French with a strong English accent, as he came in and tapped the woman on the shoulder.

He cast a knowing look back at Carlos, who replied by an assenting nod, understanding that the nabob was to keep up his part.

But the scene suddenly changed its aspect at the entrance of a person over whom neither Carlos nor Peyrade had the least power. Corentin suddenly came in. He had found the door open, and looked in as he went by to see how his old friend played his part as nabob.

"The Prefet is still bullying me!" said Peyrade in a whisper to Corentin. "He has found me out as a nabob."

"We will spill the Prefet," Corentin muttered in reply.

Then after a cool bow he stood darkly scrutinizing the magistrate.

"Stay here till I return," said Carlos; "I will go to the Prefecture. If you do not see me again, you may go your own way."

Having said this in an undertone to Peyrade, so as not to humiliate him in the presence of the waiting-maid, Carlos went away, not caring to remain under the eye of the newcomer, in whom he detected one of those fair-haired, blue-eyed men, coldly terrifying.

"That is the peace-officer sent after me by the Prefet," said Peyrade.

"That?" said Corentin. "You have walked into a trap. That man has three packs of cards in his shoes; you can see that by the place of his foot in the shoe; besides, a peace-officer need wear no disguise."

Corentin hurried downstairs to verify his suspicions: Carlos was getting into the fly.

"Hallo! Monsieur l'Abbe!" cried Corentin.

Carlos looked around, saw Corentin, and got in quickly. Still, Corentin had time to say:

"That was all I wanted to know.—Quai Malaquais," he shouted to the driver with diabolical mockery in his tone and expression.

"I am done!" said Jacques Collin to himself. "They have got me. I must get ahead of them by sheer pace, and, above all, find out what they want of us."

Corentin had seen the Abbe Carlos Herrera five or six times, and the man's eyes were unforgettable. Corentin had suspected him at once from the cut of his shoulders, then by his puffy face, and the trick of three inches of added height gained by a heel inside the shoe.

"Ah! old fellow, they have drawn you," said Corentin, finding no one in the room but Peyrade and Contenson.

"Who?" cried Peyrade, with metallic hardness; "I will spend my last days in putting him on a gridiron and turning him on it."

"It is the Abbe Carlos Herrera, the Corentin of Spain, as I suppose. This explains everything. The Spaniard is a demon of the first water, who has tried to make a fortune for that little young man by coining money out of a pretty baggage's bolster.—It is your lookout if you think you can measure your skill with a man who seems to me the very devil to deal with."

"Oh!" exclaimed Contenson, "he fingered the three hundred thousand francs the day when Esther was arrested; he was in the cab. I remember those eyes, that brow, and those marks of the smallpox."

"Oh! what a fortune my Lydie might have had!" cried Peyrade.

"You may still play the nabob," said Corentin. "To keep an eye on Esther you must keep up her intimacy with Val-Noble. She was really Lucien's mistress."

"They have got more than five hundred thousand francs out of Nucingen already," said Contenson.

"And they want as much again," Corentin went on. "The Rubempre estate is to cost a million.—Daddy," added he, slapping Peyrade on the shoulder, "you may get more than a hundred thousand francs to settle on Lydie."

"Don't tell me that, Corentin. If your scheme should fail, I cannot tell what I might not do—"

"You will have it by to-morrow perhaps! The Abbe, my dear fellow, is most astute; we shall have to kiss his spurs; he is a very superior devil. But I have him sure enough. He is not a fool, and he will knock under. Try to be a gaby as well as a nabob, and fear nothing."

In the evening of this day, when the opposing forces had met face to face on level ground, Lucien spent the evening at the Hotel Grandlieu. The party was a large one. In the face of all the assembly, the Duchess kept Lucien at her side for some time, and was most kind to him.

"You are going away for a little while?" said she.

"Yes, Madame la Duchesse. My sister, in her anxiety to promote my marriage, has made great sacrifices, and I have been enabled to repurchase the lands of the Rubempres, to reconstitute the whole estate. But I have found in my Paris lawyer a very clever man, who has managed to save me from the extortionate terms that the holders would have asked if they had known the name of the purchaser."

"Is there a chateau?" asked Clotilde, with too broad a smile.

"There is something which might be called a chateau; but the wiser plan would be to use the building materials in the construction of a modern residence."

Clotilde's eyes blazed with happiness above her smile of satisfaction.

"You must play a rubber with my father this evening," said she. "In a fortnight I hope you will be asked to dinner."

"Well, my dear sir," said the Duc de Grandlieu, "I am told that you have bought the estate of Rubempre. I congratulate you. It is an answer to those who say you are in debt. We bigwigs, like France or England, are allowed to have a public debt; but men of no fortune, beginners, you see, may not assume that privilege—"

"Indeed, Monsieur le Duc, I still owe five hundred thousand francs on my land."

"Well, well, you must marry a wife who can bring you the money; but you will have some difficulty in finding a match with such a fortune in our Faubourg, where daughters do not get large dowries."

"Their name is enough," said Lucien.

"We are only three wisk players—Maufrigneuse, d'Espard, and I—will you make a fourth?" said the Duke, pointing to the card-table.

Clotilde came to the table to watch her father's game.

"She expects me to believe that she means it for me," said the Duke, patting his daughter's hands, and looking round at Lucien, who remained quite grave.

Lucien, Monsieur d'Espard's partner, lost twenty louis.

"My dear mother," said Clotilde to the Duchess, "he was so judicious as to lose."

At eleven o'clock, after a few affectionate words with Mademoiselle de Grandlieu, Lucien went home and to bed, thinking of the complete triumph he was to enjoy a month hence; for he had not a doubt of being accepted as Clotilde's lover, and married before Lent in 1830.

On the morrow, when Lucien was smoking his cigarettes after breakfast, sitting with Carlos, who had become much depressed, M. de Saint-Esteve was announced—what a touch of irony—who begged to see either the Abbe Carlos Herrera or Monsieur Lucien de Rubempre.

"Was he told downstairs that I had left Paris?" cried the Abbe.

"Yes, sir," replied the groom.

"Well, then, you must see the man," said he to Lucien. "But do not say a single compromising word, do not let a sign of surprise escape you. It is the enemy."

"You will overhear me," said Lucien.

Carlos hid in the adjoining room, and through the crack of the door he saw Corentin, whom he recognized only by his voice, such powers of transformation did the great man possess. This time Corentin looked like an old paymaster-general.

"I have not had the honor of being known to you, monsieur," Corentin began, "but—"

"Excuse my interrupting you, monsieur, but—"

"But the matter in point is your marriage to Mademoiselle Clotilde de Grandlieu—which will never take place," Corentin added eagerly.

Lucien sat down and made no reply.

"You are in the power of a man who is able and willing and ready to prove to the Duc de Grandlieu that the lands of Rubempre are to be paid for with the money that a fool has given to your mistress, Mademoiselle Esther," Corentin went on. "It will be quite easy to find the minutes of the legal opinions in virtue of which Mademoiselle Esther was summoned; there are ways too of making d'Estourny speak. The very clever manoeuvres employed against the Baron de Nucingen will be brought to light.

"As yet all can be arranged. Pay down a hundred thousand francs, and you will have peace.—All this is no concern of mine. I am only the agent of those who levy this blackmail; nothing more."

Corentin might have talked for an hour; Lucien smoked his cigarette with an air of perfect indifference.

"Monsieur," replied he, "I do not want to know who you are, for men who undertake such jobs as these have no name—at any rate, in my vocabulary. I have allowed you to talk at your leisure; I am at home.—You seem to me not bereft of common sense; listen to my dilemma."

There was a pause, during which Lucien met Corentin's cat-like eye fixed on him with a perfectly icy stare.

"Either you are building on facts that are absolutely false, and I need pay no heed to them," said Lucien; "or you are in the right; and in that case, by giving you a hundred thousand francs, I put you in a position to ask me for as many hundred thousand francs as your employer can find Saint-Esteves to ask for.

"However, to put an end, once and for all, to your kind intervention, I would have you know that I, Lucien de Rubempre, fear no one. I have no part in the jobbery of which you speak. If the Grandlieus make difficulties, there are other young ladies of very good family ready to be married. After all, it is no loss to me if I remain single, especially if, as you imagine, I deal in blank bills to such advantage."

"If Monsieur l'Abbe Carlos Herrera—"

"Monsieur," Lucien put in, "the Abbe Herrera is at this moment on the way to Spain. He has nothing to do with my marriage, my interests are no concern of his. That remarkable statesman was good enough to assist me at one time with his advice, but he has reports to present to his Majesty the King of Spain; if you have anything to say to him, I recommend you to set out for Madrid."

"Monsieur," said Corentin plainly, "you will never be Mademoiselle Clotilde de Grandlieu's husband."

"So much the worse for her!" replied Lucien, impatiently pushing Corentin towards the door.

"You have fully considered the matter?" asked Corentin coldly.

"Monsieur, I do not recognize that you have any right either to meddle in my affairs, or to make me waste a cigarette," said Lucien, throwing away his cigarette that had gone out.

"Good-day, monsieur," said Corentin. "We shall not meet again.—But there will certainly be a moment in your life when you would give half your fortune to have called me back from these stairs."

In answer to this threat, Carlos made as though he were cutting off a head.

"Now to business!" cried he, looking at Lucien, who was as white as ashes after this dreadful interview.

IF AMONG THE SMALL NUMBER of my readers who take an interest in the moral and philosophical side of this book there should be only one capable of believing that the Baron de Nucingen was happy, that one would prove how difficult it is to explain the heart of a courtesan by any kind of physiological formula. Esther was resolved to make the poor millionaire pay dearly for what he called his day of triumph. And at the beginning of February 1830 the house-warming party had not yet been given in the "little palace."

"Well," said Esther in confidence to her friends, who repeated it to the Baron, "I shall open house at the Carnival, and I mean to make my man as happy as a cock in plaster."

The phrase became proverbial among women of her kidney.

The Baron gave vent to much lamentation; like married men, he made himself very ridiculous, he began to complain to his intimate friends, and his dissatisfaction was generally known.

Esther, meanwhile, took quite a serious view of her position as the Pompadour of this prince of speculators. She had given two or three small evening parties, solely to get Lucien into the house. Lousteau, Rastignac, du Tillet, Bixiou, Nathan, the Comte de Brambourg—all the cream of the dissipated crew—frequented her drawing-room. And, as leading ladies in the piece she was playing, Esther accepted Tullia, Florentine, Fanny Beaupre, and Florine—two dancers and two actresses—besides Madame du Val-Noble. Nothing can be more dreary than a courtesan's home without the spice of rivalry, the display of dress, and some variety of type.

In six weeks Esther had become the wittiest, the most amusing, the loveliest, and the most elegant of those female pariahs who form the class of kept women. Placed on the pedestal that became her, she enjoyed all the delights of vanity which fascinate women in general, but still as one who is raised above her caste by a secret thought. She cherished in her heart an image of herself which she gloried in, while it made her blush; the hour when she must abdicate was ever present to her consciousness; thus she lived a double life, really scorning herself. Her sarcastic remarks were tinged by the temper which was roused in her by the intense contempt felt by the Angel of Love, hidden in the courtesan, for the disgraceful and odious part played by the body in the presence, as it were, of the soul. At once actor and spectator, victim and judge, she was a living realization of the beautiful Arabian Tales, in which a noble creature lies hidden under a degrading form, and of which the type is the story of Nebuchadnezzar in the book of books—the Bible. Having granted herself a lease of life till the day after her infidelity, the victim might surely play awhile with the executioner.

Moreover, the enlightenment that had come to Esther as to the secretly disgraceful means by which the Baron had made his colossal fortune relieved her of every scruple. She could play the part of Ate, the goddess of vengeance, as Carlos said. And so she was by turns enchanting and odious to the banker, who lived only for her. When the Baron had been worked up to such a pitch of suffering that he wanted only to be quit of Esther, she brought him round by a scene of tender affection.

Herrera, making a great show of starting for Spain, had gone as far as Tours. He had sent the chaise on as far as Bordeaux, with a servant inside, engaged to play the part of master, and to wait for him at Bordeaux. Then, returning by diligence, dressed as a commercial traveler, he had secretly taken up his abode under Esther's roof, and thence, aided by Asie and Europe, carefully directed all his machinations, keeping an eye on every one, and especially on Peyrade.

About a fortnight before the day chosen for her great entertainment, which was to be given in the evening after the first opera ball, the courtesan, whose witticisms were beginning to make her feared, happened to be at the Italian opera, at the back of a box which the Baron—forced to give a box—had secured in the lowest tier, in order to conceal his mistress, and not to flaunt her in public within a few feet of Madame de Nucingen. Esther had taken her seat, so as to "rake" that of Madame de Serizy, whom Lucien almost invariably accompanied. The poor girl made her whole happiness centre in watching Lucien on Tuesdays, Thursdays, and Saturdays by Madame de Serizy's side.

At about half-past nine in the evening Esther could see Lucien enter the Countess' box, with a care-laden brow, pale, and with almost drawn features. These symptoms of mental anguish were legible only to Esther.

The knowledge of a man's countenance is, to the woman who loves him, like that of the sea to a sailor.

"Good God! what can be the matter? What has happened? Does he want to speak with that angel of hell, who is to him a guardian angel, and who lives in an attic between those of Europe and Asie?"

Tormented by such reflections, Esther scarcely listened to the music. Still less, it may be believed, did she listen to the Baron, who held one of his "Anchel's" hands in both his, talking to her in his horrible Polish-Jewish accent, a jargon which must be as unpleasant to read as it is to hear spoken.

"Esther," said he, releasing her hand, and pushing it away with a slight touch of temper, "you do not listen to me."

"I tell you what, Baron, you blunder in love as you gibber in French."

"*Der teufel!*"

"I am not in my boudoir here, I am at the opera. If you were not a barrel made by Huret or Fichet, metamorphosed into a man by some trick of nature, you would not make so much noise in a box with a woman who is fond of music. I don't listen to you? I should think not! There you sit rustling my dress like a cockchafer in a paper-bag, and making me laugh with contempt. You say to me, 'You are so pretty, I should like to eat you!' Old simpleton! Supposing I were to say to you, 'You are less intolerable this evening than you were yesterday—we will go home?'—Well, from the way you puff and sigh—for I feel you if I don't listen to you—I perceive that you have eaten an enormous dinner, and your digestion is at work. Let me instruct you—for I cost you enough to give some advice for your money now and then—let me tell you, my dear fellow, that a man whose digestion is so troublesome as yours is, is not justified in telling his mistress that she is pretty at unseemly hours. An old soldier died of that very folly 'in the arms of Religion,' as Blondet has it.

"It is now ten o'clock. You finished dinner at du Tillet's at nine o'clock, with your pigeon the Comte de Brambourg; you have millions and truffles to digest. Come to-morrow night at ten."

"Vat you are cruel!" cried the Baron, recognizing the profound truth of this medical argument.

"Cruel!" echoed Esther, still looking at Lucien. "Have you not consulted Bianchon, Desplein, old Haudry?—Since you have had a glimpse of future happiness, do you know what you seem like to me?"

"No—vat?"

"A fat old fellow wrapped in flannel, who walks every hour from his armchair to the window to see if the thermometer has risen to the degree marked '*Silkworms*,' the temperature prescribed by his physician."

"You are really an ungrateful slut!" cried the Baron, in despair at hearing a tune, which, however, amorous old men not unfrequently hear at the opera.

"Ungrateful!" retorted Esther. "What have you given me till now? A great deal of annoyance. Come, papa! Can I be proud of you? You! you are proud of me; I wear your livery and badge with an air. You paid my debts? So you did. But you have grabbed so many millions—come, you need not sulk; you admitted that to me—that you need not think twice of that. And this is your chief title to fame. A baggage and a thief—a well-assorted couple!

"You have built a splendid cage for a parrot that amuses you. Go and ask a Brazilian cockatoo what gratitude it owes to the man who placed it in a gilded cage.—Don't look at me like that; you are just like a Buddist Bonze.

"Well, you show your red-and-white cockatoo to all Paris. You say, 'Does anybody else in Paris own such a parrot? And how well it talks, how cleverly it picks its words!' If du Tillet comes in, it says at once, 'How'do, little swindler!'—Why, you are as happy as a Dutchman who has grown an unique tulip, as an old nabob pensioned off in Asia by England, when a commercial traveler sells him the first Swiss snuff-box that opens in three places.

"You want to win my heart? Well, now, I will tell you how to do it."

"Speak, speak, dere is noting I shall not do for you. I lofe to be fooled by you."

"Be young, be handsome, be like Lucien de Rubempre over there by your wife, and you shall have gratis what you can never buy with all your millions!"

"I shall go 'vay, for really you are too bat dis evening!" said the banker, with a lengthened face.

"Very well, good-night then," said Esther. "Tell Georches to make your pillows very high and place your fee low, for you look apoplectic this evening.—You cannot say, my dear, that I take no interest in your health."

The Baron was standing up, and held the door-knob in his hand.

"Here, Nucingen," said Esther, with an imperious gesture.

The Baron bent over her with dog-like devotion.

"Do you want to see me very sweet, and giving you sugar-and-water, and petting you in my house, this very evening, old monster?"

"You shall break my heart!"

"Break your heart—you mean bore you," she went on. "Well, bring me Lucien that I may invite him to our Belshazzar's feast, and you may be sure he will not fail to come. If you succeed in that little transaction, I will tell you that I love you, my fat Frederic, in such plain terms that you cannot but believe me."

"You are an enchantress," said the Baron, kissing Esther's glove. "I should be villing to listen to abuse for ein hour if alvays der vas a kiss at de ent of it."

"But if I am not obeyed, I—" and she threatened the Baron with her finger as we threaten children.

The Baron raised his head like a bird caught in a springe and imploring the trapper's pity.

"Dear Heaven! What ails Lucien?" said she to herself when she was alone, making no attempt to check her falling tears; "I never saw him so sad."

This is what had happened to Lucien that very evening.

At nine o'clock he had gone out, as he did every evening, in his brougham to go to the Hotel de Grandlieu. Using his saddle-horse and cab in the morning only, like all young men, he had hired a brougham for winter evenings, and had chosen a first-class carriage and splendid horses from one of the best job-masters. For the last month all had gone well with him; he had dined with the Grandlieus three times; the Duke was delightful to him; his shares in the Omnibus Company, sold for three hundred thousand francs, had paid off a third more of the price of the land; Clotilde de Grandlieu, who dressed beautifully now, reddened inch thick when he went into the room, and loudly proclaimed her attachment to him. Some personages of high estate discussed their marriage as a probable event. The Duc de Chaulieu, formerly Ambassador to Spain, and now for a short while Minister for Foreign Affairs, had promised the Duchesse de Grandlieu that he would ask for the title of Marquis for Lucien.

So that evening, after dining with Madame de Serizy, Lucien had driven to the Faubourg Saint-Germain to pay his daily visit.

He arrives, the coachman calls for the gate to be opened, he drives into the courtyard and stops at the steps. Lucien, on getting out, remarks four other carriages in waiting. On seeing Monsieur de Rubempre, one of the footmen placed to open and shut the hall-door comes forward and out on to the steps, in front of the door, like a soldier on guard.

"His Grace is not at home," says he.

"Madame la Duchesse is receiving company," observes Lucien to the servant.

"Madame la Duchesse is gone out," replies the man solemnly.

"Mademoiselle Clotilde—"

"I do not think that Mademoiselle Clotilde will see you, monsieur, in the absence of Madame la Duchesse."

"But there are people here," replies Lucien in dismay.

"I do not know, sir," says the man, trying to seem stupid and to be respectful.

There is nothing more fatal than etiquette to those who regard it as the most formidable arm of social law. Lucien easily interpreted the meaning of this scene, so disastrous to him. The Duke and Duchess would not admit him. He felt the spinal marrow freezing in the core of his vertebral column, and a sickly cold sweat bedewed his brow. The conversation had taken place in the presence of his own body-servant, who held the door of the brougham, doubting whether to shut it. Lucien signed to him that he was going away again; but as he stepped into the carriage, he heard the noise of people coming downstairs, and the servant called out first, "Madame la Duchesse de Chaulieu's people," then "Madame la Vicomtesse de Grandlieu's carriage!"

Lucien merely said, "To the Italian opera"; but in spite of his haste, the luckless dandy could not escape the Duc de Chaulieu and his son, the Duc de Rhetore, to whom he was obliged to bow, for they did not speak a word to him. A great catastrophe at Court, the fall of a formidable favorite, has ere now been pronounced on the threshold of a royal study, in one word from an usher with a face like a plaster cast.

"How am I to let my adviser know of this disaster—this instant—?" thought Lucien as he drove to the opera-house. "What is going on?"

He racked his brain with conjectures.

This was what had taken place. That morning, at eleven o'clock, the Duc de Grandlieu, as he went into the little room where the family all breakfasted together, said to Clotilde after kissing her, "Until further orders, my child, think no more of the Sieur de Rubempre."

Then he had taken the Duchesse by the hand, and led her into a window recess to say a few words in an undertone, which made poor

Clotilde turn pale; for she watched her mother as she listened to the Duke, and saw her expression of extreme surprise.

"Jean," said the Duke to one of his servants, "take this note to Monsieur le Duc de Chaulieu, and beg him to answer by you, Yes or No.—I am asking him to dine here to-day," he added to his wife.

Breakfast had been a most melancholy meal. The Duchess was meditative, the Duke seemed to be vexed with himself, and Clotilde could with difficulty restrain her tears.

"My child, your father is right; you must obey him," the mother had said to the daughter with much emotion. "I do not say as he does, 'Think no more of Lucien.' No—for I understand your suffering"—Clotilde kissed her mother's hand—"but I do say, my darling, Wait, take no step, suffer in silence since you love him, and put your trust in your parents' care.—Great ladies, my child, are great just because they can do their duty on every occasion, and do it nobly."

"But what is it about?" asked Clotilde as white as a lily.

"Matters too serious to be discussed with you, my dearest," the Duchess replied. "For if they are untrue, your mind would be unnecessarily sullied; and if they are true, you must never know them."

At six o'clock the Duc de Chaulieu had come to join the Duc de Grandlieu, who awaited him in his study.

"Tell me, Henri"—for the Dukes were on the most familiar terms, and addressed each other by their Christian names. This is one of the shades invented to mark a degree of intimacy, to repel the audacity of French familiarity, and humiliate conceit—"tell me, Henri, I am in such a desperate difficulty that I can only ask advice of an old friend who understands business, and you have practice and experience. My daughter Clotilde, as you know, is in love with that little Rubempre, whom I have been almost compelled to accept as her promised husband. I have always been averse to the marriage; however, Madame de Grandlieu could not bear to thwart Clotilde's passion. When the young fellow had repurchased the family estate and paid three-quarters of the price, I could make no further objections.

"But last evening I received an anonymous letter—you know how much that is worth—in which I am informed that the young fellow's fortune is derived from some disreputable source, and that he is telling lies when he says that his sister is giving him the necessary funds for his purchase. For my daughter's happiness, and for the sake of our family, I am adjured to make inquiries, and the means of doing so are suggested to me. Here, read it."

"I am entirely of your opinion as to the value of anonymous letters, my dear Ferdinand," said the Duc de Chaulieu after reading the letter. "Still, though we may contemn them, we must make use of them. We must treat such letters as we would treat a spy. Keep the young man out of the house, and let us make inquiries—

"I know how to do it. Your lawyer is Derville, a man in whom we have perfect confidence; he knows the secrets of many families, and can certainly be trusted with this. He is an honest man, a man of weight, and a man of honor; he is cunning and wily; but his wiliness is only in the way of business, and you need only employ him to obtain evidence you can depend upon.

"We have in the Foreign Office an agent of the superior police who is unique in his power of discovering State secrets; we often send him on such missions. Inform Derville that he will have a lieutenant in the case. Our spy is a gentleman who will appear wearing the ribbon of the Legion of Honor, and looking like a diplomate. This rascal will do the hunting; Derville will only look on. Your lawyer will then tell you if the mountain brings forth a mouse, or if you must throw over this little Rubempre. Within a week you will know what you are doing."

"The young man is not yet so far a Marquis as to take offence at my being 'Not at home' for a week," said the Duc de Grandlieu.

"Above all, if you end by giving him your daughter," replied the Minister. "If the anonymous letter tells the truth, what of that? You can send Clotilde to travel with my daughter-in-law Madeleine, who wants to go to Italy."

"You relieve me immensely. I don't know whether I ought to thank you."

"Wait till the end."

"By the way," exclaimed the Duc de Grandlieu, "what is your man's name? I must mention it to Derville. Send him to me to-morrow by five o'clock; I will have Derville here and put them in communication."

"His real name," said M. de Chaulieu, "is, I think, Corentin—a name you must never have heard, for my gentleman will come ticketed with his official name. He calls himself Monsieur de Saint-Something—Saint Yves—Saint-Valere?—Something of the kind.—You may trust him; Louis XVIII had perfect confidence in him."

After this confabulation the steward had orders to shut the door on Monsieur de Rubempre—which was done.

Lucien paced the waiting-room at the opera-house like a man who was drunk. He fancied himself the talk of all Paris. He had in the Duc de Rhetore one of those unrelenting enemies on whom a man must smile, as he can never be revenged, since their attacks are in conformity with the rules of society. The Duc de Rhetore knew the scene that had just taken place on the outside steps of the Grandlieus' house. Lucien, feeling the necessity of at once reporting the catastrophe to his high privy councillor, nevertheless was afraid of compromising himself by going to Esther's house, where he might find company. He actually forgot that Esther was here, so confused were his thoughts, and in the midst of so much perplexity he was obliged to make small talk with Rastignac, who, knowing nothing of the news, congratulated him on his approaching marriage.

At this moment Nucingen appeared smiling, and said to Lucien:

"Vill you do me de pleasure to come to see Montame de Champy, vat vill infite you herself to von house-varming party—"

"With pleasure, Baron," replied Lucien, to whom the Baron appeared as a rescuing angel.

"Leave us," said Esther to Monsieur de Nucingen, when she saw him come in with Lucien. "Go and see Madame du Val-Noble, whom I discover in a box on the third tier with her nabob.—A great many nabobs grow in the Indies," she added, with a knowing glance at Lucien.

"And that one," said Lucien, smiling, "is uncommonly like yours."

"And them," said Esther, answering Lucien with another look of intelligence, while still speaking to the Baron, "bring her here with her nabob; he is very anxious to make your acquaintance. They say he is very rich. The poor woman has already poured out I know not how many elegies; she complains that her nabob is no good; and if you relieve him of his ballast, perhaps he will sail closer to the wind."

"You tink ve are all tieves!" said the Baron as he went away.

"What ails you, my Lucien?" asked Esther in her friend's ear, just touching it with her lips as soon as the box door was shut.

"I am lost! I have just been turned from the door of the Hotel de Grandlieu under pretence that no one was admitted. The Duke and Duchess were at home, and five pairs of horses were champing in the courtyard."

"What! will the marriage not take place?" exclaimed Esther, much agitated, for she saw a glimpse of Paradise.

"I do not yet know what is being plotted against me—"

"My Lucien," said she in a deliciously coaxing voice, "why be worried about it? You can make a better match by and by—I will get you the price of two estates—"

"Give us supper to-night that I may be able to speak in secret to Carlos, and, above all, invite the sham Englishman and Val-Noble. That nabob is my ruin; he is our enemy; we will get hold of him, and we—"

But Lucien broke off with a gesture of despair.

"Well, what is it?" asked the poor girl.

"Oh! Madame de Serizy sees me!" cried Lucien, "and to crown our woes, the Duc de Rhetore, who witnessed my dismissal, is with her."

In fact, at that very minute, the Duc de Rhetore was amusing himself with Madame de Serizy's discomfiture.

"Do you allow Lucien to be seen in Mademoiselle Esther's box?" said the young Duke, pointing to the box and to Lucien; "you, who take an interest in him, should really tell him such things are not allowed. He may sup at her house, he may even—But, in fact, I am no longer surprised at the Grandlieus' coolness towards the young man. I have just seen their door shut in his face—on the front steps—"

"Women of that sort are very dangerous," said Madame de Serizy, turning her opera-glass on Esther's box.

"Yes," said the Duke, "as much by what they can do as by what they wish—"

"They will ruin him!" cried Madame de Serizy, "for I am told they cost as much whether they are paid or no."

"Not to him!" said the young Duke, affecting surprise. "They are far from costing him anything; they give him money at need, and all run after him."

The Countess' lips showed a little nervous twitching which could not be included in any category of smiles.

"Well, then," said Esther, "come to supper at midnight. Bring Blondet and Rastignac; let us have two amusing persons at any rate; and we won't be more than nine."

"You must find some excuse for sending the Baron to fetch Eugenie under pretence of warning Asie, and tell her what has befallen me, so that Carlos may know before he has the nabob under his claws."

"That shall be done," said Esther.

And thus Peyrade was probably about to find himself unwittingly under the same roof with his adversary. The tiger was coming into the lion's den, and a lion surrounded by his guards.

When Lucien went back to Madame de Serizy's box, instead of turning to him, smiling and arranging her skirts for him to sit by her, she affected to pay him not the slightest attention, but looked about the house through her glass. Lucien could see, however, by the shaking of her hand that the Countess was suffering from one of those terrible emotions by which illicit joys are paid for. He went to the front of the box all the same, and sat down by her at the opposite corner, leaving a little vacant space between himself and the Countess. He leaned on the ledge of the box with his elbow, resting his chin on his gloved hand; then he half turned away, waiting for a word. By the middle of the act the Countess had still neither spoken to him nor looked at him.

"I do not know," said she at last, "why you are here; your place is in Mademoiselle Esther's box—"

"I will go there," said Lucien, leaving the box without looking at the Countess.

"My dear," said Madame du Val-Noble, going into Esther's box with Peyrade, whom the Baron de Nucingen did not recognize, "I am delighted to introduce Mr. Samuel Johnson. He is a great admirer of M. de Nucingen's talents."

"Indeed, monsieur," said Esther, smiling at Peyrade.

"Oh yes, bocou," said Peyrade.

"Why, Baron, here is a way of speaking French which is as much like yours as the low Breton dialect is like that of Burgundy. It will be most amusing to hear you discuss money matters.—Do you know, Monsieur Nabob, what I shall require of you if you are to make acquaintance with my Baron?" said Esther with a smile.

"Oh!—Thank you so much, you will introduce me to Sir Baronet?" said Peyrade with an extravagant English accent.

"Yes," said she, "you must give me the pleasure of your company at supper. There is no pitch stronger than champagne for sticking men together. It seals every kind of business, above all such as you put your foot in.—Come this evening; you will find some jolly fellows.—As for you, my little Frederic," she added in the Baron's ear, "you have your carriage here—just drive to the Rue Saint-Georges and bring Europe to me here; I have a few words to say to her about the supper. I have caught Lucien; he will bring two men who will be fun.—We will draw the Englishman," she whispered to Madame du Val-Noble.

Peyrade and the Baron left the women together.

"Oh, my dear, if you ever succeed in drawing that great brute, you will be clever indeed," said Suzanne.

"If it proves impossible, you must lend him to me for a week," replied Esther, laughing.

"You would but keep him half a day," replied Madame du Val-Noble. "The bread I eat is too hard; it breaks my teeth. Never again, to my dying day, will I try to make an Englishman happy. They are all cold and selfish—pigs on their hind legs."

"What, no consideration?" said Esther with a smile.

"On the contrary, my dear, the monster has never shown the least familiarity."

"Under no circumstances whatever?" asked Esther.

"The wretch always addresses me as Madame, and preserves the most perfect coolness imaginable at moments when every man is more or less amenable. To him love-making!—on my word, it is nothing more nor less than shaving himself. He wipes the razor, puts it back in its case, and looks in the glass as if he were saying, 'I have not cut myself!'

"Then he treats me with such respect as is enough to send a woman mad. That odious Milord Potboiler amuses himself by making poor Theodore hide in my dressing-room and stand there half the day. In short, he tries to annoy me in every way. And as stingy!—As miserly as Gobseck and Gigonnet rolled into one. He takes me out to dinner, but he does not pay the cab that brings me home if I happen not to have ordered my carriage to fetch me."

"Well," said Esther, "but what does he pay you for your services?"

"Oh, my dear, positively nothing. Five hundred francs a month and not a penny more, and the hire of a carriage. But what is it? A machine such as they hire out for a third-rate wedding to carry an epicier to the Mairie, to Church, and to the Cadran bleu.—Oh, he nettles me with his respect.

"If I try hysterics and feel ill, he is never vexed; he only says: 'I wish my lady to have her own way, for there is nothing more detestable— no gentleman—than to say to a nice woman, "You are a cotton bale, a bundle of merchandise."—Ha, hah! Are you a member of the Temperance Society and anti-slavery?' And my horror sits pale, and cold, and hard while he gives me to understand that he has as much respect for me as he might have for a Negro, and that it has nothing to do with his feelings, but with his opinions as an abolitionist."

"A man cannot be a worse wretch," said Esther. "But I will smash up that outlandish Chinee."

"Smash him up?" replied Madame du Val-Noble. "Not if he does not love me. You, yourself, would you like to ask him for two sous? He would listen to you solemnly, and tell you, with British precision that would make a slap in the face seem genial, that he pays dear enough for the trifle that love can be to his poor life;" and, as before, Madame du Val-Noble mimicked Peyrade's bad French.

"To think that in our line of life we are thrown in the way of such men!" exclaimed Esther.

"Oh, my dear, you have been uncommonly lucky. Take good care of your Nucingen."

"But your nabob must have got some idea in his head."

"That is what Adele says."

"Look here, my dear; that man, you may depend, has laid a bet that he will make a woman hate him and pack him off in a certain time."

"Or else he wants to do business with Nucingen, and took me up knowing that you and I were friends; that is what Adele thinks," answered Madame du Val-Noble. "That is why I introduced him to you this evening. Oh, if only I could be sure what he is at, what tricks I could play with you and Nucingen!"

"And you don't get angry?" asked Esther; "you don't speak your mind now and then?"

"Try it—you are sharp and smooth.—Well, in spite of your sweetness, he would kill you with his icy smiles. 'I am anti-slavery,' he would say, 'and you are free.'—If you said the funniest things, he would only look at you and say, 'Very good!' and you would see that he regards you merely as a part of the show."

"And if you turned furious?"

"The same thing; it would still be a show. You might cut him open under the left breast without hurting him in the least; his internals are of tinned-iron, I am sure. I told him so. He replied, 'I am quite satisfied with that physical constitution.'"

"And always polite. My dear, he wears gloves on his soul. . .

"I shall endure this martyrdom for a few days longer to satisfy my curiosity. But for that, I should have made Philippe slap my lord's cheek—and he has not his match as a swordsman. There is nothing else left for it—"

"I was just going to say so," cried Esther. "But you must ascertain first that Philippe is a boxer; for these old English fellows, my dear, have a depth of malignity—"

"This one has no match on earth. No, if you could but see him asking my commands, to know at what hour he may come—to take me by surprise, of course—and pouring out respectful speeches like a so-called gentleman, you would say, 'Why, he adores her!' and there is not a woman in the world who would not say the same."

"And they envy us, my dear!" exclaimed Esther.

"Ah, well!" sighed Madame du Val-Noble; "in the course of our lives we learn more or less how little men value us. But, my dear, I have never been so cruelly, so deeply, so utterly scorned by brutality as I am by this great skinful of port wine.

"When he is tipsy he goes away—'not to be unpleasant,' as he tells Adele, and not to be 'under two powers at once,' wine and woman. He takes advantage of my carriage; he uses it more than I do.—Oh! if only we could see him under the table to-night! But he can drink ten bottles and only be fuddled; when his eyes are full, he still sees clearly."

"Like people whose windows are dirty outside," said Esther, "but who can see from inside what is going on in the street.—I know that property in man. Du Tillet has it in the highest degree."

"Try to get du Tillet, and if he and Nucingen between them could only catch him in some of their plots, I should at least be revenged. They would bring him to beggary!

"Oh! my dear, to have fallen into the hands of a hypocritical Protestant after that poor Falleix, who was so amusing, so good-natured, so full of chaff! How we used to laugh! They say all stockbrokers are stupid. Well, he, for one, never lacked wit but once—"

"When he left you without a sou? That is what made you acquainted with the unpleasant side of pleasure."

Europe, brought in by Monsieur de Nucingen, put her viperine head in at the door, and after listening to a few words whispered in her ear by her mistress, she vanished.

At half-past eleven that evening, five carriages were stationed in the Rue Saint-Georges before the famous courtesan's door. There was Lucien's, who had brought Rastignac, Bixiou, and Blondet; du

Tillet's, the Baron de Nucingen's, the Nabob's, and Florine's—she was invited by du Tillet. The closed and doubly-shuttered windows were screened by the splendid Chinese silk curtains. Supper was to be served at one; wax-lights were blazing, the dining-room and little drawing-room displayed all their magnificence. The party looked forward to such an orgy as only three such women and such men as these could survive. They began by playing cards, as they had to wait about two hours.

"Do you play, milord?" asked du Tillet to Peyrade.

"I have played with O'connell, Pitt, Fox, Canning, Lord Brougham, Lord—"

"Say at once no end of lords," said Bixiou.

"Lord Fitzwilliam, Lord Ellenborough, Lord Hertford, Lord—"

Bixiou was looking at Peyrade's shoes, and stooped down.

"What are you looking for?" asked Blondet.

"For the spring one must touch to stop this machine," said Florine.

"Do you play for twenty francs a point?"

"I will play for as much as you like to lose."

"He does it well!" said Esther to Lucien. "They all take him for an Englishman."

Du Tillet, Nucingen, Peyrade, and Rastignac sat down to a whist-table; Florine, Madame du Val-Noble, Esther, Blondet, and Bixiou sat round the fire chatting. Lucien spent the time in looking through a book of fine engravings.

"Supper is ready," Paccard presently announced, in magnificent livery.

Peyrade was placed at Florine's left hand, and on the other side of him Bixiou, whom Esther had enjoined to make the Englishman drink freely, and challenge him to beat him. Bixiou had the power of drinking an indefinite quantity.

Never in his life had Peyrade seen such splendor, or tasted of such cookery, or seen such fine women.

"I am getting my money's worth this evening for the thousand crowns la Val-Noble has cost me till now," thought he; "and besides, I have just won a thousand francs."

"This is an example for men to follow!" said Suzanne, who was sitting by Lucien, with a wave of her hand at the splendors of the dining-room.

Esther had placed Lucien next herself, and was holding his foot between her own under the table.

"Do you hear?" said Madame du Val-Noble, addressing Peyrade, who affected blindness. "This is how you ought to furnish a house! When a man brings millions home from India, and wants to do business with the Nucingens, he should place himself on the same level."

"I belong to a Temperance Society!"

"Then you will drink like a fish!" said Bixiou, "for the Indies are uncommon hot, uncle!"

It was Bixiou's jest during supper to treat Peyrade as an uncle of his, returned from India.

"Montame du Fal-Noble tolt me you shall have some iteas," said Nucingen, scrutinizing Peyrade.

"Ah, this is what I wanted to hear," said du Tillet to Rastignac; "the two talking gibberish together."

"You will see, they will understand each other at last," said Bixiou, guessing what du Tillet had said to Rastignac.

"Sir Baronet, I have imagined a speculation—oh! a very comfortable job—bocou profitable and rich in profits—"

"Now you will see," said Blondet to du Tillet, "he will not talk one minute without dragging in the Parliament and the English Government."

"It is in China, in the opium trade—"

"Ja, I know," said Nucingen at once, as a man who is well acquainted with commercial geography. "But de English Gover'ment hafe taken up de opium trate as a means dat shall open up China, and she shall not allow dat ve—"

"Nucingen has cut him out with the Government," remarked du Tillet to Blondet.

"Ah! you have been in the opium trade!" cried Madame du Val-Noble. "Now I understand why you are so narcotic; some has stuck in your soul."

"Dere! you see!" cried the Baron to the self-styled opium merchant, and pointing to Madame du Val-Noble. "You are like me. Never shall a millionaire be able to make a voman lofe him."

"I have loved much and often, milady," replied Peyrade.

"As a result of temperance," said Bixiou, who had just seen Peyrade finish his third bottle of claret, and now had a bottle of port wine uncorked.

"Oh!" cried Peyrade, "it is very fine, the Portugal of England."

Blondet, du Tillet, and Bixiou smiled at each other. Peyrade had the power of travestying everything, even his wit. There are very few Englishmen who will not maintain that gold and silver are better in England than elsewhere. The fowls and eggs exported from Normandy to the London market enable the English to maintain that the poultry and eggs in London are superior (very fine) to those of Paris, which come from the same district.

Esther and Lucien were dumfounded by this perfection of costume, language, and audacity.

They all ate and drank so well and so heartily, while talking and laughing, that it went on till four in the morning. Bixiou flattered himself that he had achieved one of the victories so pleasantly related by Brillat-Savarin. But at the moment when he was saying to himself, as he offered his "uncle" some more wine, "I have vanquished England!" Peyrade replied in good French to this malicious scoffer, "Toujours, mon garcon" (Go it, my boy), which no one heard but Bixiou.

"Hallo, good men all, he is as English as I am!—My uncle is a Gascon! I could have no other!"

Bixiou and Peyrade were alone, so no one heard this announcement. Peyrade rolled off his chair on to the floor. Paccard forthwith picked him up and carried him to an attic, where he fell sound asleep.

At six o'clock next evening, the Nabob was roused by the application of a wet cloth, with which his face was being washed, and awoke to find himself on a camp-bed, face to face with Asie, wearing a mask and a black domino.

"Well, Papa Peyrade, you and I have to settle accounts," said she.

"Where am I?" asked he, looking about him.

"Listen to me," said Asie, "and that will sober you.—Though you do not love Madame du Val-Noble, you love your daughter, I suppose?"

"My daughter?" Peyrade echoed with a roar.

"Yes, Mademoiselle Lydie."

"What then?"

"What then? She is no longer in the Rue des Moineaux; she has been carried off."

Peyrade breathed a sigh like that of a soldier dying of a mortal wound on the battlefield.

"While you were pretending to be an Englishman, some one else was pretending to be Peyrade. Your little Lydie thought she was with her father, and she is now in a safe place.—Oh! you will never find her! unless you undo the mischief you have done."

"What mischief?"

"Yesterday Monsieur Lucien de Rubempre had the door shut in his face at the Duc de Grandlieu's. This is due to your intrigues, and to the man you let loose on us. Do not speak, listen!" Asie went on, seeing Peyrade open his mouth. "You will have your daughter again, pure and spotless," she added, emphasizing her statement by the accent on every word, "only on the day after that on which Monsieur Lucien de Rubempre walks out of Saint-Thomas d'Aquin as the husband of Mademoiselle Clotilde. If, within ten days Lucien de Rubempre is not admitted, as he has been, to the Grandlieus' house, you, to begin with, will die a violent death, and nothing can save you from the fate that threatens you.—Then, when you feel yourself dying, you will have time before breathing your last to reflect, 'My daughter is a prostitute for the rest of her life!'

"Though you have been such a fool as give us this hold for our clutches, you still have sense enough to meditate on this ultimatum from our government. Do not bark, say nothing to any one; go to Contenson's, and change your dress, and then go home. Katt will tell you that at a word from you your little Lydie went downstairs, and has not been seen since. If you make any fuss, if you take any steps, your daughter will begin where I tell you she will end—she is promised to de Marsay.

"With old Canquoelle I need not mince matters, I should think, or wear gloves, heh?—Go on downstairs, and take care not to meddle in our concerns any more."

Asie left Peyrade in a pitiable state; every word had been a blow with a club. The spy had tears in his eyes, and tears hanging from his cheeks at the end of a wet furrow.

"They are waiting dinner for Mr. Johnson," said Europe, putting her head in a moment after.

Peyrade made no reply; he went down, walked till he reached a cabstand, and hurried off to undress at Contenson's, not saying a word to him; he resumed the costume of Pere Canquoelle, and got home by eight o'clock. He mounted the stairs with a beating heart. When the Flemish woman heard her master, she asked him:

"Well, and where is mademoiselle?" with such simplicity, that the old spy was obliged to lean against the wall. The blow was more than he could bear. He went into his daughter's rooms, and ended by fainting with grief when he found them empty, and heard Katt's story, which was that of an abduction as skilfully planned as if he had arranged it himself.

"Well, well," thought he, "I must knock under. I will be revenged later; now I must go to Corentin.—This is the first time we have met our foes. Corentin will leave that handsome boy free to marry an Empress if he wishes!—Yes, I understand that my little girl should have fallen in love with him at first sight.—Oh! that Spanish priest is a knowing one. Courage, friend Peyrade! disgorge your prey!"

The poor father never dreamed of the fearful blow that awaited him.

On reaching Corentin's house, Bruno, the confidential servant, who knew Peyrade, said:

"Monsieur is gone away."

"For a long time?"

"For ten days."

"Where?"

"I don't know.

"Good God, I am losing my wits! I ask him where—as if we ever told them—" thought he.

A few hours before the moment when Peyrade was to be roused in his garret in the Rue Saint-Georges, Corentin, coming in from his country place at Passy, had made his way to the Duc de Grandlieu's, in the costume of a retainer of a superior class. He wore the ribbon of the Legion of Honor at his button-hole. He had made up a withered old face with powdered hair, deep wrinkles, and a colorless skin. His eyes were hidden by tortoise-shell spectacles. He looked like a retired office-clerk. On giving his name as Monsieur de Saint-Denis, he was led to the Duke's private room, where he found Derville reading a letter, which he himself had dictated to one of his agents, the "number" whose business it was to write documents. The Duke took Corentin aside to tell him all he already knew. Monsieur de Saint-Denis listened coldly and respectfully, amusing himself by studying this grand gentleman, by penetrating the tufa beneath the velvet cover, by scrutinizing this being, now and always absorbed in whist and in regard for the House of Grandlieu.

"If you will take my advice, monsieur," said Corentin to Derville, after being duly introduced to the lawyer, "we shall set out this very afternoon for Angouleme by the Bordeaux coach, which goes quite as fast as the mail; and we shall not need to stay there six hours to obtain the information Monsieur le Duc requires. It will be enough—if I have understood your Grace—to ascertain whether Monsieur de Rubempre's sister and brother-in-law are in a position to give him twelve hundred thousand francs?" and he turned to the Duke.

"You have understood me perfectly," said the Duke.

"We can be back again in four days," Corentin went on, addressing Derville, "and neither of us will have neglected his business long enough for it to suffer."

"That was the only difficulty I was about to mention to his Grace," said Derville. "It is now four o'clock. I am going home to say a word to my head-clerk, and pack my traveling-bag, and after dinner, at eight o'clock, I will be—But shall we get places?" he said to Monsieur de Saint-Denis, interrupting himself.

"I will answer for that," said Corentin. "Be in the yard of the Chief Office of the Messageries at eight o'clock. If there are no places, they shall make some, for that is the way to serve Monseigneur le Duc de Grandlieu."

"Gentlemen," said the Duke most graciously, "I postpone my thanks—"

Corentin and the lawyer, taking this as a dismissal, bowed, and withdrew.

At the hour when Peyrade was questioning Corentin's servant, Monsieur de Saint-Denis and Derville, seated in the Bordeaux coach, were studying each other in silence as they drove out of Paris.

Next morning, between Orleans and Tours, Derville, being bored, began to converse, and Corentin condescended to amuse him, but keeping his distance; he left him to believe that he was in the diplomatic service, and was hoping to become Consul-General by the good offices of the Duc de Grandlieu. Two days after leaving Paris, Corentin and Derville got out at Mansle, to the great surprise of the lawyer, who thought he was going to Angouleme.

"In this little town," said Corentin, "we can get the most positive information as regards Madame Sechard."

"Do you know her then?" asked Derville, astonished to find Corentin so well informed.

"I made the conductor talk, finding he was a native of Angouleme. He tells me that Madame Sechard lives at Marsac, and Marsac is but a league away from Mansle. I thought we should be at greater advantage here than at Angouleme for verifying the facts."

"And besides," thought Derville, "as Monsieur le Duc said, I act merely as the witness to the inquiries made by this confidential agent—"

The inn at Mansle, *la Belle Etoile*, had for its landlord one of those fat and burly men whom we fear we may find no more on our return; but who still, ten years after, are seen standing at their door with as much superfluous flesh as ever, in the same linen cap, the same apron, with the same knife, the same oiled hair, the same triple chin,—all stereotyped by novel-writers from the immortal Cervantes to the immortal Walter Scott. Are they not all boastful of their cookery? have they not all "whatever you please to order"? and do not all end by giving you the same hectic chicken, and vegetables cooked with rank butter? They all boast of their fine wines, and all make you drink the wine of the country.

But Corentin, from his earliest youth, had known the art of getting out of an innkeeper things more essential to himself than doubtful dishes and apocryphal wines. So he gave himself out as a man easy to please, and willing to leave himself in the hands of the best cook in Mansle, as he told the fat man.

"There is no difficulty about being the best—I am the only one," said the host.

"Serve us in the side room," said Corentin, winking at Derville. "And do not be afraid of setting the chimney on fire; we want to thaw out the frost in our fingers."

"It was not warm in the coach," said Derville.

"Is it far to Marsac?" asked Corentin of the innkeeper's wife, who came down from the upper regions on hearing that the diligence had dropped two travelers to sleep there.

"Are you going to Marsac, monsieur?" replied the woman.

"I don't know," he said sharply. "Is it far from hence to Marsac?" he repeated, after giving the woman time to notice his red ribbon.

"In a chaise, a matter of half an hour," said the innkeeper's wife.

"Do you think that Monsieur and Madame Sechard are likely to be there in winter?"

"To be sure; they live there all the year round."

"It is now five o'clock. We shall still find them up at nine."

"Oh yes, till ten. They have company every evening—the cure, Monsieur Marron the doctor—"

"Good folks then?" said Derville.

"Oh, the best of good souls," replied the woman, "straight-forward, honest—and not ambitious neither. Monsieur Sechard, though he is very well off—they say he might have made millions if he had not allowed himself to be robbed of an invention in the paper-making of which the brothers Cointet are getting the benefit—"

"Ah, to be sure, the Brothers Cointet!" said Corentin.

"Hold your tongue," said the innkeeper. "What can it matter to these gentlemen whether Monsieur Sechard has a right or no to a patent for his inventions in paper-making?—If you mean to spend the night here—at the *Belle Etoile*—" he went on, addressing the travelers, "here is the book, and please to put your names down. We have an officer in this town who has nothing to do, and spends all his time in nagging at us—"

"The devil!" said Corentin, while Derville entered their names and his profession as attorney to the lower Court in the department of the Seine, "I fancied the Sechards were very rich."

"Some people say they are millionaires," replied the innkeeper. "But as to hindering tongues from wagging, you might as well try to stop the river from flowing. Old Sechard left two hundred thousand francs' worth of landed property, it is said; and that is not amiss for a man who began as a workman. Well, and he may have had as much again in savings, for he made ten or twelve thousand francs out of his land at last. So, supposing he were fool enough not to invest his money for ten years, that would be all told. But even if he lent it at high interest, as he is suspected of doing there would be three hundred thousand francs perhaps, and that is all. Five hundred thousand francs is a long way short of a million. I should be quite content with the difference, and no more of the *Belle Etoile* for me!"

"Really!" said Corentin. "Then Monsieur David Sechard and his wife have not a fortune of two or three millions?"

"Why," exclaimed the innkeeper's wife, "that is what the Cointets are supposed to have, who robbed him of his invention, and he does not get more than twenty thousand francs out of them. Where do you suppose such honest folks would find millions? They were very much pinched while the father was alive. But for Kolb, their manager, and Madame Kolb, who is as much attached to them as her husband, they could scarcely have lived. Why, how much had they with La Verberie!—A thousand francs a year perhaps."

Corentin drew Derville aside and said:

"In vino veritas! Truth lives under a cork. For my part, I regard an inn as the real registry office of the countryside; the notary is not better informed than the innkeeper as to all that goes on in a small neighborhood.—You see! we are supposed to know all about the Cointets and Kolb and the rest.

"Your innkeeper is the living record of every incident; he does the work of the police without suspecting it. A government should maintain two hundred spies at most, for in a country like France there are ten millions of simple-minded informers.—However, we need not trust to this report; though even in this little town something would be known about the twelve hundred thousand francs sunk in paying for the Rubempre estate. We will not stop here long—"

"I hope not!" Derville put in.

"And this is why," added Corentin; "I have hit on the most natural way of extracting the truth from the mouth of the Sechard couple. I rely upon you to support, by your authority as a lawyer, the little trick I shall employ to enable you to hear a clear and complete account of their affairs.—After dinner we shall set out to call on Monsieur Sechard," said Corentin to the innkeeper's wife. "Have beds ready for us, we want separate rooms. There can be no difficulty 'under the stars.'"

"Oh, monsieur," said the woman, "we invented the sign."

"The pun is to be found in every department," said Corentin; "it is no monopoly of yours."

"Dinner is served, gentlemen," said the innkeeper.

"But where the devil can that young fellow have found the money? Is the anonymous writer accurate? Can it be the earnings of some handsome baggage?" said Derville, as they sat down to dinner.

"Ah, that will be the subject of another inquiry," said Corentin. "Lucien de Rubempre, as the Duc de Chaulieu tells me, lives with a converted Jewess, who passes for a Dutch woman, and is called Esther van Bogseck."

"What a strange coincidence!" said the lawyer. "I am hunting for the heiress of a Dutchman named Gobseck—it is the same name with a transposition of consonants."

"Well," said Corentin, "you shall have information as to her parentage on my return to Paris."

An hour later, the two agents for the Grandlieu family set out for La Verberie, where Monsieur and Madame Sechard were living.

Never had Lucien felt any emotion so deep as that which overcame him at La Verberie when comparing his own fate with that of his brother-in-law. The two Parisians were about to witness the same scene that had so much struck Lucien a few days since. Everything spoke of peace and abundance.

At the hour when the two strangers were arriving, a party of four persons were being entertained in the drawing-room of La Verberie:

the cure of Marsac, a young priest of five-and-twenty, who, at Madame Sechard's request, had become tutor to her little boy Lucien; the country doctor, Monsieur Marron; the Maire of the commune; and an old colonel, who grew roses on a plot of land opposite to La Verberie on the other side of the road. Every evening during the winter these persons came to play an artless game of boston for centime points, to borrow the papers, or return those they had finished.

When Monsieur and Madame Sechard had bought La Verberie, a fine house built of stone, and roofed with slate, the pleasure-grounds consisted of a garden of two acres. In the course of time, by devoting her savings to the purpose, handsome Madame Sechard had extended her garden as far as a brook, by cutting down the vines on some ground she purchased, and replacing them with grass plots and clumps of shrubbery. At the present time the house, surrounded by a park of about twenty acres, and enclosed by walls, was considered the most imposing place in the neighborhood.

Old Sechard's former residence, with the outhouses attached, was now used as the dwelling-house for the manager of about twenty acres of vineyard left by him, of five farmsteads, bringing in about six thousand francs a year, and ten acres of meadow land lying on the further side of the stream, exactly opposite the little park; indeed, Madame Sechard hoped to include them in it the next year. La Verberie was already spoken of in the neighborhood as a chateau, and Eve Sechard was known as the Lady of Marsac. Lucien, while flattering her vanity, had only followed the example of the peasants and vine-dressers. Courtois, the owner of the mill, very picturesquely situated a few hundred yards from the meadows of La Verberie, was in treaty, it was said, with Madame Sechard for the sale of his property; and this acquisition would give the finishing touch to the estate and the rank of a "place" in the department.

Madame Sechard, who did a great deal of good, with as much judgment as generosity, was equally esteemed and loved. Her beauty, now really splendid, was at the height of its bloom. She was about six-and-twenty, but had preserved all the freshness of youth from living in the tranquillity and abundance of a country life. Still much in love with her husband, she respected him as a clever man, who was modest enough to renounce the display of fame; in short, to complete her portrait, it is enough to say that in her whole existence she had never felt a throb of her heart that was not inspired by her husband or her children.

The tax paid to grief by this happy household was, as may be supposed, the deep anxiety caused by Lucien's career, in which Eve Sechard suspected mysteries, which she dreaded all the more because, during his last visit, Lucien roughly cut short all his sister's questions by saying that an ambitious man owed no account of his proceedings to any one but himself.

In six years Lucien had seen his sister but three times, and had not written her more than six letters. His first visit to La Verberie had been on the occasion of his mother's death; and his last had been paid with a view to asking the favor of the lie which was so necessary to his advancement. This gave rise to a very serious scene between Monsieur and Madame Sechard and their brother, and left their happy and respected life troubled by the most terrible suspicions.

The interior of the house, as much altered as the surroundings, was comfortable without luxury, as will be understood by a glance round the room where the little party were now assembled. A pretty Aubusson carpet, hangings of gray cotton twill bound with green silk brocade, the woodwork painted to imitate Spa wood, carved mahogany furniture covered with gray woolen stuff and green gimp, with flower-stands, gay with flowers in spite of the time of year, presented a very pleasing and homelike aspect. The window curtains, of green brocade, the chimney ornaments, and the mirror frames were untainted by the bad taste that spoils everything in the provinces; and the smallest details, all elegant and appropriate, gave the mind and eye a sense of repose and of poetry which a clever and loving woman can and ought to infuse into her home.

Madame Sechard, still in mourning for her father, sat by the fire working at some large piece of tapestry with the help of Madame Kolb, the housekeeper, to whom she intrusted all the minor cares of the household.

"A chaise has stopped at the door!" said Courtois, hearing the sound of wheels outside; "and to judge by the clatter of metal, it belongs to these parts—"

"Postel and his wife have come to see us, no doubt," said the doctor.

"No," said Courtois, "the chaise has come from Mansle."

"Montame," said Kolb, the burly Alsatian we have made acquaintance with in a former volume (*Illusions perdues*), "here is a lawyer from Paris who wants to speak with monsieur."

"A lawyer!" cried Sechard; "the very word gives me the colic!"

"Thank you!" said the Maire of Marsac, named Cachan, who for twenty years had been an attorney at Angouleme, and who had once been required to prosecute Sechard.

"My poor David will never improve; he will always be absent-minded!" said Eve, smiling.

"A lawyer from Paris," said Courtois. "Have you any business in Paris?"

"No," said Eve.

"But you have a brother there," observed Courtois.

"Take care lest he should have anything to say about old Sechard's estate," said Cachan. "*He* had his finger in some very queer concerns, worthy man!"

Corentin and Derville, on entering the room, after bowing to the company, and giving their names, begged to have a private interview with Monsieur and Madame Sechard.

"By all means," said Sechard. "But is it a matter of business?"

"Solely a matter regarding your father's property," said Corentin.

"Then I beg you will allow monsieur—the Maire, a lawyer formerly at Angouleme—to be present also."

"Are you Monsieur Derville?" said Cachan, addressing Corentin.

"No, monsieur, this is Monsieur Derville," replied Corentin, introducing the lawyer, who bowed.

"But," said Sechard, "we are, so to speak, a family party; we have no secrets from our neighbors; there is no need to retire to my study, where there is no fire—our life is in the sight of all men—"

"But your father's," said Corentin, "was involved in certain mysteries which perhaps you would rather not make public."

"Is it anything we need blush for?" said Eve, in alarm.

"Oh, no! a sin of his youth," said Corentin, coldly setting one of his mouse-traps. "Monsieur, your father left an elder son—"

"Oh, the old rascal!" cried Courtois. "He was never very fond of you, Monsieur Sechard, and he kept that secret from you, the deep old dog!—Now I understand what he meant when he used to say to me, 'You shall see what you shall see when I am under the turf.'"

"Do not be dismayed, monsieur," said Corentin to Sechard, while he watched Eve out of the corner of his eye.

"A brother!" exclaimed the doctor. "Then your inheritance is divided into two!"

Derville was affecting to examine the fine engravings, proofs before letters, which hung on the drawing-room walls.

"Do not be dismayed, madame," Corentin went on, seeing amazement written on Madame Sechard's handsome features, "it is only a natural son. The rights of a natural son are not the same as those of a legitimate child. This man is in the depths of poverty, and he has a right to a certain sum calculated on the amount of the estate. The millions left by your father—"

At the word millions there was a perfectly unanimous cry from all the persons present. And now Derville ceased to study the prints.

"Old Sechard?—Millions?" said Courtois. "Who on earth told you that? Some peasant—"

"Monsieur," said Cachan, "you are not attached to the Treasury? You may be told all the facts—"

"Be quite easy," said Corentin, "I give you my word of honor I am not employed by the Treasury."

Cachan, who had just signed to everybody to say nothing, gave expression to his satisfaction.

"Monsieur," Corentin went on, "if the whole estate were but a million, a natural child's share would still be something considerable. But we have not come to threaten a lawsuit; on the contrary, our purpose is to propose that you should hand over one hundred thousand francs, and we will depart—"

"One hundred thousand francs!" cried Cachan, interrupting him. "But, monsieur, old Sechard left twenty acres of vineyard, five small farms, ten acres of meadowland here, and not a sou besides—"

"Nothing on earth," cried David Sechard, "would induce me to tell a lie, and less to a question of money than on any other.—Monsieur," he said, turning to Corentin and Derville, "my father left us, besides the land—"

Courtois and Cachan signaled in vain to Sechard; he went on:

"Three hundred thousand francs, which raises the whole estate to about five hundred thousand francs."

"Monsieur Cachan," asked Eve Sechard, "what proportion does the law allot to a natural child?"

"Madame," said Corentin, "we are not Turks; we only require you to swear before these gentlemen that you did not inherit more than five hundred thousand francs from your father-in-law, and we can come to an understanding."

"First give me your word of honor that you really are a lawyer," said Cachan to Derville.

"Here is my passport," replied Derville, handing him a paper folded in four; "and monsieur is not, as you might suppose, an inspector from the Treasury, so be easy," he added. "We had an important reason for wanting to know the truth as to the Sechard estate, and we now know it."

Derville took Madame Sechard's hand and led her very courteously to the further end of the room.

"Madame," said he, in a low voice, "if it were not that the honor and future prospects of the house of Grandlieu are implicated in this affair, I would never have lent myself to the stratagem devised by this gentleman of the red ribbon. But you must forgive him; it was necessary to detect the falsehood by means of which your brother has stolen a march on the beliefs of that ancient family. Beware now of allowing it to be supposed that you have given your brother twelve hundred thousand francs to repurchase the Rubempre estates—"

"Twelve hundred thousand francs!" cried Madame Sechard, turning pale. "Where did he get them, wretched boy?"

"Ah! that is the question," replied Derville. "I fear that the source of his wealth is far from pure."

The tears rose to Eve's eyes, as her neighbors could see.

"We have, perhaps, done you a great service by saving you from abetting a falsehood of which the results may be positively dangerous," the lawyer went on.

Derville left Madame Sechard sitting pale and dejected with tears on her cheeks, and bowed to the company.

"To Mansle!" said Corentin to the little boy who drove the chaise.

There was but one vacant place in the diligence from Bordeaux to Paris; Derville begged Corentin to allow him to take it, urging a press of business; but in his soul he was distrustful of his traveling companion, whose diplomatic dexterity and coolness struck him as being the result of practice. Corentin remained three days longer at Mansle, unable to get away; he was obliged to secure a place in the Paris coach by writing to Bordeaux, and did not get back till nine days after leaving home.

Peyrade, meanwhile, had called every morning, either at Passy or in Paris, to inquire whether Corentin had returned. On the eighth day he left at each house a note, written in their peculiar cipher, to explain to his friend what death hung over him, and to tell him of Lydie's abduction and the horrible end to which his enemies had devoted them. Peyrade, bereft of Corentin, but seconded by Contenson, still kept up his disguise as a nabob. Even though his invisible foes had discovered him, he very wisely reflected that he might glean some light on the matter by remaining on the field of the contest.

Contenson had brought all his experience into play in his search for Lydie, and hoped to discover in what house she was hidden; but as the days went by, the impossibility, absolutely demonstrated, of tracing the slightest clue, added, hour by hour, to Peyrade's despair. The old spy had a sort of guard about him of twelve or fifteen of the most experienced detectives. They watched the neighborhood of the Rue des Moineaux and the Rue Taitbout—where he lived, as a nabob, with Madame du Val-Noble. During the last three days of the term granted by Asie to reinstate Lucien on his old footing in the Hotel de Grandlieu, Contenson never left the veteran of the old general police office. And the poetic terror shed throughout the forests of America by the arts of inimical and warring tribes, of which Cooper made such good use in his novels, was here associated with the petty details of Paris life. The foot-passengers, the shops, the hackney cabs, a figure standing at a window,—everything had to the human ciphers to whom old Peyrade had intrusted his safety the thrilling interest which attaches in Cooper's romances to a beaver-village, a rock, a bison-robe, a floating canoe, a weed straggling over the water.

"If the Spaniard has gone away, you have nothing to fear," said Contenson to Peyrade, remarking on the perfect peace they lived in.

"But if he is not gone?" observed Peyrade.

"He took one of my men at the back of the chaise; but at Blois, my man having to get down, could not catch the chaise up again."

FIVE DAYS AFTER DERVILLE'S RETURN, Lucien one morning had a call from Rastignac.

"I am in despair, my dear boy," said his visitor, "at finding myself compelled to deliver a message which is intrusted to me because we are known to be intimate. Your marriage is broken off beyond all hope of reconciliation. Never set foot again in the Hotel de Grandlieu. To marry Clotilde you must wait till her father dies, and he is too selfish to die yet awhile. Old whist-players sit at table—the card-table—very late.

"Clotilde is setting out for Italy with Madeleine de Lenoncourt-Chaulieu. The poor girl is so madly in love with you, my dear fellow, that they have to keep an eye on her; she was bent on coming to see you, and had plotted an escape. That may comfort you in misfortune!"

Lucien made no reply; he sat gazing at Rastignac.

"And is it a misfortune, after all?" his friend went on. "You will easily find a girl as well born and better looking than Clotilde! Madame de Serizy will find you a wife out of spite; she cannot endure the Grandlieus, who never would have anything to say to her. She has a niece, little Clemence du Rouvre—"

"My dear boy," said Lucien at length, "since that supper I am not on terms with Madame de Serizy—she saw me in Esther's box and made a scene—and I left her to herself."

"A woman of forty does not long keep up a quarrel with so handsome a man as you are," said Rastignac. "I know something of these sunsets.— It lasts ten minutes in the sky, and ten years in a woman's heart."

"I have waited a week to hear from her."

"Go and call."

"Yes, I must now."

"Are you coming at any rate to the Val-Noble's? Her nabob is returning the supper given by Nucingen."

"I am asked, and I shall go," said Lucien gravely.

The day after this confirmation of his disaster, which Carlos heard of at once from Asie, Lucien went to the Rue Taitbout with Rastignac and Nucingen.

At midnight nearly all the personages of this drama were assembled in the dining-room that had formerly been Esther's—a drama of which the interest lay hidden under the very bed of these tumultuous lives, and was known only to Esther, to Lucien, to Peyrade, to Contenson, the mulatto, and to Paccard, who attended his mistress. Asie, without its being known to Contenson and Peyrade, had been asked by Madame du Val-Noble to come and help her cook.

As they sat down to table, Peyrade, who had given Madame du Val-Noble five hundred francs that the thing might be well done, found under his napkin a scrap of paper on which these words were written in pencil, "The ten days are up at the moment when you sit down to supper."

Peyrade handed the paper to Contenson, who was standing behind him, saying in English:

"Did you put my name here?"

Contenson read by the light of the wax-candles this "Mene, Tekel, Upharsin," and slipped the scrap into his pocket; but he knew how difficult it is to verify a handwriting in pencil, and, above all, a sentence written in Roman capitals, that is to say, with mathematical lines, since capital letters are wholly made up of straight lines and curves, in which it is impossible to detect any trick of the hand, as in what is called running-hand.

The supper was absolutely devoid of spirit. Peyrade was visibly absent-minded. Of the men about town who give life to a supper, only Rastignac and Lucien were present. Lucien was gloomy and absorbed in thought; Rastignac, who had lost two thousand francs before supper, ate and drank with the hope of recovering them later. The three women, stricken by this chill, looked at each other. Dulness deprived the dishes of all relish. Suppers, like plays and books, have their good and bad luck.

At the end of the meal ices were served, of the kind called plombieres. As everybody knows, this kind of dessert has delicate preserved fruits laid on the top of the ice, which is served in a little glass, not heaped above the rim. These ices had been ordered by Madame du Val-Noble of Tortoni, whose shop is at the corner of the Rue Taitbout and the Boulevard.

The cook called Contenson out of the room to pay the bill.

Contenson, who thought this demand on the part of the shop-boy rather strange, went downstairs and startled him by saying:

"Then you have not come from Tortoni's?" and then went straight upstairs again.

Paccard had meanwhile handed the ices to the company in his absence. The mulatto had hardly reached the door when one of the police constables who had kept watch in the Rue des Moineaux called up the stairs:

"Number twenty-seven."

"What's up?" replied Contenson, flying down again.

"Tell Papa that his daughter has come home; but, good God! in what a state. Tell him to come at once; she is dying."

At the moment when Contenson re-entered the dining-room, old Peyrade, who had drunk a great deal, was swallowing the cherry off his ice. They were drinking to the health of Madame du Val-Noble; the nabob filled his glass with Constantia and emptied it.

In spite of his distress at the news he had to give Peyrade, Contenson was struck by the eager attention with which Paccard was looking at the nabob. His eyes sparkled like two fixed flames. Although it seemed important, still this could not delay the mulatto, who leaned over his master, just as Peyrade set his glass down.

"Lydie is at home," said Contenson, "in a very bad state."

Peyrade rattled out the most French of all French oaths with such a strong Southern accent that all the guests looked up in amazement. Peyrade, discovering his blunder, acknowledged his disguise by saying to Contenson in good French:

"Find me a coach—I'm off."

Every one rose.

"Why, who are you?" said Lucien.

"Ja—who?" said the Baron.

"Bixiou told me you shammed Englishman better than he could, and I would not believe him," said Rastignac.

"Some bankrupt caught in disguise," said du Tillet loudly. "I suspected as much!"

"A strange place is Paris!" said Madame du Val-Noble. "After being bankrupt in his own part of town, a merchant turns up as a nabob or a dandy in the Champs-Elysees with impunity!—Oh! I am unlucky! bankrupts are my bane."

"Every flower has its peculiar blight!" said Esther quietly. "Mine is like Cleopatra's—an asp."

"Who am I?" echoed Peyrade from the door. "You will know ere long; for if I die, I will rise from my grave to clutch your feet every night!"

He looked at Esther and Lucien as he spoke, then he took advantage of the general dismay to vanish with the utmost rapidity, meaning to run home without waiting for the coach. In the street the spy was gripped by the arm as he crossed the threshold of the outer gate. It was Asie, wrapped in a black hood such as ladies then wore on leaving a ball.

"Send for the Sacraments, Papa Peyrade," said she, in the voice that had already prophesied ill.

A coach was waiting. Asie jumped in, and the carriage vanished as though the wind had swept it away. There were five carriages waiting; Peyrade's men could find out nothing.

On reaching his house in the Rue des Vignes, one of the quietest and prettiest nooks of the little town of Passy, Corentin, who was known there as a retired merchant passionately devoted to gardening, found his friend Peyrade's note in cipher. Instead of resting, he got into the hackney coach that had brought him thither, and was driven to the Rue des Moineaux, where he found only Katt. From her he heard of Lydie's disappearance, and remained astounded at Peyrade's and his own want of foresight.

"But they do not know me yet," said he to himself. "This crew is capable of anything; I must find out if they are killing Peyrade; for if so, I must not be seen any more—"

The viler a man's life is, the more he clings to it; it becomes at every moment a protest and a revenge.

Corentin went back to the cab, and drove to his rooms to assume the disguise of a feeble old man, in a scanty greenish overcoat and a tow wig. Then he returned on foot, prompted by his friendship for Peyrade. He intended to give instructions to his most devoted and cleverest underlings.

As he went along the Rue Saint-Honore to reach the Rue Saint-Roch from the Place Vendome, he came up behind a girl in slippers, and dressed as a woman dresses for the night. She had on a white bed-jacket and a nightcap, and from time to time gave vent to a sob and an involuntary groan. Corentin out-paced her, and turning round, recognized Lydie.

"I am a friend of your father's, of Monsieur Canquoelle's," said he in his natural voice.

"Ah! then here is some one I can trust!" said she.

"Do not seem to have recognized me," Corentin went on, "for we are pursued by relentless foes, and are obliged to disguise ourselves. But tell me what has befallen you?"

"Oh, monsieur," said the poor child, "the facts but not the story can be told—I am ruined, lost, and I do not know how—"

"Where have you come from?"

"I don't know, monsieur. I fled with such precipitancy, I have come through so many streets, round so many turnings, fancying I was being followed. And when I met any one that seemed decent, I asked my way to get back to the Boulevards, so as to find the Rue de la Paix. And at last, after walking—What o'clock is it, monsieur?"

"Half-past eleven," said Corentin.

"I escaped at nightfall," said Lydie. "I have been walking for five hours."

"Well, come along; you can rest now; you will find your good Katt."

"Oh, monsieur, there is no rest for me! I only want to rest in the grave, and I will go and wait for death in a convent if I am worthy to be admitted—"

"Poor little girl!—But you struggled?"

"Oh yes! Oh! if you could only imagine the abject creatures they placed me with—!"

"They sent you to sleep, no doubt?"

"Ah! that is it" cried poor Lydie. "A little more strength and I should be at home. I feel that I am dropping, and my brain is not quite clear.—Just now I fancied I was in a garden—"

Corentin took Lydie in his arms, and she lost consciousness; he carried her upstairs.

"Katt!" he called.

Katt came out with exclamations of joy.

"Don't be in too great a hurry to be glad!" said Corentin gravely; "the girl is very ill."

When Lydie was laid on her bed and recognized her own room by the light of two candles that Katt lighted, she became delirious. She sang scraps of pretty airs, broken by vociferations of horrible sentences she had heard. Her pretty face was mottled with purple patches. She mixed up the reminiscences of her pure childhood with those of these ten days of infamy. Katt sat weeping; Corentin paced the room, stopping now and again to gaze at Lydie.

"She is paying her father's debt," said he. "Is there a Providence above? Oh, I was wise not to have a family. On my word of honor, a child is indeed a hostage given to misfortune, as some philosopher has said."

"Oh!" cried the poor child, sitting up in bed and throwing back her fine long hair, "instead of lying here, Katt, I ought to be stretched in the sand at the bottom of the Seine!"

"Katt, instead of crying and looking at your child, which will never cure her, you ought to go for a doctor; the medical officer in the first instance, and then Monsieur Desplein and Monsieur Bianchon—We must save this innocent creature."

And Corentin wrote down the addresses of these two famous physicians.

At this moment, up the stairs came some one to whom they were familiar, and the door was opened. Peyrade, in a violent sweat, his face purple, his eyes almost blood-stained, and gasping like a dolphin, rushed from the outer door to Lydie's room, exclaiming:

"Where is my child?"

He saw a melancholy sign from Corentin, and his eyes followed his friend's hand. Lydie's condition can only be compared to that of a flower tenderly cherished by a gardener, now fallen from its stem, and crushed by the iron-clamped shoes of some peasant. Ascribe this simile to a father's heart, and you will understand the blow that fell on Peyrade; the tears started to his eyes.

"You are crying!—It is my father!" said the girl.

She could still recognize her father; she got out of bed and fell on her knees at the old man's side as he sank into a chair.

"Forgive me, papa," said she in a tone that pierced Peyrade's heart, and at the same moment he was conscious of what felt like a tremendous blow on his head.

"I am dying!—the villains!" were his last words.

Corentin tried to help his friend, and received his latest breath.

"Dead! Poisoned!" said he to himself. "Ah! here is the doctor!" he exclaimed, hearing the sound of wheels.

Contenson, who came with his mulatto disguise removed, stood like a bronze statue as he heard Lydie say:

"Then you do not forgive me, father?—But it was not my fault!"

She did not understand that her father was dead.

"Oh, how he stares at me!" cried the poor crazy girl.

"We must close his eyes," said Contenson, lifting Peyrade on to the bed.

"We are doing a stupid thing," said Corentin. "Let us carry him into his own room. His daughter is half demented, and she will go quite mad when she sees that he is dead; she will fancy that she has killed him."

Lydie, seeing them carry away her father, looked quite stupefied.

"There lies my only friend!" said Corentin, seeming much moved when Peyrade was laid out on the bed in his own room. "In all his life he never had but one impulse of cupidity, and that was for his daughter!—Let him be an example to you, Contenson. Every line of life has its code of honor. Peyrade did wrong when he mixed himself up with private concerns; we have no business to meddle with any but public cases.

"But come what may, I swear," said he with a voice, an emphasis, a look that struck horror into Contenson, "to avenge my poor Peyrade! I will discover the men who are guilty of his death and of his daughter's ruin. And as sure as I am myself, as I have yet a few days to live, which I will risk to accomplish that vengeance, every man of them shall die at four o'clock, in good health, by a clean shave on the Place de Greve."

"And I will help you," said Contenson with feeling.

Nothing, in fact, is more heart-stirring than the spectacle of passion in a cold, self-contained, and methodical man, in whom, for twenty years, no one has ever detected the smallest impulse of sentiment. It is like a molten bar of iron which melts everything it touches. And Contenson was moved to his depths.

"Poor old Canquoelle!" said he, looking at Corentin. "He has treated me many a time.—And, I tell you, only your bad sort know how to do such things—but often has he given me ten francs to go and gamble with. . ."

After this funeral oration, Peyrade's two avengers went back to Lydie's room, hearing Katt and the medical officer from the Mairie on the stairs.

"Go and fetch the Chief of Police," said Corentin. "The public prosecutor will not find grounds for a prosecution in the case; still, we will report it to the Prefecture; it may, perhaps, be of some use.

"Monsieur," he went on to the medical officer, "in this room you will see a dead man. I do not believe that he died from natural causes; you will be good enough to make a post-mortem in the presence of the Chief of the Police, who will come at my request. Try to discover some traces of poison. You will, in a few minutes, have the opinion of Monsieur Desplein and Monsieur Bianchon, for whom I have sent to examine the daughter of my best friend; she is in a worse plight than he, though he is dead."

"I have no need of those gentlemen's assistance in the exercise of my duty," said the medical officer.

"Well, well," thought Corentin. "Let us have no clashing, monsieur," he said. "In a few words I give you my opinion—Those who have just murdered the father have also ruined the daughter."

By daylight Lydie had yielded to fatigue; when the great surgeon and the young physician arrived she was asleep.

The doctor, whose duty it was to sign the death certificate, had now opened Peyrade's body, and was seeking the cause of death.

"While waiting for your patient to awake," said Corentin to the two famous doctors, "would you join one of your professional brethren in an examination which cannot fail to interest you, and your opinion will be valuable in case of an inquiry."

"Your relations died of apoplexy," said the official. "There are all the symptoms of violent congestion of the brain."

"Examine him, gentlemen, and see if there is no poison capable of producing similar symptoms."

"The stomach is, in fact, full of food substances; but short of chemical analysis, I find no evidence of poison.

"If the characters of cerebral congestion are well ascertained, we have here, considering the patient's age, a sufficient cause of death," observed Desplein, looking at the enormous mass of material.

"Did he sup here?" asked Bianchon.

"No," said Corentin; "he came here in great haste from the Boulevard, and found his daughter ruined—"

"That was the poison if he loved his daughter," said Bianchon.

"What known poison could produce a similar effect?" asked Corentin, clinging to his idea.

"There is but one," said Desplein, after a careful examination. "It is a poison found in the Malayan Archipelago, and derived from trees, as yet but little known, of the strychnos family; it is used to poison that dangerous weapon, the Malay kris.—At least, so it is reported."

The Police Commissioner presently arrived; Corentin told him his suspicions, and begged him to draw up a report, telling him where and with whom Peyrade had supped, and the causes of the state in which he found Lydie.

Corentin then went to Lydie's rooms; Desplein and Bianchon had been examining the poor child. He met them at the door.

"Well, gentlemen?" asked Corentin.

"Place the girl under medical care; unless she recovers her wits when her child is born—if indeed she should have a child—she will end her days melancholy-mad. There is no hope of a cure but in the maternal instinct, if it can be aroused."

Corentin paid each of the physicians forty francs in gold, and then turned to the Police Commissioner, who had pulled him by the sleeve.

"The medical officer insists on it that death was natural," said this functionary, "and I can hardly report the case, especially as the dead man was old Canquoelle; he had his finger in too many pies, and we should not be sure whom we might run foul of. Men like that die to order very often—"

"And my name is Corentin," said Corentin in the man's ear.

The Commissioner started with surprise.

"So just make a note of all this," Corentin went on; "it will be very useful by and by; send it up only as confidential information. The crime cannot be proved, and I know that any inquiry would be checked at the very outset.—But I will catch the criminals some day yet. I will watch them and take them red-handed."

The police official bowed to Corentin and left.

"Monsieur," said Katt. "Mademoiselle does nothing but dance and sing. What can I do?"

"Has any change occurred then?"

"She has understood that her father is just dead."

"Put her into a hackney coach, and simply take her to Charenton; I will write a note to the Commissioner-General of Police to secure her being suitably provided for.—The daughter in Charenton, the father in a pauper's grave!" said Corentin—"Contenson, go and fetch the parish hearse. And now, Don Carlos Herrera, you and I will fight it out!"

"Carlos?" said Contenson, "he is in Spain."

"He is in Paris," said Corentin positively. "There is a touch of Spanish genius of the Philip II type in all this; but I have pitfalls for everybody, even for kings."

FIVE DAYS AFTER THE NABOB's disappearance, Madame du Val-Noble was sitting by Esther's bedside weeping, for she felt herself on one of the slopes down to poverty.

"If I only had at least a hundred louis a year! With that sum, my dear, a woman can retire to some little town and find a husband—"

"I can get you as much as that," said Esther.

"How?" cried Madame du Val-Noble.

"Oh, in a very simple way. Listen. You must plan to kill yourself; play your part well. Send for Asie and offer her ten thousand francs for two black beads of very thin glass containing a poison which kills you in a second. Bring them to me, and I will give you fifty thousand francs for them."

"Why do you not ask her for them yourself?" said her friend.

"Asie would not sell them to me."

"They are not for yourself?" asked Madame du Val-Noble.

"Perhaps."

"You! who live in the midst of pleasure and luxury, in a house of your own? And on the eve of an entertainment which will be the talk of Paris for ten years—which is to cost Nucingen twenty thousand francs! There are to be strawberries in mid-February, they say, asparagus, grapes, melons!—and a thousand crowns' worth of flowers in the rooms."

"What are you talking about? There are a thousand crowns' worth of roses on the stairs alone."

"And your gown is said to have cost ten thousand francs?"

"Yes, it is of Brussels point, and Delphine, his wife, is furious. But I had a fancy to be disguised as a bride."

"Where are the ten thousand francs?" asked Madame du Val-Noble.

"It is all the ready money I have," said Esther, smiling. "Open my table drawer; it is under the curl-papers."

"People who talk of dying never kill themselves," said Madame du Val-Noble. "If it were to commit—"

"A crime? For shame!" said Esther, finishing her friend's thought, as she hesitated. "Be quite easy, I have no intention of killing anybody. I had a friend—a very happy woman; she is dead, I must follow her—that is all."

"How foolish!"

"How can I help it? I promised her I would."

"I should let that bill go dishonored," said her friend, smiling.

"Do as I tell you, and go at once. I hear a carriage coming. It is Nucingen, a man who will go mad with joy! Yes, he loves me!—Why do we not love those who love us, for indeed they do all they can to please us?"

"Ah, that is the question!" said Madame du Val-Noble. "It is the old story of the herring, which is the most puzzling fish that swims."

"Why?"

"Well, no one could ever find out."

"Get along, my dear!—I must ask for your fifty thousand francs."

"Good-bye then."

For three days past, Esther's ways with the Baron de Nucingen had completely changed. The monkey had become a cat, the cat had become a woman. Esther poured out treasures of affection on the old man; she was quite charming. Her way of addressing him, with a total absence of mischief or bitterness, and all sorts of tender insinuation, had carried conviction to the banker's slow wit; she called him Fritz, and he believed that she loved him.

"My poor Fritz, I have tried you sorely," said she. "I have teased you shamefully. Your patience has been sublime. You loved me, I see, and I will reward you. I like you now, I do not know how it is, but I should prefer you to a young man. It is the result of experience perhaps.—In the long run we discover at last that pleasure is the coin of the soul; and it is not more flattering to be loved for the sake of pleasure than it is to be loved for the sake of money.

"Besides, young men are too selfish; they think more of themselves than of us; while you, now, think only of me. I am all your life to you. And I will take nothing more from you. I want to prove to you how disinterested I am."

"Vy, I hafe gifen you notink," cried the Baron, enchanted. "I propose to gife you to-morrow tirty tousant francs a year in a Government bond. Dat is mein vedding gift."

Esther kissed the Baron so sweetly that he turned pale without any pills.

"Oh!" cried she, "do not suppose that I am sweet to you only for your thirty thousand francs! It is because—now—I love you, my good, fat Frederic."

"Ach, mein Gott! Vy hafe you kept me vaiting? I might hafe been so happy all dese tree monts."

"In three or in five per cents, my pet?" said Esther, passing her fingers through Nucingen's hair, and arranging it in a fashion of her own.

"In trees—I hat a quantity."

So next morning the Baron brought the certificate of shares; he came to breakfast with his dear little girl, and to take her orders for the following evening, the famous Saturday, the great day!

"Here, my little vife, my only vife," said the banker gleefully, his face radiant with happiness. "Here is enough money to pay for your keep for de rest of your days."

Esther took the paper without the slightest excitement, folded it up, and put it in her dressing-table drawer.

"So now you are quite happy, you monster of iniquity!" said she, giving Nucingen a little slap on the cheek, "now that I have at last accepted a present from you. I can no longer tell you home-truths, for I share the fruit of what you call your labors. This is not a gift, my poor old boy, it is restitution.—Come, do not put on your Bourse face. You know that I love you."

"My lofely Esther, mein anchel of lofe," said the banker, "do not speak to me like dat. I tell you, I should not care ven all de vorld took me for a tief, if you should tink me ein honest man.—I lofe you every day more and more."

"That is my intention," said Esther. "And I will never again say anything to distress you, my pet elephant, for you are grown as artless as a baby. Bless me, you old rascal, you have never known any innocence; the allowance bestowed on you when you came into the world was bound to come to the top some day; but it was buried so deep that it is only now reappearing at the age of sixty-six. Fished up by love's barbed hook.—This phenomenon is seen in old men.

"And this is why I have learned to love you, you are young—so young! No one but I would ever have known this, Frederic—I alone. For you were a banker at fifteen; even at college you must have lent your school-fellows one marble on condition of their returning two."

Seeing him laugh, she sprang on to his knee.

"Well, you must do as you please! Bless me! plunder the men—go ahead, and I will help. Men are not worth loving; Napoleon killed them off like flies. Whether they pay taxes to you or to the Government, what difference does it make to them? You don't make love over the budget, and on my honor!—go ahead, I have thought it over, and you are right. Shear the sheep! you will find it in the gospel according to Beranger.

"Now, kiss your Esther.—I say, you will give that poor Val-Noble all the furniture in the Rue Taitbout? And to-morrow I wish you would give her fifty thousand francs—it would look handsome, my duck. You see, you killed Falleix; people are beginning to cry out upon you, and this liberality will look Babylonian—all the women will talk about it! Oh! there will be no one in Paris so grand, so noble as you; and as the world is constituted, Falleix will be forgotten. So, after all, it will be money deposited at interest."

"You are right, mein anchel; you know the vorld," he replied. "You shall be mein adfiser."

"Well, you see," said Esther, "how I study my man's interest, his position and honor.—Go at once and bring those fifty thousand francs."

She wanted to get rid of Monsieur de Nucingen so as to get a stockbroker to sell the bond that very afternoon.

"But vy dis minute?" asked he.

"Bless me, my sweetheart, you must give it to her in a little satin box wrapped round a fan. You must say, 'Here, madame, is a fan which I hope may be to your taste.'—You are supposed to be a Turcaret, and you will become a Beaujon."

"Charming, charming!" cried the Baron. "I shall be so clever henceforth.—Yes, I shall repeat your vorts."

Just as Esther had sat down, tired with the effort of playing her part, Europe came in.

"Madame," said she, "here is a messenger sent from the Quai Malaquais by Celestin, M. Lucien's servant—"

"Bring him in—no, I will go into the ante-room."

"He has a letter for you, madame, from Celestin."

Esther rushed into the ante-room, looked at the messenger, and saw that he looked like the genuine thing.

"Tell *him* to come down," said Esther, in a feeble voice and dropping into a chair after reading the letter. "Lucien means to kill himself," she added in a whisper to Europe. "No, take the letter up to him."

Carlos Herrera, still in his disguise as a bagman, came downstairs at once, and keenly scrutinized the messenger on seeing a stranger in the ante-room.

"You said there was no one here," said he in a whisper to Europe.

And with an excess of prudence, after looking at the messenger, he went straight into the drawing-room. *Trompe-la-Mort* did not know that for some time past the famous constable of the detective force who had arrested him at the Maison Vauquer had a rival, who, it was supposed, would replace him. This rival was the messenger.

"They are right," said the sham messenger to Contenson, who was waiting for him in the street. "The man you describe is in the house; but he is not a Spaniard, and I will burn my hand off if there is not a bird for our net under that priest's gown."

"He is no more a priest than he is a Spaniard," said Contenson.

"I am sure of that," said the detective.

"Oh, if only we were right!" said Contenson.

Lucien had been away for two days, and advantage had been taken of his absence to lay this snare, but he returned this evening, and the courtesan's anxieties were allayed. Next morning, at the hour when Esther, having taken a bath, was getting into bed again, Madame du Val-Noble arrived.

"I have the two pills!" said her friend.

"Let me see," said Esther, raising herself with her pretty elbow buried in a pillow trimmed with lace.

Madame du Val-Noble held out to her what looked like two black currants.

The Baron had given Esther a pair of greyhounds of famous pedigree, which will be always known by the name of the great contemporary poet who made them fashionable; and Esther, proud of owning them, had called them by the names of their parents, Romeo and Juliet. No need here to describe the whiteness and grace of these beasts, trained for the drawing-room, with manners suggestive of English propriety. Esther called Romeo; Romeo ran up on legs so supple and thin, so strong and sinewy, that they seemed like steel springs, and looked up at his mistress. Esther, to attract his attention, pretended to throw one of the pills.

"He is doomed by his nature to die thus," said she, as she threw the pill, which Romeo crushed between his teeth.

The dog made no sound, he rolled over, and was stark dead. It was all over while Esther spoke these words of epitaph.

"Good God!" shrieked Madame du Val-Noble.

"You have a cab waiting. Carry away the departed Romeo," said Esther. "His death would make a commotion here. I have given him to you, and you have lost him—advertise for him. Make haste; you will have your fifty thousand francs this evening."

She spoke so calmly, so entirely with the cold indifference of a courtesan, that Madame du Val-Noble exclaimed:

"You are the Queen of us all!"

"Come early, and look very well—"

At five o'clock Esther dressed herself as a bride. She put on her lace dress over white satin, she had a white sash, white satin shoes, and a scarf of English point lace over her beautiful shoulders. In her hair she placed white camellia flowers, the simple ornament of an innocent girl. On her bosom lay a pearl necklace worth thirty thousand francs, a gift from Nucingen.

Though she was dressed by six, she refused to see anybody, even the banker. Europe knew that Lucien was to be admitted to her room. Lucien came at about seven, and Europe managed to get him up to her mistress without anybody knowing of his arrival.

Lucien, as he looked at her, said to himself, "Why not go and live with her at Rubempre, far from the world, and never see Paris again? I have an earnest of five years of her life, and the dear creature is one of those who never belie themselves! Where can I find such another perfect masterpiece?"

"My dear, you whom I have made my God," said Esther, kneeling down on a cushion in front of Lucien, "give me your blessing."

Lucien tried to raise her and kiss her, saying, "What is this jest, my dear love?" And he would have put his arm round her, but she freed herself with a gesture as much of respect as of horror.

"I am no longer worthy of you, Lucien," said she, letting the tears rise to her eyes. "I implore you, give me your blessing, and swear to me that you will found two beds at the Hotel-Dieu—for, as to prayers in church, God will never forgive me unless I pray myself.

"I have loved you too well, my dear. Tell me that I made you happy, and that you will sometimes think of me.—Tell me that!"

Lucien saw that Esther was solemnly in earnest, and he sat thinking.

"You mean to kill yourself," said he at last, in a tone of voice that revealed deep reflection.

"No," said she. "But to-day, my dear, the woman dies, the pure, chaste, and loving woman who once was yours.—And I am very much afraid that I shall die of grief."

"Poor child," said Lucien, "wait! I have worked hard these two days. I have succeeded in seeing Clotilde—"

"Always Clotilde!" cried Esther, in a tone of concentrated rage.

"Yes," said he, "we have written to each other.—On Tuesday morning she is to set out for Italy, but I shall meet her on the road for an interview at Fontainebleau."

"Bless me! what is it that you men want for wives? Wooden laths?" cried poor Esther. "If I had seven or eight millions, would you not marry me—come now?"

"Child! I was going to say that if all is over for me, I will have no wife but you."

Esther bent her head to hide her sudden pallor and the tears she wiped away.

"You love me?" said she, looking at Lucien with the deepest melancholy. "Well, that is my sufficient blessing.—Do not compromise yourself. Go away by the side door, and come in to the drawing-room through the ante-room. Kiss me on the forehead."

She threw her arms round Lucien, clasped him to her heart with frenzy, and said again:

"Go, only go—or I must live."

When the doomed woman appeared in the drawing-room, there was a cry of admiration. Esther's eyes expressed infinitude in which the soul sank as it looked into them. Her blue-black and beautiful hair set off the camellias. In short, this exquisite creature achieved all the effects she had intended. She had no rival. She looked like the supreme expression of that unbridled luxury which surrounded her in every form. Then she was brilliantly witty. She ruled the orgy with the cold, calm power that Habeneck displays when conducting at the Conservatoire, at those concerts where the first musicians in Europe rise to the sublime in interpreting Mozart and Beethoven.

But she observed with terror that Nucingen ate little, drank nothing, and was quite the master of the house.

By midnight everybody was crazy. The glasses were broken that they might never be used again; two of the Chinese curtains were torn; Bixiou was drunk, for the second time in his life. No one could keep his feet, the women were asleep on the sofas, and the guests were incapable of carrying out the practical joke they had planned of escorting Esther and Nucingen to the bedroom, standing in two lines with candles in their hands, and singing *Buona sera* from the *Barber of Seville*.

Nucingen simply gave Esther his hand. Bixiou, who saw them, though tipsy, was still able to say, like Rivarol, on the occasion of the Duc de Richelieu's last marriage, "The police must be warned; there is mischief brewing here."

The jester thought he was jesting; he was a prophet.

MONSIEUR DE NUCINGEN DID NOT go home till Monday at about noon. But at one o'clock his broker informed him that Mademoiselle Esther van Bogseck had sold the bond bearing thirty thousand francs interest on Friday last, and had just received the money.

"But, Monsieur le Baron, Derville's head-clerk called on me just as I was settling this transfer; and after seeing Mademoiselle Esther's real names, he told me she had come into a fortune of seven millions."

"Pooh!"

"Yes, she is the only heir to the old bill-discounter Gobseck.— Derville will verify the facts. If your mistress' mother was the handsome Dutch woman, *la Belle Hollandaise*, as they called her, she comes in for—"

"I know dat she is," cried the banker. "She tolt me all her life. I shall write ein vort to Derville."

The Baron at down at his desk, wrote a line to Derville, and sent it by one of his servants. Then, after going to the Bourse, he went back to Esther's house at about three o'clock.

"Madame forbade our waking her on any pretence whatever. She is in bed—asleep—"

"Ach der Teufel!" said the Baron. "But, Europe, she shall not be angry to be tolt that she is fery, fery rich. She shall inherit seven millions. Old

Gobseck is deat, and your mis'ess is his sole heir, for her moter vas Gobseck's own niece; and besides, he shall hafe left a vill. I could never hafe tought that a millionaire like dat man should hafe left Esther in misery!"

"Ah, ha! Then your reign is over, old pantaloon!" said Europe, looking at the Baron with an effrontery worthy of one of Moliere's waiting-maids. "Shooh! you old Alsatian crow! She loves you as we love the plague! Heavens above us! Millions!—Why, she may marry her lover; won't she be glad!"

And Prudence Servien left the Baron simply thunder-stricken, to be the first to announce to her mistress this great stroke of luck. The old man, intoxicated with superhuman enjoyment, and believing himself happy, had just received a cold shower-bath on his passion at the moment when it had risen to the intensest white heat.

"She vas deceiving me!" cried he, with tears in his eyes. "Yes, she vas cheating me. Oh, Esther, my life! Vas a fool hafe I been! Can such flowers ever bloom for de old men! I can buy all vat I vill except only yout!—Ach Gott, ach Gott! Vat shall I do! Vat shall become of me!—She is right, dat cruel Europe. Esther, if she is rich, shall not be for me. Shall I go hank myself? Vat is life midout de divine flame of joy dat I have known? Mein Gott, mein Gott!"

The old man snatched off the false hair he had combed in with his gray hairs these three months past.

A piercing shriek from Europe made Nucingen quail to his very bowels. The poor banker rose and walked upstairs on legs that were drunk with the bowl of disenchantment he had just swallowed to the dregs, for nothing is more intoxicating than the wine of disaster.

At the door of her room he could see Esther stiff on her bed, blue with poison—dead!

He went up to the bed and dropped on his knees.

"You are right! She tolt me so!—She is dead—of me—"

Paccard, Asie, every one hurried in. It was a spectacle, a shock, but not despair. Every one had their doubts. The Baron was a banker again. A suspicion crossed his mind, and he was so imprudent as to ask what had become of the seven hundred and fifty thousand francs, the price of the bond. Paccard, Asie, and Europe looked at each other so strangely that Monsieur de Nucingen left the house at once, believing that robbery and murder had been committed. Europe, detecting a packet of soft consistency, betraying the contents to be banknotes, under her mistress' pillow, proceeded at once to "lay her out," as she said.

"Go and tell monsieur, Asie!—Oh, to die before she knew that she had seven millions! Gobseck was poor madame's uncle!" said she.

Europe's stratagem was understood by Paccard. As soon as Asie's back was turned, Europe opened the packet, on which the hapless courtesan had written: "To be delivered to Monsieur Lucien de Rubempre."

Seven hundred and fifty thousand-franc notes shone in the eyes of Prudence Servien, who exclaimed:

"Won't we be happy and honest for the rest of our lives!"

Paccard made no objection. His instincts as a thief were stronger than his attachment to *Trompe-la-Mort*.

"Durut is dead," he said at length; "my shoulder is still a proof before letters. Let us be off together; divide the money, so as not to have all our eggs in one basket, and then get married."

"But where can we hide?" said Prudence.

"In Paris," replied Paccard.

Prudence and Paccard went off at once, with the promptitude of two honest folks transformed into robbers.

"My child," said Carlos to Asie, as soon as she had said three words, "find some letter of Esther's while I write a formal will, and then take the copy and the letter to Girard; but he must be quick. The will must be under Esther's pillow before the lawyers affix the seals here."

And he wrote out the following will:—

"Never having loved any one on earth but Monsieur Lucien Chardon de Rubempre, and being resolved to end my life rather than relapse into vice and the life of infamy from which he rescued me, I give and bequeath to the said Lucien Chardon de Rubempre all I may possess at the time of my decease, on condition of his founding a mass in perpetuity in the parish church of Saint-Roch for the repose of her who gave him her all, to her last thought.

ESTHER GOBSECK

"That is quite in her style," thought *Trompe-la-Mort*.

By seven in the evening this document, written and sealed, was placed by Asie under Esther's bolster.

"Jacques," said she, flying upstairs again, "just as I came out of the room justice marched in—"

"The justice of the peace you mean?"

"No, my son. The justice of the peace was there, but he had gendarmes with him. The public prosecutor and the examining judge are there too, and the doors are guarded."

"This death has made a stir very quickly," remarked Jacques Collin.

"Ay, and Paccard and Europe have vanished; I am afraid they may have scared away the seven hundred and fifty thousand francs," said Asie.

"The low villains!" said Collin. "They have done for us by their swindling game."

Human justice, and Paris justice, that is to say, the most suspicious, keenest, cleverest, and omniscient type of justice—too clever, indeed, for it insists on interpreting the law at every turn—was at last on the point of laying its hand on the agents of this horrible intrigue.

The Baron of Nucingen, on recognizing the evidence of poison, and failing to find his seven hundred and fifty thousand francs, imagined that one of two persons whom he greatly disliked—either Paccard or Europe—was guilty of the crime. In his first impulse of rage he flew to the prefecture of police. This was a stroke of a bell that called up all Corentin's men. The officials of the prefecture, the legal profession, the chief of the police, the justice of the peace, the examining judge,—all were astir. By nine in the evening three medical men were called in to perform an autopsy on poor Esther, and inquiries were set on foot.

Trompe-la-Mort, warned by Asie, exclaimed:

"No one knows that I am here; I may take an airing." He pulled himself up by the skylight of his garret, and with marvelous agility was standing in an instant on the roof, whence he surveyed the surroundings with the coolness of a tiler.

"Good!" said he, discerning a garden five houses off in the Rue de Provence, "that will just do for me."

"You are paid out, *Trompe-la-Mort*," said Contenson, suddenly emerging from behind a stack of chimneys. "You may explain to Monsieur Camusot what mass you were performing on the roof, Monsieur l'Abbe, and, above all, why you were escaping—"

"I have enemies in Spain," said Carlos Herrera.

"We can go there by way of your attic," said Contenson.

The sham Spaniard pretended to yield; but, having set his back and feet across the opening of the skylight, he gripped Contenson and flung him off with such violence that the spy fell in the gutter of the Rue Saint-Georges.

Contenson was dead on his field of honor; Jacques Collin quietly dropped into the room again and went to bed.

"Give me something that will make me very sick without killing me," said he to Asie; "for I must be at death's door, to avoid answering inquisitive persons. I have just got rid of a man in the most natural way, who might have unmasked me."

AT SEVEN O'CLOCK ON THE previous evening Lucien had set out in his own chaise to post to Fontainebleau with a passport he had procured in the morning; he slept in the nearest inn on the Nemours side. At six in the morning he went alone, and on foot, through the forest as far as Bouron.

"This," said he to himself, as he sat down on one of the rocks that command the fine landscape of Bouron, "is the fatal spot where Napoleon dreamed of making a final tremendous effort on the eve of his abdication."

At daybreak he heard the approach of post-horses and saw a britska drive past, in which sat the servants of the Duchesse de Lenoncourt-Chaulieu and Clotilde de Grandlieu's maid.

"Here they are!" thought Lucien. "Now, to play the farce well, and I shall be saved!—the Duc de Grandlieu's son-in-law in spite of him!"

It was an hour later when he heard the peculiar sound made by a superior traveling carriage, as the berline came near in which two ladies were sitting. They had given orders that the drag should be put on for the hill down to Bouron, and the man-servant behind the carriage had it stopped.

At this instant Lucien came forward.

"Clotilde!" said he, tapping on the window.

"No," said the young Duchess to her friend, "he shall not get into the carriage, and we will not be alone with him, my dear. Speak to him for the last time—to that I consent; but on the road, where we will walk on, and where Baptiste can escort us.—The morning is fine, we are well wrapped up, and have no fear of the cold. The carriage can follow."

The two women got out.

"Baptiste," said the Duchess, "the post-boy can follow slowly; we want to walk a little way. You must keep near us."

Madeleine de Mortsauf took Clotilde by the arm and allowed Lucien to talk. They thus walked on as far as the village of Grez. It was now eight o'clock, and there Clotilde dismissed Lucien.

"Well, my friend," said she, closing this long interview with much dignity, "I never shall marry any one but you. I would rather believe in you than in other men, in my father and mother—no woman ever gave greater proof of attachment surely?—Now, try to counteract the fatal prejudices which militate against you."

Just then the tramp of galloping horses was heard, and, to the great amazement of the ladies, a force of gendarmes surrounded the little party.

"What do you want?" said Lucien, with the arrogance of a dandy.

"Are you Monsieur Lucien de Rubempre?" asked the public prosecutor of Fontainebleau.

"Yes, monsieur."

"You will spend to-night in La Force," said he. "I have a warrant for the detention of your person."

"Who are these ladies?" asked the sergeant.

"To be sure.—Excuse me, ladies—your passports? For Monsieur Lucien, as I am instructed, had acquaintances among the fair sex, who for him would—"

"Do you take the Duchesse de Lenoncourt-Chaulieu for a prostitute?" said Madeleine, with a magnificent flash at the public prosecutor.

"You are handsome enough to excuse the error," the magistrate very cleverly retorted.

"Baptiste, produce the passports," said the young Duchess with a smile.

"And with what crime is Monsieur de Rubempre charged?" asked Clotilde, whom the Duchess wished to see safe in the carriage.

"Of being accessory to a robbery and murder," replied the sergeant of gendarmes.

Baptiste lifted Mademoiselle de Grandlieu into the chaise in a dead faint.

BY MIDNIGHT LUCIEN WAS ENTERING La Force, a prison situated between the Rue Payenne and the Rue des Ballets, where he was placed in solitary confinement.

The Abbe Carlos Herrera was also there, having been arrested that evening.

The End of Evil Ways

A t six o'clock next morning two vehicles with postilions, prison vans, called in the vigorous language of the populace, *paniers a salade*, came out of La Force to drive to the Conciergerie by the Palais de Justice.

Few loafers in Paris can have failed to meet this prison cell on wheels; still, though most stories are written for Parisian readers, strangers will no doubt be satisfied to have a description of this formidable machine. Who knows? A police of Russia, Germany, or Austria, the legal body of countries to whom the "Salad-basket" is an unknown machine, may profit by it; and in several foreign countries there can be no doubt that an imitation of this vehicle would be a boon to prisoners.

This ignominious conveyance, yellow-bodied, on high wheels, and lined with sheet-iron, is divided into two compartments. In front is a box-seat, with leather cushions and an apron. This is the free seat of the van, and accommodates a sheriff's officer and a gendarme. A strong iron trellis, reaching to the top, separates this sort of cab-front from the back division, in which there are two wooden seats placed sideways, as in an omnibus, on which the prisoners sit. They get in by a step behind and a door, with no window. The nickname of Salad-basket arose from the fact that the vehicle was originally made entirely of lattice, and the prisoners were shaken in it just as a salad is shaken to dry it.

For further security, in case of accident, a mounted gendarme follows the machine, especially when it conveys criminals condemned to death to the place of execution. Thus escape is impossible. The vehicle, lined with sheet-iron, is impervious to any tool. The prisoners, carefully searched when they are arrested or locked up, can have nothing but watch-springs, perhaps, to file through bars, and useless on a smooth surface.

So the *panier a salade*, improved by the genius of the Paris police, became the model for the prison omnibus (known in London as "Black Maria") in which convicts are transported to the hulks, instead of the horrible tumbril which formerly disgraced civilization, though Manon Lescaut had made it famous.

The accused are, in the first instance, despatched in the prison van from the various prisons in Paris to the Palais de Justice, to be questioned by the examining judge. This, in prison slang, is called "going up for examination." Then the accused are again conveyed from prison to the Court to be sentenced when their case is only a misdemeanor; or if, in legal parlance, the case is one for the Upper Court, they are transferred from the house of detention to the Conciergerie, the "Newgate" of the Department of the Seine.

Finally, the prison van carries the criminal condemned to death from Bicetre to the Barriere Saint-Jacques, where executions are carried out, and have been ever since the Revolution of July. Thanks to philanthropic interference, the poor wretches no longer have to face the horrors of the drive from the Conciergerie to the Place de Greve in a cart exactly like that used by wood merchants. This cart is no longer used but to bring the body back from the scaffold.

Without this explanation the words of a famous convict to his accomplice, "It is now the horse's business!" as he got into the van, would be unintelligible. It is impossible to be carried to execution more comfortably than in Paris nowadays.

At this moment the two vans, setting out at such an early hour, were employed on the unwonted service of conveying two accused prisoners from the jail of La Force to the Conciergerie, and each man had a "Salad-basket" to himself.

Nine-tenths of my readers, ay, and nine-tenths of the remaining tenth, are certainly ignorant of the vast difference of meaning in the words incriminated, suspected, accused, and committed for trial—jail, house of detention, and penitentiary; and they may be surprised to learn here that it involves all our criminal procedure, of which a clear and brief outline will presently be sketched, as much for their information as for the elucidation of this history. However, when it is said that the first van contained Jacques Collin and the second Lucien, who in a few hours had fallen from the summit of social splendor to the depths of a prison cell, curiosity will for the moment be satisfied.

The conduct of the two accomplices was characteristic; Lucien de Rubempre shrank back to avoid the gaze of the passers-by, who looked at the grated window of the gloomy and fateful vehicle on its road along the Rue Saint-Antoine and the Rue du Martroi to reach the quay and the Arch of Saint-Jean, the way, at that time, across the Place de l'Hotel de Ville. This archway now forms the entrance gate to the residence of the Prefet de la Seine in the huge municipal palace. The daring convict, on the contrary, stuck his face against the barred grating, between the officer and the gendarme, who, sure of their van, were chatting together.

The great days of July 1830, and the tremendous storm that then burst, have so completely wiped out the memory of all previous events, and politics so entirely absorbed the French during the last six months of that year, that no one remembers—or a few scarcely remember—the various private, judicial, and financial catastrophes, strange as they were, which, forming the annual flood of Parisian curiosity, were not lacking during the first six months of the year. It is, therefore, needful to mention how Paris was, for the moment, excited by the news of the arrest of a Spanish priest, discovered in a courtesan's house, and that of the elegant Lucien de Rubempre, who had been engaged to Mademoiselle Clotilde de Grandlieu, taken on the highroad to Italy, close to the little village of Grez. Both were charged as being concerned in a murder, of which the profits were stated at seven millions of francs; and for some days the scandal of this trial preponderated over the absorbing importance of the last elections held under Charles X.

In the first place, the charge had been based on an application by the Baron de Nucingen; then, Lucien's apprehension, just as he was about to be appointed private secretary to the Prime Minister, made a stir in the very highest circles of society. In every drawing-room in Paris more than one young man could recollect having envied Lucien when he was honored by the notice of the beautiful Duchesse de Maufrigneuse; and every woman knew that he was the favored attache of Madame de Serizy, the wife of one of the Government bigwigs. And finally, his handsome person gave him a singular notoriety in the various worlds that make up Paris—the world of fashion, the financial world, the world of courtesans, the young men's world, the literary world. So for two days past all Paris had been talking of these two arrests. The examining judge in whose hands the case was put regarded it as a chance for promotion; and, to proceed with the utmost rapidity, he had given orders that both the accused should be transferred from La Force to the Conciergerie as soon as Lucien de Rubempre could be brought from Fontainebleau.

As the Abbe Carlos had spent but twelve hours in La Force, and Lucien only half a night, it is useless to describe that prison, which has since been entirely remodeled; and as to the details of their consignment, it would be only a repetition of the same story at the Conciergerie.

BUT BEFORE SETTING FORTH THE terrible drama of a criminal inquiry, it is indispensable, as I have said, that an account should be given of the ordinary proceedings in a case of this kind. To begin with, its various phases will be better understood at home and abroad, and, besides, those who are ignorant of the action of the criminal law, as conceived of by the lawgivers under Napoleon, will appreciate it better. This is all the more important as, at this moment, this great and noble institution is in danger of destruction by the system known as penitentiary.

A crime is committed; if it is flagrant, the persons incriminated (inculpes) are taken to the nearest lock-up and placed in the cell known to the vulgar as the Violon—perhaps because they make a noise there, shrieking or crying. From thence the suspected persons (inculpes) are taken before the police commissioner or magistrate, who holds a preliminary inquiry, and can dismiss the case if there is any mistake; finally, they are conveyed to the Depot of the Prefecture, where the police detains them pending the convenience of the public prosecutor and the examining judge. They, being served with due notice, more or less quickly, according to the gravity of the case, come and examine the prisoners who are still provisionally detained. Having due regard to the presumptive evidence, the examining judge then issues a warrant for their imprisonment, and sends the suspected persons to be confined in a jail. There are three such jails (Maisons d'Arret) in Paris—Sainte-Pelagie, La Force, and les Madelonettes.

Observe the word inculpe, incriminated, or suspected of crime. The French Code has created three essential degrees of criminality—inculpe, first degree of suspicion; prevenu, under examination; accuse, fully committed for trial. So long as the warrant for committal remains unsigned, the supposed criminal is regarded as merely under suspicion, inculpe of the crime or felony; when the warrant has been issued, he becomes "the accused" (prevenu), and is regarded as such so long as the inquiry is proceeding; when the inquiry is closed, and as soon as the Court has decided that the accused is to be committed for trial, he becomes "the prisoner at the bar" (accuse) as soon as the superior court, at the instance of the public prosecutor, has pronounced that the charge is so far proved as to be carried to the Assizes.

Thus, persons suspected of crime go through three different stages, three siftings, before coming up for trial before the judges of the upper Court—the High Justice of the realm.

At the first stage, innocent persons have abundant means of exculpating themselves—the public, the town watch, the police. At the second state they appear before a magistrate face to face with the witnesses, and are judged by a tribunal in Paris, or by the Collective Court of the departments. At the third stage they are brought before a bench of twelve councillors, and in case of any error or informality the prisoner committed for trial at the Assizes may appeal for protection to the Supreme court. The jury do not know what a slap in the face they give to popular authority, to administrative and judicial functionaries, when they acquit a prisoner. And so, in my opinion, it is hardly possible that an innocent man should ever find himself at the bar of an Assize Court in Paris—I say nothing of other seats of justice.

The detenu is the convict. French criminal law recognizes imprisonment of three degrees, corresponding in legal distinction to these three degrees of suspicion, inquiry, and conviction. Mere imprisonment is a light penalty for misdemeanor, but detention is imprisonment with hard labor, a severe and sometimes degrading punishment. Hence, those persons who nowadays are in favor of the penitentiary system would upset an admirable scheme of criminal law in which the penalties are judiciously graduated, and they will end by punishing the lightest peccadilloes as severely as the greatest crimes.

The reader may compare in the *Scenes of Political Life* (for instance, in Une Tenebreuse affaire) the curious differences subsisting between the criminal law of Brumaire in the year IV, and that of the Code Napoleon which has taken its place.

In most trials, as in this one, the suspected persons are at once examined (and from inculpes become prevenus); justice immediately issues a warrant for their arrest and imprisonment. In point of fact, in most of such cases the criminals have either fled, or have been instantly apprehended. Indeed, as we have seen the police, which is but an instrument, and the officers of justice had descended on Esther's house with the swiftness of a thunderbolt. Even if there had not been the reasons for revenge suggested to the superior police by Corentin, there was a robbery to be investigated of seven hundred and fifty thousand francs from the Baron de Nucingen.

JUST AS THE FIRST PRISON van, conveying Jacques Collin, reached the archway of Saint-Jean—a narrow, dark passage, some block ahead compelled the postilion to stop under the vault. The prisoner's eyes shone like carbuncles through the grating, in spite of his aspect as of a dying man, which, the day before, had led the governor of La Force to believe that the doctor must be called in. These flaming eyes, free to rove at this moment, for neither the officer nor the gendarme looked round at their "customer," spoke so plain a language that a clever examining judge, M. Popinot, for instance, would have identified the man convicted for sacrilege.

In fact, ever since the "salad-basket" had turned out of the gate of La Force, Jacques Collin had studied everything on his way. Notwithstanding the pace they had made, he took in the houses with an eager and comprehensive glance from the ground floor to the attics. He saw and noted every passer-by. God Himself is not more clear-seeing as to the means and ends of His creatures than this man in observing the slightest differences in the medley of things and people. Armed with hope, as the last of the Horatii was armed with his sword, he expected help. To anybody but this Machiavelli of the hulks, this hope would have seemed so absolutely impossible to realize that he would have gone on mechanically, as all guilty men do. Not one of them ever dreams of resistance when he finds himself in the position to which justice and the Paris police bring suspected persons, especially those who, like Collin and Lucien, are in solitary confinement.

It is impossible to conceive of the sudden isolation in which a suspected criminal is placed. The gendarmes who apprehend him, the commissioner who questions him, those who take him to prison, the warders who lead him to his cell—which is actually called a cachot, a dungeon or hiding-place, those again who take him by the arms to put him into a prison-van—every being that comes near him from the moment of his arrest is either speechless, or takes note of all he says, to be repeated to the police or to the judge. This total severance, so simply effected between the prisoner and the world, gives rise to a complete overthrow of his faculties and a terrible prostration of mind, especially when the man has not been familiarized by his antecedents with the processes of justice. The duel between the judge and the criminal is all the more appalling because justice has on its side the dumbness of blank walls and the incorruptible coldness of its agents.

But Jacques Collin, or Carlos Herrera—it will be necessary to speak of him by one or the other of these names according to the circumstances of the case—had long been familiar with the methods of the police, of the jail, and of justice. This colossus of cunning and corruption had employed all his powers of mind, and all the resources of mimicry, to affect the surprise and anility of an innocent man, while giving the lawyers the spectacle of his sufferings. As has been told, Asie, that skilled Locusta, had given him a dose of poison so qualified as to produce the effects of a dreadful illness.

Thus Monsieur Camusot, the police commissioner, and the public prosecutor had been baffled in their proceedings and inquiries by the effects apparently of an apoplectic attack.

"He has taken poison!" cried Monsieur Camusot, horrified by the sufferings of the self-styled priest when he had been carried down from the attic writhing in convulsions.

Four constables had with great difficulty brought the Abbe Carlos downstairs to Esther's room, where the lawyers and the gendarmes were assembled.

"That was the best thing he could do if he should be guilty," replied the public prosecutor.

"Do you believe that he is ill?" the police commissioner asked.

The police is always incredulous.

The three lawyers had spoken, as may be imagined, in a whisper; but Jacques Collin had guessed from their faces the subject under discussion, and had taken advantage of it to make the first brief examination which is gone through on arrest absolutely impossible and useless; he had stammered out sentences in which Spanish and French were so mingled as to make nonsense.

At La Force this farce had been all the more successful in the first instance because the head of the "safety" force—an abbreviation of the title "Head of the brigade of the guardians of public safety"—Bibi-Lupin, who had long since taken Jacques Collin into custody at Madame Vauquer's boarding-house, had been sent on special business into the country, and his deputy was a man who hoped to succeed him, but to whom the convict was unknown.

Bibi-Lupin, himself formerly a convict, and a comrade of Jacques Collin's on the hulks, was his personal enemy. This hostility had its rise in quarrels in which Jacques Collin had always got the upper hand, and in the supremacy over his fellow-prisoners which *Trompe-la-Mort* had always assumed. And then, for ten years now, Jacques Collin had been the ruling providence of released convicts in Paris, their head, their adviser, and their banker, and consequently Bibi-Lupin's antagonist.

Thus, though placed in solitary confinement, he trusted to the intelligent and unreserved devotion of Asie, his right hand, and perhaps, too, to Paccard, his left hand, who, as he flattered himself, might return to his allegiance when once that thrifty subaltern had safely bestowed the seven hundred and fifty thousand francs that he had stolen. This was the reason why his attention had been so superhumanly alert all along the road. And, strange to say! his hopes were about to be amply fulfilled.

The two solid side-walls of the archway were covered, to a height of six feet, with a permanent dado of mud formed of the splashes from the gutter; for, in those days, the foot passenger had no protection from the constant traffic of vehicles and from what was called the kicking of the carts, but curbstones placed upright at intervals, and much ground away by the naves of the wheels. More than once a heavy truck had crushed a heedless foot-passenger under that archway. Such indeed Paris remained in many districts and till long after. This circumstance may give some idea of the narrowness of the Saint-Jean gate and the ease with which it could be blocked. If a cab should be coming through from the Place de Greve while a costermonger-woman was pushing her little truck of apples in from the Rue du Martroi, a third vehicle of any kind produced difficulties. The foot-passengers fled in alarm, seeking a corner-stone to protect them from the old-fashioned axles, which had attained such prominence that a law was passed at last to reduce their length.

When the prison van came in, this passage was blocked by a market woman with a costermonger's vegetable cart—one of a type which is all the more strange because specimens still exist in Paris in spite of the increasing number of green-grocers' shops. She was so thoroughly a street hawker that a Sergeant de Ville, if that particular class of police had been then in existence, would have allowed her to ply her trade without inspecting her permit, in spite of a sinister countenance that reeked of crime. Her head, wrapped in a cheap and ragged checked cotton kerchief, was horrid with rebellious locks of hair, like the bristles of a wild boar. Her red and wrinkled neck was disgusting, and her little shawl failed entirely to conceal a chest tanned brown by the sun, dust, and mud. Her gown was patchwork; her shoes gaped as though they were grinning at a face as full of holes as the gown. And what an apron! a plaster would have been less filthy. This moving and fetid rag must have stunk in the nostrils of dainty folks ten yards away. Those hands had gleaned a hundred harvest fields. Either the woman had returned from a German witches' Sabbath, or she had come out of a mendicity asylum. But what eyes! what audacious intelligence, what repressed vitality when the magnetic flash of her look and of Jacques Collin's met to exchange a thought!

"Get out of the way, you old vermin-trap!" cried the postilion in harsh tones.

"Mind you don't crush me, you hangman's apprentice!" she retorted. "Your cartful is not worth as much as mine."

And by trying to squeeze in between two corner-stones to make way, the hawker managed to block the passage long enough to achieve her purpose.

"Oh! Asie!" said Jacques Collin to himself, at once recognizing his accomplice. "Then all is well."

The post-boy was still exchanging amenities with Asie, and vehicles were collecting in the Rue du Martroi.

"Look out, there—Pecaire fermati. Souni la—Vedrem," shrieked old Asie, with the Red-Indian intonations peculiar to these female costermongers, who disfigure their words in such a way that they are transformed into a sort onomatopoeia incomprehensible to any but Parisians.

In the confusion in the alley, and among the outcries of all the waiting drivers, no one paid any heed to this wild yell, which might have been the woman's usual cry. But this gibberish, intelligible to Jacques Collin, sent to his ear in a mongrel language of their own—a mixture of bad Italian and Provencal—this important news:

"Your poor boy is nabbed. I am here to keep an eye on you. We shall meet again."

In the midst of his joy at having thus triumphed over the police, for he hoped to be able to keep up communications, Jacques Collin had a blow which might have killed any other man.

"Lucien in custody!" said he to himself.

He almost fainted. This news was to him more terrible than the rejection of his appeal could have been if he had been condemned to death.

Now that both the prison vans are rolling along the Quai, the interest of this story requires that I should add a few words about the Conciergerie, while they are making their way thither. The Conciergerie, a historical name—a terrible name,—a still more terrible thing, is inseparable from the Revolutions of France, and especially those of Paris. It has known most of our great criminals. But if it is the most interesting of the buildings of Paris, it is also the least known—least known to persons of the upper classes; still, in spite of the interest of this historical digression, it should be as short as the journey of the prison vans.

What Parisian, what foreigner, or what provincial can have failed to observe the gloomy and mysterious features of the Quai des Lunettes—a structure of black walls flanked by three round towers with conical roofs, two of them almost touching each other? This quay, beginning at the Pont du Change, ends at the Pont Neuf. A square tower—the Clock Tower, or Tour de l'Horloge, whence the signal was given for the massacre of Saint-Bartholomew—a tower almost as tall as that of Saint-Jacques de la Boucherie, shows where the Palais de Justice stands, and forms the corner of the quay.

These four towers and these walls are shrouded in the black winding sheet which, in Paris, falls on every facade to the north. About half-way along the quay at a gloomy archway we see the beginning of the private houses which were built in consequence of the construction of the Pont Neuf in the reign of Henry IV. The Place Royale was a replica of the Place Dauphine. The style of architecture is the same, of brick with binding courses of hewn stone. This archway and the Rue de Harlay are the limit line of the Palais de Justice on the west. Formerly the Prefecture de Police, once the residence of the Presidents of Parlement, was a dependency of the Palace. The Court of Exchequer and Court of Subsidies completed the Supreme Court of Justice, the Sovereign's Court. It will be seen that before the Revolution the Palace enjoyed that isolation which now again is aimed at.

This block, this island of residences and official buildings, in their midst the Sainte-Chapelle—that priceless jewel of Saint-Louis' chaplet—is the sanctuary of Paris, its holy place, its sacred ark.

For one thing, this island was at first the whole of the city, for the plot now forming the Place Dauphine was a meadow attached to the Royal demesne, where stood a stamping mill for coining money. Hence the name of Rue de la Monnaie—the street leading to the Pont Neuf. Hence, too, the name of one of the round towers—the middle one—called the Tour d'Argent, which would seem to show that money was originally coined there. The famous mill, to be seen marked in old maps of Paris, may very likely be more recent than the time when money was coined in the Palace itself, and was erected, no doubt, for the practice of improved methods in the art of coining.

The first tower, hardly detached from the Tour d'Argent, is the Tour de Montgomery; the third, and smallest, but the best preserved of the three, for it still has its battlements, is the Tour Bonbec.

The Sainte-Chapelle and its four towers—counting the clock tower as one—clearly define the precincts; or, as a surveyor would say, the perimeter of the Palace, as it was from the time of the Merovingians till the accession of the first race of Valois; but to us, as a result of certain alterations, this Palace is more especially representative of the period of Saint-Louis.

Charles V was the first to give the Palace up to the Parlement, then a new institution, and went to reside in the famous Hotel Saint-Pol, under the protection of the Bastille. The Palais des Tournelles was subsequently erected backing on to the Hotel Saint-Pol. Thus, under the later Valois, the kings came back from the Bastille to the Louvre, which had been their first stronghold.

The original residence of the French kings, the Palace of Saint-Louis, which has preserved the designation of Le Palais, to indicate the Palace of palaces, is entirely buried under the Palais de Justice; it forms the cellars, for it was built, like the Cathedral, in the Seine, and with such care that the highest floods in the river scarcely cover the lowest steps. The Quai de l'Horloge covers, twenty feet below the surface, its foundations of a thousand years old. Carriages run on the level of the capitals of the solid columns under these towers, and formerly their appearance must have harmonized with the elegance of the Palace, and have had a picturesque effect over the water, since to this day those towers vie in height with the loftiest buildings in Paris.

As we look down on this vast capital from the lantern of the Pantheon, the Palace with the Sainte-Chapelle is still the most monumental of many monumental buildings. The home of our kings, over which you tread as you pace the immense hall known as the *Salle des Pas-Perdus*, was a miracle of architecture; and it is so still to the intelligent eye of the poet who happens to study it when inspecting the Conciergerie. Alas! for the Conciergerie has invaded the home of kings. One's heart bleeds to see the way in which cells, cupboards, corridors, warders' rooms, and halls devoid of light or air, have been hewn out of that beautiful structure in which Byzantine, Gothic, and Romanesque—the three phases of ancient art—were harmonized in one building by the architecture of the twelfth century.

This palace is a monumental history of France in the earliest times, just as Blois is that of a later period. As at Blois you may admire in a single courtyard the chateau of the Counts of Blois, that of Louis XII, that of Francis I, that of Gaston; so at the Conciergerie you will find within the same precincts the stamp of the early races, and, in the Sainte-Chapelle, the architecture of Saint-Louis.

Municipal Council (to you I speak), if you bestow millions, get a poet or two to assist your architects if you wish to save the cradle of Paris, the cradle of kings, while endeavoring to endow Paris and the Supreme Court with a palace worthy of France. It is a matter for study for some years before beginning the work. Another new prison or two like that of La Roquette, and the palace of Saint-Louis will be safe.

In these days many grievances afflict this vast mass of buildings, buried under the Palais de Justice and the quay, like some antediluvian creature in the soil of Montmartre; but the worst affliction is that it is the Conciergerie. This epigram is intelligible. In the early days of the monarchy, noble criminals—for the villeins (a word signifying the peasantry in French and English alike) and the citizens came under the jurisdiction of the municipality or of their liege lord—the lords of the greater or the lesser fiefs, were brought before the king and guarded in the Conciergerie. And as these noble criminals were few, the Conciergerie was large enough for the king's prisoners.

It is difficult now to be quite certain of the exact site of the original Conciergerie. However, the kitchens built by Saint-Louis still exist, forming what is now called the mousetrap; and it is probable that the original Conciergerie was situated in the place where, till 1825, the Conciergerie prisons of the Parlement were still in use, under the archway to the right of the wide outside steps leading to the supreme Court. From thence, until 1825, condemned criminals were taken to execution. From that gate came forth all the great criminals, all the victims of political feeling—the Marechale d'Ancre and the Queen of France, Semblancay and Malesherbes, Damien and Danton, Desrues and Castaing. Fouquier-Tinville's private room, like that of the public prosecutor now, was so placed that he could see the procession of carts containing the persons whom the Revolutionary tribunal had sentenced to death. Thus this man, who had become a sword, could give a last glance at each batch.

After 1825, when Monsieur de Peyronnet was Minister, a great change was made in the Palais. The old entrance to the Conciergerie, where the ceremonies of registering the criminal and of the last toilet were performed, was closed and removed to where it now is, between the Tour de l'Horloge and the Tour de Montgomery, in an inner court entered through an arched passage. To the left is the "mousetrap," to the right the prison gates. The "salad-baskets" can drive into this irregularly shaped courtyard, can stand there and turn with ease, and in case of a riot find some protection behind the strong grating of the gate under the arch; whereas they formerly had no room to move in the narrow space dividing the outside steps from the right wing of the palace.

In our day the Conciergerie, hardly large enough for the prisoners committed for trial—room being needed for about three hundred, men and women—no longer receives either suspected or remanded criminals excepting in rare cases, as, for instance, in these of Jacques Collin and Lucien. All who are imprisoned there are committed for trial before the Bench. As an exception criminals of the higher ranks are allowed to sojourn there, since, being already disgraced by a sentence in open court, their punishment would be too severe if they served their term of imprisonment at Melun or at Poissy. Ouvrard preferred to be imprisoned at the Conciergerie rather than at Sainte-Pelagie. At this moment of writing Lehon the notary and the Prince de Bergues are serving their time there by an exercise of leniency which, though arbitrary, is humane.

As a rule, suspected criminals, whether they are to be subjected to a preliminary examination—to "go up," in the slang of the Courts—or to appear before the magistrate of the lower Court, are transferred in prison vans direct to the "mousetraps."

The "mousetraps," opposite the gate, consist of a certain number of old cells constructed in the old kitchens of Saint-Louis' building, whither prisoners not yet fully committed are brought to await the hour when the Court sits, or the arrival of the examining judge. The "mousetraps" end on the north at the quay, on the east at the headquarters of the Municipal Guard, on the west at the courtyard of the Conciergerie, and on the south they adjoin a large vaulted hall, formerly, no doubt, the banqueting-room, but at present disused.

Above the "mousetraps" is an inner guardroom with a window commanding the court of the Conciergerie; this is used by the gendarmerie of the department, and the stairs lead up to it. When the hour of trial strikes the sheriffs call the roll of the prisoners, the gendarmes go down, one for each prisoner, and each gendarme takes a criminal by the arm; and thus, in couples, they mount the stairs, cross the guardroom, and are led along the passages to a room contiguous to the hall where sits the famous sixth chamber of the law (whose functions are those of an English county court). The same road is trodden by the prisoners committed for trial on their way to and from the Conciergerie and the Assize Court.

In the *Salle des Pas-Perdus*, between the door into the first court of the inferior class and the steps leading to the sixth, the visitor must observe the first time he goes there a doorway without a door or any architectural adornment, a square hole of the meanest type. Through this the judges and barristers find their way into the passages, into the guardhouse, down into the prison cells, and to the entrance to the Conciergerie.

The private chambers of all the examining judges are on different floors in this part of the building. They are reached by squalid staircases, a maze in which those to whom the place is unfamiliar inevitably lose themselves. The windows of some look out on the quay, others on the yard of the Conciergerie. In 1830 a few of these rooms commanded the Rue de la Barillerie.

Thus, when a prison van turns to the left in this yard, it has brought prisoners to be examined to the "mousetrap"; when it turns to the right, it conveys prisoners committed for trial, to the Conciergerie. Now it was to the right that the vehicle turned which conveyed Jacques Collin to set him down at the prison gate. Nothing can be more sinister. Prisoners and visitors see two barred gates of wrought iron, with a space between them of about six feet. These are never both opened at once, and through them everything is so cautiously scrutinized that persons who have a visiting ticket pass the permit through the bars before the key grinds in the lock. The examining judges, or even the supreme judges, are not admitted without being identified. Imagine, then, the chances of communications or escape!—The governor of the Conciergerie would smile with an expression on his lips that would freeze the mere suggestion in the most daring of romancers who defy probability.

In all the annals of the Conciergerie no escape has been known but that of Lavalette; but the certain fact of august connivance, now amply proven, if it does not detract from the wife's devotion, certainly diminished the risk of failure.

The most ardent lover of the marvelous, judging on the spot of the nature of the difficulties, must admit that at all times the obstacles must have been, as they still are, insurmountable. No words can do justice to the strength of the walls and vaulting; they must be seen.

Though the pavement of the yard is on a lower level than that of the quay, in crossing this Barbican you go down several steps to enter an immense vaulted hall, with solid walls graced with magnificent columns. This hall abuts on the Tour de Montgomery—which is now part of the governor's residence—and on the Tour d'Argent, serving as a dormitory for the warders, or porters, or turnkeys, as you may prefer to call them. The number of the officials is less than might be supposed; there are but twenty; their sleeping quarters, like their beds, are in no respect different from those of the *pistoles* or private cells. The name *pistole* originated, no doubt, in the fact that the prisoners formerly paid a pistole (about ten francs) a week for this accommodation, its bareness resembling that of the empty garrets in which great men in poverty begin their career in Paris.

To the left, in the vast entrance hall, sits the Governor of the Conciergerie, in a sort of office constructed of glass panes, where he and his clerk keep the prison-registers. Here the prisoners for examination, or committed for trial, have their names entered with a full description, and are then searched. The question of their lodging is also settled, this depending on the prisoner's means.

Opposite the entrance to this hall there is a glass door. This opens into a parlor where the prisoner's relations and his counsel may speak with him across a double grating of wood. The parlor window opens on to the prison yard, the inner court where prisoners committed for trial take air and exercise at certain fixed hours.

This large hall, only lighted by the doubtful daylight that comes in through the gates—for the single window to the front court is screened by the glass office built out in front of it—has an atmosphere and a gloom that strike the eye in perfect harmony with the pictures that force themselves on the imagination. Its aspect is all the more sinister because, parallel with the Tours d'Argent and de Montgomery, you discover those mysterious vaulted and overwhelming crypts which lead to the cells occupied by the Queen and Madame Elizabeth, and to those known as the secret cells. This maze of masonry, after being of old the scene of royal festivities, is now the basement of the Palais de Justice.

Between 1825 and 1832 the operation of the last toilet was performed in this enormous hall, between a large stove which heats it and the inner gate. It is impossible even now to tread without a shudder on the paved floor that has received the shock and the confidences of so many last glances.

THE APPARENTLY DYING VICTIM ON this occasion could not get out of the horrible vehicle without the assistance of two gendarmes, who took him under the arms to support him, and led him half unconscious into the office. Thus dragged along, the dying man raised his eyes to heaven in such a way as to suggest a resemblance to the Saviour taken down from the Cross. And certainly in no picture does Jesus present a more cadaverous or tortured countenance than this of the sham Spaniard; he looked ready to breathe his last sigh. As soon as he was seated in the office, he repeated in a weak voice the speech he had made to everybody since he was arrested:

"I appeal to His Excellency the Spanish Ambassador."

"You can say that to the examining judge," replied the Governor.

"Oh Lord!" said Jacques Collin, with a sigh. "But cannot I have a breviary! Shall I never be allowed to see a doctor? I have not two hours to live."

As Carlos Herrera was to be placed in close confinement in the secret cells, it was needless to ask him whether he claimed the benefits of the pistole (as above described), that is to say, the right of having one of the rooms where the prisoner enjoys such comfort as the law permits. These rooms are on the other side of the prison-yard, of which mention will presently be made. The sheriff and the clerk calmly carried out the formalities of the consignment to prison.

"Monsieur," said Jacques Collin to the Governor in broken French, "I am, as you see, a dying man. Pray, if you can, tell that examining judge as soon as possible that I crave as a favor what a criminal must most dread, namely, to be brought before him as soon as he arrives; for my sufferings are really unbearable, and as soon as I see him the mistake will be cleared up—"

As an universal rule every criminal talks of a mistake. Go to the hulks and question the convicts; they are almost all victims of a miscarriage of justice. So this speech raises a faint smile in all who come into contact with the suspected, accused, or condemned criminal.

"I will mention your request to the examining judge," replied the Governor.

"And I shall bless you, monsieur!" replied the false Abbe, raising his eyes to heaven.

As soon as his name was entered on the calendar, Carlos Herrera, supported under each arm by a man of the municipal guard, and followed by a turnkey instructed by the Governor as to the number of the cell in which the prisoner was to be placed, was led through the subterranean maze of the Conciergerie into a perfectly wholesome room, whatever certain philanthropists may say to the contrary, but cut off from all possible communication with the outer world.

As soon as he was removed, the warders, the Governor, and his clerk looked at each other as though asking each other's opinion, and suspicion was legible on every face; but at the appearance of the second man in custody the spectators relapsed into their usual doubting frame of mind, concealed under the air of indifference. Only in very extraordinary cases do the functionaries of the Conciergerie feel any curiosity; the prisoners are no more to them than a barber's customers are to him. Hence all the formalities which appall the imagination are carried out with less fuss than a money transaction at a banker's, and often with greater civility.

Lucien's expression was that of a dejected criminal. He submitted to everything, and obeyed like a machine. All the way from Fontainebleau the poet had been facing his ruin, and telling himself that the hour of expiation had tolled. Pale and exhausted, knowing nothing of what had happened at Esther's house during his absence, he only knew that he was the intimate ally of an escaped convict, a situation which enabled him to guess at disaster worse than death. When his mind could command a thought, it was that of suicide. He must, at any cost, escape the ignominy that loomed before him like the phantasm of a dreadful dream.

Jacques Collin, as the more dangerous of the two culprits, was placed in a cell of solid masonry, deriving its light from one of the narrow yards, of which there are several in the interior of the Palace, in the wing where the public prosecutor's chambers are. This little yard is the airing-ground for the female prisoners. Lucien was taken to the same part of the building, to a cell adjoining the rooms let to misdemeanants; for, by orders from the examining judge, the Governor treated him with some consideration.

Persons who have never had anything to do with the action of the law usually have the darkest notions as to the meaning of solitary or secret confinement. Ideas as to the treatment of criminals have not yet become disentangled from the old pictures of torture chambers, of the unhealthiness of a prison, the chill of stone walls sweating tears, the coarseness of the jailers and of the food—inevitable accessories of the drama; but it is not unnecessary to explain here that these exaggerations exist only on the stage, and only make lawyers and judges smile, as well as those who visit prisons out of curiosity, or who come to study them.

For a long time, no doubt, they were terrible. In the days of the old Parlement, of Louis XIII and Louis XIV, the accused were, no doubt, flung pell-mell into a low room underneath the old gateway. The prisons were among the crimes of 1789, and it is enough only to see the cells where the Queen and Madame Elizabeth were incarcerated to conceive a horror of old judicial proceedings.

In our day, though philanthropy has brought incalculable mischief on society, it has produced some good for the individual. It is to Napoleon that we owe our Criminal Code; and this, even more than the Civil Code—which still urgently needs reform on some points—will remain one of the greatest monuments of his short reign. This new view of criminal law put an end to a perfect abyss of misery. Indeed, it may be said that, apart from the terrible moral torture which men of the better classes must suffer when they find themselves in the power of the law, the action of that power is simple and mild to a degree that would hardly be expected. Suspected or accused criminals are certainly not lodged as if they were at home; but every necessary is supplied to them in the prisons of Paris. Besides, the burden of feelings that weighs on them deprives the details of daily life of their customary value. It is never the body that suffers. The mind is in such a phase of violence that every form of discomfort or of brutal treatment, if such there were, would be easily endured in such a frame of mind. And it must be admitted that an innocent man is quickly released, especially in Paris.

So Lucien, on entering his cell, saw an exact reproduction of the first room he had occupied in Paris at the Hotel Cluny. A bed to compare with those in the worst furnished apartments of the Quartier Latin, straw chairs with the bottoms out, a table and a few utensils, compose the furniture of such a room, in which two accused prisoners are not unfrequently placed together when they are quiet in their ways, and their misdeeds are not crimes of violence, but such as forgery or bankruptcy.

This resemblance between his starting-point, in the days of his innocency, and his goal, the lowest depths of degradation and sham, was so direct an appeal to his last chord of poetic feeling, that the unhappy fellow melted into tears. For four hours he wept, as rigid in appearance as a figure of stone, but enduring the subversion of all his hopes, the crushing of all his social vanity, and the utter overthrow of his pride, smarting in each separate *I* that exists in an ambitious man—a lover, a success, a dandy, a Parisian, a poet, a libertine, and a favorite. Everything in him was broken by this fall as of Icarus.

Carlos Herrera, on the other hand, as soon as he was locked into his cell and found himself alone, began pacing it to and fro like the polar bear in his cage. He carefully examined the door and assured himself that, with the exception of the peephole, there was not a crack in it. He sounded all the walls, he looked up the funnel down which a dim light came, and he said to himself, "I am safe enough!"

He sat down in a corner where the eye of a prying warder at the grating of the peephole could not see him. Then he took off his wig, and hastily ungummed a piece of paper that did duty as lining. The side of the paper next his head was so greasy that it looked like the very texture of the wig. If it had occurred to Bibi-Lupin to snatch off the wig to establish the identity of the Spaniard with Jacques Collin, he would never have thought twice about the paper, it looked so exactly like part of the wigmaker's work. The other side was still fairly white, and clean enough to have a few lines written on it. The delicate and tiresome task of unsticking it had been begun in La Force; two hours would not have been long enough; it had taken him half of the day before. The prisoner began by tearing this precious scrap of paper so as to have a strip four or five lines wide, which he divided into several bits; he then replaced his store of paper in the same strange hiding-place, after damping the gummed side so as to make it stick again. He felt in a lock of his hair for one of those pencil leads as thin as a stout pin, then recently invented by Susse, and which he had put in with some gum; he broke off a scrap long enough to write with and small enough to hide in his ear. Having made these preparations with the rapidity and certainty of hand peculiar to old convicts, who are as light-fingered as monkeys, Jacques Collin sat down on the edge of his bed to meditate on his instructions to Asie, in perfect confidence that he should come across her, so entirely did he rely on the woman's genius.

"During the preliminary examination," he reflected, "I pretended to be a Spaniard and spoke broken French, appealed to my Ambassador, and alleged diplomatic privilege, not understanding anything I was asked, the whole performance varied by fainting, pauses, sighs—in short, all the vagaries of a dying man. I must stick to that. My papers are all regular. Asie and I can eat up Monsieur Camusot; he is no great shakes!

"Now I must think of Lucien; he must be made to pull himself together. I must get at the boy at whatever cost, and show him some plan of conduct, otherwise he will give himself up, give me up, lose all!

He must be taught his lesson before he is examined. And besides, I must find some witnesses to swear to my being a priest!"

Such was the position, moral and physical, of these two prisoners, whose fate at the moment depended on Monsieur Camusot, examining judge to the Inferior Court of the Seine, and sovereign master, during the time granted to him by the Code, of the smallest details of their existence, since he alone could grant leave for them to be visited by the chaplains, the doctor, or any one else in the world.

No human authority—neither the King, nor the Keeper of the Seals, nor the Prime Minister, can encroach on the power of an examining judge; nothing can stop him, no one can control him. He is a monarch, subject only to his conscience and the Law. At the present time, when philosophers, philanthropists, and politicians are constantly endeavoring to reduce every social power, the rights conferred on the examining judges have become the object of attacks that are all the more serious because they are almost justified by those rights, which, it must be owned, are enormous. And yet, as every man of sense will own, that power ought to remain unimpaired; in certain cases, its exercise can be mitigated by a strong infusion of caution; but society is already threatened by the ineptitude and weakness of the jury—which is, in fact, the really supreme bench, and which ought to be composed only of choice and elected men—and it would be in danger of ruin if this pillar were broken which now upholds our criminal procedure.

Arrest on suspicion is one of the terrible but necessary powers of which the risk to society is counterbalanced by its immense importance. And besides, distrust of the magistracy in general is a beginning of social dissolution. Destroy that institution, and reconstruct it on another basis; insist—as was the case before the Revolution—that judges should show a large guarantee of fortune; but, at any cost, believe in it! Do not make it an image of society to be insulted!

In these days a judge, paid as a functionary, and generally a poor man, has in the place of his dignity of old a haughtiness of demeanor that seems odious to the men raised to be his equals; for haughtiness is dignity without a solid basis. That is the vicious element in the present system. If France were divided into ten circuits, the magistracy might be reinstated by conferring its dignities on men of fortune; but with six-and-twenty circuits this is impossible.

The only real improvement to be insisted on in the exercise of the power intrusted to the examining judge, is an alteration in the conditions of preliminary imprisonment. The mere fact of suspicion ought to make no difference in the habits of life of the suspected parties. Houses of detention for them ought to be constructed in Paris, furnished and arranged in such a way as greatly to modify the feeling of the public with regard to suspected persons. The law is good, and is necessary; its application is in fault, and public feeling judges the laws from the way in which they are carried out. And public opinion in France condemns persons under suspicion, while, by an inexplicable reaction, it justifies those committed for trial. This, perhaps, is a result of the essentially refractory nature of the French.

This illogical temper of the Parisian people was one of the factors which contributed to the climax of this drama; nay, as may be seen, it was one of the most important.

To enter into the secret of the terrible scenes which are acted out in the examining judge's chambers; to understand the respective positions of the two belligerent powers, the Law and the examinee, the object of whose contest is a certain secret kept by the prisoner from the inquisition of the magistrate—well named in prison slang, "the curious man"—it must always be remembered that persons imprisoned under suspicion know nothing of what is being said by the seven or eight publics that compose *the Public*, nothing of how much the police know, or the authorities, or the little that newspapers can publish as to the circumstances of the crime.

Thus, to give a man in custody such information as Jacques Collin had just received from Asie as to Lucien's arrest, is throwing a rope to a drowning man. As will be seen, in consequence of this ignorance, a stratagem which, without this warning, must certainly have been equally fatal to the convict, was doomed to failure.

MONSIEUR CAMUSOT, THE SON-IN-LAW OF one of the clerks of the cabinet, too well known for any account of his position and connection to be necessary here, was at this moment almost as much perplexed as Carlos Herrera in view of the examination he was to conduct. He had formerly been President of a Court of the Paris circuit; he had been raised from that position and called to be a judge in Paris—one of the most coveted posts in the magistracy—by the influence of the celebrated Duchesse de Maufrigneuse, whose husband, attached to the Dauphin's person, and Colonel of a cavalry regiment of the Guards, was as much in favor with the King as she was with MADAME. In return for a very small service which he had done the Duchess—an important matter to her—on occasion of a charge of forgery brought against the young Comte d'Esgrignon by a banker of Alencon (see *La Cabinet des Antiques*; *Scenes de la vie de Province*), he was promoted from being a provincial judge to be president of his Court, and from being president to being an examining judge in Paris.

For eighteen months now he had sat on the most important Bench in the kingdom; and had once, at the desire of the Duchesse de Maufrigneuse, had an opportunity of forwarding the ends of a lady not less influential than the Duchess, namely, the Marquise d'Espard, but he had failed. (See the *Commission in Lunacy*.)

Lucien, as was told at the beginning of the Scene, to be revenged on Madame d'Espard, who aimed at depriving her husband of his liberty of action, was able to put the true facts before the Public Prosecutor and the Comte de Serizy. These two important authorities being thus won over to the Marquis d'Espard's party, his wife had barely escaped the censure of the Bench by her husband's generous intervention.

On hearing, yesterday, of Lucien's arrest, the Marquise d'Espard had sent her brother-in-law, the Chevalier d'Espard, to see Madame Camusot. Madame Camusot had set off forthwith to call on the notorious Marquise. Just before dinner, on her return home, she had called her husband aside in the bedroom.

"If you can commit that little fop Lucien de Rubempre for trial, and secure his condemnation," said she in his ear, "you will be Councillor to the Supreme Court—"

"How?"

"Madame d'Espard longs to see that poor young man guillotined. I shivered as I heard what a pretty woman's hatred can be!"

"Do not meddle in questions of the law," said Camusot.

"I! meddle!" said she. "If a third person could have heard us, he could not have guessed what we were talking about. The Marquise and I were as exquisitely hypocritical to each other as you are to me at this moment. She began by thanking me for your good offices in her suit, saying that she was grateful in spite of its having failed. She spoke of the terrible functions devolved on you by the law, 'It is fearful to have to send a man to the scaffold—but as to that man, it would be no more than justice,' and so forth. Then she lamented that such a handsome young fellow, brought to Paris by her cousin, Madame du Chatelet, should have turned out so badly. 'That,' said she, 'is what bad women like Coralie and

Esther bring young men to when they are corrupt enough to share their disgraceful profits!' Next came some fine speeches about charity and religion! Madame du Chatelet had said that Lucien deserved a thousand deaths for having half killed his mother and his sister.

"Then she spoke of a vacancy in the Supreme Court—she knows the Keeper of the Seals. 'Your husband, madame, has a fine opportunity of distinguishing himself,' she said in conclusion—and that is all."

"We distinguish ourselves every day when we do our duty," said Camusot.

"You will go far if you are always the lawyer even to your wife," cried Madame Camusot. "Well, I used to think you a goose. Now I admire you."

The lawyer's lips wore one of those smiles which are as peculiar to them as dancers' smiles are to dancers.

"Madame, can I come in?" said the maid.

"What is it?" said her mistress.

"Madame, the head lady's-maid came from the Duchesse de Maufrigneuse while you were out, and she will be obliged if you would go at once to the Hotel de Cadignan."

"Keep dinner back," said the lawyer's wife, remembering that the driver of the hackney coach that had brought her home was waiting to be paid.

She put her bonnet on again, got into the coach, and in twenty minutes was at the Hotel de Cadignan. Madame Camusot was led up the private stairs, and sat alone for ten minutes in a boudoir adjoining the Duchess' bedroom. The Duchess presently appeared, splendidly dressed, for she was starting for Saint-Cloud in obedience to a Royal invitation.

"Between you and me, my dear, a few words are enough."

"Yes, Madame la Duchesse."

"Lucien de Rubempre is in custody, your husband is conducting the inquiry; I will answer for the poor boy's innocence; see that he is released within twenty-four hours.—This is not all. Some one will ask to-morrow to see Lucien in private in his cell; your husband may be present if he chooses, so long as he is not discovered. The King looks for high courage in his magistrates in the difficult position in which he will presently find himself; I will bring your husband forward, and recommend him as a man devoted to the King even at the risk of his head. Our friend Camusot will be made first a councillor, and then the President of Court somewhere or other.—Good-bye.—I am under orders, you will excuse me, I know?

"You will not only oblige the public prosecutor, who cannot give an opinion in this affair; you will save the life of a dying woman, Madame de Serizy. So you will not lack support.

"In short, you see, I put my trust in you, I need not say—you know—"

She laid a finger to her lips and disappeared.

"And I had not a chance of telling her that Madame d'Espard wants to see Lucien on the scaffold!" thought the judge's wife as she returned to her hackney cab.

She got home in such a state of anxiety that her husband, on seeing her, asked:

"What is the matter, Amelie?"

"We stand between two fires."

She told her husband of her interview with the Duchess, speaking in his ear for fear the maid should be listening at the door.

"Now, which of them has the most power?" she said in conclusion. "The Marquise was very near getting you into trouble in the silly business of the commission on her husband, and we owe everything to the Duchess.

"One made vague promises, while the other tells you you shall first be Councillor and then President.—Heaven forbid I should advise you; I will never meddle in matters of business; still, I am bound to repeat exactly what is said at Court and what goes on—"

"But, Amelie, you do not know what the Prefet of police sent me this morning, and by whom? By one of the most important agents of the superior police, the Bibi-Lupin of politics, who told me that the Government had a secret interest in this trial.—Now let us dine and go to the Varietes. We will talk all this over to-night in my private room, for I shall need your intelligence; that of a judge may not perhaps be enough—"

Nine magistrates out of ten would deny the influence of the wife over her husband in such cases; but though this may be a remarkable exception in society, it may be insisted on as true, even if improbable. The magistrate is like the priest, especially in Paris, where the best of the profession are to be found; he rarely speaks of his business in the Courts, excepting of settled cases. Not only do magistrates' wives affect to know nothing; they have enough sense of propriety to understand that it would damage their husbands if, when they are told some secret, they allowed their knowledge to be suspected.

Nevertheless, on some great occasions, when promotion depends on the decision taken, many a wife, like Amelie, has helped the lawyer in his study of a case. And, after all, these exceptions, which, of course, are easily denied, since they remain unknown, depend entirely on the way in which the struggle between two natures has worked out in home-life. Now, Madame Camusot controlled her husband completely.

When all in the house were asleep, the lawyer and his wife sat down to the desk, where the magistrate had already laid out the documents in the case.

"Here are the notes, forwarded to me, at my request, by the Prefet of police," said Camusot.

THE ABBE CARLOS HERRERA

"This individual is undoubtedly the man named Jacques Collin, known as *Trompe-la-Mort*, who was last arrested in 1819, in the dwelling-house of a certain Madame Vauquer, who kept a common boarding-house in the Rue Nueve-Sainte-Genevieve, where he lived in concealment under the alias of Vautrin."

A marginal note in the Prefet's handwriting ran thus:

"Orders have been sent by telegraph to Bibi-Lupin, chief of the Safety department, to return forthwith, to be confronted with the prisoner, as he is personally acquainted with Jacques Collin, whom he, in fact, arrested in 1819 with the connivance of a Mademoiselle Michonneau.

"The boarders who then lived in the Maison Vauquer are still living, and may be called to establish his identity.

"The self-styled Carlos Herrera is Monsieur Lucien de Rubempre's intimate friend and adviser, and for three years past has furnished him with considerable sums, evidently obtained by dishonest means.

"This partnership, if the identity of the Spaniard with Jacques Collin can be proved, must involve the condemnation of Lucien de Rubempre.

"The sudden death of Peyrade, the police agent, is attributable to poison administered at the instigation of Jacques Collin,

Rubempre, or their accomplices. The reason for this murder is the fact that justice had for a long time been on the traces of these clever criminals."

And again, on the margin, the magistrate pointed to this note written by the Prefet himself:

"This is the fact to my personal knowledge; and I also know that the Sieur Lucien de Rubempre has disgracefully tricked the Comte de Serizy and the Public Prosecutor."

"What do you say to this, Amelie?"

"It is frightful!" repled his wife. "Go on."

"The transformation of the convict Jacques Collin into a Spanish priest is the result of some crime more clever than that by which Coignard made himself Comte de Sainte-Helene."

LUCIEN DE RUBEMPRE

"Lucien Chardon, son of an apothecary at Angouleme—his mother a Demoiselle de Rubempre—bears the name of Rubempre in virtue of a royal patent. This was granted by the request of Madame la Duchesse de Maufrigneuse and Monsieur le Comte de Serizy.

"This young man came to Paris in 182. . . without any means of subsistence, following Madame la Comtesse Sixte du Chatelet, then Madame de Bargeton, a cousin of Madame d'Espard's.

"He was ungrateful to Madame de Bargeton, and cohabited with a girl named Coralie, an actress at the Gymnase, now dead, who left Monsieur Camusot, a silk mercer in the Rue des Bourdonnais, to live with Rubempre.

"Ere long, having sunk into poverty through the insufficiency of the money allowed him by this actress, he seriously compromised his brother-in-law, a highly respected printer of Angouleme, by giving forged bills, for which David Sechard was arrested, during a short visit paid to Angouleme by Lucien. In consequence of this affair Rubempre fled, but suddenly reappeared in Paris with the Abbe Carlos Herrera.

"Though having no visible means of subsistence, the said Lucien de Rubempre spent on an average three hundred thousand francs during the three years of his second residence in Paris, and can only have obtained the money from the self-styled Abbe Carlos Herrera—but how did he come by it?

"He has recently laid out above a million francs in repurchasing the Rubempre estates to fulfil the conditions on which he was to be allowed to marry Mademoiselle Clotilde de Grandlieu. This marriage has been broken off in consequence of inquiries made by the Grandlieu family, the said Lucien having told them that he had obtained the money from his brother-in-law and his sister; but the information obtained, more especially by Monsieur Derville, attorney-at-law, proves that not only were that worthy couple ignorant of his having made this purchase, but that they believed the said Lucien to be deeply in debt.

"Moreover, the property inherited by the Sechards consists of houses; and the ready money, by their affidavit, amounted to about two hundred thousand francs.

"Lucien was secretly cohabiting with Esther Gobseck; hence there can be no doubt that all the lavish gifts of the Baron de Nucingen, the girl's protector, were handed over to the said Lucien.

"Lucien and his companion, the convict, have succeeded in keeping their footing in the face of the world longer than Coignard did, deriving their income from the prostitution of the said Esther, formerly on the register of the town."

Though these notes are to a great extent a repetition of the story already told, it was necessary to reproduce them to show the part played by the police in Paris. As has already been seen from the note on Peyrade, the police has summaries, almost invariably correct, concerning every family or individual whose life is under suspicion, or whose actions are of a doubtful character. It knows every circumstance of their delinquencies. This universal register and account of consciences is as accurately kept as the register of the Bank of France and its accounts of fortunes. Just as the Bank notes the slightest delay in payment, gauges every credit, takes stock of every capitalist, and watches their proceedings, so does the police weigh and measure the honesty of each citizen. With it, as in a Court of Law, innocence has nothing to fear; it has no hold on anything but crime.

However high the rank of a family, it cannot evade this social providence.

And its discretion is equal to the extent of its power. This vast mass of written evidence compiled by the police—reports, notes, and summaries—an ocean of information, sleeps undisturbed, as deep and calm as the sea. Some accident occurs, some crime or misdemeanor becomes aggressive,—then the law refers to the police, and immediately, if any documents bear on the suspected criminal, the judge is informed. These records, an analysis of his antecedents, are merely side-lights, and unknown beyond the walls of the Palais de Justice. No legal use can be made of them; Justice is informed by them, and takes advantage of them; but that is all. These documents form, as it were, the inner lining of the tissue of crimes, their first cause, which is hardly ever made public. No jury would accept it; and the whole country would rise up in wrath if excerpts from those documents came out in the trial at the Assizes. In fact, it is the truth which is doomed to remain in the well, as it is everywhere and at all times. There is not a magistrate who, after twelve years' experience in Paris, is not fully aware that the Assize Court and the police authorities keep the secret of half these squalid atrocities, or who does not admit that half the crimes that are committed are never punished by the law.

If the public could know how reserved the *employes* of the police are—who do not forget—they would reverence these honest men as much as they do Cheverus. The police is supposed to be astute, Machiavellian; it is, in fact most benign. But it hears every passion in its paroxysms, it listens to every kind of treachery, and keeps notes of all. The police is terrible on one side only. What it does for justice it does no less for political interests; but in these it is as ruthless and as one-sided as the fires of the Inquisition.

"Put this aside," said the lawyer, replacing the notes in their cover; "this is a secret between the police and the law. The judge will estimate its value, but Monsieur and Madame Camusot must know nothing of it."

"As if I needed telling that!" said his wife.

"Lucien is guilty," he went on; "but of what?"

"A man who is the favorite of the Duchesse de Maufrigneuse, of the Comtesse de Serizy, and loved by Clotilde de Grandlieu, is not guilty," said Amelie. "The other *must* be answerable for everything."

"But Lucien is his accomplice," cried Camusot.

"Take my advice," said Amelie. "Restore this priest to the diplomatic career he so greatly adorns, exculpate this little wretch, and find some other criminal—"

"How you run on!" said the magistrate with a smile. "Women go to the point, plunging through the law as birds fly through the air, and find nothing to stop them."

"But," said Amelie, "whether he is a diplomate or a convict, the Abbe Carlos will find some one to get him out of the scrape."

"I am only a considering cap; you are the brain," said Camusot.

"Well, the sitting is closed; give your Melie a kiss; it is one o'clock."

And Madame Camusot went to bed, leaving her husband to arrange his papers and his ideas in preparation for the task of examining the two prisoners next morning.

AND THUS, WHILE THE PRISON vans were conveying Jacques Collin and Lucien to the Conciergerie, the examining judge, having breakfasted, was making his way across Paris on foot, after the unpretentious fashion of Parisian magistrates, to go to his chambers, where all the documents in the case were laid ready for him.

This was the way of it: Every examining judge has a head-clerk, a sort of sworn legal secretary—a race that perpetuates itself without any premiums or encouragement, producing a number of excellent souls in whom secrecy is natural and incorruptible. From the origin of the Parlement to the present day, no case has ever been known at the Palais de Justice of any gossip or indiscretion on the part of a clerk bound to the Courts of Inquiry. Gentil sold the release given by Louise de Savoie to Semblancay; a War Office clerk sold the plan of the Russian campaign to Czernitchef; and these traitors were more or less rich. The prospect of a post in the Palais and professional conscientiousness are enough to make a judge's clerk a successful rival of the tomb—for the tomb has betrayed many secrets since chemistry has made such progress.

This official is, in fact, the magistrate's pen. It will be understood by many readers that a man may gladly be the shaft of a machine, while they wonder why he is content to remain a bolt; still a bolt is content— perhaps the machinery terrifies him.

Camusot's clerk, a young man of two-and-twenty, named Coquart, had come in the morning to fetch all the documents and the judge's notes, and laid everything ready in his chambers, while the lawyer himself was wandering along the quays, looking at the curiosities in the shops, and wondering within himself:—

"How on earth am I to set to work with such a clever rascal as this Jacques Collin, supposing it is he? The head of the Safety will know him. I must look as if I knew what I was about, if only for the sake of the police! I see so many insuperable difficulties, that the best plan would be to enlighten the Marquise and the Duchess by showing them the notes of the police, and I should avenge my father, from whom Lucien stole Coralie.—If I can unveil these scoundrels, my skill will be loudly proclaimed, and Lucien will soon be thrown over by his friends.—Well, well, the examination will settle all that."

He turned into a curiosity shop, tempted by a Boule clock.

"Not to be false to my conscience, and yet to oblige two great ladies— that will be a triumph of skill," thought he. "What, do you collect coins too, monsieur?" said Camusot to the Public Prosecutor, whom he found in the shop.

"It is a taste dear to all dispensers of justice," said the Comte de Granville, laughing. "They look at the reverse side of every medal."

And after looking about the shop for some minutes, as if continuing his search, he accompanied Camusot on his way down the quay without it ever occurring to Camusot that anything but chance had brought them together.

"You are examining Monsieur de Rubempre this morning," said the Public Prosecutor. "Poor fellow—I liked him."

"There are several charges against him," said Camusot.

"Yes, I saw the police papers; but some of the information came from an agent who is independent of the Prefet, the notorious Corentin, who had caused the death of more innocent men than you will ever send guilty men to the scaffold, and—But that rascal is out of your reach.— Without trying to influence the conscience of such a magistrate as you are, I may point out to you that if you could be perfectly sure that Lucien was ignorant of the contents of that woman's will, it would be self-evident that he had no interest in her death, for she gave him enormous sums of money."

"We can prove his absence at the time when this Esther was poisoned," said Camusot. "He was at Fontainebleau, on the watch for Mademoiselle de Grandlieu and the Duchesse de Lenoncourt."

"And he still cherished such hopes of marrying Mademoiselle de Grandlieu," said the Public Prosecutor—"I have it from the

Duchesse de Grandlieu herself—that it is inconceivable that such a clever young fellow should compromise his chances by a perfectly aimless crime."

"Yes," said Camusot, "especially if Esther gave him all she got."

"Derville and Nucingen both say that she died in ignorance of the inheritance she had long since come into," added Granville.

"But then what do you suppose is the meaning of it all?" asked Camusot. "For there is something at the bottom of it."

"A crime committed by some servant," said the Public Prosecutor.

"Unfortunately," remarked Camusot, "it would be quite like Jacques Collin—for the Spanish priest is certainly none other than that escaped convict—to have taken possession of the seven hundred and fifty thousand francs derived from the sale of the certificate of shares given to Esther by Nucingen."

"Weigh everything with care, my dear Camusot. Be prudent. The Abbe Carlos Herrera has diplomatic connections; still, an envoy who had committed a crime would not be sheltered by his position. Is he or is he not the Abbe Carlos Herrera? That is the important question."

And Monsieur de Granville bowed, and turned away, as requiring no answer.

"So he too wants to save Lucien!" thought Camusot, going on by the Quai des Lunettes, while the Public Prosecutor entered the Palais through the Cour de Harlay.

On reaching the courtyard of the Conciergerie, Camusot went to the Governor's room and led him into the middle of the pavement, where no one could overhear them.

"My dear sir, do me the favor of going to La Force, and inquiring of your colleague there whether he happens at this moment to have there any convicts who were on the hulks at Toulon between 1810 and 1815; or have you any imprisoned here? We will transfer those of La Force here for a few days, and you will let me know whether this so-called Spanish priest is known to them as Jacques Collin, otherwise *Trompe-la-Mort*."

"Very good, Monsieur Camusot.—But Bibi-Lupin is come. . ."

"What, already?" said the judge.

"He was at Melun. He was told that *Trompe-la-Mort* had to be identified, and he smiled with joy. He awaits your orders."

"Send him to me."

The Governor was then able to lay before Monsieur Camusot Jacques Collin's request, and he described the man's deplorable condition.

"I intended to examine him first," replied the magistrate, "but not on account of his health. I received a note this morning from the Governor of La Force. Well, this rascal, who described himself to you as having been dying for twenty-four hours past, slept so soundly that they went into his cell there, with the doctor for whom the Governor had sent, without his hearing them; the doctor did not even feel his pulse, he left him to sleep—which proves that his conscience is as tough as his health. I shall accept this feigned illness only so far as it may enable me to study my man," added Monsieur Camusot, smiling.

"We live to learn every day with these various grades of prisoners," said the Governor of the prison.

The Prefecture of police adjoins the Conciergerie, and the magistrates, like the Governor, knowing all the subterranean passages, can get to and fro with the greatest rapidity. This explains the miraculous ease with which information can be conveyed, during the sitting of the Courts, to the officials and the presidents of the Assize Courts. And by the time Monsieur Camusot had reached the top of the stairs leading to his chambers, Bibi-Lupin was there too, having come by the *Salle des Pas-Perdus*.

"What zeal!" said Camusot, with a smile.

"Ah, well, you see if it is *he*," replied the man, "you will see great fun in the prison-yard if by chance there are any old stagers here."

"Why?"

"*Trompe-la-Mort* sneaked their chips, and I know that they have vowed to be the death of him."

They were the convicts whose money, intrusted to *Trompe-la-Mort*, had all been made away with by him for Lucien, as has been told.

"Could you lay your hand on the witnesses of his former arrest?"

"Give me two summonses of witnesses and I will find you some to-day."

"Coquart," said the lawyer, as he took off his gloves, and placed his hat and stick in a corner, "fill up two summonses by monsieur's directions."

He looked at himself in the glass over the chimney shelf, where stood, in the place of a clock, a basin and jug. On one side was a bottle of water and a glass, on the other a lamp. He rang the bell; his usher came in a few minutes after.

"Is anybody here for me yet?" he asked the man, whose business it was to receive the witnesses, to verify their summons, and to set them in the order of their arrival.

"Yes, sir."

"Take their names, and bring me the list."

The examining judges, to save time, are often obliged to carry on several inquiries at once. Hence the long waiting inflicted on the witnesses, who have seats in the ushers' hall, where the judges' bells are constantly ringing.

"And then," Camusot went on, "bring up the Abbe Carlos Herrera."

"Ah, ha! I was told that he was a priest in Spanish. Pooh! It is a new edition of Collet, Monsieur Camusot," said the head of the Safety department.

"There is nothing new!" replied Camusot.

And he signed the two formidable documents which alarm everybody, even the most innocent witnesses, whom the law thus requires to appear, under severe penalties in case of failure.

BY THIS TIME JACQUES COLLIN had, about half an hour since, finished his deep meditations, and was armed for the fray. Nothing is more perfectly characteristic of this type of the mob in rebellion against the law than the few words he had written on the greasy scraps of paper.

The sense of the first—for it was written in the language, the very slang of slang, agreed upon by Asie and himself, a cipher of words—was as follows:—

"Go to the Duchesse de Maufrigneuse or Madame de Serizy: one of them must see Lucien before he is examined, and give him the enclosed paper to read. Then find Europe and Paccard; those two thieves must be at my orders, and ready to play any part I may set them.

"Go to Rastignac; tell him, from the man he met at the opera-ball, to come and swear that the Abbe Carlos Herrera has no resemblance to Jacques Collin who was apprehended at Vauquer's. Do the same with Dr. Bianchon, and get Lucien's two women to work to the same end."

On the enclosed fragment were these words in good French:

"Lucien, confess nothing about me. I am the Abbe Carlos Herrera. Not only will this be your exculpation; but, if you do not lose your head, you will have seven millions and your honor cleared."

These two bits of paper, gummed on the side of the writing so as to look like one piece, were then rolled tightly, with a dexterity peculiar to men who have dreamed of getting free from the hulks. The whole thing assumed the shape and consistency of a ball of dirty rubbish, about as big as the sealing-wax heads which thrifty women stick on the head of a large needle when the eye is broken.

"If I am examined first, we are saved; if it is the boy, all is lost," said he to himself while he waited.

His plight was so sore that the strong man's face was wet with white sweat. Indeed, this wonderful man saw as clearly in his sphere of crime as Moliere did in his sphere of dramatic poetry, or Cuvier in that of extinct organisms. Genius of whatever kind is intuition. Below this highest manifestation other remarkable achievements may be due to talent. This is what divides men of the first rank from those of the second.

Crime has its men of genius. Jacques Collin, driven to bay, had hit on the same notion as Madame Camusot's ambition and Madame de Serizy's passion, suddenly revived by the shock of the dreadful disaster which was overwhelming Lucien. This was the supreme effort of human intellect directed against the steel armor of Justice.

On hearing the rasping of the heavy locks and bolts of his door, Jacques Collin resumed his mask of a dying man; he was helped in this by the intoxicating joy that he felt at the sound of the warder's shoes in the passage. He had no idea how Asie would get near him; but he relied on meeting her on the way, especially after her promise given in the Saint-Jean gateway.

After that fortunate achievement she had gone on to the Place de Greve.

Till 1830 the name of La Greve (the Strand) had a meaning that is now lost. Every part of the river-shore from the Pont d'Arcole to the Pont Louis-Philippe was then as nature had made it, excepting the paved way which was at the top of the bank. When the river was in flood a boat could pass close under the houses and at the end of the streets running down to the river. On the quay the footpath was for the most part raised with a few steps; and when the river was up to the houses, vehicles had to pass along the horrible Rue de la Mortellerie, which has now been completely removed to make room for enlarging the Hotel de Ville.

So the sham costermonger could easily and quickly run her truck down to the bottom of the quay, and hide it there till the real owner—

who was, in fact, drinking the price of her wares, sold bodily to Asie, in one of the abominable taverns in the Rue de la Mortellerie—should return to claim it. At that time the Quai Pelletier was being extended, the entrance to the works was guarded by a crippled soldier, and the barrow would be quite safe in his keeping.

Asie then jumped into a hackney cab on the Place de l'Hotel de Ville, and said to the driver, "To the Temple, and look sharp, I'll tip you well."

A woman dressed like Asie could disappear, without any questions being asked, in the huge market-place, where all the rags in Paris are gathered together, where a thousand costermongers wander round, and two hundred old-clothes sellers are chaffering.

The two prisoners had hardly been locked up when she was dressing herself in a low, damp entresol over one of those foul shops where remnants are sold, pieces stolen by tailors and dressmakers—an establishment kept by an old maid known as La Romette, from her Christian name Jeromette. La Romette was to the "purchasers of wardrobes" what these women are to the better class of so-called ladies in difficulties—Madame la Ressource, that is to say, money-lenders at a hundred per cent.

"Now, child," said Asie, "I have got to be figged out. I must be a Baroness of the Faubourg Saint-Germain at the very least. And sharp's the word, for my feet are in hot oil. You know what gowns suit me. Hand up the rouge-pot, find me some first-class bits of lace, and the swaggerest jewelry you can pick out.—Send the girl to call a coach, and have it brought to the back door."

"Yes, madame," the woman replied very humbly, and with the eagerness of a maid waiting on her mistress.

If there had been any one to witness the scene, he would have understood that the woman known as Asie was at home here.

"I have had some diamonds offered me," said la Romette as she dressed Asie's head.

"Stolen?"

"I should think so."

"Well, then, however cheap they may be, we must do without 'em. We must fight shy of the beak for a long time to come."

It will now be understood how Asie contrived to be in the *Salle des Pas-Perdus* of the Palais de Justice with a summons in her hand, asking her way along the passages and stairs leading to the examining judge's chambers, and inquiring for Monsieur Camusot, about a quarter of an hour before that gentleman's arrival.

Asie was not recognizable. After washing off her "make-up" as an old woman, like an actress, she applied rouge and pearl powder, and covered her head with a well-made fair wig. Dressed exactly as a lady of the Faubourg Saint-Germain might be if in search of a dog she had lost, she looked about forty, for she shrouded her features under a splendid black lace veil. A pair of stays, severely laced, disguised her cook's figure. With very good gloves and a rather large bustle, she exhaled the perfume of powder a la Marechale. Playing with a bag mounted in gold, she divided her attention between the walls of the building, where she found herself evidently for the first time, and the string by which she led a dainty little spaniel. Such a dowager could not fail to attract the notice of the black-robed natives of the *Salle des Pas-Perdus*.

Besides the briefless lawyers who sweep this hall with their gowns, and speak of the leading advocates by their Christian names, as fine gentlemen address each other, to produce the impression that they are of the aristocracy of the law, patient youths are often to be seen, hangers-on of the attorneys, waiting, waiting, in hope of a case put down for the end of the day, which they may be so lucky as to be called to plead if the advocates retained for the earlier cases should not come out in time.

A very curious study would be that of the differences between these various black gowns, pacing the immense hall in threes, or sometimes in fours, their persistent talk filling the place with a loud, echoing hum—a hall well named indeed, for this slow walk exhausts the lawyers as much as the waste of words. But such a study has its place in the volumes destined to reveal the life of Paris pleaders.

Asie had counted on the presence of these youths; she laughed in her sleeve at some of the pleasantries she overheard, and finally succeeded in attracting the attention of Massol, a young lawyer whose time was more taken up by the *Police Gazette* than by clients, and who came up with a laugh to place himself at the service of a woman so elegantly scented and so handsomely dressed.

Asie put on a little, thin voice to explain to this obliging gentleman that she appeared in answer to a summons from a judge named Camusot.

"Oh! in the Rubempre case?"

So the affair had its name already.

"Oh, it is not my affair. It is my maid's, a girl named Europe, who was with me twenty-four hours, and who fled when she saw my servant bring in a piece of stamped paper."

Then, like any old woman who spends her life gossiping in the chimney-corner, prompted by Massol, she poured out the story of her woes with her first husband, one of the three Directors of the land revenue. She consulted the young lawyer as to whether she would do well to enter on a lawsuit with her son-in-law, the Comte de Gross-Narp, who made her daughter very miserable, and whether the law allowed her to dispose of her fortune.

In spite of all his efforts, Massol could not be sure whether the summons were addressed to the mistress or the maid. At the first moment he had only glanced at this legal document of the most familiar aspect; for, to save time, it is printed, and the magistrates' clerks have only to fill in the blanks left for the names and addresses of the witnesses, the hour for which they are called, and so forth.

Asie made him tell her all about the Palais, which she knew more intimately than the lawyer did. Finally, she inquired at what hour Monsieur Camusot would arrive.

"Well, the examining judges generally are here by about ten o'clock."

"It is now a quarter to ten," said she, looking at a pretty little watch, a perfect gem of goldsmith's work, which made Massol say to himself:

"Where the devil will Fortune make herself at home next!"

At this moment Asie had come to the dark hall looking out on the yard of the Conciergerie, where the ushers wait. On seeing the gate through the window, she exclaimed:

"What are those high walls?"

"That is the Conciergerie."

"Oh! so that is the Conciergerie where our poor queen—Oh! I should so like to see her cell!"

"Impossible, Madame la Baronne," replied the young lawyer, on whose arm the dowager was now leaning. "A permit is indispensable, and very difficult to procure."

"I have been told," she went on, "that Louis XVIII himself composed the inscription that is to be seen in Marie-Antoinette's cell."

"Yes, Madame la Baronne."

"How much I should like to know Latin that I might study the words of that inscription!" said she. "Do you think that Monsieur Camusot could give me a permit?"

"That is not in his power; but he could take you there."

"But his business—" objected she.

"Oh!" said Massol, "prisoners under suspicion can wait."

"To be sure," said she artlessly, "they are under suspicion.—But I know Monsieur de Granville, your public prosecutor—"

This hint had a magical effect on the ushers and the young lawyer.

"Ah, you know Monsieur de Granville?" said Massol, who was inclined to ask the client thus sent to him by chance her name and address.

"I often see him at my friend Monsieur de Serizy's house. Madame de Serizy is a connection of mine through the Ronquerolles."

"Well, if Madame wishes to go down to the Conciergerie," said an usher, "she—"

"Yes," said Massol.

So the Baroness and the lawyer were allowed to pass, and they presently found themselves in the little guard-room at the top of the stairs leading to the "mousetrap," a spot well known to Asie, forming, as has been said, a post of observation between those cells and the Court of the Sixth Chamber, through which everybody is obliged to pass.

"Will you ask if Monsieur Camusot is come yet?" said she, seeing some gendarmes playing cards.

"Yes, madame, he has just come up from the 'mousetrap.'"

"The mousetrap!" said she. "What is that?—Oh! how stupid of me not to have gone straight to the Comte de Granville.—But I have not time now. Pray take me to speak to Monsieur Camusot before he is otherwise engaged."

"Oh, you have plenty of time for seeing Monsieur Camusot," said Massol. "If you send him in your card, he will spare you the discomfort of waiting in the ante-room with the witnesses.—We can be civil here to ladies like you.—You have a card about you?"

At this instant Asie and her lawyer were exactly in front of the window of the guardroom whence the gendarmes could observe the gate of the Conciergerie. The gendarmes, brought up to respect the defenders of the widow and the orphan, were aware too of the prerogative of the gown, and for a few minutes allowed the Baroness to remain there escorted by a pleader. Asie listened to the terrible tales which a young lawyer is ready to tell about that prison-gate. She would not believe that those who were condemned to death were prepared for the scaffold behind those bars; but the sergeant-at-arms assured her it was so.

"How much I should like to see it done!" cried she.

And there she remained, prattling to the lawyer and the sergeant, till she saw Jacques Collin come out supported by two gendarmes, and preceded by Monsieur Camusot's clerk.

"Ah, there is a chaplain no doubt going to prepare a poor wretch—"

"Not at all, Madame la Baronne," said the gendarme. "He is a prisoner coming to be examined."

"What is he accused of?"

"He is concerned in this poisoning case."

"Oh! I should like to see him."

"You cannot stay here," said the sergeant, "for he is under close arrest, and he must pass through here. You see, madame, that door leads to the stairs—"

"Oh! thank you!" cried the Baroness, making for the door, to rush down the stairs, where she at once shrieked out, "Oh! where am I?"

This cry reached the ear of Jacques Collin, who was thus prepared to see her. The sergeant flew after Madame la Baronne, seized her by the middle, and lifted her back like a feather into the midst of a group of five gendarmes, who started up as one man; for in that guardroom everything is regarded as suspicious. The proceeding was arbitrary, but the arbitrariness was necessary. The young lawyer himself had cried out twice, "Madame! madame!" in his horror, so much did he fear finding himself in the wrong.

The Abbe Carlos Herrera, half fainting, sank on a chair in the guardroom.

"Poor man!" said the Baroness. "Can he be a criminal?"

The words, though spoken low to the young advocate, could be heard by all, for the silence of death reigned in that terrible guardroom. Certain privileged persons are sometimes allowed to see famous criminals on their way through this room or through the passages, so that the clerk and the gendarmes who had charge of the Abbe Carlos made no remark. Also, in consequence of the devoted zeal of the sergeant who had snatched up the Baroness to hinder any communication between the prisoner and the visitors, there was a considerable space between them.

"Let us go on," said Jacques Collin, making an effort to rise.

At the same moment the little ball rolled out of his sleeve, and the spot where it fell was noted by the Baroness, who could look about her freely from under her veil. The little pellet, being damp and sticky, did not roll; for such trivial details, apparently unimportant, had all been duly considered by Jacques Collin to insure success.

When the prisoner had been led up the higher part of the steps, Asie very unaffectedly dropped her bag and picked it up again; but in stooping she seized the pellet which had escaped notice, its color being exactly like that of the dust and mud on the floor.

"Oh dear!" cried she, "it goes to my heart.—He is dying—"

"Or seems to be," replied the sergeant.

"Monsieur," said Asie to the lawyer, "take me at once to Monsieur Camusot; I have come about this case; and he might be very glad to see me before examining that poor priest."

The lawyer and the Baroness left the guardroom, with its greasy, fuliginous walls; but as soon as they reached the top of the stairs, Asie exclaimed:

"Oh, and my dog! My poor little dog!" and she rushed off like a mad creature down the *Salle des Pas-Perdus*, asking every one where her dog was. She got to the corridor beyond (la Galerie Marchande, or Merchant's Hall, as it is called), and flew to the staircase, saying, "There he is!"

These stairs lead to the Cour de Harlay, through which Asie, having played out the farce, passed out and took a hackney cab on the Quai des Orfevres, where there is a stand; thus she vanished with the summons requiring "Europe" to appear, her real name being unknown to the police and the lawyers.

"Rue Neuve-Saint-Marc," cried she to the driver.

ASIE COULD DEPEND ON THE absolute secrecy of an old-clothes purchaser, known as Madame Nourrisson, who also called herself Madame de Saint-Esteve; and who would lend Asie not merely her personality, but her shop at need, for it was there that Nucingen had bargained for the surrender of Esther. Asie was quite at home there, for she had a bedroom in Madame Nourrisson's establishment.

She paid the driver, and went up to her room, nodding to Madame Nourrisson in a way to make her understand that she had not time to say two words to her.

As soon as she was safe from observation, Asie unwrapped the papers with the care of a savant unrolling a palimpsest. After reading the instructions, she thought it wise to copy the lines intended for Lucien on a sheet of letter-paper; then she went down to Madame Nourrisson, to whom she talked while a little shop-girl went to fetch a cab from the Boulevard des Italiens. She thus extracted the

HONORÉ DE BALZAC

addresses of the Duchesse de Maufrigneuse and of Madame de Serizy, which were known to Madame Nourrisson by her dealings with their maids.

All this running about and elaborate business took up more than two hours. Madame la Duchesse de Maufrigneuse, who lived at the top of the Faubourg Saint-Honore, kept Madame de Saint-Esteve waiting an hour, although the lady's-maid, after knocking at the boudoir door, had handed in to her mistress a card with Madame de Saint-Esteve's name, on which Asie had written, "Called about pressing business concerning Lucien."

Her first glance at the Duchess' face showed her how till-timed her visit must be; she apologized for disturbing Madame la Duchesse when she was resting, on the plea of the danger in which Lucien stood.

"Who are you?" asked the Duchess, without any pretence at politeness, as she looked at Asie from head to foot; for Asie, though she might be taken for a Baroness by Maitre Massol in the *Salle des Pas-Perdus*, when she stood on the carpet in the boudoir of the Hotel de Cadignan, looked like a splash of mud on a white satin gown.

"I am a dealer in cast-off clothes, Madame la Duchesse; for in such matters every lady applies to women whose business rests on a basis of perfect secrecy. I have never betrayed anybody, though God knows how many great ladies have intrusted their diamonds to me by the month while wearing false jewels made to imitate them exactly."

"You have some other name?" said the Duchess, smiling at a reminiscence recalled to her by this reply.

"Yes, Madame la Duchesse, I am Madame de Saint-Esteve on great occasions, but in the trade I am Madame Nourrisson."

"Well, well," said the Duchess in an altered tone.

"I am able to be of great service," Asie went on, "for we hear the husbands' secrets as well as the wives'. I have done many little jobs for Monsieur de Marsay, whom Madame la Duchesse—"

"That will do, that will do!" cried the Duchess. "What about Lucien?"

"If you wish to save him, madame, you must have courage enough to lose no time in dressing. But, indeed, Madame la Duchesse, you could not look more charming than you do at this moment. You are sweet enough to charm anybody, take an old woman's word for it! In short, madame, do not wait for your carriage, but get into my hackney coach. Come to Madame de Serizy's if you hope to avert worse misfortunes than the death of that cherub—"

"Go on, I will follow you," said the Duchess after a moment's hesitation. "Between us we may give Leontine some courage. . ."

Notwithstanding the really demoniacal activity of this Dorine of the hulks, the clock was striking two when she and the Duchesse de Maufrigneuse went into the Comtesse de Serizy's house in the Rue de la Chaussee-d'Antin. Once there, thanks to the Duchess, not an instant was lost. The two women were at once shown up to the Countess, whom they found reclining on a couch in a miniature chalet, surrounded by a garden fragrant with the rarest flowers.

"That is well," said Asie, looking about her. "No one can overhear us."

"Oh! my dear, I am half dead! Tell me, Diane, what have you done?" cried the Duchess, starting up like a fawn, and, seizing the Duchess by the shoulders, she melted into tears.

"Come, come, Leontine; there are occasions when women like us must not cry, but act," said the Duchess, forcing the Countess to sit down on the sofa by her side.

Asie studied the Countess' face with the scrutiny peculiar to those old hands, which pierces to the soul of a woman as certainly as a surgeon's instrument probes a wound!—the sorrow that engraves ineradicable lines on the heart and on the features. She was dressed without the least touch of vanity. She was now forty-five, and her printed muslin wrapper, tumbled and untidy, showed her bosom without any art or even stays! Her eyes were set in dark circles, and her mottled cheeks showed the traces of bitter tears. She wore no sash round her waist; the embroidery on her petticoat and shift was all crumpled. Her hair, knotted up under a lace cap, had not been combed for four-and-twenty hours, and showed as a thin, short plait and ragged little curls. Leontine had forgotten to put on her false hair.

"You are in love for the first time in your life?" said Asie sententiously.

Leontine then saw the woman and started with horror.

"Who is that, my dear Diane?" she asked of the Duchesse de Maufrigneuse.

"Whom should I bring with me but a woman who is devoted to Lucien and willing to help us?"

Asie had hit the truth. Madame de Serizy, who was regarded as one of the most fickle of fashionable women, had had an attachment of ten years' standing for the Marquis d'Aiglemont. Since the Marquis' departure for the colonies, she had gone wild about Lucien, and had won him from the Duchesse de Maufrigneuse, knowing nothing—

like the Paris world generally—of Lucien's passion for Esther. In the world of fashion a recognized attachment does more to ruin a woman's reputation than ten unconfessed liaisons; how much more then two such attachments? However, as no one thought of Madame de Serizy as a responsible person, the historian cannot undertake to speak for her virtue thus doubly dog's-eared.

She was fair, of medium height, and well preserved, as a fair woman can be who is well preserved at all; that is to say, she did not look more than thirty, being slender, but not lean, with a white skin and flaxen hair; she had hands, feet, and a shape of aristocratic elegance, and was as witty as all the Ronquerolles, spiteful, therefore, to women, and good-natured to men. Her large fortune, her husband's fine position, and that of her brother, the Marquis de Ronquerolles, had protected her from the mortifications with which any other woman would have been overwhelmed. She had this great merit—that she was honest in her depravity, and confessed her worship of the manners and customs of the Regency.

Now, at forty-two this woman—who had hitherto regarded men as no more than pleasing playthings, to whom, indeed, she had, strange to say, granted much, regarding love as merely a matter of sacrifice to gain the upper hand,—this woman, on first seeing Lucien, had been seized with such a passion as the Baron de Nucingen's for Esther. She had loved, as Asie had just told her, for the first time in her life.

This postponement of youth is more common with Parisian women than might be supposed, and causes the ruin of some virtuous souls just as they are reaching the haven of forty. The Duchesse de Maufrigneuse was the only person in the secret of the vehement and absorbing passion, of which the joys, from the girlish suspicion of first love to the preposterous follies of fulfilment, had made Leontine half crazy and insatiable.

True love, as we know, is merciless. The discovery of Esther's existence had been followed by one of those outbursts of rage which in a woman rise even to the pitch of murder; then came the phase of meanness, to which a sincere affection humbles itself so gladly. Indeed, for the last month the Countess would have given ten years of her life to have Lucien again for one week. At last she had even resigned herself to accept Esther as her rival, just when the news of her lover's arrest had come like the last trump on this paroxysm of devotion.

The Countess had nearly died of it. Her husband had himself nursed her in bed, fearing the betrayal of delirium, and for twenty-four hours she had been living with a knife in her heart. She said to her husband in her fever:

"Save Lucien, and I will live henceforth for you alone."

"Indeed, as Madame la Duchesse tells you, it is of no use to make your eyes like boiled gooseberries," cried the dreadful Asie, shaking the Countess by the arm. "If you want to save him, there is not a minute to lose. He is innocent—I swear it by my mother's bones!"

"Yes, yes, of course he is!" cried the Countess, looking quite kindly at the dreadful old woman.

"But," Asie went on, "if Monsieur Camusot questions him the wrong way, he can make a guilty man of him with two sentences; so, if it is in your power to get the Conciergerie opened to you, and to say a few words to him, go at once, and give him this paper.—He will be released to-morrow; I will answer for it. Now, get him out of the scrape, for you got him into it."

"I?"

"Yes, you!—You fine ladies never have a son even when you own millions. When I allowed myself the luxury of keeping boys, they always had their pockets full of gold! Their amusements amused me. It is delightful to be mother and mistress in one. Now, you—you let the men you love die of hunger without asking any questions. Esther, now, made no speeches; she gave, at the cost of perdition, soul and body, the million your Lucien was required to show, and that is what has brought him to this pass—"

"Poor girl! Did she do that! I love her!" said Leontine.

"Yes—now!" said Asie, with freezing irony.

"She was a real beauty; but now, my angel, you are better looking than she is.—And Lucien's marriage is so effectually broken off, that nothing can mend it," said the Duchess in a whisper to Leontine.

The effect of this revelation and forecast was so great on the Countess that she was well again. She passed her hand over her brow; she was young once more.

"Now, my lady, hot foot, and make haste!" said Asie, seeing the change, and guessing what had caused it.

"But," said Madame de Maufrigneuse, "if the first thing is to prevent Lucien's being examined by Monsieur Camusot, we can do that by writing two words to the judge and sending your man with it to the Palais, Leontine."

"Then come into my room," said Madame de Serizy.

THIS IS WHAT WAS TAKING place at the Palais while Lucien's protectresses were obeying the orders issued by Jacques Collin. The gendarmes placed the moribund prisoner on a chair facing the window in Monsieur Camusot's room; he was sitting in his place in front of his table. Coquart, pen in hand, had a little table to himself a few yards off.

The aspect of a magistrate's chambers is not a matter of indifference; and if this room had not been chosen intentionally, it must be owned that chance had favored justice. An examining judge, like a painter, requires the clear equable light of a north window, for the criminal's face is a picture which he must constantly study. Hence most magistrates place their table, as this of Camusot's was arranged, so as to sit with their back to the window and leave the face of the examinee in broad daylight. Not one of them all but, by the end of six months, has assumed an absent-minded and indifferent expression, if he does not wear spectacles, and maintains it throughout the examination.

It was a sudden change of expression in the prisoner's face, detected by these means, and caused by a sudden point-blank question, that led to the discovery of the crime committed by Castaing at the very moment when, after a long consultation with the public prosecutor, the magistrate was about to let the criminal loose on society for lack of evidence. This detail will show the least intelligent person how living, interesting, curious, and dramatically terrible is the conflict of an examination—a conflict without witnesses, but always recorded. God knows what remains on the paper of the scenes at white heat in which a look, a tone, a quiver of the features, the faintest touch of color lent by some emotion, has been fraught with danger, as though the adversaries were savages watching each other to plant a fatal stroke. A report is no more than the ashes of the fire.

"What is your real name?" Camusot asked Jacques Collin.

"Don Carlos Herrera, canon of the Royal Chapter of Toledo, and secret envoy of His Majesty Ferdinand VII."

It must here be observed that Jacques Collin spoke French like a Spanish trollop, blundering over it in such a way as to make his answers almost unintelligible, and to require them to be repeated. But Monsieur de Nucingen's German barbarisms have already weighted this Scene too much to allow of the introduction of other sentences no less difficult to read, and hindering the rapid progress of the tale.

"Then you have papers to prove your right to the dignities of which you speak?" asked Camusot.

"Yes, monsieur—my passport, a letter from his Catholic Majesty authorizing my mission.—In short, if you will but send at once to the Spanish Embassy two lines, which I will write in your presence, I shall be identified. Then, if you wish for further evidence, I will write to His Eminence the High Almoner of France, and he will immediately send his private secretary."

"And do you still pretend that you are dying?" asked the magistrate. "If you have really gone through all the sufferings you have complained of since your arrest, you ought to be dead by this time," said Camusot ironically.

"You are simply trying the courage of an innocent man and the strength of his constitution," said the prisoner mildly.

"Coquart, ring. Send for the prison doctor and an infirmary attendant.—We shall be obliged to remove your coat and proceed to verify the marks on your shoulder," Camusot went on.

"I am in your hands, monsieur."

The prisoner then inquired whether the magistrate would be kind enough to explain to him what he meant by "the marks," and why they should be sought on his shoulder. The judge was prepared for this question.

"You are suspected of being Jacques Collin, an escaped convict, whose daring shrinks at nothing, not even at sacrilege!" said Camusot promptly, his eyes fixed on those of the prisoner.

Jacques Collin gave no sign, and did not color; he remained quite calm, and assumed an air of guileless curiosity as he gazed at Camusot.

"I, monsieur? A convict? May the Order I belong to and God above forgive you for such an error. Tell me what I can do to prevent your continuing to offer such an insult to the rights of free men, to the Church, and to the King my master."

The judge made no reply to this, but explained to the Abbe that if he had been branded, a penalty at that time inflicted by law on all convicts sent to the hulks, the letters could be made to show by giving him a slap on the shoulder.

"Oh, monsieur," said Jacques Collin, "it would indeed be unfortunate if my devotion to the Royal cause should prove fatal to me."

"Explain yourself," said the judge, "that is what you are here for."

"Well, monsieur, I must have a great many scars on my back, for I was shot in the back as a traitor to my country while I was faithful to my King, by constitutionalists who left me for dead."

"You were shot, and you are alive!" said Camusot.

"I had made friends with some of the soldiers, to whom certain pious persons had sent money, so they placed me so far off that only spent balls reached me, and the men aimed at my back. This is a fact that His Excellency the Ambassador can bear witness to—"

"This devil of a man has an answer for everything! However, so much the better," thought Camusot, who assumed so much severity only to satisfy the demands of justice and of the police. "How is it that a man of your character," he went on, addressing the convict, "should have been found in the house of the Baron de Nucingen's mistress—and such a mistress, a girl who had been a common prostitute!"

"This is why I was found in a courtesan's house, monsieur," replied Jacques Collin. "But before telling you the reasons for my being there, I ought to mention that at the moment when I was just going upstairs I was seized with the first attack of my illness, and I had no time to speak to the girl. I knew of Mademoiselle Esther's intention of killing herself; and as young Lucien de Rubempre's interests were involved, and I have a particular affection for him for sacredly secret reasons, I was going to try to persuade the poor creature to give up the idea, suggested to her by despair. I meant to tell her that Lucien must certainly fail in his last attempt to win Mademoiselle Clotilde de Grandlieu; and I hoped that by telling her she had inherited seven millions of francs, I might give her courage to live.

"I am convinced, Monsieur le Juge, that I am a martyr to the secrets confided to me. By the suddenness of my illness I believe that I had been poisoned that very morning, but my strong constitution has saved me. I know that a certain agent of the political police is dogging me, and trying to entangle me in some discreditable business.

"If, at my request, you had sent for a doctor on my arrival here, you would have had ample proof of what I am telling you as to the state of my health. Believe me, monsieur, some persons far above our heads have some strong interest in getting me mistaken for some villain, so as to have a right to get rid of me. It is not all profit to serve a king; they have their meannesses. The Church alone is faultless."

It is impossible to do justice to the play of Jacques Collin's countenance as he carefully spun out his speech, sentence by sentence, for ten minutes; and it was all so plausible, especially the mention of Corentin, that the lawyer was shaken.

"Will you confide to me the reasons of your affection for Monsieur Lucien de Rubempre?"

"Can you not guess them? I am sixty years of age, monsieur—I implore you do not write it.—It is because—must I say it?"

"It will be to your own advantage, and more particularly to Monsieur Lucien de Rubempre's, if you tell everything," replied the judge.

"Because he is—Oh, God! he is my son," he gasped out with an effort.

And he fainted away.

"Do not write that down, Coquart," said Camusot in an undertone.

Coquart rose to fetch a little phial of "Four thieves' Vinegar."

"If he is Jacques Collin, he is a splendid actor!" thought Camusot.

Coquart held the phial under the convict's nose, while the judge examined him with the keen eye of a lynx—and a magistrate.

"Take his wig off," said Camusot, after waiting till the man recovered consciousness.

Jacques Collin heard, and quaked with terror, for he knew how vile an expression his face would assume.

"If you have not strength enough to take your wig off yourself—Yes, Coquart, remove it," said Camusot to his clerk.

Jacques Collin bent his head to the clerk with admirable resignation; but then his head, bereft of that adornment, was hideous to behold in its natural aspect.

The sight of it left Camusot in the greatest uncertainty. While waiting for the doctor and the man from the infirmary, he set to work to classify and examine the various papers and the objects seized in Lucien's rooms. After carrying out their functions in the Rue Saint-Georges at Mademoiselle Esther's house, the police had searched the rooms at the Quai Malaquais.

"You have your hand on some letters from the Comtesse de Serizy," said Carlos Herrera. "But I cannot imagine why you should have almost all Lucien's papers," he added, with a smile of overwhelming irony at the judge.

Camusot, as he saw the smile, understood the bearing of the word "almost."

"Lucien de Rubempre is in custody under suspicion of being your accomplice," said he, watching to see the effect of this news on his examinee.

"You have brought about a great misfortune, for he is as innocent as I am," replied the sham Spaniard, without betraying the smallest agitation.

"We shall see. We have not as yet established your identity," Camusot observed, surprised at the prisoner's indifference. "If you are really Don Carlos Herrera, the position of Lucien Chardon will at once be completely altered."

"To be sure, she became Madame Chardon—Mademoiselle de Rubempre!" murmured Carlos. "Ah! that was one of the greatest sins of my life."

He raised his eyes to heaven, and by the movement of his lips seemed to be uttering a fervent prayer.

"But if you are Jacques Collin, and if he was, and knew that he was, the companion of an escaped convict, a sacrilegious wretch, all the crimes of which he is suspected by the law are more than probably true."

Carlos Herrera sat like bronze as he heard this speech, very cleverly delivered by the judge, and his only reply to the words "*knew that he was*" and "*escaped convict*" was to lift his hands to heaven with a gesture of noble and dignified sorrow.

"Monsieur l'Abbe," Camusot went on, with the greatest politeness, "if you are Don Carlos Herrera, you will forgive us for what we are obliged to do in the interests of justice and truth."

Jacques Collin detected a snare in the lawyer's very voice as he spoke the words "Monsieur l'Abbe." The man's face never changed; Camusot had looked for a gleam of joy, which might have been the first indication of his being a convict, betraying the exquisite satisfaction of a criminal deceiving his judge; but this hero of the hulks was strong in Machiavellian dissimulation.

"I am accustomed to diplomacy, and I belong to an Order of very austere discipline," replied Jacques Collin, with apostolic mildness. "I understand everything, and am inured to suffering. I should be free by this time if you had discovered in my room the hiding-place where I keep my papers—for I see you have none but unimportant documents."

This was a finishing stroke to Camusot: Jacques Collin by his air of ease and simplicity had counteracted all the suspicions to which his appearance, unwigged, had given rise.

"Where are these papers?"

"I will tell you exactly if you will get a secretary from the Spanish Embassy to accompany your messenger. He will take them and be answerable to you for the documents, for it is to me a matter of confidential duty—diplomatic secrets which would compromise his late Majesty Louis XVIII—Indeed, monsieur, it would be better—

However, you are a magistrate—and, after all, the Ambassador, to whom I refer the whole question, must decide."

At this juncture the usher announced the arrival of the doctor and the infirmary attendant, who came in.

"Good-morning, Monsieur Lebrun," said Camusot to the doctor. "I have sent for you to examine the state of health of this prisoner under suspicion. He says he had been poisoned and at the point of death since the day before yesterday; see if there is any risk in undressing him to look for the brand."

Doctor Lebrun took Jacques Collin's hand, felt his pulse, asked to look at his tongue, and scrutinized him steadily. This inspection lasted about ten minutes.

"The prisoner has been suffering severely," said the medical officer, "but at this moment he is amazingly strong—"

"That spurious energy, monsieur, is due to nervous excitement caused by my strange position," said Jacques Collin, with the dignity of a bishop.

"That is possible," said Monsieur Lebrun.

At a sign from Camusot the prisoner was stripped of everything but his trousers, even of his shirt, and the spectators might admire the hairy torso of a Cyclops. It was that of the Farnese Hercules at Naples in its colossal exaggeration.

"For what does nature intend a man of this build?" said Lebrun to the judge.

The usher brought in the ebony staff, which from time immemorial has been the insignia of his office, and is called his rod; he struck it several times over the place where the executioner had branded the fatal letters. Seventeen spots appeared, irregularly distributed, but the most careful scrutiny could not recognize the shape of any letters. The usher indeed pointed out that the top bar of the letter T was shown by two spots, with an interval between of the length of that bar between the two points at each end of it, and there was another spot where the bottom of the T should be.

"Still that is quite uncertain," said Camusot, seeing doubt in the expression of the prison doctor's countenance.

Carlos begged them to make the same experiment on the other shoulder and the middle of his back. About fifteen more such scars appeared, which, at the Spaniard's request, the doctor made a note of; and he pronounced that the man's back had been so extensively seamed by wounds that the brand would not show even if it had been made by the executioner.

An office-clerk now came in from the Prefecture, and handed a note to Monsieur Camusot, requesting an answer. After reading it the lawyer went to speak to Coquart, but in such a low voice that no one could catch a word. Only, by a glance from Camusot, Jacques Collin could guess that some information concerning him had been sent by the Prefet of Police.

"That friend of Peyrade's is still at my heels," thought Jacques Collin. "If only I knew him, I would get rid of him as I did of Contenson. If only I could see Asie once more!"

After signing a paper written by Coquart, the judge put it into an envelope and handed it to the clerk of the Delegate's office.

This is an indispensable auxiliary to justice. It is under the direction of a police commissioner, and consists of peace-officers who, with the assistance of the police commissioners of each district, carry into effect orders for searching the houses or apprehending the persons of those who are suspected of complicity in crimes and felonies. These functionaries in authority save the examining magistrates a great deal of very precious time.

At a sign from the judge the prisoner was dressed by Monsieur Lebrun and the attendant, who then withdrew with the usher. Camusot sat down at his table and played with his pen.

"You have an aunt," he suddenly said to Jacques Collin.

"An aunt?" echoed Don Carlos Herrera with amazement. "Why, monsieur, I have no relations. I am the unacknowledged son of the late Duke of Ossuna."

But to himself he said, "They are burning"—an allusion to the game of hot cockles, which is indeed a childlike symbol of the dreadful struggle between justice and the criminal.

"Pooh!" said Camusot. "You still have an aunt living, Mademoiselle Jacqueline Collin, whom you placed in Esther's service under the eccentric name of Asie."

Jacques Collin shrugged his shoulders with an indifference that was in perfect harmony with the cool curiosity he gave throughout to the judge's words, while Camusot studied him with cunning attention.

"Take care," said Camusot; "listen to me."

"I am listening, sir."

"You aunt is a wardrobe dealer at the Temple; her business is managed by a demoiselle Paccard, the sister of a convict—herself a very good girl, known as la Romette. Justice is on the traces of your aunt, and in a few hours we shall have decisive evidence. The woman is wholly devoted to you—"

"Pray go on, Monsieur le Juge," said Collin coolly, in answer to a pause; "I am listening to you."

"Your aunt, who is about five years older than you are, was formerly Marat's mistress—of odious memory. From that blood-stained source she derived the little fortune she possesses.

"From information I have received she must be a very clever receiver of stolen goods, for no proofs have yet been found to commit her on. After Marat's death she seems, from the notes I have here, to have lived with a chemist who was condemned to death in the year XII for issuing false coin. She was called as witness in the case. It was from this intimacy that she derived her knowledge of poisons.

"In 1812 and in 1816 she spent two years in prison for placing girls under age upon the streets.

"You were already convicted of forgery; you had left the banking house where your aunt had been able to place you as clerk, thanks to the education you had had, and the favor enjoyed by your aunt with certain persons for whose debaucheries she supplied victims.

"All this, prisoner, is not much like the dignity of the Dukes d'Ossuna.

"Do you persist in your denial?"

Jacques Collin sat listening to Monsieur Camusot, and thinking of his happy childhood at the College of the Oratorians, where he had been brought up, a meditation which lent him a truly amazed look. And in spite of his skill as a practised examiner, Camusot could bring no sort of expression to those placid features.

"If you have accurately recorded the account of myself I gave you at first," said Jacques Collin, "you can read it through again. I cannot alter the facts. I never went to the woman's house; how should I know who her cook was? The persons of whom you speak are utterly unknown to me."

"Notwithstanding your denial, we shall proceed to confront you with persons who may succeed in diminishing your assurance"

"A man who has been three times shot is used to anything," replied Jacques Collin meekly.

Camusot proceeded to examine the seized papers while awaiting the return of the famous Bibi-Lupin, whose expedition was amazing; for at half-past eleven, the inquiry having begun at ten o'clock, the usher came in to inform the judge in an undertone of Bibi-Lupin's arrival.

"Show him in," replied M. Camusot.

Bibi-Lupin, who had been expected to exclaim, "It is he," as he came in, stood puzzled. He did not recognize his man in a face pitted with smallpox. This hesitancy startled the magistrate.

"It is his build, his height," said the agent. "Oh! yes, it is you, Jacques Collin!" he went on, as he examined his eyes, forehead, and ears. "There are some things which no disguise can alter. . . Certainly it is he, Monsieur Camusot. Jacques has the scar of a cut on his left arm. Take off his coat, and you will see. . ."

Jacques Collin was again obliged to take off his coat; Bibi-Lupin turned up his sleeve and showed the scar he had spoken of.

"It is the scar of a bullet," replied Don Carlos Herrera. "Here are several more."

"Ah! It is certainly his voice," cried Bibi-Lupin.

"Your certainty," said Camusot, "is merely an opinion; it is not proof."

"I know that," said Bibi-Lupin with deference. "But I will bring witnesses. One of the boarders from the Maison Vauquer is here already," said he, with an eye on Collin.

But the prisoner's set, calm face did not move a muscle.

"Show the person in," said Camusot roughly, his dissatisfaction betraying itself in spite of his seeming indifference.

This irritation was not lost on Jacques Collin, who had not counted on the judge's sympathy, and sat lost in apathy, produced by his deep meditations in the effort to guess what the cause could be.

The usher now showed in Madame Poiret. At this unexpected appearance the prisoner had a slight shiver, but his trepidation was not remarked by Camusot, who seemed to have made up his mind.

"What is your name?" asked he, proceeding to carry out the formalities introductory to all depositions and examinations.

Madame Poiret, a little old woman as white and wrinkled as a sweetbread, dressed in a dark-blue silk gown, gave her name as Christine Michelle Michonneau, wife of one Poiret, and her age as fifty-one years, said that she was born in Paris, lived in the Rue des Poules at the corner of the Rue des Postes, and that her business was that of lodging-house keeper.

"In 1818 and 1819," said the judge, "you lived, madame, in a boarding-house kept by a Madame Vauquer?"

"Yes, monsieur; it was there that I met Monsieur Poiret, a retired official, who became my husband, and whom I have nursed in his bed this twelvemonth past. Poor man! he is very bad; and I cannot be long away from him."

"There was a certain Vautrin in the house at the time?" asked Camusot.

"Oh, monsieur, that is quite a long story; he was a horrible man, from the galleys—"

"You helped to get him arrested?"

"That is not true sir."

"You are in the presence of the Law; be careful," said Monsieur Camusot severely.

Madame Poiret was silent.

"Try to remember," Camusot went on. "Do you recollect the man? Would you know him again?"

"I think so."

"Is this the man?"

Madame Poiret put on her "eye-preservers," and looked at the Abbe Carlos Herrera.

"It is his build, his height; and yet—no—if—Monsieur le Juge," she said, "if I could see his chest I should recognize him at once."

The magistrate and his clerk could not help laughing, notwithstanding the gravity of their office; Jacques Collin joined in their hilarity, but discreetly. The prisoner had not put on his coat after Bibi-Lupin had removed it, and at a sign from the judge he obligingly opened his shirt.

"Yes, that is his fur trimming, sure enough!—But it has worn gray, Monsieur Vautrin," cried Madame Poiret.

"What have you to say to that?" asked the judge of the prisoner.

"That she is mad," replied Jacques Collin.

"Bless me! If I had a doubt—for his face is altered—that voice would be enough. He is the man who threatened me. Ah! and those are his eyes!"

"The police agent and this woman," said Camusot, speaking to Jacques Collin, "cannot possibly have conspired to say the same thing, for neither of them had seen you till now. How do you account for that?"

"Justice has blundered more conspicuously even than it does now in accepting the evidence of a woman who recognizes a man by the hair on his chest and the suspicions of a police agent," replied Jacques Collin. "I am said to resemble a great criminal in voice, eyes, and build; that seems a little vague. As to the memory which would prove certain relations between Madame and my Sosie—which she does not blush to own—you yourself laughed at. Allow me, monsieur, in the interests of

HONORÉ DE BALZAC

truth, which I am far more anxious to establish for my own sake than you can be for the sake of justice, to ask this lady—Madame Foiret—"

"Poiret."

"Poret—excuse me, I am a Spaniard—whether she remembers the other persons who lived in this—what did you call the house?"

"A boarding-house," said Madame Poiret.

"I do not know what that is."

"A house where you can dine and breakfast by subscription."

"You are right," said Camusot, with a favorable nod to Jacques Collin, whose apparent good faith in suggesting means to arrive at some conclusion struck him greatly. "Try to remember the boarders who were in the house when Jacques Collin was apprehended."

"There were Monsieur de Rastignac, Doctor Bianchon, Pere Goriot, Mademoiselle Taillefer—"

"That will do," said Camusot, steadily watching Jacques Collin, whose expression did not change. "Well, about this Pere Goriot?"

"He is dead," said Madame Poiret.

"Monsieur," said Jacques Collin, "I have several times met Monsieur de Rastignac, a friend, I believe, of Madame de Nucingen's; and if it is the same, he certainly never supposed me to be the convict with whom these persons try to identify me."

"Monsieur de Rastignac and Doctor Bianchon," said the magistrate, "both hold such a social position that their evidence, if it is in your favor, will be enough to procure your release.—Coquart, fill up a summons for each of them."

The formalities attending Madame Poiret's examination were over in a few minutes; Coquart read aloud to her the notes he had made of the little scene, and she signed the paper; but the prisoner refused to sign, alleging his ignorance of the forms of French law.

"That is enough for to-day," said Monsieur Camusot. "You must be wanting food. I will have you taken back to the Conciergerie."

"Alas! I am suffering too much to be able to eat," said Jacques Collin.

Camusot was anxious to time Jacques Collin's return to coincide with the prisoners' hour of exercise in the prison yard; but he needed a reply from the Governor of the Conciergerie to the order he had given him in the morning, and he rang for the usher. The usher appeared, and told him that the porter's wife, from the house on the Quai Malaquais, had an important document to communicate with reference to Monsieur

Lucien de Rubempre. This was so serious a matter that it put Camusot's intentions out of his head.

"Show her in," said he.

"Beg your pardon; pray excuse me, gentlemen all," said the woman, courtesying to the judge and the Abbe Carlos by turns. "We were so worried by the Law—my husband and me—the twice when it has marched into our house, that we had forgotten a letter that was lying, for Monsieur Lucien, in our chest of drawers, which we paid ten sous for it, though it was posted in Paris, for it is very heavy, sir. Would you please to pay me back the postage? For God knows when we shall see our lodgers again!"

"Was this letter handed to you by the postman?" asked Camusot, after carefully examining the envelope.

"Yes, monsieur."

"Coquart, write full notes of this deposition.—Go on, my good woman; tell us your name and your business." Camusot made the woman take the oath, and then he dictated the document.

While these formalities were being carried out, he was scrutinizing the postmark, which showed the hours of posting and delivery, as well at the date of the day. And this letter, left for Lucien the day after Esther's death, had beyond a doubt been written and posted on the day of the catastrophe. Monsieur Camusot's amazement may therefore be imagined when he read this letter written and signed by her whom the law believed to have been the victim of a crime:—

Esther to Lucien

MONDAY, May 13th, 1830
My last day; ten in the morning

MY LUCIEN,

I have not an hour to live. At eleven o'clock I shall
be dead, and I shall die without a pang. I have paid fifty
thousand francs for a neat little black currant, containing a
poison that will kill me with the swiftness of lightning. And
so, my darling, you may tell yourself, 'My little Esther had no
suffering.'—and yet I shall suffer in writing these pages.

"The monster who has paid so dear for me, knowing
that the day when I should know myself to be his would
have no morrow—Nucingen has just left me, as drunk as
a bear with his skin full of wind. For the first and last time

in my life I have had the opportunity of comparing my old trade as a street hussy with the life of true love, of placing the tenderness which unfolds in the infinite above the horrors of a duty which longs to destroy itself and leave no room even for a kiss. Only such loathing could make death delightful.

"I have taken a bath; I should have liked to send for the father confessor of the convent where I was baptized, to have confessed and washed my soul. But I have had enough of prostitution; it would be profaning a sacrament; and besides, I feel myself cleansed in the waters of sincere repentance. God must do what He will with me.

"But enough of all this maudlin; for you I want to be your Esther to the last moment, not to bore you with my death, or the future, or God, who is good, and who would not be good if He were to torture me in the next world when I have endured so much misery in this.

"I have before me your beautiful portrait, painted by Madame de Mirbel. That sheet of ivory used to comfort me in your absence, I look at it with rapture as I write you my last thoughts, and tell you of the last throbbing of my heart. I shall enclose the miniature in this letter, for I cannot bear that it should be stolen or sold. The mere thought that what has been my great joy may lie behind a shop window, mixed up with the ladies and officers of the Empire, or a parcel of Chinese absurdities, is a small death to me. Destroy that picture, my sweetheart, wipe it out, never give it to any one—unless, indeed, the gift might win back the heart of that walking, well-dressed maypole, that Clotilde de Grandlieu, who will make you black and blue in her sleep, her bones are so sharp.—Yes, to that I consent, and then I shall still be of some use to you, as when I was alive. Oh! to give you pleasure, or only to make you laugh, I would have stood over a brazier with an apple in my mouth to cook it for you.—So my death even will be of service to you.—I should have marred your home.

"Oh! that Clotilde! I cannot understand her.—She might have been your wife, have borne your name, have never left you day or night, have belonged to you—and she could make difficulties! Only the Faubourg Saint-Germain can do that! and yet she has not ten pounds of flesh on her bones!

"Poor Lucien! Dear ambitious failure! I am thinking of your future life. Well, well! you will more than once regret your poor faithful dog, the good girl who would fly to serve you, who would have been dragged into a police court to secure your happiness, whose only occupation was to think of your pleasures and invent new ones, who was so full of love for you—in her hair, her feet, her ears—your ballerina, in short, whose every look was a benediction; who for six years has thought of nothing but you, who was so entirely your chattel that I have never been anything but an effluence of your soul, as light is that of the sun. However, for lack of money and of honor, I can never be your wife. I have at any rate provided for your future by giving you all I have.

"Come as soon as you get this letter and take what you find under my pillow, for I do not trust the people about me. Understand that I mean to look beautiful when I am dead. I shall go to bed, and lay myself flat in an attitude—why not? Then I shall break the little pill against the roof of my mouth, and shall not be disfigured by any convulsion or by a ridiculous position.

"Madame de Serizy has quarreled with you, I know, because of me; but when she hears that I am dead, you see, dear pet, she will forgive. Make it up with her, and she will find you a suitable wife if the Grandlieus persist in their refusal.

"My dear, I do not want you to grieve too much when you hear of my death. To begin with, I must tell you that the hour of eleven on Monday morning, the thirteenth of May, is only the end of a long illness, which began on the day when, on the Terrace of Saint-Germain, you threw me back on my former line of life. The soul may be sick, as the body is. But the soul cannot submit stupidly to suffering like the body; the body does not uphold the soul as the soul upholds the body, and the soul sees a means of cure in the reflection which leads to the needlewoman's resource—the bushel of charcoal. You gave me a whole life the day before yesterday, when you said that if Clotilde still refused you, you would marry me. It would have been a great misfortune for us both; I should have been still more dead, so to speak—for there are more and less bitter deaths. The world would never have recognized us.

"For two months past I have been thinking of many things, I can tell you. A poor girl is in the mire, as I was before I went into the convent; men think her handsome, they make her serve their pleasure without thinking any consideration necessary; they pack her off on foot after fetching her in a carriage; if they do not spit in her face, it is only because her beauty preserves her from such indignity; but, morally speaking they do worse. Well, and if this despised creature were to inherit five or six millions of francs, she would be courted by princes, bowed to with respect as she went past in her carriage, and might choose among the oldest names in France and Navarre. That world which would have cried Raca to us, on seeing two handsome creatures united and happy, always did honor to Madame de Stael, in spite of her 'romances in real life,' because she had two hundred thousand francs a year. The world, which grovels before money or glory, will not bow down before happiness or virtue—for I could have done good. Oh! how many tears I would have dried—as many as I have shed—I believe! Yes, I would have lived only for you and for charity.

"These are the thoughts that make death beautiful. So do not lament, my dear. Say often to yourself, 'There were two good creatures, two beautiful creatures, who both died for me ungrudgingly, and who adored me.' Keep a memory in your heart of Coralie and Esther, and go your way and prosper. Do you recollect the day when you pointed out to me a shriveled old woman, in a melon-green bonnet and a puce wrapper, all over black grease-spots, the mistress of a poet before the Revolution, hardly thawed by the sun though she was sitting against the wall of the Tuileries and fussing over a pug—the vilest of pugs? She had had footmen and carriages, you know, and a fine house! And I said to you then, 'How much better to be dead at thirty!'—Well, you thought I was melancholy, and you played all sorts of pranks to amuse me, and between two kisses I said, 'Every day some pretty woman leaves the play before it is over!'—And I do not want to see the last piece; that is all.

"You must think me a great chatterbox; but this is my last effusion. I write as if I were talking to you, and I like to talk cheerfully. I have always had a horror of a dressmaker pitying herself. You know I knew how to die decently once before, on my return from that fatal opera-ball where the men said I had been a prostitute.

"No, no, my dear love, never give this portrait to any one! If you could know with what a gush of love I have sat losing myself in your eyes, looking at them with rapture during a pause I allowed myself, you would feel as you gathered up the affection with which I have tried to overlay the ivory, that the soul of your little pet is indeed there.

"A dead woman craving alms! That is a funny idea.— Come, I must learn to lie quiet in my grave.

"You have no idea how heroic my death would seem to some fools if they could know Nucingen last night offered me two millions of francs if I would love him as I love you. He will be handsomely robbed when he hears that I have kept my word and died of him. I tried all I could still to breathe the air you breathe. I said to the fat scoundrel, 'Do you want me to love you as you wish? To promise even that I will never see Lucien again?'—'What must I do?' he asked.—'Give me the two millions for him.'—You should have seen his face! I could have laughed, if it had not been so tragical for me.

"'Spare yourself the trouble of refusing,' said I; 'I see you care more for your two millions than for me. A woman is always glad to know at what she is valued!' and I turned my back on him.

"In a few hours the old rascal will know that I was not in jest.

"Who will part your hair as nicely as I do? Pooh!—I will think no more of anything in life; I have but five minutes, I give them to God. Do not be jealous of Him, dear heart; I shall speak to Him of you, beseeching Him for your happiness as the price of my death, and my punishment in the next world. I am vexed enough at having to go to hell. I should have liked to see the angels, to know if they are like you.

"Good-bye, my darling, good-bye! I give you all the blessing of my woes. Even in the grave I am your Esther.

"It is striking eleven. I have said my last prayers. I am going to bed to die. Once more, farewell! I wish that the warmth of my hand could leave my soul there where I press a last kiss—and once more I must call you my dearest love, though you are the cause of the death of your Esther."

A vague feeling of jealousy tightened on the magistrate's heart as he read this letter, the only letter from a suicide he had ever found written with such lightness, though it was a feverish lightness, and the last effort of a blind affection.

"What is there in the man that he should be loved so well?" thought he, saying what every man says who has not the gift of attracting women.

"If you can prove not merely that you are not Jacques Collin and an escaped convict, but that you are in fact Don Carlos Herrera, canon of Toledo, and secret envoy of this Majesty Ferdinand VII," said he, addressing the prisoner "you will be released; for the impartiality demanded by my office requires me to tell you that I have this moment received a letter, written by Mademoiselle Esther Gobseck, in which she declares her intention of killing herself, and expresses suspicions as to her servants, which would seem to point to them as the thieves who have made off with the seven hundred and fifty thousand francs."

As he spoke Monsieur Camusot was comparing the writing of the letter with that of the will; and it seemed to him self-evident that the same person had written both.

"Monsieur, you were in too great a hurry to believe in a murder; do not be too hasty in believing in a theft."

"Heh!" said Camusot, scrutinizing the prisoner with a piercing eye.

"Do not suppose that I am compromising myself by telling you that the sum may possibly be recovered," said Jacques Collin, making the judge understand that he saw his suspicions. "That poor girl was much loved by those about her; and if I were free, I would undertake to search for this money, which no doubt belongs to the being I love best in the world—to Lucien!—Will you allow me to read that letter; it will not take long? It is evidence of my dear boy's innocence—you cannot fear that I shall destroy it—nor that I shall talk about it; I am in solitary confinement."

"In confinement! You will be so no longer," cried the magistrate. "It is I who must beg you to get well as soon as possible. Refer to your ambassador if you choose—"

And he handed the letter to Jacques Collin. Camusot was glad to be out of a difficulty, to be able to satisfy the public prosecutor, Mesdames de Maufrigneuse and de Serizy. Nevertheless, he studied his prisoner's face with cold curiosity while Collin read Esther's letter; in spite of the apparent genuineness of the feelings it expressed, he said to himself:

"But it is a face worthy of the hulks, all the same!"

"That is the way to love!" said Jacques Collin, returning the letter. And he showed Camusot a face bathed in tears.

"If only you knew him," he went on, "so youthful, so innocent a soul, so splendidly handsome, a child, a poet!—The impulse to sacrifice oneself to him is irresistible, to satisfy his lightest wish. That dear boy is so fascinating when he chooses—"

"And so," said the magistrate, making a final effort to discover the truth, "you cannot possibly be Jacques Collin—"

"No, monsieur," replied the convict.

And Jacques Collin was more entirely Don Carlos Herrera than ever. In his anxiety to complete his work he went up to the judge, led him to the window, and gave himself the airs of a prince of the Church, assuming a confidential tone:

"I am so fond of that boy, monsieur, that if it were needful, to spare that idol of my heart a mere discomfort even, that I should be the criminal you take me for, I would surrender," said he in an undertone. "I would follow the example of the poor girl who has killed herself for his benefit. And I beg you, monsieur, to grant me a favor—namely, to set Lucien at liberty forthwith."

"My duty forbids it," said Camusot very good-naturedly; "but if a sinner may make a compromise with heaven, justice too has its softer side, and if you can give me sufficient reasons—speak; your words will not be taken down."

"Well, then," Jacques Collin went on, taken in by Camusot's apparent goodwill, "I know what that poor boy is suffering at this moment; he is capable of trying to kill himself when he finds himself a prisoner—"

"Oh! as to that!" said Camusot with a shrug.

"You do not know whom you will oblige by obliging me," added Jacques Collin, trying to harp on another string. "You will be doing a service to others more powerful than any Comtesse de Serizy or Duchesse de Maufrigneuse, who will never forgive you for having had their letters in your chambers—" and he pointed to two packets of perfumed papers. "My Order has a good memory."

"Monsieur," said Camusot, "that is enough. You must find better reasons to give me. I am as much interested in the prisoner as in public vengeance."

"Believe me, then, I know Lucien; he has a soul of a woman, of a poet, and a southerner, without persistency or will," said Jacques Collin, who fancied that he saw that he had won the judge over. "You are convinced of the young man's innocence, do not torture him, do not question him. Give him that letter, tell him that he is Esther's heir, and restore him to freedom. If you act otherwise, you will bring despair on yourself; whereas, if you simply release him, I will explain to you—keep me still in solitary confinement—to-morrow or this evening, everything that may strike you as mysterious in the case, and the reasons for the persecution of which I am the object. But it will be at the risk of my life, a price has been set on my head these six years past. . . Lucien free, rich, and married to Clotilde de Grandlieu, and my task on earth will be done; I shall no longer try to save my skin.—My persecutor was a spy under your late King."

"What, Corentin?"

"Ah! Is his name Corentin? Thank you, monsieur. Well, will you promise to do as I ask you?"

"A magistrate can make no promises.—Coquart, tell the usher and the gendarmes to take the prisoner back to the Conciergerie.—I will give orders that you are to have a private room," he added pleasantly, with a slight nod to the convict.

Struck by Jacques Collin's request, and remembering how he had insisted that he wished to be examined first as a privilege to his state of health, Camusot's suspicions were aroused once more. Allowing his vague doubts to make themselves heard, he noticed that the self-styled dying man was walking off with the strength of a Hercules, having abandoned all the tricks he had aped so well on appearing before the magistrate.

"Monsieur!"

Jacques Collin turned round.

"Notwithstanding your refusal to sign the document, my clerk will read you the minutes of your examination."

The prisoner was evidently in excellent health; the readiness with which he came back, and sat down by the clerk, was a fresh light to the magistrate's mind.

"You have got well very suddenly!" said Camusot.

"Caught!" thought Jacques Collin; and he replied:

"Joy, monsieur, is the only panacea.—That letter, the proof of innocence of which I had no doubt—these are the grand remedy."

The judge kept a meditative eye on the prisoner when the usher and the gendarmes again took him in charge. Then, with a start like a waking man, he tossed Esther's letter across to the table where his clerk sat, saying:

"Coquart, copy that letter."

If it is natural to man to be suspicious as to some favor required of him when it is antagonistic to his interests or his duty, and sometimes even when it is a matter of indifference, this feeling is law to an examining magistrate. The more this prisoner—whose identity was not yet ascertained—pointed to clouds on the horizon in the event of Lucien's being examined, the more necessary did the interrogatory seem to Camusot. Even if this formality had not been required by the Code and by common practice, it was indispensable as bearing on the identification of the Abbe Carlos. There is in every walk of life the business conscience. In default of curiosity Camusot would have examined Lucien as he had examined Jacques Collin, with all the cunning which the most honest magistrate allows himself to use in such cases. The services he might render and his own promotion were secondary in Camusot's mind to his anxiety to know or guess the truth, even if he should never tell it.

He stood drumming on the window-pane while following the river-like current of his conjectures, for in these moods thought is like a stream flowing through many countries. Magistrates, in love with truth, are like jealous women; they give way to a thousand hypotheses, and probe them with the dagger-point of suspicion, as the sacrificing priest of old eviscerated his victims; thus they arrive, not perhaps at truth, but at probability, and at last see the truth beyond. A woman cross-questions the man she loves as the judge cross-questions a criminal. In such a frame of mind, a glance, a word, a tone of voice, the slightest hesitation is enough to certify the hidden fact—treason or crime.

"The style in which he depicted his devotion to his son—if he is his son—is enough to make me think that he was in the girl's house to keep an eye on the plunder; and never suspecting that the dead woman's pillow covered a will, he no doubt annexed, for his son, the seven hundred and fifty thousand francs as a precaution. That is why he can promise to recover the money.

"M. de Rubempre owes it to himself and to justice to account for his father's position in the world—

"And he offers me the protection of his Order—His Order!—if I do not examine Lucien—"

As has been seen, a magistrate conducts an examination exactly as he thinks proper. He is at liberty to display his acumen or be absolutely blunt. An examination may be everything or nothing. Therein lies the favor.

Camusot rang. The usher had returned. He was sent to fetch Monsieur Lucien de Rubempre with an injunction to prohibit his speaking to anybody on his way up. It was by this time two in the afternoon.

"There is some secret," said the judge to himself, "and that secret must be very important. My amphibious friend—since he is neither priest, nor secular, nor convict, nor Spaniard, though he wants to hinder his protege from letting out something dreadful—argues thus: 'The poet is weak and effeminate; he is not like me, a Hercules in diplomacy, and you will easily wring our secret from him.'—Well, we will get everything out of this innocent."

And he sat tapping the edge of his table with the ivory paper-knife, while Coquart copied Esther's letter.

How whimsical is the action of our faculties! Camusot conceived of every crime as possible, and overlooked the only one that the prisoner had now committed—the forgery of the will for Lucien's advantage. Let those whose envy vents itself on magistrates think for a moment of their life spent in perpetual suspicion, of the torments these men must inflict on their minds, for civil cases are not less tortuous than criminal examinations, and it will occur to them perhaps that the priest and the lawyer wear an equally heavy coat of mail, equally furnished with spikes in the lining. However, every profession has its hair shirt and its Chinese puzzles.

It was about two o'clock when Monsieur Camusot saw Lucien de Rubempre come in, pale, worn, his eyes red and swollen, in short, in a state of dejection which enabled the magistrate to compare nature with art, the really dying man with the stage performance. His walk from the Conciergerie to the judge's chambers, between two gendarmes, and preceded by the usher, had put the crowning touch to Lucien's despair. It is the poet's nature to prefer execution to condemnation.

As he saw this being, so completely bereft of the moral courage which is the essence of a judge, and which the last prisoner had so strongly manifested, Monsieur Camusot disdained the easy victory; and this scorn enabled him to strike a decisive blow, since it left him, on the ground, that horrible clearness of mind which the marksman feels when he is firing at a puppet.

"Collect yourself, Monsieur de Rubempre; you are in the presence of a magistrate who is eager to repair the mischief done involuntarily by the law when a man is taken into custody on suspicion that has no foundation. I believe you to be innocent, and you will soon be at liberty.—Here is the evidence of your innocence; it is a letter kept for you during your absence by your porter's wife; she has just brought it here. In the commotion caused by the visitation of justice and the news of your arrest at Fontainebleau, the woman forgot the letter which was written by Mademoiselle Esther Gobseck.—Read it!"

Lucien took the letter, read it, and melted into tears. He sobbed, and could not say a single word. At the end of a quarter of an hour, during which Lucien with great difficulty recovered his self-command, the clerk laid before him the copy of the letter and begged him to sign a footnote certifying that the copy was faithful to the original, and might be used in its stead "on all occasions in the course of this preliminary inquiry," giving him the option of comparing the two; but Lucien, of course, took Coquart's word for its accuracy.

"Monsieur," said the lawyer, with friendly good nature, "it is nevertheless impossible that I should release you without carrying out the legal formalities, and asking you some questions.—It is almost as a witness that I require you to answer. To such a man as you I think it is almost unnecessary to point out that the oath to tell the whole truth is not in this case a mere appeal to your conscience, but a necessity for your own sake, your position having been for a time somewhat ambiguous. The truth can do you no harm, be it what it may; falsehood will send you to trial, and compel me to send you back to the Conciergerie; whereas if you answer fully to my questions, you will sleep to-night in your own house, and be rehabilitated by this paragraph in the papers: 'Monsieur de Rubempre, who was arrested yesterday at Fontainebleau, was set at liberty after a very brief examination.'"

This speech made a deep impression on Lucien; and the judge, seeing the temper of his prisoner, added:

"I may repeat to you that you were suspected of being accessory to the murder by poison of this Demoiselle Esther. Her suicide is clearly proved, and there is an end of that; but a sum of seven hundred and fifty thousand francs has been stolen, which she had disposed of by will, and you are the legatee. This is a felony. The crime was perpetrated before the discovery of the will.

"Now there is reason to suppose that a person who loves you as much as you loved Mademoiselle Esther committed the theft for your benefit.—Do not interrupt me," Camusot went on, seeing that Lucien was about to speak, and commanding silence by a gesture; "I am asking you nothing so far. I am anxious to make you understand how deeply your honor is concerned in this question. Give up the false and contemptible notion of the honor binding two accomplices, and tell the whole truth."

The reader must already have observed the extreme disproportion of the weapons in this conflict between the prisoner under suspicion and the examining judge. Absolute denial when skilfully used has in its favor its positive simplicity, and sufficiently defends the criminal; but it is, in a way, a coat of mail which becomes crushing as soon as the stiletto of cross-examination finds a joint to it. As soon as mere denial is ineffectual in face of certain proven facts, the examinee is entirely at the judge's mercy.

Now, supposing that a sort of half-criminal, like Lucien, might, if he were saved from the first shipwreck of his honesty, amend his ways, and become a useful member of society, he will be lost in the pitfalls of his examination.

The judge has the driest possible record drawn up of the proceedings, a faithful analysis of the questions and answers; but no trace remains of his insidiously paternal addresses or his captious remonstrances, such as this speech. The judges of the superior courts see the results, but see nothing of the means. Hence, as some experienced persons have thought, it would be a good plan that, as in England, a jury should hear the examination. For a short while France enjoyed the benefit of this system. Under the Code of Brumaire of the year IV, this body was known as the examining jury, as distinguished from the trying jury. As to the final trial, if we should restore the examining jury, it would have to be the function of the superior courts without the aid of a jury.

"And now," said Camusot, after a pause, "what is your name?—Attention, Monsieur Coquart!" said he to the clerk.

"Lucien Chardon de Rubempre."

"And you were born—?"

"At Angouleme." And Lucien named the day, month, and year.

"You inherited no fortune?"

"None whatever."

"And yet, during your first residence in Paris, you spent a great deal, as compared with your small income?"

"Yes, monsieur; but at that time I had a most devoted friend in Mademoiselle Coralie, and I was so unhappy as to lose her. It was my grief at her death that made me return to my country home."

"That is right, monsieur," said Camusot; "I commend your frankness; it will be thoroughly appreciated."

Lucien, it will be seen, was prepared to make a clean breast of it.

"On your return to Paris you lived even more expensively than before," Camusot went on. "You lived like a man who might have about sixty thousand francs a year."

"Yes, monsieur."

"Who supplied you with the money?"

"My protector, the Abbe Carlos Herrera."

"Where did you meet him?"

"We met when traveling, just as I was about to be quit of life by committing suicide."

"You never heard him spoken of by your family—by your mother?"

"Never."

"Can you remember the year and the month when you first became connected with Mademoiselle Esther?"

"Towards the end of 1823, at a small theatre on the Boulevard."

"At first she was an expense to you?"

"Yes, monsieur."

"Lately, in the hope of marrying Mademoiselle de Grandlieu, you purchased the ruins of the Chateau de Rubempre, you added land to the value of a million francs, and you told the family of Grandlieu that your sister and your brother-in-law had just come into a considerable fortune, and that their liberality had supplied you with the money.—Did you tell the Grandlieus this, monsieur?"

"Yes, monsieur."

"You do not know the reason why the marriage was broken off?"

"Not in the least, monsieur."

"Well, the Grandlieus sent one of the most respectable attorneys in Paris to see your brother-in-law and inquire into the facts. At Angouleme this lawyer, from the statements of your sister and brother-in-law, learned that they not only had hardly lent you any money, but also that their inheritance consisted of land, of some extent no doubt, but that the whole amount of invested capital was not more than about two hundred thousand francs.—Now you cannot wonder that such people as the Grandlieus should reject a fortune of which the source is more than doubtful. This, monsieur, is what a lie has led to—"

Lucien was petrified by this revelation, and the little presence of mind he had preserved deserted him.

"Remember," said Camusot, "that the police and the law know all they want to know.—And now," he went on, recollecting Jacques Collin's assumed paternity, "do you know who this pretended Carlos Herrera is?"

"Yes, monsieur; but I knew it too late."

"Too late! How? Explain yourself."

"He is not a priest, not a Spaniard, he is—"

"An escaped convict?" said the judge eagerly.

"Yes," replied Lucien, "when he told me the fatal secret, I was already under obligations to him; I had fancied I was befriended by a respectable priest."

"Jacques Collin—" said Monsieur Camusot, beginning a sentence.

"Yes," said Lucien, "his name is Jacques Collin."

"Very good. Jacques Collin has just now been identified by another person, and though he denies it, he does so, I believe, in your interest. But I asked whether you knew who the man is in order to prove another of Jacques Collin's impostures."

Lucien felt as though he had hot iron in his inside as he heard this alarming statement.

"Do you not know," Camusot went on, "that in order to give color to the extraordinary affection he has for you, he declares that he is your father?"

"He! My father?—Oh, monsieur, did he tell you that?"

"Have you any suspicion of where the money came from that he used to give you? For, if I am to believe the evidence of the letter you have in your hand, that poor girl, Mademoiselle Esther, must have done you lately the same services as Coralie formerly rendered you. Still, for some years, as you have just admitted, you lived very handsomely without receiving anything from her."

"It is I who should ask you, monsieur, whence convicts get their money! Jacques Collin my father!—Oh, my poor mother!" and Lucien burst into tears.

"Coquart, read out to the prisoner that part of Carlos Herrera's examination in which he said that Lucien de Rubempre was his son."

The poet listened in silence, and with a look that was terrible to behold.

"I am done for!" he cried.

"A man is not done for who is faithful to the path of honor and truth," said the judge.

"But you will commit Jacques Collin for trial?" said Lucien.

"Undoubtedly," said Camusot, who aimed at making Lucien talk. "Speak out."

But in spite of all his persuasion and remonstrances, Lucien would say no more. Reflection had come too late, as it does to all men who are the slaves of impulse. There lies the difference between the poet and the man of action; one gives way to feeling to reproduce it in living images, his judgement comes in after; the other feels and judges both at once.

Lucien remained pale and gloomy; he saw himself at the bottom of the precipice, down which the examining judge had rolled him by the apparent candor which had entrapped his poet's soul. He had betrayed, not his benefactor, but an accomplice who had defended their position with the courage of a lion, and a skill that showed no flaw. Where Jacques Collin had saved everything by his daring, Lucien, the man of brains, had lost all by his lack of intelligence and reflection. This infamous lie against which he revolted had screened a yet more infamous truth.

Utterly confounded by the judge's skill, overpowered by his cruel dexterity, by the swiftness of the blows he had dealt him while making use of the errors of a life laid bare as probes to search his conscience, Lucien sat like an animal which the butcher's pole-axe had failed to kill. Free and innocent when he came before the judge, in a moment his own avowal had made him feel criminal.

To crown all, as a final grave irony, Camusot, cold and calm, pointed out to Lucien that his self-betrayal was the result of a misapprehension. Camusot was thinking of Jacques Collin's announcing himself as Lucien's father; while Lucien, wholly absorbed by his fear of seeing his confederacy with an escaped convict made public, had imitated the famous inadvertency of the murderers of Ibycus.

One of Royer-Collard's most famous achievements was proclaiming the constant triumph of natural feeling over engrafted sentiments, and defending the cause of anterior oaths by asserting that the law of hospitality, for instance, ought to be regarded as binding to the point of negativing the obligation of a judicial oath. He promulgated this theory, in the face of the world, from the French tribune; he boldly upheld conspirators, showing that it was human to be true to friendship rather than to the tyrannical laws brought out of the social arsenal to be adjusted to circumstances. And, indeed, natural rights have laws which have never been codified, but which are more effectual and better known than those laid down by society. Lucien had misapprehended, to his cost, the law of cohesion, which required him to be silent and leave Jacques Collin to protect himself; nay, more, he had accused him. In his own interests the man ought always to be, to him, Carlos Herrera.

Monsieur Camusot was rejoicing in his triumph; he had secured two criminals. He had crushed with the hand of justice one of the favorites of fashion, and he had found the undiscoverable Jacques Collin. He would be regarded as one of the cleverest of examining judges. So he left his prisoner in peace; but he was studying this speechless consternation, and he saw drops of sweat collect on the miserable face, swell and fall, mingled with two streams of tears.

"Why should you weep, Monsieur de Rubempre? You are, as I have told you, Mademoiselle Esther's legatee, she having no heirs nor near relations, and her property amounts to nearly eight millions of francs if the lost seven hundred and fifty thousand francs are recovered."

This was the last blow to the poor wretch. "If you do not lose your head for ten minutes," Jacques Collin had said in his note, and Lucien by keeping cool would have gained all his desire. He might have paid his debt to Jacques Collin and have cut him adrift, have been rich, and have married Mademoiselle de Grandlieu. Nothing could more eloquently demonstrate the power with which the examining judge is armed, as a consequence of the isolation or separation of persons under suspicion, or the value of such a communication as Asie had conveyed to Jacques Collin.

"Ah, monsieur!" replied Lucien, with the satirical bitterness of a man who makes a pedestal of his utter overthrow, "how appropriate is the phrase in legal slang 'to UNDERGO examination.' For my part, if I had to choose between the physical torture of past ages and the moral torture of our day, I would not hesitate to prefer the sufferings inflicted of old by the executioner.—What more do you want of me?" he added haughtily.

"In this place, monsieur," said the magistrate, answering the poet's pride with mocking arrogance, "I alone have a right to ask questions."

"I had the right to refuse to answer them," muttered the hapless Lucien, whose wits had come back to him with perfect lucidity.

"Coquart, read the minutes to the prisoner."

"I am the prisoner once more," said Lucien to himself.

While the clerk was reading, Lucien came to a determination which compelled him to smooth down Monsieur Camusot. When Coquart's drone ceased, the poet started like a man who has slept through a noise to which his ears are accustomed, and who is roused by its cessation.

"You have to sign the report of your examination," said the judge.

"And am I at liberty?" asked Lucien, ironical in his turn.

"Not yet," said Camusot; "but to-morrow, after being confronted with Jacques Collin, you will no doubt be free. Justice must now ascertain whether or no you are accessory to the crimes this man may have committed since his escape so long ago as 1820. However, you are no longer in the secret cells. I will write to the Governor to give you a better room."

"Shall I find writing materials?"

"You can have anything supplied to you that you ask for; I will give orders to that effect by the usher who will take you back."

Lucien mechanically signed the minutes and initialed the notes in obedience to Coquart's indications with the meekness of a resigned victim. A single fact will show what a state he was in better than the minutest description. The announcement that he would be confronted with Jacques Collin had at once dried the drops of sweat from his brow, and his dry eyes glittered with a terrible light. In short, he became, in an instant as brief as a lightning flash, what Jacques Collin was—a man of iron.

In men whose nature is like Lucien's, a nature which Jacques Collin had so thoroughly fathomed, these sudden transitions from a state of absolute demoralization to one that is, so to speak, metallic,—so extreme is the tension of every vital force,—are the most startling phenomena of mental vitality. The will surges up like the lost waters of a spring; it diffuses itself throughout the machinery that lies ready for the action of the unknown matter that constitutes it; and then the corpse is a man again, and the man rushes on full of energy for a supreme struggle.

Lucien laid Esther's letter next his heart, with the miniature she had returned to him. Then he haughtily bowed to Monsieur Camusot, and went off with a firm step down the corridors, between two gendarmes.

"That is a deep scoundrel!" said the judge to his clerk, to avenge himself for the crushing scorn the poet had displayed. "He thought he might save himself by betraying his accomplice."

"Of the two," said Coquart timidly, "the convict is the most thorough-paced."

"You are free for the rest of the day, Coquart," said the lawyer. "We have done enough. Send away any case that is waiting, to be called to-morrow.—Ah! and you must go at once to the public prosecutor's chambers and ask if he is still there; if so, ask him if he can give me a few minutes. Yes; he will not be gone," he added, looking at a common clock in a wooden case painted green with gilt lines. "It is but a quarter-past three."

THESE EXAMINATIONS, WHICH ARE SO quickly read, being written down at full length, questions and answers alike, take up an enormous amount of time. This is one of the reasons of the slowness of these preliminaries to a trial and of these imprisonments "on suspicion." To the poor this is ruin, to the rich it is disgrace; to them only immediate release can in any degree repair, so far as possible, the disaster of an arrest.

This is why the two scenes here related had taken up the whole of the time spent by Asie in deciphering her master's orders, in getting a Duchess out of her boudoir, and putting some energy into Madame de Serizy.

At this moment Camusot, who was anxious to get the full benefit of his cleverness, took the two documents, read them through, and promised himself that he would show them to the public prosecutor and take his opinion on them. During this meditation, his usher came back to tell him that Madame la Comtesse de Serizy's man-servant insisted on speaking with him. At a nod from Camusot, a servant out of livery came in, looked first at the usher, and then at the magistrate, and said, "I have the honor of speaking to Monsieur Camusot?"

"Yes," replied the lawyer and his clerk.

Camusot took a note which the servant offered him, and read as follows:—

"For the sake of many interests which will be obvious to you, my dear Camusot, do not examine Monsieur de Rubempre. We have brought ample proofs of his innocence that he may be released forthwith.

D. De Maufrigneuse

L. De Serizy

"*P. S.*—Burn this note."

Camusot understood at once that he had blundered preposterously in laying snares for Lucien, and he began by obeying the two fine ladies—he lighted a taper, and burned the letter written by the Duchess. The man bowed respectfully.

"Then Madame de Serizy is coming here?" asked Camusot.

"The carriage is being brought round."

At this moment Coquart came in to tell Monsieur Camusot that the public prosecutor expected him.

Oppressed by the blunder he had committed, in view of his ambitions, though to the better ends of justice, the lawyer, in whom seven years' experience had perfected the sharpness that comes to a man who in his practice has had to measure his wits against the grisettes of Paris, was anxious to have some shield against the resentment of two women of fashion. The taper in which he had burned the note was still alight, and he used it to seal up the Duchesse de Maufrigneuse's notes to Lucien—about thirty in all—and Madame de Serizy's somewhat voluminous correspondence.

Then he waited on the public prosecutor.

The Palais de Justice is a perplexing maze of buildings piled one above another, some fine and dignified, others very mean, the whole disfigured by its lack of unity. The *Salle des Pas-Perdus* is the largest known hall, but its nakedness is hideous, and distresses the eye. This vast Cathedral of the Law crushes the Supreme Court. The Galerie Marchande ends in two drain-like passages. From this corridor there is a double staircase, a little larger than that of the Criminal Courts, and under it a large double door. The stairs lead down to one of the Assize

Courts, and the doors open into another. In some years the number of crimes committed in the circuit of the Seine is great enough to necessitate the sitting of two Benches.

Close by are the public prosecutor's offices, the attorney's room and library, the chambers of the attorney-general, and those of the public prosecutor's deputies. All these purlieus, to use a generic term, communicate by narrow spiral stairs and the dark passages, which are a disgrace to the architecture not of Paris only, but of all France. The interior arrangement of the sovereign court of justice outdoes our prisons in all that is most hideous. The writer describing our manners and customs would shrink from the necessity of depicting the squalid corridor of about a metre in width, in which the witnesses wait in the Superior Criminal Court. As to the stove which warms the court itself, it would disgrace a cafe on the Boulevard Mont-Parnasse.

The public prosecutor's private room forms part of an octagon wing flanking the Galerie Marchande, built out recently in regard to the age of the structure, over the prison yard, outside the women's quarters. All this part of the Palais is overshadowed by the lofty and noble edifice of the Sainte-Chapelle. And all is solemn and silent.

Monsieur de Granville, a worthy successor of the great magistrates of the ancient Parlement, would not leave Paris without coming to some conclusion in the matter of Lucien. He expected to hear from Camusot, and the judge's message had plunged him into the involuntary suspense which waiting produces on even the strongest minds. He had been sitting in the window-bay of his private room; he rose, and walked up and down, for having lingered in the morning to intercept Camusot, he had found him dull of apprehension; he was vaguely uneasy and worried.

And this was why.

The dignity of his high functions forbade his attempting to fetter the perfect independence of the inferior judge, and yet this trial nearly touched the honor and good name of his best friend and warmest supporter, the Comte de Serizy, Minister of State, member of the Privy Council, Vice-President of the State Council, and prospective Chancellor of the Realm, in the event of the death of the noble old man who held that august office. It was Monsieur de Serizy's misfortune to adore his wife "through fire and water," and he always shielded her with his protection. Now the public prosecutor fully understood the terrible fuss that would be made in the world and at court if a crime should be proved against a man whose name had been so often and so malignantly linked with that of the Countess.

"Ah!" he sighed, folding his arms, "formerly the supreme authority could take refuge in an appeal. Nowadays our mania for equality"—he dared not say *for Legality*, as a poetic orator in the Chamber courageously admitted a short while since—"is the death of us."

This noble magistrate knew all the fascination and the miseries of an illicit attachment. Esther and Lucien, as we have seen, had taken the rooms where the Comte de Granville had lived secretly on connubial terms with Mademoiselle de Bellefeuille, and whence she had fled one day, lured away by a villain. (See *A Double Marriage*.)

At the very moment when the public prosecutor was saying to himself, "Camusot is sure to have done something silly," the examining magistrate knocked twice at the door of his room.

"Well, my dear Camusot, how is that case going on that I spoke of this morning?"

"Badly, Monsieur le Comte; read and judge for yourself."

He held out the minutes of the two examinations to Monsieur de Granville, who took up his eyeglass and went to the window to read them. He had soon run through them.

"You have done your duty," said the Count in an agitated voice. "It is all over. The law must take its course. You have shown so much skill, that you need never fear being deprived of your appointment as examining judge—"

If Monsieur de Granville had said to Camusot, "You will remain an examining judge to your dying day," he could not have been more explicit than in making this polite speech. Camusot was cold in the very marrow.

"Madame la Duchesse de Maufrigneuse, to whom I owe much, had desired me. . ."

"Oh yes, the Duchesse de Maufrigneuse is Madame de Serizy's friend," said Granville, interrupting him. "To be sure.—You have allowed nothing to influence you, I perceive. And you did well, sir; you will be a great magistrate."

At this instant the Comte Octave de Bauvan opened the door without knocking, and said to the Comte de Granville:

"I have brought you a fair lady, my dear fellow, who did not know which way to turn; she was on the point of losing herself in our labyrinth—"

And Comte Octave led in by the hand the Comtesse de Serizy, who had been wandering about the place for the last quarter of an hour.

"What, you here, madame!" exclaimed the public prosecutor, pushing forward his own armchair, "and at this moment! This, madame, is Monsieur Camusot," he added, introducing the judge.—"Bauvan," said he to the distinguished ministerial orator of the Restoration, "wait for me in the president's chambers; he is still there, and I will join you."

Comte Octave de Bauvan understood that not merely was he in the way, but that Monsieur de Granville wanted an excuse for leaving his room.

Madame de Serizy had not made the mistake of coming to the Palais de Justice in her handsome carriage with a blue hammer-cloth and coats-of-arms, her coachman in gold lace, and two footmen in breeches and silk stockings. Just as they were starting Asie impressed on the two great ladies the need for taking the hackney coach in which she and the Duchess had arrived, and she had likewise insisted on Lucien's mistress adopting the costume which is to women what a gray cloak was of yore to men. The Countess wore a plain brown dress, an old black shawl, and a velvet bonnet from which the flowers had been removed, and the whole covered up under a thick lace veil.

"You received our note?" said she to Camusot, whose dismay she mistook for respectful admiration.

"Alas! but too late, Madame la Comtesse," replied the lawyer, whose tact and wit failed him excepting in his chambers and in presence of a prisoner.

"Too late! How?"

She looked at Monsieur de Granville, and saw consternation written in his face. "It cannot be, it must not be too late!" she added, in the tone of a despot.

Women, pretty women, in the position of Madame de Serizy, are the spoiled children of French civilization. If the women of other countries knew what a woman of fashion is in Paris, a woman of wealth and rank, they would all want to come and enjoy that splendid royalty. The women who recognize no bonds but those of propriety, no law but the petty charter which has been more than once alluded to in this *Comedie Humaine* as the ladies' Code, laugh at the statutes framed by men. They say everything, they do not shrink from any blunder or hesitate at any folly, for they all accept the fact that they are irresponsible beings, answerable for nothing on earth but their good repute and their children. They say the most preposterous things with a laugh, and are ready on every occasion to repeat the speech made in the early days of her married life by pretty Madame de Bauvan to her husband, whom she came to fetch away from the Palais: "Make haste and pass sentence, and come away."

"Madame," said the public prosecutor, "Monsieur Lucien de Rubempre is not guilty either of robbery or of poisoning; but Monsieur Camusot has led him to confess a still greater crime."

"What is that?" she asked.

"He acknowledged," said Monsieur Camusot in her ear, "that he is the friend and pupil of an escaped convict. The Abbe Carlos Herrera, the Spaniard with whom he has been living for the last seven years, is the notorious Jacques Collin."

Madame de Serizy felt as if it were a blow from an iron rod at each word spoken by the judge, but this name was the finishing stroke.

"And the upshot of all this?" she said, in a voice that was no more than a breath.

"Is," Monsieur de Granville went on, finishing the Countess' sentence in an undertone, "that the convict will be committed for trial, and that if Lucien is not committed with him as having profited as an accessory to the man's crimes, he must appear as a witness very seriously compromised."

"Oh! never, never!" she cried aloud, with amazing firmness. "For my part, I should not hesitate between death and the disaster of seeing a man whom the world has known to be my dearest friend declared by the bench to be the accomplice of a convict.—The King has a great regard for my husband—"

"Madame," said the public prosecutor, also aloud, and with a smile, "the King has not the smallest power over the humblest examining judge in his kingdom, nor over the proceedings in any court of justice. That is the grand feature of our new code of laws. I myself have just congratulated M. Camusot on his skill—"

"On his clumsiness," said the Countess sharply, though Lucien's intimacy with a scoundrel really disturbed her far less than his attachment to Esther.

"If you will read the minutes of the examination of the two prisoners by Monsieur Camusot, you will see that everything is in his hands—"

After this speech, the only thing the public prosecutor could venture to say, and a flash of feminine—or, if you will, lawyer-like—cunning, he went to the door; then, turning round on the threshold, he added:

"Excuse me, madame; I have two words to say to Bauvan." Which, translated by the worldly wise, conveyed to the Countess: "I do not want to witness the scene between you and Camusot."

"What is this examination business?" said Leontine very blandly to Camusot, who stood downcast in the presence of the wife of one of the most important personages in the realm.

"Madame," said Camusot, "a clerk writes down all the magistrate's questions and the prisoner's replies. This document is signed by the clerk, by the judge, and by the prisoner. This evidence is the raw material of the subsequent proceedings; on it the accused are committed for trial, and remanded to appear before the Criminal Court."

"Well, then," said she, "if the evidence were suppressed—?"

"Oh, madame, that is a crime which no magistrate could possibly commit—a crime against society."

"It is a far worse crime against me to have ever allowed it to be recorded; still, at this moment it is the only evidence against Lucien. Come, read me the minutes of his examination that I may see if there is still a way of salvation for us all, monsieur. I do not speak for myself alone—I should quite calmly kill myself—but Monsieur de Serizy's happiness is also at stake."

"Pray, madame, do not suppose that I have forgotten the respect due you," said Camusot. "If Monsieur Popinot, for instance, had undertaken this case, you would have had worse luck than you have found with me; for he would not have come to consult Monsieur de Granville; no one would have heard anything about it. I tell you, madame, everything has been seized in Monsieur Lucien's lodging, even your letters—"

"What! my letters!"

"Here they are, madame, in a sealed packet."

The Countess in her agitation rang as if she had been at home, and the office-boy came in.

"A light," said she.

The boy lighted a taper and placed it on the chimney-piece, while the Countess looked through the letters, counted them, crushed them in her hand, and flung them on the hearth. In a few minutes she set the whole mass in a blaze, twisting up the last note to serve as a torch.

Camusot stood, looking rather foolish as he watched the papers burn, holding the legal documents in his hand. The Countess, who seemed absorbed in the work of destroying the proofs of her passion, studied him out of the corner of her eye. She took her time, she calculated her distance; with the spring of a cat she seized the two documents and threw them on the flames. But Camusot saved them; the Countess rushed on him and snatched back the burning papers. A struggle ensued, Camusot calling out: "Madame, but madame! This is contempt—madame!"

A man hurried into the room, and the Countess could not repress a scream as she beheld the Comte de Serizy, followed by Monsieur de Granville and the Comte de Bauvan. Leontine, however, determined to save Lucien at any cost, would not let go of the terrible stamped documents, which she clutched with the tenacity of a vise, though the flame had already burnt her delicate skin like a moxa.

At last Camusot, whose fingers also were smarting from the fire, seemed to be ashamed of the position; he let the papers go; there was nothing left of them but the portions so tightly held by the antagonists that the flame could not touch them. The whole scene had taken less time than is needed to read this account of it.

"What discussion can have arisen between you and Madame de Serizy?" the husband asked of Camusot.

Before the lawyer could reply, the Countess held the fragments in the candle and threw them on the remains of her letters, which were not entirely consumed.

"I shall be compelled," said Camusot, "to lay a complaint against Madame la Comtesse—"

"Heh! What has she done?" asked the public prosecutor, looking alternately at the lady and the magistrate.

"I have burned the record of the examinations," said the lady of fashion with a laugh, so pleased at her high-handed conduct that she did not yet feel the pain of the burns, "If that is a crime—well, monsieur must get his odious scrawl written out again."

"Very true," said Camusot, trying to recover his dignity.

"Well, well, 'All's well that ends well,'" said Monsieur de Granville. "But, my dear Countess, you must not often take such liberties with the Law; it might fail to discern who and what you are."

"Monsieur Camusot valiantly resisted a woman whom none can resist; the Honor of the Robe is safe!" said the Comte de Bauvan, laughing.

"Indeed! Monsieur Camusot was resisting?" said the public prosecutor, laughing too. "He is a brave man indeed; I should not dare resist the Countess."

And thus for the moment this serious affair was no more than a pretty woman's jest, at which Camusot himself must laugh.

But Monsieur de Granville saw one man who was not amused. Not a little alarmed by the Comte de Serizy's attitude and expression, his friend led him aside.

"My dear fellow," said he in a whisper, "your distress persuades me for the first and only time in my life to compromise with my duty."

The public prosecutor rang, and the office-boy appeared.

"Desire Monsieur de Chargeboeuf to come here."

Monsieur de Chargeboeuf, a sucking barrister, was his private secretary.

"My good friend," said the Comte de Granville to Camusot, whom he took to the window, "go back to your chambers, get your clerk to reconstruct the report of the Abbe Carlos Herrera's depositions; as he had not signed the first copy, there will be no difficulty about that. To-morrow you must confront your Spanish diplomate with Rastignac and Bianchon, who will not recognize him as Jacques Collin. Then, being sure of his release, the man will sign the document.

"As to Lucien de Rubempre, set him free this evening; he is not likely to talk about an examination of which the evidence is destroyed, especially after such a lecture as I shall give him.

"Now you will see how little justice suffers by these proceedings. If the Spaniard really is the convict, we have fifty ways of recapturing him and committing him for trial—for we will have his conduct in Spain thoroughly investigated. Corentin, the police agent, will take care of him for us, and we ourselves will keep an eye on him. So treat him decently; do not send him down to the cells again.

"Can we be the death of the Comte and Comtesse de Serizy, as well as of Lucien, for the theft of seven hundred and fifty thousand francs as yet unproven, and to Lucien's personal loss? Will it not be better for him to lose the money than to lose his character? Above all, if he is to drag with him in his fall a Minister of State, and his wife, and the Duchesse du Maufrigneuse.

"This young man is a speckled orange; do not leave it to rot.

"All this will take you about half an hour; go and get it done; we will wait for you. It is half-past three; you will find some judges about. Let me know if you can get a rule of insufficient evidence—or Lucien must wait till to-morrow morning."

Camusot bowed to the company and went; but Madame de Serizy, who was suffering a good deal from her burns, did not return his bow.

Monsieur de Serizy, who had suddenly rushed away while the public prosecutor and the magistrate were talking together, presently returned, having fetched a small jar of virgin wax. With this he dressed his wife's fingers, saying in an undertone:

"Leontine, why did you come here without letting me know?"

"My dear," replied she in a whisper, "forgive me. I seem mad, but indeed your interests were as much involved as mine."

"Love this young fellow if fatality requires it, but do not display your passion to all the world," said the luckless husband.

"Well, my dear Countess," said Monsieur de Granville, who had been engaged in conversation with Comte Octave, "I hope you may take Monsieur de Rubempre home to dine with you this evening."

This half promise produced a reaction; Madame de Serizy melted into tears.

"I thought I had no tears left," said she with a smile. "But could you not bring Monsieur de Rubempre to wait here?"

"I will try if I can find the ushers to fetch him, so that he may not be seen under the escort of the gendarmes," said Monsieur de Granville.

"You are as good as God!" cried she, with a gush of feeling that made her voice sound like heavenly music.

"These are the women," said Comte Octave, "who are fascinating, irresistible!"

And he became melancholy as he thought of his own wife. (See *Honorine*.)

As he left the room, Monsieur de Granville was stopped by young Chargeboeuf, to whom he spoke to give him instructions as to what he was to say to Massol, one of the editors of the *Gazette des Tribunaux*.

While beauties, ministers, and magistrates were conspiring to save Lucien, this was what he was doing at the Conciergerie. As he passed the gate the poet told the keeper that Monsieur Camusot had granted him leave to write, and he begged to have pens, ink, and paper. At a whispered word to the Governor from Camusot's usher a warder was instructed to take them to him at once. During the short time that it took for the warder to fetch these things and carry them up to Lucien, the hapless young man, to whom the idea of facing Jacques Collin had become intolerable, sank into one of those fatal moods in which the idea of suicide—to which he had yielded before now, but without succeeding in carrying it out—rises to the pitch of mania. According to certain mad-doctors, suicide is in some temperaments the closing phase of mental aberration; and since his arrest Lucien had been possessed by that single idea. Esther's letter, read and reread many times, increased the vehemence of his desire to die by reminding him of the catastrophe of Romeo dying to be with Juliet.

This is what he wrote:—

This is my Last Will and Testament
At the Conciergerie, May 15th, 1830

"I, the undersigned, give and bequeath to the children of my sister, Madame Eve Chardon, wife of David Sechard, formerly a printer at Angouleme, and of Monsieur David Sechard, all the property, real and personal, of which I may be possessed at the time of my decease, due deduction being made for the payments and legacies, which I desire my executor to provide for.

"And I earnestly beg Monsieur de Serizy to undertake the charge of being the executor of this my will.

"First, to Monsieur l'Abbe Carlos Herrera I direct the payment of the sum of three hundred thousand francs. Secondly, to Monsieur le Baron de Nucingen the sum of fourteen hundred thousand francs, less seven hundred and fifty thousand if the sum stolen from Mademoiselle Esther should be recovered.

"As universal legatee to Mademoiselle Esther Gobseck, I give and bequeath the sum of seven hundred and sixty thousand francs to the Board of Asylums of Paris for the foundation of a refuge especially dedicated to the use of public prostitutes who may wish to forsake their life of vice and ruin.

"I also bequeath to the Asylums of Paris the sum of money necessary for the purchase of a certificate for dividends to the amount of thirty thousand francs per annum in five per cents, the annual income to be devoted every six months to the release of prisoners for debts not exceeding two thousand francs. The Board of Asylums to select the most respectable of such persons imprisoned for debt.

"I beg Monsieur de Serizy to devote the sum of forty thousand francs to erecting a monument to Mademoiselle Esther in the Eastern cemetery, and I desire to be buried by her side. The tomb is to be like an antique tomb—square, our two effigies lying thereon, in white marble, the heads on pillows, the hands folded and raised to heaven. There is to be no inscription whatever.

"I beg Monsieur de Serizy to give to Monsieur de Rastignac a gold toilet-set that is in my room as a remembrance.

"And as a remembrance, I beg my executor to accept my library of books as a gift from me.

Lucien Chardon de Rubempre

This Will was enclosed in a letter addressed to Monsieur le Comte de Granville, Public Prosecutor in the Supreme Court at Paris, as follows:

Monsieur le Comte,

"I place my Will in your hands. When you open this letter I shall be no more. In my desire to be free, I made such cowardly replies to Monsieur Camusot's insidious questions, that, in spite of my innocence, I may find myself entangled in a disgraceful trial. Even if I were acquitted, a blameless life would henceforth be impossible to me in view of the opinions of the world.

"I beg you to transmit the enclosed letter to the Abbe Carlos Herrera without opening it, and deliver to Monsieur Camusot the formal retraction I also enclose.

"I suppose no one will dare to break the seal of a packet addressed to you. In this belief I bid you adieu, offering you my best respects for the last time, and begging you to believe that in writing to you I am giving you a token of my gratitude for all the kindness you have shown to your deceased humble servant,

Lucien de R.

To the Abbe Carlos Herrera
My Dear Abbe,

I have had only benefits from you, and I have betrayed you. This involuntary ingratitude is killing me, and when you read these lines I shall have ceased to exist. You are not here now to save me.

"You had given me full liberty, if I should find it advantageous, to destroy you by flinging you on the ground like a cigar-end; but I have ruined you by a blunder. To escape from a difficulty, deluded by a clever question from the examining judge, your son by adoption and grace went over to the side of those who aim at killing you at any cost, and insist on proving an identity, which I know to be impossible, between you and a French villain. All is said.

"Between a man of your calibre and me—me of whom you tried to make a greater man than I am capable of being—no foolish sentiment can come at the moment of final parting. You hoped to make me powerful and famous, and you have thrown me into the gulf of suicide, that is all. I have long heard the broad pinions of that vertigo beating over my head.

"As you have sometimes said, there is the posterity of Cain and the posterity of Abel. In the great human drama Cain is in opposition. You are descended from Adam through that line, in which the devil still fans the fire of which the first spark was flung on Eve. Among the demons of that pedigree, from time to time we see one of stupendous power, summing up every form of human energy, and resembling the fevered beasts of the desert, whose vitality demands the vast spaces they find there. Such men are as dangerous as lions would be in the heart of Normandy; they must have their prey, and they devour common men and crop the money of fools. Their sport is so dangerous that at last they kill the humble dog whom they have taken for a companion and made an idol of.

"When it is God's will, these mysterious beings may be a Moses, an Attila, Charlemagne, Mahomet, or Napoleon; but when He leaves a generation of these stupendous tools to rust at the bottom of the ocean, they are no more than a Pugatschef, a Fouche, a Louvel, or the Abbe Carlos Herrera. Gifted with immense power over tenderer souls, they entrap them and mangle them. It is grand, it is fine—in its way. It is the poisonous plant with gorgeous coloring that fascinates children in the woods. It is the poetry of evil. Men like you ought to dwell in caves and never come out of them. You have made me live that vast life, and I have had all my share of existence; so I may very well take my head out of the Gordian knot of your policy and slip it into the running knot of my cravat.

"To repair the mischief I have done, I am forwarding to the public prosecutor a retraction of my deposition. You will know how to take advantage of this document.

"In virtue of a will formally drawn up, restitution will be made, Monsieur l'Abbe, of the moneys belonging to your Order which you so imprudently devoted to my use, as a result of your paternal affection for me.

"And so, farewell. Farewell, colossal image of Evil and Corruption; farewell—to you who, if started on the right road, might have been greater than Ximenes, greater than Richelieu! You have kept your promises. I find myself once more just as I was on the banks of the Charente, after enjoying, by your help, the enchantments of a dream. But, unfortunately, it is not now in the waters of my native place that I shall drown the errors of a boy; but in the Seine, and my hole is a cell in the Conciergerie.

"Do not regret me: my contempt for you is as great as my admiration.

LUCIEN

Recantation

"I, the undersigned, hereby declare that I retract, without reservation, all that I deposed at my examination to-day before Monsieur Camusot.

"The Abbe Carlos Herrera always called himself my spiritual father, and I was misled by the word father used in another sense by the judge, no doubt under a misapprehension.

"I am aware that, for political ends, and to quash certain secrets concerning the Cabinets of Spain and of the Tuileries, some obscure diplomatic agents tried to show that the Abbe Carlos Herrera was a forger named Jacques Collin; but the Abbe Carlos Herrera never told me anything about the matter excepting that he was doing his best to obtain

evidence of the death or of the continued existence of
Jacques Collin.

LUCIEN DE RUBEMPRE

AT THE CONCIERGERIE, May 15th, 1830

The fever for suicide had given Lucien immense clearness of mind, and the swiftness of hand familiar to authors in the fever of composition. The impetus was so strong within him that these four documents were all written within half an hour; he folded them in a wrapper, fastened with wafers, on which he impressed with the strength of delirium the coat-of-arms engraved on a seal-ring he wore, and he then laid the packet very conspicuously in the middle of the floor.

Certainly it would have been impossible to conduct himself with greater dignity, in the false position to which all this infamy had led him; he was rescuing his memory from opprobrium, and repairing the injury done to his accomplice, so far as the wit of a man of the world could nullify the result of the poet's trustfulness.

If Lucien had been taken back to one of the lower cells, he would have been wrecked on the impossibility of carrying out his intentions, for those boxes of masonry have no furniture but a sort of camp-bed and a pail for necessary uses. There is not a nail, not a chair, not even a stool. The camp-bed is so firmly fixed that it is impossible to move it without an amount of labor that the warder would not fail to detect, for the iron-barred peephole is always open. Indeed, if a prisoner under suspicion gives reason for uneasiness, he is watched by a gendarme or a constable.

In the private rooms for which prisoners pay, and in that whither Lucien had been conveyed by the judge's courtesy to a young man belonging to the upper ranks of society, the movable bed, table, and chair might serve to carry out his purpose of suicide, though they hardly made it easy. Lucien wore a long blue silk necktie, and on his way back from examination he was already meditating on the means by which Pichegru, more or less voluntarily, ended his days. Still, to hang himself, a man must find a purchase, and have a sufficient space between it and the ground for his feet to find no support. Now the window of his room, looking out on the prison-yard, had no handle to the fastening; and the bars, being fixed outside, were divided from his reach by the thickness of the wall, and could not be used for a support.

This, then, was the plan hit upon by Lucien to put himself out of the world. The boarding of the lower part of the opening, which prevented his seeing out into the yard, also hindered the warders outside from seeing what was done in the room; but while the lower portion of the window was replaced by two thick planks, the upper part of both halves still was filled with small panes, held in place by the cross pieces in which they were set. By standing on his table Lucien could reach the glazed part of the window, and take or break out two panes, so as to have a firm point of attachment in the angle of the lower bar. Round this he would tie his cravat, turn round once to tighten it round his neck after securing it firmly, and kick the table from under his feet.

He drew the table up under the window without making any noise, took off his coat and waistcoat, and got on the table unhesitatingly to break a pane above and one below the iron cross-bar. Standing on the table, he could look out across the yard on a magical view, which he then beheld for the first time. The Governor of the prison, in deference to Monsieur Camusot's request that he should deal as leniently as possible with Lucien, had led him, as we have seen, through the dark passages of the Conciergerie, entered from the dark vault opposite the Tour d'Argent, thus avoiding the exhibition of a young man of fashion to the crowd of prisoners airing themselves in the yard. It will be for the reader to judge whether the aspect of the promenade was not such as to appeal deeply to a poet's soul.

The yard of the Conciergerie ends at the quai between the Tour d'Argent and the Tour Bonbec; thus the distance between them exactly shows from the outside the width of the plot of ground. The corridor called the Galerie de Saint-Louis, which extends from the Galerie Marchande to the Courts of Appeals and the Tour Bonbec—in which, it is said, Saint-Louis' room still exists—may enable the curious to estimate the depths of the yard, as it is of the same length. Thus the dark cells and the private rooms are under the Galerie Marchande. And Queen Marie Antoinette, whose dungeon was under the present cells, was conducted to the presence of the Revolutionary Tribunal, which held its sittings in the place where the Court of Appeals now performs its solemn functions, up a horrible flight of steps, now never used, in the very thickness of the wall on which the Galerie Marchande is built.

One side of the prison-yard—that on which the Hall of Saint-Louis forms the first floor—displays a long row of Gothic columns, between which the architects of I know not what period have built up two floors of cells to accommodate as many prisoners as possible, by choking the capitals, the arches, and the vaults of this magnificent cloister with plaster, barred loopholes, and partitions. Under the room known as the Cabinet de Saint-Louis, in the Tour Bonbec, there is a spiral stair leading to these dens. This degradation of one of the immemorial buildings of France is hideous to behold.

From the height at which Lucien was standing he saw this cloister, and the details of the building that joins the two towers, in sharp perspective; before him were the pointed caps of the towers. He stood amazed; his suicide was postponed to his admiration. The phenomena of hallucination are in these days so fully recognized by the medical faculty that this mirage of the senses, this strange illusion of the mind is beyond dispute. A man under the stress of a feeling which by its intensity has become a monomania, often finds himself in the frame of mind to which opium, hasheesh, or the protoxyde of azote might have brought him. Spectres appear, phantoms and dreams take shape, things of the past live again as they once were. What was but an image of the brain becomes a moving or a living object. Science is now beginning to believe that under the action of a paroxysm of passion the blood rushes to the brain, and that such congestion has the terrible effects of a dream in a waking state, so averse are we to regard thought as a physical and generative force. (See *Louis Lambert*.)

Lucien saw the building in all its pristine beauty; the columns were new, slender and bright; Saint-Louis' Palace rose before him as it had once appeared; he admired its Babylonian proportions and Oriental fancy. He took this exquisite vision as a poetic farewell from civilized creation. While making his arrangements to die, he wondered how this marvel of architecture could exist in Paris so utterly unknown. He was two Luciens—one Lucien the poet, wandering through the Middle Ages under the vaults and the turrets of Saint-Louis, the other Lucien ready for suicide.

Just as Monsieur de Granville had ended giving his instructions to the young secretary, the Governor of the Conciergerie came in, and the expression of his face was such as to give the public prosecutor a presentiment of disaster.

"Have you met Monsieur Camusot?" he asked.

"No, monsieur," said the Governor; "his clerk Coquart instructed me to give the Abbe Carlos a private room and to liberate Monsieur de Rubempre—but it is too late."

"Good God! what has happened?"

"Here, monsieur, is a letter for you which will explain the catastrophe. The warder on duty in the prison-yard heard a noise of breaking glass in the upper room, and Monsieur Lucien's next neighbor shrieking wildly, for he heard the young man's dying struggles. The warder came to me pale from the sight that met his eyes. He found the prisoner hanged from the window bar by his necktie."

Though the Governor spoke in a low voice, a fearful scream from Madame de Serizy showed that under stress of feeling our faculties are incalculably keen. The Countess heard, or guessed. Before Monsieur de Granville could turn round, or Monsieur de Bauvan or her husband could stop her, she fled like a flash out of the door, and reached the Galerie Marchande, where she ran on to the stairs leading out to the Rue de la Barillerie.

A pleader was taking off his gown at the door of one of the shops which from time immemorial have choked up this arcade, where shoes are sold, and gowns and caps kept for hire.

The Countess asked the way to the Conciergerie.

"Go down the steps and turn to the left. The entrance is from the Quai de l'Horloge, the first archway."

"That woman is crazy," said the shop-woman; "some one ought to follow her."

But no one could have kept up with Leontine; she flew.

A physician may explain how it is that these ladies of fashion, whose strength never finds employment, reveal such powers in the critical moments of life.

The Countess rushed so swiftly through the archway to the wicket-gate that the gendarme on sentry did not see her pass. She flew at the barred gate like a feather driven by the wind, and shook the iron bars with such fury that she broke the one she grasped. The bent ends were thrust into her breast, making the blood flow, and she dropped on the ground, shrieking, "Open it, open it!" in a tone that struck terror into the warders.

The gatekeepers hurried out.

"Open the gate—the public prosecutor sent me—to save the dead man!—"

While the Countess was going round by the Rue de la Barillerie and the Quai de l'Horloge, Monsieur de Granville and Monsieur de Serizy went down to the Conciergerie through the inner passages, suspecting Leontine's purpose; but notwithstanding their haste, they only arrived in time to see her fall fainting at the outer gate, where she was picked up by two gendarmes who had come down from the guardroom.

On seeing the Governor of the prison, the gate was opened, and the Countess was carried into the office, but she stood up and fell on her knees, clasping her hands.

"Only to see him—to see him! Oh! I will do no wrong! But if you do not want to see me die on the spot, let me look at Lucien dead or living.—Ah, my dear, are you here? Choose between my death and—"

She sank in a heap.

"You are kind," she said; "I will always love you—"

"Carry her away," said Monsieur de Bauvan.

"No, we will go to Lucien's cell," said Monsieur de Granville, reading a purpose in Monsieur de Serizy's wild looks.

And he lifted up the Countess, and took her under one arm, while Monsieur de Bauvan supported her on the other side.

"Monsieur," said the Comte de Serizy to the Governor, "silence as of the grave about all this."

"Be easy," replied the Governor; "you have done the wisest thing.—If this lady—"

"She is my wife."

"Oh! I beg your pardon. Well, she will certainly faint away when she sees the poor man, and while she is unconscious she can be taken home in a carriage."

"That is what I thought," replied the Count. "Pray send one of your men to tell my servants in the Cour de Harlay to come round to the gate. Mine is the only carriage there."

"We can save him yet," said the Countess, walking on with a degree of strength and spirit that surprised her friends. "There are ways of restoring life—"

And she dragged the gentlemen along, crying to the warder:

"Come on, come faster—one second may cost three lives!"

When the cell door was opened, and the Countess saw Lucien hanging as though his clothes had been hung on a peg, she made a spring towards him as if to embrace him and cling to him; but she fell on her face on the floor with smothered shrieks and a sort of rattle in her throat.

Five minutes later she was being taken home stretched on the seat in the Count's carriage, her husband kneeling by her side. Monsieur de Bauvan went off to fetch a doctor to give her the care she needed.

The Governor of the Conciergerie meanwhile was examining the outer gate, and saying to his clerk:

"No expense was spared; the bars are of wrought iron, they were properly tested, and cost a large sum; and yet there was a flaw in that bar."

Monsieur de Granville on returning to his room had other instructions to give to his private secretary. Massol, happily had not yet arrived.

Soon after Monsieur de Granville had left, anxious to go to see Monsieur de Serizy, Massol came and found his ally Chargeboeuf in the public prosecutor's Court.

"My dear fellow," said the young secretary, "if you will do me a great favor, you will put what I dictate to you in your *Gazette* to-morrow under the heading of Law Reports; you can compose the heading. Write now."

And he dictated as follows:—

"It has been ascertained that the Demoiselle Esther Gobseck killed herself of her own free will.

"Monsieur Lucien de Rubempre satisfactorily proved an alibi, and his innocence leaves his arrest to be regretted, all the more because just as the examining judge had given the order for his release the young gentleman died suddenly."

"I need not point out to you," said the young lawyer to Massol, "how necessary it is to preserve absolute silence as to the little service requested of you."

"Since it is you who do me the honor of so much confidence," replied Massol, "allow me to make one observation. This paragraph will give rise to odious comments on the course of justice—"

"Justice is strong enough to bear them," said the young attache to the Courts, with the pride of a coming magistrate trained by Monsieur de Granville.

"Allow me, my dear sir; with two sentences this difficulty may be avoided."

And the journalist-lawyer wrote as follows:—

"The forms of the law have nothing to do with this sad event. The post-mortem examination, which was at once made, proved that sudden death was due to the rupture of an aneurism in its last stage. If Monsieur Lucien de Rubempre had been upset by his arrest, death must have ensued sooner. But we are in a position to state that, far from being distressed at being taken into custody, the young man, whom all must lament, only laughed at it, and told those who escorted him from Fontainebleau to Paris that as soon as he was brought before a magistrate his innocence would be acknowledged."

"That saves it, I think?" said Massol.

"You are perfectly right."

"The public prosecutor will thank you for it to-morrow," said Massol slyly.

Now to the great majority, as to the more choice reader, it will perhaps seem that this Study is not completed by the death of Esther and of Lucien; Jacques Collin and Asie, Europe and Paccard, in spite of their villainous lives, may have been interesting enough to make their fate a matter of curiosity.

The last act of the drama will also complete the picture of life which this Study is intended to present, and give the issue of various interests which Lucien's career had strangely tangled by bringing some ignoble personages from the hulks into contact with those of the highest rank.

Thus, as may be seen, the greatest events of life find their expression in the more or less veracious gossip of the Paris papers. And this is the case with many things of greater importance than are here recorded.

W hat is it, Madeleine?" asked Madame Camusot, seeing her maid come into the room with the particular air that servants assume in critical moments.

"Madame," said Madeleine, "monsieur has just come in from Court; but he looks so upset, and is in such a state, that I think perhaps it would be well for you to go to his room."

"Did he say anything?" asked Madame Camusot.

"No, madame; but we never have seen monsieur look like that; he looks as if he were going to be ill, his face is yellow—he seems all to pieces—"

Madame Camusot waited for no more; she rushed out of her room and flew to her husband's study. She found the lawyer sitting in an armchair, pale and dazed, his legs stretched out, his head against the back of it, his hands hanging limp, exactly as if he were sinking into idiotcy.

"What is the matter, my dear?" said the young woman in alarm.

"Oh! my poor Amelie, the most dreadful thing has happened—I am still trembling. Imagine, the public prosecutor—no, Madame de Serizy—that is—I do not know where to begin."

"Begin at the end," said Madame Camusot.

"Well, just as Monsieur Popinot, in the council room of the first Court, had put the last signature to the ruling of 'insufficient cause' for the apprehension of Lucien de Rubempre on the ground of my report, setting him at liberty—in fact, the whole thing was done, the clerk was going off with the minute book, and I was quit of the whole business— the President of the Court came in and took up the papers. 'You are releasing a dead man,' said he, with chilly irony; 'the young man is gone, as Monsieur de Bonald says, to appear before his natural Judge. He died of apoplexy—'

"I breathed again, thinking it was sudden illness.

"'As I understand you, Monsieur le President,' said Monsieur Popinot, 'it is a case of apoplexy like Pichegru's.'

"'Gentlemen,' said the President then, very gravely, 'you must please to understand that for the outside world Lucien de Rubempre died of an aneurism.'

"We all looked at each other. 'Very great people are concerned in this deplorable business,' said the President. 'God grant for your sake, Monsieur Camusot, though you did no less than your duty, that Madame de Serizy may not go mad from the shock she has had. She was carried away almost dead. I have just met our public prosecutor in a painful state of despair.'—'You have made a mess of it, my dear Camusot,' he added in my ear.—I assure you, my dear, as I came away I could hardly stand. My legs shook so that I dared not venture into the street. I went back to my room to rest. Then Coquart, who was putting away the papers of this wretched case, told me that a very handsome woman had taken the Conciergerie by storm, wanting to save Lucien, whom she was quite crazy about, and that she fainted away on seeing him hanging by his necktie to the window-bar of his room. The idea that the way in which I questioned that unhappy young fellow—who, between ourselves, was guilty in many ways—can have led to his committing suicide has haunted me ever since I left the Palais, and I feel constantly on the point of fainting—"

"What next? Are you going to think yourself a murderer because a suspected criminal hangs himself in prison just as you were about to release him?" cried Madame Camusot. "Why, an examining judge in such a case is a general whose horse is killed under him!—That is all."

"Such a comparison, my dear, is at best but a jest, and jesting is out of place now. In this case the dead man clutches the living. All our hopes are buried in Lucien's coffin."

"Indeed?" said Madame Camusot, with deep irony.

"Yes, my career is closed. I shall be no more than an examining judge all my life. Before this fatal termination Monsieur de Granville was annoyed at the turn the preliminaries had taken; his speech to our President makes me quite certain that so long as Monsieur de Granville is public prosecutor I shall get no promotion."

Promotion! The terrible thought, which in these days makes a judge a mere functionary.

Formerly a magistrate was made at once what he was to remain. The three or four presidents' caps satisfied the ambitions of lawyers in each Parlement. An appointment as councillor was enough for a de Brosses or a Mole, at Dijon as much as in Paris. This office, in itself a fortune, required a fortune brought to it to keep it up.

In Paris, outside the Parlement, men of the long robe could hope only for three supreme appointments: those of Controller-General, Keeper of the Seals, or Chancellor. Below the Parlement, in the lower grades, the president of a lower Court thought himself quite of sufficient importance to be content to fill his chair to the end of his days.

Compare the position of a councillor in the High Court of Justice in Paris, in 1829, who has nothing but his salary, with that of a councillor to the Parlement in 1729. How great is the difference! In these days, when money is the universal social guarantee, magistrates are not required to have—as they used to have—fine private fortunes: hence we see deputies and peers of France heaping office on office, at once magistrates and legislators, borrowing dignity from other positions than those which ought to give them all their importance.

In short, a magistrate tries to distinguish himself for promotion as men do in the army, or in a Government office.

This prevailing thought, even if it does not affect his independence, is so well known and so natural, and its effects are so evident, that the law inevitably loses some of its majesty in the eyes of the public. And, in fact, the salaries paid by the State makes priests and magistrates mere *employes*. Steps to be gained foster ambition, ambition engenders subservience to power, and modern equality places the judge and the person to be judged in the same category at the bar of society. And so the two pillars of social order, Religion and Justice, are lowered in this nineteenth century, which asserts itself as progressive in all things.

"And why should you never be promoted?" said Amelie Camusot.

She looked half-jestingly at her husband, feeling the necessity of reviving the energies of the man who embodied her ambitions, and on whom she could play as on an instrument.

"Why despair?" she went on, with a shrug that sufficiently expressed her indifference as to the prisoner's end. "This suicide will delight Lucien's two enemies, Madame d'Espard and her cousin, the Comtesse du Chatelet. Madame d'Espard is on the best terms with the Keeper of the Seals; through her you can get an audience of His Excellency and tell him all the secrets of this business. Then, if the head of the law is on your side, what have you to fear from the president of your Court or the public prosecutor?"

"But, Monsieur and Madame de Serizy?" cried the poor man. "Madame de Serizy is gone mad, I tell you, and her madness is my doing, they say."

"Well, if she is out of her mind, O judge devoid of judgment," said Madame Camusot, laughing, "she can do you no harm.—Come, tell me all the incidents of the day."

"Bless me!" said Camusot, "just as I had cross-questioned the unhappy youth, and he had deposed that the self-styled Spanish priest is really Jacques Collin, the Duchesse de Maufrigneuse and Madame de Serizy sent me a note by a servant begging me not to examine him. It was all over!—"

"But you must have lost your head!" said Amelie. "What was to prevent you, being so sure as you are of your clerk's fidelity, from calling Lucien back, reassuring him cleverly, and revising the examination?"

"Why, you are as bad as Madame de Serizy; you laugh justice to scorn," said Camusot, who was incapable of flouting his profession. "Madame de Serizy seized the minutes and threw them into the fire."

"That is the right sort of woman! Bravo!" cried Madame Camusot.

"Madame de Serizy declared she would sooner see the Palais blown up than leave a young man who had enjoyed the favors of the Duchesse de Maufrigneuse and her own to stand at the bar of a Criminal court by the side of a convict!"

"But, Camusot," said Amelie, unable to suppress a superior smile, "your position is splendid—"

"Ah! yes, splendid!"

"You did your duty."

"But all wrong; and in spite of the jesuitical advice of Monsieur de Granville, who met me on the Quai Malaquais."

"This morning!"

"This morning."

"At what hour?"

"At nine o'clock."

"Oh, Camusot!" cried Amelie, clasping and wringing her hands, "and I am always imploring you to be constantly on the alert.—Good heavens! it is not a man, but a barrow-load of stones that I have to drag on!—Why, Camusot, your public prosecutor was waiting for you.—He must have given you some warning."

"Yes, indeed—"

"And you failed to understand him! If you are so deaf, you will indeed be an examining judge all your life without any knowledge whatever of the question.—At any rate, have sense enough to listen to me," she went on, silencing her husband, who was about to speak. "You think the matter is done for?" she asked.

Camusot looked at his wife as a country bumpkin looks at a conjurer.

"If the Duchesse de Maufrigneuse and Madame de Serizy are compromised, you will find them both ready to patronize you," said Amelie. "Madame de Serizy will get you admission to the Keeper of the Seals, and you will tell him the secret history of the affair; then he will amuse the King with the story, for sovereigns always wish to see the wrong side of the tapestry and to know the real meaning of the events the public stare at open-mouthed. Henceforth there will be no cause to fear either the public prosecutor or Monsieur de Serizy."

"What a treasure such a wife is!" cried the lawyer, plucking up courage. "After all, I have unearthed Jacques Collin; I shall send him to his account at the Assize Court and unmask his crimes. Such a trial is a triumph in the career of an examining judge!"

"Camusot," Amelie began, pleased to see her husband rally from the moral and physical prostration into which he had been thrown by Lucien's suicide, "the President told you that you had blundered to the wrong side. Now you are blundering as much to the other—you are losing your way again, my dear."

The magistrate stood up, looking at his wife with a stupid stare.

"The King and the Keeper of the Seals will be glad, no doubt, to know the truth of this business, and at the same time much annoyed at seeing the lawyers on the Liberal side dragging important persons to the bar of opinion and of the Assize Court by their special pleading—such people as the Maufrigneuses, the Serizys, and the Grandlieus, in short, all who are directly or indirectly mixed up with this case."

"They are all in it; I have them all!" cried Camusot.

And Camusot walked up and down the room like Sganarelle on the stage when he is trying to get out of a scrape.

"Listen, Amelie," said he, standing in front of his wife. "An incident recurs to my mind, a trifle in itself, but, in my position, of vital importance.

"Realize, my dear, that this Jacques Collin is a giant of cunning, of dissimulation, of deceit.—He is—what shall I say?—the Cromwell of the hulks!—I never met such a scoundrel; he almost took me in.—But in examining a criminal, a little end of thread leads you to find a ball, is a clue to the investigation of the darkest consciences and obscurest facts.—When Jacques Collin saw me turning over the letters seized in Lucien de Rubempre's lodgings, the villain glanced at them with the evident intention of seeing whether some particular packet were among them, and he allowed himself to give a visible expression of satisfaction.

This look, as of a thief valuing his booty, this movement, as of a man in danger saying to himself, 'My weapons are safe,' betrayed a world of things.

"Only you women, besides us and our examinees, can in a single flash epitomize a whole scene, revealing trickery as complicated as safety-locks. Volumes of suspicion may thus be communicated in a second. It is terrifying—life or death lies in a wink.

"Said I to myself, 'The rascal has more letters in his hands than these!'—Then the other details of the case filled my mind; I overlooked the incident, for I thought I should have my men face to face, and clear up this point afterwards. But it may be considered as quite certain that Jacques Collin, after the fashion of such wretches, has hidden in some safe place the most compromising of the young fellow's letters, adored as he was by—"

"And yet you are afraid, Camusot? Why, you will be President of the Supreme Court much sooner than I expected!" cried Madame Camusot, her face beaming. "Now, then, you must proceed so as to give satisfaction to everybody, for the matter is looking so serious that it might quite possibly be snatched from us.—Did they not take the proceedings out of Popinot's hands to place them in yours when Madame d'Espard tried to get a Commission in Lunacy to incapacitate her husband?" she added, in reply to her husband's gesture of astonishment. "Well, then, might not the public prosecutor, who takes such keen interest in the honor of Monsieur and Madame de Serizy, carry the case to the Upper Court and get a councillor in his interest to open a fresh inquiry?"

"Bless me, my dear, where did you study criminal law?" cried Camusot. "You know everything; you can give me points."

"Why, do you believe that, by to-morrow morning, Monsieur de Granville will not have taken fright at the possible line of defence that might be adopted by some liberal advocate whom Jacques Collin would manage to secure; for lawyers will be ready to pay him to place the case in their hands!—And those ladies know their danger quite as well as you do—not to say better; they will put themselves under the protection of the public prosecutor, who already sees their families unpleasantly close to the prisoner's bench, as a consequence of the coalition between this convict and Lucien de Rubempre, betrothed to Mademoiselle de Grandlieu—Lucien, Esther's lover, Madame de Maufrigneuse's former lover, Madame de Serizy's darling. So you must conduct the affair in such a way as to conciliate the favor of your public prosecutor, the gratitude of Monsieur de Serizy, and that of the Marquise d'Espard and the Comtesse du Chatelet, to reinforce Madame de Maufrigneuse's influence by that of the Grandlieus, and to gain the complimentary approval of your President.

"I will undertake to deal with the ladies—d'Espard, de Maufrigneuse, and de Grandlieu.

"You must go to-morrow morning to see the public prosecutor. Monsieur de Granville is a man who does not live with his wife; for ten years he had for his mistress a Mademoiselle de Bellefeuille, who bore him illegitimate children—didn't she? Well, such a magistrate is no saint; he is a man like any other; he can be won over; he must give a hold somewhere; you must discover the weak spot and flatter him; ask his advice, point out the dangers of attending the case; in short, try to get him into the same boat, and you will be—"

"I ought to kiss your footprints!" exclaimed Camusot, interrupting his wife, putting his arm round her, and pressing her to his heart. "Amelie, you have saved me!"

"I brought you in tow from Alencon to Mantes, and from Mantes to the Metropolitan Court," replied Amelie. "Well, well, be quite easy!—I intend to be called Madame la Presidente within five years' time. But, my dear, pray always think over everything a long time before you come to any determination. A judge's business is not that of a fireman; your papers are never in a blaze, you have plenty of time to think; so in your place blunders are inexcusable."

"The whole strength of my position lies in identifying the sham Spanish priest with Jacques Collin," the judge said, after a long pause. "When once that identity is established, even if the Bench should take the credit of the whole affair, that will still be an ascertained fact which no magistrate, judge, or councillor can get rid of. I shall do like the boys who tie a tin kettle to a cat's tail; the inquiry, whoever carries it on, will make Jacques Collin's tin kettle clank."

"Bravo!" said Amelie.

"And the public prosecutor would rather come to an understanding with me than with any one else, since I am the only man who can remove the Damocles' sword that hangs over the heart of the Faubourg Saint-Germain.

"Only you have no idea how hard it will be to achieve that magnificent result. Just now, when I was with Monsieur de Granville in his private office, we agreed, he and I, to take Jacques Collin at his own valuation—a canon of the Chapter of Toledo, Carlos Herrera. We consented to recognize his position as a diplomatic envoy, and allow him to be claimed by the Spanish Embassy. It was in consequence of this plan that I made out the papers by which Lucien de Rubempre was released, and revised the minutes of the examinations, washing the prisoners as white as snow.

"To-morrow, Rastignac, Bianchon, and some others are to be confronted with the self-styled Canon of Toledo; they will not recognize him as Jacques Collin who was arrested in their presence ten years ago in a cheap boarding-house, where they knew him under the name of Vautrin."

There was a short silence, while Madame Camusot sat thinking.

"Are you sure your man is Jacques Collin?" she asked.

"Positive," said the lawyer, "and so is the public prosecutor."

"Well, then, try to make some exposure at the Palais de Justice without showing your claws too much under your furred cat's paws. If your man is still in the secret cells, go straight to the Governor of the Conciergerie and contrive to have the convict publicly identified. Instead of behaving like a child, act like the ministers of police under despotic governments, who invent conspiracies against the monarch to have the credit of discovering them and making themselves indispensable. Put three families in danger to have the glory of rescuing them."

"That luckily reminds me!" cried Camusot. "My brain is so bewildered that I had quite forgotten an important point. The instructions to place Jacques Collin in a private room were taken by Coquart to Monsieur Gault, the Governor of the prison. Now, Bibi-Lupin, Jacques Collin's great enemy, has taken steps to have three criminals, who know the man, transferred from La Force to the Conciergerie; if he appears in the prison-yard to-morrow, a terrific scene is expected—"

"Why?"

"Jacques Collin, my dear, was treasurer of the money owned by the prisoners in the hulks, amounting to considerable sums; now, he is supposed to have spent it all to maintain the deceased Lucien in luxury, and he will be called to account. There will be such a battle, Bibi-Lupin tells me, as will require the intervention of the warders, and the secret will be out. Jacques Collin's life is in danger.

"Now, if I get to the Palais early enough I may record the evidence of identity."

"Oh, if only his creditors should take him off your hands! You would be thought such a clever fellow!—Do not go to Monsieur de Granville's room; wait for him in his Court with that formidable great gun. It is a loaded cannon turned on the three most important families of the Court and Peerage. Be bold: propose to Monsieur de Granville that he should relieve you of Jacques Collin by transferring him to La Force, where the convicts know how to deal with those who betray them.

"I will go to the Duchesse de Maufrigneuse, who will take me to the Grandlieus. Possibly I may see Monsieur de Serizy. Trust me to sound the alarm everywhere. Above all, send me a word we will agree upon to let me know if the Spanish priest is officially recognized as Jacques Collin. Get your business at the Palais over by two o'clock, and I will have arranged for you to have an interview with the Keeper of the Seals; perhaps I may find him with the Marquise d'Espard."

Camusot stood squarely with a look of admiration that made his knowing wife smile.

"Now, come to dinner and be cheerful," said she in conclusion. "Why, you see! We have been only two years in Paris, and here you are on the highroad to be made Councillor before the end of the year. From that to the Presidency of a court, my dear, there is no gulf but what some political service may bridge."

This conjugal sitting shows how greatly the deeds and the lightest words of Jacques Collin, the lowest personage in this drama, involved the honor of the families among whom he had planted his now dead protege.

At the Conciergerie Lucien's death and Madame de Serizy's incursion had produced such a block in the wheels of the machinery that the Governor had forgotten to remove the sham priest from his dungeon-cell.

Though more than one instance is on record of the death of a prisoner during his preliminary examination, it was a sufficiently rare event to disturb the warders, the clerk, and the Governor, and hinder their working with their usual serenity. At the same time, to them the important fact was not the handsome young fellow so suddenly become a corpse, but the breakage of the wrought-iron bar of the outer prison gate by the frail hands of a fine lady. And indeed, as soon as the public prosecutor and Comte Octave de Bauvan had gone off with Monsieur de Serizy and his unconscious wife, the Governor, clerk, and turnkeys gathered round the gate, after letting out Monsieur Lebrun, the prison doctor, who had been called in to certify to Lucien's death, in concert with the "death doctor" of the district in which the unfortunate youth had been lodging.

In Paris, the "death doctor" is the medical officer whose duty it is in each district to register deaths and certify to their causes.

With the rapid insight for which he was known, Monsieur de Granville had judged it necessary, for the honor of the families concerned, to have the certificate of Lucien's death deposited at the Mairie of the district in which the Quai Malaquais lies, as the deceased had resided there, and to have the body carried from his lodgings to the Church of Saint-Germain des Pres, where the service was to be held. Monsieur de Chargeboeuf, Monsieur de Granville's private secretary, had orders to this effect. The body was to be transferred from the prison during the night. The secretary was desired to go at once and settle matters at the Mairie with the parish authorities and with the official undertakers. Thus, to the world in general, Lucien would have died at liberty in his own lodgings, the funeral would start from thence, and his friends would be invited there for the ceremony.

So, when Camusot, his mind at ease, was sitting down to dinner with his ambitious better-half, the Governor of the Conciergerie and Monsieur Lebrun, the prison doctor, were standing outside the gate bewailing the fragility of iron bars and the strength of ladies in love.

"No one knows," said the doctor to Monsieur Gault, "what an amount of nervous force there is in a man wound up to the highest pitch of passion. Dynamics and mathematics have no formulas or symbols to express that power. Why, only yesterday, I witnessed an experiment which gave me a shudder, and which accounts for the terrible strength put forth just now by that little woman."

"Tell me about it," said Monsieur Gault, "for I am so foolish as to take an interest in magnetism; I do not believe in it, but it mystifies me."

"A physician who magnetizes—for there are men among us who believe in magnetism," Lebrun went on, "offered to experiment on me in proof of a phenomenon that he described and I doubted. Curious to see with my own eyes one of the strange states of nervous tension by which the existence of magnetism is demonstrated, I consented.

"These are the facts.—I should very much like to know what our College of Medicine would say if each of its members in turn were subjected to this influence, which leaves no loophole for incredulity.

"My old friend—this doctor," said Doctor Lebrun parenthetically, "is an old man persecuted for his opinions since Mesmer's time by all the faculty; he is seventy or seventy-two years of age, and his name is Bouvard. At the present day he is the patriarchal representative of the theory of animal magnetism. This good man regards me as a son; I owe my training to him.—Well, this worthy old Bouvard it was who proposed to prove to me that nerve-force put in motion by the magnetizer was, not indeed infinite, for man is under immutable laws, but a power acting like other powers of nature whose elemental essence escapes our observation.

"'For instance,' said he, 'if you place your hand in that of a somnambulist who, when awake, can press it only up to a certain average of tightness, you will see that in the somnambulistic state—as it is stupidly termed—his fingers can clutch like a vise screwed up by a blacksmith.'—Well, monsieur, I placed my hand in that of a woman, not asleep, for Bouvard rejects the word, but isolated, and when the old man bid her squeeze my wrist as long and as tightly as she could, I begged him to stop when the blood was almost bursting from my finger tips. Look, you can see the marks of her clutch, which I shall not lose for these three months."

"The deuce!" exclaimed Monsieur Gault, as he saw a band of bruised flesh, looking like the scar of a burn.

"My dear Gault," the doctor went on, "if my wrist had been gripped in an iron manacle screwed tight by a locksmith, I should not have felt the bracelet of metal so hard as that woman's fingers; her hand was of unyielding steel, and I am convinced that she could have crushed my bones and broken my hand from the wrist. The pressure, beginning almost insensibly, increased without relaxing, fresh force being constantly added to the former grip; a tourniquet could not have been more effectual than that hand used as an instrument of torture.—To me, therefore, it seems proven that under the influence of passion, which is the will concentrated on one point and raised to an incalculable power of animal force, as the different varieties of electric force are also, man may direct his whole vitality, whether for attack or resistance, to one of his organs.—Now, this little lady, under the stress of her despair, had concentrated her vital force in her hands."

"She must have a good deal too, to break a wrought-iron bar," said the chief warder, with a shake of the head.

"There was a flaw in it," Monsieur Gault observed.

"For my part," said the doctor, "I dare assign no limits to nervous force. And indeed it is by this that mothers, to save their children, can magnetize lions, climb, in a fire, along a parapet where a cat would not venture, and endure the torments that sometimes attend childbirth. In this lies the secret of the attempts made by convicts and prisoners to regain their liberty. The extent of our vital energies is as yet unknown; they are part of the energy of nature itself, and we draw them from unknown reservoirs."

"Monsieur," said the warder in an undertone to the Governor, coming close to him as he was escorting Doctor Lebrun as far as the outer gates of the Conciergerie, "Number 2 in the secret cells says he is ill, and needs the doctor; he declares he is dying," added the turnkey.

"Indeed," said the Governor.

"His breath rattles in his throat," replied the man.

"It is five o'clock," said the doctor; "I have had no dinner. But, after all, I am at hand. Come, let us see."

"Number 2, as it happens, is the Spanish priest suspected of being Jacques Collin," said Monsieur Gault to the doctor, "and one of the persons suspected of the crime in which that poor young man was implicated."

"I saw him this morning," replied the doctor. "Monsieur Camusot sent for me to give evidence as to the state of the rascal's health, and I may assure you that he is perfectly well, and could make a fortune by playing the part of Hercules in a troupe of athletes."

"Perhaps he wants to kill himself too," said Monsieur Gault. "Let us both go down to the cells together, for I ought to go there if only to transfer him to an upper room. Monsieur Camusot has given orders to mitigate this anonymous gentleman's confinement."

Jacques Collin, known as *Trompe-la-Mort* in the world of the hulks, who must henceforth be called only by his real name, had gone through terrible distress of mind since, after hearing Camusot's order, he had been taken back to the underground cell—an anguish such as he had never before known in the course of a life diversified by many crimes, by three escapes, and two sentences at the Assizes. And is there not something monstrously fine in the dog-like attachment shown to the man he had made his friend by this wretch in whom were concentrated all the life, the powers, the spirit, and the passions of the hulks, who was, so to speak, their highest expression?

Wicked, infamous, and in so many ways horrible, this absolute worship of his idol makes him so truly interesting that this Study, long as it is already, would seem incomplete and cut short if the close of this criminal career did not come as a sequel to Lucien de Rubempre's end. The little spaniel being dead, we want to know whether his terrible playfellow the lion will live on.

In real life, in society, every event is so inevitably linked to other events, that one cannot occur without the rest. The water of the great river forms a sort of fluid floor; not a wave, however rebellious, however high it may toss itself, but its powerful crest must sink to the level of the mass of waters, stronger by the momentum of its course than the revolt of the surges it bears with it.

And just as you watch the current flow, seeing in it a confused sheet of images, so perhaps you would like to measure the pressure exerted by social energy on the vortex called Vautrin; to see how far away the rebellious eddy will be carried ere it is lost, and what the end will be of this really diabolical man, human still by the power of loving—so hardly can that heavenly grace perish, even in the most cankered heart.

This wretched convict, embodying the poem that has smiled on many a poet's fancy—on Moore, on Lord Byron, on Mathurin, on Canalis—the demon who has drawn an angel down to hell to refresh him with dews stolen from heaven,—this Jacques Collin will be seen, by the reader who has understood that iron soul, to have sacrificed his own life for seven years past. His vast powers, absorbed in Lucien, acted solely for Lucien; he lived for his progress, his loves, his ambitions. To him, Lucien was his own soul made visible.

It was *Trompe-la-Mort* who dined with the Grandlieus, stole into ladies' boudoirs, and loved Esther by proxy. In fact, in Lucien he saw Jacques Collin, young, handsome, noble, and rising to the dignity of an ambassador.

Trompe-la-Mort had realized the German superstition of a doppelganger by means of a spiritual paternity, a phenomenon which will be quite intelligible to those women who have ever truly loved, who have felt their soul merge in that of the man they adore, who have lived his life, whether noble or infamous, happy or unhappy, obscure or brilliant; who, in defiance of distance, have felt a pain in their leg if he were wounded in his; who if he fought a duel would have been aware of it; and who, to put the matter in a nutshell, did not need to be told he was unfaithful to know it.

As he went back to his cell Jacques Collin said to himself, "The boy is being examined."

And he shivered—he who thought no more of killing a man than a laborer does of drinking.

"Has he been able to see his mistresses?" he wondered. "Has my aunt succeeded in catching those damned females? Have the Duchesses and Countesses bestirred themselves and prevented his being examined? Has Lucien had my instructions? And if ill-luck will have it that he is cross-questioned, how will he carry it off? Poor boy, and I have brought him to this! It is that rascal Paccard and that sneak Europe who have caused all this rumpus by collaring the seven hundred and fifty thousand francs for the certificate Nucingen gave Esther. That precious pair tripped us up at the last step; but I will make them pay dear for their pranks.

"One day more and Lucien would have been a rich man; he might have married his Clotilde de Grandlieu.—Then the boy would have been all my own!—And to think that our fate depends on a look, on a blush of Lucien's under Camusot's eye, who sees everything, and has all a judge's wits about him! For when he showed me the letters we tipped each other a wink in which we took each other's measure, and he guessed that I can make Lucien's lady-loves fork out."

This soliloquy lasted for three hours. His torments were so great that they were too much for that frame of iron and vitriol; Jacques Collin, whose brain felt on fire with insanity, suffered such fearful thirst that he unconsciously drank up all the water contained in one of the pails with which the cell was supplied, forming, with the bed, all its furniture.

"If he loses his head, what will become of him?—for the poor child has not Theodore's tenacity," said he to himself, as he lay down on the camp-bed—like a bed in a guard-room.

A WORD MUST HERE BE said about this Theodore, remembered by Jacques Collin at such a critical moment. Theodore Calvi, a young Corsican, imprisoned for life at the age of eighteen for eleven murders, thanks to the influential interference paid for with vast sums, had been made the fellow convict of Jacques Collin, to whom he was chained, in 1819 and 1820. Jacques Collin's last escape, one of his finest inventions—for he had got out disguised as a gendarme leading Theodore Calvi as he was, a convict called before the commissary of police—had been effected in the seaport of Rochefort, where the convicts die by dozens, and where, it was hoped, these two dangerous rascals would have ended their days. Though they escaped together, the difficulties of their flight had forced them to separate. Theodore was caught and restored to the hulks.

Indeed, a life with Lucien, a youth innocent of all crime, who had only minor sins on his conscience, dawned on him as bright and glorious as a summer sun; while with Theodore, Jacques Collin could look forward to no end but the scaffold after a career of indispensable crimes.

The thought of disaster as a result of Lucien's weakness—for his experience of an underground cell would certainly have turned his brain—took vast proportions in Jacques Collin's mind; and, contemplating the probabilities of such a misfortune, the unhappy man felt his eyes fill with tears, a phenomenon that had been utterly unknown to him since his earliest childhood.

"I must be in a furious fever," said he to himself; "and perhaps if I send for the doctor and offer him a handsome sum, he will put me in communication with Lucien."

At this moment the turnkey brought in his dinner.

"It is quite useless my boy; I cannot eat. Tell the governor of this prison to send the doctor to see me. I am very bad, and I believe my last hour has come."

Hearing the guttural rattle that accompanied these words, the warder bowed and went. Jacques Collin clung wildly to this hope; but when he saw the doctor and the governor come in together, he perceived that the attempt was abortive, and coolly awaited the upshot of the visit, holding out his wrist for the doctor to feel his pulse.

"The Abbe is feverish," said the doctor to Monsieur Gault, "but it is the type of fever we always find in inculpated prisoners—and to me," he added, in the governor's ear, "it is always a sign of some degree of guilt."

Just then the governor, to whom the public prosecutor had intrusted Lucien's letter to be given to Jacques Collin, left the doctor and the prisoner together under the guard of the warder, and went to fetch the letter.

"Monsieur," said Jacques Collin, seeing the warder outside the door, and not understanding why the governor had left them, "I should think nothing of thirty thousand francs if I might send five lines to Lucien de Rubempre."

"I will not rob you of your money," said Doctor Lebrun; "no one in this world can ever communicate with him again—"

"No one?" said the prisoner in amazement. "Why?"

"He has hanged himself—"

No tigress robbed of her whelps ever startled an Indian jungle with a yell so fearful as that of Jacques Collin, who rose to his feet as a tiger rears to spring, and fired a glance at the doctor as scorching as the flash of a falling thunderbolt. Then he fell back on the bed, exclaiming:

"Oh, my son!"

"Poor man!" said the doctor, moved by this terrific convulsion of nature.

In fact, the first explosion gave way to such utter collapse, that the words, "Oh, my son," were but a murmur.

"Is this one going to die in our hands too?" said the turnkey.

"No; it is impossible!" Jacques Collin went on, raising himself and looking at the two witnesses of the scene with a dead, cold eye. "You are mistaken; it is not Lucien; you did not see. A man cannot hang himself in one of these cells. Look—how could I hang myself here? All Paris shall answer to me for that boy's life! God owes it to me."

The warder and the doctor were amazed in their turn—they, whom nothing had astonished for many a long day.

On seeing the governor, Jacques Collin, crushed by the very violence of this outburst of grief, seemed somewhat calmer.

"Here is a letter which the public prosecutor placed in my hands for you, with permission to give it to you sealed," said Monsieur Gault.

"From Lucien?" said Jacques Collin.

"Yes, monsieur."

"Is not that young man—"

"He is dead," said the governor. "Even if the doctor had been on the spot, he would, unfortunately, have been too late. The young man died—there—in one of the rooms—"

"May I see him with my own eyes?" asked Jacques Collin timidly. "Will you allow a father to weep over the body of his son?"

"You can, if you like, take his room, for I have orders to remove you from these cells; you are no longer in such close confinement, monsieur."

The prisoner's eyes, from which all light and warmth had fled, turned slowly from the governor to the doctor; Jacques Collin was examining them, fearing some trap, and he was afraid to go out of the cell.

"If you wish to see the body," said Lebrun, "you have no time to lose; it is to be carried away to-night."

"If you have children, gentlemen," said Jacques Collin, "you will understand my state of mind; I hardly know what I am doing. This blow is worse to me than death; but you cannot know what I am saying. Even if you are fathers, it is only after a fashion—I am a mother too—I—I am going mad—I feel it!"

By going through certain passages which open only to the governor, it is possible to get very quickly from the cells to the private rooms. The two sets of rooms are divided by an underground corridor formed of two massive walls supporting the vault over which Galerie Marchande, as it is called, is built. So Jacques Collin, escorted by the warder, who took his arm, preceded by the governor, and followed by the doctor, in a few minutes reached the cell where Lucien was lying stretched on the bed.

On seeing the body, he threw himself upon it, seizing it in a desperate embrace with a passion and impulse that made these spectators shudder.

"There," said the doctor to Monsieur Gault, "that is an instance of what I was telling you. You see that man clutching the body, and you do not know what a corpse is; it is stone—"

"Leave me alone!" said Jacques Collin in a smothered voice; "I have not long to look at him. They will take him away to—"

He paused at the word "bury him."

"You will allow me to have some relic of my dear boy! Will you be so kind as to cut off a lock of his hair for me, monsieur," he said to the doctor, "for I cannot—"

"He was certainly his son," said Lebrun.

"Do you think so?" replied the governor in a meaning tone, which made the doctor thoughtful for a few minutes.

The governor gave orders that the prisoner should be left in this cell, and that some locks of hair should be cut for the self-styled father before the body should be removed.

At half-past five in the month of May it is easy to read a letter in the Conciergerie in spite of the iron bars and the close wire trellis that guard the windows. So Jacques Collin read the dreadful letter while he still held Lucien's hand.

The man is not known who can hold a lump of ice for ten minutes tightly clutched in the hollow of his hand. The cold penetrates to the very life-springs with mortal rapidity. But the effect of that cruel chill, acting like a poison, is as nothing to that which strikes to the soul from the cold, rigid hand of the dead thus held. Thus Death speaks to Life; it tells many dark secrets which kill many feelings; for in matters of feeling is not change death?

As we read through once more, with Jacques Collin, Lucien's last letter, it will strike us as being what it was to this man—a cup of poison:—

To the Abbe Carlos Herrera
MY DEAR ABBE,

I have had only benefits from you, and I have betrayed you. This involuntary ingratitude is killing me, and when you read these lines I shall have ceased to exist. You are not here now to save me.

"You had given me full liberty, if I should find it advantageous, to destroy you by flinging you on the ground like a cigar-end; but I have ruined you by a blunder. To escape from a difficulty, deluded by a clever question from the examining judge, your son by adoption and grace went over to the side of those who aim at killing you at any cost, and insist on proving an identity, which I know to be impossible, between you and a French villain. All is said.

"Between a man of your calibre and me—me of whom you tried to make a greater man than I am capable of being—no foolish sentiment can come at the moment of final parting. You hoped to make me powerful and famous, and you have thrown me into the gulf of suicide, that is all. I have long heard the broad pinions of that vertigo beating over my head.

"As you have sometimes said, there is the posterity of Cain and the posterity of Abel. In the great human drama Cain is in opposition. You are descended from Adam through that line, in which the devil still fans the fire of which the first spark was flung on Eve. Among the demons of that pedigree, from time to time we see one of stupendous power, summing up every form of human energy, and resembling the fevered beasts of the desert, whose vitality demands the vast spaces they find there. Such men are as dangerous as lions would be in the heart of Normandy; they must have their prey, and they devour common men and crop the money of fools. Their sport is so dangerous that at last they kill the humble dog whom they have taken for a companion and made an idol of.

"When it is God's will, these mysterious beings may be a Moses, an Attila, Charlemagne, Mahomet, or Napoleon;

but when He leaves a generation of these stupendous tools to rust at the bottom of the ocean, they are no more than a Pugatschef, a Fouche, a Louvel, or the Abbe Carlos Herrera. Gifted with immense power over tenderer souls, they entrap them and mangle them. It is grand, it is fine—in its way. It is the poisonous plant with gorgeous coloring that fascinates children in the woods. It is the poetry of evil. Men like you ought to dwell in caves and never come out of them. You have made me live that vast life, and I have had all my share of existence; so I may very well take my head out of the Gordian knot of your policy and slip it into the running knot of my cravat.

"To repair the mischief I have done, I am forwarding to the public prosecutor a retraction of my deposition. You will know how to take advantage of this document.

"In virtue of a will formally drawn up, restitution will be made, Monsieur l'Abbe, of the moneys belonging to your Order which you so imprudently devoted to my use, as a result of your paternal affection for me.

"And so, farewell. Farewell, colossal image of Evil and Corruption; farewell—to you who, if started on the right road, might have been greater than Ximenes, greater than Richelieu! You have kept your promises. I find myself once more just as I was on the banks of the Charente, after enjoying, by your help, the enchantments of a dream. But, unfortunately, it is not now in the waters of my native place that I shall drown the errors of a boy; but in the Seine, and my hole is a cell in the Conciergerie.

"Do not regret me: my contempt for you is as great as my admiration.

LUCIEN

A little before one in the morning, when the men came to fetch away the body, they found Jacques Collin kneeling by the bed, the letter on the floor, dropped, no doubt, as a suicide drops the pistol that has shot him; but the unhappy man still held Lucien's hand between his own, and was praying to God.

On seeing this man, the porters paused for a moment, for he looked like one of those stone images, kneeling to all eternity on a mediaeval tomb, the work of some stone-carver's genius. The sham priest, with eyes as bright as a tiger's, but stiffened into supernatural rigidity, so impressed the men that they gently bid him rise.

"Why?" he asked mildly. The audacious *Trompe-la-Mort* was as meek as a child.

The governor pointed him out to Monsieur de Chargeboeuf; and he, respecting such grief, and believing that Jacques Collin was indeed the priest he called himself, explained the orders given by Monsieur de Granville with regard to the funeral service and arrangements, showing that it was absolutely necessary that the body should be transferred to Lucien's lodgings, Quai Malaquais, where the priests were waiting to watch by it for the rest of the night.

"It is worthy of that gentleman's well-known magnanimity," said Jacques Collin sadly. "Tell him, monsieur, that he may rely on my gratitude. Yes, I am in a position to do him great service. Do not forget these words; they are of the utmost importance to him.

"Oh, monsieur! strange changes come over a man's spirit when for seven hours he has wept over such a son as he—And I shall see him no more!"

After gazing once more at Lucien with an expression of a mother bereft of her child's remains, Jacques Collin sank in a heap. As he saw Lucien's body carried away, he uttered a groan that made the men hurry off. The public prosecutor's private secretary and the governor of the prison had already made their escape from the scene.

What had become of that iron spirit; of the decision which was a match in swiftness for the eye; of the nature in which thought and action flashed forth together like one flame; of the sinews hardened by three spells of labor on the hulks, and by three escapes, the muscles which had acquired the metallic temper of a savage's limbs? Iron will yield to a certain amount of hammering or persistent pressure; its impenetrable molecules, purified and made homogeneous by man, may become disintegrated, and without being in a state of fusion the metal had lost its power of resistance. Blacksmiths, locksmiths, tool-makers sometimes express this state by saying the iron is retting, appropriating a word applied exclusively to hemp, which is reduced to pulp and fibre by maceration. Well, the human soul, or, if you will, the threefold powers of body, heart, and intellect, under certain repeated shocks, get into such a condition as fibrous iron. They too are disintegrated. Science and law and the public seek a thousand causes for the terrible catastrophes on railways caused by the rupture of an iron rail, that of Bellevue being a famous instance; but no one has asked the evidence of real experts in such matters, the blacksmiths, who all say the same thing, "The iron was stringy!" The danger cannot be foreseen. Metal that has gone soft, and metal that has preserved its tenacity, both look exactly alike.

Priests and examining judges often find great criminals in this state. The awful experiences of the Assize Court and the "last toilet" commonly produce this dissolution of the nervous system, even in the strongest natures. Then confessions are blurted by the most firmly set lips; then the toughest hearts break; and, strange to say, always at the moment when these confessions are useless, when this weakness as of death snatches from the man the mask of innocence which made Justice uneasy—for it always is uneasy when the criminal dies without confessing his crime.

Napoleon went through this collapse of every human power on the field of Waterloo.

At eight in the morning, when the warder of the better cells entered the room where Jacques Collin was confined, he found him pale and calm, like a man who has collected all his strength by sheer determination.

"It is the hour for airing in the prison-yard," said the turnkey; "you have not been out for three days; if you choose to take air and exercise, you may."

Jacques Collin, lost in his absorbing thoughts, and taking no interest in himself, regarding himself as a garment with no body in it, a perfect rag, never suspected the trap laid for him by Bibi-Lupin, nor the importance attaching to his walk in the prison-yard.

The unhappy man went out mechanically, along the corridor, by the cells built into the magnificent cloisters of the Palace of the Kings, over which is the corridor Saint-Louis, as it is called, leading to the various purlieus of the Court of Appeals. This passage joins that of the better cells; and it is worth noting that the cell in which Louvel was imprisoned, one of the most famous of the regicides, is the room at the right angle formed by the junction of the two corridors. Under the pretty room in the Tour Bonbec there is a spiral staircase leading from the dark passage, and serving the prisoners who are lodged in these cells to go up and down on their way from or to the yard.

Every prisoner, whether committed for trial or already sentenced, and the prisoners under suspicion who have been reprieved from the closest cells—in short, every one in confinement in the Conciergerie takes exercise in this narrow paved courtyard for some hours every day, especially the early hours of summer mornings. This recreation ground, the ante-room to the scaffold or the hulks on one side, on the other still clings to the world through the gendarme, the examining judge, and the Assize Court. It strikes a greater chill perhaps than even the scaffold. The scaffold may be a pedestal to soar to heaven from; but the prison-yard is every infamy on earth concentrated and unavoidable.

Whether at La Force or at Poissy, at Melun or at Sainte-Pelagie, a prison-yard is a prison-yard. The same details are exactly repeated, all but the color of the walls, their height, and the space enclosed. So this Study of Manners would be false to its name if it did not include an exact description of this Pandemonium of Paris.

Under the mighty vaulting which supports the lower courts and the Court of Appeals there is, close to the fourth arch, a stone slab, used by Saint-Louis, it is said, for the distribution of alms, and doing duty in our day as a counter for the sale of eatables to the prisoners. So as soon as the prison-yard is open to the prisoners, they gather round this stone table, which displays such dainties as jail-birds desire—brandy, rum, and the like.

The first two archways on that side of the yard, facing the fine Byzantine corridor—the only vestige now of Saint-Louis' elegant palace—form a parlor, where the prisoners and their counsel may meet, to which the prisoners have access through a formidable gateway—a double passage, railed off by enormous bars, within the width of the third archway. This double way is like the temporary passages arranged at the door of a theatre to keep a line on occasions when a great success brings a crowd. This parlor, at the very end of the vast entrance-hall of the Conciergerie, and lighted by loop-holes on the yard side, has lately been opened out towards the back, and the opening filled with glass, so that the interviews of the lawyers with their clients are under supervision. This innovation was made necessary by the too great fascinations brought to bear by pretty women on their counsel. Where will morality stop short? Such precautions are like the ready-made sets of questions for self-examination, where pure imaginations are defiled by meditating on unknown and monstrous depravity. In this parlor, too, parents and friends may be allowed by the authorities to meet the prisoners, whether on remand or awaiting their sentence.

The reader may now understand what the prison-yard is to the two hundred prisoners in the Conciergerie: their garden—a garden without trees, beds, or flowers—in short, a prison-yard. The parlor, and the stone of Saint-Louis, where such food and liquor as are allowed are dispensed, are the only possible means of communication with the outer world.

The hour spent in the yard is the only time when the prisoner is in the open air or the society of his kind; in other prisons those who are sentenced for a term are brought together in workshops; but in the Conciergerie no occupation is allowed, excepting in the privileged cells. There the absorbing idea in every mind is the drama of the Assize Court, since the culprit comes only to be examined or to be sentenced.

This yard is indeed terrible to behold; it cannot be imagined, it must be seen.

In the first place, the assemblage, in a space forty metres long by thirty wide, of a hundred condemned or suspected criminals, does not constitute the cream of society. These creatures, belonging for the most part to the lowest ranks, are poorly clad; their countenances are base or horrible, for a criminal from the upper sphere of society is happily, a rare exception. Peculation, forgery, or fraudulent bankruptcy, the only crimes that can bring decent folks so low, enjoy the privilege of the better cells, and then the prisoner scarcely ever quits it.

This promenade, bounded by fine but formidable blackened walls, by a cloister divided up into cells, by fortifications on the side towards the quay, by the barred cells of the better class on the north, watched by vigilant warders, and filled with a herd of criminals, all meanly suspicious of each other, is depressing enough in itself; and it becomes terrifying when you find yourself the centre of all those eyes full of hatred, curiosity, and despair, face to face with that degraded crew. Not a gleam of gladness! all is gloom—the place and the men. All is speechless—the walls and men's consciences. To these hapless creatures danger lies everywhere; excepting in the case of an alliance as ominous as the prison where it was formed, they dare not trust each other.

The police, all-pervading, poisons the atmosphere and taints everything, even the hand-grasp of two criminals who have been intimate. A convict who meets his most familiar comrade does not know that he may not have repented and have made a confession to save his life. This absence of confidence, this dread of the nark, marks the liberty, already so illusory, of the prison-yard. The "nark" (in French, le Mouton or le coqueur) is a spy who affects to be sentenced for some serious offence, and whose skill consists in pretending to be a chum. The "chum," in thieves' slang, is a skilled thief, a professional who has cut himself adrift from society, and means to remain a thief all his days, and continues faithful through thick and thin to the laws of the swell-mob.

Crime and madness have a certain resemblance. To see the prisoners of the Conciergerie in the yard, or the madmen in the garden of an asylum, is much the same thing. Prisoners and lunatics walk to and fro, avoiding each other, looking up with more or less strange or vicious glances, according to the mood of the moment, but never cheerful, never grave; they know each other, or they dread each other. The anticipation of their sentence, remorse, and apprehension give all these men exercising, the anxious, furtive look of the insane. Only the most consummate criminals have the audacity that apes the quietude of respectability, the sincerity of a clear conscience.

As men of the better class are few, and shame keeps the few whose crimes have brought them within doors, the frequenters of the prison-yard are for the most part dressed as workmen. Blouses, long and short, and velveteen jackets preponderate. These coarse or dirty garments, harmonizing with the coarse and sinister faces and brutal manner—somewhat subdued, indeed, by the gloomy reflections that weigh on men in prison—everything, to the silence that reigns, contributes to strike terror or disgust into the rare visitor who, by high influence, has obtained the privilege, seldom granted, of going over the Conciergerie.

Just as the sight of an anatomical museum, where foul diseases are represented by wax models, makes the youth who may be taken there more chaste and apt for nobler and purer love, so the sight of the Conciergerie and of the prison-yard, filled with men marked for the hulks or the scaffold or some disgraceful punishment, inspires many, who might not fear that Divine Justice whose voice speaks so loudly to the conscience, with a fear of human justice; and they come out honest men for a long time after.

As the men who were exercising in the prison-yard, when *Trompe-la-Mort* appeared there, were to be the actors in a scene of crowning importance in the life of Jacques Collin, it will be well to depict a few of the principal personages of this sinister crowd.

Here, as everywhere when men are thrown together, here, as at school even, force, physical and moral, wins the day. Here, then, as on the hulks, crime stamps the man's rank. Those whose head is doomed are the aristocracy. The prison-yard, as may be supposed, is a school of criminal law, which is far better learned there than at the Hall on the Place du Pantheon.

A never-failing pleasantry is to rehearse the drama of the Assize Court; to elect a president, a jury, a public prosecutor, a counsel, and to go through the whole trial. This hideous farce is played before almost every great trial. At this time a famous case was proceeding in the Criminal Court, that of the dreadful murder committed on the persons of Monsieur and Madame Crottat, the notary's father and mother, retired farmers who, as this horrible business showed, kept eight hundred thousand francs in gold in their house.

One of the men concerned in this double murder was the notorious Dannepont, known as la Pouraille, a released convict, who for five years had eluded the most active search on the part of the police, under the protection of seven or eight different names. This villain's disguises were so perfect, that he had served two years of imprisonment under the name of Delsouq, who was one of his own disciples, and a famous thief, though he never, in any of his achievements, went beyond the jurisdiction of the lower Courts. La Pouraille had committed no less than three murders since his dismissal from the hulks. The certainty that he would be executed, not less than the large fortune he was supposed to have, made this man an object of terror and admiration to his fellow-prisoners; for not a farthing of the stolen money had ever been recovered. Even after the events of July 1830, some persons may remember the terror caused in Paris by this daring crime, worthy to compare in importance with the robbery of medals from the Public Library; for the unhappy tendency of our age is to make a murder the more interesting in proportion to the greater sum of money secured by it.

La Pouraille, a small, lean, dry man, with a face like a ferret, forty-five years old, and one of the celebrities of the prisons he had successively lived in since the age of nineteen, knew Jacques Collin well, how and why will be seen.

Two other convicts, brought with la Pouraille from La Force within these twenty-four hours, had at once acknowledged and made the whole prison-yard acknowledge the supremacy of this past-master sealed to the scaffold. One of these convicts, a ticket-of-leave man, named Selerier, alias l'Avuergnat, Pere Ralleau, and le Rouleur, who in the sphere known to the hulks as the swell-mob was called Fil-de-Soie (or silken thread)—a nickname he owed to the skill with which he slipped through the various perils of the business—was an old ally of Jacques Collin's.

Trompe-la-Mort so keenly suspected Fil-de-Soie of playing a double part, of being at once in the secrets of the swell-mob and a spy laid by the police, that he had supposed him to be the prime mover of his arrest in the Maison Vauquer in 1819 (*Le Pere Goriot*). Selerier, whom we must call Fil-de-Soie, as we shall also call Dannepont la Pouraille, already guilty of evading surveillance, was concerned in certain well-known robberies without bloodshed, which would certainly take him back to the hulks for at least twenty years.

The other convict, named Riganson, and his kept woman, known as la Biffe, were a most formidable couple, members of the swell-mob. Riganson, on very distant terms with the police from his earliest years, was nicknamed le Biffon. Biffon was the male of la Biffe—for nothing is sacred to the swell-mob. These fiends respect nothing, neither the law nor religions, not even natural history, whose solemn nomenclature, it is seen, is parodied by them.

Here a digression is necessary; for Jacques Collin's appearance in the prison-yard in the midst of his foes, as had been so cleverly contrived by Bibi-Lupin and the examining judge, and the strange scenes to ensue, would be incomprehensible and impossible without some explanation as to the world of thieves and of the hulks, its laws, its manners, and above all, its language, its hideous figures of speech being indispensable in this portion of my tale.

So, first of all, a few words must be said as to the vocabulary of sharpers, pickpockets, thieves, and murderers, known as Argot, or thieves' cant, which has of late been introduced into literature with so much success that more than one word of that strange lingo is familiar on the rosy lips of ladies, has been heard in gilded boudoirs, and become the delight of princes, who have often proclaimed themselves "done brown" (floue)! And it must be owned, to the surprise no doubt of many persons, that no language is more vigorous or more vivid than that of this underground world which, from the beginnings of countries with capitals, has dwelt in cellars and slums, in the third limbo of society everywhere (le troisieme dessous, as the expressive and vivid slang of the theatres has it). For is not the world a stage? Le troisieme dessous is the lowest cellar under the stage at the Opera where the machinery is kept and men stay who work it, whence the footlights are raised, the ghosts, the blue-devils shot up from hell, and so forth.

Every word of this language is a bold metaphor, ingenious or horrible. A man's breeches are his kicks or trucks (montante, a word that need not be explained). In this language you do not sleep, you snooze, or doze (pioncer—and note how vigorously expressive the word is of the sleep of the hunted, weary, distrustful animal called a thief, which as soon as it is in safety drops—rolls—into the gulf of deep slumber so necessary under the mighty wings of suspicion always hovering over it; a fearful sleep, like that of a wild beast that can sleep, nay, and snore, and yet its ears are alert with caution).

In this idiom everything is savage. The syllables which begin or end the words are harsh and curiously startling. A woman is a trip or a moll (une largue). And it is poetical too: straw is la plume de Beauce, a farmyard feather bed. The word midnight is paraphrased by twelve leads striking—it makes one shiver! Rincer une cambriole is to "screw the shop," to rifle a room. What a feeble expression is to go to bed in comparison with "to doss" (piausser, make a new skin). What picturesque imagery! Work your dominoes (jouer des dominos) is to eat; how can men eat with the police at their heels?

And this language is always growing; it keeps pace with civilization, and is enriched with some new expression by every fresh invention. The potato, discovered and introduced by Louis XVI and Parmentier, was at once dubbed in French slang as the pig's orange (Orange a Cochons) [the Irish have called them bog oranges]. Banknotes are invented; the "mob" at once call them Flimsies (fafiots garotes, from "Garot," the name of the cashier whose signature they bear). Flimsy! (fafiot.) Cannot you hear the rustle of the thin paper? The thousand franc-note is male flimsy (in French), the five hundred franc-note is the female; and convicts will, you may be sure, find some whimsical name for the hundred and two hundred franc-notes.

In 1790 Guillotin invented, with humane intent, the expeditious machine which solved all the difficulties involved in the problem of capital punishment. Convicts and prisoners from the hulks forthwith investigated this contrivance, standing as it did on the monarchical borderland of the old system and the frontier of modern legislation; they instantly gave it the name of *l'Abbaye de Monte-a-Regret*. They looked at the angle formed by the steel blade, and described its action as repeating (faucher); and when it is remembered that the hulks are called the meadow (le pre), philologists must admire the inventiveness of these horrible vocables, as Charles Nodier would have said.

The high antiquity of this kind of slang is also noteworthy. A tenth of the words are of old Romanesque origin, another tenth are the old Gaulish French of Rabelais. Effondrer, to thrash a man, to give him what for; otolondrer, to annoy or to "spur" him; cambrioler, doing anything in a room; aubert, money; Gironde, a beauty (the name of a river of Languedoc); fouillousse, a pocket—a "cly"—are all French of the fourteenth and fifteenth centuries. The word affe, meaning life, is of the highest antiquity. From affe anything that disturbs life is called affres (a rowing or scolding), hence affreux, anything that troubles life.

About a hundred words are derived from the language of Panurge, a name symbolizing the people, for it is derived from two Greek words signifying All-working.

Science is changing the face of the world by constructing railroads. In Argot the train is le roulant Vif, the Rattler.

The name given to the head while still on the shoulders—la Sorbonne—shows the antiquity of this dialect which is mentioned by very early romance-writers, as Cervantes, the Italian story-tellers, and Aretino. In all ages the moll, the prostitute, the heroine of so many old-world romances, has been the protectress, companion, and comfort of the sharper, the thief, the pickpocket, the area-sneak, and the burglar.

Prostitution and robbery are the male and female forms of protest made by the natural state against the social state. Even philosophers, the innovators of to-day, the humanitarians with the communists and Fourierists in their train, come at last, without knowing it, to the same conclusion—prostitution and theft. The thief does not argue out questions of property, of inheritance, and social responsibility, in sophistical books; he absolutely ignores them. To him theft is appropriating his own. He does not discuss marriage; he does not complain of it; he does not insist, in printed Utopian dreams, on the mutual consent and bond of souls which can never become general; he pairs with a vehemence of which the bonds are constantly riveted by the hammer of necessity. Modern innovators write unctuous theories, long drawn, and nebulous or philanthropical romances; but the thief acts. He is as clear as a fact, as logical as a blow; and then his style!

Another thing worth noting: the world of prostitutes, thieves, and murders of the galleys and the prisons forms a population of about sixty to eighty thousand souls, men and women. Such a world is not to be disdained in a picture of modern manners and a literary reproduction of the social body. The law, the gendarmerie, and the police constitute a body almost equal in number; is not that strange? This antagonism of persons perpetually seeking and avoiding each other, and fighting a vast and highly dramatic duel, are what are sketched in this Study. It has been the same thing with thieving and public harlotry as with the stage, the police, the priesthood, and the gendarmerie. In these six walks of life the individual contracts an indelible character. He can no longer be himself. The stigmata of ordination are as immutable as those of the soldier are. And it is the same in other callings which are strongly in opposition, strong contrasts with civilization. These violent, eccentric, singular signs—sui generis—are what make the harlot, the robber, the murderer, the ticket-of-leave man, so easily recognizable by their foes, the spy and the police, to whom they are as game to the sportsman: they have a gait, a manner, a complexion, a look, a color, a smell—in short, infallible marks about them. Hence the highly-developed art of disguise which the heroes of the hulks acquire.

One word yet as to the constitution of this world apart, which the abolition of branding, the mitigation of penalties, and the silly leniency of furies are making a threatening evil. In about twenty years Paris will be beleaguered by an army of forty thousand reprieved criminals; the department of the Seine and its fifteen hundred thousand inhabitants being the only place in France where these poor wretches can be hidden. To them Paris is what the virgin forest is to beasts of prey.

The swell-mob, or more exactly, the upper class of thieves, which is the Faubourg Saint-Germain, the aristocracy of the tribe, had, in 1816, after the peace which made life hard for so many men, formed an association called les grands fanandels—the Great Pals—consisting of the most noted master-thieves and certain bold spirits at that time bereft of any means of living. This word pal means brother, friend, and comrade all in one. And these "Great Pals," the cream of the thieving fraternity, for more than twenty years were the Court of Appeal, the Institute of Learning, and the Chamber of Peers of this community. These men all had their private means, with funds in common, and a code of their own. They knew each other, and were pledged to help and succor each other in difficulties. And they were all superior to the tricks or snares of the police, had a charter of their own, passwords and signs of recognition.

From 1815 to 1819 these dukes and peers of the prison world had formed the famous association of the Ten-thousand (see le Pere Goriot), so styled by reason of an agreement in virtue of which no job was to be undertaken by which less than ten thousand francs could be got.

At that very time, in 1829-30, some memoirs were brought out in which the collective force of this association and the names of the leaders were published by a famous member of the police-force. It was terrifying to find there an army of skilled rogues, male and female; so numerous, so clever, so constantly lucky, that such thieves as Pastourel, Collonge, or Chimaux, men of fifty and sixty, were described as outlaws from society from their earliest years! What a confession of the ineptitude of justice that rogues so old should be at large!

Jacques Collin had been the cashier, not only of the "Ten-thousand," but also of the "Great Pals," the heroes of the hulks. Competent authorities admit that the hulks have always owned large sums. This curious fact is quite conceivable. Stolen goods are never recovered but in very singular cases. The condemned criminal, who can take nothing with him, is obliged to trust somebody's honesty and capacity, and to deposit his money; as in the world of honest folks, money is placed in a bank.

Long ago Bibi-Lupin, now for ten years a chief of the department of Public Safety, had been a member of the aristocracy of "Pals." His treason had resulted from offended pride; he had been constantly set aside in favor of *Trompe-la-Mort's* superior intelligence and prodigious strength. Hence his persistent vindictiveness against Jacques Collin. Hence, also, certain compromises between Bibi-Lupin and his old companions, which the magistrates were beginning to take seriously.

So in his desire for vengeance, to which the examining judge had given play under the necessity of identifying Jacques Collin, the chief of the "Safety" had very skilfully chosen his allies by setting la Pouraille, Fil-de-Soie, and le Biffon on the sham Spaniard—for la Pouraille and Fil-de-Soie both belonged to the "Ten-thousand," and le Biffon was a "Great Pal."

La Biffe, le Biffon's formidable trip, who to this day evades all the pursuit of the police by her skill in disguising herself as a lady, was at liberty. This woman, who successfully apes a marquise, a countess, a baroness, keeps a carriage and men-servants. This Jacques Collin in petticoats is the only woman who can compare with Asie, Jacques Collin's right hand. And, in fact, every hero of the hulks is backed up by a devoted woman. Prison records and the secret papers of the law courts will tell you this; no honest woman's love, not even that of the bigot for her spiritual director, has ever been greater than the attachment of a mistress who shares the dangers of a great criminal.

With these men a passion is almost always the first cause of their daring enterprises and murders. The excessive love which—constitutionally, as the doctors say—makes woman irresistible to them, calls every moral and physical force of these powerful natures into action. Hence the idleness which consumes their days, for excesses of passion necessitate sleep and restorative food. Hence their loathing of all work, driving these creatures to have recourse to rapid ways of getting money. And yet, the need of a living, and of high living, violent as it is, is but a trifle in comparison with the extravagance to which these generous Medors are prompted by the mistress to whom they want to give jewels and dress, and who—always greedy—love rich food. The baggage wants a shawl, the lover steals it, and the woman sees in this a proof of love.

This is how robbery begins; and robbery, if we examine the human soul through a lens, will be seen to be an almost natural instinct in man.

Robbery leads to murder, and murder leads the lover step by step to the scaffold.

Ill-regulated physical desire is therefore, in these men, if we may believe the medical faculty, at the root of seven-tenths of the crimes committed. And, indeed, the proof is always found, evident, palpable at the post-mortem examination of the criminal after his execution. And these monstrous lovers, the scarecrows of society, are adored by their mistresses. It is this female devotion, squatting faithfully at the prison gate, always eagerly balking the cunning of the examiner, and incorruptibly keeping the darkest secrets which make so many trials impenetrable mysteries.

In this, again, lies the strength as well as the weakness of the accused. In the vocabulary of a prostitute, to be honest means to break none of the laws of this attachment, to give all her money to the man who is nabbed, to look after his comforts, to be faithful to him in every way, to undertake anything for his sake. The bitterest insult one of these women can fling in the teeth of another wretched creature is to accuse her of infidelity to a lover in quod (in prison). In that case such a woman is considered to have no heart.

La Pouraille was passionately in love with a woman, as will be seen.

Fil-de-Soie, an egotistical philosopher, who thieved to provide for the future, was a good deal like Paccard, Jacques Collin's satellite, who had fled with Prudence Servien and the seven hundred and fifty thousand francs between them. He had no attachment, he condemned women, and loved no one but Fil-de-Soie.

As to le Biffon, he derived his nickname from his connection with la Biffe. (La Biffe is scavenging, rag-picking.) And these three distinguished members of *la haute pegre*, the aristocracy of roguery, had a reckoning to demand of Jacques Collin, accounts that were somewhat hard to bring to book.

No one but the cashier could know how many of his clients were still alive, and what each man's share would be. The mortality to which the depositors were peculiarly liable had formed a basis for *Trompe-la-Mort's* calculations when he resolved to embezzle the funds for Lucien's benefit. By keeping himself out of the way of the police and of his pals for nine years, Jacques Collin was almost certain to have fallen heir, by the terms of the agreement among the associates, to two-thirds of the depositors. Besides, could he not plead that he had repaid the pals who had been scragged? In fact, no one had any hold over these *Great Pals*. His comrades trusted him by compulsion, for the hunted life led by convicts necessitates the most delicate confidence between the gentry of this crew of savages. So Jacques Collin, a defaulter for a hundred thousand crowns, might now possibly be quit for a hundred thousand francs. At this moment, as we see, la Pouraille, one of Jacques Collin's creditors, had but ninety days to live. And la Pouraille, the possessor of a sum vastly greater, no doubt, than that placed in his pal's keeping, would probably prove easy to deal with.

ONE OF THE INFALLIBLE SIGNS by which prison governors and their agents, the police and warders, recognize old stagers (chevaux de retour), that is to say, men who have already eaten beans (les gourganes, a kind of haricots provided for prison fare), is their familiarity with prison ways; those who have been *in* before, of course, know the manners and customs; they are at home, and nothing surprises them.

And Jacques Collin, thoroughly on his guard, had, until now, played his part to admiration as an innocent man and stranger, both at La Force and at the Conciergerie. But now, broken by grief, and by two deaths—for he had died twice over during that dreadful night—he was Jacques Collin once more. The warder was astounded to find that the Spanish priest needed no telling as to the way to the prison-yard. The perfect actor forgot his part; he went down the corkscrew stairs in the Tour Bonbec as one who knew the Conciergerie.

"Bibi-Lupin is right," said the turnkey to himself; "he is an old stager; he is Jacques Collin."

At the moment when *Trompe-la-Mort* appeared in the sort of frame to his figure made by the door into the tower, the prisoners, having made their purchases at the stone table called after Saint-Louis, were scattered about the yard, always too small for their number. So the newcomer was seen by all of them at once, and all the more promptly, because nothing can compare for keenness with the eye of a prisoner, who in a prison-yard feels like a spider watching in its web. And this comparison is mathematically exact; for the range of vision being limited on all sides by high dark walls, the prisoners can always see, even without looking at them, the doors through which the warders come and go, the windows of the parlor, and the stairs of the Tour Bonbec— the only exits from the yard. In this utter isolation every trivial incident is an event, everything is interesting; the tedium—a tedium like that of a tiger in a cage—increases their alertness tenfold.

It is necessary to note that Jacques Collin, dressed like a priest who is not strict as to costume, wore black knee breeches, black stockings, shoes with silver buckles, a black waistcoat, and a long coat of dark-brown cloth of a certain cut that betrays the priest whatever he may do, especially when these details are completed by a characteristic style of haircutting. Jacques Collin's wig was eminently ecclesiastical, and wonderfully natural.

"Hallo!" said la Pouraille to le Biffon, "that's a bad sign! A rook! (sanglier, a priest). How did he come here?"

"He is one of their 'narks'" (trucs, spies) "of a new make," replied Fil-de-Soie, "some runner with the bracelets" (marchand de lacets— equivalent to a Bow Street runner) "looking out for his man."

The gendarme boasts of many names in French slang; when he is after a thief, he is "the man with the bracelets" (marchand de lacets); when he has him in charge, he is a bird of ill-omen (hirondelle de la Greve); when he escorts him to the scaffold, he is "groom to the guillotine" (hussard de la guillotine).

To complete our study of the prison-yard, two more of the prisoners must be hastily sketched in. Selerier, alias l'Auvergnat, alias le Pere Ralleau, called le Rouleur, alias Fil-de-Soie—he had thirty names, and as many passports—will henceforth be spoken of by this name only, as he was called by no other among the swell-mob. This profound philosopher, who saw a spy in the sham priest, was a brawny fellow of about five feet eight, whose muscles were all marked by strange bosses. He had an enormous head in which a pair of half-closed eyes sparkled like fire—the eyes of a bird of prey, with gray, dull, skinny eyelids. At first glance his face resembled that of a wolf, his jaws were so broad, powerful, and prominent; but the cruelty and even ferocity suggested by this likeness were counterbalanced by the cunning and eagerness of his face, though it was scarred by the smallpox. The margin of each scar being sharply cut, gave a sort of wit to his expression; it was seamed with ironies. The life of a criminal—a life of danger and thirst, of nights spent bivouacking on the quays and river banks, on bridges and streets, and the orgies of strong drink by which successes are celebrated—had laid, as it were, a varnish over these features. Fil-de-Soie, if seen in his undisguised person, would have been marked by any constable or gendarme as his prey; but he was a match for Jacques Collin in the arts of make-up and dress. Just now Fil-de-Soie, in undress, like a great actor who is well got up only on the stage, wore a sort of shooting jacket bereft of buttons, and whose ripped button-holes showed the white lining, squalid green slippers, nankin trousers now a dingy gray, and on his head a cap without a peak, under which an old bandana was tied, streaky with rents, and washed out.

Le Biffon was a complete contrast to Fil-de-Soie. This famous robber, short, burly, and fat, but active, with a livid complexion, and deep-set black eyes, dressed like a cook, standing squarely on very bandy legs, was alarming to behold, for in his countenance all the features predominated that are most typical of the carnivorous beast.

Fil-de-Soie and le Biffon were always wheedling la Pouraille, who had lost all hope. The murderer knew that he would be tried, sentenced, and executed within four months. Indeed, Fil-de-Soie and le Biffon, la Pouraille's chums, never called him anything but *le Chanoine de l'Abbaye de Monte-a-Regret* (a grim paraphrase for a man condemned to the guillotine). It is easy to understand why Fil-de-Soie and le Biffon should fawn on la Pouraille. The man had somewhere hidden two hundred and fifty thousand francs in gold, his share of the spoil found in the house of the Crottats, the "victims," in newspaper phrase. What a splendid fortune to leave to two pals, though the two old stagers would be sent back to the galleys within a few days! Le Biffon and Fil-de-Soie would be sentenced for a term of fifteen years for robbery with violence, without prejudice to the ten years' penal servitude on a former sentence, which they had taken the liberty of cutting short. So, though one had twenty-two and the other twenty-six years of imprisonment to look forward to, they both hoped to escape, and come back to find la Pouraille's mine of gold.

But the "Ten-thousand man" kept his secret; he did not see the use of telling it before he was sentenced. He belonged to the "upper ten" of the hulks, and had never betrayed his accomplices. His temper was well known; Monsieur Popinot, who had examined him, had not been able to get anything out of him.

This terrible trio were at the further end of the prison-yard, that is to say, near the better class of cells. Fil-de-Soie was giving a lecture to a young man who was IN for his first offence, and who, being certain of ten years' penal servitude, was gaining information as to the various convict establishments.

"Well, my boy," Fil-de-Soie was saying sententiously as Jacques Collin appeared on the scene, "the difference between Brest, Toulon, and Rochefort is—"

"Well, old cock?" said the lad, with the curiosity of a novice.

This prisoner, a man of good family, accused of forgery, had come down from the cell next to that where Lucien had been.

"My son," Fil-de-Soie went on, "at Brest you are sure to get some beans at the third turn if you dip your spoon in the bowl; at Toulon you never get any till the fifth; and at Rochefort you get none at all, unless you are an old hand."

Having spoken, the philosopher joined le Biffon and la Pouraille, and all three, greatly puzzled by the priest, walked down the yard, while Jacques Collin, lost in grief, came up it. *Trompe-la-Mort*, absorbed in terrible meditations, the meditations of a fallen emperor, did not think of himself as the centre of observation, the object of general attention, and he walked slowly, gazing at the fatal window where Lucien had hanged himself. None of the prisoners knew of this catastrophe, since, for reasons to be presently explained, the young forger had not mentioned the subject. The three pals agreed to cross the priest's path.

"He is no priest," said Fil-de-Soie; "he is an old stager. Look how he drags his right foot."

It is needful to explain here—for not every reader has had a fancy to visit the galleys—that each convict is chained to another, an old one and a young one always as a couple; the weight of this chain riveted to a ring above the ankle is so great as to induce a limp, which the convict never loses. Being obliged to exert one leg much more than the other to drag this fetter (manicle is the slang name for such irons), the prisoner inevitably gets into the habit of making the effort. Afterwards, though he no longer wears the chain, it acts upon him still; as a man still feels an amputated leg, the convict is always conscious of the anklet, and can never get over that trick of walking. In police slang, he "drags his right." And this sign, as well known to convicts among themselves as it is to the police, even if it does not help to identify a comrade, at any rate confirms recognition.

In *Trompe-la Mort*, who had escaped eight years since, this trick had to a great extent worn off; but just now, lost in reflections, he walked at such a slow and solemn pace that, slight as the limp was, it was strikingly evident to so practiced an eye as la Pouraille's. And it is quite intelligible that convicts, always thrown together, as they must be, and never having any one else to study, will so thoroughly have watched each other's faces and appearance, that certain tricks will have impressed them which may escape their systematic foes—spies, gendarmes, and police-inspectors.

Thus it was a peculiar twitch of the maxillary muscles of the left cheek, recognized by a convict who was sent to a review of the Legion of the Seine, which led to the arrest of the lieutenant-colonel of that corps, the famous Coignard; for, in spite of Bibi-Lupin's confidence, the police could not dare believe that the Comte Pontis de Sainte-Helene and Coignard were one and the same man.

"He is our boss" (dab or master) said Fil-de-Soie, seeing in Jacques Collin's eyes the vague glance a man sunk in despair casts on all his surroundings.

"By Jingo! Yes, it is *Trompe-la-Mort*," said le Biffon, rubbing his hands. "Yes, it is his cut, his build; but what has he done to himself? He looks quite different."

"I know what he is up to!" cried Fil-de-Soie; "he has some plan in his head. He wants to see the boy" (sa tante) "who is to be executed before long."

The persons known in prison as tantes or aunts may be best described in the ingenious words of the governor of one of the great prisons to the late Lord Durham, who, during his stay in Paris, visited every prison. So curious was he to see every detail of French justice, that he even persuaded Sanson, at that time the executioner, to erect the scaffold and decapitate a living calf, that he might thoroughly understand the working of the machine made famous by the Revolution. The governor having shown him everything—the yards, the workshops, and the underground cells—pointed to a part of the building, and said, "I need not take your Lordship there; it is the quartier des tantes."—"Oh," said Lord Durham, "what are they!"—"The third sex, my Lord."

"And they are going to scrag Theodore!" said la Pouraille, "such a pretty boy! And such a light hand! such cheek! What a loss to society!"

"Yes, Theodore Calvi is yamming his last meal," said le Biffon. "His trips will pipe their eyes, for the little beggar was a great pet."

"So you're here, old chap?" said la Pouraille to Jacques Collin. And, arm-in-arm with his two acolytes, he barred the way to the new arrival. "Why, Boss, have you got yourself japanned?" he went on.

"I hear you have nobbled our pile" (stolen our money), le Biffon added, in a threatening tone.

"You have just got to stump up the tin!" said Fil-de-Soie.

The three questions were fired at him like three pistol-shots.

"Do not make game of an unhappy priest sent here by mistake," Jacques Collin replied mechanically, recognizing his three comrades.

"That is the sound of his pipe, if it is not quite the cut of his mug," said la Pouraille, laying his hand on Jacques Collin's shoulder.

This action, and the sight of his three chums, startled the "Boss" out of his dejection, and brought him back to a consciousness of reality; for during that dreadful night he had lost himself in the infinite spiritual world of feeling, seeking some new road.

"Do not blow the gaff on your Boss!" said Jacques Collin in a hollow threatening tone, not unlike the low growl of a lion. "The reelers are here; let them make fools of themselves. I am faking to help a pal who is awfully down on his luck."

He spoke with the unction of a priest trying to convert the wretched, and a look which flashed round the yard, took in the warders under the archways, and pointed them out with a wink to his three companions.

"Are there not narks about? Keep your peepers open and a sharp lookout. Don't know me, Nanty parnarly, and soap me down for a priest, or I will do for you all, you and your molls and your blunt."

"What, do you funk our blabbing?" said Fil-de-Soie. "Have you come to help your boy to guy?"

"Madeleine is getting ready to be turned off in the Square" (the Place de Greve), said la Pouraille.

"Theodore!" said Jacques Collin, repressing a start and a cry.

"They will have his nut off," la Pouraille went on; "he was booked for the scaffold two months ago."

Jacques Collin felt sick, his knees almost failed him; but his three comrades held him up, and he had the presence of mind to clasp his hands with an expression of contrition. La Pouraille and le Biffon respectfully supported the sacrilegious *Trompe-la-Mort*, while Fil-de-Soie ran to a warder on guard at the gate leading to the parlor.

"That venerable priest wants to sit down; send out a chair for him," said he.

And so Bibi-Lupin's plot had failed.

Trompe-la-Mort, like a Napoleon recognized by his soldiers, had won the submission and respect of the three felons. Two words had done it. Your molls and your blunt—your women and your money—epitomizing every true affection of man. This threat was to the three convicts an indication of supreme power. The Boss still had their fortune in his hands. Still omnipotent outside the prison, their Boss had not betrayed them, as the false pals said.

Their chief's immense reputation for skill and inventiveness stimulated their curiosity; for, in prison, curiosity is the only goad of these blighted spirits. And Jacques Collin's daring disguise, kept up even under the bolts and locks of the Conciergerie, dazzled the three felons.

"I have been in close confinement for four days and did not know that Theodore was so near the Abbaye," said Jacques Collin. "I came in to save a poor little chap who scragged himself here yesterday at four o'clock, and now here is another misfortune. I have not an ace in my hand—"

"Poor old boy!" said Fil-de-Soie.

"Old Scratch has cut me!" cried Jacques Collin, tearing himself free from his supporters, and drawing himself up with a fierce look. "There comes a time when the world is too many for us! The beaks gobble us up at last."

The governor of the Conciergerie, informed of the Spanish priest's weak state, came himself to the prison-yard to observe him; he made him sit down on a chair in the sun, studying him with the keen acumen which increases day by day in the practise of such functions, though hidden under an appearance of indifference.

"Oh! Heaven!" cried Jacques Collin. "To be mixed up with such creatures, the dregs of society—felons and murders!—But God will not desert His servant! My dear sir, my stay here shall be marked by deeds of charity which shall live in men's memories. I will convert these unhappy creatures, they shall learn they have souls, that life eternal awaits them, and that though they have lost all on earth, they still may win heaven—Heaven which they may purchase by true and genuine repentance."

Twenty or thirty prisoners had gathered in a group behind the three terrible convicts, whose ferocious looks had kept a space of three feet between them and their inquisitive companions, and they heard this address, spoken with evangelical unction.

"Ay, Monsieur Gault," said the formidable la Pouraille, "we will listen to what this one may say—"

"I have been told," Jacques Collin went on, "that there is in this prison a man condemned to death."

"The rejection of his appeal is at this moment being read to him," said Monsieur Gault.

"I do not know what that means," said Jacques Collin, artlessly looking about him.

"Golly, what a flat!" said the young fellow, who, a few minutes since, had asked Fil-de-Soie about the beans on the hulks.

"Why, it means that he is to be scragged to-day or to-morrow."

"Scragged?" asked Jacques Collin, whose air of innocence and ignorance filled his three pals with admiration.

"In their slang," said the governor, "that means that he will suffer the penalty of death. If the clerk is reading the appeal, the executioner will no doubt have orders for the execution. The unhappy man has persistently refused the offices of the chaplain."

"Ah! Monsieur le Directeaur, this is a soul to save!" cried Jacques Collin, and the sacrilegious wretch clasped his hands with the expression of a despairing lover, which to the watchful governor seemed nothing less than divine fervor. "Ah, monsieur," *Trompe-la-Mort* went on, "let me prove to you what I am, and how much I can do, by allowing me to incite that hardened heart to repentance. God has given me a power of speech which produces great changes. I crush men's hearts; I open them.—What are you afraid of? Send me with an escort of gendarmes, of turnkeys—whom you will."

"I will inquire whether the prison chaplain will allow you to take his place," said Monsieur Gault.

And the governor withdrew, struck by the expression, perfectly indifferent, though inquisitive, with which the convicts and the prisoners on remand stared at this priest, whose unctuous tones lent a charm to his half-French, half-Spanish lingo.

"How did you come in here, Monsieur l'Abbe?" asked the youth who had questioned Fil-de-Soie.

"Oh, by a mistake!" replied Jacques Collin, eyeing the young gentleman from head to foot. "I was found in the house of a courtesan who had died, and was immediately robbed. It was proved that she had killed herself, and the thieves—probably the servants—have not yet been caught."

"And it was for that theft that your young man hanged himself?"

"The poor boy, no doubt, could not endure the thought of being blighted by his unjust imprisonment," said *Trompe-la-Mort*, raising his eyes to heaven.

"Ay," said the young man; "they were coming to set him free just when he had killed himself. What bad luck!"

"Only innocent souls can be thus worked on by their imagination," said Jacques Collin. "For, observe, he was the loser by the theft."

"How much money was it?" asked Fil-de-Soie, the deep and cunning.

"Seven hundred and fifty thousand francs," said Jacques Collin blandly.

The three convicts looked at each other and withdrew from the group that had gathered round the sham priest.

"He screwed the moll's place himself!" said Fil-de-Soie in a whisper to le Biffon, "and they want to put us in a blue funk for our cartwheels" (thunes de balles, five-franc pieces).

"He will always be the boss of the swells," replied la Pouraille. "Our pieces are safe enough."

La Pouraille, wishing to find some man he could trust, had an interest in considering Jacques Collin an honest man. And in prison, of all places, a man believes what he hopes.

"I lay you anything, he will come round the big Boss and save his chum!" said Fil-de-Soie.

"If he does that," said le Biffon, "though I don't believe he is really God, he must certainly have smoked a pipe with old Scratch, as they say."

"Didn't you hear him say, 'Old Scratch has cut me'?" said Fil-de-Soie.

"Oh!" cried la Pouraille, "if only he would save my nut, what a time I would have with my whack of the shiners and the yellow boys I have stowed."

"Do what he bids you!" said Fil-de Soie.

"You don't say so?" retorted la Pouraille, looking at his pal.

"What a flat you are! You will be booked for the Abbaye!" said le Biffon. "You have no other door to budge, if you want to keep on your pins, to yam, wet your whistle, and fake to the end; you must take his orders."

"That's all right," said la Pouraille. "There is not one of us that will blow the gaff, or if he does, I will take him where I am going—"

"And he'll do it too," cried Fil-de-Soie.

THE LEAST SYMPATHETIC READER, WHO has no pity for this strange race, may conceive of the state of mind of Jacques Collin, finding himself between the dead body of the idol whom he had been bewailing during five hours that night, and the imminent end of his former comrade— the dead body of Theodore, the young Corsican. Only to see the boy would demand extraordinary cleverness; to save him would need a miracle; but he was thinking of it.

For the better comprehension of what Jacques Collin proposed to attempt, it must be remarked that murderers and thieves, all the men who people the galleys, are not so formidable as is generally supposed. With a few rare exceptions these creatures are all cowards, in consequence no doubt, of the constant alarms which weigh on their spirit. The faculties being perpetually on the stretch in thieving, and the success of a stroke of business depending on the exertion of every vital force, with a readiness of wit to match their dexterity of hand, and an alertness which exhausts the nervous system; these violent exertions of will once over, they become stupid, just as a singer or a dancer drops quite exhausted after a fatiguing pas seul, or one of those tremendous duets which modern composers inflict on the public.

Malefactors are, in fact, so entirely bereft of common sense, or so much oppressed by fear, that they become absolutely childish. Credulous to the last degree, they are caught by the bird-lime of the simplest snare. When they have done a successful *job*, they are in such a state of prostration that they immediately rush into the debaucheries they crave for; they get drunk on wine and spirits, and throw themselves madly into the arms of their women to recover composure by dint of exhausting their strength, and to forget their crime by forgetting their reason.

Then they are at the mercy of the police. When once they are in custody they lose their head, and long for hope so blindly that they believe anything; indeed, there is nothing too absurd for them to accept it. An instance will suffice to show how far the simplicity of a criminal who has been *nabbed* will carry him. Bibi-Lupin, not long before, had extracted a confession from a murderer of nineteen by making him believe that no one under age was ever executed. When this lad was transferred to the Conciergerie to be sentenced after the rejection of his appeal, this terrible man came to see him.

"Are you sure you are not yet twenty?" said he.

"Yes, I am only nineteen and a half."

"Well, then," replied Bibi-Lupin, "you may be quite sure of one thing—you will never see twenty."

"Why?"

"Because you will be scragged within three days," replied the police agent.

The murderer, who had believed, even after sentence was passed, that a minor would never be executed, collapsed like an omelette soufflee.

Such men, cruel only from the necessity for suppressive evidence, for they murder only to get rid of witnesses (and this is one of the arguments adduced by those who desire the abrogation of capital punishment),—these giants of dexterity and skill, whose sleight of hand, whose rapid sight, whose every sense is as alert as that of a savage, are heroes of evil only on the stage of their exploits. Not only do their difficulties begin as soon as the crime is committed, for they are as much bewildered by the need for concealing the stolen goods as they were depressed by necessity—but they are as weak as a woman in childbed. The vehemence of their schemes is terrific; in success they become like children. In a word, their nature is that of the wild beast—easy to kill when it is full fed. In prison these strange beings are men in dissimulation and in secretiveness, which never yields till the last moment, when they are crushed and broken by the tedium of imprisonment.

It may hence be understood how it was that the three convicts, instead of betraying their chief, were eager to serve him; and as they suspected he was now the owner of the stolen seven hundred and fifty thousand francs, they admired him for his calm resignation, under bolt and bar of the Conciergerie, believing him capable of protecting them all.

When Monsieur Gault left the sham priest, he returned through the parlor to his office, and went in search of Bibi-Lupin, who for twenty minutes, since Jacques Collin had gone downstairs, had been on the watch with his eye at a peephole in a window looking out on the prison-yard.

"Not one of them recognized him," said Monsieur Gault, "and Napolitas, who is on duty, did not hear a word. The poor priest all through the night, in his deep distress, did not say a word which could imply that his gown covers Jacques Collin."

"That shows that he is used to prison life," said the police agent.

Napolitas, Bibi-Lupin's secretary, being unknown to the criminals then in the Conciergerie, was playing the part of the young gentlemen imprisoned for forgery.

"Well, but he wishes to be allowed to hear the confession of the young fellow who is sentenced to death," said the governor.

"To be sure! That is our last chance," cried Bibi-Lupin. "I had forgotten that. Theodore Calvi, the young Corsican, was the man chained to Jacques Collin; they say that on the hulks Jacques Collin made him famous pads—"

The convicts on the galleys contrive a kind of pad to slip between their skin and the fetters to deaden the pressure of the iron ring on their ankles and instep; these pads, made of tow and rags, are known as patarasses.

"Who is warder over the man?" asked Bibi-Lupin.

"Coeur la Virole."

"Very well, I will go and make up as a gendarme, and be on the watch; I shall hear what they say. I will be even with them."

"But if it should be Jacques Collin are you not afraid of his recognizing you and throttling you?" said the governor to Bibi-Lupin.

"As a gendarme I shall have my sword," replied the other; "and, besides, if he is Jacques Collin, he will never do anything that will risk his neck; and if he is a priest, I shall be safe."

"Then you have no time to lose," said Monsieur Gault; "it is half-past eight. Father Sauteloup has just read the reply to his appeal, and Monsieur Sanson is waiting in the order room."

"Yes, it is to-day's job, the 'widow's huzzars'" (les hussards de la veuve, another horrible name for the functionaries of the guillotine) "are ordered out," replied Bibi-Lupin. "Still, I cannot wonder that the prosecutor-general should hesitate; the boy has always declared that he is innocent, and there is, in my opinion, no conclusive evidence against him."

"He is a thorough Corsican," said Monsieur Gault; "he has not said a word, and has held firm all through."

The last words of the governor of the prison summed up the dismal tale of a man condemned to die. A man cut off from among the living by law belongs to the Bench. The Bench is paramount; it is answerable to nobody, it obeys its own conscience. The prison belongs to the Bench, which controls it absolutely. Poetry has taken possession of this social theme, "the man condemned to death"—a subject truly apt to strike the imagination! And poetry has been sublime on it. Prose has no resource but fact; still, the fact is appalling enough to hold its own against verse. The existence of a condemned man who has not confessed his crime, or betrayed his accomplices, is one of fearful torment. This is no case of iron boots, of water poured into the stomach, or of limbs racked by hideous machinery; it is hidden and, so to speak, negative torture. The condemned wretch is given over to himself with a companion whom he cannot but trust.

The amiability of modern philanthropy fancies it has understood the dreadful torment of isolation, but this is a mistake. Since the abolition of torture, the Bench, in a natural anxiety to reassure the too sensitive consciences of the jury, had guessed what a terrible auxiliary isolation would prove to justice in seconding remorse.

Solitude is void; and nature has as great a horror of a moral void as she has of a physical vacuum. Solitude is habitable only to a man of genius who can people it with ideas, the children of the spiritual world; or to one who contemplates the works of the Creator, to whom it is bright with the light of heaven, alive with the breath and voice of God. Excepting for these two beings—so near to Paradise—solitude is to the mind what torture is to the body. Between solitude and the torture-chamber there is all the difference that there is between a nervous malady and a surgical disease. It is suffering multiplied by infinitude. The body borders on the infinite through its nerves, as the spirit does through thought. And, in fact, in the annals of the Paris law courts the criminals who do not confess can be easily counted.

This terrible situation, which in some cases assumes appalling importance—in politics, for instance, when a dynasty or a state is involved—will find a place in the HUMAN COMEDY. But here a description of the stone box in which after the Restoration, the law shut up a man condemned to death in Paris, may serve to give an idea of the terrors of a felon's last day on earth.

Before the Revolution of July there was in the Conciergerie, and indeed there still is, a condemned cell. This room, backing on the governor's office, is divided from it by a thick wall in strong masonry, and the other side of it is formed by a wall seven or eight feet thick, which supports one end of the immense *Salle des Pas-Perdus*. It is entered through the first door in the long dark passage in which the eye loses itself when looking from the middle of the vaulted gateway. This ill-omened room is lighted by a funnel, barred by a formidable grating, and hardly perceptible on going into the Conciergerie yard, for it has been pierced in the narrow space between the office window close to the railing of the gateway, and the place where the office clerk sits—a den like a cupboard contrived by the architect at the end of the entrance court.

This position accounts for the fact that the room thus enclosed between four immensely thick walls should have been devoted, when the Conciergerie was reconstituted, to this terrible and funereal service. Escape is impossible. The passage, leading to the cells for solitary confinement and to the women's quarters, faces the stove where gendarmes and warders are always collected together. The air-hole, the only outlet to the open air, is nine feet above the floor, and looks out on the first court, which is guarded by sentries at the outer gate. No human power can make any impression on the walls. Besides, a man sentenced to death is at once secured in a straitwaistcoat, a garment which precludes all use of the hands; he is chained by one foot to his camp bed, and he has a fellow prisoner to watch and attend on him. The room is paved with thick flags, and the light is so dim that it is hard to see anything.

It is impossible not to feel chilled to the marrow on going in, even now, though for sixteen years the cell has never been used, in consequence of the changes effected in Paris in the treatment of criminals under sentence. Imagine the guilty man there with his remorse for company, in silence and darkness, two elements of horror, and you will wonder how he ever failed to go mad. What a nature must that be whose temper can resist such treatment, with the added misery of enforced idleness and inaction.

And yet Theodore Calvi, a Corsican, now twenty-seven years of age, muffled, as it were, in a shroud of absolute reserve, had for two months held out against the effects of this dungeon and the insidious chatter of the prisoner placed to entrap him.

These were the strange circumstances under which the Corsican had been condemned to death. Though the case is a very curious one, our account of it must be brief. It is impossible to introduce a long digression at the climax of a narrative already so much prolonged, since its only interest is in so far as it concerns Jacques Collin, the vertebral column, so to speak, which, by its sinister persistency, connects *Le Pere Goriot* with *Illusions perdues*, and *Illusions perdues* with this Study. And, indeed, the reader's imagination will be able to work out the obscure case which at this moment was causing great uneasiness to the jury of the sessions, before whom Theodore Calvi had been tried. For a whole week, since the criminal's appeal had been rejected by the Supreme Court, Monsieur de Granville had been worrying himself over the case, and postponing from day to day the order for carrying out the sentence, so anxious was he to reassure the jury by announcing that on the threshold of death the accused had confessed the crime.

A poor widow of Nanterre, whose dwelling stood apart from the township, which is situated in the midst of the infertile plain lying between Mount-Valerian, Saint-Germain, the hills of Sartrouville, and Argenteuil, had been murdered and robbed a few days after coming into her share of an unexpected inheritance. This windfall amounted to three thousand francs, a dozen silver spoons and forks, a gold watch and chain and some linen. Instead of depositing the three thousand francs in Paris, as she was advised by the notary of the wine-merchant who had left it her, the old woman insisted on keeping it by her. In the first place, she had never seen so much money of her own, and then she distrusted everybody in every kind of affairs, as most common and country folk do. After long discussion with a wine-merchant of Nanterre, a relation of her own and of the wine-merchant who had left her the money, the widow decided on buying an annuity, on selling her house at Nanterre, and living in the town of Saint-Germain.

The house she was living in, with a good-sized garden enclosed by a slight wooden fence, was the poor sort of dwelling usually built by small landowners in the neighborhood of Paris. It had been hastily constructed, with no architectural design, of cement and rubble, the materials commonly used near Paris, where, as at Nanterre, they are extremely abundant, the ground being everywhere broken by quarries open to the sky. This is the ordinary hut of the civilized savage. The house consisted of a ground floor and one floor above, with garrets in the roof.

The quarryman, her deceased husband, and the builder of this dwelling, had put strong iron bars to all the windows; the front door was remarkably thick. The man knew that he was alone there in the open country—and what a country! His customers were the principal master-masons in Paris, so the more important materials for his house, which stood within five hundred yards of his quarry, had been brought out in his own carts returning empty. He could choose such as suited him where houses were pulled down, and got them very cheap. Thus the window frames, the iron-work, the doors, shutters, and wooden fittings were all derived from sanctioned pilfering, presents from his customers, and good ones, carefully chosen. Of two window-frames, he could take the better.

The house, entered from a large stable-yard, was screened from the road by a wall; the gate was of strong iron-railing. Watch-dogs were kept in the stables, and a little dog indoors at night. There was a garden of more than two acres behind.

His widow, without children, lived here with only a woman servant. The sale of the quarry had paid off the owner's debts; he had been dead about two years. This isolated house was the widow's sole possession, and she kept fowls and cows, selling the eggs and milk at Nanterre. Having no stableboy or carter or quarryman—her husband had made them do every kind of work—she no longer kept up the garden; she only gathered the few greens and roots that the stony ground allowed to grow self-sown.

The price of the house, with the money she had inherited, would amount to seven or eight thousand francs, and she could fancy herself living very happily at Saint-Germain on seven or eight hundred francs a year, which she thought she could buy with her eight thousand francs. She had had many discussions over this with the notary at Saint-Germain, for she refused to hand her money over for an annuity to the wine-merchant at Nanterre, who was anxious to have it.

Under these circumstances, then, after a certain day the widow Pigeau and her servant were seen no more. The front gate, the house door, the shutters, all were closed. At the end of three days, the police, being informed, made inquisition. Monsieur Popinot, the examining judge, and the public prosecutor arrived from Paris, and this was what they reported:—

Neither the outer gate nor the front door showed any marks of violence. The key was in the lock of the door, inside. Not a single bar

HONORÉ DE BALZAC

had been wretched; the locks, shutters, and bolts were all untampered with. The walls showed no traces that could betray the passage of the criminals. The chimney-posts, of red clay, afforded no opportunity for ingress or escape, and the roofing was sound and unbroken, showing no damage by violence.

On entering the first-floor rooms, the magistrates, the gendarmes, and Bibi-Lupin found the widow Pigeau strangled in her bed and the woman strangled in hers, each by means of the bandana she wore as a nightcap. The three thousand francs were gone, with the silver-plate and the trinkets. The two bodies were decomposing, as were those of the little dog and of a large yard-dog.

The wooden palings of the garden were examined; none were broken. The garden paths showed no trace of footsteps. The magistrate thought it probable that the robber had walked on the grass to leave no footprints if he had come that way; but how could he have got into the house? The back door to the garden had an outer guard of three iron bars, uninjured; and there, too, the key was in the lock inside, as in the front door.

All these impossibilities having been duly noted by Monsieur Popinot, by Bibi-Lupin, who stayed there a day to examine every detail, by the public prosecutor himself, and by the sergeant of the gendarmerie at Nanterre, this murder became an agitating mystery, in which the Law and the Police were nonplussed.

This drama, published in the *Gazette des Tribunaux*, took place in the winter of 1828-29. God alone knows what excitement this puzzling crime occasioned in Paris! But Paris has a new drama to watch every morning, and forgets everything. The police, on the contrary, forgets nothing.

Three months after this fruitless inquiry, a girl of the town, whose extravagance had invited the attention of Bibi-Lupin's agents, who watched her as being the ally of several thieves, tried to persuade a woman she knew to pledge twelve silver spoons and forks and a gold watch and chain. The friend refused. This came to Bibi-Lupin's ears, and he remembered the plate and the watch and chain stolen at Nanterre. The commissioners of the Mont-de-Piete, and all the receivers of stolen goods, were warned, while Manon la Blonde was subjected to unremitting scrutiny.

It was very soon discovered that Manon la Blonde was madly in love with a young man who was never to be seen, and was supposed to be deaf to all the fair Manon's proofs of devotion. Mystery on mystery. However, this youth, under the diligent attentions of police spies, was soon seen and identified as an escaped convict, the famous hero of the Corsican vendetta, the handsome Theodore Calvi, known as Madeleine.

A man was turned on to entrap Calvi, one of those double-dealing buyers of stolen goods who serve the thieves and the police both at once; he promised to purchase the silver and the watch and chain. At the moment when the dealer of the Cour Saint-Guillaume was counting out the cash to Theodore, dressed as a woman, at half-past six in the evening, the police came in and seized Theodore and the property.

The inquiry was at once begun. On such thin evidence it was impossible to pass a sentence of death. Calvi never swerved, he never contradicted himself. He said that a country woman had sold him these objects at Argenteuil; that after buying them, the excitement over the murder committed at Nanterre had shown him the danger of keeping this plate and watch and chain in his possession, since, in fact, they were proved by the inventory made after the death of the wine merchant, the widow Pigeau's uncle, to be those that were stolen from her. Compelled at last by poverty to sell them, he said he wished to dispose of them by the intervention of a person to whom no suspicion could attach.

And nothing else could be extracted from the convict, who, by his taciturnity and firmness, contrived to insinuate that the wine-merchant at Nanterre had committed the crime, and that the woman of whom he, Theodore, had bought them was the wine-merchant's wife. The unhappy man and his wife were both taken into custody; but, after a week's imprisonment, it was amply proved that neither the husband nor the wife had been out of their house at the time. Also, Calvi failed to recognize in the wife the woman who, as he declared, had sold him the things.

As it was shown that Calvi's mistress, implicated in the case, had spent about a thousand francs since the date of the crime and the day when Calvi tried to pledge the plate and trinkets, the evidence seemed strong enough to commit Calvi and the girl for trial. This murder being the eighteenth which Theodore had committed, he was condemned to death for he seemed certainly to be guilty of this skilfully contrived crime. Though he did not recognize the wine-merchant's wife, both she and her husband recognized him. The inquiry had proved, by the evidence of several witnesses, that Theodore had been living at Nanterre for about a month; he had worked at a mason's, his face whitened with plaster, and his clothes very shabby. At Nanterre the lad was supposed to be about eighteen years old, for the whole month he must have been nursing that brat (nourri ce poupon, i.e. hatching the crime).

The lawyers thought he must have had accomplices. The chimney-pots were measured and compared with the size of Manon la Blonde's body to see if she could have got in that way; but a child of six could not have passed up or down those red-clay pipes, which, in modern buildings, take the place of the vast chimneys of old-fashioned houses. But for this singular and annoying difficulty, Theodore would have been executed within a week. The prison chaplain, it has been seen, could make nothing of him.

ALL THIS BUSINESS, AND THE name of Calvi, must have escaped the notice of Jacques Collin, who, at the time, was absorbed in his single-handed struggle with Contenson, Corentin, and Peyrade. It had indeed been a point with *Trompe-la-Mort* to forget as far as possible his chums and all that had to do with the law courts; he dreaded a meeting which should bring him face to face with a pal who might demand an account of his boss which Collin could not possibly render.

The governor of the prison went forthwith to the public prosecutor's court, where he found the Attorney-General in conversation with Monsieur de Granville, who had spent the whole night at the Hotel de Serizy, was, in consequence of this important case, obliged to give a few hours to his duties, though overwhelmed with fatigue and grief; for the physicians could not yet promise that the Countess would recover her sanity.

After speaking a few words to the governor, Monsieur de Granville took the warrant from the attorney and placed it in Gault's hands.

"Let the matter proceed," said he, "unless some extraordinary circumstances should arise. Of this you must judge. I trust to your judgment. The scaffold need not be erected till half-past ten, so you still have an hour. On such an occasion hours are centuries, and many things may happen in a century. Do not allow him to think he is reprieved; prepare the man for execution if necessary; and if nothing comes of that, give Sanson the warrant at half-past nine. Let him wait!"

As the governor of the prison left the public prosecutor's room, under the archway of the passage into the hall he met Monsieur Camusot, who was going there. He exchanged a few hurried words with the examining judge; and after telling him what had been done at the Conciergerie with regard to Jacques Collin, he went on to witness the meeting of *Trompe-la-Mort* and Madeleine; and he did not allow the so-called priest to see the condemned criminal till Bibi-Lupin, admirably disguised as a gendarme, had taken the place of the prisoner left in charge of the young Corsican.

No words can describe the amazement of the three convicts when a warder came to fetch Jacques Collin and led him to the condemned cell! With one consent they rushed up to the chair on which Jacques Collin was sitting.

"To-day, isn't it, monsieur?" asked Fil-de-Soie of the warder.

"Yes, Jack Ketch is waiting," said the man with perfect indifference.

Charlot is the name by which the executioner is known to the populace and the prison world in Paris. The nickname dates from the Revolution of 1789.

The words produced a great sensation. The prisoners looked at each other.

"It is all over with him," the warder went on; "the warrant has been delivered to Monsieur Gault, and the sentence has just been read to him."

"And so the fair Madeleine has received the last sacraments?" said la Pouraille, and he swallowed a deep mouthful of air.

"Poor little Theodore!" cried le Biffon; "he is a pretty chap too. What a pity to drop your nut" (eternuer dans le son) "so young."

The warder went towards the gate, thinking that Jacques Collin was at his heels. But the Spaniard walked very slowly, and when he was getting near to Julien he tottered and signed to la Pouraille to give him his arm.

"He is a murderer," said Napolitas to the priest, pointing to la Pouraille, and offering his own arm.

"No, to me he is an unhappy wretch!" replied Jacques Collin, with the presence of mind and the unction of the Archbishop of Cambrai. And he drew away from Napolitas, of whom he had been very suspicious from the first. Then he said to his pals in an undertone:

"He is on the bottom step of the Abbaye de Monte-a-Regret, but I am the Prior! I will show you how well I know how to come round the beaks. I mean to snatch this boy's nut from their jaws."

"For the sake of his breeches!" said Fil-de-Soie with a smile.

"I mean to win his soul to heaven!" replied Jacques Collin fervently, seeing some other prisoners about him. And he joined the warder at the gate.

"He got in to save Madeleine," said Fil-de-Soie. "We guessed rightly. What a boss he is!"

"But how can he? Jack Ketch's men are waiting. He will not even see the kid," objected le Biffon.

"The devil is on his side!" cried la Pouraille. "He claim our blunt! Never! He is too fond of his old chums! We are too useful to him! They wanted to make us blow the gaff, but we are not such flats! If he saves his Madeleine, I will tell him all my secrets."

The effect of this speech was to increase the devotion of the three convicts to their boss; for at this moment he was all their hope.

Jacques Collin, in spite of Madeleine's peril, did not forget to play his part. Though he knew the Conciergerie as well as he knew the hulks in the three ports, he blundered so naturally that the warder had to tell him, "This way, that way," till they reached the office. There, at a glance, Jacques Collin recognized a tall, stout man leaning on the stove, with a long, red face not without distinction: it was Sanson.

"Monsieur is the chaplain?" said he, going towards him with simple cordiality.

The mistake was so shocking that it froze the bystanders.

"No, monsieur," said Sanson; "I have other functions."

Sanson, the father of the last executioner of that name—for he has recently been dismissed—was the son of the man who beheaded Louis XVI After four centuries of hereditary office, this descendant of so many executioners had tried to repudiate the traditional burden. The Sansons were for two hundred years executioners at Rouen before being promoted to the first rank in the kingdom, and had carried out the decrees of justice from father to son since the thirteenth century. Few families can boast of an office or of nobility handed down in a direct line during six centuries.

This young man had been captain in a cavalry regiment, and was looking forward to a brilliant military career, when his father insisted on his help in decapitating the king. Then he made his son his deputy when, in 1793, two guillotines were in constant work—one at the Barriere du Trone, and the other in the Place de Greve. This terrible functionary, now a man of about sixty, was remarkable for his dignified air, his gentle and deliberate manners, and his entire contempt for Bibi-Lupin and his acolytes who fed the machine. The only detail which betrayed the blood of the mediaeval executioner was the formidable breadth and thickness of his hands. Well informed too, caring greatly for his position as a citizen and an elector, and an enthusiastic florist, this tall, brawny man with his low voice, his calm reserve, his few words, and a high bald forehead, was like an English nobleman rather than an executioner. And a Spanish priest would certainly have fallen into the mistake which Jacques Collin had intentionally made.

"He is no convict!" said the head warder to the governor.

"I begin to think so too," replied Monsieur Gault, with a nod to that official.

Jacques Collin was led to the cellar-like room where Theodore Calvi, in a straitwaistcoat, was sitting on the edge of the wretched camp bed. *Trompe-la-Mort*, under a transient gleam of light from the passage, at once recognized Bibi-Lupin in the gendarme who stood leaning on his sword.

"Io sono Gaba-Morto. Parla nostro Italiano," said Jacques Collin very rapidly. "Vengo ti salvar."

"I am *Trompe-la-Mort*. Talk our Italian. I have come to save you."

All the two chums wanted to say had, of course, to be incomprehensible to the pretended gendarme; and as Bibi-Lupin was left in charge of the prisoner, he could not leave his post. The man's fury was quite indescribable.

Theodore Calvi, a young man with a pale olive complexion, light hair, and hollow, dull, blue eyes, well built, hiding prodigious strength under the lymphatic appearance that is not uncommon in Southerners, would have had a charming face but for the strongly-arched eyebrows and low forehead that gave him a sinister expression, scarlet lips of savage cruelty, and a twitching of the muscles peculiar to Corsicans, denoting that excessive irritability which makes them so prompt to kill in any sudden squabble.

Theodore, startled at the sound of that voice, raised his head, and at first thought himself the victim of a delusion; but as the experience of two months had accustomed him to the darkness of this stone box, he looked at the sham priest, and sighed deeply. He did not recognize Jacques Collin, whose face, scarred by the application of sulphuric acid, was not that of his old boss.

"It is really your Jacques; I am your confessor, and have come to get you off. Do not be such a ninny as to know me; and speak as if you were making a confession." He spoke with the utmost rapidity. "This young fellow is very much depressed; he is afraid to die, he will confess everything," said Jacques Collin, addressing the gendarme.

Bibi-Lupin dared not say a word for fear of being recognized.

"Say something to show me that you are he; you have nothing but his voice," said Theodore.

"You see, poor boy, he assures me that he is innocent," said Jacques Collin to Bibi-Lupin, who dared not speak for fear of being recognized.

"Sempre mi," said Jacques, returning close to Theodore, and speaking the word in his ear.

"Sempre ti," replied Theodore, giving the countersign. "Yes, you are the boss—"

"Did you do the trick?"

"Yes."

"Tell me the whole story, that I may see what can be done to save you; make haste, Jack Ketch is waiting."

The Corsican at once knelt down and pretended to be about to confess.

Bibi-Lupin did not know what to do, for the conversation was so rapid that it hardly took as much time as it does to read it. Theodore hastily told all the details of the crime, of which Jacques Collin knew nothing.

"The jury gave their verdict without proof," he said finally.

"Child! you want to argue when they are waiting to cut off your hair—"

"But I might have been sent to spout the wedge.—And that is the way they judge you!—and in Paris too!"

"But how did you do the job?" asked *Trompe-la-Mort*.

"Ah! there you are.—Since I saw you I made acquaintance with a girl, a Corsican, I met when I came to Paris."

"Men who are such fools as to love a woman," cried Jacques Collin, "always come to grief that way. They are tigers on the loose, tigers who blab and look at themselves in the glass.—You were a gaby."

"But—"

"Well, what good did she do you—that curse of a moll?"

"That duck of a girl—no taller than a bundle of firewood, as slippery as an eel, and as nimble as a monkey—got in at the top of the oven, and opened the front door. The dogs were well crammed with balls, and as dead as herrings. I settled the two women. Then when I got the swag, Ginetta locked the door and got out again by the oven."

"Such a clever dodge deserves life," said Jacques Collin, admiring the execution of the crime as a sculptor admires the modeling of a figure.

"And I was fool enough to waste all that cleverness for a thousand crowns!"

"No, for a woman," replied Jacques Collin. "I tell you, they deprive us of all our wits," and Jacques Collin eyed Theodore with a flashing glance of contempt.

"But you were not there!" said the Corsican; "I was all alone—"

"And do you love the slut?" asked Jacques Collin, feeling that the reproach was a just one.

"Oh! I want to live, but it is for you now rather than for her."

"Be quite easy, I am not called *Trompe-la-Mort* for nothing. I undertake the case."

"What! life?" cried the lad, lifting his swaddled hands towards the damp vault of the cell.

"My little Madeleine, prepare to be lagged for life (penal servitude)," replied Jacques Collin. "You can expect no less; they won't crown you with roses like a fatted ox. When they first set us down for Rochefort, it was because they wanted to be rid of us! But if I can get you ticketed for Toulon, you can get out and come back to Pantin (Paris), where I will find you a tidy way of living."

A sigh such as had rarely been heard under that inexorable roof struck the stones, which sent back the sound that has no fellow in music, to the ear of the astounded Bibi-Lupin.

"It is the effect of the absolution I promised him in return for his revelations," said Jacques Collin to the gendarme. "These Corsicans, monsieur, are full of faith! But he is as innocent as the Immaculate Babe, and I mean to try to save him."

"God bless you, Monsieur l'Abbe!" said Theodore in French.

Trompe-la-Mort, more Carlos Herrera, more the canon than ever, left the condemned cell, rushed back to the hall, and appeared before Monsieur Gault in affected horror.

"Indeed, sir, the young man is innocent; he has told me who the guilty person is! He was ready to die for a false point of honor—he is a Corsican! Go and beg the public prosecutor to grant me five minutes' interview. Monsieur de Granville cannot refuse to listen at once to a Spanish priest who is suffering so cruelly from the blunders of the French police."

"I will go," said Monsieur Gault, to the extreme astonishment of all the witnesses of this extraordinary scene.

HONORÉ DE BALZAC

"And meanwhile," said Jacques, "send me back to the prison-yard where I may finish the conversion of a criminal whose heart I have touched already—they have hearts, these people!"

This speech produced a sensation in all who heard it. The gendarmes, the registry clerk, Sanson, the warders, the executioner's assistant—all awaiting orders to go and get the scaffold ready—to rig up the machine, in prison slang—all these people, usually so indifferent, were agitated by very natural curiosity.

Just then the rattle of a carriage with high-stepping horses was heard; it stopped very suggestively at the gate of the Conciergerie on the quay. The door was opened, and the step let down in such haste, that every one supposed that some great personage had arrived. Presently a lady waving a sheet of blue paper came forward to the outer gate of the prison, followed by a footman and a chasseur. Dressed very handsomely, and all in black, with a veil over her bonnet, she was wiping her eyes with a floridly embroidered handkerchief.

Jacques Collin at once recognized Asie, or, to give the woman her true name, Jacqueline Collin, his aunt. This horrible old woman—worthy of her nephew—whose thoughts were all centered in the prisoner, and who was defending him with intelligence and mother-wit that were a match for the powers of the law, had a permit made out the evening before in the name of the Duchesse de Maufrigneuse's waiting-maid by the request of Monsieur de Serizy, allowing her to see Lucien de Rubempre, and the Abbe Carlos Herrera so soon as he should be brought out of the secret cells. On this the Colonel, who was the Governor-in-Chief of all the prisons had written a few words, and the mere color of the paper revealed powerful influences; for these permits, like theatre-tickets, differ in shape and appearance.

So the turnkey hastened to open the gate, especially when he saw the chasseur with his plumes and an uniform of green and gold as dazzling as a Russian General's, proclaiming a lady of aristocratic rank and almost royal birth.

"Oh, my dear Abbe!" exclaimed this fine lady, shedding a torrent of tears at the sight of the priest, "how could any one ever think of putting such a saintly man in here, even by mistake?"

The Governor took the permit and read, "Introduced by His Excellency the Comte de Serizy."

"Ah! Madame de San-Esteban, Madame la Marquise," cried Carlos Herrera, "what admirable devotion!"

"But, madame, such interviews are against the rules," said the good old Governor. And he intercepted the advance of this bale of black watered-silk and lace.

"But at such a distance!" said Jacques Collin, "and in your presence—" and he looked round at the group.

His aunt, whose dress might well dazzle the clerk, the Governor, the warders, and the gendarmes, stank of musk. She had on, besides a thousand crowns of lace, a black India cashmere shawl, worth six thousand francs. And her chasseur was marching up and down outside with the insolence of a lackey who knows that he is essential to an exacting princess. He spoke never a word to the footman, who stood by the gate on the quay, which is always open by day.

"What do you wish? What can I do?" said Madame de San-Esteban in the lingo agreed upon by this aunt and nephew.

This dialect consisted in adding terminations in ar or in or, or in al or in i to every word, whether French or slang, so as to disguise it by lengthening it. It was a diplomatic cipher adapted to speech.

"Put all the letters in some safe place; take out those that are most likely to compromise the ladies; come back, dressed very poorly, to the *Salle des Pas-Perdus*, and wait for my orders."

Asie, otherwise Jacqueline, knelt as if to receive his blessing, and the sham priest blessed his aunt with evengelical unction.

"Addio, Marchesa," said he aloud. "And," he added in their private language, "find Europe and Paccard with the seven hundred and fifty thousand francs they bagged. We must have them."

"Paccard is out there," said the pious Marquise, pointing to the chasseur, her eyes full of tears.

This intuitive comprehension brought not merely a smile to the man's lips, but a gesture of surprise; no one could astonish him but his aunt. The sham Marquise turned to the bystanders with the air of a woman accustomed to give herself airs.

"He is in despair at being unable to attend his son's funeral," said she in broken French, "for this monstrous miscarriage of justice has betrayed the saintly man's secret.—I am going to the funeral mass.— Here, monsieur," she added to the Governor, handing him a purse of gold, "this is to give your poor prisoners some comforts."

"What slap-up style!" her nephew whispered in approval.

Jacques Collin then followed the warder, who led him back to the yard.

Bibi-Lupin, quite desperate, had at last caught the eye of a real gendarme, to whom, since Jacques Collin had gone, he had been addressing significant "Ahems," and who took his place on guard in the condemned cell. But *Trompe-la-Mort's* sworn foe was released too late to see the great lady, who drove off in her dashing turn-out, and whose voice, though disguised, fell on his ear with a vicious twang.

"Three hundred shiners for the boarders," said the head warder, showing Bibi-Lupin the purse, which Monsieur Gault had handed over to his clerk.

"Let's see, Monsieur Jacomety," said Bibi-Lupin.

The police agent took the purse, poured out the money into his hand, and examined it curiously.

"Yes, it is gold, sure enough!" said he, "and a coat-of-arms on the purse! The scoundrel! How clever he is! What an all-round villain! He does us all brown—and all the time! He ought to be shot down like a dog!"

"Why, what's the matter?" asked the clerk, taking back the money.

"The matter! Why, the hussy stole it!" cried Bibi-Lupin, stamping with rage on the flags of the gateway.

The words produced a great sensation among the spectators, who were standing at a little distance from Monsieur Sanson. He, too, was still standing, his back against the large stove in the middle of the vaulted hall, awaiting the order to crop the felon's hair and erect the scaffold on the Place de Greve.

On re-entering the yard, Jacques Collin went towards his chums at a pace suited to a frequenter of the galleys.

"What have you on your mind?" said he to la Pouraille.

"My game is up," said the man, whom Jacques Collin led into a corner. "What I want now is a pal I can trust."

"What for?"

La Pouraille, after telling the tale of all his crimes, but in thieves' slang, gave an account of the murder and robbery of the two Crottats.

"You have my respect," said Jacques Collin. "The job was well done; but you seem to me to have blundered afterwards."

"In what way?"

"Well, having done the trick, you ought to have had a Russian passport, have made up as a Russian prince, bought a fine coach with a coat-of-arms on it, have boldly deposited your money in a bank, have got a letter of credit on Hamburg, and then have set out posting to

Hamburg with a valet, a ladies' maid, and your mistress disguised as a Russian princess. At Hamburg you should have sailed for Mexico. A chap of spirit, with two hundred and eighty thousand francs in gold, ought to be able to do what he pleases and go where he pleases, flathead!"

"Oh yes, you have such notions because you are the boss. Your nut is always square on your shoulders—but I—"

"In short, a word of good advice in your position is like broth to a dead man," said Jacques Collin, with a serpentlike gaze at his old pal.

"True enough!" said la Pouraille, looking dubious. "But give me the broth, all the same. If it does not suit my stomach, I can warm my feet in it—"

"Here you are nabbed by the Justice, with five robberies and three murders, the latest of them those of two rich and respectable folks. . . Now, juries do not like to see respectable folks killed. You will be put through the machine, and there is not a chance for you."

"I have heard all that," said la Pouraille lamentably.

"My aunt Jacqueline, with whom I have just exchanged a few words in the office, and who is, as you know, a mother to the pals, told me that the authorities mean to be quit of you; they are so much afraid of you."

"But I am rich now," said La Pouraille, with a simplicity which showed how convinced a thief is of his natural right to steal. "What are they afraid of?"

"We have no time for philosophizing," said Jacques Collin. "To come back to you—"

"What do you want with me?" said la Pouraille, interrupting his boss.

"You shall see. A dead dog is still worth something."

"To other people," said la Pouraille.

"I take you into my game!" said Jacques Collin.

"Well, that is something," said the murderer. "What next?"

"I do not ask you where your money is, but what you mean to do with it?"

La Pouraille looked into the convict's impenetrable eye, and Jacques coldly went on: "Have you a trip you are sweet upon, or a child, or a pal to be helped? I shall be outside within an hour, and I can do much for any one you want to be good-natured to."

La Pouraille still hesitated; he was delaying with indecision. Jacques Collin produced a clinching argument.

"Your whack of our money would be thirty thousand francs. Do you leave it to the pals? Do you bequeath it to anybody? Your share is safe; I can give it this evening to any one you leave it to."

The murderer gave a little start of satisfaction.

"I have him!" said Jacques Collin to himself. "But we have no time to play. Consider," he went on in la Pouraille's ear, "we have not ten minutes to spare, old chap; the public prosecutor is to send for me, and I am to have a talk with him. I have him safe, and can ring the old boss' neck. I am certain I shall save Madeleine."

"If you save Madeleine, my good boss, you can just as easily—"

"Don't waste your spittle," said Jacques Collin shortly. "Make your will."

"Well, then—I want to leave the money to la Gonore," replied la Pouraille piteously.

"What! Are you living with Moses' widow—the Jew who led the swindling gang in the South?" asked Jacques Collin.

For *Trompe-la-Mort*, like a great general, knew the person of every one of his army.

"That's the woman," said la Pouraille, much flattered.

"A pretty woman," said Jacques Collin, who knew exactly how to manage his dreadful tools. "The moll is a beauty; she is well informed, and stands by her mates, and a first-rate hand. Yes, la Gonore has made a new man of you! What a flat you must be to risk your nut when you have a trip like her at home! You noodle; you should have set up some respectable little shop and lived quietly.—And what does she do?"

"She is settled in the Rue Sainte-Barbe, managing a house—"

"And she is to be your legatee? Ah, my dear boy, this is what such sluts bring us to when we are such fools as to love them."

"Yes, but don't you give her anything till I am done for."

"It is a sacred trust," said Jacques Collin very seriously.

"And nothing to the pals?"

"Nothing! They blowed the gaff for me," answered la Pouraille vindictively.

"Who did? Shall I serve 'em out?" asked Jacques Collin eagerly, trying to rouse the last sentiment that survives in these souls till the last hour. "Who knows, old pal, but I might at the same time do them a bad turn and serve you with the public prosecutor?"

The murderer looked at his boss with amazed satisfaction.

"At this moment," the boss replied to this expressive look, "I am playing the game only for Theodore. When this farce is played out, old boy, I might do wonders for a chum—for you are a chum of mine."

"If I see that you really can put off the engagement for that poor little Theodore, I will do anything you choose—there!"

"But the trick is done. I am sure to save his head. If you want to get out of the scrape, you see, la Pouraille, you must be ready to do a good turn—we can do nothing single-handed—"

"That's true," said the felon.

His confidence was so strong, and his faith in the boss so fanatical, that he no longer hesitated. La Pouraille revealed the names of his accomplices, a secret hitherto well kept. This was all Jacques needed to know.

"That is the whole story. Ruffard was the third in the job with me and Godet—"

"Arrache-Laine?" cried Jacques Collin, giving Ruffard his nickname among the gang.

"That's the man.—And the blackguards peached because I knew where they had hidden their whack, and they did not know where mine was."

"You are making it all easy, my cherub!" said Jacques Collin.

"What?"

"Well," replied the master, "you see how wise it is to trust me entirely. Your revenge is now part of the hand I am playing.—I do not ask you to tell me where the dibs are, you can tell me at the last moment; but tell me all about Ruffard and Godet."

"You are, and you always will be, our boss; I have no secrets from you," replied la Pouraille. "My money is in the cellar at la Gonore's."

"And you are not afraid of her telling?"

"Why, get along! She knows nothing about my little game!" replied la Pouraille. "I make her drunk, though she is of the sort that would never blab even with her head under the knife.—But such a lot of gold—!"

"Yes, that turns the milk of the purest conscience," replied Jacques Collin.

"So I could do the job with no peepers to spy me. All the chickens were gone to roost. The shiners are three feet underground behind some wine-bottles. And I spread some stones and mortar over them."

"Good," said Jacques Collin. "And the others?"

"Ruffard's pieces are with la Gonore in the poor woman's bedroom, and he has her tight by that, for she might be nabbed as accessory after the fact, and end her days in Saint-Lazare."

"The villain! The reelers teach a thief what's what," said Jacques.

"Godet left his pieces at his sister's, a washerwoman; honest girl, she may be caught for five years in La Force without dreaming of it. The pal raised the tiles of the floor, put them back again, and guyed."

"Now do you know what I want you to do?" said Jacques Collin, with a magnetizing gaze at la Pouraille.

"What?"

"I want you to take Madeleine's job on your shoulders."

La Pouraille started queerly; but he at once recovered himself and stood at attention under the boss' eye.

"So you shy at that? You dare to spoil my game? Come, now! Four murders or three. Does it not come to the same thing?"

"Perhaps."

"By the God of good-fellowship, there is no blood in your veins! And I was thinking of saving you!"

"How?"

"Idiot, if we promise to give the money back to the family, you will only be lagged for life. I would not give a piece for your nut if we keep the blunt, but at this moment you are worth seven hundred thousand francs, you flat."

"Good for you, boss!" cried la Pouraille in great glee.

"And then," said Jacques Collin, "besides casting all the murders on Ruffard—Bibi-Lupin will be finely cold. I have him this time."

La Pouraille was speechless at this suggestion; his eyes grew round, and he stood like an image.

He had been three months in custody, and was committed for trial, and his chums at La Force, to whom he had never mentioned his accomplices, had given him such small comfort, that he was entirely hopeless after his examination, and this simple expedient had been quite overlooked by these prison-ridden minds. This semblance of a hope almost stupefied his brain.

"Have Ruffard and Godet had their spree yet? Have they forked out any of the yellow boys?" asked Jacques Collin.

"They dare not," replied la Pouraille. "The wretches are waiting till I am turned off. That is what my moll sent me word by la Biffe when she came to see le Biffon."

"Very well; we will have their whack of money in twenty-four hours," said Jacques Collin. "Then the blackguards cannot pay up, as you will; you will come out as white as snow, and they will be red with all that blood! By my kind offices you will seem a good sort of fellow led away by them. I shall have money enough of yours to prove alibis on the other counts, and when you are back on the hulks—for you are bound to go there—you must see about escaping. It is a dog's life, still it is life!"

La Pouraille's eyes glittered with suppressed delirium.

"With seven hundred thousand francs you can get a good many drinks," said Jacques Collin, making his pal quite drunk with hope.

"Ay, ay, boss!"

"I can bamboozle the Minister of Justice.—Ah, ha! Ruffard will shell out to do for a reeler. Bibi-Lupin is fairly gulled!"

"Very good, it is a bargain," said la Pouraille with savage glee. "You order, and I obey."

And he hugged Jacques Collin in his arms, while tears of joy stood in his eyes, so hopeful did he feel of saving his head.

"That is not all," said Jacques Collin; "the public prosecutor does not swallow everything, you know, especially when a new count is entered against you. The next thing is to bring a moll into the case by blowing the gaff."

"But how, and what for?"

"Do as I bid you; you will see." And *Trompe-la-Mort* briefly told the secret of the Nanterre murders, showing him how necessary it was to find a woman who would pretend to be Ginetta. Then he and la Pouraille, now in good spirits, went across to le Biffon.

"I know how sweet you are on la Biffe," said Jacques Collin to this man.

The expression in le Biffon's eyes was a horrible poem.

"What will she do while you are on the hulks?"

A tear sparkled in le Biffon's fierce eyes.

"Well, suppose I were to get her lodgings in the Lorcefe des Largues" (the women's La Force, i.e. les Madelonnettes or Saint-Lazare) "for a stretch, allowing that time for you to be sentenced and sent there, to arrive and to escape?"

"Even you cannot work such a miracle. She took no part in the job," replied la Biffe's partner.

"Oh, my good Biffon," said la Pouraille, "our boss is more powerful than God Almighty."

"What is your password for her?" asked Jacques Collin, with the assurance of a master to whom nothing can be refused.

"Sorgue a Pantin (night in Paris). If you say that she knows you have come from me, and if you want her to do as you bid her, show her a five-franc piece and say Tondif."

"She will be involved in the sentence on la Pouraille, and let off with a year in quod for snitching," said Jacques Collin, looking at la Pouraille.

La Pouraille understood his boss' scheme, and by a single look promised to persuade le Biffon to promote it by inducing la Biffe to take upon herself this complicity in the crime la Pouraille was prepared to confess.

"Farewell, my children. You will presently hear that I have saved my boy from Jack Ketch," said *Trompe-la-Mort*. "Yes, Jack Ketch and his hairdresser were waiting in the office to get Madeleine ready.—There," he added, "they have come to fetch me to go to the public prosecutor."

And, in fact, a warder came out of the gate and beckoned to this extraordinary man, who, in face of the young Corsican's danger, had recovered his own against his own society.

It is worthy of note that at the moment when Lucien's body was taken away from him, Jacques Collin had, with a crowning effort, made up his mind to attempt a last incarnation, not as a human being, but as a *thing*. He had at last taken the fateful step that Napoleon took on board the boat which conveyed him to the Bellerophon. And a strange concurrence of events aided this genius of evil and corruption in his undertaking.

But though the unlooked-for conclusion of this life of crime may perhaps be deprived of some of the marvelous effect which, in our day, can be given to a narrative only by incredible improbabilities, it is necessary, before we accompany Jacques Collin to the public prosecutor's room, that we should follow Madame Camusot in her visits during the time we have spent in the Conciergerie.

One of the obligations which the historian of manners must unfailingly observe is that of never marring the truth for the sake of dramatic arrangement, especially when the truth is so kind as to be in itself romantic. Social nature, particularly in Paris, allows of such freaks of chance, such complications of whimsical entanglements, that it constantly outdoes the most inventive imagination. The audacity of facts, by sheer improbability or indecorum, rises to heights of "situation" forbidden to art, unless they are softened, cleansed, and purified by the writer.

Madame Camusot did her utmost to dress herself for the morning almost in good taste—a difficult task for the wife of a judge who for six years has lived in a provincial town. Her object was to give no hold for criticism to the Marquise d'Espard or the Duchesse de Maufrigneuse, in a call so early as between eight and nine in the morning. Amelie Cecile Camusot, nee Thirion, it must be said, only half succeeded; and in a matter of dress is this not a twofold blunder?

Few people can imagine how useful the women of Paris are to ambitious men of every class; they are equally necessary in the world of fashion and the world of thieves, where, as we have seen, they fill a most important part. For instance, suppose that a man, not to find himself left in the lurch, must absolutely get speech within a given time with the high functionary who was of such immense importance under the Restoration, and who is to this day called the Keeper of the Seals—a man, let us say, in the most favorable position, a judge, that is to say, a man familiar with the way of things. He is compelled to seek out the presiding judge of a circuit, or some private or official secretary, and prove to him his need of an immediate interview. But is a Keeper of the Seals ever visible "that very minute"? In the middle of the day, if he is not at the Chamber, he is at the Privy Council, or signing papers, or hearing a case. In the early morning he is out, no one knows where. In the evening he has public and private engagements. If every magistrate could claim a moment's interview under any pretext that might occur to him, the Supreme Judge would be besieged.

The purpose of a private and immediate interview is therefore submitted to the judgment of one of those mediatory potentates who are but an obstacle to be removed, a door that can be unlocked, so long as it is not held by a rival. A woman at once goes to another woman; she can get straight into her bedroom if she can arouse the curiosity of mistress or maid, especially if the mistress is under the stress of a strong interest or pressing necessity.

Call this female potentate Madame la Marquise d'Espard, with whom a Minister has to come to terms; this woman writes a little scented note, which her man-servant carries to the Minister's man-servant. The note greets the Minister on his waking, and he reads it at once. Though the Minister has business to attend to, the man is enchanted to have a reason for calling on one of the Queens of Paris, one of the Powers of the Faubourg Saint-Germain, one of the favorites of the Dauphiness, of MADAME, or of the King. Casimir Perier, the only real statesman of the

Revolution of July, would leave anything to call on a retired Gentleman of the bed-chamber to King Charles X.

This theory accounts for the magical effect of the words:

"Madame,—Madame Camusot, on very important business, which she says you know of," spoken in Madame d'Espard's ear by her maid, who thought she was awake.

And the Marquise desired that Amelie should be shown in at once.

The magistrate's wife was attentively heard when she began with these words:

"Madame la Marquise, we have ruined ourselves by trying to avenge you—"

"How is that, my dear?" replied the Marquise, looking at Madame Camusot in the dim light that fell through the half-open door. "You are vastly sweet this morning in that little bonnet. Where do you get that shape?"

"You are very kind, madame.—Well, you know that Camusot's way of examining Lucien de Rubempre drove the young man to despair, and he hanged himself in prison."

"Oh, what will become of Madame de Serizy?" cried the Marquise, affecting ignorance, that she might hear the whole story once more.

"Alas! they say she is quite mad," said Amelie. "If you could persuade the Lord Keeper to send for my husband this minute, by special messenger, to meet him at the Palais, the Minister would hear some strange mysteries, and report them, no doubt, to the King. . . Then Camusot's enemies would be reduced to silence."

"But who are Camusot's enemies?" asked Madame d'Espard.

"The public prosecutor, and now Monsieur de Serizy."

"Very good, my dear," replied Madame d'Espard, who owed to Monsieur de Granville and the Comte de Serizy her defeat in the disgraceful proceedings by which she had tried to have her husband treated as a lunatic, "I will protect you; I never forget either my foes or my friends."

She rang; the maid drew open the curtains, and daylight flooded the room; she asked for her desk, and the maid brought it in. The Marquise hastily scrawled a few lines.

"Tell Godard to go on horseback, and carry this note to the Chancellor's office.—There is no reply," said she to the maid.

The woman went out of the room quickly, but, in spite of the order, remained at the door for some minutes.

"There are great mysteries going forward then?" asked Madame d'Espard. "Tell me all about it, dear child. Has Clotilde de Grandlieu put a finger in the pie?"

"You will know everything from the Lord Keeper, for my husband has told me nothing. He only told me he was in danger. It would be better for us that Madame de Serizy should die than that she should remain mad."

"Poor woman!" said the Marquise. "But was she not mad already?"

Women of the world, by a hundred ways of pronouncing the same phrase, illustrate to attentive hearers the infinite variety of musical modes. The soul goes out into the voice as it does into the eyes; it vibrates in light and in air—the elements acted on by the eyes and the voice. By the tone she gave to the two words, "Poor woman!" the Marquise betrayed the joy of satisfied hatred, the pleasure of triumph. Oh! what woes did she not wish to befall Lucien's protectress. Revenge, which nothing can assuage, which can survive the person hated, fills us with dark terrors. And Madame Camusot, though harsh herself, vindictive, and quarrelsome, was overwhelmed. She could find nothing to say, and was silent.

"Diane told me that Leontine went to the prison," Madame d'Espard went on. "The dear Duchess is in despair at such a scandal, for she is so foolish as to be very fond of Madame de Serizy; however, it is comprehensible: they both adored that little fool Lucien at about the same time, and nothing so effectually binds or severs two women as worshiping at the same altar. And our dear friend spent two hours yesterday in Leontine's room. The poor Countess, it seems, says dreadful things! I heard that it was disgusting! A woman of rank ought not to give way to such attacks.—Bah! A purely physical passion.—The Duchess came to see me as pale as death; she really was very brave. There are monstrous things connected with this business."

"My husband will tell the Keeper of the Seals all he knows for his own justification, for they wanted to save Lucien, and he, Madame la Marquise, did his duty. An examining judge always has to question people in private at the time fixed by law! He had to ask the poor little wretch something, if only for form's sake, and the young fellow did not understand, and confessed things—"

"He was an impertinent fool!" said Madame d'Espard in a hard tone.

The judge's wife kept silence on hearing this sentence.

"Though we failed in the matter of the Commission in Lunacy, it was not Camusot's fault, I shall never forget that," said the Marquise after a pause. "It was Lucien, Monsieur de Serizy, Monsieur de Bauvan, and Monsieur de Granville who overthrew us. With time God will be on my side; all those people will come to grief.—Be quite easy, I will send the Chevalier d'Espard to the Keeper of the Seals that he may desire your husbands's presence immediately, if that is of any use."

"Oh! madame—"

"Listen," said the Marquise. "I promise you the ribbon of the Legion of Honor at once—to-morrow. It will be a conspicuous testimonial of satisfaction with your conduct in this affair. Yes, it implies further blame on Lucien; it will prove him guilty. Men do not commonly hang themselves for the pleasure of it.—Now, good-bye, my pretty dear—"

Ten minutes later Madame Camusot was in the bedroom of the beautiful Diane de Maufrigneuse, who had not gone to bed till one, and at nine o'clock had not yet slept.

However insensible duchesses may be, even these women, whose hearts are of stone, cannot see a friend a victim to madness without being painfully impressed by it.

And besides, the connection between Diane and Lucien, though at an end now eighteen months since, had left such memories with the Duchess that the poor boy's disastrous end had been to her also a fearful blow. All night Diane had seen visions of the beautiful youth, so charming, so poetical, who had been so delightful a lover—painted as Leontine depicted him, with the vividness of wild delirium. She had letters from Lucien that she had kept, intoxicating letters worthy to compare with Mirabeau's to Sophie, but more literary, more elaborate, for Lucien's letters had been dictated by the most powerful of passions—Vanity. Having the most bewitching of duchesses for his mistress, and seeing her commit any folly for him—secret follies, of course—had turned Lucien's head with happiness. The lover's pride had inspired the poet. And the Duchess had treasured these touching letters, as some old men keep indecent prints, for the sake of their extravagant praise of all that was least duchess-like in her nature.

"And he died in a squalid prison!" cried she to herself, putting the letters away in a panic when she heard her maid knocking gently at her door.

"Madame Camusot," said the woman, "on business of the greatest importance to you, Madame la Duchesse."

Diane sprang to her feet in terror.

"Oh!" cried she, looking at Amelie, who had assumed a duly condoling air, "I guess it all—my letters! It is about my letters. Oh, my letters, my letters!"

She sank on to a couch. She remembered now how, in the extravagance of her passion, she had answered Lucien in the same vein, had lauded the man's poetry as he has sung the charms of the woman, and in what a strain!

"Alas, yes, madame, I have come to save what is dearer to you than life—your honor. Compose yourself and get dressed, we must go to the Duchesse de Grandlieu; happily for you, you are not the only person compromised."

"But at the Palais, yesterday, Leontine burned, I am told, all the letters found at poor Lucien's."

"But, madame, behind Lucien there was Jacques Collin!" cried the magistrate's wife. "You always forget that horrible companionship which beyond question led to that charming and lamented young man's end. That Machiavelli of the galleys never loses his head! Monsieur Camusot is convinced that the wretch has in some safe hiding-place all the most compromising letters written by you ladies to his—"

"His friend," the Duchess hastily put in. "You are right, my child. We must hold council at the Grandlieus'. We are all concerned in this matter, and Serizy happily will lend us his aid."

Extreme peril—as we have observed in the scenes in the Conciergerie—has a hold over the soul not less terrible than that of powerful reagents over the body. It is a mental Voltaic battery. The day, perhaps, is not far off when the process shall be discovered by which feeling is chemically converted into a fluid not unlike the electric fluid.

The phenomena were the same in the convict and the Duchess. This crushed, half-dying woman, who had not slept, who was so particular over her dressing, had recovered the strength of a lioness at bay, and the presence of mind of a general under fire. Diane chose her gown and got through her dressing with the alacrity of a grisette who is her own waiting-woman. It was so astounding, that the lady's-maid stood for a moment stock-still, so greatly was she surprised to see her mistress in her shift, not ill pleased perhaps to let the judge's wife discern through the thin cloud of lawn a form as white and as perfect as that of Canova's Venus. It was like a gem in a fold of tissue paper. Diane suddenly remembered where a pair of stays had been put that fastened in front, sparing a woman in a hurry the ill-spent time and fatigue of being laced. She had arranged the lace trimming of her shift and the fulness of the bosom by the time the maid had fetched her petticoat, and crowned the work by putting on her gown. While Amelie, at a sign from the maid, hooked the bodice behind, the woman brought out a pair of thread stockings, velvet boots, a shawl, and a bonnet. Amelie and the maid each drew on a stocking.

"You are the loveliest creature I ever saw!" said Amelie, insidiously kissing Diane's elegant and polished knee with an eager impulse.

"Madame has not her match!" cried the maid.

"There, there, Josette, hold your tongue," replied the Duchess.— "Have you a carriage?" she went on, to Madame Camusot. "Then come along, my dear, we can talk on the road."

And the Duchess ran down the great stairs of the Hotel de Cadignan, putting on her gloves as she went—a thing she had never been known to do.

"To the Hotel de Grandlieu, and drive fast," said she to one of her men, signing to him to get up behind.

The footman hesitated—it was a hackney coach.

"Ah! Madame la Duchesse, you never told me that the young man had letters of yours. Otherwise Camusot would have proceeded differently. . ."

"Leontine's state so occupied my thoughts that I forgot myself entirely. The poor woman was almost crazy the day before yesterday; imagine the effect on her of this tragical termination. If you could only know, child, what a morning we went through yesterday! It is enough to make one forswear love!—Yesterday Leontine and I were dragged across Paris by a horrible old woman, an old-clothes buyer, a domineering creature, to that stinking and blood-stained sty they call the Palace of Justice, and I said to her as I took her there: 'Is not this enough to make us fall on our knees and cry out like Madame de Nucingen, when she went through one of those awful Mediterranean storms on her way to Naples, "Dear God, save me this time, and never again—!"'

"These two days will certainly have shortened my life.—What fools we are ever to write!—But love prompts us; we receive pages that fire the heart through the eyes, and everything is in a blaze! Prudence deserts us—we reply—"

"But why reply when you can act?" said Madame Camusot.

"It is grand to lose oneself utterly!" cried the Duchess with pride. "It is the luxury of the soul."

"Beautiful women are excusable," said Madame Camusot modestly. "They have more opportunities of falling than we have."

The Duchess smiled.

"We are always too generous," said Diane de Maufrigneuse. "I shall do just like that odious Madame d'Espard."

"And what does she do?" asked the judge's wife, very curious.

"She has written a thousand love-notes—"

"So many!" exclaimed Amelie, interrupting the Duchess.

"Well, my dear, and not a word that could compromise her is to be found in any one of them."

"You would be incapable of maintaining such coldness, such caution," said Madame Camusot. "You are a woman; you are one of those angels who cannot stand out against the devil—"

"I have made a vow to write no more letters. I never in my life wrote to anybody but that unhappy Lucien.—I will keep his letters to my dying day! My dear child, they are fire, and sometimes we want—"

"But if they were found!" said Amelie, with a little shocked expression.

"Oh! I should say they were part of a romance I was writing; for I have copied them all, my dear, and burned the originals."

"Oh, madame, as a reward allow me to read them."

"Perhaps, child," said the Duchess. "And then you will see that he did not write such letters as those to Leontine."

This speech was woman all the world over, of every age and every land.

MADAME CAMUSOT, LIKE THE FROG in la Fontaine's fable, was ready to burst her skin with the joy of going to the Grandlieus' in the society of the beautiful Diane de Maufrigneuse. This morning she would forge one of the links that are so needful to ambition. She could already hear herself addressed as Madame la Presidente. She felt the ineffable gladness of triumphing over stupendous obstacles, of which the greatest was her husband's ineptitude, as yet unrevealed, but to her well known. To win success for a second-rate man! that is to a woman— as to a king—the delight which tempts great actors when they act a bad play a hundred times over. It is the very drunkenness of egoism. It is in a way the Saturnalia of power.

Power can prove itself to itself only by the strange misapplication which leads it to crown some absurd person with the laurels of success while insulting genius—the only strong-hold which power cannot touch. The knighting of Caligula's horse, an imperial farce, has been, and always will be, a favorite performance.

In a few minutes Diane and Amelie had exchanged the elegant disorder of the fair Diane's bedroom for the severe but dignified and splendid austerity of the Duchesse de Grandlieu's rooms.

She, a Portuguese, and very pious, always rose at eight to attend mass at the little church of Sainte-Valere, a chapelry to Saint-Thomas d'Aquin, standing at that time on the esplanade of the Invalides. This chapel, now destroyed, was rebuilt in the Rue de Bourgogne, pending the building of a Gothic church to be dedicated to Sainte-Clotilde.

On hearing the first words spoken in her ear by Diane de Maufrigneuse, this saintly lady went to find Monsieur de Grandlieu, and brought him back at once. The Duke threw a flashing look at Madame Camusot, one of those rapid glances with which a man of the world can guess at a whole existence, or often read a soul. Amelie's dress greatly helped the Duke to decipher the story of a middle-class life, from Alencon to Mantes, and from Mantes to Paris.

Oh! if only the lawyer's wife could have understood this gift in dukes, she could never have endured that politely ironical look; she saw the politeness only. Ignorance shares the privileges of fine breeding.

"This is Madame Camusot, a daughter of Thirion's—one of the Cabinet ushers," said the Duchess to her husband.

The Duke bowed with extreme politeness to the wife of a legal official, and his face became a little less grave.

The Duke had rung for his valet, who now came in.

"Go to the Rue Saint-Honore: take a coach. Ring at a side door, No. 10. Tell the man who opens the door that I beg his master will come here, and if the gentleman is at home, bring him back with you.—Mention my name, that will remove all difficulties."

"And do not be gone more than a quarter of an hour in all."

Another footman, the Duchess' servant, came in as soon as the other was gone.

"Go from me to the Duc de Chaulieu, and send up this card."

The Duke gave him a card folded down in a particular way. When the two friends wanted to meet at once, on any urgent or confidential business which would not allow of note-writing, they used this means of communication.

Thus we see that similar customs prevail in every rank of society, and differ only in manner, civility, and small details. The world of fashion, too, has its argot, its slang; but that slang is called style.

"Are you quite sure, madame, of the existence of the letters you say were written by Mademoiselle Clotilde de Grandlieu to this young man?" said the Duc de Grandlieu.

And he cast a look at Madame Camusot as a sailor casts a sounding line.

"I have not seen them, but there is reason to fear it," replied Madame Camusot, quaking.

"My daughter can have written nothing we would not own to!" said the Duchess.

"Poor Duchess!" thought Diane, with a glance at the Duke that terrified him.

"What do you think, my dear little Diane?" said the Duke in a whisper, as he led her away into a recess.

"Clotilde is so crazy about Lucien, my dear friend, that she had made an assignation with him before leaving. If it had not been for little Lenoncourt, she would perhaps have gone off with him into the forest of Fontainebleau. I know that Lucien used to write letters to her which were enough to turn the brain of a saint.—We are three daughters of Eve in the coils of the serpent of letter-writing."

The Duke and Diane came back to the Duchess and Madame Camusot, who were talking in undertones. Amelie, following the advice of the Duchesse de Maufrigneuse, affected piety to win the proud lady's favor.

"We are at the mercy of a dreadful escaped convict!" said the Duke, with a peculiar shrug. "This is what comes of opening one's house to people one is not absolutely sure of. Before admitting an acquaintance, one ought to know all about his fortune, his relations, all his previous history—"

This speech is the moral of my story—from the aristocratic point of view.

"That is past and over," said the Duchesse de Maufrigneuse. "Now we must think of saving that poor Madame de Serizy, Clotilde, and me—"

"We can but wait for Henri; I have sent to him. But everything really depends on the man Gentil is gone to fetch. God grant that man may be in Paris!—Madame," he added to Madame Camusot, "thank you so much for having thought of us—"

This was Madame Camusot's dismissal. The daughter of the court usher had wit enough to understand the Duke; she rose. But the Duchess de Maufrigneuse, with the enchanting grace which had won her so much friendship and discretion, took Amelie by the hand as if to show her, in a way, to the Duke and Duchess.

"On my own account," said she, "to say nothing of her having been up before daybreak to save us all, I may ask for more than a remembrance for my little Madame Camusot. In the first place, she has already done me such a service as I cannot forget; and then she is wholly devoted to our side, she and her husband. I have promised that her Camusot shall have advancement, and I beg you above everything to help him on, for my sake."

"You need no such recommendation," said the Duke to Madame Camusot. "The Grandlieus always remember a service done them. The King's adherents will ere long have a chance of distinguishing themselves; they will be called upon to prove their devotion; your husband will be placed in the front—"

Madame Camusot withdrew, proud, happy, puffed up to suffocation. She reached home triumphant; she admired herself, she made light of the public prosecutor's hostility. She said to herself:

"Supposing we were to send Monsieur de Granville flying—"

It was high time for Madame Camusot to vanish. The Duc de Chaulieu, one of the King's prime favorites, met the bourgeoise on the outer steps.

"Henri," said the Duc de Grandlieu when he heard his friend announced, "make haste, I beg of you, to get to the Chateau, try to see the King—the business of this;" and he led the Duke into the window-recess, where he had been talking to the airy and charming Diane.

Now and then the Duc de Chaulieu glanced in the direction of the flighty Duchess, who, while talking to the pious Duchess and submitting to be lectured, answered the Duc de Chaulieu's expressive looks.

"My dear child," said the Duc de Grandlieu to her at last, the *aside* being ended, "do be good! Come, now," and he took Diane's hands, "observe the proprieties of life, do not compromise yourself any more, write no letters. Letters, my dear, have caused as much private woe as public mischief. What might be excusable in a girl like Clotilde, in love for the first time, had no excuse in—"

"An old soldier who has been under fire," said Diane with a pout.

This grimace and the Duchess' jest brought a smile to the face of the two much-troubled Dukes, and of the pious Duchess herself.

"But for four years I have never written a billet-doux.—Are we saved?" asked Diane, who hid her curiosity under this childishness.

"Not yet," said the Duc de Chaulieu. "You have no notion how difficult it is to do an arbitrary thing. In a constitutional king it is what infidelity is in a wife: it is adultery."

"The fascinating sin," said the Duc de Grandlieu.

"Forbidden fruit!" said Diane, smiling. "Oh! how I wish I were the Government, for I have none of that fruit left—I have eaten it all."

"Oh! my dear, my dear!" said the elder Duchess, "you really go too far."

The two Dukes, hearing a coach stop at the door with the clatter of horses checked in full gallop, bowed to the ladies and left them, going into the Duc de Grandlieu's study, whither came the gentleman from the Rue Honore-Chevalier—no less a man than the chief of the King's private police, the obscure but puissant Corentin.

"Go on," said the Duc de Grandlieu; "go first, Monsieur de Saint-Denis."

Corentin, surprised that the Duke should have remembered him, went forward after bowing low to the two noblemen.

"Always about the same individual, or about his concerns, my dear sir," said the Duc de Grandlieu.

"But he is dead," said Corentin.

"He has left a partner," said the Duc de Chaulieu, "a very tough customer."

"The convict Jacques Collin," replied Corentin.

"Will you speak, Ferdinand?" said the Duke de Chaulieu to his friend.

"That wretch is an object of fear," said the Duc de Grandlieu, "for he has possessed himself, so as to be able to levy blackmail, of the letters written by Madame de Serizy and Madame de Maufrigneuse to Lucien Chardon, that man's tool. It would seem that it was a matter of system in the young man to extract passionate letters in return for his own, for I am told that Mademoiselle de Grandlieu had written some—at least, so we fear—and we cannot find out from her—she is gone abroad."

"That little young man," replied Corentin, "was incapable of so much foresight. That was a precaution due to the Abbe Carlos Herrera."

Corentin rested his elbow on the arm of the chair on which he was sitting, and his head on his hand, meditating.

"Money!—The man has more than we have," said he. "Esther Gobseck served him as a bait to extract nearly two million francs from that well of gold called Nucingen.—Gentlemen, get me full legal powers, and I will rid you of the fellow."

"And—the letters?" asked the Duc de Grandlieu.

"Listen to me, gentlemen," said Corentin, standing up, his weasel-face betraying his excitement.

He thrust his hands into the pockets of his black doeskin trousers, shaped over the shoes. This great actor in the historical drama of the day had only stopped to put on a waistcoat and frock-coat, and had not changed his morning trousers, so well he knew how grateful men can be for immediate action in certain cases. He walked up and down the room quite at his ease, haranguing loudly, as if he had been alone.

"He is a convict. He could be sent off to Bicetre without trial, and put in solitary confinement, without a soul to speak to, and left there to die.—But he may have given instructions to his adherents, foreseeing this possibility."

"But he was put into the secret cells," said the Duc de Grandlieu, "the moment he was taken into custody at that woman's house."

"Is there such a thing as a secret cell for such a fellow as he is?" said Corentin. "He is a match for—for me!"

"What is to be done?" said the Dukes to each other by a glance.

"We can send the scoundrel back to the hulks at once—to Rochefort; he will be dead in six months! Oh! without committing any crime," he added, in reply to a gesture on the part of the Duc de Grandlieu. "What do you expect? A convict cannot hold out more than six months of a hot summer if he is made to work really hard among the marshes of the Charente. But this is of no use if our man has taken precautions with regard to the letters. If the villain has been suspicious of his foes, and that is probable, we must find out what steps he has taken. Then, if the present holder of the letters is poor, he is open to bribery. So, no, we must make Jacques Collin speak. What a duel! He will beat me. The better plan would be to purchase those letters by exchange for another document—a letter of reprieve—and to place the man in my gang. Jacques Collin is the only man alive who is clever enough to come after me, poor Contenson and dear old Peyrade both being dead! Jacques Collin killed those two unrivaled spies on purpose, as it were, to make a place for himself. So, you see, gentlemen, you must give me a free hand. Jacques Collin is in the Conciergerie. I will go to see Monsieur de Granville in his Court. Send some one you can trust to meet me there, for I must have a letter to show to Monsieur de Granville, who knows nothing of me. I will hand the letter to the President of the Council, a very impressive sponsor. You have half an hour before you, for I need half an hour to dress, that is to say, to make myself presentable to the eyes of the public prosecutor."

"Monsieur," said the Duc de Chaulieu, "I know your wonderful skill. I only ask you to say Yes or No. Will you be bound to succeed?"

"Yes, if I have full powers, and your word that I shall never be questioned about the matter.—My plan is laid."

This sinister reply made the two fine gentlemen shiver. "Go on, then, monsieur," said the Duc de Chaulieu. "You can set down the charges of the case among those you are in the habit of undertaking."

Corentin bowed and went away.

Henri de Lenoncourt, for whom Ferdinand de Grandlieu had a carriage brought out, went off forthwith to the King, whom he was privileged to see at all times in right of his office.

Thus all the various interests that had got entangled from the highest to the lowest ranks of society were to meet presently in Monsieur de Granville's room at the Palais, all brought together by necessity embodied in three men—Justice in Monsieur de Granville, and the family in Corentin, face to face with Jacques Collin, the terrible foe who represented social crime in its fiercest energy.

What a duel is that between justice and arbitrary wills on one side and the hulks and cunning on the other! The hulks—symbolical of that daring which throws off calculation and reflection, which avails itself of any means, which has none of the hyprocrisy of high-handed justice, but is the hideous outcome of the starving stomach—the swift and bloodthirsty pretext of hunger. Is it not attack as against self-protection, theft as against property? The terrible quarrel between the social state and the natural man, fought out on the narrowest possible ground! In short, it is a terrible and vivid image of those compromises, hostile to social interests, which the representatives of authority, when they lack power, submit to with the fiercest rebels.

When Monsieur Camusot was announced, the public prosecutor signed that he should be admitted. Monsieur de Granville had foreseen this visit, and wished to come to an understanding with the examining judge as to how to wind up this business of Lucien's death. The end could no longer be that on which he had decided the day before in agreement with Camusot, before the suicide of the hapless poet.

"Sit down, Monsieur Camusot," said Monsieur de Granville, dropping into his armchair. The public prosecutor, alone with the inferior judge, made no secret of his depressed state. Camusot looked at Monsieur de Granville and observed his almost livid pallor, and such utter fatigue, such complete prostration, as betrayed greater suffering perhaps than that of the condemned man to whom the clerk had announced the rejection of his appeal. And yet that announcement, in the forms of justice, is a much as to say, "Prepare to die; your last hour has come."

"I will return later, Monsieur le Comte," said Camusot. "Though business is pressing—"

"No, stay," replied the public prosecutor with dignity. "A magistrate, monsieur, must accept his anxieties and know how to hide them. I was in fault if you saw any traces of agitation in me—"

Camusot bowed apologetically.

"God grant you may never know these crucial perplexities of our life. A man might sink under less! I have just spent the night with one of my most intimate friends.—I have but two friends, the Comte Octave de Bauvan and the Comte de Serizy.—We sat together, Monsieur de Serizy, the Count, and I, from six in the evening till six this morning, taking it in turns to go from the drawing-room to Madame de Serizy's bedside, fearing each time that we might find her dead or irremediably insane. Desplein, Bianchon, and Sinard never left the room, and she has two nurses. The Count worships his wife. Imagine the night I have spent, between a woman crazy with love and a man crazy with despair. And a statesman's despair is not like that of an idiot. Serizy, as calm as if he were sitting in his place in council, clutched his chair to force himself to show us an unmoved countenance, while sweat stood over the brows bent by so much hard thought.—Worn out by want of sleep, I dozed from five till half-past seven, and I had to be here by half-past eight to warrant an execution. Take my word for it, Monsieur Camusot, when a judge has been toiling all night in such gulfs of sorrow, feeling the heavy hand of God on all human concerns, and heaviest on noble souls, it is hard to sit down here, in front of a desk, and say in cold blood, 'Cut off a head at four o'clock! Destroy one of God's creatures full of life, health, and strength!'— And yet this is my duty! Sunk in grief myself, I must order the scaffold—

"The condemned wretch cannot know that his judge suffers anguish equal to his own. At this moment he and I, linked by a sheet of paper—I, society avenging itself; he, the crime to be avenged—embody the same duty seen from two sides; we are two lives joined for the moment by the sword of the law.

"Who pities the judge's deep sorrow? Who can soothe it? Our glory is to bury it in the depth of our heart. The priest with his life given to God, the soldier with a thousand deaths for his country's sake, seem to me far happier than the magistrate with his doubts and fears and appalling responsibility.

"You know who the condemned man is?" Monsieur de Granville went on. "A young man of seven-and-twenty—as handsome as he who killed himself yesterday, and as fair; condemned against all our anticipations, for the only proof against him was his concealment of the stolen goods. Though sentenced, the lad will confess nothing! For seventy days he has held out against every test, constantly declaring that he is innocent. For two months I have felt two heads on my shoulders! I would give a year of my life if he would confess, for juries need encouragement; and imagine what a blow it would be to justice if some day it should be discovered that the crime for which he is punished was committed by another.

"In Paris everything is so terribly important; the most trivial incidents in the law courts have political consequences.

"The jury, an institution regarded by the legislators of the Revolution as a source of strength, is, in fact, an instrument of social ruin, for it fails in action; it does not sufficiently protect society. The jury trifles with its functions. The class of jurymen is divided into two parties, one averse to capital punishment; the result is a total upheaval of true equality in administration of the law. Parricide, a most horrible crime, is in some departments treated with leniency, while in others a common murder, so to speak, is punished with death. [There are in penal servitude twenty-three parricides who have been allowed the benefit of *extenuating circumstances*.] And what would happen if here in Paris, in our home district, an innocent man should be executed!"

"He is an escaped convict," said Monsieur Camusot, diffidently.

"The Opposition and the Press would make him a paschal lamb!" cried Monsieur de Granville; "and the Opposition would enjoy white-washing him, for he is a fanatical Corsican, full of his native notions, and his murders were a *Vendetta*. In that island you may kill your enemy, and think yourself, and be thought, a very good man.

"A thorough-paced magistrate, I tell you, is an unhappy man. They ought to live apart from all society, like the pontiffs of old. The world should never see them but at fixed hours, leaving their cells, grave, and old, and venerable, passing sentence like the high priests of antiquity, who combined in their person the functions of judicial and sacerdotal authority. We should be accessible only in our high seat.—As it is, we are to be seen every day, amused or unhappy, like other men. We are to be found in drawing-rooms and at home, as ordinary citizens, moved by our passions; and we seem, perhaps, more grotesque than terrible."

This bitter cry, broken by pauses and interjections, and emphasized by gestures which gave it an eloquence impossible to reduce to writing, made Camusot's blood run chill.

"And I, monsieur," said he, "began yesterday my apprenticeship to the sufferings of our calling.—I could have died of that young fellow's death. He misunderstood my wish to be lenient, and the poor wretch committed himself."

"Ah, you ought never to have examined him!" cried Monsieur de Granville; "it is so easy to oblige by doing nothing."

"And the law, monsieur?" replied Camusot. "He had been in custody two days."

"The mischief is done," said the public prosecutor. "I have done my best to remedy what is indeed irremediable. My carriage and servants are following the poor weak poet to the grave. Serizy has sent his too; nay, more, he accepts the duty imposed on him by the unfortunate boy, and will act as his executor. By promising this to his wife he won from her a gleam of returning sanity. And Count Octave is attending the funeral in person."

"Well, then, Monsieur le Comte," said Camusot, "let us complete our work. We have a very dangerous man on our hands. He is Jacques Collin—and you know it as well as I do. The ruffian will be recognized—"

"Then we are lost!" cried Monsieur de Granville.

"He is at this moment shut up with your condemned murderer, who, on the hulks, was to him what Lucien has been in Paris—a favorite protege. Bibi-Lupin, disguised as a gendarme, is watching the interview."

"What business has the superior police to interfere?" said the public prosecutor. "He has no business to act without my orders!"

"All the Conciergerie must know that we have caught Jacques Collin.—Well, I have come on purpose to tell you that this daring felon has in his possession the most compromising letters of Lucien's correspondence with Madame de Serizy, the Duchesse de Maufrigneuse, and Mademoiselle Clotilde de Grandlieu."

"Are you sure of that?" asked Monsieur de Granville, his face full of pained surprise.

"You shall hear, Monsieur le Comte, what reason I have to fear such a misfortune. When I untied the papers found in the young man's rooms, Jacques Collin gave a keen look at the parcel, and smiled with satisfaction in a way that no examining judge could misunderstand. So deep a villain as Jacques Collin takes good care not to let such a weapon slip through his fingers. What is to be said if these documents should be placed in the hands of counsel chosen by that rascal from among the foes of the government and the aristocracy!—My wife, to whom the Duchesse de Maufrigneuse has shown so much kindness, is gone to warn her, and by this time they must be with the Grandlieus holding council."

"But we cannot possibly try the man!" cried the public prosecutor, rising and striding up and down the room. "He must have put the papers in some safe place—"

"I know where," said Camusot.

These words finally effaced every prejudice the public prosecutor had felt against him.

"Well, then—" said Monsieur de Granville, sitting down again.

"On my way here this morning I reflected deeply on this miserable business. Jacques Collin has an aunt—an aunt by nature, not putative—a woman concerning whom the superior police have communicated a report to the Prefecture. He is this woman's pupil and idol; she is his father's sister, her name is Jacqueline Collin. This wretched woman carries on a trade as a wardrobe purchaser, and by the connection this business has secured her she gets hold of many family secrets. If Jacques Collin has intrusted those papers, which would be his salvation, to any one's keeping, it is to that of this creature. Have her arrested."

The public prosecutor gave Camusot a keen look, as much as to say, "This man is not such a fool as I thought him; he is still young, and does not yet know how to handle the reins of justice."

"But," Camusot went on, "in order to succeed, we must give up all the plans we laid yesterday, and I came to take your advice—your orders—"

The public prosecutor took up his paper-knife and tapped it against the edge of the table with one of the tricky movements familiar to thoughtful men when they give themselves up to meditation.

"Three noble families involved!" he exclaimed. "We must not make the smallest blunder!—You are right: as a first step let us act on Fouché's principle, 'Arrest!'—and Jacques Collin must at once be sent back to the secret cells."

"That is to proclaim him a convict and to ruin Lucien's memory!"

"What a desperate business!" said Monsieur de Granville. "There is danger on every side."

At this instant the governor of the Conciergerie came in, not without knocking; and the private room of a public prosecutor is so well guarded, that only those concerned about the courts may even knock at the door.

"Monsieur le Comte," said Monsieur Gault, "the prisoner calling himself Carlos Herrera wishes to speak with you."

"Has he had communication with anybody?" asked Monsieur de Granville.

"With all the prisoners, for he has been out in the yard since about half-past seven. And he has seen the condemned man, who would seem to have talked to him."

A speech of Camusot's, which recurred to his mind like a flash of light, showed Monsieur de Granville all the advantage that might be taken of a confession of intimacy between Jacques Collin and Theodore Calvi to obtain the letters. The public prosecutor, glad to have an excuse for postponing the execution, beckoned Monsieur Gault to his side.

"I intend," said he, "to put off the execution till to-morrow; but let no one in the prison suspect it. Absolute silence! Let the executioner seem to be superintending the preparations.

"Send the Spanish priest here under a strong guard; the Spanish Embassy claims his person! Gendarmes can bring up the self-styled Carlos by your back stairs so that he may see no one. Instruct the men each to hold him by one arm, and never let him go till they reach this door.

"Are you sure, Monsieur Gault, that this dangerous foreigner has spoken to no one but the prisoners!"

"Ah! just as he came out of the condemned cell a lady came to see him—"

The two magistrates exchanged looks, and such looks!

"What lady was that!" asked Camusot.

"One of his penitents—a Marquise," replied Gault.

"Worse and worse!" said Monsieur de Granville, looking at Camusot.

"She gave all the gendarmes and warders a sick headache," said Monsieur Gault, much puzzled.

"Nothing can be a matter of indifference in your business," said the public prosecutor. "The Conciergerie has not such tremendous walls for nothing. How did this lady get in?"

"With a regular permit, monsieur," replied the governor. "The lady, beautifully dressed, in a fine carriage with a footman and a chasseur, came to see her confessor before going to the funeral of the poor young man whose body you had had removed."

"Bring me the order for admission," said Monsieur de Granville.

"It was given on the recommendation of the Comte de Serizy."

"What was the woman like?" asked the public prosecutor.

"She seemed to be a lady."

"Did you see her face?"

"She wore a black veil."

"What did they say to each other?"

"Well—a pious person, with a prayer-book in her hand—what could she say? She asked the Abbe's blessing and went on her knees."

"Did they talk together a long time?"

"Not five minutes; but we none of us understood what they said; they spoke Spanish no doubt."

"Tell us everything, monsieur," the public prosecutor insisted. "I repeat, the very smallest detail is to us of the first importance. Let this be a caution to you."

"She was crying, monsieur."

"Really weeping?"

"That we could not see, she hid her face in her handkerchief. She left three hundred francs in gold for the prisoners."

"That was not she!" said Camusot.

"Bibi-Lupin at once said, 'She is a thief!'" said Monsieur Gault.

"He knows the tribe," said Monsieur de Granville.—"Get out your warrant," he added, turning to Camusot, "and have seals placed on everything in her house—at once! But how can she have got hold of Monsieur de Serizy's recommendation?—Bring me the order—and go, Monsieur Gault; send me that Abbe immediately. So long as we have him safe, the danger cannot be greater. And in the course of two hours' talk you get a long way into a man's mind."

"Especially such a public prosecutor as you are," said Camusot insidiously.

"There will be two of us," replied Monsieur de Granville politely.

And he became discursive once more.

"There ought to be created for every prison parlor, a post of superintendent, to be given with a good salary to the cleverest and most energetic police officers," said he, after a long pause. "Bibi-Lupin ought to end his days in such a place. Then we should have an eye and ear on the watch in a department that needs closer supervision than it gets.— Monsieur Gault could tell us nothing positive."

"He has so much to do," said Camusot. "Still, between these secret cells and us there lies a gap which ought not to exist. On the way from the Conciergerie to the judges' rooms there are passages, courtyards, and stairs. The attention of the agents cannot be unflagging, whereas the prisoner is always alive to his own affairs.

"I was told that a lady had already placed herself in the way of Jacques Collin when he was brought up from the cells to be examined. That woman got into the guardroom at the top of the narrow stairs from the mousetrap; the ushers told me, and I blamed the gendarmes."

"Oh! the Palais needs entire reconstruction," said Monsieur de Granville. "But it is an outlay of twenty to thirty million francs! Just try asking the Chambers for thirty millions for the more decent accommodation of Justice."

The sound of many footsteps and a clatter of arms fell on their ear. It would be Jacques Collin.

The public prosecutor assumed a mask of gravity that hid the man. Camusot imitated his chief.

The office-boy opened the door, and Jacques Collin came in, quite calm and unmoved.

"You wished to speak to me," said Monsieur de Granville. "I am ready to listen."

"Monsieur le Comte, I am Jacques Collin. I surrender!"

Camusot started; the public prosecutor was immovable.

"As you may suppose, I have my reasons for doing this," said Jacques Collin, with an ironical glance at the two magistrates. "I must inconvenience you greatly; for if I had remained a Spanish priest, you would simply have packed me off with an escort of gendarmes as far as the frontier by Bayonne, and there Spanish bayonets would have relieved you of me."

The lawyers sat silent and imperturbable.

"Monsieur le Comte," the convict went on, "the reasons which have led me to this step are yet more pressing than this, but devilish personal to myself. I can tell them to no one but you.—If you are afraid—"

"Afraid of whom? Of what?" said the Comte de Granville.

In attitude and expression, in the turn of his head, his demeanor and his look, this distinguished judge was at this moment a living embodiment of the law which ought to supply us with the noblest examples of civic courage. In this brief instant he was on a level with the magistrates of the old French Parlement in the time of the civil wars, when the presidents found themselves face to face with death, and stood, made of marble, like the statues that commemorate them.

"Afraid to be alone with an escaped convict!"

"Leave us, Monsieur Camusot," said the public prosecutor at once.

"I was about to suggest that you should bind me hand and foot," Jacques Collin coolly added, with an ominous glare at the two gentlemen. He paused, and then said with great gravity:

"Monsieur le Comte, you had my esteem, but you now command my admiration."

"Then you think you are formidable?" said the magistrate, with a look of supreme contempt.

"*Think* myself formidable?" retorted the convict. "Why think about it? I am, and I know it."

Jacques Collin took a chair and sat down, with all the ease of a man who feels himself a match for his adversary in an interview where they would treat on equal terms.

At this instant Monsieur Camusot, who was on the point of closing the door behind him, turned back, came up to Monsieur de Granville, and handed him two folded papers.

"Look!" said he to Monsieur de Granville, pointing to one of them.

"Call back Monsieur Gault!" cried the Comte de Granville, as he read the name of Madame de Maufrigneuse's maid—a woman he knew.

The governor of the prison came in.

"Describe the woman who came to see the prisoner," said the public prosecutor in his ear.

"Short, thick-set, fat, and square," replied Monsieur Gault.

"The woman to whom this permit was given is tall and thin," said Monsieur de Granville. "How old was she?"

"About sixty."

"This concerns me, gentlemen?" said Jacques Collin. "Come, do not puzzle your heads. That person is my aunt, a very plausible aunt, a woman, and an old woman. I can save you a great deal of trouble. You will never find my aunt unless I choose. If we beat about the bush, we shall never get forwarder."

"Monsieur l'Abbe has lost his Spanish accent," observed Monsieur Gault; "he does not speak broken French."

"Because things are in a desperate mess, my dear Monsieur Gault," replied Jacques Collin with a bitter smile, as he addressed the Governor by name.

Monsieur Gault went quickly up to his chief, and said in a whisper, "Beware of that man, Monsieur le Comte; he is mad with rage."

Monsieur de Granville gazed slowly at Jacques Collin, and saw that he was controlling himself; but he saw, too, that what the governor said was true. This treacherous demeanor covered the cold but terrible nervous irritation of a savage. In Jacques Collin's eyes were the lurid fires of a volcanic eruption, his fists were clenched. He was a tiger gathering himself up to spring.

"Leave us," said the Count gravely to the prison governor and the judge.

"You did wisely to send away Lucien's murderer!" said Jacques Collin, without caring whether Camusot heard him or no; "I could not contain myself, I should have strangled him."

Monsieur de Granville felt a chill; never had he seen a man's eyes so full of blood, or cheeks so colorless, or muscles so set.

"And what good would that murder have done you?" he quietly asked.

"You avenge society, or fancy you avenge it, every day, monsieur, and you ask me to give a reason for revenge? Have you never felt vengeance throbbing in surges in your veins? Don't you know that it was that idiot of a judge who killed him?—For you were fond of my Lucien, and he loved you! I know you by heart, sir. The dear boy would tell me everything at night when he came in; I used to put him to bed as a nurse tucks up a child, and I made him tell me everything. He confided everything to me, even his least sensations!

"The best of mothers never loved an only son so tenderly as I loved that angel! If only you knew! All that is good sprang up in his heart as flowers grow in the fields. He was weak; it was his only fault, weak as the string of a lyre, which is so strong when it is taut. These are the most beautiful natures; their weakness is simply tenderness, admiration, the power of expanding in the sunshine of art, of love, of the beauty God has made for man in a thousand shapes!—In short, Lucien was a woman spoiled. Oh! what could I not say to that brute beast who had just gone out of the room!

"I tell you, monsieur, in my degree, as a prisoner before his judge, I did what God A'mighty would have done for His Son if, hoping to save Him, He had gone with Him before Pilate!"

A flood of tears fell from the convict's light tawny eyes, which just now had glared like those of a wolf starved by six months' snow in the plains of the Ukraine. He went on:

"That dolt would listen to nothing, and he killed the boy!—I tell you, sir, I bathed the child's corpse in my tears, crying out to the Power I do not know, and which is above us all! I, who do not believe in God!— (For if I were not a materialist, I should not be myself.)

"I have told everything when I say that. You don't know—no man knows what suffering is. I alone know it. The fire of anguish so dried up my tears, that all last night I could not weep. Now I can, because I feel that you can understand me. I saw you, sitting there just now, an Image of Justice. Oh! monsieur, may God—for I am beginning to believe in Him—preserve you from ever being as bereft as I am! That cursed judge has robbed me of my soul, Monsieur le Comte! At this moment they are burying my life, my beauty, my virtue, my conscience, all my powers! Imagine a dog from which a chemist had extracted the blood.—That's me! I am that dog—

"And that is why I have come to tell you that I am Jacques Collin, and to give myself up. I made up my mind to it this morning when they came and carried away the body I was kissing like a madman—like a mother—as the Virgin must have kissed Jesus in the tomb.

"I meant then to give myself up to justice without driving any bargain; but now I must make one, and you shall know why."

"Are you speaking to the judge or to Monsieur de Granville?" asked the magistrate.

The two men, Crime and Law, looked at each other. The magistrate had been strongly moved by the convict; he felt a sort of divine pity for the unhappy wretch; he understood what his life and feelings were. And besides, the magistrate—for a magistrate is always a magistrate— knowing nothing of Jacques Collin's career since his escape from prison, fancied that he could impress the criminal who, after all, had only been sentenced for forgery. He would try the effect of generosity

HONORÉ DE BALZAC

on this nature, a compound, like bronze, of various elements, of good and evil.

Again, Monsieur de Granville, who had reached the age of fifty-three without ever having been loved, admired a tender soul, as all men do who have not been loved. This despair, the lot of many men to whom women can only give esteem and friendship, was perhaps the unknown bond on which a strong intimacy was based that united the Comtes de Bauvan, de Granville, and de Serizy; for a common misfortune brings souls into unison quite as much as a common joy.

"You have the future before you," said the public prosecutor, with an inquisitorial glance at the dejected villain.

The man only expressed by a shrug the utmost indifference to his fate.

"Lucien made a will by which he leaves you three hundred thousand francs."

"Poor, poor chap! poor boy!" cried Jacques Collin. "Always too honest! I was all wickedness, while he was goodness—noble, beautiful, sublime! Such lovely souls cannot be spoiled. He had taken nothing from me but my money, sir."

This utter and complete surrender of his individuality, which the magistrate vainly strove to rally, so thoroughly proved his dreadful words, that Monsieur de Granville was won over to the criminal. The public prosecutor remained!

"If you really care for nothing," said Monsieur de Granville, "what did you want to say to me?"

"Well, is it not something that I have given myself up? You were getting warm, but you had not got me; besides, you would not have known what to do with me—"

"What an antagonist!" said the magistrate to himself.

"Monsieur le Comte, you are about to cut off the head of an innocent man, and I have discovered the culprit," said Jacques Collin, wiping away his tears. "I have come here not for their sakes, but for yours. I have come to spare you remorse, for I love all who took an interest in Lucien, just as I will give my hatred full play against all who helped to cut off his life—men or women!

"What can a convict more or less matter to me?" he went on, after a short pause. "A convict is no more in my eyes than an emmet is in yours. I am like the Italian brigands—fine men they are! If a traveler is worth ever so little more than the charge of their musket, they shoot him dead.

"I thought only of you.—I got the young man to make a clean breast of it; he was bound to trust me, we had been chained together. Theodore is very good stuff; he thought he was doing his mistress a good turn by undertaking to sell or pawn stolen goods; but he is no more guilty of the Nanterre job than you are. He is a Corsican; it is their way to revenge themselves and kill each other like flies. In Italy and Spain a man's life is not respected, and the reason is plain. There we are believed to have a soul in our own image, which survives us and lives for ever. Tell that to your analyst! It is only among atheistical or philosophical nations that those who mar human life are made to pay so dearly; and with reason from their point of view—a belief only in matter and in the present.

"If Calvi had told you who the woman was from whom he obtained the stolen goods, you would not have found the real murderer; he is already in your hands; but his accomplice, whom poor Theodore will not betray because she is a woman—Well, every calling has its point of honor; convicts and thieves have theirs!

"Now, I know the murderer of those two women and the inventors of that bold, strange plot; I have been told every detail. Postpone Calvi's execution, and you shall know all; but you must give me your word that he shall be sent safe back to the hulks and his punishment commuted. A man so miserable as I am does not take the trouble to lie—you know that. What I have told you is the truth."

"To you, Jacques Collin, though it is degrading Justice, which ought never to condescend to such a compromise, I believe I may relax the rigidity of my office and refer the case to my superiors."

"Will you grant me this life?"

"Possibly."

"Monsieur, I implore you to give me your word; it will be enough."

Monsieur Granville drew himself up with offended pride.

"I hold in my hand the honor of three families, and you only the lives of three convicts in yours," said Jacques Collin. "I have the stronger hand."

"But you may be sent back to the dark cells: then, what will you do?" said the public prosecutor.

"Oh! we are to play the game out then!" said Jacques Collin. "I was speaking as man to man—I was talking to Monsieur de Granville. But if the public prosecutor is my adversary, I take up the cards and hold them close.—And if only you had given me your word, I was ready to give you back the letters that Mademoiselle Clotilde de Grandlieu—"

This was said with a tone, an audacity, and a look which showed Monsieur de Granville, that against such an adversary the least blunder was dangerous.

"And is that all you ask?" said the magistrate.

"I will speak for myself now," said Jacques. "The honor of the Grandlieu family is to pay for the commutation of Theodore's sentence. It is giving much to get very little. For what is a convict in penal servitude for life? If he escapes, you can so easily settle the score. It is drawing a bill on the guillotine! Only, as he was consigned to Rochefort with no amiable intentions, you must promise me that he shall be quartered at Toulon, and well treated there.

"Now, for myself, I want something more. I have the packets of letters from Madame de Serizy and Madame de Maufrigneuse.—And what letters!—I tell you, Monsieur le Comte, prostitutes, when they write letters, assume a style of sentiment; well, sir, fine ladies, who are accustomed to style and sentiment all day long, write as prostitutes behave. Philosophers may know the reasons for this contrariness. I do not care to seek them. Woman is an inferior animal; she is ruled by her instincts. To my mind a woman has no beauty who is not like a man.

"So your smart duchesses, who are men in brains only, write masterpieces. Oh! they are splendid from beginning to end, like Piron's famous ode!—"

"Indeed!"

"Would you like to see them?" said Jacques Collin, with a laugh.

The magistrate felt ashamed.

"I cannot give them to you to read. But, there; no nonsense; this is business and all above board, I suppose?—You must give me back the letters, and allow no one to play the spy or to follow or to watch the person who will bring them to me."

"That will take time," said Monsieur de Granville.

"No. It is half-past nine," replied Jacques Collin, looking at the clock; "well, in four minutes you will have a letter from each of these ladies, and after reading them you will countermand the guillotine. If matters were not as they are, you would not see me taking things so easy.—The ladies indeed have had warning."—Monsieur de Granville was startled.—"They must be making a stir by now; they are going to bring the Keeper of the Seals into the fray—they may even appeal to the King, who knows?—Come, now, will you give me your word that you will forget all that has passed, and neither follow, nor send any one to follow, that person for a whole hour?"

"I promise it."

"Very well; you are not the man to deceive an escaped convict. You are a chip of the block of which Turennes and Condes are made, and would keep your word to a thief.—In the *Salle des Pas-Perdus* there is at this moment a beggar woman in rags, an old woman, in the very middle of the hall. She is probably gossiping with one of the public writers, about some lawsuit over a party-wall perhaps; send your office messenger to fetch her, saying these words, 'Dabor ti Mandana' (the Boss wants you). She will come.

"But do not be unnecessarily cruel. Either you accept my terms or you do not choose to be mixed up in a business with a convict.—I am only a forger, you will remember!—Well, do not leave Calvi to go through the terrors of preparation for the scaffold."

"I have already countermanded the execution," said Monsieur de Granville to Jacques Collin. "I would not have Justice beneath you in dignity."

Jacques Collin looked at the public prosecutor with a sort of amazement, and saw him ring his bell.

"Will you promise not to escape? Give me your word, and I shall be satisfied. Go and fetch the woman."

The office-boy came in.

"Felix, send away the gendarmes," said Monsieur de Granville.

Jacques Collin was conquered.

In this duel with the magistrate he had tried to be the superior, the stronger, the more magnanimous, and the magistrate had crushed him. At the same time, the convict felt himself the superior, inasmuch as he had tricked the Law; he had convinced it that the guilty man was innocent, and had fought for a man's head and won it; but this advantage must be unconfessed, secret and hidden, while the magistrate towered above him majestically in the eye of day.

As Jacques Collin left Monsieur de Granville's room, the Comte des Lupeaulx, Secretary-in-Chief of the President of the Council, and a deputy, made his appearance, and with him a feeble-looking, little old man. This individual, wrapped in a puce-colored overcoat, as though it were still winter, with powdered hair, and a cold, pale face, had a gouty gait, unsteady on feet that were shod with loose calfskin boots; leaning on a gold-headed cane, he carried his hat in his hand, and wore a row of seven orders in his button-hole.

"What is it, my dear des Lupeaulx?" asked the public prosecutor.

"I come from the Prince," replied the Count, in a low voice. "You have carte blanche if you can only get the letters—Madame de Serizy's, Madame de Maufrigneuse's and Mademoiselle Clotilde de Grandlieu's. You may come to some arrangement with this gentleman—"

"Who is he?" asked Monsieur de Granville, in a whisper.

"There are no secrets between you and me, my dear sir," said des Lupeaulx. "This is the famous Corentin. His Majesty desires that you will yourself tell him all the details of this affair and the conditions of success."

"Do me the kindness," replied the public prosecutor, "of going to tell the Prince that the matter is settled, that I have not needed this gentleman's assistance," and he turned to Corentin. "I will wait on His Majesty for his commands with regard to the last steps in the matter, which will lie with the Keeper of the Seals, as two reprieves will need signing."

"You have been wise to take the initiative," said des Lupeaulx, shaking hands with the Comte de Granville. "On the very eve of a great undertaking the King is most anxious that the peers and the great families should not be shown up, blown upon. It ceases to be a low criminal case; it becomes an affair of State."

"But tell the Prince that by the time you came it was all settled."

"Really!"

"I believe so."

"Then you, my dear fellow, will be Keeper of the Seals as soon as the present Keeper is made Chancellor—"

"I have no ambition," replied the magistrate.

Des Lupeaulx laughed, and went away.

"Beg of the Prince to request the King to grant me ten minutes' audience at about half-past two," added Monsieur de Granville, as he accompanied the Comte des Lupeaulx to the door.

"So you are not ambitious!" said des Lupeaulx, with a keen look at Monsieur de Granville. "Come, you have two children, you would like at least to be made peer of France."

"If you have the letters, Monsieur le Procureur General, my intervention is unnecessary," said Corentin, finding himself alone with Monsieur de Granville, who looked at him with very natural curiosity.

"Such a man as you can never be superfluous in so delicate a case," replied the magistrate, seeing that Corentin had heard or guessed everything.

Corentin bowed with a patronizing air.

"Do you know the man in question, monsieur?"

"Yes, Monsieur le Comte, it is Jacques Collin, the head of the 'Ten Thousand Francs Association,' the banker for three penal settlements, a convict who, for the last five years, has succeeded in concealing himself under the robe of the Abbe Carlos Herrera. How he ever came to be intrusted with a mission to the late King from the King of Spain is a question which we have all puzzled ourselves with trying to answer. I am now expecting information from Madrid, whither I have sent notes and a man. That convict holds the secrets of two kings."

"He is a man of mettle and temper. We have only two courses open to us," said the public prosecutor. "We must secure his fidelity, or get him out of the way."

"The same idea has struck us both, and that is a great honor for me," said Corentin. "I am obliged to have so many ideas, and for so many people, that out of them all I ought occasionally to meet a clever man."

He spoke so drily, and in so icy a tone, that Monsieur de Granville made no reply, and proceeded to attend to some pressing matters.

Mademoiselle Jacqueline Collin's amazement on seeing Jacques Collin in the *Salle des Pas-Perdus* is beyond imagining. She stood square on her feet, her hands on her hips, for she was dressed as a costermonger. Accustomed as she was to her nephew's conjuring tricks, this beat everything.

"Well, if you are going to stare at me as if I were a natural history show," said Jacques Collin, taking his aunt by the arm and leading her out of the hall, "we shall be taken for a pair of curious specimens; they may take us into custody, and then we should lose time."

And he went down the stairs of the Galerie Marchande leading to the Rue de la Barillerie. "Where is Paccard?"

"He is waiting for me at la Rousse's, walking up and down the flower market."

"And Prudence?"

"Also at her house, as my god-daughter."

"Let us go there."

"Look round and see if we are watched."

La Rousse, a hardware dealer living on the Quai aux Fleurs, was the widow of a famous murderer, one of the "Ten Thousand." In 1819, Jacques Collin had faithfully handed over twenty thousand francs and odd to this woman from her lover, after he had been executed. *Trompe-la-Mort* was the only person who knew of his pal's connection with the girl, at that time a milliner.

"I am your young man's boss," the boarder at Madame Vauquer's had told her, having sent for her to meet him at the Jardin des Plantes. "He may have mentioned me to you, my dear.—Any one who plays me false dies within a year; on the other hand, those who are true to me have nothing to fear from me. I am staunch through thick and thin, and would die without saying a word that would compromise anybody I wish well to. Stick to me as a soul sticks to the Devil, and you will find the benefit of it. I promised your poor Auguste that you should be happy; he wanted to make you a rich woman, and he got scragged for your sake.

"Don't cry; listen to me. No one in the world knows that you were mistress to a convict, to the murderer they choked off last Saturday; and I shall never tell. You are two-and-twenty, and pretty, and you have twenty-six thousand francs of your own; forget Auguste and get married; be an honest woman if you can. In return for peace and quiet, I only ask you to serve me now and then, me, and any one I may send you, but without stopping to think. I will never ask you to do anything that can get you into trouble, you or your children, or your husband, if you get one, or your family.

"In my line of life I often want a safe place to talk in or to hide in. Or I may want a trusty woman to carry a letter or do an errand. You will be one of my letter-boxes, one of my porters' lodges, one of my messengers, neither more nor less.

"You are too red-haired; Auguste and I used to call you la Rousse; you can keep that name. My aunt, an old-clothes dealer at the Temple, who will come and see you, is the only person in the world you are to obey; tell her everything that happens to you; she will find you a husband, and be very useful to you."

And thus the bargain was struck, a diabolical compact like that which had for so long bound Prudence Servien to Jacques Collin, and which the man never failed to tighten; for, like the Devil, he had a passion for recruiting.

In about 1821 Jacques Collin found la Rousse a husband in the person of the chief shopman under a rich wholesale tin merchant. This head-clerk, having purchased his master's house of business, was now a prosperous man, the father of two children, and one of the district Maire's deputies. La Rousse, now Madame Prelard, had never had the smallest ground for complaint, either of Jacques Collin or of his aunt; still, each time she was required to help them, Madame Prelard quaked in every limb. So, as she saw the terrible couple come into her shop, she turned as pale as death.

"We want to speak to you on business, madame," said Jacques Collin.

"My husband is in there," said she.

"Very well; we have no immediate need of you. I never put people out of their way for nothing."

"Send for a hackney coach, my dear," said Jacqueline Collin, "and tell my god-daughter to come down. I hope to place her as maid to a very great lady, and the steward of the house will take us there."

A shop-boy fetched the coach, and a few minutes later Europe, or, to be rid of the name under which she had served Esther, Prudence Servien, Paccard, Jacques Collin, and his aunt, were, to la Rousse's great joy, packed into a coach, ordered by *Trompe-la-Mort* to drive to the Barriere d'Ivry.

Prudence and Paccard, quaking in presence of the boss, felt like guilty souls in the presence of God.

"Where are the seven hundred and fifty thousand francs?" asked the boss, looking at them with the clear, penetrating gaze which so effectually curdled the blood of these tools of his, these ames damnees, when they were caught tripping, that they felt as though their scalp were set with as many pins as hairs.

"The seven hundred and *thirty* thousand francs," said Jacqueline Collin to her nephew, "are quite safe; I gave them to la Romette this morning in a sealed packet."

"If you had not handed them over to Jacqueline," said *Trompe-la-Mort*, "you would have gone straight there," and he pointed to the Place de Greve, which they were just passing.

Prudence Servien, in her country fashion, made the sign of the Cross, as if she had seen a thunderbolt fall.

"I forgive you," said the boss, "on condition of your committing no more mistakes of this kind, and of your being henceforth to me what these two fingers are of my right hand," and he pointed to the first and middle fingers, "for this good woman is the thumb," and he slapped his aunt on the shoulder.

"Listen to me," he went on. "You, Paccard, have nothing more to fear; you may follow your nose about Pantin (Paris) as you please. I give you leave to marry Prudence Servien."

Paccard took Jacques Collin's hand and kissed it respectfully.

"And what must I do?" said he.

"Nothing; and you will have dividends and women, to say nothing of your wife—for you have a touch of the Regency about you, old boy!— That comes of being such a fine man!"

Paccard colored under his sultan's ironical praises.

"You, Prudence," Jacques went on, "will want a career, a position, a future; you must remain in my service. Listen to me. There is a very good house in the Rue Sainte-Barbe belonging to that Madame de Saint-Esteve, whose name my aunt occasionally borrows. It is a very good business, with plenty of custom, bringing in fifteen to twenty thousand francs a year. Saint-Esteve puts a woman in to keep the shop—"

"La Gonore," said Jacqueline.

"Poor la Pouraille's moll," said Paccard. "That is where I bolted to with Europe the day that poor Madame van Bogseck died, our mis'ess."

"Who jabbers when I am speaking?" said Jacques Collin.

Perfect silence fell in the coach. Paccard and Prudence did not dare look at each other.

"The shop is kept by la Gonore," Jacques Collin went on. "If that is where you went to hide with Prudence, I see, Paccard, that you have wit enough to dodge the reelers (mislead the police), but not enough to puzzle the old lady," and he stroked his aunt's chin. "Now I see how she managed to find you.—It all fits beautifully. You may go back to la Gonore.—To go on: Jacqueline will arrange with Madame Nourrisson to purchase her business in the Rue Sainte-Barbe; and if you manage well, child, you may make a fortune out of it," he said to Prudence. "An Abbess at your age! It is worthy of a Daughter of France," he added in a hard tone.

Prudence flung her arms round *Trompe-la-Mort's* neck and hugged him; but the boss flung her off with a sharp blow, showing his extraordinary strength, and but for Paccard, the girl's head would have struck and broken the coach window.

"Paws off! I don't like such ways," said the boss stiffly. "It is disrespectful to me."

"He is right, child," said Paccard. "Why, you see, it is as though the boss had made you a present of a hundred thousand francs. The shop is worth that. It is on the Boulevard, opposite the Gymnase. The people come out of the theatre—"

"I will do more," said *Trompe-la-Mort*; "I will buy the house."

"And in six years we shall be millionaires," cried Paccard.

Tired of being interrupted, *Trompe-la-Mort* gave Paccard's shin a kick hard enough to break it; but the man's tendons were of india-rubber, and his bones of wrought iron.

"All right, boss, mum it is," said he.

"Do you think I am cramming you with lies?" said Jacques Collin, perceiving that Paccard had had a few drops too much. "Well, listen. In the cellar of that house there are two hundred and fifty thousand francs in gold—"

Again silence reigned in the coach.

"The coin is in a very hard bed of masonry. It must be got out, and you have only three nights to do it in. Jacqueline will help you.—A hundred thousand francs will buy up the business, fifty thousand will pay for the house; leave the remainder."

"Where?" said Paccard.

"In the cellar?" asked Prudence.

"Silence!" cried Jacqueline.

"Yes, but to get the business transferred, we must have the consent of the police authorities," Paccard objected.

"We shall have it," said *Trompe-la-Mort*. "Don't meddle in what does not concern you."

Jacqueline looked at her nephew, and was struck by the alteration in his face, visible through the stern mask under which the strong man generally hid his feelings.

"You, child," said he to Prudence Servien, "will receive from my aunt the seven hundred and fifty thousand francs—"

"Seven hundred and thirty," said Paccard.

"Very good, seven hundred and thirty then," said Jacques Collin. "You must return this evening under some pretext to Madame Lucien's house. Get out on the roof through the skylight; get down the chimney into your miss'ess' room, and hide the packet she had made of the money in the mattress—"

"And why not by the door?" asked Prudence Servien.

"Idiot! there are seals on everything," replied Jacques Collin. "In a few days the inventory will be taken, and you will be innocent of the theft."

"Good for the boss!" cried Paccard. "That is really kind!"

"Stop, coachman!" cried Jacques Collin's powerful voice.

The coach was close to the stand by the Jardin des Plantes.

"Be off, young 'uns," said Jacques Collin, "and do nothing silly! Be on the Pont des Arts this afternoon at five, and my aunt will let you know if there are any orders to the contrary.—We must be prepared for everything," he whispered to his aunt. "To-morrow," he went on, "Jacqueline will tell you how to dig up the gold without any risk. It is a ticklish job—"

Paccard and Prudence jumped out on to the King's highway, as happy as reprieved thieves.

"What a good fellow the boss is!" said Paccard.

"He would be the king of men if he were not so rough on women."

"Oh, yes! He is a sweet creature," said Paccard. "Did you see how he kicked me? Well, we deserved to be sent to old Nick; for, after all, we got him into this scrape."

"If only he does not drag us into some dirty job, and get us packed off to the hulks yet," said the wily Prudence.

"Not he! If he had that in his head, he would tell us; you don't know him.—He has provided handsomely for you. Here we are, citizens at large! Oh, when that man takes a fancy to you, he has not his match for good-nature."

"Now, my jewel," said Jacques Collin to his aunt, "you must take la Gonore in hand; she must be humbugged. Five days hence she will be taken into custody, and a hundred and fifty thousand francs will be found in her rooms, the remains of a share from the robbery and murder of the old Crottat couple, the notary's father and mother."

"She will get five years in the Madelonnettes," said Jacqueline.

"That's about it," said the nephew. "This will be a reason for old Nourrisson to get rid of her house; she cannot manage it herself, and a manager to suit is not to be found every day. You can arrange all that. We shall have a sharp eye there.—But all these three things are secondary to the business I have undertaken with regard to our letters. So unrip your gown and give me the samples of the goods. Where are the three packets?"

"At la Rousse's, of course."

"Coachman," cried Jacques Collin, "go back to the Palais de Justice, and look sharp—

"I promised to be quick, and I have been gone half an hour; that is too much.—Stay at la Rousse's, and give the sealed parcels to the office clerk, who will come and ask for Madame *de* Saint-Esteve; the *de* will be the password. He will say to you, 'Madame, I have come from the public prosecutor for the things you know of.' Stand waiting outside the door, staring about at what is going on in the Flower-Market, so as not to arouse Prelard's suspicions. As soon as you have given up the letters, you can start Paccard and Prudence."

"I see what you are at," said Jacqueline; "you mean to step into Bibi-Lupin's shoes. That boy's death has turned your brain."

"And there is Theodore, who was just going to have his hair cropped to be scragged at four this afternoon!" cried Jacques Collin.

"Well, it is a notion! We shall end our days as honest folks in a fine property and a delightful climate—in Touraine."

"What was to become of me? Lucien has taken my soul with him, and all my joy in life. I have thirty years before me to be sick of life in, and I have no heart left. Instead of being the boss of the hulks, I shall be a Figaro of the law, and avenge Lucien. I can never be sure of demolishing Corentin excepting in the skin of a police agent. And so long as I have a man to devour, I shall still feel alive.—The profession a man follows in the eyes of the world is a mere sham; the reality is in the idea!" he added, striking his forehead.—"How much have we left in the cash-box?" he asked.

"Nothing," said his aunt, dismayed by the man's tone and manner. "I gave you all I had for the boy. La Romette has not more than twenty thousand francs left in the business. I took everything from Madame Nourrisson; she had about sixty thousand francs of her own. Oh! we are lying in sheets that have been washed this twelve months past. That boy had all the pals' blunt, our savings, and all old Nourrisson's."

"Making—?"

"Five hundred and sixty thousand."

"We have a hundred and fifty thousand which Paccard and Prudence will pay us. I will tell you where to find two hundred thousand more. The remainder will come to me out of Esther's money. We must repay old Nourrisson. With Theodore, Paccard, Prudence, Nourrisson, and you, I shall soon have the holy alliance I require.—Listen, now we are nearly there—"

"Here are the three letters," said Jacqueline, who had finished unsewing the lining of her gown.

"Quite right," said Jacques Collin, taking the three precious documents—autograph letters on vellum paper, and still strongly scented. "Theodore did the Nanterre job."

"Oh! it was he."

"Don't talk. Time is precious. He wanted to give the proceeds to a little Corsican sparrow named Ginetta. You must set old Nourrisson to find her; I will give you the necessary information in a letter which Gault will give you. Come for it to the gate of the Conciergerie in two hours' time. You must place the girl with a washerwoman, Godet's sister; she must seem at home there. Godet and Ruffard were concerned with la Pouraille in robbing and murdering the Crottats.

"The four hundred and fifty thousand francs are all safe, one-third in la Gonore's cellar—la Pouraille's share; the second third in la Gonore's bedroom, which is Ruffard's; and the rest is hidden in Godet's sister's house. We will begin by taking a hundred and fifty thousand francs out of la Pouraille's whack, a hundred thousand of Godet's, and a hundred thousand of Ruffard's. As soon as Godet and Ruffard are nabbed, they will be supposed to have got rid of what is missing from their shares. And I will make Godet believe that I have saved a hundred thousand francs for him, and that la Gonore has done the same for la Pouraille and Ruffard.

"Prudence and Paccard will do the job at la Gonore's; you and Ginetta—who seems to be a smart hussy—must manage the job at Godet's sister's place.

"And so, as the first act in the farce, I can enable the public prosecutor to lay his hands on four hundred thousand francs stolen from the Crottats, and on the guilty parties. Then I shall seem to have shown up the Nanterre murderer. We shall get back our shiners, and are behind the scenes with the police. We were the game, now we are the hunters—that is all.

"Give the driver three francs."

The coach was at the Palais. Jacqueline, speechless with astonishment, paid. *Trompe-la-Mort* went up the steps to the public prosecutor's room.

A COMPLETE CHANGE OF LIFE is so violent a crisis, that Jacques Collin, in spite of his resolution, mounted the steps but slowly, going up from the Rue de la Barillerie to the Galerie Marchande, where, under the gloomy peristyle of the courthouse, is the entrance to the Court itself.

Some civil case was going on which had brought a little crowd together at the foot of the double stairs leading to the Assize Court, so that the convict, lost in thought, stood for some minutes, checked by the throng.

To the left of this double flight is one of the mainstays of the building, like an enormous pillar, and in this tower is a little door. This door opens on a spiral staircase down to the Conciergerie, to which the public prosecutor, the governor of the prison, the presiding judges, King's council, and the chief of the Safety department have access by this back way.

It was up a side staircase from this, now walled up, that Marie Antoinette, the Queen of France, was led before the Revolutionary tribunal which sat, as we all know, in the great hall where appeals are now heard before the Supreme Court. The heart sinks within us at the sight of these dreadful steps, when we think that Marie Therese's daughter, whose suite, and head-dress, and hoops filled the great staircase at Versailles, once passed that way! Perhaps it was in expiation of her mother's crime—the atrocious division of Poland. The sovereigns who commit such crimes evidently never think of the retribution to be exacted by Providence.

When Jacques Collin went up the vaulted stairs to the public prosecutor's room, Bibi-Lupin was just coming out of the little door in the wall.

The chief of the "Safety" had come from the Conciergerie, and was also going up to Monsieur de Granville. It was easy to imagine Bibi-Lupin's surprise when he recognized, in front of him, the gown of Carlos Herrera, which he had so thoroughly studied that morning; he ran on to pass him. Jacques Collin turned round, and the enemies were face to face. Each stood still, and the self-same look flashed in both pairs of eyes, so different in themselves, as in a duel two pistols go off at the same instant.

"This time I have got you, rascal!" said the chief of the Safety Department.

"Ah, ha!" replied Jacques Collin ironically.

It flashed through his mind that Monsieur de Granville had sent some one to watch him, and, strange to say, it pained him to think the magistrate less magnanimous than he had supposed.

Bibi-Lupin bravely flew at Jacques Collin's throat; but he, keeping his eye on the foe, gave him a straight blow, and sent him sprawling on his back three yards off; then *Trompe-la-Mort* went calmly up to Bibi-Lupin, and held out a hand to help him rise, exactly like an English boxer who, sure of his superiority, is ready for more. Bibi-Lupin knew better than to call out; but he sprang to his feet, ran to the entrance to the passage, and signed to a gendarme to stand on guard. Then, swift as lightning, he came back to the foe, who quietly looked on. Jacques Collin had decided what to do.

"Either the public prosecutor has broken his word, or he had not taken Bibi-Lupin into his confidence, and in that case I must get the matter explained," thought he.—"Do you mean to arrest me?" he asked his enemy. "Say so without more ado. Don't I know that in the heart of this place you are stronger than I am? I could kill you with a well-placed kick, but I could not tackle the gendarmes and the soldiers. Now, make no noise. Where to you want to take me?"

"To Monsieur Camusot."

"Come along to Monsieur Camusot," replied Jacques Collin. "Why should we not go to the public prosecutor's court? It is nearer," he added.

Bibi-Lupin, who knew that he was out of favor with the upper ranks of judicial authorities, and suspected of having made a fortune at the expense of criminals and their victims, was not unwilling to show himself in Court with so notable a capture.

"All right, we will go there," said he. "But as you surrender, allow me to fit you with bracelets. I am afraid of your claws."

And he took the handcuffs out of his pocket.

Jacques Collin held out his hands, and Bibi-Lupin snapped on the manacles.

"Well, now, since you are feeling so good," said he, "tell me how you got out of the Conciergerie?"

"By the way you came; down the turret stairs."

"Then have you taught the gendarmes some new trick?"

"No, Monsieur de Granville let me out on parole."

"You are gammoning me?"

"You will see. Perhaps it will be your turn to wear the bracelets."

Just then Corentin was saying to Monsieur de Granville:

"Well, monsieur, it is just an hour since our man set out; are you not afraid that he may have fooled you? He is on the road to Spain perhaps by this time, and we shall not find him there, for Spain is a whimsical kind of country."

"Either I know nothing of men, or he will come back; he is bound by every interest; he has more to look for at my hands than he has to give."

Bibi-Lupin walked in.

"Monsieur le Comte," said he, "I have good news for you. Jacques Collin, who had escaped, has been recaptured."

"And this," said Jacques Collin, addressing Monsieur de Granville, "is the way you keep your word!—Ask your double-faced agent where he took me."

"Where?" said the public prosecutor.

"Close to the Court, in the vaulted passage," said Bibi-Lupin.

"Take your irons off the man," said Monsieur de Granville sternly. "And remember that you are to leave him free till further orders.—Go!— You have a way of moving and acting as if you alone were law and police in one."

The public prosecutor turned his back on Bibi-Lupin, who became deadly pale, especially at a look from Jacques Collin, in which he read disaster.

"I have not been out of this room. I expected you back, and you cannot doubt that I have kept my word, as you kept yours," said Monsieur de Granville to the convict.

"For a moment I did doubt you, sir, and in my place perhaps you would have thought as I did, but on reflection I saw that I was unjust. I bring you more than you can give me; you had no interest in betraying me."

The magistrate flashed a look at Corentin. This glance, which could not escape *Trompe-la-Mort*, who was watching Monsieur de Granville, directed his attention to the strange little old man sitting in an armchair in a corner. Warned at once by the swift and anxious instinct that scents the presence of an enemy, Collin examined this figure; he saw at a glance that the eyes were not so old as the costume would suggest, and he detected a disguise. In one second Jacques Collin was revenged on Corentin for the rapid insight with which Corentin had unmasked him at Peyrade's.

"We are not alone!" said Jacques Collin to Monsieur de Granville.

"No," said the magistrate drily.

"And this gentleman is one of my oldest acquaintances, I believe," replied the convict.

He went forward, recognizing Corentin, the real and confessed originator of Lucien's overthrow.

Jacques Collin, whose face was of a brick-red hue, for a scarcely perceptible moment turned white, almost ashy; all his blood rushed to his heart, so furious and maddening was his longing to spring on this dangerous reptile and crush it; but he controlled the brutal impulse, suppressing it with the force that made him so formidable. He put on a polite manner and the tone of obsequious civility which he had practised since assuming the garb of a priest of a superior Order, and he bowed to the little old man.

"Monsieur Corentin," said he, "do I owe the pleasure of this meeting to chance, or am I so happy as to be the cause of your visit here?"

Monsieur de Granville's astonishment was at its height, and he could not help staring at the two men who had thus come face to face. Jacques Collin's behavior and the tone in which he spoke denoted a crisis, and he was curious to know the meaning of it. On being thus suddenly and miraculously recognized, Corentin drew himself up like a snake when you tread on its tail.

"Yes, it is I, my dear Abbe Carlos Herrera."

"And are you here," said *Trompe-la-Mort*, "to interfere between monsieur the public prosecutor and me? Am I so happy as to be the object of one of those negotiations in which your talents shine so brightly?—Here, Monsieur le Comte," the convict went on, "not to waste time so precious as yours is, read these—they are samples of my wares."

And he held out to Monsieur de Granville three letters, which he took out of his breast-pocket.

"And while you are studying them, I will, with your permission, have a little talk with this gentleman."

"You do me great honor," said Corentin, who could not help giving a little shiver.

"You achieved a perfect success in our business," said Jacques Collin. "I was beaten," he added lightly, in the tone of a gambler who has lost his money, "but you left some men on the field—your victory cost you dear."

"Yes," said Corentin, taking up the jest, "you lost your queen, and I lost my two castles."

"Oh! Contenson was a mere pawn," said Jacques Collin scornfully; "you may easily replace him. You really are—allow me to praise you to your face—you are, on my word of honor, a magnificent man."

"No, no, I bow to your superiority," replied Corentin, assuming the air of a professional joker, as if he said, "If you mean humbug, by all means humbug! I have everything at my command, while you are single-handed, so to speak."

"Oh! Oh!" said Jacques Collin.

"And you were very near winning the day!" said Corentin, noticing the exclamation. "You are quite the most extraordinary man I ever met in my life, and I have seen many very extraordinary men, for those I have to work with me are all remarkable for daring and bold scheming.

"I was, for my sins, very intimate with the late Duc d'Otranto; I have worked for Louis XVIII when he was on the throne; and, when he was exiled, for the Emperor and for the Directory. You have the tenacity of Louvel, the best political instrument I ever met with; but you are as supple as the prince of diplomates. And what auxiliaries you have! I would give many a head to the guillotine if I could have in my service the cook who lived with poor little Esther.—And where do you find such beautiful creatures as the woman who took the Jewess' place for Monsieur de Nucingen? I don't know where to get them when I want them."

"Monsieur, monsieur, you overpower me," said Jacques Collin. "Such praise from you will turn my head—"

"It is deserved. Why, you took in Peyrade; he believed you to be a police officer—he!—I tell you what, if you had not that fool of a boy to take care of, you would have thrashed us."

"Oh! monsieur, but you are forgetting Contenson disguised as a mulatto, and Peyrade as an Englishman. Actors have the stage to help them, but to be so perfect by daylight, and at all hours, no one but you and your men—"

"Come, now," said Corentin, "we are fully convinced of our worth and merits. And here we stand each of us quite alone; I have lost my old friend, you your young companion. I, for the moment, am in the stronger position, why should we not do like the men in *l'Auberge des Adrets*? I offer you my hand, and say, 'Let us embrace, and let bygones be bygones.' Here, in the presence of Monsieur le Comte, I propose to give you full and plenary absolution, and you shall be one of my men, the chief next to me, and perhaps my successor."

"You really offer me a situation?" said Jacques Collin. "A nice situation indeed!—out of the fire into the frying-pan!"

"You will be in a sphere where your talents will be highly appreciated and well paid for, and you will act at your ease. The Government police are not free from perils. I, as you see me, have already been imprisoned twice, but I am none the worse for that. And we travel, we are what we choose to appear. We pull the wires of political dramas, and are treated with politeness by very great people.—Come, my dear Jacques Collin, do you say yes?"

"Have you orders to act in this matter?" said the convict.

"I have a free hand," replied Corentin, delighted at his own happy idea.

"You are trifling with me; you are very shrewd, and you must allow that a man may be suspicious of you.—You have sold more than one man by tying him up in a sack after making him go into it of his own accord. I know all your great victories—the Montauran case, the Simeuse business—the battles of Marengo of espionage."

"Well," said Corentin, "you have some esteem for the public prosecutor?"

"Yes," said Jacques Collin, bowing respectfully, "I admire his noble character, his firmness, his dignity. I would give my life to make him happy. Indeed, to begin with, I will put an end to the dangerous condition in which Madame de Serizy now is."

Monsieur de Granville turned to him with a look of satisfaction.

"Then ask him," Corentin went on, "if I have not full power to snatch you from the degrading position in which you stand, and to attach you to me."

"It is quite true," said Monsieur de Granville, watching the convict.

"Really and truly! I may have absolution for the past and a promise of succeeding to you if I give sufficient evidence of my intelligence?"

"Between two such men as we are there can be no misunderstanding," said Corentin, with a lordly air that might have taken anybody in.

"And the price of the bargain is, I suppose, the surrender of those three packets of letters?" said Jacques Collin.

"I did not think it would be necessary to say so to you—"

"My dear Monsieur Corentin," said *Trompe-la-Mort*, with irony worthy of that which made the fame of Talma in the part of Nicomede, "I beg to decline. I am indebted to you for the knowledge of what I am worth, and of the importance you attach to seeing me deprived of my weapons—I will never forget it.

"At all times and for ever I shall be at your service, but instead of saying with Robert Macaire, 'Let us embrace!' I embrace you."

He seized Corentin round the middle so suddenly that the other could not avoid the hug; he clutched him to his heart like a doll, kissed him on both cheeks, carried him like a feather with one hand, while with the other he opened the door, and then set him down outside, quite battered by this rough treatment.

"Good-bye, my dear fellow," said Jacques Collin in a low voice, and in Corentin's ear: "the length of three corpses parts you from me; we have measured swords, they are of the same temper and the same length. Let us treat each other with due respect; but I mean to be your equal, not your subordinate. Armed as you would be, it strikes me you would be too dangerous a general for your lieutenant. We will place a grave between us. Woe to you if you come over on to my territory!

"You call yourself the State, as footmen call themselves by their master's names. For my part, I will call myself Justice. We shall often meet; let us treat each other with dignity and propriety—all the more because we shall always remain—atrocious blackguards," he added in a whisper. "I set you the example by embracing you—"

Corentin stood nonplussed for the first time in his life, and allowed his terrible antagonist to wring his hand.

"If so," said he, "I think it will be to our interest on both sides to remain chums."

"We shall be stronger each on our own side, but at the same time more dangerous," added Jacques Collin in an undertone. "And you will allow me to call on you to-morrow to ask for some pledge of our agreement."

"Well, well," said Corentin amiably, "you are taking the case out of my hands to place it in those of the public prosecutor. You will help him to promotion; but I cannot but own to you that you are acting wisely.—Bibi-Lupin is too well known; he has served his turn; if you get his place, you will have the only situation that suits you. I am delighted to see you in it—on my honor—"

"Till our next meeting, very soon," said Jacques Collin.

On turning round, *Trompe-la-Mort* saw the public prosecutor sitting at his table, his head resting on his hands.

"Do you mean that you can save the Comtesse de Serizy from going mad?" asked Monsieur de Granville.

"In five minutes," said Jacques Collin.

"And you can give me all those ladies' letters?"

"Have you read the three?"

"Yes," said the magistrate vehemently, "and I blush for the women who wrote them."

"Well, we are now alone; admit no one, and let us come to terms," said Jacques Collin.

"Excuse me, Justice must first take its course. Monsieur Camusot has instructions to seize your aunt."

"He will never find her," said Jacques Collin.

"Search is to be made at the Temple, in the shop of a demoiselle Paccard who superintends her shop."

"Nothing will be found there but rags, costumes, diamonds, uniforms—However, it will be as well to check Monsieur Camusot's zeal."

Monsieur de Granville rang, and sent an office messenger to desire Monsieur Camusot to come and speak with him.

"Now," said he to Jacques Collin, "an end to all this! I want to know your recipe for curing the Countess."

"Monsieur le Comte," said the convict very gravely, "I was, as you know, sentenced to five years' penal servitude for forgery. But I love my liberty.—This passion, like every other, had defeated its own end, for lovers who insist on adoring each other too fondly end by quarreling. By dint of escaping and being recaptured alternately, I have served seven years on the hulks. So you have nothing to remit but the added terms I earned in quod—I beg pardon, in prison. I have, in fact, served my time, and till some ugly job can be proved against me,—which I defy Justice to do, or even Corentin—I ought to be reinstated in my rights as a French citizen.

"What is life if I am banned from Paris and subject to the eye of the police? Where can I go, what can I do? You know my capabilities. You have seen Corentin, that storehouse of treachery and wile, turn ghastly pale before me, and doing justice to my powers.—That man has bereft me of everything; for it was he, and he alone, who overthrew the edifice of Lucien's fortunes, by what means and in whose interest I know not.— Corentin and Camusot did it all—"

"No recriminations," said Monsieur de Granville; "give me the facts."

"Well, then, these are the facts. Last night, as I held in my hand the icy hand of that dead youth, I vowed to myself that I would give up the mad contest I have kept up for twenty years past against society at large.

"You will not believe me capable of religious sentimentality after what I have said of my religious opinions. Still, in these twenty years I have seen a great deal of the seamy side of the world. I have known its back-stairs, and I have discerned, in the march of events, a Power which you call Providence and I call Chance, and which my companions call Luck. Every evil deed, however quickly it may hide its traces, is overtaken by some retribution. In this struggle for existence, when the game is going well—when you have quint and quartorze in your hand and the lead— the candle tumbles over and the cards are burned, or the player has a fit of apoplexy!—That is Lucien's story. That boy, that angel, had not committed the shadow of a crime; he let himself be led, he let things go! He was to marry Mademoiselle de Grandlieu, to be made marquis; he had a fine fortune;—well, a prostitute poisons herself, she hides the price of a certificate of stock, and the whole structure so laboriously built up crumbles in an instant.

"And who is the first man to deal a blow? A man loaded with secret infamy, a monster who, in the world of finance, has committed such crimes that every coin of his vast fortune has been dipped in the tears of a whole family [see *la Maison Nucingen*]—by Nucingen, who has been a legalized Jacques Collin in the world of money. However, you know as well as I do all the bankruptcies and tricks for which that man deserves hanging. My fetters will leave a mark on all my actions, however virtuous. To be a shuttlecock between two racquets—one called the hulks, and the other the police—is a life in which success means never-ending toil, and peace and quiet seem quite impossible.

"At this moment, Monsieur de Granville, Jacques Collin is buried with Lucien, who is being now sprinkled with holy water and carried away to Pere-Lachaise. What I want is a place not to live in, but to die in. As things are, you, representing Justice, have never cared to make the released convict's social status a concern of any interest. Though the law may be satisfied, society is not; society is still suspicious, and does all it can to justify its suspicions; it regards a released convict as an impossible creature; it ought to restore him to his full rights, but, in fact, it prohibits his living in certain circles. Society says to the poor wretch, 'Paris, which is the only place you can be hidden in; Paris and its suburbs for so many miles round is the forbidden land, you shall not live there!' and it subjects the convict to the watchfulness of the police. Do you think that life is possible under such conditions? To live, the convict must work, for he does not come out of prison with a fortune.

"You arrange matters so that he is plainly ticketed, recognized, hedged round, and then you fancy that his fellow-citizens will trust him, when society and justice and the world around him do not. You condemn him to starvation or crime. He cannot get work, and is inevitably dragged into his old ways, which lead to the scaffold.

"Thus, while earnestly wishing to give up this struggle with the law, I could find no place for myself under the sun. One course alone is open to me, that is to become the servant of the power that crushes us; and as soon as this idea dawned on me, the Power of which I spoke was shown in the clearest light. Three great families are at my mercy. Do not suppose I am thinking of blackmail—blackmail is the meanest form of murder. In my eyes it is baser villainy than murder. The murderer needs, at any rate, atrocious courage. And I practise what I preach; for the letters which are my safe-conduct, which allow me to address you thus, and for the moment place me on an equality with you—I, Crime, and you, Justice—those letters are in your power. Your messenger may fetch them, and they will be given up to him.

"I ask no price for them; I do not sell them. Alas! Monsieur le Comte, I was not thinking of myself when I preserved them; I thought that Lucien might some day be in danger! If you cannot agree to my request, my courage is out; I hate life more than enough to make me blow out my own brains and rid you of me!—Or, with a passport, I can go to America and live in the wilderness. I have all the characteristics of a savage.

"These are the thoughts that came to me in the night.—Your clerk, no doubt, carried you a message I sent by him. When I saw what precautions you took to save Lucien's memory from any stain, I dedicated my life to you—a poor offering, for I no longer cared for it; it seemed to me impossible without the star that gave it light, the happiness that glorified it, the thought that gave it meaning, the prosperity of the young poet who was its sun—and I determined to give you the three packets of letters—"

Monsieur de Granville bowed his head.

"I went down into the prison-yard, and there I found the persons guilty of the Nanterre crime, as well as my little chain companion within an inch of the chopper as an involuntary accessory after the fact," Jacques Collin went on. "I discovered that Bibi-Lupin is cheating the authorities, that one of his men murdered the Crottats. Was not this providential, as you say?—So I perceived a remote possibility of doing good, of turning my gifts and the dismal experience I have gained to account for the benefit of society, of being useful instead of mischievous, and I ventured to confide in your judgment, your generosity."

The man's air of candor, of artlessness, of childlike simplicity, as he made his confession, without bitterness, or that philosophy of vice which had hitherto made him so terrible to hear, was like an absolute transformation. He was no longer himself.

"I have such implicit trust in you," he went on, with the humility of a penitent, "that I am wholly at your mercy. You see me with three roads open to me—suicide, America, and the Rue de Jerusalem. Bibi-Lupin is rich; he has served his turn; he is a double-faced rascal. And if you set me to work against him, I would catch him red-handed in some trick within a week. If you will put me in that sneak's shoes, you will do society a real service. I will be honest. I have every quality that is needed in the profession. I am better educated than Bibi-Lupin; I went through my schooling up to rhetoric; I shall not blunder as he does; I have very good manners when I choose. My sole ambition is to become an instrument of order and repression instead of being the incarnation of corruption. I will enlist no more recruits to the army of vice.

"In war, monsieur, when a hostile general is captured, he is not shot, you know; his sword is returned to him, and his prison is a large town; well, I am the general of the hulks, and I have surrendered.—I am beaten, not by the law, but by death. The sphere in which I crave to live and act is the only one that is suited to me, and there I can develop the powers I feel within me.

"Decide."

And Jacques Collin stood in an attitude of diffident submission.

"You place the letters in my hands, then?" said the public prosecutor.

"You have only to send for them; they will be delivered to your messenger."

"But how?"

Jacques Collin read the magistrate's mind, and kept up the game.

"You promised me to commute the capital sentence on Calvi for twenty years' penal servitude. Oh, I am not reminding you of that to drive a bargain," he added eagerly, seeing Monsieur de Granville's expression; "that life should be safe for other reasons, the lad is innocent—"

"How am I to get the letters?" asked the public prosecutor. "It is my right and my business to convince myself that you are the man you say you are. I must have you without conditions."

"Send a man you can trust to the Flower Market on the quay. At the door of a tinman's shop, under the sign of Achilles' shield—"

"That house?"

"Yes," said Jacques Collin, smiling bitterly, "my shield is there.—Your man will see an old woman dressed, as I told you before, like a fish-woman who has saved money—earrings in her ears, and clothes like a rich market-woman's. He must ask for Madame de Saint-Esteve. Do not omit the DE. And he must say, 'I have come from the public prosecutor to fetch you know what.'—You will immediately receive three sealed packets."

"All the letters are there?" said Monsieur de Granville.

"There is no tricking you; you did not get your place for nothing!" said Jacques Collin, with a smile. "I see you still think me capable of testing you and giving you so much blank paper.—No; you do not know me," said he. "I trust you as a son trusts his father."

"You will be taken back to the Conciergerie," said the magistrate, "and there await a decision as to your fate."

Monsieur de Granville rang, and said to the office-boy who answered:

"Beg Monsieur Garnery to come here, if he is in his room."

Besides the forty-eight police commissioners who watch over Paris like forty-eight petty Providences, to say nothing of the guardians of Public Safety—and who have earned the nickname of quart d'oeil, in thieves' slang, a quarter of an eye, because there are four of them to each district,—besides these, there are two commissioners attached equally to the police and to the legal authorities, whose duty it is to undertake delicate negotiation, and not frequently to serve as deputies to the examining judges. The office of these two magistrates, for police commissioners are also magistrates, is known as the Delegates' office; for they are, in fact, delegated on each occasion, and formally empowered to carry out inquiries or arrests.

These functions demand men of ripe age, proved intelligence, great rectitude, and perfect discretion; and it is one of the miracles wrought by Heaven in favor of Paris, that some men of that stamp are always forthcoming. Any description of the Palais de Justice would be incomplete without due mention of these *preventive* officials, as they may be called, the most powerful adjuncts of the law; for though it must be owned that the force of circumstances has abrogated the ancient pomp and wealth of justice, it has materially gained in many ways. In Paris especially its machinery is admirably perfect.

Monsieur de Granville had sent his secretary, Monsieur de Chargeboeuf, to attend Lucien's funeral; he needed a substitute for this business, a man he could trust, and Monsieur Garnery was one of the commissioners in the Delegates' office.

"Monsieur," said Jacques Collin, "I have already proved to you that I have a sense of honor. You let me go free, and I came back.—By this time the funeral mass for Lucien is ended; they will be carrying him to the grave. Instead of remanding me to the Conciergerie, give me leave to follow the boy's body to Pere-Lachaise. I will come back and surrender myself prisoner."

"Go," said Monsieur de Granville, in the kindest tone.

"One word more, monsieur. The money belonging to that girl—Lucien's mistress—was not stolen. During the short time of liberty you allowed me, I questioned her servants. I am sure of them as you are of your two commissioners of the Delegates' office. The money paid for the certificate sold by Mademoiselle Esther Gobseck will certainly be found in her room when the seals are removed. Her maid remarked to me that the deceased was given to mystery-making, and very distrustful; she no doubt hid the banknotes in her bed. Let the bedstead be carefully examined and taken to pieces, the mattresses unsewn—the money will be found."

"You are sure of that?"

"I am sure of the relative honesty of my rascals; they never play any tricks on me. I hold the power of life and death; I try and condemn them and carry out my sentence without all your formalities. You can see for yourself the results of my authority. I will recover the money stolen from Monsieur and Madame Crottat; I will hand you over one of Bibi-Lupin's men, his right hand, caught in the act; and I will tell you the secret of the Nanterre murders. This is not a bad beginning. And if you only employ me in the service of the law and the police, by the end of a year you will be satisfied with all I can tell you. I will be thoroughly all that I ought to be, and shall manage to succeed in all the business that is placed in my hands."

"I can promise you nothing but my goodwill. What you ask is not in my power. The privilege of granting pardons is the King's alone, on the recommendation of the Keeper of the Seals; and the place you wish to hold is in the gift of the Prefet of Police."

"Monsieur Garnery," the office-boy announced.

At a nod from Monsieur de Granville the Delegate commissioner came in, glanced at Jacques Collin as one who knows, and gulped down his astonishment on hearing the word "Go!" spoken to Jacques Collin by Monsieur de Granville.

"Allow me," said Jacques Collin, "to remain here till Monsieur Garnery has returned with the documents in which all my strength lies, that I may take away with me some expression of your satisfaction."

This absolute humility and sincerity touched the public prosecutor.

"Go," said he; "I can depend on you."

Jacques Collin bowed humbly, with the submissiveness of an inferior to his master. Ten minutes later, Monsieur de Granville was in possession of the letters in three sealed packets that had not been opened! But the importance of this point, and Jacques Collin's avowal, had made him forget the convict's promise to cure Madame de Serizy.

WHEN ONCE HE WAS OUTSIDE, Jacques Collin had an indescribable sense of satisfaction. He felt he was free, and born to a new phase of life. He walked quickly from the Palais to the Church of Saint-Germain-des-Pres, where mass was over. The coffin was being sprinkled with holy water, and he arrived in time thus to bid farewell, in a Christian fashion, to the mortal remains of the youth he had loved so well. Then he got into a carriage and drove after the body to the cemetery.

In Paris, unless on very exceptional occasions, or when some famous man has died a natural death, the crowd that gathers about a funeral diminishes by degrees as the procession approaches Pere-Lachaise. People make time to show themselves in church; but every one has his business to attend to, and returns to it as soon as possible. Thus of ten mourning carriages, only four were occupied. By the time they reached Pere-Lachaise there were not more than a dozen followers, among whom was Rastignac.

"That is right; it is well that you are faithful to him," said Jacques Collin to his old acquaintance.

Rastignac started with surprise at seeing Vautrin.

"Be calm," said his old fellow-boarder at Madame Vauquer's. "I am your slave, if only because I find you here. My help is not to be despised; I am, or shall be, more powerful than ever. You slipped your cable, and you did it very cleverly; but you may need me yet, and I will always be at your service.

"But what are you going to do?"

"To supply the hulks with lodgers instead of lodging there," replied Jacques Collin.

Rastignac gave a shrug of disgust.

"But if you were robbed—"

Rastignac hurried on to get away from Jacques Collin.

"You do not know what circumstances you may find yourself in."

They stood by the grave dug by the side of Esther's.

"Two beings who loved each other, and who were happy!" said Jacques Collin. "They are united.—It is some comfort to rot together. I will be buried here."

When Lucien's body was lowered into the grave, Jacques Collin fell in a dead faint. This strong man could not endure the light rattle of the spadefuls of earth thrown by the gravediggers on the coffin as a hint for their payment.

Just then two men of the corps of Public Safety came up; they recognized Jacques Collin, lifted him up, and carried him to a hackney coach.

"What is up now?" asked Jacques Collin when he recovered consciousness and had looked about him.

He saw himself between two constables, one of whom was Ruffard; and he gave him a look which pierced the murderer's soul to the very depths of la Gonore's secret.

"Why, the public prosecutor wants you," replied Ruffard, "and we have been hunting for you everywhere, and found you in the cemetery, where you had nearly taken a header into that boy's grave."

Jacques Collin was silent for a moment.

"Is it Bibi-Lupin that is after me?" he asked the other man.

"No. Monsieur Garnery sent us to find you."

"And he told you nothing?"

The two men looked at each other, holding council in expressive pantomime.

"Come, what did he say when he gave you your orders?"

"He bid us fetch you at once," said Ruffard, "and said we should find you at the Church of Saint-Germain-des-Pres; or, if the funeral had left the church, at the cemetery."

"The public prosecutor wants me?"

"Perhaps."

"That is it," said Jacques Collin; "he wants my assistance."

And he relapsed into silence, which greatly puzzled the two constables.

At about half-past two Jacques Collin once more went up to Monsieur de Granville's room, and found there a fresh arrival in the person of Monsieur de Granville's predecessor, the Comte Octave de Bauvan, one of the Presidents of the Court of Appeals.

"You forgot Madame de Serizy's dangerous condition, and that you had promised to save her."

"Ask these rascals in what state they found me, monsieur," said Jacques Collin, signing to the two constables to come in.

"Unconscious, monsieur, lying on the edge of the grave of the young man they were burying."

"Save Madame de Serizy," said the Comte de Bauvan, "and you shall have what you will."

"I ask for nothing," said Jacques Collin. "I surrendered at discretion, and Monsieur de Granville must have received—"

"All the letters, yes," said the magistrate. "But you promised to save Madame de Serizy's reason. Can you? Was it not a vain boast?"

"I hope I can," replied Jacques Collin modestly.

"Well, then, come with me," said Comte Octave.

"No, monsieur; I will not be seen in the same carriage by your side—I am still a convict. It is my wish to serve the Law; I will not begin by discrediting it. Go back to the Countess; I will be there soon after you. Tell her Lucien's best friend is coming to see her, the Abbe Carlos Herrera; the anticipation of my visit will make an impression on her and favor the cure. You will forgive me for assuming once more the false part of a Spanish priest; it is to do so much good!"

"I shall find you there at about four o'clock," said Monsieur de Granville, "for I have to wait on the King with the Keeper of the Seals."

Jacques Collin went off to find his aunt, who was waiting for him on the Quai aux Fleurs.

"So you have given yourself up to the authorities?" said she.

"Yes."

"It is a risky game."

"No; I owed that poor Theodore his life, and he is reprieved."

"And you?"

"I—I shall be what I ought to be. I shall always make our set shake in their shoes.—But we must get to work. Go and tell Paccard to be off as fast as he can go, and see that Europe does as I told her."

"That is a trifle; I know how to deal with la Gonore," said the terrible Jacqueline. "I have not been wasting my time here among the gilliflowers."

"Let Ginetta, the Corsican girl, be found by to-morrow," Jacques Collin went on, smiling at his aunt.

"I shall want some clue."

"You can get it through Manon la Blonde," said Jacques.

"Then we meet this evening," replied the aunt, "you are in such a deuce of a hurry. Is there a fat job on?"

"I want to begin with a stroke that will beat everything that Bibi-Lupin has ever done. I have spoken a few words to the brute who killed Lucien, and I live only for revenge! Thanks to our positions, he and I shall be equally strong, equally protected. It will take years to strike the blow, but the wretch shall have it straight in the heart."

"He must have vowed a Roland for your Oliver," said the aunt, "for he has taken charge of Peyrade's daughter, the girl who was sold to Madame Nourrisson, you know."

"Our first point must be to find him a servant."

"That will be difficult; he must be tolerably wide-awake," observed Jacqueline.

"Well, hatred keeps one alive! We must work hard."

JACQUES COLLIN TOOK A CAB and drove at once to the Quai Malaquais, to the little room he lodged in, quite separate from Lucien's apartment. The porter, greatly astonished at seeing him, wanted to tell him all that had happened.

"I know everything," said the Abbe. "I have been involved in it, in spite of my saintly reputation; but, thanks to the intervention of the Spanish Ambassador, I have been released."

He hurried up to his room, where, from under the cover of a breviary, he took out a letter that Lucien had written to Madame de Serizy after that lady had discarded him on seeing him at the opera with Esther.

Lucien, in his despair, had decided on not sending this letter, believing himself cast off for ever; but Jacques Collin had read the little masterpiece; and as all that Lucien wrote was to him sacred, he had treasured the letter in his prayer-book for its poetical expression of a passion that was chiefly vanity. When Monsieur de Granville told him of Madame de Serizy's condition, the keen-witted man had very wisely concluded that this fine lady's despair and frenzy must be the result of the quarrel she had allowed to subsist between herself and Lucien. He knew women as magistrates know criminals; he guessed the most secret impulses of their hearts; and he at once understood that the Countess probably ascribed Lucien's death partly to her own severity, and reproached herself bitterly. Obviously a man on whom she had shed her love would never have thrown away his life!—To know that he had loved her still, in spite of her cruelty, might restore her reason.

If Jacques Collin was a grand general of convicts, he was, it must be owned, a not less skilful physician of souls.

This man's arrival at the mansion of the Serizys was at once a disgrace and a promise. Several persons, the Count, and the doctors were assembled in the little drawing-room adjoining the Countess' bedroom; but to spare him this stain on his soul's honor, the Comte de Bauvan dismissed everybody, and remained alone with his friend. It was bad enough even then for the Vice-President of the Privy Council to see this gloomy and sinister visitor come in.

Jacques Collin had changed his dress. He was in black with trousers, and a plain frock-coat, and his gait, his look, and his manner were all that could be wished. He bowed to the two statesmen, and asked if he might be admitted to see the Countess.

"She awaits you with impatience," said Monsieur de Bauvan.

"With impatience! Then she is saved," said the dreadful magician.

And, in fact, after an interview of half an hour, Jacques Collin opened the door and said:

"Come in, Monsieur le Comte; there is nothing further to fear."

The Countess had the letter clasped to her heart; she was calm, and seemed to have forgiven herself. The Count gave expression to his joy at the sight.

"And these are the men who settle our fate and the fate of nations," thought Jacques Collin, shrugging his shoulders behind the two men. "A female has but to sigh in the wrong way to turn their brain as if it were a glove! A wink, and they lose their head! A petticoat raised a little higher, dropped a little lower, and they rush round Paris in despair! The whims of a woman react on the whole country. Ah, how much stronger is a man when, like me, he keeps far away from this childish tyranny, from honor ruined by passion, from this frank malignity, and wiles worthy of savages! Woman, with her genius for ruthlessness, her talent for torture, is, and always will be, the marring of man. The public prosecutor, the minister—here they are, all hoodwinked, all moving the spheres for some letters written by a duchess and a chit, or to save the reason of a woman who is more crazy in her right mind than she was in her delirium."

And he smiled haughtily.

"Ay," said he to himself, "and they believe in me! They act on my information, and will leave me in power. I shall still rule the world which has obeyed me these five-and-twenty years."

Jacques Collin had brought into play the overpowering influence he had exerted of yore over poor Esther; for he had, as has often been shown, the mode of speech, the look, the action which quell madmen, and he had depicted Lucien as having died with the Countess' image in his heart.

No woman can resist the idea of having been the one beloved.

"You now have no rival," had been this bitter jester's last words.

He remained a whole hour alone and forgotten in that little room. Monsieur de Granville arrived and found him gloomy, standing up, and lost in a brown study, as a man may well be who makes an 18th Brumaire in his life.

The public prosecutor went to the door of the Countess' room, and remained there a few minutes; then he turned to Jacques Collin and said:

"You have not changed your mind?"

"No, monsieur."

"Well, then, you will take Bibi-Lupin's place, and Calvi's sentence will be commuted."

"And he is not to be sent to Rochefort?"

"Not even to Toulon; you may employ him in your service. But these reprieves and your appointment depend on your conduct for the next six months as subordinate to Bibi-Lupin."

WITHIN A WEEK BIBI-LUPIN'S NEW deputy had helped the Crottat family to recover four hundred thousand francs, and had brought Ruffard and Godet to justice.

The price of the certificates sold by Esther Gobseck was found in the courtesan's mattress, and Monsieur de Serizy handed over to Jacques Collin the three hundred thousand francs left to him by Lucien de Rubempre.

The monument erected by Lucien's orders for Esther and himself is considered one of the finest in Pere-Lachaise, and the earth beneath it belongs to Jacques Collin.

After exercising his functions for about fifteen years Jacques Collin retired in 1845.

A Note About the Author

Honoré de Balzac (1799–1850) was a French novelist and playwright active during the mid-19th century. Balzac made attempts at many professions, including publishing, business, politics, and law, before he found his best fit as a writer. Balzac was very dedicated to his work, often writing for fifteen hours a day. Because of his attention to detail and unfiltered representation of reality, Balzac is regarded as the founder of realism within the European literary canon.

A Note from the Publisher

Spanning many genres, from non-fiction essays to literature classics to children's books and lyric poetry, Mint Edition books showcase the master works of our time in a modern new package. The text is freshly typeset, is clean and easy to read, and features a new note about the author in each volume. Many books also include exclusive new introductory material. Every book boasts a striking new cover, which makes it as appropriate for collecting as it is for gift giving. Mint Edition books are only printed when a reader orders them, so natural resources are not wasted. We're proud that our books are never manufactured in excess and exist only in the exact quantity they need to be read and enjoyed.

Discover more of your favorite classics with Bookfinity™.

- Track your reading with custom book lists.
- Get great book recommendations for your personalized Reader Type.
- Add reviews for your favorite books.
- AND MUCH MORE!

Visit **bookfinity.com** and take the fun Reader Type quiz to get started.

Enjoy our classic and modern companion pairings!